A New Ally

A New Ally

Dragon's Blood

Book II

Magdalena Marków

Table of Contents

CHAPTER 1

Looking at Neila walking in front of him, Drasan had a stronger and stronger impression that he had been looking for her for so long. She did not have the beauty and position of all those sophisticated ladies from good houses, but she certainly had something they did not have - a sense of self-dignity. He knew perfectly well that each of these wealthy snobs wanted him not for his personality but for his crown.

Neila turned out to be quite different.

Though she pretended to despise him, she couldn't hide her true feelings when he got close. With more sensitive senses, he was able to catch what was invisible to others. As soon as they were alone, her heart accelerated rapidly, her breathing shallow.

Reaching the city, they entered a narrow alleyway, and Alder lifted the half-dragon's spell. However, he still had to concentrate on hiding his presence from all magical beings. The mercenary led them deeper and deeper, passing the few inhabitants hurrying to their homes. Nobody paid any attention to them, although it must be admitted that they looked quite peculiar. All but the woman were wrapped in thick coats with hoods pulled over their foreheads so that it was impossible to recognize their faces.

The girl was walking quickly, not once looking at them, and the snow covering the cobbled streets effectively muffled the sound of her steps. Several taverns from which a cheerful buzz was heard passed. The smell of roast invaded Drasan's nostrils. His stomach immediately reacted with a sharp twist, reminding him of how hungry he was. They only stopped at the corner, right in front of the dingy building. Rusty chains held a faded sign above his door. Proclaiming that they were at the entrance to the inn called "Under the Black Sail."

Neila stood in front of the door and turned to face her companions. Drasan picked up her tension involuntarily, and something else: the typical scent emitted by a victim cornered - fear.

"Okay," she spoke to them for the first time since they were in town. "This is a dive with a nasty reputation for the worst scum in town." She took a deep breath, clearly trying to calm the tension in her voice. "I just want to ask you, as it concerns mainly you, Drasan..." she turned to the half-dragon. "...to remain calm, even if it gets hotter. Alder must stay outside, because if the red-haired bitch of Alt'ar is here somewhere, she must have already sensed him. It's safer for him and us, if he hangs around and watches what is happening on the street," she said all this in one breath, clearly trying to hide her emotions.

"Relax," Drasan said, knowing that the girl was simply afraid. "I'll try not to reveal my identity until absolutely necessary," he added with a slight smile.

Neila just shook her head.

"You don't understand," she said softly. "By bringing you here, I exposed myself to the wrath of the most powerful man in the city after Bal'zar. He hated me before, and now I just stepped into his territory. We will be lucky if we can make it out alive. The old wolf does not like uninvited guests."

"Wolf?" Drasan asked, raising an eyebrow.

"Oh, that's what they sometimes call him because he's known to walk with a wolf at his feet. But it doesn't matter," she took a deep breath again. "They say he can sense magic from kilometer, just like some animals do.

The closer you get to him, the more likely he will expose you, so please don't do anything stupid."

There was silence after this speech. They stared into each other's eyes. This time the girl completely gave up the badness she used in relation to him. There was genuine concern in her gaze.

"Hold on to me and don't talk unnecessarily," she added, then pushed the massive wing open. The door opened with a loud creak announcing their arrival.

As soon as they moved, Drasan was enveloped in a wave of a strong odor, dominated by the musty smell, vomit and digested alcohol. Even that could not mask the smell of another predator. Originally, he couldn't sense it, but as he changed each day his senses became more sensitive than humans, so that now he could smell a scent that no one else could smell.

He stepped back and growled softly.

Neila had no such resistance and boldly crossed the threshold of the room drowning in the twilight, followed by Velwel.

The room was not large, most of it was occupied by four long tables with clunky benches. It was occupied by the worst crowd Drasan had ever encountered. Most did not hide their weapons at all. Swords, knives, sabers, and even bows and crossbows stood leaned against the beams or lay on tables so that the owners could reach for them at any time. The slayers seemed to be oblivious to the visitors, busy playing cards or sipping beer from earthenware mugs.

The half-dragon saw them surreptitiously glared at Neila as she walked over to the counter as if nothing had happened and, resting her elbows on it, looked at the innkeeper, who was taller than her.

"Hello, Vick!" She said in a tone of carefree chat. "I'm looking for the old Wolf. Maybe you know where to find him?"

The man watched her carefully with bloodshot eyes, then replied hoarsely:

"You're not very welcome here."

As soon as he spoke these words, the man sitting at the nearest table got up and walked over to the girl. He was taller than her, had a square jaw, small eyes, and a shaved bald head. His movements showed that, despite his bulky figure, he was able to move with the grace of a dancer. He wore a long-curved saber at his waist. Drasan noticed his fingers caressing her hilt. The bully put a huge paw on Neila's shoulder and turned her face to him in one move. He didn't have to use too much force for it, because the mercenary jumped up instantly, reaching for the sword. The innkeeper behind her grabbed her wrist. She froze, pinned to the counter.

"Don't even try, Hereth," she snapped through gritted teeth, struggling to keep her voice from trembling.

The bully laughed, and it was a very unpleasant laugh. Drasan reacted instinctively. In an instant, he yanked his sword out and aimed its tip at the bully's throat. He wanted to tear it open with his bare hands. The power was flowing through his body in waves, causing more and more hot flashes. He couldn't afford to use it here. He had to stay in control.

The smile on Hereth's face was immediately replaced by a grim grimace.

"Put the weapon down, son," he growled without even turning to face him. Apparently, he didn't care at all about the threat of the half-dragon, at best he was slightly irritated by his attitude.

The young man, still not taking the blade from the bully's throat, looked around the room. All the men who had seemed completely engrossed in their activities until then were getting up and reaching for their weapons. He could kill them without even moving, but he preferred not to. Such a show would not go unnoticed, and he did not care about publicity. Not only that, he preferred no one to find out about his presence in the city. The situation was saved, as usual, by Neila. She took her hand out of the innkeeper's grasp, pushed Hereth away, walked over to the half-dragon and, soothingly, placed her hand on his shoulder.

"Do what he says," she said in a voice that could not bear the objection, then looked at Velwel, who was also standing with a drawn sword in his hand. "And you too!" she added.

Drasan hesitated a long time before he finally obeyed her orders. He did so reluctantly and never take his eyes off the bald man. The man smiled broadly, displaying a lot of missing teeth.

"Well, well..." He purred, eyeing the half-dragon as if he had a thoroughbred horse in front of him. He walked around him, judging. "He's crazy, people like him wouldn't live for long," he said matter-of-factly, then added, "I can see that it has changed a bit. Did you like teamwork? Not good, oh, not good." He shook his finger at her, then added in a much more serious tone, "Now tell those little boys to drop their toys before they hurt themselves. Come on!"

The prince looked at the assassin, and when she nodded slightly, he let go of the sword, which fell with a noise to the dust-covered floor. Velwel did the same. As soon as they did so, at Hereth's gesture, the other thugs surrounded them in a semicircle, cutting off the only way out. They are trapped.

"I think you forgot something, sweetheart," the bully said in a velvety voice, rubbing a dirty finger across Neila's cheek. From the depths of Drasan's throat came a soft, warning hiss, the thug apparently did not hear it, because he continued: "You were supposed to never show yourself here again, and certainly not bring strangers."

Neila snorted like an enraged kitten and angrily pushed his hand away.

"And what, I should be scared of a foul-smelling hog like you?" She asked contemptuously.

She regretted the words immediately. Hereth quickly proved that despite his size, he can move really fast. Before the mercenary could move, he pinned her to the counter again, simultaneously grabbing both wrists and pinning them in an iron grip.

A low, guttural growl erupted from the half-dragon's throat, and the muscles tightened to fight. He lost all his composure, his eyes turned from human to reptile. He could see Neila's lips forming to scream. She didn't want him to come out. Unfortunately. Orange-red flames just enveloped his body, a sphere the size of a human head materialized in his hand. The assassins began to step back, having no idea what was happening.

"Enough!" An imperious voice rang out.

A woman appeared in the doorway. It took Drasan one look to realize she was a witch. She had it written all over her face, with somewhat sharp, predatory features and large dark green eyes underlined with a black pencil. It was even hidden in a mysterious half smile. The hair was a deep auburn color, and it fell freely to the back. The tight leather outfit emphasized every advantage of the figure, the effect was complemented by horse riding boots reaching above the knees.

As soon as she entered the room, the assassins stepped aside, lowering their weapons. Then Drasan felt a slight breeze of magic on his skin and hissed softly, revealing a little fang, now completely unlike human fangs.

The witch stopped in front of him, the power swirling around her, hugging her like a protective cocoon. Her eyes flashed like two emeralds as she formed a small ball of energy in front of her with a few motions of her slim hands. Directed by the will of the newcomer, she sped towards Drasan. He merely closed his eyes and immediately a protective circle of flames, reaching his waist, burst out around him. Though he was in control, he was eager to fight. He wanted to tear his enemies to shreds and burn the debris.

"Fire magic is forbidden," it echoed in his mind. "Fire is an element so unpredictable that it is impossible to control it."

Drasan just smiled and stoked the flames so that they now reached his chest, only to make them engulf him a moment later.

"I'm not human," he communicated to her, letting the roaring power within him engulf her as well, lifting every hair on her body. He felt himself tremble and only then let the flames fall to his feet. He had no doubts that his show had exactly the effect he had expected - it terrified her.

"Who are you then?" Asked the witch, stepping back involuntarily.

The half-dragon unleashed a power that left him with his murderous fury. He smiled at the witch, who preferred to keep a safe distance.

"I want to see Alt'ar," he said bluntly.

The woman scanned the room with a stern gaze, spotted Neila, and her eyes narrowed dangerously. Without hesitating, she moved towards her, but Drasan blocked her way.

"She's with me," he growled, and formed a small fireball in his hand to emphasize his words.

"What do you want?" She asked immediately, changing sides, anger in her voice.

Drasan took a step forward, this time she did not back away. She boldly looked him in the eye. Still smiling, she gestured to Hereth, who took a long, ugly looking knife from his belt and put it to Neila's throat.

"Rodian," because now he had no doubts who he was dealing with - she smiled wickedly.

"I am Alt'ar's right-hand, and before I admit anyone to him, he must confess to me first." She propped up her hips and continued. "Until you used my power, I didn't feel your presence. So, I conclude that you can disguise yourself. You are not a mage, as neither of them can control the energy of fire, nor are you an elf, because your countenance does not resemble that of this vile race. So, who you are remains an intriguing mystery."

Drasan looked first at Neila, then at Velwel. He couldn't put any of them at risk now, and his only chance of survival was here among these people. So, he made the only right decision.

"You're right," he said, ignoring the mercenary's pleading gaze. "I'm not human, at least not entirely." He clenched his still-burning fist. The ball turned to smoke, then vanished. "I'm a half-dragon, pupil of Queen Vaya of Sheardon. And I came here despite the risks to ask your leader for help."

"Then it's you," the witch blurted out, her emerald eyes becoming as large as saucers. "The king himself and his witch are looking for you. If they find out you're here..."

"They will kill anyone in their way. Just to catch me," Drasan finished with a sour smile.

"Why shouldn't I hand you over to them?" She asked, her voice trembling with anger.

"Because it won't save you or anyone else. Besides, you won't stick your nose out of the safe hole you've crawled into, and just like me, you don't want to become anyone's slave. When Dhalia catches me, she will make me an instrument of destruction. It will be the end of everything you know."

He talked and saw Rodian's face slowly spread to understanding. She knew what it meant to be someone else's slave, there were still marks from the handcuffs on her soul. He risked all the cards, but had no choice.

"Good," said the witch at last. "I will take you to Alt'ar on one condition. You will go there unarmed. You and your companions."

"I'll only do it if you promise not to let a single hair fall off their heads," replied Drasan.

Neila laughed ironically.

"She won't guarantee you that. She would be glad to see me dead, and Velwel is indifferent to her." She said, ignoring the knife to her throat.

"You shouldn't have come here," Rodian retorted, moving toward her, the thud of her heels echoing in the silence that followed. "You know he doesn't give you a second chance."

Drasan looked from one to the other, trying to decipher what they meant. He had guessed before that Neila must have had some trouble with the red-haired witch. But he did not think that it also applied to Alt'ar.

"I'm not going to ask for it," the girl growled, boldly looking into the eyes of the redhead.

"So why did you come back?" Rodian asked, crossing her arms over her chest.

"At his request," the girl replied, nodding at Drasan.

The witch looked at the man carefully. Like every adept of black magic, she had an amazing beauty, but he had known for a long time that it was only an illusion. Camouflage to entrap the victim. He had developed immunity to it in the Kahaer dungeons. It was there that Dhalia proved to him that outer beauty can hide a rotten interior.

"He must mean a lot to you, since for him, you have gone where everyone dreams of breaking your neck," she said a little calmer, although there was still tension in her voice. "Well then," she brought a smile to her face again, "the four of us will go there, though I cannot vouch for Alt'ar himself."

After these words, the assassin named Hereth released Neila and returned to the others, who had never gone back to their current activities. The freed mercenary walked over to Drasan, massaging her sore wrists.

"I hope you know what you're doing," she said, softly enough that only he heard it.

"I hope so too," he replied.

Later they did not have much opportunity to talk, because Rodian went deeper into the room without a word, and they had to follow her, whether they wanted it or not. The woman passed the tables and passed through the hidden door. Behind them was a room that looked like a pantry. There she walked for a while, her heels tapping on the wooden floor over and over again, until it made a hollow noise. Then she stopped and wiped some dust off with the toe of her shoe. Only then the clear outline of the hatch appeared behind which, as they guessed, the descent to the basement must have been hidden. There appeared a narrow stone staircase sinking in deep darkness. It blew damp and musty.

Drasan looked down uncertainly. There was nothing, no suspicious odor, which made him even more concerned. Rodian at this time conjured up a small ball of energy to light their way as they made their way down the dark tunnel. She was the first to descend, with a half-dragon behind her back. Neila and Velwel were the last to go. The passage, as they guessed, led to a cellar filled with squat barrels, the sweet smell of fermented grapes in the air.

Rodian selected one of the barrels and pushed it effortlessly aside. Their eyes saw another passage carved in the stone wall with remarkable precision. As the witch pulled on the empty torch holder, the stone door swiveled with a soft screech and followed her into a round chamber, almost regal-styled. There were two velvet-covered armchairs, a few poufs, and cushioned chairs. The floor was covered with wolf and bear skins and hand-knotted carpets. One wall was adorned with a magnificent, carefully crafted map of Lineland.

Men and women of different ages sat on chairs, armchairs, and pouffes. There were ten of them altogether. At the sight of the new arrivals, some of them jumped up from their seats, instinctively reaching for their weapons. Only at the gesture of the man occupying the largest seat, they sat down again, reassured. The new arrivals had no doubt that they were facing Alt'ar alone.

His age was difficult to determine, for he seemed neither young nor old. His blond hair was cropped close, as was his beard and mustache, and his deep blue eyes looked at them almost with amusement. He was thin and wiry, and he didn't seem particularly strong, and he had something of predator in him. He wore a black shirt, a laced leather jacket, and matching knee-length pants and boots. At his feet lay an enormous wolf with silvery gray hair and amber eyes.

Instincts urged Drasan to be careful, though the incense sticks lit in the room effectively masked any suspicious odors. Nobody said anything, but the air was thick with tension.

When the blond got up from his seat and, with the wolf at his feet, he walked towards them, everyone parted from him to the sides, bowing their heads respectfully. Then Drasan felt it: a slight impulse of magic, even a prickle. It woke a faint warning hiss deep in his throat. The man's eyes narrowed into slits, and a wide smile, devoid of any cheerfulness, reached his mouth.

"All the fuss because of you," he said, rather than asking, taking another step forward. "Hello, Drasan," he added, extending a thin, callused hand.

Drasan stepped back, giving the man the field involuntarily.

"How do you know my name?" He asked, though it seemed obvious. Dhalia made a lot of effort to capture him.

"There is probably no one else who does not know you. Your fame has even overshadowed mine. I think all the bounty hunters around here are looking for you, because the king spared no effort to capture you. One hundred thousand gold crowns. A lot of my men would sell their own mother, sister, and brother for that much." He smiled slightly, still keeping his narrowed eyes on the half-dragon. "And you just came to me, the best-paid assassin in all of Riden, infamous Bloody Alt'ar."

The half-dragon looked around involuntarily at the men of the Underworld Prince. They surrounded them in silence, in a semicircle waiting for the command of their leader. They are trapped. If they were to come out alive, he would have to take the challenge in that strange game the Wolf was playing with him.

"What are you going to do?" He asked with a grim smile.

"That's the problem: I don't know what to do with you." He sighed with exaggerated affection. "As you can see, I have no shortage of gold," he added, making a wide gesture with his hand and smiling slyly. "I'm fed up with people too, when you only have the two behind you. So I am the master of the situation. I would have saved myself a lot of trouble if I had handed you over, but..." He paused and smiled again. "Before I make a decision, I'd love to hear your offer."

Drasan stared at him. He knew he was treading on very thin ice. He had to convince the man that fighting Dhalia and Bal'zar was also in his interest, and something told him that it would not be easy.

"Well, now that we've settled some things, let's get down to business." Their host said, smiling a little artificially. "Why don't you sit down?" He suggested pointing to empty seats.

This unexpected courtesy made Drasan suspicious of him. He still didn't know if he could trust Alt'ar.

"I'll stand," he growled softly, taking a step forward and crossing his arms over his chest. He had assumed a dominant attitude in the human world and was now waiting for a reaction.

The response from the leader of the assassins' guild was not what he had expected. A soft warning snarl escaped from the man's throat, muscles tensing like ties in an instant. No one even moved as he crossed the space separating him from Drasan with a few quick strides, the irises of his eyes flooded with blood red. The wolf at his feet immediately fell to the ground, baring his fangs to the gums.

There was a silence as Drasan and Alt'ar looked at each other, assessing their chances in a direct battle. The half-dragon's eyes became reptilian under the influence of anger, a hiss like that of an enraged serpent heard from deep in his throat.

Seeing what was going on, Rodian whispered the formula of the spell, erecting a barrier between them strong enough to stop any act of aggression against her superior. Drasan was trembling with rage. He could not and did not want to accept the fact that he was in the territory of another predator - a werewolf.

All this fury had to find an outlet.

"Why didn't you warn me!" He roared, turning to look at Neila.

The girl met the gaze of inhuman eyes.

"I tried, but you didn't listen to me," she replied.

"You could have said it straight, instead of twisting!" He growled, splashing saliva on her. He was losing whatever composure he had left, which must have resulted in a change, and he couldn't let that happen. Such an outburst of magic would only get them into trouble.

"It's not her fault," Velwel unexpectedly defended Neila. Thus, he made him understand that he himself knew nothing of the second nature of the king of the underworld. He gained so much that he temporarily distracted Drasan from the mercenary and directed it at himself. "She risked a lot anyway when she agreed to bring you here."

"You both know my attitude towards werewolves," he growled, though the anger that had burned in him so far had faded somewhat.

"So I'm listening," Alt'ar said in a voice not much louder than a whisper, but it sounded clearly in the silence that followed. "What does your ducal majesty have to do with other misfits?"

Drasan turned to face him in a flash, his anger flared up in him again.

"Werewolves are twisted monsters!" He roared so that everyone shuddered. "They don't stop at killing, they take physical delight in inflicting unbearable torment on the victim. They hunt not to satisfy their hunger, but to satisfy their bloody lust."

Alt'ar stiffened at the insult. Anger boiled in him, but he held back the change. His eyes burned with the lust for murder, and the vein in his temple pulsed furiously. He contented himself with taking a few stiff steps toward the magic barrier that separated him from the half-dragon.

"You don't know anything about us," he said through clenched teeth. - You judge the whole race by prejudices and superstition, not by hard facts. How many of my kind have you met to make such accusations?

"One," the half-dragon growled. "I've seen enough to know what monsters like you are capable of."

Alt'ar snorted a mirthless laugh.

"Like me?" He repeated, his voice trembling with anger. Better look at you. You are an even greater misfit, half-human, half-dragon. If you came out you would be treated with as much hatred as me. You hunt and kill to survive, just like me. What makes you all the better, Drasan?" He continued, pacing back and forth in front of the barrier. "Your position? Title? I have heard the rumors. You are nobody without your kingdom."

"At least I don't hunt humans like your race," growled Drasan, his arguments running out. In fact, most of his news of werewolves came from dusty volumes in the Sheardon library. He met only Boris on his way, it was he who caused him to develop an aversion to the whole nation.

"I don't do that either!" Alt'ar roared furiously. The wolf slowly but surely crawled out of the human skin. If the Guild leader would change, Drasan would have to do the same, and that would attract the witch's attention. He had no choice: he was in werewolf territory, and if he did not want to bring them all down, he had to submit.

Therefore, he did exactly what no one would expect from him. He fell to his knees and bowed his neck, demonstrating complete submission.

"Accept my apology, Alt'ar," he spoke to the floor, forcing himself to keep his tone calm. Muscles tensed, causing excruciating pain.

The air flickered as the witch behind him removed the barrier so that Alt'ar could finally approach the kneeling Drasan. The nervousness evident in the assassin's every move was by no means fading away, though the eyes regained their natural steel-blue color.

"I accept your apology," he said softly.

The half-dragon stood up without looking up. The werewolf's body still exuded unnatural heat, which meant that he had not yet regained full control of his wolf self.

Alt'ar walked slowly around him, making a soft hum unlike the sounds humans usually make. From time to time, it exposed the upper lip, showing canines similar to dogs, but not associated with humans. He finally calmed down enough to step forward against the half-dragon. He dared to look up.

"So I'm listening," he said, his voice warmer, though his jaws were still twitching. "What was it that forced you to take the risk of being discovered by those who wish you death and seeking help from someone like me?"

Drasan took a deep breath, he had to think carefully about each word so as not to enchant the werewolf on the verge of endurance.

"I'm desperate," he replied, resolving to tell the truth. "I'm being hunted by a pair of the most powerful mages. The worst thing is, they're not going to kill me." He smiled wryly. "Only to enslave and transform into a tool of destruction. I'm also aware of Dhalia's plans for werewolves, and I know that if she fails to enslave you, she will annihilate your entire kind. So, we have a choice either to fight together, or to come to terms with our fate and idly look at the slow destruction of everything we know."

Alt'ar was silent for a long moment, thoughtfully scratching his wolf behind the ear. He seemed to consider Drasan's words from every angle, until he finally sighed heavily.

"You put me in a difficult position," he said wearily, then returned to his chair and sat down, gesturing for the prince to do the same. This time he did it without resistance. "You come here to tell me what I have known for a long time. Humans have been hunting werewolves since the dawn of time. They consider us, like you, soulless monsters." He smiled sourly. "I've heard a lot of rumors about you, some certainly can be put into fairy tales right away, and others aroused in me just curiosity. The prince who turns out to be a beast..." He laughed ironically, "almost like in a children's story, except that this story does not have a happy ending."

Alt'ar reached for an ornate decanter of amber liquid and poured little by little into two goblets. He pushed one of them to Drasan and drank from the other one.

The prince reached for the cup and sniffed the drink distrustfully - it turned out to have a pleasant, sweet, spicy smell. He took a sip and immediately felt warmth spread over his body.

The werewolf at that time leaned back, sinking into the soft backrest. He narrowed his eyes as he relished the effect of the wine.

"Let's get down to business," he said suddenly. "What exactly do you expect from me?"

The question surprised Drasan completely, so that he froze with the cup halfway to his mouth, then carefully set it down on the table. He heard Neila take a deep breath behind him, maybe she was about to say something. He no longer remembered her presence. He focused his full attention on the werewolf sitting across from him.

"Dhalia and Bal'zar are gathering an army," he said finally, trying in vain to succumb to the relaxing effects of alcohol. "If I don't stop their actions now, they'll go to Antua or Earden with the first thaws. My guess is that, like me, you are also not satisfied with the current regime."

After his words there was a silence in which loud panting of the wolf was heard. Alt'ar scratched his chin thoughtfully, his gaze unreadable.

"You don't seem to understand my question, Drasan," he said slowly, emphasizing each word. "I asked: what do you want from me?"

"Help in destroying the witch," replied the prince. "I'm the only person who resisted her magic. That's why she decided to break me, starting by destroying everything I knew and loved. She hopes that I will crawl over to her on my knees and will happily allow her to put on my slave chains!" He almost shouted the last words.

"It's your problem, I won't gain anything from it," Alt'ar said quietly. "You're bringing trouble to my neck. In addition, you bring someone to my hideout who is not welcome here," his gaze fell on Neila, who at these words seemed to shrink, trying to hide behind Drasan's chair. "I'm not in the habit of giving traitors a second chance."

"I'm not going into what happened between you and Neila," Drasan said, trying to speak clearly. "But know that she has my full trust."

He reached over the back of the chair and squeezed Neila's forearm tightly, making her understand that he would not let her hurt her. The girl withdrew her hand and, to the surprise of those present, she faced Alt'ar.

"I didn't cheat on you, you self-righteous bastard," she said through clenched teeth. "I was protecting your ass by risking my own life, while you thought my visit to court was an act of treason. I didn't say a word then or now. I have exposed myself to the wrath of someone ten times more powerful than you." She glanced over her shoulder at Drasan. "And as for all those werewolf control games, know that I've never bent my neck in front of anyone, and neither will I be in front of you."

Alt'ar stood up so quickly that it made Drasan shiver involuntarily. He preferred not to move. Instead, he summoned power and wrapped the mercenary in a protective circle of flames that reached her waist. The werewolf stepped back, snarling softly, then without a moment's thought headed straight for the seated half-dragon.

Drasan knew he was agitated again but had already decided not to fight back. It could destroy any chances of an alliance.

"Why are you defending her?" The assassin asked in a low, trembling voice. The anger flared up in him again. "That saucy bitch should learn a lesson at last," he continued in the same tone.

The contempt in his voice made Drasan jump up from his seat. His body was instantly enveloped in flames.

"It's not up to you to discipline her," he growled.

"Are you threatening me?" The werewolf snapped back, his jaw twitching menacingly.

"No, just a reminder of who you're dealing with," the half-dragon replied softly but emphatically.

Alt'ar looked into his eyes. This time Drasan did not look away.

"You love her?" He asked.

This question took the prince by surprise. He glanced at Neila, unsure what to say. What exactly did he feel for her? He couldn't tell yet, and his instincts kept telling him that he should protect her.

"Where did this question come from?" He asked.

The assassin folded his arms over his chest, which clearly meant he wouldn't let go that easily.

"Simple question, simple answer," he drawled through gritted teeth. "Do you love her or not?"

"Does it matter how I feel about her?" Drasan said. "She belongs to my people, and therefore I am bound to defend her, just as you defend each of your own."

To his surprise, Alt'ar laughed and said:

"You entered my territory with a woman whom I personally forbade to come here. You brought the royal soldiers to my neck. I wouldn't be surprised if they were storming my door right now. On top of that, you didn't show me the proper respect."

In response to his words, the hidden door suddenly swung open and the bulky silhouette of the already familiar assassin, Hereth, appeared. At the sight of Drasan and his company, he grimaced and clenched his huge hands into fists.

"There are the royal guard upstairs," he grunted in his thick voice, glaring unfriendly at Drasan. "They're searching the inn."

Drasan sprang to his feet, but Alt'ar pushed him back into his chair even faster.

"What a coincidence," he drawled. "For twenty years I've managed to hide from the king quite well. He didn't find me until the day you entered my fortress. I suggest you explain, otherwise I'll pass you on in pieces."

Drasan looked at him coolly. He did not believe that Alt'ar would hand him over to a witch. Rather, he was the type to settle scores on his own.

"It's Dhalia, she must have sensed my presence," he replied as calmly as he could.

At the sound of that name, Rodian walked over to him, her heels tapping on the stone floor.

"What did you say?" She asked, frowning.

"Dhalia is a witch just like you. She can sense my presence when she wants to."

"Impossible here," she said, shaking her head until her thick red hair rippled. "This room is secured against magical penetration, I personally cast protective spells..." She suddenly fell silent, staring at him with wide eyes. "Unless someone else knows..."

"I trust mine," growled Drasan. He liked it less and less. If Rodian was telling the truth, then someone must have betrayed. But he was sure it was none of his people.

"This is a serious problem," the werewolf said. "Someone sold you." His eyes fell on Neila, who huddled behind the half-dragon chair.

"None of mine," the half-dragon growled softly, trying to get up again. This time he couldn't even move. He hissed furiously, barely felt Rodian cast a spell.

The witch stood nearby, her arms folded over her chest, watching him with her eyes narrowed to slits. The werewolf started circling again, he was furious.

"You're not leaving," he growled, stabbing the half-dragon in the chest. It was evident that he was barely in control of himself. "They're looking for you, so I only have two options. Either I hand you over or hide you, risking not only my reputation but my own life as well. The question is what can you give me in return."

Drasan stopped fighting the spell for a moment and looked straight into the eyes of the leader of the Assassins' Guild. He understood that Alt'ar would not hesitate to hand him over, as long as he saved himself and his people from the noose in this way. Unfortunately, he wasn't sure if handing them the half-dragon would make Bal'zar suddenly forget about himself. He wanted a guarantee that this one could keep them safe.

"Dhalia is desperate," he said slowly, weighing each word. "She will not hesitate to kill anyone who has had or has contact with me. Even if you hand us over, it won't guarantee you inviolability, only a neck loop if you're lucky." He took a deep breath and continued. "I, although I cannot promise you that you will be safe, I'm able to slightly extend the life of you and your people, if only you agree to help me in the campaign against the witch and her helper."

Before he could twitch, the werewolf's hand shot toward him like a snake attacking. Claw-like fingers gripped Drasan's throat with the force of an iron vise, nearly crushing his throat. The half-dragon snarled hoarsely, but as the assassin tightened his grip, he fell silent.

"I see you're too used to giving orders," he panted in his face. "Therefore, I would like to remind you that you are in my territory, and here it is me, not you, who is both Alpha and Omega. Your life is in my hands right now, so please kindly shut your mouth." He released him.

Drasan coughed, rubbing his throat as it slowly healed. He couldn't speak, so his eyes just followed the werewolf pacing on the carpet.

"As strange as it may seem to you, I also didn't have love for the current king, and even less for his mage friend," he blurted out his words in a low, growl-like voice. "The simplest solution is to bind you like a ram and return to his majesty, respecting his royal majesty. However, it would draw unnecessary attention to my humble person. So, for now, I have decided to let you enjoy my hospitality. As for the alliance... At the moment, with the royal guard swarming at the threshold of my hideout, I cannot give you any answer."

Drasan felt relieved. At the same time, the magical bonds loosened and he could assume a more comfortable position, but he avoided the assassin's gaze, guessing that he was still extremely close to transforming. He would have liked to do it himself, although he understood that in the present situation it was not the most sensible solution.

***

Bal'zar tore a large chunk from the deer leg and lazily tossed the dog sitting next to the table. It grabbed the flesh in flight, snapping its jaw loudly. The young ruler stuck his teeth into the piece of roast he held in his hand, then, ignoring Dhalia's disapproving gaze, wiped his mouth with the back of his hand.

The witch regarded him with her cool pale blue eyes. Contrary to the young man, she looked gorgeous as always: dressed in a green gown with a deep neckline, decorated with a diamond ruff, and with black hair pinned up at the top of her head in a refined bun. An empty plate stood in front of her, and a set of gilded cutleries lay in a row next to it, slightly gleaming.

Suddenly, Shirza raised an enormous head from above the gnawed bone and growled softly. Bal'zar showed no surprise, not even a hint of interest. Even when a tall bald man dressed in a long black coat emerged from the darkness in the corner of the room. The stranger bowed to the ruler, then made the same gesture in front of the stunned witch.

Dhalia stood up so abruptly that she knocked over her chair. It fell to the floor with a loud thud that echoed through the empty dining-room. The woman walked past them, slightly lifting the hem of the dress. She walked briskly towards the head of the table, where Bal'zar was sitting, still unconcerned with the unexpected visitor's visit.

"Who is he?" She asked in a cool voice, not trying to be polite.

As if casually, Bal'zar put down the cutlery in his hands and looked up at her.

"It's just Alder. A spy, who I placed close enough to your favorite reptile to report to me of his every move," he announced in a calm tone as if he was explaining to her that after night comes day.

Dhalia gave the mage a cursory glance, then turned to the king again. He was playing with the chewed bone, closely watched by the wolfhound lying at his feet. Finally, he tossed her aside, and the dog grabbed it, crushing it in its powerful jaws.

"Then please explain to me what your spy is doing here at dinner time. They say the walls are so closely guarded that the mouse won't slip through?" She asked softly.

The ruler smiled slightly.

"Alder is exactly where your pet Drasan is. Since he had come here, that damned lizard must have found a way to deceive the guards at the city gate," he replied in the same, infuriating, calm tone.

"It's impossible," she snapped, instantly turning purple with anger. "He couldn't come in here, even invisible. I would sense his presence."

"Now that you mentioned it, I was the one who helped Drasan get to the city." The mage said with a sly smile. "That's how I gained his trust. With this one simple trick, I can still be around him without fear of breaking my neck or burning me alive."

Bal'zar clapped his hands, summoning a servant in velvet green livery with a decanter of wine. He generously filled three goblets before he left without a word.

"Sit down, my friend," he offered the mage a seat by his side.

Dhalia stiffened. The young ruler did not allow her to be so close. Anyway, even if he did, she would not have accepted the invitation. The waves of power emanating from him made her skin tingling unpleasantly. He turned out to be a powerful mage, taking minimal advantage of it. He didn't need all the talent. And so he controlled not only the castle service, but also most of the army.

Alder sat down carefully on the edge of the chair, sniffed the wine, then took a small sip while still staring at the witch standing nearby.

"Well…" Bal'zar began, setting the empty cup aside and leaning back comfortably on the back. "What's our scaly friend up to?"

"As far as I know, he's going to try to get support from the local band of thugs calling themselves the Assassins' Guild," replied the mage, reaching for one of the chicken legs without asking. "He wants them to help him fight against you, my lord," he added with a slight smile.

"Ah..." Bal'zar snorted dismissively. "Alt'ar. I could guess it, he was always salt in my father's eye. He gathered the best paid cutters in all Riden. So far, however, he had not dared to crawl out of his safe den. I even tried to remind him gently why it was not worth messing with me by sending a squad of guards there."

"So," Dhalia interjected, her fingers gripping the back of the chair in front of her so tightly her knuckles turned white. "As usual, everything happened without my knowledge. By disregarding Drasan's abilities, you are making a great mistake."

"There is nothing he can do to me," Bal'zar said calmly. "I want to see his reaction when I finally corner him and cut off the only escape route."

"If you really count on it being that simple, then you're a fool," hissed Dhalia. "You aren't yet ready for a direct battle with him, his power and skills are constantly growing."

"Mine, too," Bal'zar replied, showing signs of annoyance for the first time. He quickly regained his composure, and a dismissive smile returned to his lips. "Don't worry, my dear. I don't want to permanently damage your precious prey. Although, in my opinion, eliminating him would make things easier. However, I believe that it is worth teaching him a lesson so that he knows who he is dealing with."

Dhalia was already opening her mouth to answer, but he silenced her with a single gesture, as if he were brushing off the intrusive fly.

"That's why I invited dear Alder here. I'm sure he has an interesting story for us about all the weaknesses of our dragon prince," the king said, smiling encouragingly at the mage.

CHAPTER 2

Winter in the north was much harsher than elsewhere on the peninsula. People dragged from the fields and pastures to wait out the frosty months in the warm rooms of their homes. Merchant caravans appeared on the routes less and less frequently. No wonder that the sight of a rider traveling alone turned out to be something unusual and filled the population with panic. Probably a thief, bandit or deserter. Everyone gave him a wide berth as he tirelessly headed east. Right towards Riden.

Yarred Cordydian took only the necessary items with him, knowing that too much weight would unnecessarily slow him down. He wished he could take Mary, unfortunately her condition precluded a journey so far. The girl tried not to let her show how sad this unexpected separation had made her feel. She obviously didn't want to worry him. He left Miral in her care. The boy endured more than he should, and no one was surprised that he had lost his mind.

The key to unraveling the whole mystery was the queen's letter to Drasan. He was taking the parcel with him, safely hidden in the saddlebags. The captain wasn't sure what it might contain. He guessed that there was no less, no more, just an explanation of what happened. What else could prove so important that the queen was in control of the messenger's life? After all, she knew the kingdom was in decline. There was another explanation, but Yarred instinctively flinched at the thought. Someone from the close circle of the ruler could have betrayed, bringing misfortune on everyone.

Yarred shook his head. Drasan had too many enemies to pinpoint the culprit. However... Suddenly everything became clear and transparent, like water in a mountain stream. The Queen learned the traitor's identity and dispatched a messenger to warn both him and the prince before returning to Sheardon. It is possible that this apostate, like that smelly goofy Darius, had been working with Dhalia as a spy for years.

This theory, while explaining a lot, made no sense in a situation where the deceased, beautiful Ulrica was used as a decoy. The spy could be a woman, perhaps even one of those whose heart the young man broke. Neither of these assumptions seemed logical enough. It would be easier to punch the prince with a dagger in the heart while he was asleep, or to sprinkle poison in the wine. But whoever gave up his soul to that damned witch was definitely not going to kill him. He wanted to punish him in the cruelest possible way.

In this situation, it is easy to understand the motives of such a person. Driven by envy or a desire to take revenge for grievances, she spread the rumor that the heir to the Sheardon's throne, could wield fire. This rumor goes to Darius, who in turn sells it to Dhalia. This in turn causes an avalanche of disasters, from the capture of Drasan to the destruction of Sheardon. Such a person must not only know the queen and her ward well, but also inspire their trust. Unfortunately, only one person came to mind for Captain Cordydian - Mirian.

She was a royal adviser at one time. She knew Drasan from the cradle, and the queen trusted her. She could inform the principal about everything that was happening at court. This explained how Dhalia knew about the prince's weakness for the fair sex and why she knew his habits. She also seemed well informed about the friendship between the captain of the guard and the young heir to the throne.

Who would have suspected sweet plump, red-faced Mirian with a freckled nose and big green eyes? Fate shook her beauty. In return, bestowing a character that not only inspired confidence, but also perfectly masked her true intentions. She was able to hide in the court of Queen Vaya for years and work as a spy for Dhalia. It so happened that the ruler finally discovered the traitor's identity. Then the witch struck, sending troops of the merciless Doars into the defenseless kingdom. Knowing that she had little time, Vaya made two letters in which she included a warning.

These and other thoughts tormented Yarred as he headed straight for Riden. He trusted that this was where he would find all the answers.

***

The visit of unexpected guests turned out to be a drop that filled the goblet. For the first time in more than fifty years, the Alt'ar was barely in control. He himself no longer knew why Drasan's presence was so irritating to him. Perhaps it was because there was another, no less dangerous predator walking on its territory. Rather, he relied on arrogance and an almost complete lack of humility. Not only did he come uninvited, but he also did not show him the respect he deserved. Nay! He brought on the killer's head trouble which, because of his second nature, he preferred to avoid. Since becoming leader of the Assassins' Guild, he no longer had to worry about his own safety. Others did it for him. The call of murder was satisfied without the need to use fangs and claws, a sword or a pair of knives were enough.

When Drasan entered its doorstep, dual nature became a problem. The constant tension caused irritation that was difficult to control. He somehow endured the others, although he had to admit that a young killer named Velwel irritated him a little with his incessant chatter. He chose to ignore Neila. Although he had come across her several times due to the same profession, somehow, they never liked each other. What surprised him, however, was what company she found herself in. As far as he knew, she always preferred to work alone, liked independence, and disliked men.

Meanwhile, today she showed up with the typical alpha male. If he didn't know her, he would have thought she was in love.

The mercenary's love dilemmas were among the least of his worries. Knowing that now there is no other way out, he was trying hard to solve the situation. He needed a good plan. He used to have several different hiding places in case someone spotted him. Now that he has become the leader of one of the largest and highest-paid guilds, he no longer needs them. He's never smuggled anyone before.

He could, however, hand over to the royal guard both Drasan and his companions. True, that wouldn't solve any of his problems. He was too much under the skin of the current ruler to just let him go. Therefore, he knew perfectly well that as soon as he pushed his nose out of the safe hiding place, the king would happily pass judgment on both him and his people.

There was nothing left to do here and think. If only he could hunt, his head would light up immediately. Unfortunately, with the guards on the doorstep, he didn't even have that luxury.

***

Drasan also had trouble with composure. As a half-dragon, he had a fiery temper. And his male ego could hardly bear the werewolf's presence. On top of that, he couldn't concentrate his thoughts because Neila was constantly muttering under her breath. Like him, the girl hated idleness, which she demonstrated in every possible way.

"I don't like it," she muttered.

"We have no choice," replied Drasan. There was a strain in his voice, though his face was like a stone mask. "We have to wait here until we can safely leave town."

"It will take ages," the girl grumbled. Minute by minute her mood was getting worse, making him more nervous.

"Stop it," Velwel muttered, daringly playing the role of a peacemaker.

Drasan's jaw tightened dangerously, he was about to say something, but he bit his tongue. He was also not amused by the situation. He was trapped. The leader of the Guild could hand him over to the guards at any moment, relieving the trouble. All the assembled assassins glared at him unfriendly. The witch seemed to be the only one to understand the seriousness of the situation and wisely kept aloof. Ready to react if any of Alt'ar's people lose their patience and decide to bring the culprit to justice themselves.

Like the Guild leader, Rodian knew that when it got hotter, Drasan was their only bargaining chip. However, they preferred to play it without the participation of the king and his subordinates. Until then, they also had in mind not to over-inflame the heir to the Sheardon throne.

Fortunately, the problem resolved as night fell. A fifteen-year-old teenager burst into the hidden chamber and, looking for Alt'ar, ran to him.

"They retreated!" He announced in a happy voice. "Everyone withdrew to the palace! They only left the two we've already dealt with. Ram'a waiting outside with horses saddled."

Alt'ar nodded, not even gesturing how pleased he was at the news. He understood why Ram'a sent the boy instead of showing up alone. The Noai'dirian was one of the finest warriors in stealth combat. He was great with both a saber and a shortbow, although he preferred to fight with a knife.

"So, it would be best if we left immediately," he said, then, looking at Drasan eloquently, he added, "Before his Majesty has changed his mind and sent more people here."

The half-dragon decided it would be wiser to ignore the remark, especially with the thirty eyes watching him closely. Alt'ar's assassins had not only the advantage of numbers, but also the support of a lurking witch. So, they felt much more confident than he did.

Looking at him, Prince of the Underworld had a stronger and stronger impression that he saw himself from several decades ago, even before he became a werewolf. Then he too believed that he would conquer the whole world. And then everything changed.

He knew well how it would end for the pampered prince. He certainly had no idea what he had gotten himself into. He may have had the will to rule, but he lacked experience. There was a lot to learn, and the Blood Hunter lacked the patience to be a good teacher.

The low growl of the wolf crouching at his feet snapped him out of his thoughts, and a sudden gust of magic lifted all the hair on his neck. Rodian took a deep breath. She felt the touch too, not much stronger than the brush. Everyone shuddered violently. The strangest reaction turned out to be Drasan's.

He fell to his knees, grasping his temples. It was as if he heard a very high-pitched noise or...

"Rodian." Alt'ar instinctively looked at the witch, and she shook her head no.

The protective shield surrounding the site remained intact. Except that the half-dragon's demeanor made it clear that someone was attacking his consciousness. He recognized it by observing his frozen face, squeezed eyelids and tight jaws.

None of his companions knew what was going on. They were in the same daze as everyone else.

Neila was the first to find the courage and knelt down in front of him, trying to take his hand in hers. He broke free from her, snarling furiously. His eyes flushed with blood, and saliva seeped from between the tightly clenched jaws. He looked terrifying.

"Rodian," the werewolf repeated, more sharply this time. "He's about to change, and then he'll kill us all."

The witch awoke from lethargy. She looked first at her leader, then shifted her gaze to the kneeling half-dragon. She walked towards him fearlessly, slowly forming a ball of frosty air in her hands. She knew it was the only way to fire a fiery attack.

"Stand back," she said to Neila, her eyes never leaving Drasan.

The girl did not immediately obey the order. This moment was enough for the prince, he pushed her aside and, with a roar of rage, rushed towards the red-haired, standing still. In a fit of panic, she threw an ice ball at him. She missed, which made him even more furious.

Alt'ar made an instant assessment of the situation. He jumped towards the young man and struck him on the jaw with his fist. The momentum of the blow knocked the other man off his feet without knocking him unconscious. The werewolf had to bet on the advantage of strength. He rolled over to face his opponent, then took a swing and struck him in the face, swinging his nose in the process. Drasan was covered in blood, but instead of his expected weakness, it made him even more angry. Moreover, his wounds healed in no time. They could hit each other for hours. This embarrassment was interrupted by the witch by joining the fight. She formed another ball and threw it at the prince. She managed to hit his temple, knocking him unconscious.

The Guild leader wasted no time. When one of his men handed him a coil of rope, he immediately set about restraining Drasan's wrists and ankles.

"What are you doing?" The mercenary asked him indignantly.

"What is needed," he said, continuing his work.

"You don't have to kill him," Velwel replied, pushing aside the terrified Neila.

"I do not intend to..." His further words were drowned out by a loud growl. It's hard to believe that a similar sound can come out of a human throat.

Alt'ar decided to act. He did not want to kill, but he had to knock the prince unconscious again before he unleashed the destructive energy of fire. Using his superhuman strength with panache, he struck him on the temple with his fist. He managed to gain some time with this.

"Your turn," he gasped as he addressed Rodian. "Put the bastard to sleep. I must have time to think."

The witch nodded silently. She rolled up her sleeves and was about to start, but then the black-haired girl once again proved her loyalty, covering the half-dragon.

"Do you realize it's dangerous?" Rodian asked, giving her a disgusted look. "He's not exactly human, if he wakes up, he'll tear us all apart."

"He won't hurt me," the girl said calmly. "He has had many opportunities and I know he will not. Even now."

"A spell has been put on him, you dumb idiot!" Rodian shouted, losing all her composure. "It's a miracle that he resisted him at all, because the one who was throwing him wished us death. However, it awakened in him the need for protection, which in turn put aside all human emotions. He's dangerous to all of us now."

Neila wasn't going to move, so Velwel walked over and gently pulled her aside.

"Rodian," Alt'ar growled, flexing his muscles as the half-dragon's heat began to beat. His skin was almost burning. "That son of a bitch is about to change."

The witch began to chant the spell's formula softly, trying not to take her eyes off the half-dragon's tense and distorted face. As the sleep spell began to work, his muscles gradually relaxed, his body went limp. Finally, Duke of Underworld loosened his grip and slowly backed away for Rodian to complete the incantation.

The assassins stood as far as possible from the sleeping young man, though now he looked quite innocent. To be sure, the redhead repeated the formula and surrounded him in a protective circle resembling a colorless dome.

Alt'ar smiled bitterly and said:

"Well, then we are totally blown away."

"That's not true," Neila muttered. "He'll get over it. It won't stay like this forever."

"We don't know the power of the charm cast on him, and therefore we don't know what the consequences are for someone who is not human," replied Rodian.

"There is someone who will know what to do," Velwel said, astonishing everyone. "But getting him here is practically impossible."

"You mean Gaenor?" Neila asked incredulously.

"This is the only representative of his species known to us. Why should we not use his help?" Replied the young man.

"Because he doesn't like Drasan too much," the mercenary retorted.

Alt'ar didn't speak. He didn't like bringing another reptile here, seeing the slim chance of another half-dragon incapacitation. He nodded, expressing his approval.

"If he can help, all you have to do is mentally contact him," said Rodian. "He doesn't have to come here in person, he can direct me."

"How?" Neila and Velwel asked simultaneously.

The witch smiled slightly.

"If you have magical abilities yourself, in extreme cases it may happen that someone else takes control of your body for a while. However, hosting an alien in your mind is not pleasant and carries the risk of it discovering too much. Therefore, few of the talented decide to do so. I am ready to allow it on one condition - you leave us alone."

"Forget it," Neila snapped. "I don't believe in your pure intentions."

"Believe me or not, this combination requires full focus. Nothing can distract me during this time, because it involves a serious risk." She said, not losing her composure. "Besides, it's very intimate and I'm not sure if it will work out for sure."

"There has to be another way," the mercenary did not give up.

"Oh, there are plenty of them," Alt'ar said sarcastically. "You can cut his throat, cut his heart, or chop off his head. A lot of choices, unless we intend to keep him alive. There are no other options, you have to obey Rodian."

This comment finally shut the girl's mouth. The witch slowly and carefully walked around the slightly shimmering dome to make sure that the half-dragon was still deeply asleep, then walked over to Velwel.

"I need your help," she said. Wasting no time to explain further, she took his hands in hers and closed her eyes.

For a moment she searched persistently, skimming through hundreds of minds until she hit the barrier. Then she opened her eyes, she was unwaveringly certain that she had found the dragon.

"He's not admitting me," she choked, releasing Velwel's hands and rubbing her temples.

Velwel scratched his head in confusion.

"Or maybe let one of us speak," he suggested. "He should recognize a known voice."

Surprised by the proposal, the woman grabbed his hands again.

"Close your eyes," she ordered calmly, then did it herself. "Relax. Let me lead you," she added.

The young assassin did not follow her orders immediately, because it's hard to relax when you feel someone's presence in your head. In the end, he managed to calm down as much as the task set before him required.

Listen to my voice. Focus on it. – this time Rodian's voice echoed directly in his head. – You should feel the barrier by now.

According to her words, the killer's mind hit something like a wall. As irrational as it seemed, he tried to get through it. To his surprise, the obstacle disappeared and he found himself in something like a huge room with no windows or doors.

Who you are and what you want? – thundered in his thoughts a voice he recognized easily.

Velwel gathered himself to put his thoughts into words.

I am Velwel, friend of Drasan. He's in trouble himself. Your help is needed.

The dragon was silent for a long time.

How can I help you while you are in a city ruled by our enemies?

I'll talk to him – the witch's voice rang out.

Who is there?! – the angry dragon growled.

I am Rodian, and who I am does not matter now. We have a problem with your kinsman here. I know you cannot come in person, but there is a way for you to guide me – she took a deep breath. – I want you to take over my body temporarily.

For a while, nothing happened. Rodian released Velwel's hands, then stepped back a few steps. Suddenly a shiver ran through her, and a painful scream erupted from her throat. Alt'ar sprang to the woman, ready to intervene, but the scream ceased as suddenly as it had begun. She opened her eyes, now they looked like a reptile's eyes the color of poisonous yellow.

"How dare you disturb my peace?" The voice coming from Rodian's throat didn't sound like hers at all.

"We would not have summoned you if it had not been necessary," Alt'ar said, stepping forward.

Gaenor's yellow eyes focused on him for a moment, and his nostrils twitched as the reptile in the witch's body tried to find out who he was dealing with.

"You're a werewolf," he said disgustedly.

"Who I am doesn't matter now. I was told only you can help. We seem to have a little problem with one of your species here." He nodded at the half-dragon in magical sleep.

Rodian's lips curled into a kind of crooked smile as Gaenor led her way slowly around the protective sphere. She even dared to brush her fingers lightly.

"Why did you put him to sleep?" He asked softly.

"He has become unpredictable under the spell someone tried to cast on him," Neila explained quietly. "One moment he was acting normally, and the next he was furious. He would have killed us if we hadn't overpowered him."

"It's all clear then," the dragon muttered to himself, then added. "You have to wake him up."

"Just like that?" Velwel asked incredulously.

"Just like that," Gaenor repeated. "Until we do, we won't know if he managed to counter the spell's effects. If it turned out to be as strong as you claim it could unleash primal wild instincts. In such a state, the dragon loses itself, it is then aggressive and unpredictable. He will defend himself against anyone who poses a potential threat to his life."

"So, he's now..." The rest of the sentence didn't want to pass the terrified Neila down her throat.

"...beast, monster, animal," Gaenor finished after her, his eyes glittering. "With age, we learn to control it to behave in a more civilized way. But a very young dragon, when guided solely by instinct, poses a serious threat to anyone it deems an enemy at that time." He looked eloquently at Alt'ar. "In fact, waking him up while he is in this state is a very big risk. He could kill us in the midst of the transformation itself."

"Then why do you want to do this?" Alt'ar asked, separating the dragon from the dome with the sleeping Drasan.

"Because only I can stop him from annihilating you all," replied the dragon, tilting his head slightly to meet the werewolf's blazing eyes.

"Even in this body?" The assassin asked incredulously.

"The body is irrelevant, it is the strength of the mind that counts, not the muscles," Gaenor replied calmly.

"But how are you going to wake him up without Rodian's help?" Velwel asked reasonably.

"It's easy. The dreamlike charm works on the principle of a trance, so taking it off is a matter of skillfully waking up from it. However, I will not be able to do it myself, I need the help of the only person whom this audacious reptile will not kill immediately." He looked at Neila eloquently.

"Me?" The surprised girl took a step back.

"Ironically, only you can get near him," said the dragon with a wry smile.

"Are you crazy?!" She growled, crossing her arms over her chest. "Only a complete lunatic would decide to do it."

Gaenor flesh Rodian smiled wickedly.

"Whatever you want. Of course, there is another, more violent way that will not require your intervention," he said casually, looking the girl straight in the eye. Watching the fear clearly drawn in them, he already knew: he had hit a weak point.

Now Alt'ar was also watching closely the mercenary's reaction, now pale. He felt her heart pounding, a sign of an outburst of emotion. Apparently, Drasan is not indifferent to her, moreover, the reptile temporarily residing in the witch's body knew it perfectly well.

"You want to kill him?" She asked in a slightly trembling voice.

"Yes," replied the dragon without hesitating for a moment. "But not here, not now, and certainly not like that."

"So, what do you expect from me?" The moment of hesitation passed and Neila resumed her mask of "strong and independent".

"You just have to go over and wake him up," Gaenor explained. "If my observations are correct, it won't hurt you. If not, we're always around to stop him in time."

"What if you're wrong?" this question in turn was asked by Velwel. The young man, who looked rather slack at first, turned out to be much sharper than anyone expected.

"I don't think so," Gaenor snorted, the witch's beautiful face contorted with contemptuous expression.

Alt'ar stood and looked at the three of them, who silently dagger their eyes. He decided not to interfere until the need arose. But he saw Neila cast hesitant glances at the sleeping half-dragon. Something about her was struggling to get a say. Finally, slowly but firmly, she made her way towards the magic dome. Strangely enough, the shield let her pass.

The girl knelt beside Drasan, bent down, and placed a gentle but firm kiss on his pursed lips. For a moment, all those present froze in anticipation. Suddenly, Neila stepped back as if burned. Before the others realized what was causing it, the werewolf's sharp eyes noticed the movement. Just a twitching of the eyelids and a slight grimace on the so far immobile face... and then everything happened in a flash.

Drasan's eyelids opened so suddenly and unexpectedly that everyone flinched. They were still nothing human, and they shone like two oil lamps. It was as if there was a flame of unbridled anger behind them. Like a wild animal trapped in a cage, it looked at everyone present until it came across... Neila.

The mercenary was a step away from him in a slight kneeling, ready to flee immediately. As he stuck those terrifying reptilian eyes into her, she froze, unable to move or even breathe deeply. She felt like a doe surrounded by a hungry wolf.

The half-dragon stood up. He did it in one move, which scared her even more. In her mind's eye, she saw the muscles under her clothes flex. Perhaps he was getting ready to jump straight at the victim paralyzed by fear. He did something that she completely did not expect. He took a step and knelt beside her. Now his face was dangerously close to hers. She just didn't know why her stupid heart started pounding furiously. She looked straight into the reptilian eyes, devoid of that anger and wildness. There was warmth and something else. Like last time, she was absolutely sure that she would not hurt her.

In some strange and incomprehensible way, even as he turned from human to a formidable beast, he still felt the need to protect her. She couldn't deny that it flattered her.

She smiled, unsure if she could move. His face, however, remained the same stone, only a blind glow lurked somewhere in the depths. She decided to seize the moment. She leaned down and kissed him, and he returned the kiss with equal enthusiasm, entwining his hands into her hair.

Now is the time to act. Both Alt'ar and Gaenor, with the terrified Velwel behind them, started towards the protective dome. Before they took the first few steps, around the half-dragon and the girl, a ring of flames fired from the ground, separating them from the others.

***

As the flames flared around them, a startled Neila moved away from Drasan. He wouldn't let her get up; his strong arms wrapped around her waist like iron vices. She had no idea what to do in such a situation, so just in case she did not move. Instead, she tried to get his gaze back on her. In vain.

The half-dragon concentrated on holding the fiery barrier. His eyes shone like fireballs. She had to distract him, the problem was, she didn't know how. She shivered. She felt himself flinch, apparently responding to her physical discomfort.

Maybe that was it.

"I'm scared," she whispered softly.

At first, he did not react to her words. I think he let them go deafening. Only after a moment did he turn, focusing his eyes on her again. If only in this look, she had found any signs of humanity, perhaps she would have known what to do. Unfortunately, what temporarily took over his "I" turned out to be very far from what she knew. She couldn't predict how she would react to the sudden attack from her, but she had no choice.

She threw her full weight at him.

***

If Alt'ar had not seen it with his own eyes, he would never have believed it. Here is the curtain of flames - so far successfully separating both him and others from the half-dragon and mercenary - has fallen rapidly. It turned out that the frail girl attacked the prince and began furiously punching him. She didn't bother that it didn't make the slightest impression on him. Just like in a frenzy, she attacked his body with more and more stubbornness.

The werewolf decided to seize the moment and began to slowly creep towards the pair. Perhaps he could have gotten close enough to attack himself, had it not been for the dragon...

Gaenor, who apparently had a private plan, strode straight to the point where the one-sided struggle was underway. Drasan did not actually defend himself against the attack of the slender girl. He lay under her, seemingly completely motionless, only his eyes moved, following the approaching enemies.

Suddenly he pushed off the mercenary of himself and sprang to his feet. Two fireballs instantly materialized in his hands. He seemed ready to attack.

Alt'ar stopped and gestured for Gaenor to do the same. He didn't want to expose Rodian to being burned alive. The dragon who had complete control of her body for the time being did not obey. His yellow eyes followed his brother's movements stoically. He was not afraid of him. He seemed confident.

He was not going to use physical strength at all. Continuing to move forward, he fixed his piercing gaze on his younger relative. At first, Alt'ar had the strange feeling that the dragon intended to set him on fire.

Nothing like that happened.

The silent struggle of the will continued. Only one whose mind proves to be strong enough to endure physical pain could win. It grew with every moment of resistance.

Suddenly a spasm ran through the half-dragon's body, and something between a scream and a screech escaped its throat. The fire quickly died out as the young man made a desperate attempt to protect his mind from the intruder.

In this one, Gaenor turned out to be not only better, but also stronger. Drasan was clearly losing his strength, which was mainly due to the massive dose of pain flowing through his body. Neila watched in horror, not in doubt that it was a real pleasure for the dragon to torment the young man. Though she didn't like the method at all, she had to admit that it worked.

As the prince's resistance weakened, his eyes regained their human appearance. Everyone felt a sigh of relief. Only the werewolf remained alert and tense. Fortunately, his interference turned out to be unnecessary, as suddenly the half-dragon fell to his knees. Blood was oozing from his nose, but he seemed to be himself again.

Neila was the first to approach him. She might have left that privilege to Gaenor, but Drasan now looked like a helpless child who had no idea what had happened. He needed her.

"Are you okay?" She asked softly.

He looked up at her.

"What happened?" He asked. His voice was slightly hoarse. Apparently, he didn't remember anything.

"You're totally crazy, man!" Emboldened Velvel came closer.

Drasan looked from Neila's face to him. He seemed to be trying to remember recent events.

"Don't treat him like a baby. From the point of view of my species, he is a fully mature male," Gaenor, who was still visiting in the body of the red-haired witch, looked at Drasan, his head tilted slightly. "It happened the second time in a short period of time, and in both cases..." he shifted his gaze to Neila, "...she was present," he added after a short thought.

The girl met the gaze of the yellow eyes.

"And it's my fault again," she snapped. "The cause of all troubles! And you might not have thought that it was your old friend's doing!"

"Shut up!" Gaenor hissed. The memory of Dhalia seemed to upset him. "Magic doesn't work on him. Most spells he fought easily, others after a while. I don't quite know how he does it, but I don't think there is anyone who can threaten him with magic. It seems logical, then, that one of you must have provoked him after defeating the spell."

"You say it as if I'm the only one responsible for this mess," the mercenary retorted.

"It's possible," muttered the dragon.

"Wait a minute," Drasan stepped behind Neila, staring straight into the dragon's yellow eyes. "What are you two talking about?!"

There was no doubt that the half-dragon was unaware of what he was up to when he lost control. The mercenary, somewhat emboldened by his presence behind her back, boldly stepped forward.

"I think you should explain everything to him now."

"That won't be necessary," Gaenor said calmly. As soon as he said it, the violent spasm rocked his body again. She closed her eyes and clenched her jaw, not suppressing the groan of pain that escaped her throat moments later. The witch stumbled as if drunk, and she would have probably fallen if Alt'ar hadn't grabbed her in half and sat her down on one of the surviving armchairs. Then she blinked her eyelids and opened her eyes wide, which in the meantime had regained their natural green color. She looked at Neila, and then at Drasan, standing one step behind her. A faint smile touched her pale lips.

"So, it worked," she said, then passed out.

CHAPTER 3

Many days passed before the first human settlements replaced the universal whiteness of the Antuan plains. Most were fenced off by a tall, thick log palisade, guarded by surly mercenaries. These, in turn, turned out to be extremely reluctant to trust the two elves. On this side of the peninsula, people were not so afraid of witchcraft as they simply distrusted all representatives of the magical races. Incidents in the neighboring kingdom of Sheardon strengthened the belief that it is best to avoid all kinds of aliens practicing this art.

As a high-ranking Master, Ashkan was able to tame the three elements. It belonged to water, earth and air. Its natural feature turned out to be the ability to heal any wounds. Elemental magic, unlike blood magic, also known as the black arts, was based on extremely simple principles. It was enough to find the source and draw as much power from it as necessary when, for example, you need to warm yourself. Unfortunately, it also had limitations: it was impossible to create anything material with it. Water could be summoned, but not a vessel in which it could be stored. Usually, mages preferred to use this type of witchcraft only. Mainly out of fear of the consequences that awaited those who used black art, even if they acted in good faith.

Having lost its title and rank, the unicorn did not break the law. Still, he felt disgusted with himself as he reached for blood magic. His veins were filled with raw energy, so all he had to do was take advantage of it, unleashing incredible power. He had to do so, for it turned out that none of the taverns he passed were going to host either him or Nolan. He himself could have survived for days without food, but his companion as a half-human did not have this privilege. The prohibition on killing living creatures did not allow them to hunt any animal. It was necessary to be content with what Ashkan created with the help of black art, i.e. a loaf of bread, three apples and a handful of wild raspberries.

This modest meal was enough for Nolan to rejuvenate his strength, weakened by the frost. In a valley of the elves that were magically sheltered from winter, he had never experienced it. So he didn't know how to protect himself from it, which resulted in a few frostbitten fingers. The shoes made of thin material did not protect him from the cold. Despite the inconvenience of the temperature, the half-elf did not manage to lose his serenity, only occasionally stared intently at the sky. Perhaps he expected Drasan to come back for them. Knowing its pupil and the best student at the same time, the unicorn was aware that this would not happen.

Finally, when they stopped one day to give the horses a break, Nolan couldn't hold back and asked a question that had clearly haunted him for a long time:

"Drasan won't come back for us, will he?"

To Ashkan, the answer seemed clear. He personally ordered the former apprentice to fly as far away from Michandrell as possible. If he had stayed there, he would have surely died. Of course, then he was not sure if he would listen to it at all, because too much hot blood was flowing in his veins. Only when the half-dragon flew away did he understand that this time he had managed to dissuade him from taking revenge on the pale-faced torturers.

Ashkan, like many of his fellows, realized that for a dragon, food plays a key role in life. Therefore, a hungry dragon, like a hungry werewolf, easily lost control. Drasan's severe training in his youth has helped somewhat. The unicorn used the method of its own race here. It was based on the law of survival. The grown foals were left alone in the mountains. This was to check whether they would survive the final transformation into an adult individual. Such a youngster had to learn not only how to control the magic flowing through his body, but also how to survive in rigorous conditions without the help of his mother or a master. Left in the depths of the Wolf's Forest, the only twelve-year-old prince received only a knife. It was to serve as a tool for him and for possible defense against wild animals. Harnessing magic and controlling it was also essential.

It was this training that made him survive in both the Kahaer dungeons and the Ertan Tower. None of these prisons had managed to drive him insane because he had learned to contain his lust, thirst, and hunger. This also proved to be the key reason why Dhalia so desired to destroy him. He alone withstood the might of her charm. As a witch, she then suffered a disastrous defeat. Ashkan taught him to look deeper, beyond the deceptive illusion of what the eyes can see.

The unicorn knew perfectly well what this maddened hag was capable of. In the old days it was she who contributed to the fall of one of the greatest kingdoms, the last reminder of the times when dragons ruled the peninsula. When she poisoned Gaenor's mind, the ancient race ultimately cursed the land. All her wealth turned to dust in a few years. All the great cities have fallen, and the people have either starved to death or fled far from the cursed earth. Only the palace of Illariss remained, and it was on its ruins that the dragon and his bride built the Kahaer - which literally translated the language of the ancient runes means "lamentation."

For hundreds of years, the people of Lineland had been able to enjoy peace, until the vision the witch had in her dream. The vision of a child with a dragon heart, able to overcome it. The first half-blood dragon to start a new royal lineage.

Ashkan was not going to explain this to Nolan. Not now, with hope for a better tomorrow still lingering in his heart. Instead, he raised a warm smile on his face and said:

"I think we'll see him soon."

He told the first lie in his life, but he had no choice. In fact, they might not wait for the next sunrise. Especially if the witch's spies already know of their presence near the borders of Riden.

***

Drasan paced the room back and forth, fists clenched in helpless rage. Alt'ar locked all three of them here and went to confer with the people. Of course, such a door would not be an obstacle for the half-dragon if Rodian had not cast a series of spells on him. Now he wouldn't scratch them even if he hit the wood with all his might. The room in which they were locked turned out to be something like a vault. Huge iron crates occupied most of them. Neila sat in one of them, staring blankly at her shoes. Velwel was leaning against the wall next to a huge mirror in a gilded frame. Nobody wanted to meet his eyes.

He wasn't surprised by them. Having lost control, he could kill everyone. The power of the spell Dhalia was trying to cast on him must have been considerable for he managed to defend himself from her by relying on his animal half. According to Rodian and Alt'ar's stories, Neila was the only person he allowed to approach him. At the moment he didn't want to think about what that might mean. Especially since they had much more trouble on their minds.

After his performance, more soldiers appeared, patrolling all the streets near the inn. They could have been hiding in this basement for months, as they had plenty of supplies. Drasan doubted that Alt'ar had the patience to bear him that long. In addition, he was concerned about Alder. Were his wits enough to hide from the guards? Or maybe they have already captured him and interrogated him? He wished he could mentally contact him. The risk of overhearing such a conversation was too great now.

All this made him feel the true burden of leadership for the first time. He had no one to help him out. His foster mother died trying to protect him, and his current mentor and guardian was too far away to offer advice and help. He had to deal with himself. Usually, those he loved died as soon as they got in Dhalia's path. He couldn't let any of his people fall into her clutches. Turning to Alt'ar for help, he made a decision. He revealed himself. The witch knew he was here and waited patiently for his move. She was playing a sophisticated game in which the stakes were the lives of all those determined to help him. He was treading on boggy ground. One false move, and everything he has fought for will turn to dust.

"What are you going to do?" Velwel's calm voice snapped him out of his gloomy thoughts and recalled him to reality.

"I don't know yet," he said, not looking at his friend.

"We're like trapped rats," Neila muttered, not looking at either of them. "We can't get out of here; they've got us like a fork. We need some sort of plan of action before Alt'ar finally decides it's better to trade us in and get out of trouble."

"He will not," said the prince calmly. "I know this type of people, it's about his honor. He won't hand us over to Dhalia, he'd rather kill us himself. However, it is not just his skin that is at stake, which means that he cannot make decisions too hastily."

"Our presence did not make it easier for him, and that's why he chose to lock us up here," Velwel said, still calmly, though without a bit of his usual serenity. "Making a decision in such a situation is choosing on whose side you are. Theoretically, he could hand us over to the guards, but since he has not yet done so, it means that he has already made this decision. He only hesitates to confess the truth. He is not going to bow his neck to you or acknowledge your leadership."

"I don't expect that of him," growled Drasan. His control hung by a thread.

"Then tell him." Neila stood up abruptly, and though she was shorter than a half-dragon, she somehow towered above him this time. "Stand in front of his Wolf Highness and say that you do not want him to crawl in front of you. Though I don't think it will help you to reach an agreement. When you face each other, you look as if one is about to throw himself down the other's throat. Do you want an alliance? So stop playing dominance games." Saying that, she stabbed the young man in the chest. "If we're going to get out of this alive, you've got to do something about it, because you put us in this mess."

She was right. He should do something about it, because he was the only one responsible for what happened.

"You know that the only way to keep our heads would be by my voluntary surrender to Dhalia." He said gloomily. "Then you would have enough time to escape..."

"Don't even think about it," Neila said. "We don't all stick our neck out for you here, just to let you hand yourself over to this bitch voluntarily."

"Neila is right," Velwel said. "That's no solution."

The lock clicked in response to his words, and Rodian stood in the open door.

"Come on," she said, handing them back the weapons.

Drasan took his sword and threw it over his back. The fact that the Alt'ar had decided to hand them over the weapons was something of a trust. It didn't mean he had decided about an alliance, but it was a good sign in itself.

They followed the witch, which led them to an underground chamber, now partially demolished by the half-dragon. A few of the precious furniture splintered, a few were burned, and rugs and skins were rolled up against the wall. Apparently, the Guild leader didn't want anything else in his collection to suffer.

Most of the assassins stood or sat on the surviving chairs and armrests. They all looked at the three with hostile eyes, and many seemed ready to fight. Each of them had more than one corpse, so a few more made no difference. It only took one nod from Alt'ar for them to retreat to the side, making way for Drasan and his companions. Rodian stood right behind the back of the high chair occupied by her boss. The half-dragon stopped in the center of the room, with a couple of assassins behind him.

A vein in his temple pulsed at the sight of him, and his hands tightened on the armrests of the chair. The face was still like a stone mask, impossible to read.

"I have made up my mind," he said shortly. He got up and walked slowly towards Drasan. "Though you caused me trouble, I must admit that you also made quite an impression. We are both predators, so let's talk as one predator to the other. We will go hunting together to kill the witch and her helper. When that happens, however, everyone will go their own way, and never again will get in the other's way. Remember, if I must kill you, I won't hesitate. Our alliance is valid only until we defeat our common enemies. I think you will also like this arrangement."

The prince smiled, then shook Alt'ar's hand tightly.

"So, this is only a temporary truce," he said rather than asked, looking into the Guild leader's blue eyes.

"It's the only thing that makes sense," said the werewolf. "Friendship between us has no right to exist."

"I never counted on your friendship," the half-dragon replied. "I just thought you wouldn't like the rule of a ruthless pair of despots either."

"I never paid attention to governments. Demiworld Prince snorted dismissively. "The bias against my race won't just go away. Werewolves are monsters, and nothing will change that."

"Then why did you decide to make an alliance?" Asked the prince, frowning.

"I'm not doing it for myself, but for my people," the assassin replied. "Mercenaries will always be needed. Under Bal'zar, the military began to hunt us like rabid dogs. Within a month, this crowned brat had killed fifteen of mine, and the other five, using blackmail and torture, forced him into the army. We crumble because they have the advantage and are everywhere. We can hide or fight, but the latter option is definitely more my style."

Drasan looked gloomy. He still wasn't sure if or how much he could trust the Guild leader. If he masked his second nature so well for so many years, he could turn out to be a gifted actor. The question was: what would he do if he led him out of the way? At the same time, he knew perfectly well that he had to choose his words not only carefully but also with caution. He had no doubt that Alt'ar would have killed him without hesitation if he had accused him of lying.

"What's your plan?" He asked finally, trying to keep his face straight.

The Bloody Hunter laughed.

"I assumed that when you came here you knew exactly what you were doing," he said, rising from his seat and taking a few steps towards the prince. "As you can see, I was wrong."

"This is your city," Drasan replied, keeping his calm composure. "I thought that since we agreed on the terms of our alliance..."

"Then I will do your every whim... Your Highness," Alt'ar's eyes glowed dangerously.

"Boys," seeing what was going to happen, Rodian stepped between the two men. "If you want to play together, you have to stick to the established rules. First, no magic, she shot a scolding glance at the half-dragon, whose body was unknowingly covered in flames, and second, behave in a civilized manner, that is, no growling at each other."

Alt'ar looked at her, then gave the prince a murderous glare.

"I'm only willing to agree to it on the condition that this brat stops acting as if we were his property," he said, keeping his voice under control.

Drasan took control of his emotions by an enormous effort of his will. He knew it wouldn't be easy for him to keep control in the presence of a werewolf. Especially since he didn't seem thrilled with the prospect of becoming his ally. Unfortunately, if they wanted to avoid capture, they had to cooperate.

"Forgive Alt'ar," he said, lowering his gaze. "I know I can't order you. So what are you proposing? I would love to hear what you have to say because, as you have pointed out, we are in your territory."

The Guild leader looked at him, then gestured for one of his men to come to him. A youngster with pale, almost white hair and small black eyes resembling a rat. He approached him with a vigorous step with his chest proudly stuck out.

"Jero, tell me how many guards are patrolling the area of the inn?" The werewolf asked.

"Two are hanging around the entrance, two in the back. The other four or five are at the end of the street leading to the market square." The boy recited, very pleased with himself.

"So, there will be no more than ten of them in total," Alt'ar said, not addressing anyone in particular. "It looks like the king set an ambush on the assumption that I will let myself be approached."

"So, let's give them exactly what they're looking for," said Rodian, smiling slightly. "If a dragon appeared in the area..."

"The king's soldiers would have too much on their heads to bother us..." finished the werewolf, glancing at the half-dragon. "It could work."

As he stood to the side and listened, Drasan felt more and more insecure. Yes, he was partly to blame for the fact that the area was swarming with armed men. He assumed that as leader of the Guild, Alt'ar had an escape plan ready for the occasion. Unfortunately, he was wrong. By agreeing to the conditions set for him, he did not know that he would have to play the role of bait. What if the werewolf's idea gets stuck in the head and the soldiers don't fall for it? Anyway, he was risking not only his freedom but also the lives of his friends.

Alt'ar, meanwhile, had made his decision, and was apparently getting ready to lay out the details of his plan.

"So, we have two options," he said calmly. "Either I will hand you over to the soldiers and demand inviolability in return," he smiled broadly enough to show his fangs, "or you do exactly what I tell you to do."

"Looks like I have no choice," the half-dragon grumbled.

"Oh, yes," said Rodian, giving him a long look. "You can accept our plan or not. However, know that every decision you make will have consequences not only for you."

"So, what is your plan?" Drasan asked, ignoring Neila's loud grunt.

"If you changed form and flew over the city, you'd distract the guards," Rodian hastened to explain. "As far as I know, no arrow will penetrate your skin. You can maul a few soldiers and fly over the walls, making a little fuss. It would distract us and allow us to reach the tunnel."

"What tunnel?" The half-dragon asked, frowning.

"There are several tunnels underneath the city leading beyond the walls," Alt'ar explained. "In the old days, these were the only options in the event of a siege of the city. Some of them have collapsed, but I know one used by smugglers. It is two streets away on the west side of the city. So someone has to distract the guards long enough for us to slip past."

Drasan's eyes narrowed. Alt'ar and Rodian's plan was simple, but it ran the risk of failure. First, Dhalia might not have fallen for this clever ruse. Capturing his comrades was better. Either way, she had him in hand.

Before he could open his mouth to speak, Neila did it for him.

"This is your wonderful plan?" She asked, not hiding her irritation. "Save your own skin at the expense of someone else's?"

Drasan grabbed her arm, but she broke free and took two steps forward towards Alt'ar. She looked him straight in the eyes. She obviously had no idea she was challenging him on his own territory in this way.

"This situation is entirely his fault," the werewolf growled, baring his teeth. His blue irises turned to ruby ones. One of the arms was covered with white and gray fur and the nails turned into long black claws.

The half-dragon has once again proved that he can pride himself on superhuman reflexes. Before the huge paw, armed with razor-sharp claws, stripped the girl's head, he pulled her to the floor, covering her with his body. Surprised, Neila looked from him to the werewolf, panting loudly. Apparently, it was only now that she realized that she had almost lost her life because of her bad tongue.

The prince helped her to her feet and placed her behind his back.

"I'll agree on one condition," he said emphatically. "No one of my companions should have a hair off their head."

"I guess you mean mostly that saucy bitch," Alt'ar growled, watching his hand slowly revert to human appearance. Few of the werewolves had the control to do only a partial transformation.

This, in turn, not only impressed Drasan, but also made him think. He had never tried it himself. His transformations happened spontaneously and regardless of the phases of the moon. He was born half a dragon, and when the time was right, the transformation was entirely natural. It did not cause any pain or discomfort in any way. It felt like a snake shedding its skin to thread itself with a new one. It used up a lot of energy, however, so that he felt an irresistible urge to feed himself afterwards. Even though it happened that he also wanted ... carnal pleasures. Being a prince, he treated sex as a kind of active and informal entertainment. This made him a frequent visitor to brothels and taverns. Using his beauty and position, he easily won the hearts of girls.

Now something has changed. The stay in Kahaer made him realize that beauty is a powerful weapon. Dhalia turned out to be as beautiful as evil, perverse and even cruel. So, he stopped missing the female body... for a while. When he met Neila on his way, and this one turned out to be different. He was irritated at first, used to having women worship him.

The mercenary was extremely resistant. He came out of his skin to please her; she constantly ignored his advances. At first, he thought it was because of the scars that disfigured him, but after noticing the way he was looking at him several times, he quickly abandoned the absurd idea. The problem was probably his somewhat possessive demeanor. Unfortunately, he couldn't help but be angry at the mere thought of someone even scratching her. In some strange and not fully understood way, she has now become the center of his world.

Perhaps under different circumstances, he would have ignored the fact that Alt'ar was just trying to kill a woman he felt something for. Before he knew it, he was already an inch from the werewolf, covered in a halo of flames, a soft, malevolent hiss coming from the depths of his throat. The Guild leader jumped back, snarling and baring his fangs. They would both be at each other's throats, but Rodian again acted as peacemaker. Without fear, she stepped between them, creating a magical barrier that protected her from the heat emanating from the half-dragon.

"You are simply unbearable." She said, slowly drawing her words. "Then why don't you postpone this killing of each other to some other date, because one more explosion like this could bring all the mages under Bal'zar on our heads."

She was right. Drasan knew he had to yield. Otherwise, there is bound to be a bloodshed that will shatter their already fragile alliance. With an enormous effort of his will, he controlled his anger and fell to his knees, assuming a submissive attitude in the world of predators. Half-transformed Alt'ar walked towards him, growling softly. One of his massive paws' rests on his neck. His teeth were still bared, and his eyes glowed red.

The Guild leader calmed down slowly. You could tell by the muscles in his hands, now like a bear's paws. They loosened until he finally released his grip and allowed Drasan to stand up. The half-dragon chose not to look up until Alt'ar was fully human again. As long as the wolf lurked on the surface, it would be unwise to do it too fast. Fortunately, neither Neila nor Velwel thought of taking up a weapon.

The mercenary barely realized that she had miraculously escaped death. All she could understand was the sight of a giant werewolf resting a paw on the half-dragon's neck. He could bet it was an unusual sight for her. Especially that in dragon form it is much larger than Alt'ar. He didn't want to risk a fight.

He got up and had Neila by his side. The expression on her face made it clear that she had something to say to him.

"We need to talk to you in private," she said in a voice that could not bear any objection, thus confirming his assumptions.

Drasan cast an uncertain glance at Alt'ar, but Alt'ar only shrugged. So he followed the girl to the nearest door. As it turned out, the room was an armory, and it was the best equipped room the prince had ever seen. Under other circumstances, he would have liked to have a close look at the collection here, but not today.

"You're crazy," she growled at the outset. She didn't even bother to lower her voice to a whisper, though she had to be aware that Alt'ar could hear every word. "You entrust your life to this monster? Have you seen what he is capable of? Then imagine it is only a small percentage of his skill. In some circles, they call him "Bloody Hunter" and it is not for nothing that he earned this nickname. He's the most dangerous man on the peninsula, and you've made an alliance with him?"

Drasan stoically listened to the flow of words, then asked without hiding his amusement:

"That's all?"

"This is no time for jokes, you dumb buffoon!" She snapped at him and added sarcastically, "Maybe you need to explain it to you, like a child. Alt'ar is a cold, ruthless murderer who cares only about the interests of his peers. The guild does not accept mediocre thugs into its ranks, it is the most effective and bloody band you have ever seen in your life. There is no room for pity or scruples among them, so if they want to set you up, they will do it without hesitation. You're something of a "security" to them, and in case it gets hot, they'll sell you to Dhalia..."

This time the girl has gone too far. After all, he had grown up from childhood a long time ago and did not need a nanny. If Alt'ar's men turned out to be as good as he bragged, they had a chance, a small one, but it's always better than nothing. He admitted to himself that they needed strategy and armed support from one of the monarchs. A bit of luck and they will manage to stop the doom which will eventually be led by Dhalia and Bal'zar.

"Now you listen," he growled at her. "Maybe the whole campaign does not make sense and we will be annihilated anyway. However, I'm not going to wait idly. As long as I'm alive, I want to at least try to stop it. Until now, I had only been hiding, waiting for her to move. But that's the end of it, because of my passivity she practically wiped Sheardon off the face of the earth. I have their blood on my hands and I can't help it. If Vaya has taught me anything, it is certainly not to "look back." I cannot change the past; I only influence the present. It is for this reason that I am not going to hide anymore. I'm going to show this mad witch that I'm not afraid of her."

"What if you die? After all, you are not unbeaten," Neila whispered.

Drasan took her chin.

"I will not die, I can promise you one thing," he said, stroking her cheek with his thumb. "But when the worst comes to the worst and I am captured, don't try to save me. Run as far as you can. Get on any ship and leave Lineland."

"We will not leave you," the girl replied in a rebellious tone.

The prince laughed bitterly.

"I was expecting such an answer," he said, then became suddenly serious. "So, you must promise me that you will leave without looking back. Dhalia won't kill me; she will turn me into something worse than you can imagine. If she succeeds, I'll be your worst nightmare, okay?" While Neila was still shaking her head, he took her chin again so that she looked straight into his eyes, then whispered fondly, "I know you love me. I also know that you will never admit it. So please do not take unnecessary risks and then I will be calm. But you have to swear it to me."

"I can't," the girl groaned in a tormented voice.

"You have to. That's all I ask," he said firmly, though the sight of her pained face was almost physical in him. "In return, I can promise you that I will not give up so easily. I will fight even when there is no more hope."

"It can kill you?" She said softly.

"If it were possible, I would welcome the Lady of the Dead with open arms," Drasan replied ironically. "Better death than what awaits me at the hands of Dhalia," he added with a crooked smile. "I don't know if you've ever seen what magicians call "rebirth". In practice, it is about slowly destroying the personality of the gifted person. They torture you until you forget who you were. Eventually you turn into a passive puppet. Completely submissive and utterly devoted to whoever broke you. Now do you understand? The magic flowing in my veins made me stronger and more resilient, so even the worst torments will not kill me. They can weaken me, destroy me, but certainly not kill me."

"You speak all this with such calm as if you have already come to terms with your fate," she said.

Drasan smiled slightly.

"No," he replied with daring mock nonchalance. "Not yet."

Neila hesitated for a moment, then she pressed against his chest as he stroked her back. He couldn't afford to show fear. Dhalia's passivity meant that he was preparing something. If she appears in the city, she can fall straight into the trap she has set. After all, the witch turned out to be cunning as a lurking snake and was not to be taken lightly. It only surprised him that Bal'zar had not yet resorted to the help of mages. He could have easily chased them out of here, so why hadn't he?

***

As she walked the enormous marble steps towards the royal chambers, Dhalia had to be very careful. The expensive dress she was wearing was made of body-tight silk and finished with red lace, starting above the knees and ending below the ankles. The dress might not be too comfortable, but it turned out to be worth the effect it produced. She found not a single courtier who did not follow her with greedy eyes. Still, no one dared look her straight in the eye. Everyone, both the servants and the guards, hurried out of her way, not wanting in any way to disturb the sorceress with the status of royal adviser.

As she reached the double dark wood inlaid with gold doors, the guards quickly moved aside to make room for her. She slammed into the royal sleeping chamber. Fortunately, Bal'zar was fully clothed, and moreover, he was not alone. At the sight of her, the two half-naked concubines accompanying him quickly disappeared through the door of the dressing room.

Dhalia didn't care. Rage was driving her.

"Cancel orders!" She screamed from the threshold.

The Ruler brushed invisible dust from his immaculate green tunic. He gave her a long look, which lingered for a long time at the exceptionally plunging cleavage and half-exposed calves.

"I don't want to," he said, calmly lifting her gaze. "I'm going to chase this reptile out from under the stone under which he crawled, disposing of Alt'ar in the process. This way I will kill two birds with one stone."

"It's not that simple," she growled, coming closer. "You think he's a fool and you think he's just going to get you caught. Meanwhile, he was trained by a unicorn and a witch with extraordinary magical abilities. Disregard it and it will tear your heart out of your chest before you can utter the spell."

Bal'zar stood up, his clenched fists showing that Dhalia had said too much.

"You're the one who underestimates me," he said in an angry voice. "You have me for a crowned brat. Meanwhile, it was I who thought about placing a spy in the ranks of the enemy. And no one else, but I found Drasan without difficulty. I almost managed to cast a spell on him! If it weren't for this red-haired Alt'ar whore, he would have succumbed to me!"

Dhalia froze, staring at him wide-eyed. The goddamn shit made her dumbfounded. She had tried to cast any spell on the half-dragon for so long, and nothing, and he almost got it right the first time.

"How?" She gasped, sitting on one of the cushioned chairs.

Bal'zar smiled, then showed her a roll of blood-stained cloth.

"This rag is steeped in his magic." He replied, adding conscientiously, "Your reptile is not careful enough. If he had been, he would have burned anything on which even a drop of his blood fell on him. It seems he forgot the most important rule. You can defend yourself against someone else's power, but not your own."

Dhalia silently took the bloody tunic from him and studied it for a moment. The stains looked old, but she could still feel the magic in them. She had never thought of it, and yet it had seemed so simple. The blood of any magical creature can be used to cast a spell, that was the basis of primordial magic. Of course, under certain conditions.

"How did you get through the barrier?" She asked. More than once she has tried to find Drasan. With no result.

"Just as easy," he replied, smiling slyly. "I just destroyed it, but so that the red-haired bitch would not guess that she was gone. It wasn't easy for me to deceive her, but I did it."

"How?!" A note of uncertainty crept into Dhalia's confident voice. "The barrier protects everyone from outside influences, it is impossible to bypass or break through it."

"It may be difficult, but not impossible. You can remove it and then create a convincing illusion that gives you a false sense of security."

"It takes a lot of energy for that," she wanted to grab his shoulders and shake him hard. How did he lead to the impossible? Suddenly she looked at the crumpled rag lying on the carpet at her feet. She picked it up and examined it closely. A large part was missing, and though the material reeked of blood and magic, something seemed wrong. She scanned the room and then noticed a small round table in the corner of the room, with a stone basin on it surrounded by four black candles. Slowly, on soft legs, she walked over to the altar and peered into the vessel. It contained the largest piece of bloody cloth, along with a tuft of black hair that no doubt belonged to Drasan. Below, on the floor, were the runes that encircle the altar, inscribed in blood-browned blood.

"You used his blood," she whispered, not believing he was saying it. She would never risk that. The power that pulsed in Drasan could tear her apart.

"Why are you so surprised?" The young man asked, raising his eyebrows slightly. "It's basically the easiest way to get rid of the blockage. If the bitch hadn't intervened, he would have been mine. I had him in my hand. He resisted, but he wouldn't have slipped away anymore."

"What spell did you try to cast?" Dhalia asked. Suddenly her mouth was dry. Could she have created the basis for and chords of the monster?

"Summoner," he replied, smiling maliciously, "He would come to me even if he had to hack his way out with a sword."

"It is impossible. He's damn immune to magic," Dhalia wanted to convince herself that she wasn't weaker than Bal'zar.

"Not really, my dear. Maybe you couldn't take him, but I could. Of course, if I had bled him like a piglet earlier and used his juice to cast a spell," the king replied calmly, leaning back and exposing his teeth in a wide, satisfied smile.

At that time, Dalya's mind was working at high speed. The brat has gotten too powerful to be allowed to live. He could threaten her position. Drasan had to wait, she had another problem on her mind now.

CHAPTER 4

The roof of the inn overlooked the deserted streets of Washmorth. Thanks to Rodian's tricks, it was possible to deceive the closest guards for a short while. As a result, both Drasan and his companion Alt'ar remained invisible. The prince stood on the very edge and looked down. The pavement was much closer than he had expected. Given that the building was in decline, he was not sure if the beams supporting the roof would be able to bear its weight when it turned into a great reptile. He had two options: jump to the ground and cause a little confusion, or transform in the air, which would certainly attract the attention of not only soldiers but also city residents.

"Remember not to fly too low," the werewolf instructed. "They have great crossbows and net launchers on the walls. Attack the western gate, it should distract the soldiers from this part of the city and give us a safe passage to the tunnels."

Drasan nodded his understanding. He only focused on one thing now - he had to shield his friends from escaping. That was all that mattered.

He looked around the city once more. Before dawn, it seemed so quiet, except for the soldiers, no one leaned over the thresholds of the houses. Despite the unpleasantly biting cold, both he and the Guild leader stood on the roof, stripped to their waist. As a result, they had greater freedom of movement in case they had to fight.

The werewolf looked up at the grayed sky, inhaled sharply through his swollen nostrils.

"Dawn," he looked at his companion. "You are ready?"

The half-dragon nodded in reply. He closed his eyes focusing on the pulsating energy filling him. Flames enveloped his body. Then he took two steps forward and jumped. The transformation on the fly was not easy. Its limbs continued to widen as it deftly landed in the narrow alley, flooding it with a stream of fire. Several guards had died from the heat. He swept another three with a single wave of his tail. One of the soldiers screamed in awe and, dropping his long spear, ran away. The half-dragon leapt, pinning him to the ground with his massive body and crushing his ribs. The scream died in the man's chest.

Overwhelmed with anger, Drasan lunged at the others, but they managed to raise the alarm by blowing their trumpets. In this way, they could bring back the entire garrison. Drasan growled and, unable to spread his wings, climbed onto one of the buildings. The support beams groaned in protest but held out before he could take off. Arrows were quickly launched at him, ricocheting off the hard-shell armor without doing any harm. It rose higher, then dove toward the north wall. Feverish bustle began. A group of slanted-eyed men in funny, pointed cones boiled launchers, putting on the largest spear he had ever seen.

They did not make it.

Drasan grasped the machine effortlessly, rose with it, knocking down several dragon hunters in the process. Once he was high enough, he released her. The launcher crashed to the ground, shattering to pieces. This allowed him to achieve the intended goal. All the soldiers focused solely on him. And since it flew mostly over the west side of the city, Alt'ar and the rest had a safe passage.

***

Amid the cacophony of loud vengeance on the king and curses, nearly all rushed to leave, any order forgotten. The only person who was admirably cold-blooded turned out to be Neila. Perhaps because she was holding her breath constantly, listening to the sound of a huge body hitting the pavement.

So far, Drasan has proved that he is second to none in the air attack. Even so, Alt'ar was concerned that neither Bal'zar nor Dhalia paid any attention to the confusion. They remained passive even when the half-dragon smashed one of the watchtowers at the west gate.

Something was up. Before the Guild leader had time to think about it, suddenly a bluish-purple ball appeared in the sky and it hovered over the city.

Rodian was at his side in no time, observing the phenomenon with concern. She obviously didn't know what she was dealing with, nor did she see Drasan. For a moment they stood shoulder to shoulder looking up at the sky. The rest of the killers froze, staring mesmerized at the spectacle. Then there was a deafening roar. The ball exploded, flooding everyone with a blinding wave of light. Alt'ar squeezed his eyes shut, but the glare nearly thrust his eyeballs into his skull. The others were hiding from the glare of what fell, cursing their voice at the same time.

Blinding spell.

No one was surprised by a hoarse roar or the sound of a huge body that suddenly fell on a building, turning it into a pile of rubble and broken wood. The dazzled half-dragon hastily shifted to human form. His clothes were frayed and his naked torso was covered with great bruises and abrasions. Before his companions ran up to him, they had completely disappeared, but he still did not open his eyes.

Alt'ar guessed why. He was probably close to the ball when it exploded. Since his eyesight was much more sensitive, the explosion must have blinded him. As a werewolf, the leader of the guild had little trouble tossing the inert body over his back and carrying it back to his hideout.

The plan has failed. They needed to improvise.

Neila and Rodian were the first to run to him as he laid the limp prince on the table. The witch gently pulled back one of her eyelids and hissed.

"If he were human, the spell would burn his eyes," she said. "Fortunately, just like you, he has an accelerated regeneration. This may take time, so it would be better if he remained unconscious until the end of this process."

"And what now?" Neila asked, deeply shaken by what had happened.

"Nothing," Alt'ar replied hollowly. "We're back to square one. We must get out of here before Bal'zar sends the entire garrison. All we need are fast horses and a safe ride."

"Isn't it too late for that? Now that they saw him..."

"Not if you shut up and obey me," the Guild leader growled. "Before the king sends reinforcements here, we'll be able to make our way into the tunnel. The only condition is that Drasan remains unconscious."

In response to his words, the prince suddenly moved, clenched his fists and hissed in pain. Alt'ar leapt up to him and slammed his fist on the mold.

"That'll give us some time to wake up again," he said to the pair of mercenaries staring at him in bewilderment.

A horse was brought to him, a tall steel gray stallion. The assassin lifted Drasan's limp body and placed it in front of the saddle, then bound his wrists with a rather thick thong with remarkable agility. His wolf appeared beside him silently as a ghost. Alt'ar glanced at him, then nodded at two of his men - the tall Noai'dirian and the swarthy dark-haired youth. They both approached him without a word.

"You will go first as recon," he instructed them. "Ars will run ahead, he will show you safe passage through the city. In case someone gets in your way," he paused for a moment to emphasize the importance of the next words, "kill him before he raises the alarm."

The men silently mounted their horses and followed the wolf. Only then did Alt'ar take his seat himself in the saddle, right behind the half-dragon slung over it. Neila and Velwel did so as well, taking their places to either side of him.

"We will go in groups of no more than five," Alt'ar said. "I'll meet you at the tunnel entrance." With that, he sprung his mount and took the lead while Rodian, Neila, Velwel and the other Noai'dir galloped after him.

The rested horses rushed forward, showing no sign of effort. They drove the first few streets without any problems. Hooves chimed steadily on the cobblestones, but none of the townspeople even looked to glimpse the commotion. After Drasan's performance, this did not surprise anyone. The dragon must have scared people quite a bit. In any case, the Guild leader took it at face value as it gave them more room for maneuver.

They drove to the market square at a gallop, they had two more streets to go. To get there as quickly as possible, they increased the pace every now and then. As expected, it was there that they encountered their first obstacle. Two wagons were stacked across the entrance to the street, with four crossbowmen waiting in front of them.

At the sight of them, they knelt down, preparing to shoot. Alt'ar leapt from his horse without even slowing down or changing form. He sped towards them like lightning. The soldiers stunned, only one fired in panic, but the bolt barely scratched the werewolf's forearm without slowing it down. The first soldier was struck by a skillfully thrown knife that hit him in the throat, another was stabbed in the stomach. The last two, seeing what was happening, abandoned their weapons and rushed to flee, but Velwel cut them off. One of them was slashed in the neck, while the other was hit in the middle of the back with a knife and fell like a thunderbolt.

The slayers dragged the carts aside, leaving a pathway for another group to burst into the marketplace. They passed them without releasing. Alt'ar re-mounted his horse and led the way forward. They rode at a steady pace, squeezing as much of their mounts as possible. This is how they crossed another street, entering a narrow alley that seemed to be blind at first. Scouts sent earlier by the werewolf were waiting for them there. They were accompanied by a short, thin gentleman with a pointed beard and watery blue eyes. He greeted the new arrivals with a sly smile.

Alt'ar started his horse right in front of him.

"We need to get to the tunnel, Tregor," he said bluntly, dropping to the ground.

The smuggler's eyes narrowed dangerously. His gaze fell on the still unconscious Drasan slung like a sack of flour over his saddle. In the depths of the cunning mind, a light immediately went on.

"Seems the king's soldiers are looking for him all over town," he said, rather than asking. "Must be worth a lot," he added to himself.

"He paid me for my safe passage," Alt'ar said through clenched teeth. "I don't think I need to remind you that endangering me is a symptom of extreme recklessness, Tregor. The boy must get out of here alive. I am responsible for its safety," he added to emphasize the earlier words.

More killers were coming. It started to get crowded in a narrow alley. Seeing the growing number of opponents, the smuggler hesitated. He didn't own that many people, so he wouldn't have survived this clash. But he had another ace up his sleeve.

"You have to pay me for the safe passage through the tunnel," he said suddenly, his eyes lit with cunning sparks. "Hard times have come for those like us, Altar, you know. It is getting harder and harder to make a living from smuggling alone. The army is patrolling not only the highways, but also the side roads."

Alt'ar muttered something that sounded like a curse under his breath, then took three gold coins from a pouch attached to his belt. Without delaying a moment, he placed them on the man's outstretched hand. He stared at the small fortune for a moment, hurriedly stuffing it into his coat pocket.

Tregor bowed and hit the wall three times with his fist. To the surprise of Neila and Velwel, after a while, a passage began to appear in it. It looked a bit like a ramp on which barrels of wine roll into the cellars. As Alt'ar led his horse towards her, the others immediately followed him, disappearing into the tunnel as quickly as possible. Some of the mounts didn't seem thrilled to be forced into a dark and musty corridor. Then their owners tied scarves in front of them and led the dumb animals down.

Once underground, Rodian conjured up a small ball of pure energy to illuminate their path. She started, dragging the mare with her punishment. The others followed her goose, as the passage was too narrow to go in pairs.

The tunnel led a slight slope deeper and deeper. They sensed even more moisture there. It grew so cold that almost everyone wrapped their cloaks and capes tighter. Nobody said anything, but they stayed in a tight group. They were moving forward at a slow pace. The horses remained restless but submitted to their masters' will without protest.

It took a long time for the first rays of daylight to creep into the surrounding darkness. Then Rodian removed the sphere, and Alt'ar released the wolf forward without a word. The predator flashed away like a silver arrow. He returned a moment later with drops of molten snow deposited on his fur. Everyone brightened visibly, because that meant the exit was not far away. The horses also raised their heads and began to inhale the fresh, frosty air into their nostrils.

Finally, the tunnel ended and they saw an exit somewhat reminiscent of the one they got here, though it had been covered with a thick layer of fresh snow for a change. Ars ran through them first, and Alt'ar, leaving his horse, followed him. They both went straight into the blinding rays of the morning sun. The man and the wolf stood for a moment, squinting their eyes, which gradually got used to the brightness that prevailed around them. The others slowly followed.

Neila and Velwel were the last to emerge from the snow. The girl stared at the werewolf standing still for a long time, before she finally decided to approach him. She stood with her legs wide apart and her arms folded across her chest.

"Perhaps you would have set him free already." She gestured to the restrained Drasan, by the efforts of Rodian still unconscious.

Alt'ar shook his head slowly, not even looking at her.

"It's too risky, we're too close," he replied.

As soon as he said it, they all realized that the threat was not over yet. The hill where someone had knocked out of the tunnel long ago was perilously close to the city walls, and there was still the feverish bustle of the dragon's attack.

Neila opened her mouth, but changed her mind and, closing it, turned to Velwel, who was standing, horse reins in his hands. Unlike her, he didn't care too much about the fact that he barely got away. Relaxing and smiling from ear to ear, he tried to get Rodian's attention. She ignored his aspirations with equal determination. Poor man. If only he knew how dangerous the game was. Women like her never paid any attention to freaks like him. A miracle would have to happen for them to pair up.

For some reason, her thoughts turned to Drasan. What did they have in common? In fact, the answer was: nothing at all. So why was she reacting to him this way? This question has remained unanswered so far. She could still play hard and inaccessible in front of the others, but somehow, he saw the true face in some incomprehensible way. The same one she decided to hide a long time ago.

Her deliberations were interrupted by a long, drawn-out wolf howl cutting through the silence like a knife. Alt'ar looked toward the nearby hill, and a similar sound came out of his throat. Nobody cared about it. Girl shivered. Here she found herself in a world where the monsters of legends wandered carelessly around the world, and no one was surprised.

Alt'ar's wolf materialized at its master's leg. He yelped softly, licked his hand, and waved his tail, lowered low. The Guild Leader awoke from his trance, reminding himself that they should continue their journey. He grabbed the horse and with one agile movement was in the saddle. In response, the stallion started at a long trot, wading through the thick snow. The other killers followed his example.

Nobody said anything, so there was silence for a long moment. The werewolf led the horsemen's column to the west. He wanted to get as far away from Washmorth as possible, then turn south and follow the river to Rihn. Before they got there, he knew they had to separate. Such a large group going in the same direction could attract the attention of the villagers, who would alert the army. It seemed wise to divide into small divisions of no more than five to ten people.

As if reading his mind, Rodian suddenly caught up with him, which was met with a strong protest from her mare. The witch ignored her and turned to the leader of the Guild, raising a topic uncomfortable for him.

"We can't keep him unconscious. The spell blinded him. He must change and hunt to recover, she said, glancing at the unconscious prince."

"Not here, and not right now," he replied in a calm tone concealed by a hidden command.

The woman was silent for a moment, then unexpectedly changed the subject.

"You think there's something between them?" She asked casually.

Of course, she meant Drasan and Neila.

Alt'ar huffed, but after a while he thought more about it. Neila wasn't one of the salon beauties. She also lacked any special gift. What could it have been about a pampered, capricious bastard who had grown up in the royal court? Where must he have tasted luxuries, and where every lady of a good home was just waiting for his nod? Had he really misjudged him and had something more to him than haughtiness, shoe and arrogance? Someone like him would certainly not pay the slightest attention to such a ragged and unfortunate creature as a mercenary. And yet the way he looked at her only made one impression - he was in love.

"I'm not sure," he said finally, without taking his eyes off the horizon.

Rodian decided not to pursue the topic as finished. Instead, she decided to move another one.

"Have you made your decision yet?" She asked in a barely audible whisper.

He nodded, wondering if the witch knew what it cost him. Until now, he has remained passive. Choosing one of the parties to the conflict resulted in a death sentence. Still, he knew he was doing the right thing, and his second nature had nothing to do with it, rather his human sense of decency and, above all, honor. He had no army of his own like Bal'zar, only a handful of men willing to follow him even into the fire. Unlike Drasan, he knew the burden of leadership.

***

Ashkan spent the following days teaching Nolan - the half-elf seemed curious about everything. It turned out that he never left Isterl and everything around him was completely new to him. As he was used to the frost and snow, he was amazed at such simple things as a mill powered by river water. He also looked at dogs and other farm animals with real fascination. The elves never bred them. He also wondered how people could live without heat and sun.

More villages passed, and more and more disturbing news reached them. In one of them, the gray-haired old man told those who would listen to him about a huge army on its way from Alikorn to Riden. In another village, he came across a conversation between two merchants who were seriously considering moving their families south. Apparently, news of the war in the air had made it north. The townspeople kept getting out of their way as if the sight of two unfriendly races moving towards Riden was disturbing.

A few days after leaving Michandrell, they were on the shores of Lake Falan. There, Ashkan decided to stop to give the horses a rest. Tarssen was visible from afar, the first major city on their route. They weren't going to go there. Having unsaddled the horses, they spread their blankets on the snow, and for the first time since their escape from the magical valley, they dared to light a small fire. From his saddlebags, Nolan pulled out a sack of dried fruit and a wineskin of sweet wine they had bought from the merchant selling the merchandise. They shared this simple meal and then spread it out in the snow. Nolan was staring at the sky as always.

Ashkan thought about what Drasan was up to now. He had been trying to make contact with him for a long time, but to no avail. The prolonged silence disturbed him, but he couldn't help it. Along with his position in the Council, he lost many of the privileges he had been entitled to. His magical powers were now limited to healing - and most of his fellows did. He still had the gift of longevity, but he didn't want that life at all.

"They're great, aren't they?" Nolan asked.

Ashkan, lost in his own thoughts, had forgotten about him. His companion was staring at the patch of starry sky visible in the gap between the clouds. The unicorn didn't even notice when night fell. He was confused but decided not to bother his friend with problems. He was now acting like a child learning about the world.

"Oh yes, they're beautiful," he muttered.

"It's amazing how much we lose by hiding from the world. There are so many wonderful things here, and people aren't as bad as they say," Nolan dreamed.

"At least not all are like that," the unicorn said matter-of-factly. "But they are remarkable despite their short lives."

"Strange, they must value them very much. For some of us death would be a salvation, and they avoid it in every way," the elf said thoughtfully. "Your pupil is half human, right?" He asked unexpectedly.

At the mention of Drasan, Ashkan felt his stomach clench unpleasantly. Until now, he was protecting the half-dragon, though the dragon was unaware of it. Now he realized once again that he would not be able to do this anymore, and he grew overwhelmed. It did not go unnoticed by the elf lying next to him, who asked:

"Did something happen?"

Ashkan shook his head. In fact, he didn't feel like talking about it. Until now, he had not considered whether he would even take part in the coming war. Yes, open rebellion against the law binding all unicorns amounted to a denial of everything he had believed in so far. He was not sure if his people, especially the Council of Elders, were not making a mistake by sticking to their principles. After all, what could harm the balance more than the rule of Dhalia?

* * *

A few feet away, Yarred stopped his mount in one of the small settlements. He was going to buy some provisions and fodder for the horse before he continued his journey. He had covered a long distance already, but he knew the boundaries of Riden were several days of hard driving through snowy roads. Bruen has been doing great so far. A month's rest in Hearen's stables did him good. The stallion's coat glistened again, the sides filled, and its freshly-shod hooves ripped the frozen snow with surprising ease.

He was still uneasy with him. He left his loved ones far behind him, to the west of the peninsula. Where he thought they were safe. Unfortunately, the increasingly frequent rumors about the huge army that the newly crowned King of Riden was gathering around him made him doubt about his decision. He might have turned back to Hearen and abandoned the thought of finding Drasan. After all, he wasn't even sure if his friend was still alive.

Something like a sense of duty drove him forward with far more force than his longing for Mara. So, he pressed on, not knowing if he would ever succeed. He could only have an unwavering faith that he knew his friend much better than he realized. Drasan was never sensible, but neither was he a fool. So, he must have realized that Bal'zar was getting ready to occupy new territories. It therefore seemed logical that Antua would be the first kingdom on the route of his troops.

Antua, in which Yarred left his loved ones, naively believing that they were safe there.

The next days passed for the captain on the way. He only paused briefly to give his horse a respite and moisten his throat with a few drops of wine before moving forward. Eventually the area grew wilder, the last settlements disappeared, and in front of it was a flat plain, covered with snow sparkling in the sun. Yarred let Bruen slow to the walk, which he gratefully accepted after long hours of incessant galloping. Driven by the sun, they turned south, deviating from the beaten path. The horse's legs sagged into soft fluff up to the knees, but he pushed forward bravely.

"Come on, old man," Yarred patted the horse's neck. "We've got a long distance to go before we reach the next village."

Bruen grunted and shook his head. The man gently nudged his sides with his heels and the horse moved to the trot. His legs were stuck in the thick snow and he was quickly covered in sweat, and flakes of foam fell from his mouth. Seeing this, the captain allowed him to slow down. After a while he stopped his horse, staring in disbelief at some distant point clearly visible against the white background.

The black spot was moving very fast, which seemed unusual given the conditions. The stallion grunted and pushed his ears back. The man touched his neck and felt his muscles tense. The strange cloud was already close - and it turned out that it was not a cloud at all! It looked like a bunch of birds, but they didn't feel like ordinary animals. They were scarcely above Yarred, suspended in the air, and a loud hum was heard. It sounded like the buzzing of hundreds of angry bees. Bruen reared up. The surprised captain with a thud fell to the ground, and the frightened horse rushed to a panicked run.

A swarm of strange humming birds circled overhead for a moment, then headed south. Yarred got up, brushed the snow off his cloak and looked sadly at the place where his mount had disappeared, then, with his head full of disturbing speculations, he followed his trace.

CHAPTER 5

Driving on uneven terrain, in addition covered with a layer of thick sticky snow, was not pleasant. Soon Alt'ar ordered a halt, for both the mounts and the humans deserved a rest. As they managed to find the soldiers on the wall out of sight, Neila decided to try again to speak to the leader of the Guild. This time, he had no excuse.

She reached him a moment after unsaddling his horse. She glanced uncertainly at Rodian, leaning over the half-dragon lying motionless. She was whispering some formulas. Alt'ar looked at her, and then she froze, like a sheep that a starving wolf looks at. She quickly remembered why she had come here and, shaking herself, took two more steps, keeping a safe distance.

"I'll anticipate your question," said Alt'ar, whose only voice seemed calm. You could see, she violated some important point of the werewolf etiquette. Just in case, she took a step back. "The Prince will regain consciousness in a few minutes, which does not mean regaining full sharp vision. He was treated with a spell that literally burns people's eyeballs. If he was lucky, he would regain his sight in a few days."

In response to these words, Drasan's throat released a soft hiss, accompanied by the opening of his fists. As he opened his eyes, Neila fully realized the importance of Alt'ar's words. Drasan's eyes, usually green with a hint of yellow, were now a milky blue, like those of a blind man. She realized that the blind man must follow his other senses.

The witch handed the half-dragon a water bag. He grabbed it so violently that he almost crushed her fingers. He drank long and greedily, and when he was finished; he threw down the empty pot and began to sniff. Alt'ar must have figured out what he meant this time, for he himself offered him a few strips of dried meat. No one was surprised by the enthusiasm with which he took up a meal that was extremely modest for his needs. Having finished instinctively, he felt for more around him.

"We don't have much meat," Alt'ar said. "To regain your strength and your eyesight, you have to hunt big game."

Drasan followed the source of the voice, then replied, with difficulty uttering the individual words:

"I would have to change," it sounded like a hoarse grunt, too soft for anyone other than Alt'ar to understand.

"Let's go then," said the werewolf.

Drasan's blurry eyes unexpectedly rested on the mercenary, and his nostrils twitched, inhaling the familiar scent.

"Neila..." he grunted, then got to his feet without any effort. His muscular torso now looked like a lump of marble. In spite of the bitter cold, he didn't care at all about the lack of a shirt.

The girl felt a familiar thrill piercing her every time she had the opportunity to look at the dragon. In a peculiar and quite natural way, it made her unable to take her eyes off him. For some reason, fear still dominated this hot feeling. Above all, Drasan turned out to be deadly, and his every move resembled the majestic steps of a natural predator. The muscles playing beneath the scarred skin were like iron gears that moved a perfect killer mechanism. That's why Neila felt uncomfortable with him and Alt'ar. Their characters differed, but their movements were identical. Two monsters and she: so fragile and vulnerable among them.

"Hi," she muttered, blushing like a peony. When he got so close to her, the extraordinary warmth emanating from his naked torso hit her.

He smiled in response, showing teeth with two unnaturally long fangs. And she felt her heart speed up rapidly. Both in human and dragon form, Drasan was able to rip the victim's throat with these teeth. Still, there was no aggression or domination in his smile. He seemed so ordinary, almost human.

"If that's okay with you, I'd like you to use my "eyes" for the hunt," he said without smiling, almost deadly seriously.

With the tongue temporarily failing to obey her, Neila just grunted.

At the sound, Drasan smiled again and offered her his arm. She froze, not knowing what to do, then gently, as if afraid of being burned, took his hand. Instantly a wave of heat spread over her body.

The half-dragon pulled her aside. Of course, he had to change after all. Despite his temporary handicap, his remaining senses served him remarkably well. Unlike her, stumbling over the bumps hidden under a thick layer of snow, he moved with the grace of a dancer. At last, he stopped and, releasing her hand, walked a few steps away, then, spreading his arms, he burst into the flames.

Though she had had the opportunity to watch this spectacle more than once, Neila flinched as always, terrified as the fire literally took over his body, stretching it to unbelievable dimensions. Just the fact that she managed not to scream when he appeared next to him in the form of a giant brown beast seemed quite a success. He turned his head and grinned in what was probably meant to symbolize a smile. She shuddered violently at the sight of the fangs, each as long as her hand. She was glad the prince could not see her reaction. After a few seconds, she took a deep breath and stepped closer.

"What now?" She asked softly.

"We have to look for the right prey," he said.

The mercenary sighed in resignation. What was it supposed to do for him now? After all, he had no equal in tracking and killing. Suddenly she remembered that he was now almost blind. He needed her not to track or hunt, sooner to warn him in time in the event of an emergency.

When he started sniffing, sniffing the icy air into his wide nostrils, she just stood there waiting for him to catch the trail. At last, he froze like a stone statue, then suddenly dropped to his forepaws and started forward with astonishing speed. Neila almost had to run to keep track of him.

When he finally stopped, she was slightly out of breath, but she immediately understood what the rush was for. The victim, or rather what was left of it in the form of carcasses not eaten by the wolves, rested in a small valley. It was guarded by two huge wolfs. Drasan hissed, his whole-body springing to spring. The smell of an imminent feast made him so excited that he trembled. The pair of gray beasts were no obstacles to him on the way to victory.

As he froze, crouching, Neila held her breath. Even though she had watched or participated in more than one carnage, the very fact that she was about to see the truly primal struggle for survival caused her not so much fear as excitement.

Drasan slid his belly across the snow, inch by inch closer to the gray beasts guarding their prey. Finally, one of the wolves smelled the unknown scent and sprang to his feet. His companion did the same, and both predators bared their teeth up to their gums, ready to defend their food. The prince jumped in flight, spreading his wings to soften the fall from a considerable height. None of the wolf players had a chance against him. He grabbed the first of the attackers and crushed him in his powerful jaws, the second tried to flee, but one of the front legs of the giant reptile, equipped with long talons, pinned him to the ground. The wolf struggled to break free, whimpering desperately, but it did not last long, for soon the dragon tightened its grip, cracking its ribs. He treated this unequal struggle as having fun. He quickly shook off the excitement she had brought him and turned his head towards the prey.

It turned out to be the carcass of a large deer, partially devoured by wolves, but some meat remained on it for a hungry reptile. Drasan approached him, savoring his victory, for though he still could not see anything, he was guided by his sense of smell.

As he pounced on the remains of the wolf's feast, Neila could barely contain her disgust. She still couldn't get used to the idea that her companion eats mostly raw meat. Watching him hunting and fighting was different but hearing the crackle of crushing bones and loud smacking was beyond her strength. She sat down in the snow as far away from the two dead wolves as possible and tried to ignore the sounds of the dragon eating.

She could bear the company of Drasan in both forms, provided he did not act like an animal. She had a hard time accepting that she could change form as easily as she drew her sword. Fire turned out to be his element, and not only because he had full power over him. His every touch and gaze gave her hot flashes. If only she could accept the fact that they are more than just friends. Unfortunately, his arrogance and overconfidence acted on her like a rag for a bull. So she was wondering how someone so deadly could be so ignorant. After all, she was giving him clear signals that it would be fine. He should, therefore, go off and look for another prey. Why didn't he do that? Was there a grain of truth in what Gaenor was saying? If so, how the hell was she going to deal with such possessive protectiveness? Common sense told her that she should back down while she still had a chance. Still, the very thought of never seeing him again made her feel tight.

No, there had to be a compromise, she thought, trying to drown out the vision of Drasan holding her heart in his bloody claws.

The dragon finished eating before the approaching dusk cast long shadows on the valley. He seemed very pleased. His eyes were no longer milky white, they turned slightly bluish.

"How's your eyes?" She asked, trying to dismiss a problem that was embarrassing for both of them.

"My eyesight has improved. Instead of a dark spot, I see a light spot," he said with a smile. "There were also vague outlines, as if shadows," he added after a moment, laughing again in that peculiar reptilian way.

Neila somehow managed not to snort.

"Then Alt'ar was right, you were helped by character change."

"It's possible," he said carefully.

They were walking side by side now, a young woman and a great reptile. The mercenary knew that no one would see them in this wasteland. So, they could feel at ease. Finally, Drasan decided to bring up a topic she was trying to avoid.

"I know you fear me, but your fear is completely irrational," he said soothingly. This was probably what a mother spoke to when she was scared of the storm. "I never treated you as a threat. On the contrary, in both dragon and human skin, I feel responsible for you. It strengthens the feeling that I should protect you as best I can."

Neila had no idea what to say to him. It made her truly embarrassed. Finally, when she was sure the prince would add nothing, she sighed heavily and leaned against his side.

"It's not that I'm afraid of you anymore," she said, though the words struggled through her throat. "Though I can't deny that you scare me sometimes, especially when you turn into..." She searched for the right word for a moment, and when she didn't find it, she just added, "...this."

"You mean my true nature," he said, didn't ask. He clearly became sad. "Unfortunately, I can't help it." He added much softer, so that it sounded like a hollow murmur.

"I didn't mean to put it that way," the girl defended, trying to control the trembling of her voice. "I just don't feel very comfortable with you being so big and with fangs and claws to top it off..." She broke off as she had clothed her thoughts wrong again. She decided to fix it. "I prefer when you're more human."

"Was that a compliment?" He huffed, lines of steam escaping from his nostrils.

"Understand, until recently, I took creatures like you and Alt'ar as characters from legends. I never expected to stand face to face with them," she was nervously talking through her hat. Drasan listened in complete silence. "And suddenly bang, you show up and my whole idea of the world so far is in ruins. In addition, you can be as sweet and innocent as a lost puppy while being a wild beast inside. I'm not afraid that you will kill me, and more so that I will eventually succumb to you. When it is over, it will turn out that I am just another conquest of your bloated ego. Unexpectedly yours. So, I advise you to look for another victim, because I have had enough of this. I'm not the party for you, dragon prince, so stop fawning at me. The sooner you do it, the better."

She knew she was hurting him, but at the moment she didn't care. As long as he quit this strange game he was playing.

To her surprise, Drasan stopped suddenly and lay down in the snow. It took a few seconds for her to realize that she was shaking all over with a giggle. Irritated, Neila punched him as hard as she could. He probably even felt it, while she ripped her knuckles almost to her bone. He was laughing at her? He was just making fun of her words? He didn't take it seriously at all. Taking a deep breath, she decided to wait out this sudden mirthful attack.

When Drasan managed to compose himself enough to stand up, she immediately approached him.

"Are you done?" She asked irritably.

"It's been a long time since I laughed like that," he muttered, in that deep, velvety voice that made her shudder. "I especially liked that bit about my bloated ego. Where do such sophisticated words come from in a simple mercenary?"

Her heart was pounding with difficulty and she frowned at him angrily.

"You're impossible," she said, crossing her arms defensively in front of her.

He grinned as if he had heard a compliment. She passed him without a word, hiding her wounded and bleeding hand under her arm, and walked briskly towards the camp. She figured he was going to catch up with her anyway, so she didn't even look in his direction.

In her mind, she could already see Rodian's malicious gaze and Velwel's stupid smile. She shook her head to clear the image and quickened her pace. Of course, he caught up with her in a few strides, in human form.

"Are you mad at me?" He asked in a somewhat apologetic tone.

Neila huffed and looked to the side.

You're acting like an offended child, she mentally scolded herself and brought a forced smile to her face.

"Do you see anything else?" She asked, deliberately changing the subject. At the same time, she glanced at him.

To her great surprise, she met the gaze of familiar olive-green eyes, still somewhat hazy. It took her breath away. She hadn't expected the charm of that gaze to hit her again so quickly.

"It's much better, although the world still looks like a fog," he replied, a smile lighting his face that made her heart beat three times as fast. He was far too close, and the warmth emanating from him kept her from thinking straight.

"Don't look at me like that," she whispered.

"How?" He murmured, smiling in that characteristic mischievous way.

"As if I were the only creature in the world," she tried to move away from him, but her legs refused to obey.

He leaned forward slightly. His face was only inches from hers, then he brushed his lips against her forehead. He made a gesture so gentle you could hardly read anything more than a friendly kiss. Why couldn't she control the trembling? Drasan moved away from her far too quickly. She quickly understood the reason. He was only a few feet from them. Alt'ar's Silver Wolf.

The half-dragon muttered what sounded like a "goddamn mongrel" and walked briskly towards the camp. She had to speed up again to keep up with him. His good mood disappeared forever.

When they reached the edge of the camp, Velwel ran to meet them. He seemed very excited about something. This turned out to be quite unusual, considering the fact that most of the killers were either already in their saddles or standing next to the horses.

"We have to turn south!" He exclaimed as soon as he caught his breath. "Two scouts have returned with the news that Bal'zar has released his "hounds" after us. A small unit, about twenty horses, so we could have faced them if it were not for the witch accompanying them."

Neila shot a quick glance at Drasan, but even if he felt fear, he clearly wasn't going to let it show.

"How close are they?" He asked in an emotionless voice.

"The thing is, they'll be here soon, which is why Alt'ar gave the order to march. We will divide into groups; each will go in a different direction."

The prince shook his head.

"It won't do anything; it won't even slow them down."

"So, what are you suggesting?" At the sound of Alt'ar's voice, the mercenary jumped, but the half-dragon kept the same stoic calm.

"Send as many people as you can, leave a few of the best with you," Drasan ordered, then turned to Velwel. "Get Neila out of here and go south as far as you can so that you don't get betrayed by your thoughts."

"No way!" The girl exclaimed. "Should I run away while you stick your neck out? Rather, you should get out of here and get out of here asap, because that bitch is hunting you."

The deathly gravity on the prince's face was instantly lit by the shadow of a smile that suddenly faded.

"That's why it's nobody else, and I must stay and cover your escape," he said calmly, but in a voice that resisted. "I will recover from almost every wound, unfortunately you do not. I will hide my thoughts from her, and yours will be like an open book for her. So grant my request and go as far as you can without looking back. It'll be easier for me to fight if I know you're safe."

His calmness and confidence made Neila bristle. He didn't treat her like a fighter! More like a lady in a lace dress who can't tell one end of a sword from the other. Under other circumstances, she might have taken it as a compliment, but not today, not now. Before she could open her mouth to protest, Drasan made some simple gesture that made her tongue go limp.

"Please hear me out," he asked in the same velvety voice she loved so much. "You have no idea what will happen to you if she catches you and, worse, reads your thoughts. If Dhalia discovers our connection, she will use you to manipulate me. She has done it once and will not hesitate to use it again if you or Velwel accidentally come within her range. Neither of you are allowed to be around when she shows up."

After these words, he revoked the spell and the girl regained her speech ability. She knew he was right, but because of her rebelliousness, she was unable to accept her. By what right was he ordering her?! After all, she has made it clear that she is not and does not intend to become anyone's property. She could fight, and it was no worse than him. And considering he hadn't fully regained his sharp vision yet, she would probably have done better than that. Besides, after seeing the scars on his body, she just couldn't let the witch get to him again.

"We don't have much time," Alt'ar reminded them. His voice sounded impatient.

"Send your men away, then," the half-dragon repeated, never taking his eyes off Neila's face.

As the werewolf left, the tension on his face gave way to a little uncertainty. Apparently, he was just playing cool and confident. He approached her and placed his broad hands on her waist. He said nothing, just stared at her as if nothing else mattered to him. She hated it when he did it because then she knew she couldn't resist him.

"You have to go," he said quietly and calmly, raising his hand and stroking her cheek.

The touch, though so gentle, made her shudder suddenly.

The heart sped up, reacting to its proximity more intensely than ever before. She didn't protest as he took her chin and placed a gentle kiss on her lips. So different, because devoid of possessiveness, light as a brush. He pushed her shoulder distance and, still looking deep into her eyes, whispered:

"I'll be back."

When he walked away in the direction Alt'ar had disappeared a moment ago, Neila was still standing where he had left her, trembling like aspen. The body completely refused to obey her. Fortunately, Velwel appeared next to her, holding two mounts by the reins. He didn't say anything; no words were needed. She mounted her horse and, as Drasan wished, left without looking back.

***

Drasan watched the departing companions for a long time before finally deciding to think back to the encounter that awaited him. As expected, Alt'ar left only the best of the people with him. He recognized the two Nai'dirians, the two sullen Ridenians, and the one swarthy Alikornian. Six in total against a much larger squad led by a witch. To his surprise, the leader of the Guild sent Rodian away, though her support would probably be of use.

The werewolf and his companions were crouched in a small pine grove, so after a moment's hesitation he decided to join them.

"How much time do we have?" He directed the question to Alt'ar, who has not only the best hearing but also the best eyesight of all of them.

"They're over that hill," he replied, without taking his eyes off a nearby hill. "We should see them soon."

A single rider appeared in response to these words, and then another. They looked like a scout. They looked around carefully for a moment, then turned back to report their observations to their commander. There was no doubt that this was what they were looking for.

Ars growled softly as Alt'ar sprang to his feet. Drasan followed his steps. After a while, they were both standing shoulder to shoulder, staring at the horizon. Finally, single black silhouettes materialized on the hill. It looked so peculiar that it would seem that they appear out of nowhere.

Drasan frowned. Something was wrong.

His eyes, which were not fully regenerated, still caused him a lot of difficulties. Instinct said it was some clever trick. First, the riders behaved very strangely. He had already had the opportunity to see the black-armored Dhalia warriors up close, and therefore the manner of the steel seemed suspicious to him. They looked like stone statues.

"Something's wrong," he said, directing the words to Alt'ar.

Alarmed by his words, the killer began to look more closely at his opponents. From the mars on his forehead, Drasan recognized that he, too, had noticed the extremely inhuman behavior of the Doars.

"Do you want to back out?" The werewolf whispered.

Drasan shook his head.

"It's too late for that," he replied. "At least two of them are human. The rest may turn out to be a mere illusion. However, this does not exclude the presence of a real squad on the other side of the hill."

"I think there's only one way to find out," Alt'ar said, reaching for his sword and gesturing for the people to follow his example.

The half-dragon also took a weapon. As his fingers tightened on the cool hilt, he immediately felt more confident.

The leader of the Assassins' Guild gave him a short but searching glance.

"How are your eyes?" He asked suddenly, intending to assess the prince's usefulness in the fight.

"I can handle it," Drasan replied, partly because he didn't need his sympathy, and second, because he didn't want to show his weakness. He had to be careful.

The assassin nodded, though he clearly didn't believe him. He focused his eyes on his opponents again. Knowing it was just a witch's stratagem, he kept vigilant anyway. His unshakable calm and self-confidence made a considerable impression on the prince. Alt'ar was undoubtedly born to lead.

Drasan smirked. Here, his only ally and companion in arms was the werewolf. The smile slipped from his face as he spotted a lone rider heading towards them.

The Guild Leader cursed under his breath, then muttered more to himself than to his companion:

"Mage."

Drasan cursed as well and began to look more closely at the intruder wearing - like those on the hill - black armor. Moments later, he noticed a silhouette that was more feminine than the rest. When he removed the helmet, he knew who he was dealing with.

"Dhalia," he hissed, showing his teeth involuntarily.

He could have guessed who Bal'zar would send after him. After all, it was she who was one of the most powerful aces up his sleeve.

In response to his unspoken thoughts, the witch smiled broadly. Triumph shone in her eyes.

Here was a woman who transformed his life into one great series of misfortunes. The woman he swore to die.

"Are you looking for death, witch?" He asked in a low, malevolent voice. His muscles tightened in anticipation of an attack.

"Nice to see you, too," replied the witch. Her gaze fell on Alt'ar, and a smile was replaced by a contemptuous grimace. "I see that you are taking everybody as your allies, considering the company of the garbage you deal with."

Alt'ar growled in response, the corners of his lips twitched dangerously as if he were trying to bare his teeth. Fortunately, he could keep the beast in check, otherwise they would be doomed.

Drasan regarded him anxiously.

Thank the gods the killer realized the gravity of the situation. A few deep breaths allowed him to control himself enough to stop the shivering.

"Give up this talk," the prince hissed, throwing the raven-haired glare. "That's not what you're here for, is it?" He added with a crooked smile. So let's end this idiotic performance before my companion sinks his fangs into your throat.

Dhalia's beautiful face returned to a smile that would have made many men heart pound.

"I can see you've learned a lot from our last meeting," she said calmly. "You can hide your thoughts and keep your emotions in check. You've become much more powerful than I expected."

Drasan withstood the magnetic force of her gaze. At the same time, he took a tiny fraction of the energy filling him and sent it towards the hand, still clenched on the hilt of his sword. As expected, flames crept along the blade. To his surprise and annoyance, it did not get the reaction he had anticipated.

His performance brought an indulgent smile to the witch's face.

"Forget those market tricks, Drasan," she said. "I know well that you are not at full strength. The more it surprises me that you are left behind.

Did you really think you could measure up to me?" She looked at him thoughtfully.

"I said give up," growled the prince. "Your tricks don't work for me, so let's end this."

In fact, he didn't know what was more irritating to him: her self-confidence or her outright ignorance. No other creature aroused such negative emotions in him. Well, maybe apart from Saruviel.

Something about the witch's posture told him that she was only teasing him. Apparently, she was hoping her talk would provoke him. He was much too smart for that.

The smile disappeared from the brunette's face. It has been replaced with an expression of deep concentration. Drasan knew it too well, so he managed to erect the fiery barrier before the first stream of pure energy burst from between her fingers.

"Congratulations on your reflex," she praised him. She walked around the circle looking for a weak point. She was like a sneaking panther, graceful and deadly.

Drasan knew they did not have much time. The barrier he hastily encircled himself and Alt'ara slowly but relentlessly exhausted the small reserves of energy he had accumulated. To get her back, he will have to hunt again. He glanced at the man standing by his side and noticed that his face twisted in a strange grimace, jaws clenched tightly. The transformation could come soon.

The two comrades in arms exchanged glances, and when the prince nodded slightly in agreement, the Guild leader fell to his knees. His body arched, the skin on his hands and face turned gray. The half-dragon stepped back a moment before Alt'ar was struck by a violent wave of shivers that in turn tore a truly inhuman yelp of pain from his throat. His clothes split open under the influence of rapidly growing limbs, and his bare skin was covered with thick, silvery fur. The werewolf twisted and winded, clawing the snow with its claws. It underwent a process of transformation that made it one of the most dangerous monsters to inhabit the peninsula.

The transformation was exactly as Drasan had imagined hearing the chilling tales of the sons of the moon - short, violent, and extremely painful. The opposite of what he himself went through whenever he turned into a dragon. He realized that the metamorphosis process was as ordinary as breathing for him. In the case of Alt'ar, this has proved to be a monstrous reaction to the venom that circulates through the veins, causing nothing but violence, aggression and brutality. Werewolfing turned out to be a curse.

When the transformation was complete, a strange combination of a human and a wolf lay in the place of a tall man with a lithe body and undefined age. The head and torso looked decidedly wolf, and the arms and legs looked like human, even for their size and hair growing on them. The werewolf stood unsteadily and growled, baring impressively long fangs. His red eyes rested on Drasan.

"Alt'ar?" The half-dragon asked, backing away because he wasn't sure if it would manage to control it.

Suddenly he felt a presence on the edge of his consciousness. He stiffened, considering that the witch would do anything to know his thoughts. Still, something told him it wasn't her. So he allowed the creature to penetrate beyond the protective barrier. He shuddered violently as Alt'ar's voice echoed in his head.

Unlike you, after the transformation, I am unable to speak, so this is the only way I can communicate with you.

Drasan breathed a sigh of relief. He preferred to give up mental communication for a while. Dhalia could easily overhear their conversation. He made sure his mind shield was still protecting his thoughts effectively, then turned his attention back to the confrontation that lay ahead. With a werewolf by his side, he might have had a better chance, but it was clear that his opponent was much more powerful and had many aces up his sleeve.

So far, there was no indication that Dhalia was leading any branch. He admired her concentration. Maintaining such a complicated illusion required a great deal of magical energy and maximum concentration. What was the purpose of that, actually? After all, she didn't think he was stupid enough to fall for it?

Today was a great opportunity to avenge Sheardon. It was enough just to think clearly and not be guided by emotions. Dhalia was able to use them to torment her victims. So, he had to hide his anger and vengeance deep. Keep cool. Clear his mind as he did before each fight, stay cool as the steel of the sword he held in his hand.

Easier said than done.

"Ready," he muttered to Alt'ar.

A low snarl answered him. He beckoned to the other killers, who emerged from the grove silently as ghosts. Drasan lowered the flames so that they could pass safely.

"The attacker is outnumbered. They are hardened and disciplined warriors of the barbaric Doar tribe," the prince began, trying to be serious. "So you have to show not so much skill in combat as clever. Me and Alt'ar take care of the witch. Remember to stay close enough for one of us to support you. That's all. Good luck."

The assassins nodded, then mounted their horses. Drasan focused again, this time to remove the fiery shield. He did not expect an attack from Dhalia. As it turned out, this assumption turned out to be a mistake. The witch struck so quickly that he barely managed to dodge and roll across the snow. He sprang to his feet hastily and counterattacked.

She laughed, swiftly raising the barrier in front of her. The fireball crashed into it without doing any harm.

He must have distracted her somehow.

"Is that all you can do?" He asked with a slight mockery in his voice.

He didn't have to wait long for a response as another missile hit the snow just a foot away.

"Oh, it's just a small rehearsal." She said, playing with the light ball. "I know you're almost blind." A broad smile appeared on her lips. "The spell Bal'zar used was extremely powerful," she explained to the slightly confused young man. "You probably literally burned out your eyes."

A light spell, Drasan thought. He should have figured it out.

But he preferred to keep his tongue down. He was tired of the game. Dhalia, like him, avoided open combat. She wasn't going to attack, she waited for him to do it first. He looked at Alt'ar, the werewolf clearly refusing to wait. His killers silently followed the witch's movements.

He glanced at the illusion. It still felt all too real.

He could send a fireball or two at her and see the reaction. So Drasan, without thinking much, concentrated on drawing the power to execute the two missiles, then hurled them one by one directly at the motionless riders. As he expected: none of them reached their destination, they were stopped by Dhalia's magic shield. He realized that in order to destroy the illusion, he would have to face this calculating bitch first. Let it be that way.

He drew his power again, this time creating a projectile twice as large. He sent it towards the witch. As he thought, she hadn't had time to prepare herself. However, she deviated his path. The fire charred her left arm slightly before it struck straight at the riders she had created. The illusion flickered and disappeared.

This minor victory turned out to be the signal for the others to start the offensive. The assassins surrounded the witch, wanting to cut off her escape route, while Drasan, side by side with Alt'ar, launched an attack. Neither of them expected her reaction.

The first light missile hit the werewolf right in the chest, throwing him far away and hurling him into the snowdrift. The second was intended for Drasan, but despite his poor eyesight, he managed to dodge and roll over the snow. Dhalia smiled encouragingly, as if to wish her opponent's luck. The half-dragon snarled, baring his teeth. He intended to use the right moment to renew his attack.

The witch chuckled mockingly, materializing the single-edged black blade. It looked a bit like a Noai'dir saber. She marked a few blows with it, then grasped the gun with both hands, standing slightly astride. Drasan looked at her and smiled. So far, he had not met a swordsman who could match him in a sword fight. He calmly took a stance with the blade at an angle to his body and the weight resting on his left leg. He intended to attack with a roundhouse. He just waited for her first move.

Dhalia attacked as nimbly as a panther: a blow from above that would normally behead an opponent. The half-dragon had superhuman reflexes, after all, he had been taught by the swordsman king. He managed to dodge and quickly counterattacked, aiming at the witch's exposed side. This one managed to block herself. Pushing his blade aside, she showered him with a veritable barrage of blows. As if she wasn't holding a piece of metal in her hand, but a thin reed. Pushed to the defense, Drasan had to show not only reaction time, but also strength.

He finally managed to push her away from him, but it took a lot of effort. They jumped away from each other and circled, watching each other like two wolves ready to attack. Then Alt'ar appeared, still in its shaggy form. His fur showed burn marks. He gave up his jump, standing at Drasan's side. They both knew they had to work as a team to get out of this alive. They began to circle the witch on both sides.

Dhalia smiled at the sight.

"You're both worth each other. An outlaw with an overgrown ego and a werewolf who pretended to be a human," she said calmly.

"This is your new tactic," Drasan mocked, hoping he could infuriate her enough to make her commit a mistake. "Now, instead of complimenting us, will you insult us? What a nice change, I was sick of the sweetness already."

"You'll miss it yet," she attacked, still smiling, proving that she could use a saber no worse than he could with a sword. The blow was aimed at his left shoulder, but he managed to dodge. The blade grazed his hand harmlessly.

"A point for me," she muttered with satisfaction that quickly turned to a scowl. It was Alt'ar who decided to join the fight.

The werewolf wanted to throw himself on her back, but she had time to prepare for it. She turned to him, saber ready, smiling vindictively. Alt'ar jumped back, snarling furiously, and Drasan took the opportunity to put his sword to the side of her neck.

Bloody retaliation flared up in him with renewed vigor. Here he was finally able to avenge all the wrongs for which the witch was responsible. All it took was the smooth movement of the blade to shorten her head and end this nightmare. Before he decided to do this, he felt the cold blade just under his left shoulder blade. One thrust and an attacker behind him would pierce his heart.

"Drop your gun and withdraw your shaggy sidekick," growled a familiar, slightly hoarse voice that made Drasan's neck bristle. Still, he didn't release his sword.

Boris! He could have guessed that the werewolf would accompany the witch. He looked into the eyes of the Rider's killer standing in front of him. Alt'ar was still seething with murder, it was enough to take advantage of it. Unfortunately, it's hard to make any sense when you feel the coldness of steel on your back.

The witch's minion was not patient, so the half-dragon felt a slight thrust. The blade cut smoothly through the skin, penetrating the flesh.

"Your Lady won't be delighted if you kill me," he said, trying to keep a cool head. Meanwhile, he hoped Alt'ar would have time to come up with something.

"You are on the brink of death once, dragonspawn, and yet you are still alive. Maybe this time you will be able to slip out of the hands of the Lady of the Dead?" Replied the werewolf and pressed even harder on the prince's body.

The young Sheardonian had no choice. He knew that if he slit Dhalia's throat, Boris would pierce him. All he could do was surrender and hope his comrades could rescue him. With that thought he loosened his grip, releasing the sword from his hand. Barely able to do so, Dhalia turned to him with a radiant smile. Ahead of them, Alt'ar continued to circulate, seeking an opportunity to attack.

"Call the dog away," she muttered softly.

"You call yours away first," he growled in response. He exchanged knowing looks with Alt'ar, trying to find his awareness and send him a silent warning.

Run, he repeated in his mind. Get out of here before they kill you.

Alt'ar hesitated for a moment, but as he realized that neither Dhalia nor Boris showed any interest in him, he dropped to his feet and set off for a run. Nobody was chasing him. Only then did Drasan realize something was wrong.

Where are the other assassins?

On a hunch, he turned to survey the valley. All he could see were the traces of blood that stood out clearly against the whiteness of the snow. No bodies. Alt'ar's men were taken by surprise by the werewolf.

He cursed ugly and looked straight into the witch's cold blue eyes. She did not need a detachment, all she needed was a faithful servant.

"So it's just a bluff," he said, jaw clenching in helpless anger. How could he be so stupid? It wasn't the first time that he allowed her to be led out of the field. In addition, he endangered not only himself, but also the Bloody Hunter.

Dhalia smirked.

"Of course. And you took the bait as always," she said. "I've got to know you well enough to know that you won't put your comrades at unnecessary risk."

And he hesitated so long about slitting a bitch's throat! Too long. He should have done it when he had the opportunity to do so. Feeling Boris's breath against his neck, he forced himself to control his anger. Meanwhile, Dhalia calmly approached the horse and took two items out of her packs - a small bag and a silver canteen. Without taking her eyes off Drasan, she poured the white powder into the bottle and mixed it several times, then handed the prince with the words:

"Drink it."

The half-dragon didn't even flinch. In time he remembered the werewolf behind him, still holding the blade buried in his body. So he accepted the canteen without pouring it into his mouth.

"You prefer me to pour it down your throat?" She asked with exaggerated sweetness.

"Don't provoke me, witch," he snapped back, casting a hateful glance.

Dhalia pursed her lips into a narrow line, then said in a voice devoid of all emotion:

"Boris... Our prisoner does not want to cooperate..."

In his mind's eye Drasan saw the disfigured face of the werewolf stretch into a broad, sadistic smile. With his free hand, he grabbed the hair on the nape of his neck and with a brutal jerk forced him to tilt his head back. Meanwhile, with his other hand, he rotated the blade embedded in the youth's body. Pain wrenched a short scream from the half-dragon's chest that forced him to open his mouth. It was enough for the witch to pour the entire contents of the canteen into them, then she magically closed his mouth and stuffed his nose, forcing him to swallow the bitter solution.

As soon as the liquid ran down his throat, the prince felt a strange numbness, and a wave of violent shivers ran through his body. Boris let go of him, making sure he would not threaten anyone again. Drasan fell to his knees, choking and coughing. He only had one chance, and although he knew it would weaken him, he had to risk a transformation. He tried to ignore the dull ache in his temples and the nausea and the sickness that came with it. He focused on the magic filling his body. Though he concentrated as hard as he could, he felt nothing. Even the familiar hot flashes. Instead, a terrible headache struck him, and his stomach tightened in a tight loop. After a while, to his own surprise, he vomited profusely.

"You think I'm stupid enough to let you transform?" Dhalia asked, leaning over him. "I just gave you powdered gaudalum root. It just so happens that in Riden it is a very popular drug. Apparently, it helps to relax. I have discovered by accident that this drug has a slightly different effect on anyone who shows even a faint magical talent. Well, during its operation, the abilities disappear or become significantly dulled. Every supernatural being becomes someone quite ordinary."

Drasan felt the blood drain from his face. She planned it all, step by step. He felt like a fly caught in a spider's web. Dhalia had a considerable advantage over him, as the seer she could predict his every move. And now she had taken his chance to defend himself. Which meant she could do anything, read his mind easily. He would find out about Velwel and... Neila. And if she found out what he had in common with this girl... The mere thought seized him with fear.

What will they do if they find out that I have been captured? He swallowed nervously because his mouth was dry. Unable to use her abilities, she will not be able to defend any of them.

Throughout all this deluge of thought, he was barely aware that he was still kneeling in the snow and that his nose was constantly dripping with blood. It must be the effect of the hideous thing that Dhalia gave him. He tried to get up, which caused another bout of nausea. So he decided it would be safer to stay in that position at least until they passed.

"I would advise you not to do it again," said the witch, as if she had already read his mind. "You got a real megadose. The seller said that you only need a pinch to feel the effect." She smiled wickedly, then knelt in front of him and pressed her hands to his temple.

He tried to push her away, unsuccessfully. She laughed at his attempts to resist and glanced urgently at the helper.

"Boris."

He didn't have to wait long for a reaction. The werewolf was obviously just waiting for it, because in no time he was behind him. He grabbed one of his arms and painfully twisted it backwards. Drasan was unable to suppress a cry of pain. He knew all too well that this sadistic bastard would like to see any attempt to protest and break his arm with genuine delight. Calmly, Dhalia repeated the deed, pressed her hands to his temples, and closed her eyes. He did not have to wait long for the effect of these actions. In an instant, he felt the cold tentacles of her mind encroach upon his consciousness. More images flashed before his eyes. This time he couldn't oppose it. He clenched his jaws, waiting for the witch to finish. She had no intention of stopping her activities. As a result, the dull throbbing intensified, and blood spurted from the nose again.

He only breathed a sigh of relief when Dhalia backed off. For a moment he couldn't shake himself. The mere thought of what she had learned from his memories terrified him. Luckily for him, Boris seemed to think he had done his job, so he let go of him and walked away. Drasan didn't even have the strength to crawl. He just knelt in the snow for a long time, trying to come up with some sensible way out of the situation.

The hope is that his companions will take the warning seriously and will disappear before Dhalia decides it is worth getting them so that she can manipulate him. Unfortunately, knowing Neila, he knew exactly what she was going to do.

***

The murderous pace imposed by Rodian turned out to be tiring not only for the horses, but also for the riders. When they stopped, Neila felt grateful that she hadn't frozen to the saddle. Muscles had become stiff from the constant shaking. Nobody spokes all the way. Even Velwel was gloomy and silent. The girl decided that he also did not like to leave his companions to the witch's favor. Aside from the fact that the half-dragon has yet to regain full sharp vision, it may well be that both he and Alt'ar have greatly overestimated their abilities.

When they all got off their horses, Rodian made a gesture of her hand that she wanted her to come over. The mercenary had no idea why, but she did.

"For some time now, I have the intention of asking you about something," the woman said, giving her an appraising look. "What exactly is between you and Drasan?"

Neila was speechless. She hadn't expected such a direct question. Moreover, she did not think it would be asked by Rodian.

"Why you ask that?" she cut herself off.

The redhead shrugged.

"I'm just curious. I don't know if you noticed that he is deadly handsome. People like him don't usually like girls like you."

The mercenary looked at her incredulously for a long moment. It's clear that she had an appetite for Drasan, because what normal woman wouldn't? True, she did not expect a beauty like Rodian to treat her as a rival.

For some reason, the mere thought of it triggered an uncontrolled burst of merriment. Before she knew it, she was already standing in front of the stunned witch, croaking like a frog.

She did not care at all that the redhead's face was red with anger. She knew he would not dare to touch her; she was too afraid of Drasan's reaction. After all, he stood up for her more than once. Fortunately, before she angered her for good, Velwel appeared and gently pulled her aside.

She looked at him, wanting to find out what he thought about it. His face looked serious and concerned. She had never seen such an expression on his face before.

"What's up?" She asked, because she didn't like it a bit.

Instead of answering, he pointed his hand at the horizon. Neila followed his gaze without a word, and her heart skipped a beat. Here, of the six comrades, only two returned. She did not find Drasan.

She felt her knees buckle under her, but the young assassin caught her in time and held her up. Exactly what she had predicted happened. The prince and the werewolf overestimated their own abilities. The witch turned out to be cleverer than they had assumed.

The riders stopped the foamed horses and dismounted. They looked wounded and terrified. Alt'ar was scarred and - more amazingly - furious.

Wasting no time explaining, he walked over to Rodian.

"She set a trap," he growled at the outset. "It seems she knows our prince better than I thought. She knew exactly what to do to outsmart him."

Neila didn't know why she was doing this. Her legs carried her to the assassin.

"You left him alone?" She asked with an angry note in her voice. "Knowing what that bitch is going to do with him?"

"I had no choice," Bloodhunter growled, his hands unconsciously clenched into fists. "She had another werewolf there. In his eyes, I could see that he would not hesitate to pierce Drasan if he even tried to save him."

"How convenient, right?" The mercenary no longer heeded the words. "You sacrificed him to save your own skin. You would be much more noble to stab a knife through his heart."

"Calm down," Velwel hissed at her, trying to gently pull away from Alt'ar.

She broke away angrily.

"It's so typical of you! Tuck your tail under you and run away. It never crossed your mind that the witch was just digging his head and discovering your alliance anyway. This time you will have nowhere to hide..."

To the astonishment of those present, Alt'ar listened to her words with stoic calm, though judging by the intense throbbing of the vein in his temple, it was hard for him to do so.

"You're the last person to tell me what to do," he growled softly. "The only reason I tolerate you at all is because of your relationship with Drasan! And I don't care what you think about it," he added, seeing the girl open her mouth to deny it. "There is no room for rash action in this situation. Each decision must be carefully considered, because the witch will take advantage of even the smallest mistake."

After these words he turned his back to her and turned to Rodian.

"Do you have any idea?"

The witch frowned.

"Here we must act quickly," she said finally. "If we're lucky, they'll stay where they are, at least until that female dog recovers enough energy to open a teleporter to Rosher."

"Poor consolation," Velwel muttered.

Neila thought the same thing. So far, their luck has not been theirs. It is unknown why Drasan has not been able to free himself so far. After all, he hadn't used up all his energy in the fight. Or maybe he has used up? The very thought made her feel cold.

"You wouldn't be able to do anything," Velwel whispered, as if he could read minds. "If Alt'ar couldn't, then you wouldn't have done it any more. He is a werewolf; you are only human."

The mercenary was no longer listening to him because she had just realized something. Since Drasan has been captured and possibly incapacitated, this witch must have read his thoughts. And since she did, she knew that they had something in common. Just the thought of what she would do with that knowledge made her stomach twitch.

Velwel looked at her anxiously, expecting some stupid movement on her part. Neila had no intention of further insulting the Guild leader. Instead, she walked over to Rodian. At the sight of her, the witch raised her eyebrows so high that they were close to disappearing under thick hair. The girl calmly endured her mocking gaze and, clearing her throat, said:

"We can't sit here idly. We are just wasting valuable time."

He and Alt'ar both looked at her as if she was suddenly speaking a foreign language.

"What do you mean?" Rodian asked.

"We should develop a plan of action and at least try to free him," the mercenary announced, not doing anything to the redheaded attitude.

Rodian exchanged a knowing glance with her leader, and when the latter nodded almost imperceptibly, she turned to the mercenary and said:

"We had an action plan in advance. I assumed that it would not be needed, but as you can see, fate can be malicious." She laughed, which sounded a bit too artificial. "Since your attempt to recapture the half-dragon may fail, it would be better if some of you stay here." She looked at Neila and Velwel standing one step behind her. "The rest will go with me and Alt'ar to investigate the situation. If the opportunity arises, we will free our companion, if not, we will withdraw. If we hadn't come back, don't wait for us, just go as far south as possible."

The girl gave her a scowl.

"If you think I will stay here while you save him, then you are wrong," she grunted, looking at Alt'ar.

It's obvious she wasn't going to sit back. The only man she cared about was kidnapped. Though she wouldn't admit it to him for any treasures in the world. She liked him, maybe even more than she should. Not enough, however, to conceive romantic visions about marriage and life together. The best she could do was dream that one day, when this nightmare was over, Drasan would still be interested in her.

Alt'ar sighed in resignation. Apparently, he had prepared himself for such a reaction in advance.

"I don't need your presence for anything, but I know all too well that you will follow us anyway." He said calmly, then turned to the others. "We will go there in no more than ten people. If my observations are correct, the witch did not move. We just need to approach her without noticing any of us."

"How can you be sure she's not out of there?" The mercenary asked skeptically.

The leader of the Assassins' Guild raised his eyebrows as if the answer to that question were obvious:

"We think she used up a lot of magic energy during the fight. Much of it was spent just sustaining the illusion. I think she is exhausted," he replied.

"Why didn't Drasan just transform?" She asked because it suddenly occurred to her.

"I suppose he didn't want to risk losing his strength," suggested Velwel shyly. "If he changed form, he would have exhausted what little power he would need to defend himself."

Alt'ar nodded silently, apparently having nothing to add.

"We have to move immediately. It's getting dark and we have no news of Drasan's condition," Rodian said.

Neila swallowed nervously. She guessed what the Guild leader's redheaded companion might be. Presumably, Dhalia knew that there were ways to torture, not to require violence. Perhaps that was what she was using now. She hastily dismissed the thought and accepted the reins Velwel was handing her. The young man looked into her eyes. She sensed his unease. She wanted to say something to cheer him up, but no sound came out of her lump in her throat.

"Take care of yourself," he whispered.

The girl could do nothing but nod her head. Alt'ar's men had already lined up, so she hastily mounted her horse to join them. She tried not to think about what she feared most.

***

Dhalia clearly did not expect anyone to try to rescue the prince. After reading his mind, she felt at ease enough to light a small fire. Boris disappeared somewhere, probably went hunting for the inhabitants of a nearby village. The mere thought of it made Drasan sick. He preferred to focus on what was going on with his body. He managed to regain his eyesight enough to see more details. He could recognize the deep thought on the witch's face now. He was still trying unsuccessfully to draw power, if only enough to burn through the bonds. Unsuccessfully. All he gained was an even bigger headache.

The little freedom that the oppressor left him was of no help. Although he was not bound, he was a prisoner anyway. The woman only seemingly stopped paying attention to him, he felt her eyes on him constantly. He knew she was exhausted, too, for she avoided using magic. She did not surround them with a protective shield, she even lit a fire in a human way. As long as he could not use his own abilities, it gave no hope of regaining his freedom. There was hope that Alt'ar would come back for him. However, he avoided thinking openly about it. After all, Dhalia might want to "look into his head" again at any moment.

So, he took advantage of the fact that he was not embarrassed and kept as far away from her as possible. It did not help to keep him warm. After a short time in the frost, he discovered with horror that it was not only his ability to control fire to fail. The natural tendency to maintain body temperature has also become dulled. As a result, he was shaking with cold, his temples throbbing with furious pain. His only consolation was that Dhalia was saving power and was not even trying to torment him. Even so, he was irritated by the strange silence on her part. Was she afraid that the werewolf would try to take him back and preferred not to betray it just in case? Taking away his hope could prove to be her most powerful weapon.

If she really feared an attack by a group of killers, would it be so easy to get Boris out of here? She would have to be absolutely sure of her advantage before dismissing the servant. Unless she had reason to suspect that he might cheat on her. It might turn out that, despite his brutal and wild nature, the werewolf refused to fight his kin, it would outweigh the scales of victory on the side of the Guild Leader. So it was logical to chase him away so that he would not cause problems during a possible match.

The thought filled him with hope. Alt'ar might have hated him, but if war broke out, he would sooner slit his throat personally than let it fall into enemy hands. Plus, there was a chance that, despite prior reluctance, the other killers appreciated his fighting prowess. Maybe he even gained some respect in their eyes?

Suddenly, Dhalia got up and walked away from the fire, staring at the surrounding darkness illuminated by the white of the snow. She stood there listening to the sounds of the night for a while, then turned back to the victim.

"Time to have fun," she said with a demonic smile.

She stood behind his back and grasped the hair on the back of his neck, forcing him to tilt her head, and aimed a kick at the very center of his spine. Sharp burning pain wrenched the man's throat with an inhuman whine of pain.

The damned bitch knew well that once at her command, he had been whipped on the back until he passed out. Many of the scars still felt at the most unexpected moment.

Moments later, the prince flinched violently as he felt icy tentacles entwine his consciousness. It wasn't painful yet, but unpleasant enough. The pain came after a moment as the woman dragged out one of his worst memories, making him relive it. He gritted his teeth, knowing he couldn't take it long, then screamed. It was a terrifying sound, almost the howl of a tortured being, cutting the night's silence like the crack of a whip.

***

Alt'ar felt a shiver run down his spine as a scream reached his ears, undoubtedly from the throat of the tormented prince. It meant that Dhalia was still here, not going to hide at all, but this time the assassin had no intention of letting himself be caught in a trap. There was no sign of the half-dragon. What troubled him more was that Drasan had failed to defeat her, despite the fact that she had almost exhausted her power. He did not think that a few small fireballs would have undermined his strength so badly. So the witch had to find another way to neutralize him.

This, in turn, forced the Guild leader to think longer about his plan of action. He couldn't risk people's lives so stupidly. Neilia lacked such inhibitions, perhaps because she had no idea what was going to happen to her. It cost him a lot to get her to stay hidden for as long as possible. The girl was ready to fight, as if she was going to tear the witch to shreds herself. This reinforced his suspicions about the fact that there was something between her and the prince.

He looked at Rodian. As one of the few of his people, she had a genuine sympathy for Drasan, and it was not only due to her fascination with his abilities. Others regarded him with fear or resentment, though some appeared to be a bit hesitant. The witch gave him a slight half-smile to signal that they were in no danger of anything terrible enough to make them withdraw. They had known each other long enough that they could communicate without words.

Alt'ar moved towards the thin line of smoke cutting through the trees, and his men followed, stretching into a long line. For some reason, Rodian and Neila took their seats on either side of him, as if they were trying to reassure him of their usefulness. He knew from experience that the red-haired friend was trying to protect him, and the mercenary was hoping to confront the witch. As they entered the circle of light, the assassin felt his stomach clench unkindly.

Dhalia and Drasan were alone. The woman used his body as a shield. In addition, the face of the young man, distorted with pain, testified to real torture. At the sight of Alt'ar and his companions, a faint glimmer of hope flashed deep within his eyes.

The leader of the Guild had seen a look like that before, belonging to someone just as young. He still remembered Garot, whom he had looked after since the brat had been fatally wounded by a werewolf. However, the moment of his death, to which he became an involuntary witness, stuck in his mind the most. The young werewolf had exactly the same expression in his eyes. Then the killer hesitated for a moment, which was enough for the torturer to literally gut the boy. Sometimes his tortured face and that look still came back to him in his dreams: terrified and yet full of hope.

Looking at Drasan, he couldn't help feeling that he was in a similar situation. Except this time, he wasn't going to hesitate. With that in mind, he took a step forward, appearing before his companions.

"I can see you don't trust your sidekick very much," he said calmly, but his gaze remained alert. He tried to connect with the half-dragon consciousness, but the pain it felt was too great to maintain the connection.

Dhalia made no reply, just clung tighter to Drasan. Despite the fact that she daringly pretended to be composed, there was fear in the depths of her eyes. Seeing Neila creeping toward her, she smirked.

As a result, she made the mistake of focusing solely on the girl. The Guild leader used this moment to launch an attack. He started forward, drawing his sword on the run. He saw the witch's eyes widen with terror as his intentions reached her. Before he got closer, she made a simple gesture that made the snow curtain come up. She pushed Drasan away from her and rushed to her horse. Before anyone could react to this unusual development, Dhalia was already racing down the slope, sparing no whip for her mount.

Alt'ar sheathed his sword and looked at Drasan. The kid was trying to lick into shape. He didn't look very good. Even despite the dried-up traces of blood around his nose and ears, his movements lacked the usual energy. As if he had no strength for anything.

"Thank you for coming back for me," he whispered without looking up.

The assassin smiled in that distinctive, ironic way.

"I had no choice," he said, giving Neila a meaningful glance. "As someone once said: we may hate each other, but we need each other."

Drasan smiled too, but weakly and without conviction, and a moment later all trace of mirth vanished from his face. Alt'ar didn't have to look back to understand who was causing it. So, he pulled himself to his feet and, without saying a word, withdrew towards Rodian and the other killers. Out of the corner of his eye, he saw the two standing uncertainly opposite each other, avoiding each other's gaze. After a while the girl unexpectedly threw herself on the young man's neck with such force that she almost knocked him off his feet.

***

After several moments of frantic driving, Dhalia was finally in front of the west gate. Upon seeing her, the guards hastened to open the mighty gates. She ran through them without slowing down and without gaining a single glance. Then she galloped through the city, throwing away those townspeople who turned out to be reckless enough to get in her way. She only slowed down when she was near the entrance to the castle courtyard. The guards opened the gates, lifted the grate, and let it pass without a word. The stable man jumped to collect her horse.

The witch almost ran across the castle square and headed straight for the double gates. There was only one thought in her head.

She had to find Bal'zar.

She found him neither in the throne room, nor in the library, nor in his chambers. The enraged woman checked all the rooms one by one, but he was nowhere to be found. Resigned, she went to the great window overlooking the royal gardens and her eyes widened with astonishment. In a great square covered with grass, two opponents armed with swords faced each other. In one of them, Dhalia recognized Bal'zar.

She was about to go down to him when something caught her attention again. The young ruler's rival looked strangely familiar. She began to watch the mock struggle with the mounting tension.

The king made a short lunge, but his opponent blocked the blow with incredible ease, then smiled in the characteristic way she knew so well. Pale shoulder-length hair, eyes like liquid gold, a neatly trimmed goatee...

It's Arano! A young and ambitious magician whom she personally condemned to death.

She felt her heart leap into her throat. It is impossible! She saw them being led to the stake. She later left because she didn't want him to figure out that it was no one else, and she had betrayed him.

Had he changed with someone at the last moment? If so, where has he been hiding all these years?

Suddenly, another thought struck her.

What if he knew the traitor's identity? Maybe he came back only to take revenge on his ex-lover?

She shook her head to chase these ideas away. If he was really Arano, she couldn't show with a single gesture that she was afraid of him. The mage would take advantage of this immediately, as would his exotic beauty. For a moment, she even thought that she was in love with him, but she quickly shook off the feeling. She didn't want him to discover her weaknesses.

Just like Bal'zar.

Realizing this, she felt a sudden chill. The presence of Arano made it all complicated. Now for nothing she could admit that Drasan had eluded her again. Nor could she reveal that she used all her power to capture him. So, she had to kill some unfortunate prisoner and use his blood to strengthen herself.

Yes, that was what should have been done before meeting Arano. Besides... Her gaze suddenly fell on the reflection in the glass pane and she flinched. She looked terrible. She also had to draw power, visit a bathhouse, and then put on the appropriate clothes.

With that in mind, she quickly moved away from the window and ran down the stairs. In her mind's eye, she could still see the smiling face of her former lover.

CHAPTER 6

After driving a few miles, Alt'ar finally stopped and ordered a short stop. He sent two men ahead to notify the others of the success of their mission. Drasan remained silent all the way. Even to Neila, who was not far from him now. Some of the killers, who had so far treated him rather with cold forced courtesy, approached him and slapped him sympathetically on the back. He paid no attention to it. Honestly, he would appreciate a little loneliness, so he could sort things out. He was trying to summon power all the time. So far to no avail.

He was in such a foul mood that he refused to eat, though his stomach twisted with hunger. He sat down in the snow away from the others. The mercenary slapped beside him, of course, but he ignored her. He didn't even dare to meet her eyes; it was much easier to look at your feet.

Finally, impatient with his behavior, the girl decided to speak first:

"How long are you going to feel so sorry for yourself?" She asked.

He did not answer. The anger at himself grew even deeper. He didn't feel sorry, he just resented himself for letting himself be so stupid. Dhalia read his mind and now she knew his every weak point.

Neila was by no means going to give up.

"You are pathetic with your idiotic guilt, even Alt'ar was deceived," she said, trying in vain to get him to look at her.

She doesn't understand, he thought, shocked and terrified at the same time. "She cannot comprehend what threatens her now."

Drasan took a deep breath, intending to disclose the facts, but suddenly changed his mind. He couldn't do that, not yet. He tried to smile, but judging from the expression on her face, he didn't quite get it.

"I'll be honest with you," he said, though the words hardly passed his throat. "It may be best for you not to be friends with me."

To his surprise and annoyance, Neila snorted.

"And since when are we friends?" She asked skeptically. "The annoying, arrogant bastard with an overgrown ego is the last person I would call a friend. You look more like burr stuck to me. You are extremely difficult to get rid of, but I have gotten used to your presence."

"Interesting metaphor," Alt'ar had the annoying habit of moving noiselessly, which always made it pop out of the ground. He remained completely serious when he handed Drasan the small bottle, though his eyes were gleaming merrily. "Rodian says this will alleviate some of the effects of too much gaudalum."

The prince accepted the unexpected gift, muttering "thank you," under his breath, and the assassin withdrew as suddenly as he had appeared.

Neila studied the vessel in the half-dragon's hands, her eyes narrowed suspiciously. The man saw no reason not to take advantage of the gift. He slowly unscrewed the lid and wrinkled his nose as the pungent smell of some herbs hit him. Still, he took a sip. The liquid tasted unpleasantly bitter and burned in the throat, but the inconvenience was bearable. So Drasan took another sip, screwed on the lid, and put the vessel in the wide pocket of his coat.

"Do you have anything else to tell me?" The mercenary asked irritably as it became clear that Drasan had no intention of resuming the interrupted conversation.

Before he could answer her, their camp was in turmoil. Everyone rushed to the horses, and after a while there were choral shouts of greeting. The killers recognized their own. More than twenty riders, headed by Velwel, stopped their mounts. The young man himself began to look around, and when he saw the familiar faces, he immediately rode up to them.

"Hello," he said, his voice so serious he didn't seem to suit him at all. "I'm glad to see you all safe and sound."

"Likewise," muttered the prince, raising an eyebrow in mock surprise. "Something happened that I don't know?"

Neila looked as if she was choking with laughter, but she managed to control herself and replied before Velwel opened his mouth.

"Oh, that's nothing," she said. "It seems our friend has settled down for good among the members of the" Guild," she added, still struggling to control the gaiety.

"That's not true," Velwel said, sounding like before. "I'm just trying to fit in with the company, that's all," he shrugged and smiled. "I prefer to be with you guys," he absentmindedly scratched his bald head. "They're so..." he searched for the right word for a moment, "...serious."

Neila snorted.

"Seriously?" She asked in an ironic tone, and then without waiting for an answer added: "And what did you expect from such a gang? After all, they are the murderers and villains from under the dark star."

Fortunately, before Velwel could think of an answer, Alt'ar announced it was time to move.

With everyone in the saddle, Drasan sped his horse and caught up with the werewolf. Since their escape, the sorcerers had no chance to discuss any further plans. The assassin looked at him and almost smiled, and Rodian, riding beside him, gave him a coquettish look. The prince ignored her and turned to the leader of the Guild.

"What now?" He asked, even though the question seemed trivial.

Alt'ar didn't answer right away, he seemed lost in his own thoughts.

"We seem to have a major change of plan ahead," he said, not looking at the half-dragon. "My people are tired of playing cat and mouse with the king and his henchmen. The most sensible thing to do would be to go straight south towards the Haerral Mountains, but..." He paused for a moment. "...by following the straightest possible road in that direction, we will become too visible."

"In my opinion, the best we do is get out of sight for a while," replied Drasan.

Alt'ar shook his head, then leaned forward and reached for the wooden tube he was carrying by the saddle. He took one end off and pulled out a roll of parchment. When he unfolded it, it turned out to be a map of the peninsula with all the mercantile routes and royal roads marked.

"We're here," he pointed to a group of hills near Washmorth. "And this is one of the royal roads leading to the southeast." He pointed to one of the lines marked in brown, "In order to avoid encountering the troops wandering everywhere, avoid the main routes and choose only paths known to hunters and minor trade routes."

Rodian looked over his shoulder and pointed to one of the roads marked in gray leading to the northeast.

"This road seems to be rarely traveled. It passes several villages. We could drive it for a long time..." She tapped the dot with the name of the city with her finger. "Ram'ar is a city so far south that our king has no interest in it at all." It is a real asylum for people like us. There you can replenish your supplies and talk to the population. And here..." She pointed to a group of hills outside the city "...there are several abandoned hunting lodges in the valley. We can hide there for a while."

Drasan looked at the place and frowned. It is clearly marked on the map that the valley is surrounded on all sides by quite high hills, and that it can only be accessed through the narrow gorge of the gorge. There was also a lake, one of the small ones, but very deep. A natural trap.

Alt'ar stared at the map for a long time before finally sighed, or rather gasped.

"We have no choice," he said, gently rolling the parchment and putting it back into the tube. "To survive, we must find a hiding place as far from Washmorth as possible, renew supplies, and gather as many people as possible. But I will go to Ram'ar alone." He glanced at Drasan as if expecting a protest. When that did not happen, he continued. "This is the most sensible solution. More mercenaries armed to the teeth could raise suspicions. If we are not careful, Bal'zar will easily figure out our plans and begin exterminating the assassins all over the peninsula, which we don't want to do. If we're lucky enough to reach Noai'dir safely, we can spread news of the plans for the new King Riden there."

"What if we fail?" Asked the prince, who liked less and less the fact that Alt'ar was clearly going to remove him from making more important decisions.

"It's going to be improv," said the assassin. "For now, we're sticking to my plan as long as possible."

It did not escape Drasan's attention that the assassin had clearly underlined the word "mine." He stifled his anger with great difficulty. He silently promised himself that she would talk to him about it under more favorable circumstances. In its present state, challenging a werewolf was suicide. He must have discharged in a slightly different way, so he resumed his attempts to summon the power. Though he put all his will into it, he failed to resurrect even a spark.

***

Wading in the thick, sticky snow was not pleasant. Yarred had the opportunity to find out for himself when he had to follow his trail after an unfortunate fall from a horse. At first, he hoped the panicked animal hadn't gone far. He was wrong. After an hour's walk, he paused, resigned, and looked back.

It was starting to get dark, and he unfortunately kept everything except his sword in his saddlebags. He knew that at any moment snow could start falling from the low suspended clouds, effectively preventing him from further searching. He cursed himself and Bruen several times, but to no avail. His horse had never acted like this before. All the Guardian horses came from the best Antuan studs and were trained to obey them from the foal. So, something like this should not have happened. But...

"Those strange birds," he said to himself.

It seemed they had intentionally scared his horse away. But why? What could they have done in this and who sent them? They didn't act like ordinary animals, they acted like flying spies. It was as if someone was controlling them with a powerful spell.

He shook his head to ward off those thoughts.

I must be going insane, he thought, and quickly resumed his search. It seemed unlikely that the stallion would have run that far.

The night came earlier than he had expected, but as he had suspected it had started snowing. The dense petals quickly formed a dense white curtain through which it is difficult to see anything. Captain Cordydian let out a long whistle, but he did not hear the expected pounding and welcoming neighing of his mount. He began to feel uneasy.

What if wolves or some stray bear or mountain lion caught him? After all, the mount always came back to him. What could have terrified him so much that he had run this far?

Soon it was impossible to follow the horse's trail any longer. Chilled and exhausted, the man leaned against the trunk of a great oak tree that stood alone in the white plain. He decided to wait out the storm and move on with the advent of dawn. Fortunately, he had a tinder with him, and it was much more difficult to find dry wood. How much would he give in such a situation to have Drasan next to him. His friend could summon fire at his command, and he certainly never felt cold. Unfortunately, at the moment he was too far away to use his help. He had to deal with himself.

He didn't know how he managed to make a small fire, but he mentally thanked all the gods he knew for it. Holding his naked sword in his lap, he sat down under the tree and began to gaze unconsciously at the whirling petals in the air.

He closed his eyes and recalled Mary. Her face with flushed cheeks and gorgeous blue eyes... Her fiery red hair curls into soft locks and cascades down to the waist. This was what he forever imprinted on his mind, and that was what he wanted to see her again.

Smiling at his thoughts, Yarred covered himself with his cloak, then, curled up, fell into a restless sleep.

***

The village, situated in a hidden valley, turned out to be very small. Several huts made of moss-sealed wooden tubs, and one half-fallen barn. The absence of a living soul did not surprise Alt'ar in any way. People probably heard about the dragon and decided to seek shelter within the city walls. Nevertheless, recent events demanded caution, after all, they still did not know where the witch's servant had gone. He could be lurking around here waiting for them to run into a trap. Luckily, he had Ars.

He stopped at the edge of the buildings and gestured for the others to do the same. Then he dismounted and called the wolf with a soft whistle. He appeared almost immediately and sat down across from his master. Alt'ar stared at the pet's amber eyes for a moment, then gave the order:

"Search."

The predator, without delaying with a slight jog, moved towards the buildings. The reconnaissance took only a moment, he returned to the assassin clutching some bloody rag in his mouth. When he got closer, it turned out to be... a human arm.

The gruesome find did not scare the guild leader. But he had a very bad feeling about the village. Unfortunately, one of them had to go there to replenish supplies. So he sighed and turned to the others.

"The villagers were probably murdered." He said, deciding to tell the truth. "We do not know who or what attacked them, so it will be safer for all of us if I go to the settlement alone." He looked at the people's faces. None of them would dare to question his opinion, but as his eyes fixed on Drasan, he understood that he was not going to be silent. He could just ignore him and do his thing, but he figured he wouldn't obey his orders anyway. So it seemed safer to take him with him. "But I need someone to come with me and watch the rear."

As expected, Drasan quickly jumped off his horse and stood at his side, with Neil following him like a shadow.

The assassin gasped in exasperation, then, without waiting for either of them, lunged forward, followed by Ars.

***

This blatantly disrespectful attitude from the Guild leader irritated Drasan. He wanted to snarl at him, but with a last effort of his will he managed to suppress the urge. Instead, he followed him briskly. Neila almost had to run to keep up with him.

As he still hadn't fully recovered his strength, Alt'ar insisted on keeping his head down. The almost complete inaction drove him mad. He was unaccustomed to obeying orders, and so any order the assassin gave him was causing him increasing frustration. He drank the drink Rodian had made steadfastly, hoping that he might finally be able to transform himself and go hunting. He was starting to get hungry, which increased his aggression and awakened the dormant beast. As a result, more and more often, instead of talking, he growled or hissed, and he was starting to feel sick from the strips of dried mutton. He did not think that after another day on the meager rations he had to settle for, he would still be able to control himself.

To top it off, gaudalum continued to block most of his natural abilities. Besides not being able to change, he was also unable to focus his thoughts, which made mental contact impossible. For this reason, he began to resemble a wild beast more and more. Hunger triggered instincts. His behavior in a short time became so unbearable that the only person who could endure in his company was Neila. The mercenary insisted on accompanying him everywhere, which meant he didn't have even a bit of privacy.

Now she followed him too, though Alt'ar watched with genuine disapproval. Drasan remained silent, fearing that his voice might betray him. Instinct, extremely alert to the presence of a potential prey, told him that there was something nearby that could serve as a meal from poverty. It could even be a carcass now, and it would have rushed at it only to satisfy its visceral hunger.

As they approached the buildings, it became more and more difficult to control his instincts that drove him towards the ruined barn. Something was there...

There was a promise of a future feast in it. Unfortunately, Alt'ar has targeted the largest hut in the center of the village.

Irritated and furious, Drasan stopped and Neila did the same.

The assassin paused, and after a moment's thought, he slowly turned to look at them. Apparently, he was not used to outright disregarding his instructions. It was evident that he did not like the prince's attitude at all.

The young man ignored him. The predator's instincts prevailed over human reason, and before he knew it, he was already walking towards the barn. His sense of smell told him that he would find meat there.

He didn't react when Alt'ar called his name, and ignored the mercenary who, in her habit, followed him. His senses focused on only one. He walked amok straight to the source of the seductive smell. When he got close to the target, he accelerated to get there as quickly as possible. Reaching the barn door, he opened it with a flourish and stopped at the threshold.

Walls, ceiling, floor... There was blood everywhere... It looked as if someone had chased all the inhabitants of the settlement here and then slaughtered them like pigs. Worst of all, it didn't stop there. Most of the bodies had been dismembered and some had been gutted.

The anger and rage sparked a long-awaited response.

The fire flooded his body with one violent wave of heat, stretching his limbs and covering his body in a tight cocoon. The transformation happened much faster than anyone could have expected, including himself. Survival instinct finally defeated the drug, unleashing the magic in one violent blast.

***

The enormous reptile into which Drasan had transformed took a defensive posture, and a loud growl emerged from his throat. The muscles tightened and the jaws opened, exposing the teeth.

Alt'ar's Wolf bared his fangs as well and looked at his master as if awaiting a command from him. The killer's face turned into a stone mask in the blink of an eye, and the eyes turned from plain gray-blue to blood red. But the Guild leader somehow managed to keep his composure. Not only did he not change, he even spoke in a voice in which was the hidden command of the born alpha:

"Stand back, you idiot!"

He was directing these words to Neila, who was frozen in mid-step, staring at the dragon with wide eyes, unable to make any movement. But the gaze of the great eyes fell on Alt'ar.

The girl held her breath at the sight of two deadly predators staring at each other. She stood between them paralyzed with fear. She prayed silently that neither of them would decide to fight.

Drasan's reaction was as unpredictable as his character. Unexpectedly for those present, he tensed a part of his torso vertically, resting the weight of his huge body on his hind legs only, and hissed like an enraged snake.

Neila wasn't sure if this was just a warning or a challenge to the werewolf. She looked at the other uncertainly.

Fortunately, Alt'ar kept his composure this time. He not only managed to keep the wolf part of his nature in check, but he also had no problems controlling people. And they showed up as soon as it became clear that something was wrong.

"Don't make any sudden movements," he growled at them. "He's not attacking yet, and so long as you keep your distance. It is primarily a hungry predator. His instincts took over, so he would defend himself against anyone who gets too close.

Everyone instantly turned into stone statues. No one dared move or even glance in the direction of the enraged reptile. It worked. Drasan stopped snarling and dropped to his front paws, causing a slight shock. He continued to watch them with slightly narrowed eyes, with a silent warning that seemed to say: stay out or I'll kill you.

The mercenary didn't know why she was doing it, but her legs carried her up to the dragon. The reptile did not move, did not even blink. There was no indication that the human half of his personality had regained control of the half-maddened beast. Even so, Neila, ignoring Alt'ar's warning growls, made her way toward him step by step.

"Drasan," she said, her voice soft, gentle, not much louder than a whisper. She guessed he could hear her anyway. "I know you can control yourself; you just have to try a little." Speaking like that, unexpectedly for everyone she was just a foot in front of his mouth. Close enough that the heat emanating from him began to burn her skin unpleasantly. One of the great eyes with vertical pupils glared at her menacingly.

Slowly, very slowly, she reached out and touched the hot scales, dangerously close to her dilated nostrils. Drasan didn't move an inch as she ran her fingers over them, scalding her fingertips. Neila took a deep breath as the dragon suddenly opened its mouth. Now she could see each tooth separately. It took a good few moments to realize the half-dragon was smiling. The heat emanating from him no longer burned, but radiated a pleasant warmth. The girl leaned against his face with a sigh of relief.

"And I was afraid you would eat me," she said.

Drasan didn't answer, just wrapped himself around her and sighed deeply as well.

"I wish you'd go back to human form. They are all very scared," she continued, pleased that her companion was showing no sign of aggression. "We could talk then..." She broke off and shuddered slightly as she felt someone's presence on the edge of consciousness. She stiffened, not knowing what to do. She relaxed as a familiar voice echoed in her head:

Forgive me if I scared you with this, but this is the only way to communicate now.

Neila took a deep breath to control herself, then asked in the calmest tone she could do:

"What happened?"

The half-dragon made a deep grunt, then came the words:

When I transformed, a certain change took place in me, my senses went crazy. I can't control myself enough to take my human form again. On top of that, the dragon half of my personality treats everyone around me as a potential threat, which means I can attack any of you at any time.

"But not me," added the mercenary.

In response to this short sentence, from the depths of Drasan's gut came a hoarse growl that might have been a laugh. He shook his head as if trying to push something away, and when he chose to speak again, his voice was tense.

This is not entirely true. Even now, when you are so close, I find it hard to resist the hypnotic music played by your heart or the scent of the blood pulsating in your veins. You must remember that I am primarily a predator and one of the most dangerous in the world.

Neila flinched violently as his hot breath enveloped her. Before she could answer, he spoke again:

Hear me out now, because it's very important and I really don't have much time. I don't know how much longer I can control myself. You must go back now and tell Alt'ar my words. He sighed deeply. Let him take his men as far as possible, but back off slowly, because the prey-seeking instinct may take over me. No one, including you, can stay here. Take my horse as well, because I don't know how long I will spend in dragon form. I will try to get back to you as soon as possible. For now, my senses are over-aroused and focused on hunting. As soon as my hunger is satisfied, I believe that my former balance will return and I will be able to transform myself. Until that happens, however, stay away from me. He paused for a moment, then shifted so that he could look at her. It will be better when you go...

Neila hesitated, unsure what to do. The air felt suddenly thick and the temperature so high that breathing became a torment. And then, inch by inch, Drasan began to move his enormous body in such a way that she could finally take a deeper breath. Even so, she was still afraid to twitch.

Get out! He roared in her mind.

This finally motivated her to take her first shy steps back because she was afraid to turn her back on him now. As she stepped outside, she was lit by the warm rays of the setting sun. Apparently, she had spent more time mentally talking to Drasan than she had expected. Alt'ar found herself in the exact same place she had left him. He and his killers stood in a row, staring at her with fear, uncertainty, and anger.

The mercenary ignored it. Now the most important thing was to convey to the Guild leader what Drasan had asked her to do. She tried her best to remain completely calm. Once she was far enough from the barn to be sure the half-dragon wouldn't rush at her, she decided to turn to face Alt'ar and quickened her pace.

The Guild leader didn't look thrilled, but he didn't say a word.

Neila breathed a sigh of relief imperceptibly. And she was afraid he would inundate her with questions. She didn't feel like explaining the complicated relationship between her and Drasan. The fact that he didn't kill her was mainly due to his feelings for her. It might even sparkle, but she preferred not to get too much of her hopes.

She gathered her strength and looked straight into the killer's cool blue eyes.

"Drasan told me to tell you that it would be best if we all leave immediately. He also emphasized that it should not look like a panic escape. At the moment, he is not fully in control of himself and guided by his instincts, he can attack us. He also hinted that he should take his horse, as he is not sure how much longer it will remain in the dragon's skin." She blurted it out in one breath, as if fearing that someone might interrupt her at a crucial moment, and she preferred to get it over with.

"How do you know this, since he hasn't had a word with you?" Asked the witch suspiciously.

Neila gasped in irritation. She had expected such a reaction from her, so she had an answer ready.

"He found a way to convey it to me without words," she replied, lifting her chin proudly and looking into the red-haired beauty's green eyes.

"If we leave, he will be on his own," Alt'ar was addressing to no one in particular. It might seem that he is just thinking aloud. "Dhalia's return cannot be ruled out. He can take more people with him or even a second mage to help," he continued the monologue, before suddenly turning to Neila. "We can't go too far. Besides, someone has to finally notify the rest of your "allies"." He smirked. "It would be safer if they joined us in Ram'ar. It will be a kind of an excursion camp and we will all meet there."

Neila took a deep breath. So they had to separate. She and Velwel were to go in search of Gaenor and Alder, if the latter managed to get out of Washmorth. There will be no problem with the dragon. Drasan will find him himself when he recovers. As for Alder, the girl had serious doubts as to whether he had managed to come out alive. Especially after all the fuss the half-dragon has made.

"I'm not sure it's a good idea," she decided to voice her doubts aloud. "Of our allies, one may be dead, and the other may be anywhere because of the fact that he has wings. We don't have any news about the others, because we split up quite a long time ago."

Alt'ar frowned.

"Then we'll go straight to the Ram'ar. We'll get out of sight and gather as many people as we can. If Drasan gets in order, he can join us, but," he hesitated for a moment and looked at her carefully, "someone must stay near him in case the witch reappeared on the horizon."

Neila just nodded. She ignored Rodian's hateful look. She, too, realized that there was something between her and Drasan. And judging by her increasingly contemptuous treatment of the girl, she didn't like it at all.

***

The snow-white unicorn was nervously tearing the frozen ground with his hooves. The half-elf standing next to him tried in vain to calm his horse. The black stallion struggled and screamed, his ears back against him. The reason for their anxiety turned out to be a strange cloud that was moving very fast towards them. It did not appear to be a natural phenomenon. As Nolan rightly pointed out: she was flying too fast and against the wind. It was only this that made Ashkan appear in his natural form, ready to stand up for his friend. However, the black shape stopped above them only for a moment. There was a strange noise like the buzzing of a swarm of bees. On closer inspection, they saw that it was made up of hundreds of small birds with beaded eyes. And the sound seemed to be made by their wings, moving so fast that they were blurred in their eyes. The creatures circled and flew off towards the Unicorn Mountains.

"What was that?" Nolan asked as the strange creatures vanished from sight.

Ashkan shook his head but didn't answer. He was still staring where they had appeared.

I have no idea, he said truthfully.

Nolan, still trying to calm the clearly scared steed, sighed heavily.

"It didn't seem like a natural phenomenon," he said, a long line wrinkle across his normally smooth forehead. "I have lived in this world for quite a long time and have seen many things, but not something similar yet. These birds... acted like one organism..."

"It's not that what worries me, but the fact that they are kind of scouts." Ashkan replied, returning to the form of a tall, silver-haired elf. "For animals can be trained to serve only those who have magical control over them. You need a gift to have power over lower creatures." He frowned, then added, "I only knew two people who could do it, and one of them is dead."

"What do you mean by that?" His companion asked softly, frowning.

"That we must be on our guard from now on," he thought again and began to circle back and forth. "It changes a lot, actually everything. If I contact Drasan, he will realize that something is wrong and will be here immediately. In turn, if I do not do it, it may turn out that..." He paused for a moment. "...I missed something extremely important."

Ashkan blurted out the words faster and faster that Nolan, who was watching him, no longer understood. He mechanically stroked the black stallion on the neck and stared fearfully at his companion.

The unicorn stopped abruptly and looked skyward, a single wrinkle appearing on its smooth forehead. He looked as if he was thinking deeply about something. After a while his gray eyes lit up, maybe he came up with the solution of some extremely difficult riddle, and his features were contorted with an ironic grimace.

"It's obvious," he said, more to himself than to his companion. "I could have figured it out a long time ago. But you see, I've been around people for too long, and my senses have gone dull. If she had acted alone, she wouldn't have been able to..." He broke off and looked directly into the half-elf's eyes widened with fear. "Saruviel," he said the name like an extremely foul curse. Without waiting for his companion's reaction, he added, slowly drawing his words. "It must be theirs. He smiled sadly, then turned to Nolan. "I'm afraid, my friend, we're not safe here, and we'd better move on," he said calmly. "I owe you an explanation, but not here."

They got their horses and started walking.

Nolan stared at his companion with a mixture of interest and fear.

"In order for you to understand everything, we have to go back a few centuries. Until the dragons left Lineland, leaving power to the people," Ashkan began, his gray eyes flashing. "That era was called the Golden Age by the people. For years, wise and just rulers passed their power down from generation to generation. They had no armies, no wars were fought, and groups of knights called Nihil'imi were formed to keep the peace. Each of the kings chose one of their favorite animals as their guardian and protector."

The bear became the coat of arms of Riden because the people there valued strength and endurance; Alikorn chose the osprey because the bird symbolized patience and persistence; Sheardon the wolf, for they took courage; Earden the horse, because they treated these animals like soul mates; And Antua wanted the eagle, symbolizing wisdom, to become their icon; Noai'dir chose the fox, an allegory of cunning; and Thoran chose the mountain lion as his protector because he combined strength, speed and endurance.

"The mages living on the peninsula, both men and women, used elemental magic at that time, no one knew or used the darkest of arts - the magic of the Ancients, commonly known as black magic or blood magic. As you can imagine, the blood of all living things has some magical properties, but for centuries no one has dared to break the law against bloody rituals..." Ashkan sighed heavily. "The rulers of the time forgot, however, that what is forbidden is an irresistible temptation. Black art began to tempt young and ambitious women. They craved power far beyond their natural abilities. This is how witches were born. At first, no one saw anything wrong with this new method. It was only when these women began to show an unrestrained lust for power that sages like Thorret realized their mistake. Unfortunately, by that time many of these women had gained a significant position thanks to their beauty. The kings, at the urging of their beautiful wives or mistresses, began to fight for the land," Ashkan paused for a moment, his face twisted with a grimace of pain, as if these memories had left a permanent mark on his memory. "Many of them led to a fall, others even to death. Their lovely spouses, possessing both power and power, began to compete with each other in their midst. Many of them began to search for gifted girls and boys in order to accept them into their ranks or to draw power from their blood." He smiled wryly. "The children they trained, especially boys, found their way to royal courts and slowly sipped venom into the hearts of the rulers. People poisoned by it became greedy and cruel, attacked each other and began to despise each other. The small but highly influential kingdom beyond the unicorn mountains was the first to fall, and my ancestors made this once fertile and beautiful land a barren desert. Some lands, including Sheardon, have managed to remain neutral by refusing to participate in the fratricidal war. At the same time, the elves began to avoid humans, and in time to hate them and treat them as vermin that should be exterminated. Bloody fights lasted for years and took many lives..." He broke off, as if further words would not pass through his throat. There was scorn in his voice when he finally broke it. "Of course, when the repentant witches came back, when they stopped, and many kings gladly accepted their help. Not all of them had evil hearts. Some, like Vaya, wanted the old order back. Most only wanted power. As you can imagine, one of them turned out to be Dhalia. To the surprise of her sisters, she chose the farthest, barren wasteland of Rosher. She quickly captured the heart and mind of the young dragon Gaenor."

"Wait, isn't that the same one, who...?" Nolan interrupted impatiently.

"Listen to the end," Ashkan looked at him sternly, then resumed his story as if nothing had happened. "So Gaenor, deluded by Dhalia's spell, attacked and killed the king next door to Ardan, then proclaimed himself sole ruler. Of course, he, too, ruled only apparently. The other witches were less successful, but waited patiently for their chance. There aren't many of them left, so we figured they didn't pose a threat. We were only following Dhalia. As long as she didn't extend her power beyond this gloomy wasteland, we didn't take her seriously." His mouth twitched in a grim grimace. "It turned out to be our biggest mistake as a result, and when we realized what he was up to... it turned out to be too late. The witch had long-term plans for a child. Worse, she knew exactly where to find him. After all, she had the gift of foresight, we should remember that. She found a young Shantaryanka named Ayla. She knew the girl would give birth to a boy with dragon's blood flowing through his veins. She decided to do anything to get her hands on him. She sent Boris for this. At her request, he was to bring the future mother to Kahaer. However, not everything went as it should, because instead of finding a defenseless woman, he encountered a fearless warrior, ready to defend his unborn child. The future mother did not come out unscathed. I found her almost at the last moment, because the enraged werewolf was going to kill her. I managed to neutralize him and take the badly injured princess to Sheardon. Initially, we managed to confuse Dhalia. Convinced that the child had died with her mother, she gave up her search. "He sighed heavily. We did our best with Vaya to make her believe that Ayla died before giving birth. For many years we've successfully concealed the boy's existence from the witch, or so we thought. Unfortunately, due to his explosive temperament, accidents involving the use of powers that he himself could not control more and more often happened. Sooner or later, all this masquerade would have to come to light. With Dhalia still not making her presence known, it seemed to me that the news of these incidents had yet to reach her ears. Unfortunately, fate plays ugly tricks," he smiled bitterly, "because you see, Drasan himself did not know who he was. If he had known this, perhaps he wouldn't have slipped out of our vigilant protection so often and fell right into the hands of this mad woman. She was obsessed with him from the beginning. She knew perfectly well how powerful he would be once he reached his full potential. With him by her side, she could get everything that her greedy and power-hungry heart has long desired..."

Listening to his story, Nolan did not even seem to notice that it was dusk and that a bright crescent moon appeared in the sky.

"What happened next..." Ashkan continued in the same sombre tone. "...it's actually my only fault. I did not treat this witch as a real threat. Plus, like the rest of Lineland, I've long forgotten that she's not the only one. There are still like hers in the world. I don't know how many there are, but each is dangerous in its own way. From what I have read in the old scrolls, there are witches who have a gift that allows them to freely influence the weather, as well as those who are able to control animals. The worst, however, are the ones that can put pressure on weaker minds, as Ertan does..." He paused for a moment and frowned as if he was considering something. "Saruviel also seems to have a purely mental gift..."

Nolan flinched violently, as if the mere sound of the elf's name made him shudder.

"Saruviel is not an elven sorceress, she is a monster with a beautiful face," he whispered, looking around fearfully. "She even loves to use her talent against the weak. She enjoys tormenting prisoners almost physically. That's what she was doing with your student before we interrupted her."

The unicorn looked at him completely speechless. Saruviel? No it is not possible! After all, Ertan would sense it, he would surely... Suddenly something hit him. How blind and idiot he had turned out to never see it before?! You can see the elf was trained by one of the escaped witches, and she did it so well that she led everyone around, including the same elven leader from the Michanderell valley. And since she disguised herself so well, others will come out soon, too. Lured by the success of Dhalia, they will fly like ravens blowing the scent of carcass.

This information hit him like a bolt from the blue. Suddenly he realized that he had been deceived and deceived like a child. He couldn't see the truth, though he had it before his eyes. And now it might be too late. Drasan has no idea that he will have to fight not only with Dhalia herself, but also with the others whom she may have already called for help. If so, he must warn him, even if he was to pay for it with his life.

Nolan, unaware of the decision he had just made, stared at him intently, but for the time being Ashkan was unable to tell him how deadly they were.

Unfortunately, it turned out that he wouldn't have to explain it at all. The sky above them suddenly darkened sharply, extinguishing the light from the moon and stars. The worried horses began to perch on their hindquarters and neigh. Ashkan didn't even have to turn around, he could see his companion's pale face and eyes widened with fear. A gust of magic hit him like a tide and crashed into the invisible shield he raised around them at the last moment.

One of the otherworldly beautiful women gave a sinister hiss. The unicorn turned its mount towards the attackers just as another sent a luminous bolt of pure energy towards it, which also crashed against the shield. Ashkan looked at the first of the witches, the one with liquid gold eyes and straight black hair. Mariv - assigning a name to the sharp features of his face was easy for him. Though she must have been a good six hundred years old, her sixteen-year-old body hadn't even aged a day. The black birds turned out to be her "children" - as she used to call all the creatures she ruled - and now they circled over her head like a swarm of angry bees. The other attacker also recognized... Saruviel. There was no way to mistake her face for any other, because they were all pale compared to her beauty. Unfortunately, it went hand in hand with the contempt and cruelty that lay deep within the blue eyes. The third striker looked even older than her companions, so old that he had wondered about her identity for a long time.

Anar - the Lady of the Elements and one of the first adepts. She must have been well over a thousand years old! Even so, her porcelain and white face looked the same as the day she became a witch, and her cold black eyes resembled the depths of the Abyss itself. The black cloud obscuring the sky is definitely her work. Unlike her sisters, she didn't grace Ashkan with a single glance.

The witches stopped at a certain distance from the shield he was creating. Nolan let out a soft groan.

Saruviel was the first to step forward.

"Surprised?" She asked in a mocking tone. "I would advise you to lower your shield, you stand no chance against our power." She smiled coldly.

"Who are you?" Ashkan asked softly, never taking his eyes off the elf.

"Haven't you figured it out yet?" She asked in mock surprise, and Mariv, standing next to her, laughed derisively. "I'm an apprentice of Harav - one of the most powerful elven witches. She had come to Michandrell a long time ago, and she was able to disguise herself so well that she led Ertan himself out of the way, who, moreover, could not resist her. He was the first to visit her bed and even then, he did not discover how much talent he had." She snorted contemptuously. "I was sixteen when Harav sensed that she had strong magical abilities. My mother never let me learn magic, and that was because she herself was one of the few elves completely devoid of powers." She narrowed her eyes with delight. "Oh, what a wonderful feeling it was to kill that cold bitch. And when Harav found out that I was stronger than her, I slit her throat in her sleep and burned what was left."

Mariv chuckled sneeringly again.

Ashkan tried very hard to remain calm, though inside he was trembling with rage. Saruviel misled not only Ertan, but also him. Suddenly, another thought occurred to him.

"I should have guessed from what I saw in Isterl," he drawled.

Saruviel smirked.

"How's your crossbreed? I hope he's still alive. Maybe I can play with him one more time." As she said that, her face suddenly brightened and an expression of exultation appeared on her. "Yeah... that was really great entertainment: watching him squirm at my feet, howling in pain. He'd probably go mad from it in the end, like everyone else, and then I'd kill him slowly, so that he would be aware of the coming end..."

The unicorn remained calm. He knew the witch was playing with him and trying to provoke him, but he was not going to let that happen. Drasan was safe, otherwise he would have felt if something had happened to him.

"Dhalia would not like it very much. He has other plans for the boy, he said coldly, knowing that he was hitting a weak point. Most of these surviving witches had an open aversion to the black-haired beauty."

A mocking smile returned to Saruviel's beautiful face, but it was clearly meant to mask the anger.

"Dhalia will be pleased with the information I got under the torture," she replied with haughty nonchalance. "She will probably be surprised by what I discovered. Ultimately, her crossbreed is still in one piece. Besides, it's not about that pathetic student of yours anymore." She smiled predatory. "I had a different prey for myself."

Ashkan felt an involuntary chill, caught Nolan's fearful gaze out of the corner of his eye, and in the blink of an eye made his decision.

Run! he instructed him in his mind, and he jumped off his horse, getting ready to fight.

The half-elf didn't move, just, with a trembling hand, reached for the crossbow. Apparently, he had no intention of abandoning his companion to his fate. Ashkan sighed heavily. Usually he avoided fighting, it was not in the nature of his kind. Therefore, he took it only when he found no other way out.

Saruviel was staring at him, head tilted slightly, as if curious about the outcome of the internal struggle he had to fight with himself. Now at last he understood why Vaya would rather commit suicide than give Dhalia what she wanted. The dead have no voice or memories, so they can't reveal anything anymore. By deliberating so, he finally made a decision. A fight seemed inevitable, although he knew he would not be able to win this time. At the same time, he could not allow this cold bitch to celebrate his victory.

Hesitantly, he lowered his shield and reached for his sword. He knew the blade would not protect him, but he had a different plan entirely. He only regretted Nolan, for a terrible death was waiting for him. He was never afraid of her himself. When a person lives that long, annihilation is nothing terrifying to him. So before any of the women around him could even think about casting a spell, he deliberately knelt and thrust his sword in his chest. A wave of cold flooded his body and his eyes grew misty. He smiled, knowing that was not what they expected.

Nolan let out a deafening howl, then without hesitation he lunged at the witches.

Ashkan didn't care about that anymore. Life was slowly pouring out of him, though he had clearly missed a heartbeat. He must have punctured one of his lungs and now it was flooded with blood. He had only a few moments of existence ahead of him. He wanted to notify Drasan so that his former apprentice would understand that he would be on his own from now on, but he lacked the strength. He could barely understand what was happening next door. He could hear the deafening screams of Nolan squirming in agony, and there was no way he could help him.

His heart beat slower and slower, but he managed to catch the gaze of the only being with intelligence to whom he could convey what he wanted. Ernil, staring at him, froze as he made his last effort pouring his death memories into him. He hoped that the horse would find its master like hundreds of times before. The stallion climbed up on his hind legs, threw his head and grunted, then ran away.

Ashkan was relieved to finally close his eyes. He listened for a moment as his heart made its last sounds, to finally be silent forever. And then there was an explosion. A wave of pure magical energy spread in all directions, blinding the three attackers.

CHAPTER 7

A short wolf howl cut the silence. At this signal, Alt'ar emerged from the small grove, dragging his mount with him. He did not find a living soul on the road. Ars gave him a glance of eyes glittering in the twilight and trotted forward. He jumped into the saddle and followed him towards the darkening hills on the horizon. He quietly hoped that the recent outburst of magic had attracted no attention and that he would not have to fight back. He rode slower than his habit on one of the less traveled trade routes, and his horse's hooves were stuck in slush. The thaw that had lasted for several days did not arouse enthusiasm, and he was no exception.

Three days had passed since he left Drasan in that village. Even so, he was starting to feel uneasy. Most of his people, like himself, were not overly fond of the half-dragon, but they had gotten used to him. Some even considered staying nearby in case the arrogant prince was about to join them. The only person who insisted on doing so turned out to be Velwel and the idea quickly expired. Neila, as was her custom, decided to make up her own mind and was the only one to stay in the village.

The wolf ran along the road, his nose to the ground, and the Guild leader, trusting in his unmatched instincts, followed him. In Ram'ar, he expected to find most of his subjects. Such border towns were famous for their many fun houses and taverns. Many of them said that in some of these places it is possible to order a half-elf woman for a bag of Riga crowns. Alt'ar didn't really believe this, for the elves were not in the habit of interbreeding with people they considered an inferior and weaker race. Indeed, it is not difficult to convince a very tipsy and horny gentleman just stupidity. The leader of the Guild did not shy away from this type of entertainment but preferred to keep it in moderation. Above all, as a werewolf he was violent, and the alcohol deprived him of all inhibitions. He had to drink thoughtfully enough to stay in control and not allow himself to change.

Like many poorer cities, Ram'ar was fenced with a palisade of rough logs. In front of her, refugees from other parts of the kingdom were camping in carelessly constructed shacks. Alt'ar lightly nudged the mount's sides and moved a little faster into the cluster. The sight of men, women and children in dirty and torn clothes did not surprise him at all. He'd been seeing them more than usual lately. He suspected that the reason for this was the rule of the king. There were rumors of increased taxes ruining many lesser merchants. They lost everything.

At the sight of a lonely traveler, some beggars would emerge, reaching out for alms. Young girls, less than twelve years old, offered their charms for a mediocre copper, and dirty children clung to the harness. As soon as he reached the gate, everyone fled in a panic.

Two shaved bald mercenaries with identical rectangular faces and small black eyes regarded the assassin with not very friendly glances.

"What?" Growled one of them, stepping forward and lifting a slightly iron-clad wooden truncheon.

Alt'ar looked up at the powerfully built hog, looking like an overgrown hog.

"I want to go into town," he said in a relaxed, carefree tone.

The bully scratched his bald head. You see, thinking was very difficult for him.

"Nobody's coming in," he said finally, his face threatening. "Order of the steward."

The leader of the Assassins' Guild was not in the least impressed. He knew the steward here well and knew that at this time of day he was probably too busy emptying another pitcher of wine to be interested in his arrival. Besides, he feared him more than the priest's demon.

Not bothering himself with the guard's threatening face, he rode a little closer.

"You mean that fat hog, Garod?" He asked contemptuously, casually revealing the gleaming hilt of his sword. "I think his skin is so dear to him that he would not dare to refuse me hospitality," he added with a hint of menace.

The second of the thugs backed away at the sight of the weapon and gripped the long spear tighter in his hand. He was not used to threats.

"Who are you by the way?" He asked less hesitantly.

Alt'ar broke free in the saddle.

"Someone you wouldn't want to offend," he replied calmly.

Bullyboy hesitated. Alt'ar saw what was going on in his head. The little pig's eyes constantly looked fearfully at him, then at his sword. Finally, he tapped a ham-like fist on the gate wing. At this signal, the heavy gates moved and began to slowly open.

The assassin passed the guard and rode into the city, followed by Ars like a silvery gray shadow. The horse's hooves sank down to the hocks in the mud mixed with a thick layer of faeces. These, in turn, gave off an unbearable stench. Alt'ar directed the horse into one of the wider streets, where the inn "Under the One-Eyed Witch" was located. It was there that he expected to find Falk - a trickster, drunk and whoremonger, who was also a kind of "king" of the local underworld.

The assassin stopped his horse in front of a slightly neglected building with dirty glass from which a faint light spilled. Most of the paint has fallen off from the stooped figure on the old sign. He had no doubt that he had come to the right address. Especially when an old man staggered out of there without a single leg and, ignoring him, let out a stream of urine up the mossy stairs. The leader of the Assassins' Guild winced as the sharp smell of the cripple hit him. Unfortunately, the stench coming from inside the room turned out to be much worse. As a werewolf, he had a much more acute sense of smell, which turned out to be a curse at times like this.

As he entered the tabernacle, Alt'ar still looked disgusted. As he expected, the room was filled with customers in various states of intoxication. On the threshold he was greeted by a huge bouncer who acted as a bouncer, but at the sight of the huge wolf he backed away. Most of the tables in the spacious room were occupied. The two maidens swarmed like boiling water, trying to serve the very cheerful guys in no time. Among them, it was easy to recognize who he was looking for. So he immediately headed for one of the long benches.

On it sat a short, broad-shouldered man with a shaved bald head and slightly dazed black eyes. He was surrounded by a small group of scantily dressed young ladies of average beauty. On the wooden table, among the emptied wine jars, there were nibbled chicken bones. Another vessel was in his hand, the other was embraced around the waist of a plump blonde with generous breasts.

"Having fun?" Asked the assassin, facing him.

The man smiled, revealing a lot of missing teeth, and saluted with the jug he was holding.

"Look who came here!" He exclaimed, drawing the attention of all the guests. "What also brings you to such a crap?"

The killer appraised him critically. Falko was about thirty years old, though it is difficult to estimate by looking at his deeply furrowed and scarred face. He was dressed so dirty and worn that it differed little from a beggar. Nevertheless, his attitude and self-confidence made him feel a certain amount of respect in people.

Alt'ar was not human. So, the first thing he did was wrinkle his nose. The scent emanating from his interlocutor, which was a mixture of the stench of a long unwashed body, digested alcohol and urine, was barely bearable. Nevertheless, he mastered the revulsion that rose in him, and replied in a cool voice:

"Business."

He wasn't going to betray this bald imbecile any more. He had to be constantly on guard lest it be prematurely revealed that he openly opposed the royal authority. Especially since he intended to help overthrow it. He did not think that Falko was dipping his dirty fingers in politics. Unfortunately, it was possible that one of his men was a spy.

Falko looked at him slightly blurry. Apparently, he not only drank a lot this evening, but also took Gaudalum. And the killer had too fresh a picture of what the "harmless" drug had done to the half-dragon. He wasn't going to find out for himself what it was like.

"And we are celebrating, as you can see," the man said, his other hand drawing the redhead with a sow-like face to him. "The king either forgot about us, or he simply has the southernmost lands in his veil. At least, no patrol has been seen here for months, which is very good for my business." He smiled slightly. "But I see that something is bothering you in turn, old friend. What also could have prompted you to leave the capital at such a low time?"

The Guild leader frowned. He did not know yet how much he could trust Falko, and the risk was too great.

"I suppose you've heard the rumors of a rebellion in the north, as many have," he said carefully, studying his face carefully.

Falko frowned, pondered the answer, sighed in resignation and said:

"Eh, Alt'ar. I didn't think you'd ever get involved in politics, because it's a really nasty swamp and extremely smelly..." He trailed off his voice and lowered it to a conspiratorial whisper. "I've heard more than rumors. I know from a good source that something is going and that is why the king brings all the armed to the capital. Not only that, compulsory salaries have started. Any man capable of carrying weapons must join the ranks of the royal army. It looks like you're getting ready for a conquest or a war, but the matter stinks from afar, because the opposite side is said to be led by a real dragon."

Alt'ar listened to these revelations calmly. It did not surprise him that people had heard rumors of a dragon. After all, Drasana in its natural form could not be overlooked. The discovery of the amassing of troops and compulsory conscription was also nothing new to him, the news spread extremely quickly in Riden. Nevertheless, it worried him that nobody was worried about it, they all lived as they used to, which was proved all too well by Falko's attitude. Even in the face of such a threat, he did not give up smuggling goods across the Noai'dir border, on the contrary: he was glad that the king was busy with something completely different. Will it then be possible to convince him and other mercenaries to abandon their comfortable life in favor of an unequal struggle with an opponent that is a hundred times more numerous?

He forced a smile and said, weighing every word:

"And I came to Ram'ar just to make you an offer, dear friend. I'm sure you will find it interesting."

The bald man's eyebrows rose and his enthusiasm visibly waned.

"Forgive Alt'ar, by your face I conclude that the matter is serious. I'd rather not talk about it here, you understand..." He winked knowingly. "Tomorrow I will send someone for you, and tonight I encourage you to celebrate with me." To confirm the end of the conversation, he reached for another jug and started emptying it.

Alt'ar sighed deeply and perched on the edge of the wide bench, and the wolf lay at his feet. The killer leaned down and plunged his hand into the thick fur on the animal's neck.

"We have a hard mission ahead of us, my friend," he said.

Ars looked at him with amber eyes and whined softly.

* * *

Standing in front of the great mirror in his chamber, Bal'zar turned once again, admiring the work of the best armorer in the city. The armor fit perfectly, and at the same time it turned out to be incredibly light, and it did not restrict movement. A bear standing on its hind legs - the symbol of Riden - is embossed on the breastplate. The young king yanked his sword away and hissed through the air several times. It used to belong to his father in the past. Until now it lay unused in the vault, he thought he would make it a symbol of his power. Anyway, this weapon deserved to be carried at the belt by someone who would prove to be a ruler.

Dhalia watched the display through narrowed eyes. It had long since stopped amusing her. The little jerky little bastard was starting to irritate her. He intended to lead the army into battle personally. There was no point in taking anything from him as long as he did not launch himself against the two dragons. He wouldn't have listened anyway. .

But it wasn't his endeavors that kept her awake at night, but the last confrontation with Drasan. She couldn't deny that he was getting stronger with each passing moment. She probably found a way to neutralize it for a while. Gaudalum turned out to be even more effective than she had expected. She kept it to herself for now. Should it be revealed that he had slipped out of her hands despite her obvious advantage, Bal'zar might question her competence. And so she could argue that it was the fault of insufficient information given to them by his informer.

Ultimately, she did not fail completely. She managed to discover the greatest weakness of the half-dragon. It turned out to be a girl and his feelings towards her. She could turn out to be the source of his defeat. Nevertheless, it was still necessary to wait and play it skillfully.

Lost in thought, she focused on Drasan and closed her eyes, recalling images from his future. As always, she saw mostly pain and death in it, but there was something else. She saw clearly how the prince understood this girl to be his wife. Now he had a great gap in the armor he had made for himself.

Dhalia smiled at her thoughts before opening her eyes to meet Bal'zar's. He was staring at her as intensely as if he had seen her mind. She felt uncomfortable. Did he know what pleased her so much?

He confirmed her guesses as he unexpectedly made his way toward her.

"What are you thinking about?" He asked in a velvety voice, gently stroking her neck with his fingers. A slight shiver ran through her. She looked at him. It is true that he lacked Drasan's beauty, but his features turned from childhood to masculine. He even had stubble.

The woman sighed slightly and with remarkable skill, worthy of the best royal courtesan, wrapped her legs around his waist and pulled him towards her. With satisfaction she heard his breathing become twice as fast. He fell into the trap of her beauty. She effortlessly rose to meet his eyes.

"We're close, Bal'zar," she whispered seductively, running her hand over his breastplate. "It's enough to remove the last obstacle and we will gain power you never dreamed of."

The young ruler shook his head, barely concentrating on what she was saying.

"You mean someone or something?" He asked, not fully understanding.

Dhalia pushed him slightly away from her. She stood up and stretched, tautening her body like a kitten after a long nap. She heard the youth's dreamy sigh. He now had a perfect view of her almost naked body covered with a silk petticoat.

"You grow stronger every day, but he grows stronger, too," she said, turning to look at him.

"Drasan," he said the name like something filthy and disgusting.

She smiled slightly at the sight of the scorn on his face. She went to the dressing table and began to brush her long hair while still watching him. She waited for him to come to her.

He did not do it.

"You know we should kill him," he said casually. "His actions may threaten our joint plans."

She smiled.

"Why kill a dragon when it can be tame," she said. "It's enough to find one weak point and we will have it in hand."

"If so, why have you failed so far?" He asked slyly, taking a few steps towards her. "You did not succumb," he added with a gleam of triumph in his eyes. "He's the only one who has not fallen into the trap of your beauty. It's probably frustrating to have the power of fire at your fingertips and not be able to take advantage of it."

Dhalia stopped smiling. Her lips formed a narrow line.

"What are you getting at?" She asked.

He laughed softly, malevolently.

"You had your chance, you failed. The beast you wanted to tame is out of control. You have to put him back in the cage, neutralize or kill him. You don't need magic for that, just the right tactics."

"I'm afraid I still don't understand," she said softly.

"You will understand everything the moment I reveal my plan to you. There is a new pawn in our game - a girl. She can make us win or lose. From what Alder has told me, our young friend has feelings for her. He certainly wouldn't let anything bad happen to her. So my idea is this: we will get her, and he will come to us."

"It's not that simple, my dear. The girl is still too close to her scaly defender. We have to wait for the appropriate moment. One that will support the rest of our plans. Therefore, for now, let's focus on current affairs. For example, the band of thugs that Alt'ar gathers around him." She pointed out the error and now waited for a reaction.

Bal'zar winced slightly, but then a steel gleam appeared in his eyes.

"Leave Alt'ar me. I'll soon remind him why it's not worth messing with me."

* * *

The big fat man sitting behind the cluttered pile of papers scowled at the leader of the Killers' Guild standing in front of him. After a moment, a wide, false smile spread across his piggy face.

"Hello, Alt'ar," he said in a loud voice. "'What brings you to our town?"

The killer sat down in the only available chair.

"Not your business," he replied, and to emphasize the words threw his legs up onto the desk.

There was a menacing gleam in the steward's little pig eyes, but Alt'ar ignored it.

"It's all my business here," Garod said, his fake smile still going on. "You are in my yard and my rules are the only ones." He clearly underlined the word "my" in each sentence.

The Guild leader leaned towards him; a soft growl sounded from under the table. The steward looked anxiously at the great gray beast sitting at his feet.

"Get that brute out of here!" He growled, the smile fading from his face, giving way to panicky fear. "Guard!" He roared towards the door.

Alt'ar got up and swiftly turned towards the entrance, in which stood two men armed with short swords. They looked around the room for a moment, perhaps not fully understanding why they had been summoned. Seeing an inconspicuous man with a huge wolf hiding at his feet, ready to attack at any moment, they lowered their weapons and smiled dismissively.

"What are you waiting for, you fool?" Asked the steward. "Get him!"

The guards slowly moved towards Alt'ar, but Alt'ar only smiled. From the scabbards hidden in the sleeves with a gentle tug he took out two short daggers and with a smooth movement threw one in the direction of the approaching men. To his satisfaction, he saw the first of them collapse in half a step, and it was clear from the expression on his face that he had no idea what had happened. Realization came a moment later when he saw the hilt protruding from his chest.

The assassin cast a brief glance at the wolf lurking at his feet, then instructed him:

"Look after!"

His companion resumed his seat at the base of the desk and watched the scene unfolding calmly.

The second of the guards clearly lost heart. He must have realized that he was not dealing with an ordinary robber, as he was now slowly backing towards the door. Alt'ar rose from the chair in one fluid movement, his eyes never leaving the lad. The other looked nervously from him to his employer. Finally, he dropped his weapon and hurried to the door. However, he did not have time to reach them, as the blade thrown by the leader of the Guild pierced the very center of his back. The bully roared like a wounded buffalo and fell to the floor. The killer jumped up to him and with one point of the sword he finished the work, thus shortening the torment of his victim.

As he checked for anything outside, indicating that reinforcements were coming, Alt'ar turned to the steward with a mocking smile:

"You could have tried a little harder." He pointed to the two dead bodies on the floor. "Is there no one in the area better suited to defend your fat body?" He added, clearly emphasizing the last four words.

Garod wiped the sweat from his brow. For a moment he thoughtlessly stared at the bloodstain soaking into the priceless carpet, his little pig eyes staring at the Alt'ar again.

"What do you want?" He asked as he pulled a handkerchief from his silk jacket pocket and wiped his face with it.

"Only one," Alt'ar replied, deftly walking around the two bodies stretched out on the floor. "Don't try to interfere in my affairs."

The steward stood up. He did it with some difficulty, because his enormous body did not fit on the velvet chair. He walked slowly, swaying from side to side, to the assassin, taking care not to splash the blood on his high-gloss polished shoes.

"Agreed," he said, and a broad smile flashed across his round face again, as if the events from before were meaningless.

Alt'ar slapped his thigh vigorously, and the wolf ran up to him. He did not take his amber eyes off the huge man, staggering into the corridor. What he saw there he did not like at all. About a dozen of his men were disarmed and incapacitated by four killers. In one of the attackers, he recognized Thal - his son. He was a tall and slender young man, not resembling his father at all. He had straight black hair flowing down his shoulders and brown eyes. He wore a sleeveless leather caftan, straight pants, and knee-high riding boots.

The steward's forehead was once again covered with thick beads of sweat, and his ring-shaped fingers began to mindlessly tug at the large thick mustache. He swallowed loudly and turned back to the Guild leader, fear lurking in his eyes.

"Why?" He groaned, nodding his head at Thal.

Alt'ar smiled. He knew he had it at hand.

"Your son has talent," he said calmly. "He came to see me himself, he heard a lot about the Guild, and he wanted to join our ranks."

"He's still young," said Garod. "And his mother..." His voice cracked.

"I understand that you are willing to pay dearly for the life of your only son," Alt'ar said with a sly smile on his face.

"I'll do what you want," the man stammered, staring at the firstborn and wringing a handkerchief in his fingers.

Alt'ar nodded and began to speak:

"A large group of my people will be here soon, many of them you would like to see dangling on the scaffold, but..." He paused and added with a vindictive smile, "...if you want your son to be alive, you will do nothing. You will keep your thugs away from my killers. Understand?"

The steward nodded eagerly, his little eyes still on Thal, who avoided his gaze with equal determination.

"Besides, I don't advise you to try to interfere in my affairs in any way. You will squeeze into your den, and you will not lean out of it until I leave town."

Garod nodded again, making his three chins tremble.

Alt'ar smiled in satisfaction.

"Okay, that would be it." He patted the stunned man on his massive back and started toward the exit of the building. After a while he changed his mind, as he paused, turned on his heel and threw aside, "Have a nice day."

He left the terrified steward, still staring in disbelief at his son until he and the rest of the killers disappeared through the door.

***

How I got into all of this? Mara thought, going down slowly up the rickety wooden stairs to the musty basement.

Not more than two days ago, one of the innkeeper's guests informed the dumbfounded visitors of the inn that, for some unknown reason, the young king of Radzina had begun to gather a truly powerful army. It was quite unusual, as it was still winter on the peninsula, and the freezing ice and bitter frost were not conducive to conquests. Rumors were beginning to circulate that the Rideen would start with the first thaws.

The girl understood that if she wanted to do something, she had to start now. The journey in its present state seemed like sheer madness, after all it was with hope. However, no force could dissuade her from her intended endeavors. It has long been heard of the dire condition of the aging king of Antua, as well as the fact that the ruler would die childless. Now was the last chance to claim inheritance.

Despite the lack of a proper upbringing, Mara knew full well that only this would save her and her unborn child from certain death. Yarred was too far away, she couldn't count on him, and she understood from the many stories of the local women that one in three had a draconian childbirth. With such an alternative, the girl had to break a given word and set off on a long and dangerous journey to the capital. She had no choice.

She knew all too well that riding a horse was not a good idea. Fortunately, the money Captain Cordydian left her was enough to buy a sledge. The landlord provided her with provisions for the road, and his wife with a few thick sheepskins to keep her from freezing. She knew that before leaving her current asylum, she had to at least try to establish mental contact with Drasan.

It was for this purpose that she descended into that foul cellar, as far as possible from prying ears and eyes. She wasn't sure if she would succeed. After all, she had never tried to do this before. Unfortunately, it was her duty. She had to tell the only person she trusted after Yarred.

Trying not to think about where she was, Mara focused on trying to find the half-dragon. Along the way, she saw many clusters pulsating with power, but she steadfastly avoided them until she finally found the consciousness she was looking for. She took a deep breath and began to form her thoughts into intelligible words:

Drasan! If you can hear me, know I have to abandon my safe hiding place. As you had suggested earlier, I am going to go to King Valden's court. It is rumored that he is dying. Perhaps this is my last chance to secure my child's future. If I succeed, I will do my best to help you!

Despite no reply, Mara withdrew slowly. She took a few deep breaths, trying to get back into balance. It is true that she did not achieve exactly what she wanted, but it calmed her conscience enough to start thinking about the most important again.

She stroked her belly tenderly and whispered:

"I'll do anything to keep you safe."

***

When Yarred opened his eyes, the sun was high. He mentally chided himself for taking a nap. Fresh snow covered the horse's trail. Now he couldn't tell in which direction the pet had run away. He got up, brushed off his coat, and looked around. He was amazed to discover that he had reached the shores of the lake.

There was no living soul around, but a distinct trail of sled runners ran through the center of the enormous sheet of ice. The captain said it would be safest to go this way. After all, he had to find some sort of human abode. There he will buy a mount and think about what to do next. It was not easy for him to come to terms with the loss of Bruen, but he knew that he would not be able to find him now.

The lake was huge, from the place where the man was standing, the opposite shore could not be seen at all. Slowly and carefully, he stepped onto the frozen pane. Snow creaked under his boots. He thought it would be best if he followed the trail, it gave him hope that he would be on the other side before dusk fell.

Suddenly he stopped and pricked his ears. After a while, he had no doubt he heard the dull thud of horses' hooves. Someone was driving towards him. He looked around but saw no one. Had he misheard? After a moment he heard the same noise, but much closer. He turned and a smile lit his face. Bruen was trotting towards him. He gasped at the sight of you and quickened his pace. Yarred grabbed the reins and examined his friend, wanting to make sure he was real.

"Ah, old man," he sighed, stroking the horse's neck. "I thought you were done."

He checked the saddlebags and pulled out a piece of dried bread and a handful of dried fruit. He began to devour this meager meal greedily to drown the hunger a little. When he had eaten, he took a handful of hemlock from another sack and held it under the mount's mouth. The stallion ate in the blink of an eye and nudged the captain with his mouth, hoping for more, but Yarred shook his head and said:

"I'm sorry, my friend, but we have a long way to go, we must save provisions." He patted the horse's neck and climbed into the saddle.

They trotted along the track of the runners. Regaining his friend, and better humor with him, Yarred began humming an old military song. Bruen's ears twitched and he gasped at the familiar tune.

***

Neila cursed, repeatedly unsuccessfully trying to spark a spark. Neither hands, nor bitter winds helped in this. Drasan went hunting in his enormous and formidable reptilian form. Although he hadn't spoken at all since their brief mental discussion, his presence was somehow reassuring. If he had been around, he would have warmed her with his body, she wouldn't have to worry about lighting the fire.

Now that her companion has disappeared, she was forced to fend for herself. It wasn't going very well in this soulless wilderness. Since leaving the massacred settlement, they avoided all traces of human existence. This quickly resulted in an empty lunch bag. Neil understood Drasan's noble motives, but it irritated her a little that he didn't include her in his plans. He would often disappear for hours, either hunting or patrolling the immediate area in search of another hideout.

The mercenary was waiting for him at that time, doubting his return. He seemed wilder and wilder every day. She was slowly losing hope that she would ever turn back to a human. Worse: on one occasion he might have treated it as a snack.

Giving up on trying to make a fire, Neila scanned the horizon, hoping to see a familiar shape. After a while she gave up. Drasan did not intend to make a spectacle of himself. He was probably hiding somewhere above the dark gray clouds covering the sky. The girl went back to her horse and took one of the last pieces of dried meat out of the sack. As she chewed it slowly, she tried to ignore the persistent growl in her stomach. At such moments, she wished she were a hunter. She might have asked the prince to bring her a small scrap of prey, but she was afraid that his instinct to defend his food would take over him.

The familiar noise of great wings snapped her out of her gloomy contemplation. Drasan returned to their hideout, all covered in blood as usual. This time it carried what looked to be half a deer or a deer in its mouth. He laid the "snack" on the ground, lay down in the snow, as was his habit, and began to clean the claws of his forepaws of debris.

"As I can see, the hunt is a success," the girl said carefully, keeping a safe distance.

A soft murmur answered her. There was no hint of aggression in him, sounds he made when he was content.

"It's been three days. I would be grateful if you started to behave in the old way," she continued her monologue, undeterred by the lack of reaction on the part of her companion. "I mean human transformation," she added quickly.

Drasan stopped licking the blood from his claws for a moment and glared at her with one eye. Thus, she was sure that she could hear and understand her.

"You're starting to scare me a little," she continued. "You look and act like a wild beast, and you don't say anything about it." This is a little pissy, you know? Especially since we are alone in this wilderness. Alt'ar and his entourage are long gone, there is no danger. Why don't you try to change?"

To her surprise, the half-dragon stood up. He was now imposing, as tall as three workhorses. It was really huge. However, that wasn't what surprised Neila, but something else: he suddenly spoke to her in his usual voice.

"It didn't occur to you that I just don't want to change yet?" He lowered his head so that it was level with her eyes. "My needs as a reptile are much simpler and my life is much less complicated. When I'm hungry, I go hunting. When I feel sleepy, I curl up in a ball and drift away. When I feel a threat, I look for a suitable hiding place to wait it out safely. Maybe I'm fed up with taking responsibility for all of you? Enough that everyone puts their trust in me. Above all, I want a little peace to sort it all out. As a dragon, I have the best chance."

Neila was stunned, staring into one of her green eyes from extremely close range. Indeed, none of that had even crossed her mind. She kept telling herself it was the effect of Gaudalum.

"Ah..." she began, but she bit her tongue and finished it much more gently. "If I understand correctly, you're just hiding."

She regretted those words, because Drasan suddenly turned and started walking.

"Wait!" She shouted after him in one last desperate attempt to find out what was going on.

He stopped and let her come closer.

"I'm afraid I still don't understand," she added, leaning against his rough side. "What are you running from?"

Unknowingly, she made another mistake. A hoarse growl rose in the dragon's throat.

"I'm running away?!" He repeated furiously. "I'm trying to protect you by keeping aloof. You don't understand anything! I made one mistake too many and..." He broke off, his jaw twitching menacingly. "...now you can all pay for it," he said through gritted teeth.

Understanding all too well, Neila slowly circled the enormous body to face it.

"What are you actually talking about?" She asked in a whisper.

Drasan sighed heavily and fell back down in the snow.

"Dhalia..." he began and paused. "Has anyone been playing with your mind?" He asked unexpectedly gently.

The mercenary shook her head slowly.

"The first time she caught and tortured me, she often broke into my mind..." He broke off and gritted his teeth. "...then I was able to fight her, although it had poor results and caused unbearable pain... Last time it was different..." He took a deep breath and hissed through clenched teeth: "...the last time I was unable to defend myself. Dhalia could go deeper than before. Now she knows all my weaknesses, knows where to strike to hurt the most. The worst part is that she found out about you."

"About me?" Neila was stunned. She didn't know how to understand it.

The prince snorted, but he was far from laughing.

"It's not about you, it's about my feelings for you," he replied bluntly.

Neila was stunned. Well, if the cursed witch rummaged in his head, she could learn about their extraordinary bond. She had a hook on him.

Drasan was silent for a long time. She felt he hesitated. It took a great deal of self-denial and courage to utter these words aloud. Finally, he took a deep breath and whispered so softly it was like a breath of wind:

"I exposed myself too much. I shouldn't interfere with my private affairs. I should suppress this feeling, forget normality. To accept that loneliness is meant for me, he continued, his voice swollen with suffering."

"What?!" At first, Neila didn't understand what he meant. After all, he was definitely not talking about...

Meanwhile, Drasan continued in the same tone as before, but much louder:

"It's stupid, I know. I chose a really bad moment for this confession, but I can't hide it anymore. You should know." He paused, raised his head and looked into her eyes. "I... have more than just friendship for you."

Neila felt her face flush with a scarlet blush.

"Drasan, I... I..." She broke off. She didn't know what to say to that. She was a mercenary, not a courtesan. She had no idea about love. Since her mother's death, her father had raised her, and he was very harsh and strict. He had never come to terms with the fact that his wife had died without bearing a son to him. He did his best to gain an heir - for example, by forcing his fourteen-year-old daughter to marry a much older man. Neila had no idea what it meant to be loved.

"Now do you understand?" He asked. "I needed time. I had to think about it, consider all the possibilities. Consider what to do next."

When the first surprise passed, the girl felt only anger.

"When were you going to tell me about this?" She asked, raising her voice. "For three days I have been worried about your strange behavior and you are just avoiding responsibility. You must be a selfish asshole!" She finished, glaring at him at the same time.

To her surprise and annoyance, the half-dragon didn't react at all. He stared intently at the horizon, as if he saw something there that he did not expect to see. Resigned, she followed his gaze and froze, unable to make any movement. A column of riders headed straight towards them. If her eyesight was right, there were over twenty of them.

In an instant, her knees buckled under her and she had to lean against one of her massive paws to keep from falling. Drasan's muscles tightened, ready to fend off any attack, and a furious hiss was born in his throat. The riders were close enough to be recognized. They were by no means part of the Rift army. They could be a mercenary group or a local gang of thugs. There was little chance that they had not come here to capture or kill them.

Neila glanced uncertainly at her companion, who kept his eyes on the approaching enemies. She also decided to pull herself together and reached for a gun. The chill of the hilt restored her confidence. She stood beside the dragon; sword raised to hip level.

One of the newcomers, the leader, saw them first. He trotted towards them, while his companions stopped the horses some distance from the strange pair. Apparently, they had realized what they were dealing with and preferred to stay away just in case.

"Hey, you there!" He exclaimed, stopping his horse. "I don't think you know that..." He suddenly stopped talking and his eyes widened.

Drasan grinned, displaying a full set of teeth. Neila knew this heralded trouble.

"Seems no one has taught you to choose your opponents wisely. I advise you to get out of here while you still have a chance," he said in a strangely indulgent tone.

The head of the gang did not know what to do. He had apparently taken Drasan for a large boulder of an unprecedented shape before. The mercenary did not have to look to predict accidents. Drasan simply launched himself at the lone rider, and before the rider could start the horse to run, he grabbed him by the half and crushed him in his huge jaws. The rest of the gang was more than enough. They quickly turned their mounts and ran away. The half-dragon spat what was left of their leader to the ground and turned back. It was obvious that his mood immediately improved.

CHAPTER 8

Alt'ar watched with satisfaction as the people gathered in the square. They came from the farthest corners of the kingdom, obeying his call. He looked at the faces of the best of the best - many of them had the worst associations with their ugly scars. Among them stood out tall red-haired Antuans, swarthy-eyed and slant-eyed Alikorians, and low, tattooed Noai'dirians. The latter caused the greatest panic among the local population. Although by nature they were a people of peace, mainly engaged in fishing, their warriors looked like figures from a nightmare.

So far, nearly a hundred of them have arrived and they caused quite a sensation. A large group of onlookers had gathered in the main town square, mostly filthy children who had escaped from their mothers' care, and were now staring at the men with flushed faces, one of whom looked weirder than the other. There were also townspeople. The latter watched the whole crowd with growing anxiety. Some people looked anxiously for the city guard, and this one was nowhere to be seen.

One of the riders who made the townspeople the most panic both with his impressive height and with a nasty burn scar that covered half of his face, jumped off his horse and walked over to Alt'ar. The men shook hands.

The big man spoke in a thudding bass:

"Hello, Alt'ar. I'm glad to see you again."

"Hello, Boran," replied the assassin, looking fearlessly into the huge man's black eyes.

He knew perfectly well that this one could twist the neck of a mountain bear with his bare hands. The mercenaries nicknamed him "iron fist" because he was able to knock out a large husband with one blow.

"What is this urgent task?" Asked the giant assassin, adjusting both belts with swords slung diagonally across his back. "You've probably got all the cutters in the neighborhood here. There are rumors that you are preparing for a war with the king." He smiled as if to be a good joke, but then he became serious again.

The Guild leader thought about it. The eyes of all the killers stared at him expectantly. Alt'ar decided it was better not to beat around the bush. He jumped on a lonely wagon so that all the gathered could see him well.

"The rumors are true," he began, trying to make his voice authoritative. "Our demented lord is getting ready to go to war with the rest of the peninsula. Its main goal is to create its own Empire on the ruins of the other kingdoms. Put simply, it will walk over the corpses of your mothers, wives, daughters, sons, brothers and sisters, just to achieve a goal."

He looked sternly at all faces, continued, "He won't hesitate to enslave you or destroy everything you once knew. The former order of things will crumble, swallowed up by a cruel tyrant's lust for power." He paused, waiting for any comment, but everyone was silent. Even the townspeople looked at him in horror. Alt'ar smiled sourly, resumed the interrupted monologue. "I'm going to fight him because I think it's the most appropriate. I dare not ask any of you for support. The decision is yours; you can remain passive and wait for the inevitable destruction of the world you know..." Here he looked menacingly at the killers surrounding him in a semicircle. "Or with me and my allies, throw the gauntlet directly at the tyrant's feet. Who will go with me?!" He shouted the last words.

All assassins assembled reached for their weapons to raise in support of their leader.

Meanwhile, Alt'ar went on, still in his tone:

"We are all pursued without exception by what His Majesty calls "the justice system". The same thing awaits us all..." He paused again, "...a short dance on the loop. We have nothing to lose and much to gain. Some of you have families." Here he looked at a few of the Noai'dirians, who nodded silently. "...ask yourself: Do you want your children henceforth to live in poverty under the tyrant's rule or perish during the conquest? And your wives, mothers, daughters have become free entertainment for his soldiers? This is what is coming and the only hope in us and our actions! We all remember how Sheardon ended, and by the gods, let's not let the same happen to your hometowns and villages!" This time, all the killers gathered in the square raised their weapons, and from their throats came a consistent roar of support for his words. The townspeople, timid and distrustful at first, also listened to his speech as if they were hypnotized. "I'm calling you to fight! Everyone, even those who have been undecided so far. Soon the royal army will be knocking on your door to take your sons and force them to fight! The king will send your children to their deaths, to him they are worth less than a herd of cows. They are called "dog meat", "raven food". They always go in the front line and they are hit by the first impetus of the enemy forces." At the sound of the insulting name that the infantry carried in Riden's army, an uproar broke out among the crowd of townspeople. Many of them openly cursed the king, regardless of the fact that such audacity is punishable by death.

The Guild leader looked at it all with undisguised satisfaction. He has been able to hypnotize many interlocutors with his speech for a long time, but he has never had the opportunity to speak to such crowds before. In the eyes of both his killers and ordinary gray people, he could see that they were ready to follow him to his death.

***

"No matter what they think of me, I won't wear it anymore," Drasan replied. He was slowly losing both patience and good humor. The whole discussion was about the pile of rags Neila had miraculously obtained in a nearby village.

After transforming back into a human, it turned out that his current garment was by no means suitable for wearing. The tunic and shirt were shredded, and the pants were streaked with dirt and blood. Though the prince had long forgotten the touch of silk or any other expensive material he used to wear, he had no intention of wearing begging rags. From a distance they smelled as if their previous owner had recently taken a bath in the city's gutter. He preferred his old outfit.

"You cannot show up near any human settlement in this outfit." The mercenary did not give up. "They're definitely looking for you."

Drasan briefly snorted at this. He didn't regret the fact that he had made a pulp out of the local warlord's chief. It was a lot of fun for him: watching thugs blow with their tails tucked up. Anyway, he and Neila made every effort to ensure that no one would find the bastard, burying his charred remains a few feet under the snow.

Unfortunately, the girl did not share his optimism.

"I don't think anyone would believe them," said the young man tiredly, as they had been talking about the subject for a good few hour. "So far, no one has come to look for confirmation of the words of a few bandits."

"It must be a deliberate act," replied the girl. She was furious that he hadn't taken care of it properly. "They won't send an infantry regiment against you, or you would have swept them away with a single wave of your tail. So maybe they sent a messenger to the nearest town? And I don't think I need to remind you which one is closest, wolly?" She asked, without waiting for an answer, she added, "Washmorth. If I were in the witch's shoes, I would be doing the second attempt right now, with armed support."

"Where does this pessimism come from?" Drasan asked, unable to bear this distrust any longer. "I have explained to you what is keeping me here. We are in a complete seclusion, there is at least a day's drive to the nearest town, and only if you can change horses frequently. We have ample time for the soldiers to arrive."

Neila took a deep breath to soothe her nerves and began to speak, slowly drawing the words out:

"The nearby village has recently suffered an air raid by Riden troops. They plundered everything that could be of use to the army, including horses. Even the train ones. Not to mention chickens and other farm animals. They raped a few women and drove towards the capital, driving both livestock and peasants capable of carrying weapons. They have been a hair since the discovery of our hideout in what you say is a remote wilderness."

Drasan did not seem surprised by this. Bal'zar's strength grew steadily, and he did not hesitate to plunder the villagers for this purpose. He finally pursued the longed-for goal of power over the entire peninsula. He needed a whole lot of supplies to feed such a huge army. There was one serious drawback to doing so, which neither the young ruler nor the Dhalia took into account - the repressed population could revolt at any moment. They were now like a freshly prepared pile drenched in olive oil, and it was enough to spark a spark to set it on fire. The prince knew that with only peasants armed with scythes and pitchforks behind him, he would not win this war. He had to have a real army.

"It makes no sense to attack me now," he said, deciding to keep his thoughts to himself. "The last time, not only for me, turned out to be a valuable lesson. Dhalia understood that I had made a powerful ally for myself, and she would be very careful now."

He wasn't really sure about it at all, but he preferred not to arouse an attack of hysteria in the already jittery mercenary. They both had to focus on finding the others now. Alt'ar, as far as he could remember, was going to go to the Ram'ar, but he certainly did not succeed in having all of his people there. He probably left at least some of them. Before they could continue their journey, Drasan faced one more serious conversation, which he did not feel like.

It didn't take long for him to concentrate his mind and find Gaenor. The dragon was nearby, waiting for news.

What do you want? the greeting of his older brother was as harsh as always, but the prince had got used to it.

And I greet you, Gaenor. I would like you to honor us with your presence so that we can discuss the plans without the risk of being overheard. Drasan replied, forcing himself to maintain official etiquette. Otherwise, he knew the dragon would simply ignore him.

As you wish, Your Majesty. He stated with a hint of sarcasm and broke off contact.

Drasan opened his eyes and looked into Neila's glowing eyes.

"I hate it when you do that," she snapped at him.

"You know I have no choice," he retorted, adding in a somber voice, "Besides, digging into my head, Dhalia found out everything anyway. There is no point in hiding from her any further."

Neila scowled to protest, but gave it up as she turned on her heel and walked briskly towards the overhang. There she sat down with her back to him, not saying a word.

Drasan wasn't going to worry about it. He was used to such treatment by the girl. He sat down in the snow nearby and stared at the horizon. He did not have to wait long, because he noticed the familiar figure after a while. Probably the older dragon was much closer than he expected. Gaenor was almost three times smaller than he was, which gave him a grace in the air that he did not possess. The dimensions did not allow him to do so. Landing was also much easier for him than for his younger brother.

The gaze of the yellow eyes, as usual, made the young man shiver, for although Gaenor was now one of his allies, he certainly would not have missed the opportunity to give him a decent smack.

"How are the negotiations, Your Majesty?" He asked, folding his wings and making himself as comfortable as possible.

"I think we've gained one ally," Drasan replied evasively. He did not intend to report on his confrontation with Dhalia for the time being. She will tell him about it in more favorable circumstances. "Alder showed up?" He asked, changing the subject.

"No," Gaenor did not hide how much he was irritated by the sudden change of subject. It is possible that he was tempted to make a little punch on the younger confrere. "Judging by your expression, not everything went right." There was no concern in his tone, rather a virulent malice.

Knowing that the dragon was going to provoke him again, Drasan ignored the taunts and said in the most calm tone possible:

"You must have had a good view of the area by flying here. I would like to know how many troops are nearby and how to avoid them?"

The dragon snorted softly with obvious contempt.

"I saw only meager infantry units and one light cavalry, less than two hundred men in total. However, this is not what will interest you." He smirked maliciously. "The main forces of the Riden army are concentrated on Lake Una, and the headquarters is located near Washmorth itself. This is not the end of the revelation. It is said that the commander-in-chief is not the king, but one of his mages. I haven't had a chance to look too closely at it, but even from a distance it looked oddly familiar."

Drasan frowned.

"What do you mean?" He asked with a strange certainty that what he was about to hear he would not like at all.

"In my humble opinion it was Alder," replied the elder dragon. "The same one who traveled with you for months. He turned out to be an exceptionally clever spy on Bal'zar."

Drasan felt an icy chill in his heart. He seemed to disregard the real threat by focusing on watching Gaenor. Alder, who had rather meager magical abilities, did not seem threatening to him. He treated his interest in supernatural beings as a strange hobby. He also ignored the fact that the sorcerer had disappeared shortly after they got into the city. He naively believed in a fairy tale about the alleged removal from the court. Meanwhile, he was holding a poisonous snake, which was just waiting for the right moment to attack.

"What now, Drasan?" The dragon asked, not hiding his irony. "The enemy knows all our plans. He knows what kind of move we are going to make in front of us. We don't have any army, and even if we somehow get armed support, we have no chance of surviving it."

"What do you suggest?!" The half-dragon exploded, unexpectedly for himself. "Should I give up? Walk politely towards Washmorth and let yourself be turned into a passive slave? Forgive me, but I'd rather die, preferably in a fight!"

"That's not what I meant, arrogant brat," the dragon hissed. "I want you to think a little for a change, instead of going to the element. Coolly, without emotions, calculate the odds with a handful of people against the entire army. Who will help us? Antuans? Eardenes? Or are you going to ask the southern barbarians for it? Look at what happened to Sheardon and learn from it. You have nothing left to fight for, and timely retreat is no disgrace. Our time is long gone, Drasan, let people decide their own fate."

"You want me to run away with my tail curled up," growled the prince, feeling his anger rise again. "Like a cowardly rat, you demand that I escape from a sinking ship? Unfortunately, that's not how I was brought up, that's not what I was taught..."

"Open your eyes at last, you stupid puppy!" Gaenor yelled at him. "Your teachers have failed! Even your beloved mentor Ashkan, a great fan of the Old Codex, to whom his own race has become stuck! You have been to the Sanctuary and you have seen with your own eyes how much unicorns care about the fate of mankind! Finally, learn to lose! Dhalia and Bal'zar have won, you have failed! That's the end!"

This was too much for Drasan. He was overcome with anger so much that he was close to transforming. Red flames enveloped his body. He was getting ready to pounce on Gaenor, but Neila showed up just in time.

"What are you guys doing?!" She screamed at them. "Your quarrel will bring all the soldiers in the area to our necks!"

Drasan mastered his anger with difficulty and turned his reptilian eyes to her.

"Don't interfere," he hissed through clenched teeth.

"And don't try to direct me," the mercenary retorted, standing in front of him with her hands on her hips. "I thought we were primarily not to draw attention to ourselves. Meanwhile, the whole neighborhood heard your little quarrel."

The prince considered it most appropriate in this situation to calm down. It was not easy for him, considering that he had spent the last few days as a giant reptile.

He finally managed to stifle his anger. He noticed that Gaenor was smiling in an oddly mocking way. Drasan snarled at him. There was nothing more degrading than a woman commanding him. Probably, as in the world of werewolves, dragons were of the opinion that the female was always lower in the hierarchy.

It was his custom to twist his father's ring on his finger in such a situation, twirling nervously back and forth. He considered the possibilities, but leaving the peninsula was in last place. He tried to ignore Gaenor, because whenever he looked at him, his anger returned. He was tired of waiting for Dhalia and Bal'zar to gather enough strength to attack. From what he understood from military training, the best line of defense is a pre-emptive attack. So, he could either wait a while, or go to Dhalia with the forces at his disposal, and count on the fact that infantry composed mainly of the force of conscripted peasants would fall apart at the first encounter. After all, he had to reach Alt'ar and find out how many men he had gathered before deciding anything.

With that in mind, he finally managed to find a solution. He had to risk mental contact with Rodian. It was she who played the role of Alt'ar's right hand, in his absence he had to consult everything with her.

He stopped and closed his eyes. He didn't look long; it was indeed nearby. He waited calmly for her to speak first.

Drasan. Her voice sounded uncertain, maybe she didn't know what to say.

We don't have much time for discussion, he announced without saying hello. I need to know how far your camp is from here.

Nearby. She sent him an image of two twin hills and a small valley in the center. You have to be careful, because the army is swarming around.

Drasan was not surprised by this, given that they were dangerously close to Lake Una, over which the enemy had located their main forces. It was impossible to slip away unnoticed, unless...

Could you open a teleport for us?

Rodian was silent a long moment, weighing up the pros and cons.

If I open the door for you, I will draw your attention to it. Such a strong spell will not go unnoticed. This is a very risky move, considering what has happened recently...

We don't have time, interrupted Drasan. We've attracted too much attention to ourselves anyway.

This is another argument against, she said, clearly not enthusiastic about his idea.

Will you do it or not?! The prince was slowly losing his composure.

Yes, but you need to give me some time to focus, she replied, and broke off contact before he answered her.

Drasan opened his eyes and looked at Gaenor.

"Our ally will create a portal for us..." he began, but was interrupted by a furious hiss. The self-possessed dragon suddenly bristled.

"Since when do you fraternize with witches?" He asked incredulously.

"I did what was necessary," the half-dragon growled. He had resumed his ready-to-fight stance.

This time Neila was not going to interfere, which Drasan took as a good sign. Staring into his fellow man's yellow eyes, he allowed himself to be overwhelmed by power. The transformation, as always, was quick and without any problems. As he faced Gaenor, preparing to fight, Gaenor began to back away. Perhaps he did not expect that the young kinsman had grown significantly since the last meeting. The prince exposed his teeth slightly. It was not an act of aggression, but rather a purely demonstrative gesture.

"Dhalia and Bal'zar are gearing up to attack Antua!" He thundered. "And while you probably won't support it, I'm going to do everything in my power to prevent it. You can either join me or wait for this bitch to crush the entire world you know."

Before the older dragon understood the insult contained in this sentence, an oval circle of light shone in the air in front of them, and after a while it took the form of a stationary mirror surface. Neila breathed a sigh of relief when a slender red-haired witch emerged from him, propping herself up on her hips and looking defiantly at both reptiles.

"I'm sorry to interrupt your carefree chat, boys," said Rodian coldly, facing Drasan and staring fearlessly into one of the wild staring eyes. "I have news from Alt'ar. He managed to assemble about nine hundred of the best killers from all over the peninsula. Now he is waiting for us on the mountain pass near Ram'ar. If you hurry up, we have a chance to get there before dark."

Gaenor snorted contemptuously, looking at Drasan as if he were insane.

"Nine hundred?!" He rumbled Neila involuntarily backed away, and Rodian instinctively raised her shields around her. "This is your army?! Are you facing a handful against tens of thousands? Then maybe give up right away! You'll save the work for gravediggers."

"I'm trying my best," Drasan snapped back.

"And nothing comes of it, Your Majesty," the dragon bit back, grinning at him. "Your stupidity is beyond even ego. Bal'zar will crush you like a bear crushes a fly that bothers him! But maybe this will teach you something at last, you smart brat! Maybe the sight of people dying under your command will finally open your eyes!"

Drasan understood instantly what Gaenor was striving for. The elder dragon was still trying to provoke him. He might have accepted the challenge, but it was not the right time.

"Perhaps you're right," he drawled, trying to contain his anger. "History will judge one day what commander I was."

Gaenor dismissed it with another contemptuous huff, but this time he was silent.

Taking advantage of the moment of silence, Drasan turned his back to his rival and started towards the portal. Neila followed him. Out of the corner of his eye, he saw Gaenor spread his wings again in preparation for flight.

CHAPTER 9

A small black bird flew through the open window of the chamber and landed on Dhalia's shoulder. The witch took a roll of parchment off his leg and scanned him quickly. Bal'zar tried to read the text over her shoulder. Before he could do it, the woman rolled the letter up and stood up. She looked happy.

The ruler frowned. Shirza lying at his feet raised his head and fixed a greedy look at the bird sitting on the witch's shoulder.

"This is very good news for us," she said, as if reading his mind. "It seems that all is not lost yet and the mistake you made will be corrected."

"What are you talking about?" Bal'zar daringly pretended to be politely surprised. He was getting way too brazen. The witch choked back her anger.

"You know exactly what I'm talking about," she said coldly, wrapping the letter in her clenched hand. "Do you think I don't know about the two light banners and three shelves of infantry that you sent to complete crap on the pretext of putting down a peasant rebellion? We both know there is no rebellion!"

"What do you mean?" Asked the youth arrogantly. "It's a remote place, full of great places to hide. I bet that's where that flea fighter Alt'ar hid with his rogue gang. I can beat them to their feet there, and after the problem. Then your reptile will have no armed support. The easier it will be to track him down and capture him."

He saw the witch hesitate. He clearly surprised her with his insight. Maybe she even guessed the truth, which he tried to keep from her for as long as he needed it. The truth that he is much more powerful than she is. As a result, he had to be more careful than before. Everything should be carried out according to the plan prepared for hundreds of years in the prison in which he was to remain until the end of the world.

He smiled at her to ease the tension. It would be much better if he impersonated someone with a beauty resembling that dark charm of his brother. He could wrap any woman. And Bal'zar had to be content with this weak body in his opinion. And while he knew it was just a shell, he felt that he deserved something much better.

As he smiled, lost in his own thoughts, he suddenly noticed that the witch was staring at him, brow furrowed. He should watch out better.

"We must act with caution, my dear King," Dhalia said, her voice dripping with artificial sweetness. "We need Drasan alive, and so do Alt'ar. They have to be neutralized, not killed. Your idiots will not take this into account and they will murder all the "rebels". Meanwhile, both the half-dragon, his girlfriend, and the werewolf must survive. Be a patient hunter and do not be glad that you can shoot a deer, since it is worth hiding a little in hiding and catching a wolf and a bear at the same time," at the end her voice hit a tender tone.

The young ruler gave her an irritated look, but remained silent. There was no point in explaining to her now that he had given his men clear and distinct orders. Neutralize the reptile and the werewolf, and kill the rest without mercy. This was not the time for sentiment. They had plans to declare war on the rest of Lineland's kingdoms.

Dhalia smiled at him. Perhaps she sensed his tension. He hoped she still thought him an inexperienced little boy.

"Fortunately, your mistakes can still be corrected," continued the witch in the same indulgent tone. "Someone who had a great influence on Drasan was removed. His mentor and friend, Ashkan." She laughed softly. "My three confreres told me that he preferred to commit suicide than to be taken alive. It's a pity, priceless information has been lost with it..."

"Wait a minute," Bal'zar interrupted, rising abruptly from his seat. "There are more of you?"

"Ah, have I forgotten to mention it to you?" Now it was Dhalia who pretended to be politely surprised. "They will come here soon to help us fight for a new world order."

"And who was all this Ashkan?" Asked the young lord, feigning interest.

"A unicorn," replied the witch in a perfunctory tone. "It doesn't matter who he was. The most important thing is that it will never get in the way. Even more importantly, the enemy has lost a powerful ally."

"A unicorn?" Bal'zar snorted with a seething smile. But these were only appearances, because deep down he knew who he was talking about and he hated the race with all his heart. "But this is a myth, if these creatures existed at all, they have not been on the ground for a long time."

"Your ignorance amazes me," Dhalia replied, undeterred by the mockery in his voice. "I don't want to remind you that your opponent is a creature from legends."

"That proves nothing," Bal'zar said in the same mocking tone, returning to his seat and lounging back in his chair. "Besides, your pet is only half a dragon. He will never be equal to his ancestors. Nevertheless, it may turn out to be a valuable gain, and therefore I will let it live."

Dhalia smiled slightly.

"Don't underestimate him, my dear," she said, her eyes shining like stars. "For his veins undoubtedly contain the blood of Magot himself - the lord of all dragons. I've only seen a fraction of his power, and it grows with every moment. After all, you know that he will not reach his full potential until he is thirty."

Bal'zar blinked rapidly, as his imagination took him over too. He saw himself in it, sinking a knife into the heart of the dragon that had imprisoned him. Oh yes, revenge might be the best reward. He will destroy the last descendant of the royal blood, putting an end to the entire family. He struggled to keep from laughing.

He looked into Dhalia's eyes. He saw in them exactly what he had expected - the thirst for power. The witch turned out to be dangerous, and should be disposed of as soon as the opportunity presented itself. It's a plan for later. Now it was flypaper. The bait for that goddamn dragon that kept slipping out of his hands.

She thought he hadn't noticed the roll of parchment she had tucked stealthily behind the ribbon tied to the bird's leg, turned her back and faced the window.

"Getting back to the topic," she continued, sitting down on the edge of the stone sill and letting the bird outside. "Ashkan is dead. Drasan probably doesn't know it yet, and when he does, the bloodthirsty demon will awaken in him again. It will be worth taking advantage of this moment and giving him exactly what he wants. Revenge. Let him avenge his master and friend. Let him think that victory is his, then deal him a crushing blow." The elated expression returned to her face. "Boris will be pleased to be able to taste his blood."

At the mention of that name, Bal'zar shuddered slightly. He hated werewolves. They were as useful as extremely difficult to keep in check.

"And where is your disgusting minion now?" He made the question sound indifferent.

"Ah, Boris is doing an important task for me, but he will certainly come back to me," replied Dhalia with a wry smile. It was obvious that she didn't like him either.

Bal'zar was bored of this conversation. He had a wild desire to drag the witch to the bed and tear that damn gown off her. She was one of the truly beautiful women, and at the same time turned out to be a passionate lover. It gave him a delight he hadn't felt in ages. Her body was the essence of perfection: from full breasts and a slim waist to curvy hips. He could run her around forever, and he would never get enough of it.

Desire was written all over his face, because her full lips suddenly parted in a smile. She effortlessly unlaced the bodice of her dress and pushed it off her shoulders, letting the fabric fall down to her feet.

***

The chain of hills near Ram'ar protruded like the teeth of a giant beast. Most of them were too steep to climb. There was a narrow gorge below that looked like a dry riverbed. The road, which was a long-forgotten trade route, led straight to the valley. A large lake reigned there, and a little further it turned into a narrow and steep path.

Alt'ar understood perfectly well why the merchants had given up this path. It turned out not only dangerous, it also made it impossible to defend against attack from above. A natural trap, from which there was only one way out - the other was, of course, the risky climb up the waterfall over the rocks slick with moisture.

Unfortunately, the presence of the military in this wasteland left him little choice. He had to find a safe haven for himself and his people. There were only a handful of them against tens of thousands. The Guild leaders could only count on Drasan as sole heir to the throne of Sheardon to make influential friends at the courts of Antua and Earden. Otherwise, the shortest campaign in the history of the peninsula awaited them. They might have incited a revolt among the peasants, but not many men were left capable of carrying any weapon of any kind among the common people.

To his anger and annoyance, Falko interrupted his gloomy mental debate. He rode up to him on a giant stallion, more like a farm animal than a horse, and spoke in a tone of carefree chat.

"I understand that you are devising some complicated combat strategy that will get us out of the swamp you put us into."

Alt'ar gave him a gloomy look. He wasn't sure what to say. In fact, he hoped the military wasn't here to slaughter them all, but might be gathering volunteers again, or looking for mercenaries willing to sell their souls for a handful of gold coins. This hope quickly faded when it turned out that the soldiers chased after them like hounds unleashed.

"Have a little faith," he murmured finally.

The smuggler nodded.

"I told you this case stinks from afar." He scratched his chin. "Better not to risk yourself to the king. They say it's a demonspawn and a sorcerer. There is no way to do such, brother, you have to curl your tail and run away to the other end of the peninsula."

Alt'ar gave an ironic laugh. He knew that sooner or later people would question his decision, but he didn't care. All that mattered was that gut feeling about what was right, in accordance with one's own conscience. Drasan may not have been a great leader, and he had no idea of strategy. Moreover, he was a regrettable idealist. He probably had potential, but there was no doubt that he didn't know how to use it properly. And the enemies were still on their heels.

"I'm not a miracle worker, Falko," he said finally. "But at last, I feel that what I am doing is right. Maybe we'll finally have to fight for more than a purse of gold. I can't explain it in words..." He trailed off as the commotion behind him caught his attention.

Someone was trying to get to the head of the column. On horseback. It was accompanied by shouts of horror and numerous curses. Finally, a young man less than ten years old, riding on a bony mare, emerged from the crowd of riders.

"Lord... army..." he panted in one breath. "...the royal army is on its way here!"

Alt'ar looked at him, frowning.

"Are you sure?" He asked, trying to stay cool.

The boy nodded vigorously, almost falling off the horse's bony back.

"Yes, lord, they wear green tunics with a bear mark and riding blue ones with an osprey mark. They passed the Ram'ar and headed right here, towards the gorge..."

The Guild leader felt the blood drain from his face. He couldn't panic. His people, as always, counted on him to make sober and logical decisions.

"If this is really a royal army, then we have no choice." He replied calmly, while he scanned the walls of the ravine for the archers hidden there. "We have to prepare for the fight. I don't think we can count on the grace of our ruler in this situation." He laughed sarcastically, and several of his killers echoed him. "Many will probably agree with me," he made a semicircle with his hand, "that this ravine is not suitable for defense. We have to get out of it into the open space."

The mob of assassins surged, many of whom drew their weapons and rested them on the saddle-pommel. Their faces were so tight as if it was about to do another job. Alt'ar knew he could rely on them this time as well. They showed no fear at the mention of the overwhelming advantage of the enemy and were ready to face him.

Ars ran forward and effortlessly climbed the ledge. From there he looked at his master as if to make him understand that it was a pity to waste precious time. Alt'ar looked into his friend's amber eyes and smiled slightly, enough to make his heart glow with a ray of hope. After all, he had the best killers in all of Lineland behind him. Driven by this thought, he stabbed the mount with his heels and headed for the clear opening - the exit from the ravine. The others followed.

The horses' hooves hitting the frozen ground made a dormant echo. The inhabitants of nearby villages listening to this must have believed that an army of ten thousand was going there. At the head was the wolf of Alt'ar, pausing every now and then to watch the rest, as if to make sure they were following him. The leader of the Guild made it his goal to get out of the ravine as quickly as possible. They couldn't stay here, because if the king's soldiers accidentally had the idea to climb the mountain, they would fire them like ducks, and if they didn't even think about it, they could crush them by pressing them against the walls. Their only chance was to bring soldiers to the area known to them. Immediately beyond this rocky bed was the valley where he would meet Drasan. In fact, he hoped the reptile had already arrived there.

***

Drasan stopped at the top of a small mound, and the women with him did the same. The valley where he would meet Alt'ar lay below. Right next to them, a waterfall rolled with a crash, plunging straight into a small lake. Next to it was a very narrow path leading down. To the side were several hunting lodges that looked deserted. On the other side of the valley a narrow gorge was clearly visible. The place was completely unprofitable! There was a thick coniferous forest on one side and a steep rock wall on the other.

The enemy could easily plant on them in the forest or place archers on the rocks. They would have shot them in the blink of an eye! As soon as he thought about it, he heard the thud of hooves at the mouth of the gorge. There was also a wolf. The prince recognized him - a favorite of the leader of the Assassins' Guild. Anyway, shortly after him, the riders, led by Alt'ar, emerged one by one. They poured out from there like a river, scattering across the valley.

Neila, who watched it, frowned.

"It looks like they are getting ready to fight," she said.

Indeed, the Guild leader rode among the scattered assassins, testing their readiness. Even at this distance, his nervousness was evident, but he did not lose control. In fact, this is not the first time Drasan has admired the discipline and discipline of his people. Such respect for the commander would be sought in vain among the royal soldiers.

The mercenaries in the blink of an eye lined up facing the mouth of the gorge. At last, it became clear what they were waiting for as the clear sound of a horn echoed above the roar of the waterfall, echoing off the valley walls. The presence of the military could only mean one thing - Bal'zar had learned of his alliance with the Assassins' Guild.

The prince held his breath. He had never seen a real battle before, much less take part in it. He felt both excitement and fear as he looked down at the people below. As he thought about it, the first ranks of infantry appeared at the mouth of the gorge, over which the banner with the Riden emblem was flown - a black bear on a green background. They marched in tight ranks, each armed with a long spear and holding shields in front of them. They poured out of the gorge like a green river. Alt'ar watched them stoically, as did his killers. Probably cold to judge their chances. Rodian was the first to shake her shock at what was happening.

"Come on! We have to do something!" She looked at the half-dragon, fear in her eyes.

Drasan thought frantically. The only thing that could happen to him at that moment was to fly down. There was a possibility that at the sight of the dragon, the army would lose its enthusiasm for the fight, and maybe even withdraw from it. He glanced at Neila.

The prince glanced at her automatically. The assassin seemed calmer than she wanted to show. She tried to keep an appearance of self-control. Even so, it was revealed by the tremor of her fisted hands.

Did he understand that he had to decide something? He has never avoided fighting, but had never dealt with such a large number of opponents before. The Ridean advantage seemed obvious, while Alt'ar's men were only a handful.

Rodian was not a patient person. Without waiting for them, she whispered the formula of the spell and then jumped from the cliff into the lake. But instead of falling into the water like a stone, she spread her arms and swam gently, landing on the shore, just behind the line of killers.

Then the Sheardonian made a decision. Regardless of the outcome of this encounter, he had no choice but to fight alongside Alt'ar.

He glanced at Neila again and lay flat on the ground, signaling to her that she should mount him.

"Are you crazy?!" She asked, half scared, half angry. "I'm not going to mount you; I can go down the same path as Rodian." She looked down into the foaming lake water and swallowed nervously.

Drasan had no time for her frills. Before she could protest, he grabbed her half in one of her front paws and, ignoring the loud protest, he ducked sharply down, spreading his wings at the last moment and landing on the shore of the lake.

Before she cooled down enough to scold him, the killers cheered for him. He couldn't help but let out a loud roar. This one turned out to be the best battle song for them. Only the horses did not like the proximity of a predatory reptile, and the rest of them would carry it in their arms if they could.

Embarrassed Neila marched somewhere to the side, but he did not even notice where, because he was immediately caught by the joyful Velwel, who did not bother himself with the opponents.

Alt'ar greeted him with a polite nod, as he was still busy arguing with Rodian. Drasan settled at his side, pleased that his arrival had improved the morale of the killers.

For a moment it seemed that the Ridean infantry had lost their spirits. Some of them stepped back as if they wanted to be as far away from Drasan as possible at all costs. Seeing this, the half-dragon let out another roar, and the cheerful slayers echoed him. Velwel and Neila had grown up at his side, though the latter still avoided his gaze.

Suddenly there was silence, broken from time to time by a horse's snort. The killers stared at their opponents with grim determination, and they owed them no more. They had recovered from the shock of the enormous reptile and were now closing ranks again.

"It begins," Alt'ar muttered softly.

Indeed, after a short organization, the first unit moved forward, led by one of the commanders riding a large fighting stallion. They marched in tight formation and did not look scared at all. I guess they realized that they had an overwhelming numerical advantage.

Alt'ar looked at them contemptuously and raised his hand up. At this signal, the assassins rushed wildly at the enemy.

The Rideans stopped, unsure what to do, only the more awake raised their spears. Before the commanders could give an order, speeding horsemen attacked them from both sides. The air filled with the clash of weapons and the screams of royal soldiers who, against orders, scattered in panic in all directions. Some were trampled, others fell down with a sword or an ax.

Soon the valley was in turmoil. The footmen, at first so sure of their superiority in numbers, now ran in panic. Some even tried to climb the rocks, but fell from there quickly. Drasan, who was furious in the heat of battle, from time-to-time puked streams of fire at his opponents. Then the air was filled with acrid black smoke and the stench of burning meat.

Alt'ar fought next to him, and it must be admitted that he was second to none. His opponents fell like flies, not fully realizing what had stung them. Every now and then his huge wolf would jump out of the clouds of smoke, throwing himself at the unsuspecting soldiers.

Most of the killers were in their element. Also, Velwel, who was one of the few lefts in the saddle. At full gallop, he suddenly fell into the crowd of fighters and with his sword cut off the heads of the Rideans. His straitjacket was all flecked with blood. Somewhere in the middle of the battlefield there was a huge man with a horned helmet and a great ax that could easily split the skulls of soldiers much smaller than he was. A large pile of dead bodies had grown around him.

Neila and Rodian did not worse, as they probably decided to forget about their mutual prejudices during the battle and fought side by side. The assassin raged with a sword that looked like a silvery streak while the witch hurled energy balls at the men attacking them.

All around echoed the wild screams of Alt'ar's teammates possessed with murderous frenzy, mingled with the groans of the dying and the squeal of terrified horses. It was a real shamble. The remnants of the infantry squad abandoned their weapons and ran to panic in order to die under the hooves of horses or to be burned alive by dragon fire.

Everything indicated that the scales of victory were on the Guild's side. Unfortunately, they soon doubted it, because suddenly, above all the noise of the battle, there was once again the clear sound of the horn.

Drasan released the shapeless mass of flesh that had until recently been a Ridean's footman and looked towards the mouth of the ravine. Hardly visible now, for the entire valley was drowned in black smoke. Alt'ar and the other killers did the same. Even the Rideans ceased their attack. Everyone watched in amazement as the single rider emerged from the crack. In his arms he carried a huge banner with an osprey on a blue background - the symbol of Alikorn. He stopped the gray horse at the edge of the battlefield and shuddered slightly at the sight of the piles of corpses lying in the bloodied snow. He quickly mastered his fear and pulled a scroll out of the long tube by his saddle. He unwrapped it, cleared his throat, and began to read:

"By order of King Bal'zar, who reigns graciously, I command you to lay down your arms and surrender. You are accused of treason and inciting rebellion against His Majesty, for which the king punishes with death. However, in his boundless mercy, His Majesty is ready to forgive you for all your sins and to reward you handsomely. The condition is that a certain Drasan, an exceptionally dangerous criminal, be handed over to him. Anyone who does not obey this ordinance will be sentenced to death."

The killers stared at the herald for a moment in silent astonishment, all of them roared with mocking laughter in unison. Drasan did not take his eyes off the man dressed in the colors of the kingdom of Alikorn.

"Rogues, barbarians and monsters!" He exclaimed, a purple flush of indignation flushing across his cheeks. "There will be no mercy on you, you bastards..."

Nobody heard his further words, because they were drowned in a loud roar that sounded somewhere above. Everyone, including the messenger, looked up and watched the black dragon as it landed neatly at Drasan's side. The half-dragon looked at him with a mixture of surprise and indignation.

"You're late," he muttered.

Gaenor looked at him as if he had just seen him now.

"I'm not your minion," he growled. "I'll come and go when I like it. Plus, the real fun is just getting started."

This was not the best time for verbal skirmishes, Drasan simply ignored the words, though unfortunately it was not without a few chuckles at the remark. Even the usually serious Alt'ar smiled. Fortunately, the dragon had someone to survive on.

The stunned herald was suddenly speechless as he looked from reptile to reptile. Probably no one would deign to inform him that he would be dealing with two dragons. The prince understood his fear perfectly well. Dragons were not a fact in Lineland, but a myth long forgotten and obliterated in human memory. The appearance of two representatives of a race considered long extinct at once must have made quite an impression.

Drasan was not going to wait for the king's envoy to regain his speech. He stepped forward and announced in a voice full of open contempt:

"I also have a proposition for you. Take your proud butts and return to your king. Do not forget to tell him that he is a coward who hides behind safe walls, sending his people to certain death. The true king stands at the head of his armies and dies with them if destiny so decides. Bal'zar is not a king, but a self-proclaimed usurper who tore the crown from his dying father's hands. As if that were not enough, he ordered to kill him himself. Give him these contemptuous words. For I despise him as much as the filthy whore he has in his service."

The killers roared with laughter at the sight of the herald who, despite the gravity of the situation, was still trying to adopt a dignified attitude.

As soon as the laughter ceased, Drasan walked through the battlefield, ignoring the fact that he was treading the dead bodies into the snow:

"If you want to live, you will leave immediately, because we will surely show no mercy to you and we will kill you all." He paused in front of the messenger who was trying in vain to control the panicked mount. "We give you a choice: stay and perish, or return to your ruler and convey my words to him. If he kept hiding from me, he wouldn't only lose his army. I will drag him out of his hiding place, even if I have to take Washmorth apart stone by stone."

Again there was laughter, even louder and more derisive. Some of the killers appeared in a semicircle around Drasan, still holding the bloody weapon in their hands.

The herald squirmed, trying to keep at least the appearance of dignity.

"You..." He broke off, unable to find the right word for a great reptile. Instead, he turned his horse around and disappeared again into the gorge entrance.

"Prepare yourselves," Drasan muttered to the killers around him.

Alt'ar's men looked at each other and lined up. The Guild leader himself mounted his horse and rode over to Drasan.

"You think they're gonna attack?" He asked in a relaxed tone, as if it were about the weather.

"I'm not sure," replied the prince. "Alikorians aren't cowardly, but they'll think carefully about their tactics before they strike."

Ars suddenly appeared next to them. His silvery gray fur was also stained with blood. Following the wolf, Velwel rode up to them, deprived of his usual smile.

"Neila's hurt," he said in a grave tone.

Drasan hoped the friend was joking. Unfortunately, the young man was far from laughing.

In an instant the prince felt the metal forceps clenching his chest. He changed so quickly that he felt dizzy and, if not for Velwel, he would have collapsed into a snowdrift. He followed him as if in a dream, the gigantic red stain in his mind. As soon as he noticed the slender figure of Rodian kneeling in the bloodied snow and bending over the inert body of the mercenary, his knees softened and his legs failed.

The witch recited spells with trembling hands, drawing strange symbols in the snow. Suddenly she looked up and their eyes met. In Rodian's eyes he saw exactly what he feared - the wound was too heavy.

He kept shuffling on. These suddenly resembled two iron poles. He fell to his knees beside the limp body lying in a pool of blood. One glance at the gaping wound in her side was enough for him to understand that it was too late. The spear went under the ribs, breaking at least one of them, and though it didn't reach the heart, it pierced one of the lungs. Even without being a magician or a healer, the prince knew such injuries were fatal. It is impossible to remove the tip, because a sudden violent hemorrhage would surely kill the girl. Either way, she was probably going to die.

Feeling helpless, Drasan pushed the blood-stained hair from the unconscious mercenary's forehead and groaned at the sight of her pearly-pale complexion. He wanted to howl.

The witch got up from her knees, her face a marble mask.

The wound is too deep and the point is stuck between the ribs. I can't even get him out with magic, because that will surely kill her. I slowed the bleeding and relieved the pain, but she didn't have much time left. Here you need knowledge, which unfortunately I do not have - her voice reached the young man as if from behind a thick wall.

He nodded, because his voice was temporarily stuck in his throat. He only came to his senses when he saw the huge red drops dripping on the snow, and only then did he realize that he was also hurt. Blood flowed from under the left epaulette in a narrow stream.

His own blood filled with the power of fire!

In an instant he understood what he should do. Feeling that he had little time, he took Rodian's hand and pulled him toward him.

"You know the blood ritual?' He croaked in an uneasy voice.

She hesitated, replied so softly that only he would hear:

"Yes, but it doesn't change anything. I can't get enough..."

"Use my blood," he cut her off in mid-words. He sounded like a madman, and before she could protest, he took a sharp, flat stone from under the snow and cut the palm of his hand deep enough so that the wound would not close immediately. "But do it quickly," he hissed through gritted teeth.

The witch stared at him for only a moment before the meaning of his words reached her. She rolled up her sleeves, grabbed one of the infantry's helmets, and began to collect blood for it. Drasan repeated the cut from time to time so that she could gather enough of it. Then he watched with blurry eyes as he drew a circle around the immobile mercenary, consisting of strange symbols written in the snow with his blood. It was a frighteningly long time. Finally, the circle closed around the three of them, and Rodian knelt in the center, making strange serpentine movements and reciting the spell in an undertone.

The runic circle glowed with a ruby glow. Then flames erupted around them. The blood in the snow hissed and crackled as the monotonous song recited by the witch rose and fell.

Neila lay as still as a boulder, her face like a stone. Drasan, on the other hand, remained lethargic, staring at the bizarre serpentine movements of the entranced witch. He jerked suddenly when he saw the shaft of the spear in the girl's side extend inch by inch, and finally, with a terrible crunch, the triangular point also came out. Rodian continued her strange song, and then a fist-sized wound began to close. It took an awfully long time. The Sheardon's eyelids began to weigh heavily.

He did not realize how exhausted he was... It seemed to him that he had lost quite a lot of blood this day. In addition, the hypnotic song Rodian made him sleepy. The blood-streaked snow suddenly felt as soft as a down comforter. He fought the sleepiness for a moment, only to finally lean his forehead against Neila's chest.

It turned out so warm, so soft, so alive...

He wished this dream would never end...

In that dream, her body suddenly twitched as she took a sharp breath. This one made her heart beat much faster. He tried to lift his head to look at her, but his body felt as if it were made of iron.

"You never give up, do you?" Her faint whisper came to him as if from another world.

He had no strength to answer, darkness pressed against him on all sides. He didn't know if it was a dream or a reality? He just lay still, inhaling her scent. He didn't protest when strong arms grabbed him under his armpits and pulled him aside. Or when the staggering Rodian had somehow reached him and whispered in a soft, inaudible whisper:

"He will live..."

Moments later, she fell into the snow beside him, like a puppet with cut strings.

Someone tall and thin he had seen through the haze bent down and put two fingers to her neck.

Someone else shook his own shoulder several times, and when he didn't react, left him alone. He was grateful to them for that, for he wanted nothing more than solitude now. He wanted to curl up in a ball as he did when he was a boy. He wanted to cry. Its members still refused to obey. He felt as if he had left his soul behind Neila's still body.

He remained in such lethargy for a long time.

Very long...

It seemed like ages before he could open his eyes. The first thing he saw was not the face of Neila or Velwell, but the half-stern, half-concerned face of Alt'ar. The Slayer looked at him for a long moment, his brow furrowed, but when he spoke, there was no anger in his voice:

"What you two did was not only stupid and dangerous." Suddenly his face seemed to Drasan much older than it really was. "Black magic and blood rites weren't banned for nothing. Witches, falling into a trance and summoning the power of the strongest runes, use the energy of any living creature inside the circle." As he spoke, he made one of the more complex signs in the snow. "This is rah'ki or life, one of the most powerful runes. It drains the life of the giver, that is, the person whose blood was used. You're lucky the spell didn't kill you. Rodian channeled the power of the runes so that they only took some of your energy to heal Neila's wounds."

"Is she alive?" Asked the prince hoarsely.

"She's alive but unconscious." The Guild leader replied. "We have to get out of here before the Alikorians arrive. We are lucky that we were attacked by the Rideans infantry first, because the ride would have torn us apart. If the scouts are to be believed, there are five light alikorn and three heavy Ridean flags coming at us. There will be over a thousand in total, and we are in this damned basin, the exit from which only leads through the ravine."

"How much time do we have?" Drasan asked, trying to force his aching body to move.

"Until sunset." The slightly distorted assassin replied. "But if they blocked the mouth of the ravine, we don't stand a chance. They can knock us out with minimal losses. We can try to fight here, but success is negligible. With the lake and the waterfall behind our backs, we have little room for maneuver."

"You're right," Drasan replied, still rubbing his temples for the pain in his head would not ease off.

He stood there for a moment, trying to collect his thoughts. The situation seemed to have no way out. He himself was as weak as a child, he needed a huge dose of sleep and a whole mountain of meat. And he had only a few hours until the sun went below the horizon and plunges the valley into twilight.

"So, what do you propose?" Alt'ar was clearly losing his patience.

The prince, with a tremendous effort, looked up to meet his face.

"I don't know," he said finally.

He felt that the situation was beyond him. Neither he nor Rodian were temporarily fit to fight, not to mention Neila and many other wounded. They had no choice but to hoist the white flag and count, in the worst case, on handcuffs and slavery in Washmorth.

"We have to surrender," he said, amazed at his own words.

"I don't believe it," Gaenor's voice cut through the air like the crack of a whip. The dragon stood nearby, staring at him with eyes like glittering red and yellow jewels. "Your attitude is truly noble. You are forgetting one small detail: Dhalia and Bal'zar only want you alive. They'll kill the rest."

"What am I supposed to do then?" The young man asked, feeling that in a moment he would lose consciousness and slide into darkness.

"Fight," growled the dragon through gritted teeth. "There's no other way. As an alternative you have of course become Dhalia's slave."

"They will tear us up," groaned the prince.

"Move your brain instead of swinging your sword," Gaenor replied. "They sent the infantry first for a reason."

"Are you suggesting it was a provocation?" Drasan asked calmly.

"I think Bal'zar wanted to see who he was dealing with," the Guild leader replied.

Drasan felt his head ache again from the multitude of thoughts and conjectures.

"I guess it's high time you let us know your plan," Alt'ar said, crossing his arms over his chest.

"Not here," Drasan hissed shortly. "We need to get out of here as soon as possible."

"How?" Gaenor asked skeptically. "At least thirty people have been seriously injured to the extent that they are unable to drive for several days. You yourself need some time to recharge your batteries. And the only way out of the gorge, which is guarded by the enemy army, is the steep path up the waterfall..."

"Still, we're not safe here," the half-dragon interrupted impatiently. "Alt'ar is right, it could have been a simple provocation. That is why they sent the weakest link, the infantry, to fight us. The loss of these few troops did not matter to the king. If we spend more than a few hours here, which we have to devote to the organization, they will come back here in a much greater force and will crush us to the dust."

"Time is a luxury we've just got stumbled upon," Alt'ar said sarcastically. "If we're lucky, we'll take a moment to catch our breath before they come back to finish their work."

"So, what are you suggesting?" Drasan asked softly. He was sick of this. He needed a short nap to recharge his batteries. Meanwhile, the real battle was yet to begin, which means that he would not be allowed to wink until at least dawn.

"We have to regroup and face them. I don't see any other choice. Hopefully the sight of two dragons will have some impact on the morale of their army. If not, we're dead anyway," the killer replied.

It cut off any further discussion, and Drasan did not have the strength to protest. His eyelids felt heavy as if they were made of lead. Finally, fatigue took over, and he plunged into something like a restless nap.

***

When he opened his eyes, the sun had hidden behind the neighboring hills. Meanwhile, the valley was boiling over. The wounded were placed on a makeshift stretcher, and the dead were placed in rows and covered with rugs.

Drasan stood up and was relieved to find that he did not feel dizzy. He did not seem surprised that during his sleep he was transferred to a hastily made field infirmary, where he sat among the more severely wounded. Two beds away was Rodian, white as linen but conscious. Neila was stacked even further - she was still unconscious but alive.

He headed towards her, passing several more seriously wounded on the way. He knew at least a few of them would not survive the night.

The girl was lying on the bed as motionless as a boulder, her side covered with tears. The young man fell to his knees beside her bedding. He could feel hot tears under his eyelids, yet he couldn't even cry. He rested his forehead against her motionless body and lasted a long moment.

"You look terrible," her weak voice was the sweetest tune to him.

He rose, uncertain if it was a dream resulting from total exhaustion. Neila looked at him quite conscious, though her face was still pale.

Drasan forced a weak smile. There was no doubt that, although he had not been injured, his clothes were stained with the blood of the killed Rideans. Even on his face - especially around his mouth - he could feel the hardened blood. It had to look really picturesque.

"You look great," he replied in a relaxed tone.

"Don't lie," She corrected herself and winced in pain. "I know I look terrible too. But that's okay, it has been much worse. But you could use a decent bath, because you smell like a slaughterhouse."

The half-dragon laughed harshly.

"It looks like we're even," he said, amused.

Neila suddenly grew serious and looked into his eyes.

"Velwel told me what you did for me. You must know that it was extremely stupid and reckless..." She paused for the meaning of the words to reach him, "...but I'm glad you did," she finished smiling uncertainly.

Drasan sat down across from him and only stared at her for a moment. Until now, he hadn't had a chance to notice that her eyes were amazingly blue, or that when she smiled, her cheeks appeared fuller than usual. This time it was different. She showed no fear in front of him or made any biting remarks.

"Never before..." he began, but paused as he felt her curious gaze upon him. And again, he was speechless. He swallowed nervously, but that didn't help. "...it's not so simple..."

"I know what you want to say," she interrupted, suddenly taking his face in her hands and pulling him towards her. Gently and timidly, she placed a kiss on his lips.

Drasan was so shocked by this that he was speechless for a moment. He continued for a moment, his heart pounding against his chest, feeling the warmth of her skin beneath him.

"Please don't say anything," she whispered, brushing her lips against his ear. "Let me enjoy this moment."

The prince felt that he was trembling and he did not know whether it was from lust or exhaustion. It was so beautiful it was unreal. He took a deep breath again.

"I just want to tell you..." The rest of the speech was drowned in the loud roar of an enraged dragon.

Drasan sprang to his feet and instinctively reached over his left shoulder, gripping his hand on the cool hilt and yanking the sword out. He looked around to locate the source of this confusion. After a while his eyes widened with fear.

Gaenor roared furiously and spat streams of pale blue fire, but was completely powerless, pinned to the ground by a metal mesh. The fight flared up around him again, though most looked as surprised as the prince.

Troops in the colors of Alikorn poured in through the narrow isthmus like a rushing river. Some of the killers died right away under the hooves of their rushing mounts, others gathered around the immobilized Gaenor. Alt'ar stood at their head. Unfortunately, after his expression, he noticed that he, too, did not expect such a turn of events.

They were trapped...

CHAPTER 10

Drasan could not believe what his eyes saw. For a moment he stared at the scene unfolding before him. Gallons of water spilled behind him with deafening thunder. No wonder they didn't hear the clatter of hooves, muffled by the snow everywhere. He looked up and saw archers spread out in the hills surrounding the valley. It was from there that the net was cast on Gaenor.

The cavalry formed a semicircle, pushing the remaining rebels to the shores of the lake. Their commander came to the fore. The prince recognized him by the red plume on top of his helmet. He knew that this time there would be no negotiation and the soldiers would attack them like hungry wolves at a cornered deer. That was the end and all he had left was to stand for that final fight alongside his comrades.

The horses tore the snow nervously with their hooves and shook their heads. Their riders silently watched the small group of people huddled around the immobilized dragon. Their leader Alt'ar showed no sign of fear for a moment. Even with the Guild members gathered around him, there was only a handful against the well-armed Alikornian cavalry. He had four banners in front of him, each of them consisting of at least a hundred fine warriors with swarthy, sun-tanned and sea-winded faces. They had thick spears in their hands, and short, curved sabers at their belts. Full armor was carried by a commander who Drasan recognized as one of the princes of the Alikorn, perhaps a royal son. The others were dressed in light half-armor.

Drasan covered the distance quickly and stood at Alt'ar's side. The leader of the Guild gave him a brief glance, looked back at the silent riders. The half-dragon knew he was judging their chances against well-trained soldiers who were three times ahead. The assassins gathered around him also looked at them with grim expressions.

The joy after the recent victory has evaporated. Everyone knew they were staring death in the eye. Even Velwel looked at peace with his fate.

You can still save them, said the familiar, venomous whisper in the half-dragon's head.

Only now did he remember that he felt so relaxed that he forgot to shield his mind.

What do you want? He asked, furious with himself for allowing himself to be surprised.

Dhalia laughed.

Get out of my head! He growled and used all his willpower to push her out of his mind. Before he could do that, he could feel a deep sense of satisfaction overwhelming her - she knew she had hit a sore spot.

He looked at Alt'ar, but he avoided his eyes, clearly trying to focus on the task at hand. The great gray wolf growled hollowly, and the sun setting over the valley was reflected in its amber eyes.

And at the same moment Drasan had a crazy thought:

The Alikorians did not attack, they were waiting for the sunset! And when it does, the valley will be plunged into twilight. What if Boris had formed an army of werewolves at the behest of Dhalia? What were their chances against bloodthirsty beasts of superhuman strength and speed?

Velwel, standing next to him, seemed to think the same, with the difference that he dared to express his concerns aloud.

"You don't think they are preparing against us..." The word "werewolf" clearly didn't want to pass through his throat. "...something inhuman?" He finished, staring at Drasan, hoping he would deny it.

But the prince remained silent, watching the sun disappear behind the hills. The valley was slowly plunging into darkness. Beside him, Alt'ar's assassins also stared ahead, not quite understanding why their opponents were not attacking, but were blocking their escape route. Some of the Bloodhunter's men looked around anxiously, hoping to find the cause of their enemies' strange behavior.

The last rays of sunlight had barely disappeared, and the valley was plunged into darkness, something moved in the hills. Some dark shapes broke away from the rocks one by one and fell straight into the lake. The killers watched with growing anxiety. Gaenor, lying motionless so far, began to struggle furiously, as if fear had given him strength. Drasan followed the figures emerging from the lake without a word.

Most of them looked wildly with bloodshot eyes, saliva trickling from their mouths. They moved slowly and as if in hypnosis. They were all half undressed, and the remnants of their clothes were dirty and frayed. There were about twenty of them - men and women. Some had lost the rest of their human qualities and were on all fours, snarling, snorting, and grinning yellowed teeth. They surrounded their victims in the way that a pack of wolves usually does.

Boris emerged from among them, a smile that was inseparable from his scarred face. The werewolves backed away from him, bending their necks respectfully - there was no doubt they considered him their leader. Somehow, he managed to become the alpha.

Drasan stared at the werewolf, feeling nothing but disgust. The grim creatures circled around, making strange gurgling noises and snapping their jaws. However, they did not dare to attack the half-dragon without orders.

Above their heads, the sky was slowly turning a deep navy blue, and after a while a pale circle of the moon appeared on it, shining like a great lantern. As soon as its glow fell on the figures huddled around Boris, they began to change rapidly, accompanied by a bloodcurdling whine unlike anything else. Drasan had seen this change once, and unlike his fellow men driven by fear, he stood unfazed by the sight. Alt'ar looked composed as well, but he reached under his cloak and gripped the hilt of one of his daggers. Beside him, Ars growled dully at the monstrous creatures, and long fangs flashed from beneath his curled lips.

The half-dragon and his comrades-in-arms realized they were trapped. There was a crowd of monsters in front of them, followed by the Alikornians riders who now looked like a silver wall. There was no time to think about any strategy. There was nowhere to run. All that's left to do is stay and face the inevitable...

***

Mara didn't really know why she was doing it. Two months have passed since the birth of her son. It was just that long that she needed to organize a trip to the capital of Antua. After another week of preparation and making sure she had everything she needed, news came unexpectedly from the south - Bal'zar had dispatched troops to massacre the alleged rebels. Praying to all known deities that Yarred would not be among these "rebels", she decided to leave immediately.

Now she walked the streets of An'thil, bundle in her arms, where Lender slept safe and free from all worries. This name was given to her son by Miral: it is said that one of the heroes of a well-known fairy tale carried it. Ahead of her, in the distance, loomed a palace surrounded by a high white wall. The girl paused for a moment and looked ahead at the gate embedded in the wall. The two guarding guards watched her suspiciously. She straightened with dignity and pressed the bundle to her breast even tighter. She tried to look like one of those noble virgins sometimes seen on the streets of Athar.

Unfortunately, the men guarding the gate were not convinced by this, and when she came closer, one of them blocked her way with a halberd in his hand.

"What are you looking for here, you stray?" He asked harshly.

He was big and stout. Mara had to tilt her head up to face him. She resembled the work of a not very precise sculptor. The features were too pronounced and hewn, and the eyes, completely hidden in a tangle of thick eyebrows, were like two pieces of coal. Half of his teeth were missing from his mouth stretched out in a mocking smile.

"I want to see your king." She tried to keep her voice firm and confident. "I'm an ambassador to the Duke of Sheardon." She added, straightening herself with dignity.

The second guard, who looked like a giant ape, looked at her and laughed harshly. There was no doubt that he was not taking her seriously.

At such moments, the girl wished that Tanara had managed to teach her anything - she would have thrown some spell at those thugs. Instead, she had to pull a bulky purse from her coat - the last one Yarred had left her. At the sound of the clink of gold coins, a disgusted smile appeared on the trollish guard's face. He measured her with a long gaze, lingering on the bundle she was squeezing, in which the unaware Lender slept.

Seeing this, Mara took a step back, ready to defend her son with the ferocity of a lioness.

As if reading her mind, the guard furrowed his bushy eyebrows and, pointing to the bundle, asked, abandoning the polite tone for good:

"What have you got there?"

Mara took another step back, glancing surreptitiously down the empty street - no one was there. At this time of day, the city should be bustling with life. Instead, the girl found rows of locked houses. Several inns had boarded up windows and doors. But she couldn't show that she was afraid. These two were just waiting for it. Straightening up, she straightened her bundle and looked superiorly at the nearest man.

"I'm here on a diplomatic mission, which means you can't hurt me," she said with dignity. "And I have the right to ask for an audience with your lord."

"The king is dead," the guard said dryly. "His successor has not been crowned yet."

Mara cursed silently. She might have expected it, Valden wasn't young, after all. Nevertheless, she decided to go perfectly informed about the situation.

"I know that the king is dead," she said calmly. "I also know that during a free election the power is exercised by his supreme adviser and it is him that I want to talk to."

The guards looked at each other, one of them shrugged and struck the iron gates three times. At this pre-arranged signal, the gate slowly began to open. Mara found herself in the castle courtyard, where two guards were waiting for her. They were very different from the guards guarding the gate. Each was wearing a spotless blue caftan with an eagle embroidered in gold thread over the chain mail. They held halberds in their hands and short swords on their belts. They were even of similar height.

They bowed stiffly and, wordlessly, led her across the courtyard towards the ornate arch and on to the wide staircase leading to another iron-forged door.

The castle was a rather crude structure, built on a circular plan with two towers. One clearly functioned as a prison, because there were bars in the windows, and the entrance was guarded by two guards like those at the gate. The entrance hall was dimmed by the light of several torches. The guards briskly passed her and found themselves in front of another gate. These, the girl guessed, led to the throne room. She recognized it by the golden eagle emblem on both door leaves and by the guards standing in front of them.

The gates swung open noiselessly, and the three of them entered the enormous hall. It was completely empty except for an elderly man sitting on a gilded throne. As Mara stepped over the threshold, he gave her a short stare of steel gray eyes. She bowed to him and walked closer.

The old man watched her through frozen lids, smiling slightly. As she stood a few steps away from him, he spoke in a clear, sonorous voice:

"I was expecting you."

Mara froze, unable to move, staring at the strange man.

"Yes, I know who you are and who sent you here," the man continued, glancing at her with his steel-gray eyes. "I also know that you gave birth to a son two weeks ago, a descendant of the family of Valden and the only rightful heir to the throne of Antua."

Instinctively, Mara pressed the bundle to her chest.

"Who are you?" She asked.

The man laughed.

"And will you believe if I tell you that I'm very similar to your friend?" he replied, and seeing that the girl did not understand any of it, he added in a voice full of bitterness: "I'm a hybrid, that is, according to the law in force in the place where my mother came from, a creature unworthy of existence. That's why they condemned her to death right after I was born."

"Are you a half-elf?" Mara asked, still not understanding.

"Close," the man smiled bitterly. "But no. I'm not a half-elf, though it might be fine, because elves are a haughty and proud race. Unfortunately, unicorns are no less proud and no less haughty, and at the same time cruel."

Mara looked at him as if he was crazy. For was it not by chance that the unicorn was Drasan's mentor and friend of Yarred? Are all the stories about unicorns just a cleverly veiled lie designed to hide a cruel truth?

No, it's impossible, she scolded herself

"It can't be," she said aloud. "I know a unicorn that wouldn't be capable of anything like this..." She hesitated. After all, she didn't know Ashkan that well.

But Yarred knew him, and he seemed to have respect and appreciation. A man so righteous and honorable could not worship a cruelty.

"Indeed, not all representatives of this race are like that," admitted the man. "Unfortunately for most, the very fact that I'm half-blood makes me something worse. Something disgusting. But I was lucky because, even though I was left to die, a lonely hunter found me. As you may have guessed, it was quite a mystery to see a baby dumped so high in the mountains. He took me to Antua where I grew up under the care of his aged wife. When I grew up, I began to show my magical abilities. My adoptive parents were simple people and realized that they would not provide proper care for me. They made sure that I would go to the teachings of the old magician..."

"Wait a minute," Mara said, because there was something wrong with her story. "Aren't unicorns forever young? Don't they live for hundreds or even thousands of years?"

"Good point." He smiled at her. "My present appearance is a kind of camouflage. Thanks to this, I can live among you without any obstacles. I claim to be a magician, and I am talented enough to attend royal courts. But I don't have to hide my true face from you..."

Before her eyes, the wrinkled face began to smooth out, his jaws became smooth and hair darkened. The stooped old man who sat in front of her turned into a handsome young man. The eyes and voice remained the same, for when he spoke again it was still clear and resonant:

"This is what I have looked like for over a thousand years, so every now and then I have to pretend my death and come back in a different form..." He broke off and looked at her much more piercingly than before. "But you didn't come here to hear the story about me, which I have pleased you anyway."

Mara, who had been staring at him so far with her mouth half open, shook herself as she realized that she had not asked the unusual interlocutor's name. Before she opened her mouth to ask him a question, he said:

"I'm Culiaro. That's my real name, that's what my mother gave me. However, I have used many others. I'm now known as Tharon, and I would like to ask you to call me that."

"Tharon," the girl repeated, perhaps wanting to check the sound of the name. She quickly recovered as she found her staring at him wide-eyed. "Well, you first stated that you knew the reason for my coming..."

"Of course, it's obvious," Tharon interrupted gently. "You want me to help you get your son on the throne of Antua." He smiled. "I must warn you that it will not be easy, because according to the well-known information Valden died childless. It won't be easy to prove your right to the throne, especially since the heir may be a male heir..."

"I know the law," Mara interrupted impatiently, "I mean, Lender... my son, he is..."

"Unique," the half-unicorn finished for her, standing up and walking over to her. He held out his hands, and the girl hesitantly handed him the bundle.

Tharon smiled warmly at her and unrolled the blankets. It turned out that Lender was awake and was staring at him with wide eyes the color of pure blue. He showed no fear at all.

"It didn't occur to you that if you weren't developing the gift, your power might pass to the child?" He asked, still staring at the little boy with red curls that looked so much like his mother's hair.

"No," Mara said truthfully, because she hadn't really thought about it. Lender exuded such a strong charm around him that everyone fell in love with him immediately, and he seemed to be over-developed.

Tharon nodded as if the answer explained it all.

"It happens sometimes," he said, lifting the boy a little and studying him curiously. "For example, I inherited a gift from my mother, although I look more like my father." He gave Mara a long look. "By the way, you too look like your father. Same red hair, same hard look..."

Mara did not dare to deny it, though she had never before wondered who she looked like. She did not know her father, and her mother died when she was little herself. Sometimes she remembered her beautiful but sad face...

"I didn't know my mother either," Tharon said unexpectedly, and Mara jumped at the sound of his voice. She was so deeply immersed in her memories that she completely forgot about the presence of the man. "I was not able to remember her appearance. They killed her shortly after I was born," he finished, and there was a hint of sadness in his eyes.

"So you understand me, don't you?" She asked.

"Yes. And I'll try to help you as far as I can," he replied, handing Lender back to her.

Mara took the baby from him and smiled. The unbearable weight in her chest that she had felt since she came to the capital had slightly eased. If she had an ally here, maybe it would be much easier for her than she had anticipated?

***

Drasan and Alt'ar stood side by side, watching their enemies form a silent wall around them, and in the case of Boris' servants a moving circle. The werewolves paced back and forth along the lake shore, snarling and snapping their teeth. Boris stood still, watching the half-dragon with his one eye.

"What are they waiting for?" The Guild leader asked half-mouth.

Drasan shook his head to show that he didn't know the answer to that question. His head was totally confused, making it difficult for him to focus on anything. He frantically tried to clear his mind, as he always had before a fight. Unfortunately, this time it made it difficult for him to feel that whatever he decided, they would fail anyway. The opponents had an overwhelming advantage. This was not taught to him in any training. He was not ready for such a great deal of responsibility.

Automatically he took his father's ring out of his pocket and began to twist it between his fingers. The chill of the metal gave him some confidence. He clenched his fist and pressed it to his lips as if it might help him find a way out of this death trap.

Then came the revelation. And it was such an obvious solution that he wondered for a moment why he hadn't thought of it before - Gaenor. The elder dragon certainly knew Dhalia better than anyone, except maybe Boris.

He pivoted on his heel and, without a word of explanation, walked towards the immobilized dragon. He felt that everyone was watching him, but he did not want to give them hope yet, which might prove to be deceptive.

He took a deep breath only when he faced the reptilian head of his older brother.

Gaenor had long stopped struggling. He had to understand that a spell had been cast on the bonds that bound him, preventing him from freeing himself. He lay motionless, staring at Drasan with large yellow eyes with a completely wild expression.

"Would you believe me if I admitted I was a fool?" He asked bluntly.

Gaenor slowly raised his head as far as the heavy net would allow. The look on his face showed all too clearly that he was quite amused.

"I'm glad you understood this in time. As you can see, you're not completely out of your mind," he said, not being polite.

Drasan was not at all surprised by the tone of his voice. On the contrary, he expected much harsher treatment from a much older and more experienced dragon.

"I came to ask for your advice," he felt the words struggling through his throat.

The dragon blinked in mock disbelief.

"Do I hear you right?" He smiled broadly, presenting a suit of sharp as knives teeth. "Our great, fearless leader needs advice from someone like me?"

The half-dragon grimaced as his pride stung painfully. He would not have been able to bear Gaenor's mockery otherwise, but he had no choice. He needed it. He forced a parody of a smile.

"No time for jokes. If you haven't noticed yet, we have a serious problem here," he said through gritted teeth. "And you seem to be the only thing that can get us out of this."

"Where did this conclusion come from?" Gaenor asked, still in the same mocking tone.

Drasan sighed heavily in impotent anger. He was heartily fed up with these games, but he had to grit his teeth, bear the mockery, and choose his words carefully, knowing that if he said something wrong, Gaenor might refuse to cooperate further.

"You see," he said slowly, trying to speak calmly. "You have been with Dhalia for hundreds of years, and that means your knowledge is worth its weight in gold.

Gaenor's smile widened even more.

"Ah, that's it," he said, and added, "It finally dawned on you that you are not dealing with a dull witch, but with a cunning woman like a snake who will not stop on her way to the throne..." He broke off, clearly enjoying the pain and helpless anger on the face of his younger kindred. He was always trying to provoke him with something.

Drasan struggled to keep from hitting Gaenor with the fireball.

"I got it," he said impatiently.

"Those human emotions again," the dragon snorted contemptuously. "Learn to silence them, because they make you weak and vulnerable to manipulation."

Drasan's jaws twitched menacingly. It took a lot of self-control to ignore his words. He was sick of hearing that he was weak because of his half human nature and his ability to feel emotions. He couldn't or even didn't want to get rid of them. Gaenor might despise himself humans, but so far only they had resisted. There was no doubt that they were stronger than the races who considered themselves "superior" believed.

"Stop these enigmatic statements and be clear about what you mean," he said with the last of his strength, forcing himself to calm down as he seethed with anger inside.

Gaenor regarded him with a long stare of venomously yellow eyes, clearly savoring the disturbance of the half-dragon. Drasan clenched his fists with such force that his nails dug into the palm of his hand. He ignored the throbbing pain and focused on the dragon still watching him with interest.

"I wouldn't have come to you for help if it weren't absolutely necessary," he gasped at last, forcing himself to calm down. "So please, please stop testing my patience, especially in the moment of the inevitable battle with the enemy."

"Okay then," Gaenor said calmly, getting serious and straightening up as much as the net would allow. "Let me tell you something few of us know. This knowledge was lost long ago, but Dhalia knows it and secretly fears it. Magical beings like us can sometimes take advantage of "self-connection". This is as difficult as it is dangerous, because sometimes the connection cannot be broken, and the two selves may remain trapped in one body forever. When combined, you gain both the power and skill of the person with whom you connect."

For a moment the meaning of these words did not reach Drasan. Only when he repeated them in his mind did he understand what the older dragon meant.

"You mean our consciousness?" He asked, wanting to be sure.

Gaenor shifted uneasily.

"Yes," he replied hesitantly. "But connecting the self requires full discipline of the mind, purifying it of all thoughts and emotions. Jamming the rest of the world and focusing completely on your own essence. It won't be difficult for me, but for you..."

"I can do it," the half-dragon interrupted impatiently. To tell the truth, he wasn't so sure, but he had no choice. He had to trust Gaenor because now his life depended on him alone.

"You must set me free, then," the dragon said calmly.

Drasan shook himself from his own thoughts and looked at him in utter amazement.

"How am I supposed to do this?" He asked skeptically.

"Concentrate. You are able to do this because you have much more power than Dhalia. First, control your anger, use its energy. You can melt and break these chains..."

Drasan did not hear the rest of his words, for he focused on the chains with his whole being. He was staring at them intensely, trying to control his tormenting emotions. And suddenly the links, one by one, began to snap with a loud crash. Gaenor spread his wings and roared loudly.

He has been freed!

The half-dragon stared at the melted links in disbelief and mounting excitement. He didn't even know he was capable of it. He looked around and was surprised to find that everyone was staring at him.

Suddenly, the clear sound of the horn broke the silence. At this sound, the first row of the Alikornian ride began to move forward. The assassins made the wall tight again, led by Gaenor, Drasan, Alt'ar, and Velwel.

Drasan was still gripping the ring with all his strength, as if hoping that it would somehow inexplicably protect him. Closer and closer, the riders could clearly hear the crunch of frozen snow crushed by the horses' hooves. A huge assassin stood beside the half-dragon, holding a menacing-looking butcher's ax in his hands. The front of his doublet was stained with dried blood, which was more than enough evidence that he could wield this peculiar weapon.

The soldiers were within an inch of the magic shield. Unlike the Ridenian infantry, they did not scream at them, on the contrary - they behaved with cold determination, giving the impression that they had nothing to lose.

Because we have much more to lose, Drasan thought, gripping his hand tighter on the hilt of his sword. He closed his eyes, trying to calm his mind.

Focus on the fight. Focus on the fight. Focus on the fight, he told himself.

And then the light Alikornian ride collided with them with a deafening rumble, accompanied by the screeching of horses and screams of pain from the first wounded. Above all this noise for a moment rose the triumphant roar of Gaenor, which burst into flame directly at the knights charging at him. Drasan didn't have time to look at it any longer, as two others rushed straight at him.

The blade glowed, reflecting the moonlight as he lifted it to eye level. He was ready to deliver the killing blow. Before he could make another move, something silvery gray jumped on the chest of one of the riders, knocking him off the horse to the ground. The other did not hesitate for a moment. His mount leapt over the body of his dead companion and lunged at the half-dragon, striking his chest with the spear's edge. Drasan jumped and before the other could turn his horse, he bounced off the ground and jumped on his back. They both collapsed right into the lake, where they fought fiercely for a while, exchanging punches of fists. Finally, the prince tightened his hands around the knight's throat and squeezed them, crushing his throat.

He got out of the water and felt his sword blindly. Only when the hand tightened again on the cool hilt did he feel a rush of mad joy. It was a strange feeling... Unlike anything else, it was as if he had finally found his place in the tumult of battle.

Alt'ar was also in his element. He rode his horse at full gallop across the battlefield, beheading his enemies. The red cloak fluttered behind him like a bloody pennant. This giant also fought nearby, towering above the others, and around him a dozen other killers, including Velwel, who obtained a bay stallion from somewhere and circled the battlefield, helping in the struggle.

Drasan had a strange reflection. After all, not so long ago he had been ready to chase this peculiar young man into four winds, and now they were fighting side by side.

Suddenly, with a hunch, he started looking for Neila. He had a vague feeling that the girl needed his help now. Fortunately, he found her without much trouble. She, too, fought in the saddle and looked like a mythical goddess of war. Her leather jerkin was stained with blood, and thankfully she hadn't received any new wounds. There was always something growing in his chest at the sight of her and filling his whole body with inner warmth.

He might deceive himself, but he couldn't hide the fact that he was madly in love with her.

His thoughts were interrupted by a violent attack. One of the Alikornian knights charged at him with full force. Drasan parried the slash easily, and before his opponent could raise his sword to the blow again, he slashed it diagonally across his chest. A fountain of blood splattered his face, and a frightened steed reared up, throwing off the body. Drasan efficiently grabbed the reins, jumped on the saddle and screamed and urged the horse to run. In the prevailing turmoil of battle, he once again lost sight of the mercenary.

He was just starting to find her when a hoarse snarl set him in place. Out of the darkness before him emerged a shaggy beast the size of a large bear. Red eyes blazed with murder, and the snout wrinkled to reveal yellowed fangs. The monster moved neither human nor animal. Two huge paws hung strangely above the ground.

The frightened horse reared again, but the prince managed to stay in the saddle. He sheathed his sword, because werewolves were sensitive to silver. Instead, he drew a long spear from a soldier's carcass. The beast growled in its throats, attacking with such extreme speed that it strongly contradicted its size. Drasan leaned slightly in the saddle and gripped the shaft tighter, jerked the reins, turning the horse sideways to the charging werewolf, and threw the spear at him with all his might. The arrowhead plunged into the creature's massive chest, forcing it to stop. The monster roared with rage and pain, broke the shaft like a thin twig, and renewed its attack with even greater ferocity.

Drasan jumped off his horse and, tapping his back, took him out of the way, focused on creating two fireballs. One by one, he threw them at the advancing werewolf. They both reached their target, accompanied by a howl of pain and the stench of burnt hair. In the blink of an eye the beast burst into flames and thrashed over and over again, howling in pain. Drasan couldn't look at it, he wasn't cruel. He walked over to the creature squirming with pain, and in one fluid movement shortened it by a head.

Somehow the battle had moved to the other end of the valley. From there he saw plumes of bright blue fire fired by Gaenor. Drasan caught one of the loose steeds and skillfully climbed onto its back. In the patch of moonlight, he could see the shadows of Boris' servants moving, and Boris himself had disappeared. He stabbed the horse with his heels and trotted along the shore of the lake, passing piles of bodies piled up everywhere. The horse, to his relief, showed no fear, he must have seen more than one battle and it did not make the slightest impression on him.

The snow was ruby red all over the place. Under the circumstances, he saw nothing unusual about it, but his insides twisted at the sight of it. Among the corpses, he recognized a giant who had been doing so well in hand-to-hand combat. Judging by the fifteen quills sticking out of his chest, he was killed with a bow or crossbow.

Stinky cowards, he thought disgustedly as he passed the body.

From then on, he forced himself not to look at the faces of the dead. Instead, he stared ahead and found himself very close to the battle rage. One of the soldiers saw him, too, and started toward him, a bloody spear clutched in his fist. Drasan remembered the giant and, with a roar of fury, rushed to meet him. The other hesitated, but before he could make up his mind, his head flew a few feet away and landed in the snow. Velwel grinned at the stunned prince, passed him and disappeared among the fighters.

Drasan followed his example. On the way, he pierced one of the crossbowmen who had been targeting Alt'ar's wolf. Then, without even slowing down, he cracked the skull of another soldier with the flat of his sword. Now that he was back in the fray, he couldn't complain about the lack of opponents. They threw themselves at him like rabid dogs. He also found, with some surprise, that killing them was not difficult for him. In moments of respite, he looked around for Neila, but was nowhere to be seen.

Suddenly, from a distance, he caught a glimpse of Alt'ar's red cloak. Without hesitating any longer, he walked towards him, making his way between the fighters. The Guild leader fought five soldiers at once. He still carried two swords and handled them with skill. One of the opponents charged at him, intending to stab him with a spear, but the assassin only smiled and jumped aside without much trouble. The rider passed him, and then Alt'ar threw one of his knives. This one struck the center of the poor man's back. The second attacked him with a sword, but also this time the killer showed off with excellent fencing skills. He whirled in a pirouette and slapped the knight across his chest, almost cutting him in half. He remained in motion all the time, deceiving his opponents with the movements of two blades. From time to time he would inflict an unexpected blow, and one of the soldiers surrounding him fell from his horse to the ground. His movements proved so quick and precise that

Drasan had no doubt that even if he fell in this battle, his fame would endure in songs for centuries.

Before the prince cut his way to him, the assassin had dealt with all the soldiers and was now tearing his precious knives out of the carcass. He smiled slightly when he saw the half-dragon. At the same time, he looked very pleased. Drasan admired his composure. He did not know if he would retain control of the beast in such a situation. He himself did not change, because it would take the remnants of his miraculously regained strength from him.

After collecting and clearing the weapons, Alt'ar found and mounted his own horse. He looked at Drasan, and without a word it drove like a wedge between the combatants, and his wolf chased after him. The prince smiled too. They were both in their natural element. They both needed a fight to live.

The prince hammered his heels into the mount's sides and, with a wild scream, he burst among the fighters, slashing with his sword amok filled with bloodlust. Few could match him when he wielded a sword. The fight was permanently inscribed in his dragon's heart. Unfortunately, the enemy still had too significant an advantage to defeat him in battle without resorting to magic, so he decided it would be best to find Gaenor.

With that in mind, he urged his horse away. Finding the older kinsman turned out to be very easy, because his path was marked by piles of burnt bodies of people and horses. As he got closer to him, it turned out that he needed his help. It was surrounded and propped up against the crest of the hill. His furious roars echoed far away. To his horror, Drasan noticed that the dragon's left wing was torn apart. There were also a dozen broken bolts in it, which made the wound deeper. People around him repeatedly shot him with crossbows. Most of them glided over hard scales, but some hit the wings pressed against the sides, preventing the reptile from taking flight.

Anger gave the prince strength. He dismounted from his horse and started toward the crossbowmen. In motion, he turned into a fireball and attacked the surprised soldiers in this form. Most died right away, engulfed by the blood-red flames, the rest were torn apart by sharp claws. Already in dragon form, Drasan approached his older kindred.

Gaenor was panting. The fight almost exhausted his strength. The half-dragon approached him, trampling on the charred debris. The elder dragon looked at him with a mixture of gratitude and surprise. Despite the hoarse protests, Drasan sent energy deep into his body. Only a warning snarl brought him back to reality.

Five soldiers galloped towards them.

He hissed, baring his teeth, his body automatically springing into the fight. He looked at Gaenor and nodded silently. The elder dragon did the same to show that he understood. Feeling that the act might cost him his life, he closed his eyes and focused all of himself on the magical energy pulsing within him. He understood what Gaenor meant when he said that cleansing the mind is essential to fuse the self. His head was as confused as it had been on the battlefield.

Concentrate, Gaenor admonished him. I told you it was not easy. You need absolute peace of mind.

Drasan let everything fade from his thoughts except the awareness of his own power, and this turned out to be huge. For a moment he was so fascinated by this discovery that he almost lost himself in his own thoughts.

Focus! Gaenor growled in his mind. Now you need to find my energy ball.

The half-dragon concentrated now on looking for this ball, and to his great surprise, he found it very quickly. The elder dragon's power turned out to be much smaller.

Now the hardest part awaits us. We will merge our minds into one.

Concentrating on Gaenor's self-had come much easier than he had expected. But knowing that it was now in his head was not pleasant. Sudden power surge is another thing.

Now we can act as one. Woe to our enemies, because we are much stronger together. But remember not to use up all your energy, because that will kill both of us.

Moments later, the sense of someone else's presence vanished, though the awareness of his own power remained. Suddenly, the people at his feet seemed like little ants that he could crush. He took a deep breath and roared as the frightened horses knocked the riders off their backs and began to run away in panic.

He moved forward, ignoring the fact that he was tripping people into the ground. He threw fire right at the Alice knights, who retreated from him fearfully. The werewolves whined away from him and fell hit by the assassins emboldened by this sudden turn of events.

With the battlefield cleared, Gaenor slowly retreated from his mind. Only then did he discover how exhausted he was. He could barely stand on his feet. Right next to his legs he saw the familiar face of Velwell, brightened in a smile, who, like the others, was roaring as much as he could in his lungs. Unable to help himself, Drasan also let out a triumphant roar. After a while Gaenor also echoed him.

The euphoria caused by the victory subsided somewhat and the prince began to look for another, much dearer to him, person. He sighed in relief as he finally fished it out of the hundreds of faces staring at him. She was standing on a sword blade. She didn't look injured, but she remained sickly pale. When their eyes met, she smiled as his heart somersaulted. He could hardly resist the urge to approach her and hug her with all his might. The awareness of being a reptile helped, and she had been badly injured recently.

Only Gaenor's quiet snarl managed to bring him back to reality. He realized that they both had duties to perform. After all, it was necessary to clear the battlefield of the remnants of the enemy army.

***

Bruen croaked in warning. Yarred, trusting in his friend's infallible senses, pulled the reins and looked for the source of his anxiety. Around him, as far as the eye could see, stretched an undulating plain, covered in a thick layer of snow glistening in the sun. And suddenly he heard the sound of the galloping horse's hooves. Bruen pricked his ears and grunted softly. For a moment the pulse stopped, they heard a loud neighing.

The captain jumped a few inches and turned. A beautiful black stallion stood a few steps behind them. Yarred recognized him - it was Ernil. The man looked at him without understanding. The mount was not saddled, with a thin rope tied to the harness, its end appeared to be broken.

Yarred jumped off his horse and clapped on his friend's mount, but the latter did not move. The captain knew that Drasan had trained him so that no one but him could ride. He took a step forward, reaching out to him. Ernil lowered his ears and snapped his teeth in warning. The captain withdrew his hand and whistled softly.

The stallion pricked his ears.

The man smiled and whistled again. Then the horse advanced a few steps and stopped a few inches from him. This time his ears weren't closed as Yarred reached out to touch the soft nostrils.

The captain grabbed the rope and looked at it carefully. It was thin but looked quite strong. He realized that he must have rubbed himself. Still stroking Ernil, he began to watch him looking for cuts or other injuries, but his coat was as smooth and shiny as ever.

"How did you get here?" He wondered aloud as the stallion nibbled at the sleeve of his doublet.

There weren't many settlements in the area, so Yarred had no trouble avoiding unwanted company. He gave up the road, because it was swarming with patrols by the Ridean guards. Traveling off-road may not have been the most comfortable, but it was safer.

Along the way, he came across several wanted letters with a portrait of Drasan next to posters of men and women he did not know. The prize was tempting, they offered 1,000 crowns for each wanted person. In one of the villages, he also saw a proclamation saying that anyone who joins the rebels will be hanged without trial.

Still remembering his last encounter with the Ridean watching him suspiciously, he looked around to make sure no one was watching him, grabbed a rope and fastened it to Bruen's saddle. He mounted his horse and started trotting. Ernil obediently followed him. He knew he had to be even more careful now. Soldiers will certainly not buy a story that he has just found such a beautiful horse, but they will happily accuse him of theft and hang him. Owning a horse like this was as dangerous now as it was openly saying that you wanted to join Drasan, who was being hunted down by the commander-in-chief of the rebellion.

"The sooner we find your master's hideout, the better," he whispered to Ernil.

CHAPTER 11

The dawn rising over the valley showed an image that would be remembered once and for all. Heaps of corpses were piled up everywhere as far as the eye could see, their dead eyes staring at the slowly glowing sky where flocks of ravens and crows were gathering. The sullen stench of death poisoned the air. Drasan stood and watched the sight, knowing that he would never be able to erase it from his memory. He would still be haunted by the death cries of the dying and the pleading groans of those forced to fight against their will and to be killed. Some turned out to be younger than him. He only wanted one thing right now: to stop thinking about what he had done, focus on the here and now, but he couldn't. Meditation and trying to clear the mind did not help.

He decided to explore the battlefield alone, but the sight of the piles of bodies did little to help him think rationally. Suddenly he felt the familiar cool breeze on the back of his neck, which made his hair stand on end. He paused for a moment and looked around - she was standing there bent over the body of a soldier who had died from the blow of a knotty club - as evidenced by the bloody pulp that had once been his face.

As if that were not enough, she took the form of an innocent child.

Ghostly child, he corrected himself.

The girl turned her pale face towards him and curled her colorless lips in a smile. The Sheardonian did not even bother to reply the same. He stared at her for a moment, then looked away quickly because his skin ached from that cold gaze.

"I wonder..." He smirked. "...do you act this way on everyone?" He finished, trying not to look at her.

"I honor the few alive with my presence," replied the Lady of the Dead, placing a kiss on the forehead of some nameless soldier.

"And might I know why you chose me?" He asked in the same ironic tone, realizing how ridiculous it looked to stand here talking to himself.

"Isn't it obvious, Chosen One?" She replied with a question.

He winced at the name.

"Don't call me that," he growled.

The nightmare girl smiled sweetly, and her black eyes sparkled.

"And why do you not like this name?" She asked.

Drasan forced himself to look into those cold, empty eyes.

"I'm not any Chosen One," he said louder than he intended, and several heads turned to look at him with interest.

"You will not escape your destiny," replied the Lady of the Dead, smiling even wider. That smile made skin prickle and shivers down spine.

The prince kicked his helmet angrily, feeling more and more stupid. The goddess continued to walk at his side. Suddenly he remembered something. A question that has been haunting him for a long time.

"I should be dead," he said blankly. "Why am I still alive?"

"You made your choice," she said, as if that explained it all.

"That's no answer," he said, trying to keep his voice as low as possible, even though he felt his anger building up in him.

The Lady of the Dead did not reply immediately. For a moment she bent over another body, fixed her empty black eyes on it, and spoke in a voice vibrating with power:

"This was and will always be your destiny, Drasan. You can rebel against it, you can run away from it, but it will always find you." She pointed a pale finger at his chest, her face darkening rapidly. The bones of the face stood out under the stretched skin. "You can't avoid it, you're marked."

Drasan flinched at the sight but was not going to let go so easily. He needed to know the answer.

"I was destined to die when Boris hurt me," he said, his voice trembling with rage. "What would you do if I decided to go further?" He asked, knowing he was pushing the point.

The colorless lips of the Goddess stretched out in a mirthless smile.

"You really want it?" She asked, stepping closer and forcing him back a few steps. Her face suddenly lengthened to take the shape of a wolf's face and covered in shiny black fur. "Do you want to go to the other side?" Now her voice sounded like Boris's.

Drasan stepped back, but his foot caught one of the bodies and he stretched out long. The Lady of the Dead smiled, showing her yellowed fangs, and said:

"There will be time for you too, Chosen One. But before your days are finished, you must fulfill your mission," after these words she turned into a shiver of gray smoke and disappeared in the air.

Drasan lay on the ground for a moment, unable to move, his heart beating against his ribs and his lungs starting to ache from holding his breath. He got up, knowing he was ghastly pale and feeling hundreds of curious stares on him. As if that were not enough, Velwel was striding towards him, his face very concerned. The half-dragon cursed under his breath and, forcing his numb limbs to move, came to meet him. He knew he had to come up with something quickly, because if he had told the truth, they would have found him insane. After all, what normal person is talking to the Goddess of Death?

Velwel stood in front of him. The close-up wound on the left cheek, recently patched by Rodian, was all too conspicuous. The assassin flatly refused to get rid of her witchcraft, stubbornly claiming that the scar was proud and proud of it.

"What happened? You look paler than usual." He remarked in a concerned tone.

Drasan tried to smile, but he could tell from his friend's expression that he had failed. He decided he needed to get rid of his company as soon as possible.

"Do I ask too much when I want a little loneliness?" He asked ironically.

"Well," Velwel was clearly confused. "Actually, Alt'ar told me to find you. He mentioned something about the conference."

Drasan looked at his friend, trying to convey to him without words that he was incapable of clear thinking now, but he gave up, seeing that he was still staring at him with fear. He probably expected a violent outburst.

He sighed resignedly.

"So, come on."

The young assassin breathed a sigh of relief to see that the half-dragon had no intention of unloading himself on him, and a shy smile appeared on his lips.

"So, um... are you not mad at me?" He asked.

Drasan frowned.

"And why should I be angry with you?" He asked, not hiding his irritation. In fact, he was only angry with himself, but he was not going to share this observation with anyone.

Velwel was confused again.

"Well, um... I thought there was something between you and Neila..." he began sluggishly. "...and she... I really didn't want to tell her!" He blurted, stopping so abruptly that Drasan almost ran into him.

"Tell what?" The half-dragon asked again, not quite understanding where his friend was going.

"She wanted to know what happened... you know, when you and Rodian... this whole magic ritual..." Velwel explained lame. "...you scared us all."

"What are you raving about?!" Drasan asked, grabbing his shoulders and shaking him violently.

"You mean you don't remember anything?" Velwel asked, sincerely surprised, not realizing that his feet had lost contact with the ground. "You looked and acted crazy, we had to force you away from her."

Drasan pulled him to his feet and tried to calm down. He was convinced that he had passed out then. After all, it took a lot of sacrifice for him to heal Neila's wounds. He tried to recall that moment but couldn't. As if it never happened.

"What I did?" He asked with a sigh.

The young killer looked confused.

"First you yelled at Rodian, then you cut your arm open..."

"I still remember that, but what did I do later?!" The prince broke in on his word.

"You performed some extremely difficult ritual with the witch, which depleted you both completely. And then you were delirious." He smiled sheepishly. "Sorry, but it looked like you were speaking to someone invisible. You groaned not to take it from you. You kept saying that you would give up everything. Even..." He swallowed. "...your soul. You really scared us all."

Drasan stood petrified. The words of the Lady of the Dead echoed in his mind: "You have made a choice." He didn't understand it then. He thought it was another puzzling answer. Now he had grasped its meaning - Neila's life in exchange for his service. That was his destiny. No matter how much he tries to avoid it, it is always on his heels.

Eventually the surprise passed and the bitterness of helpless anger replaced it. She made him take an oath. He was to be the messenger of the Goddess of Death. She ordered him, and he could not oppose her as there were serious consequences. He clenched his fists, forgetting Velwel's presence and the fact that everyone was staring at him. He wanted to scream out what was in his heart. With an enormous effort of his will, he restrained himself, knowing that the last thing he needed was to cause even more confusion among the handful of allies.

He moved forward with such vigor that Velwel could hardly keep pace with him. He knew he had to concentrate on the conference awaiting him, but unfortunately his thoughts were still haunted by the vision of the Lady of the Dead's smile - she mocked him. She knew she would obey anyway.

They finally reached one of the abandoned huts where the Guild leader had set up a kind of headquarters. Everything that could be useful was also collected there: food, maps and weapons.

At the sight of them, Alt'ar looked up from the map spread out on the table. From his expression, Drasan concluded that he was not thrilled. Rodian sat next to him, still very pale and silent. In the far corner, near the old hearth, where the fire had burned for the first time in years, Gaenor lurked, dressed as usual in a silk loincloth. The dragon was in a sort of semi-trance, but its eyes were wide open. Neila sat in one of the few stools, cleaning her throwing knives vigorously, ostentatiously ignoring new arrivals. The only person who seemed to be completely unconcerned was one of the killer's men - a shaven bald man with a sullen look and a strange ironic smile on his lips.

Drasan walked over to Alt'ar, who frowned menacingly at the sight of him.

"Well, finally you honor us with your presence," he said ironically. "I think it would be worth doing something more useful than counting the corpses."

The prince stiffened. He stared at the assassin for a moment, trying to make him look away. This one did not bend.

"It was worth checking if there was a spy somewhere who could tell the king how many of us were left," he replied coldly.

"That's quite a trivial reason. We have much more serious problems," said the Bloody Hunter firmly. "I have five hundred men left to raise a gun. Over fifty are injured, twenty of whom are seriously injured. We lack horses, supplies, clean cloth for dressing wounds... In return I have a whole heap of worthless iron and several hundred horses suitable only for a butcher's knife."

The half-dragon felt like a disciplined schoolboy, but he forced an ironic smile.

"So, find out that I'm aware of the situation we are in. I have spent the last few hours devising some sensible way out of this impasse," he replied. He lied as hard as he could, but he couldn't let himself lose face to Alt'ar. He and his killers still needed him. He knew the Guild leader wouldn't be delighted with what he heard in a moment. "I'm sorry, but we can't afford a long delay. Bal'zar can send us new regiments of infantry at any time..."

The muscles in the werewolf's jaws twitched menacingly, and there were red flashes in his eyes.

"You want to tell me..." he drawled through gritted teeth. "...that this is your wonderful plan? Shall I leave my badly injured men here who fought for you?" He got up, and then Drasan realized that he was much taller than he was. "If you think I will obey your order, then you are wrong. I'm not the king's subject, much less yours. My people were risking their lives in not their struggle..." He broke off, staring at him in disgust. "We could hand you over to them and walk away with a clear conscience." He pointed a trembling finger at his chest.

The half-dragon knew he was right. Unfortunately, he also realized that even if he had voluntarily surrendered, he would not have saved the lives of Alt'ar and his killers. He knew Dhalia too well.

"You're right," he said resignedly. "But only partially. Dhalia would have slaughtered you anyway. We should not argue with each other, we must unite on a common cause. Believe me, it's the only way out."

"I'll agree with him here," Gaenor interjected.

Drasan turned to face him. He was one of the last people from whom he expected support.

The dragon got up and stretched as if after a long nap.

"We have to unite, otherwise one day it will turn out that we all dream the same nightmare from which it's impossible to wake up. You're all too young to remember what witches are capable of. Dhalia is an incarnation of chaos clothed in a beautiful body, and you are just looking at the only being completely immune to her power." He nodded at his kindred. "And that means only he can destroy her. But he won't be able to get through to it by himself. She had built up a wall of hundreds of innocents lives between herself and him, as she had always done. We cannot avoid war, but we can turn it to our advantage."

"He makes sense," Neila agreed. "Drasan cannot defeat Bal'zar's army by himself. You are stuck with each other at least until this war is over." She gave the half-dragon a defiant glare, expecting an objection.

Drasan was silent. He knew his next words would determine the fate of this campaign. He had to be careful.

"You're all right," he said finally. "I'm a lousy leader," he smiled bitterly. "But I must admit that no one has prepared me for war before. I was trained to fight, prepared for the role of a ruler, but to this day I didn't really realize how much responsibility this entails." No one was eager to deny it, so he continued. "Perhaps my actions seem rash and reckless to you."

This time everyone, including Neila, nodded in agreement, and he grimaced. Though he mentally prepared himself for a similar reaction, his pride stung painfully. He withstood Alt'ar's scorching gaze and Gaenor's scornful huff. Now the most important thing is to convince them that they can learn from their mistakes.

"Don't think that I underestimate your sacrifice." He looked at Alt'ar, who nodded silently, jaws still clenched. "As Gaenor said: we must unite against a common enemy. I would be a fool to try to fight alone, those times are gone. Now I know that I can't do anything myself." Suddenly he realized that everyone was listening to his speech with their mouths half open. They surprised him with this reaction so much that he stood motionless for a moment, unable to utter a word more.

Finally, he felt a hand on his shoulder. He shook it off impatiently, without even turning around. He took a few steps forward but stopped at the sight of Alt'ar's expression. The leader of the Assassins' Guild hadn't calmed down yet, his eyebrows still furrowed, and the vein in his temple was throbbing slightly.

"Oh, give me a break with that childishness!" Neila said unexpectedly, looking up at them. "You are both being extremely frivolous for the two strongest races. Learn to cooperate because it is the only way out."

The half-dragon felt pleasantly flattered that she was defending him. It was extremely difficult to look away from her, and he needed all of his willpower to do so. When he finally succeeded, he focused on Altar again. He decided to do as she advised him and was the first to reach out to him. The killer hesitated, but finally embraced her.

"So, I'm turning into ears. What's your next move?" He said, sitting down on the bench again and moving the map closer to him. For a moment he pretended to be watching her with interest. But Drasan saw the Guild leader smiling.

Perhaps these were the beginnings of a friendlier relationship between them.

***

Neila was walking towards the lake with the firm determination that this time Drasan and she would explain everything to each other. She was sick and tired of suppressing all the feelings he was evoking in her. She could deceive everyone around her at will, but by the demon horde, she couldn't deceive her own heart anymore. There was something between them. Something she tried to silence for fear of rejection. Years ago, she had sworn to herself that she would never open up to any man. Now she was going to break that promise.

Before her eyes appeared the lake, she sensed someone's presence behind her. She turned sharply to chase the intruder off, but it only took one look into the furiously wide yellow eyes for her to freeze. Gaenor charged at her with a low growl, pinning her against the rocks behind her back.

"I've been watching you for a long time," he said in that thrilling, impassive voice. "I can also see how he looks at you, his gaze speaking for itself."

Neila summoned her courage and looked into those reptilian eyes.

"What's it to you?" She asked proudly.

The dragon brought his face closer to her and hissed through clenched teeth:

"The fact that you are making him weaker and weaker every day. One look of yours and he melts like hot wax. I must not let his human emotions take precedence over the strength of a dragon's heart."

"You must not let?" She tried to push him away, but he wouldn't let her.

"I'm not stupid enough to let you do this," he growled, pushing her even tighter against the rock wall. "You're supposed to alienate him, and I don't care how you do it!"

"What?" She couldn't believe her own ears. What's that supposed to mean?! Why did Gaenor suddenly become concerned about Drasan's heart affairs? He hated it, after all.

Gaenor smiled showing his teeth at the same time, and these did not resemble human ones at all.

"You humans lose so much with your dull senses," he said, more to himself than to her. "When you are around him, he changes, he becomes warmer, more caring and definitely more human than usual. This is unacceptable in the current situation. Drasan cannot afford weakness, and you are that weakness."

The mercenary did not believe her ears. Not that she wasn't flattered by that, since Duke Sheardon was handsome, but she wasn't quite ready to make such a confession.

Meanwhile Gaenor continued in the same tone:

"When Dhalia finds out about your bond, she will use you against him. You will be forced to watch him suffer torment, because our nature is not conducive to submission, but we are also loyal to our partners. And we choose these once in a lifetime."

Neila held her breath. Was Gaenor right and Drasan's strange behavior supposed to show her how he felt about her? She had sensed a weakness for her before, but she didn't think it was more than infatuation. Or was she just deceiving herself because she refused to accept that feeling into consciousness?

"You must understand that he cannot allow himself to be weak," continued the dragon mercilessly. "He must be strong. Strong enough to send Dhalia and Bal'zar back into the depths of the abyss. You make him reveal himself too much, he can be distracted, and he reveals his emotions to everyone, which is a mistake. Dhalia will use this weakness to her advantage and break it with one well-aimed blow. All she has to do is get you."

"Should I hurt him?" She asked in a low, slightly tearful voice. She didn't want to do this.

"You have to to break his heart," Gaenor replied mercilessly. "Then he will become stronger because he will stop letting emotions speak. Maybe then he will be able to fight for us, because so far he is far too weak for that."

"This is cruel," she said, feeling her plans just crumble.

"It is necessary," he replied firmly. "There is no room for feelings in war."

Neila knew there was no point in arguing against such strong arguments. She felt sorry for Drasan because she knew how much it would hurt him, probably as badly as she did, but she had no choice. Gaenor was right: Duke Sheardon could not allow himself to be weak.

***

Drasan stood on the edge of the lake and began to remove more pieces of his bent and damaged armor. Finally, he also took off his tunic. He stood there for a moment, undressed to the waist, enjoying the refreshing chill of the air and listening to the sound of the waterfall - it was soothing to his troubled thoughts.

Finally, as if he had been getting ready for a long time, he entered the stream of icy water. He was relieved to wash away dried blood and dirt, and it was such an invigorating experience that he could do it for hours. Unfortunately, there was not enough time for this.

When he finished, still dripping with water, he stepped out from under the waterfall and sat on a nearby rock, brushing cold drops off his hair. He studied his reflection in the lake critically. He rubbed his chin, feeling that he had gotten quite thick stubble, and ran a hand through his hair. They were a little below his shoulders now, and their raven blackness was streaked here and there with individual gray streaks - a reminder of a stay in the Kahaer dungeons. He tensed his muscles, pleased to see that they had regained their former form. Even the scars weren't so visible anymore. It was partly due to the nature of the dragons. Thanks to her, all wounds healed in the blink of an eye.

At the sound of footsteps, he turned around, instinctively reaching over his left shoulder. He swore softly as he remembered the sword was a few feet away. Where the gloomy remnants of armor and the rest of his garments.

Neila froze, holding her breath. As always, the sight of her acted on him like a soothing balm. He smiled at her and ran a hand through his hair. The girl was still standing in the same place, as if she had grown into the ground. It took a moment for him to realize that he was standing in front of her, stripped down to the waist, which gave her a much better view of his scarred torso.

"You could get dressed..." she choked out after a long moment of embarrassing silence.

He grinned in a smug smile. The embarrassment of his nakedness clearly tickled his vain ego. Women always liked to watch him, and he willingly let them.

"Sorry, baby..." he purred in a seductive tone, winking at her mischievously, "I still forget how I act on women."

Neila snorted with obvious irritation.

"You have a really vivid imagination, Your Highness," she growled through clenched teeth, propping herself up to her hips. "And you can leave such texts for those sleek ladies who faint at the sight of you. I only feel disgust."

For some reason, her agitation only excited him. He really didn't know women who were not physically attracted to him. Most drooled at the sight of him, even when he was fully clothed. Neila was different.

"I'm trying to figure you out all the time." He took a few steps forward.

Neila stepped back, keeping his distance.

"Maybe get dressed first so we can talk in a civilized way," she said.

The half-dragon grinned in a sly smile.

"Do you feel embarrassed by my nakedness?" He asked aggressively.

The mercenary was clearly in no mood for jokes today. Instead, she grimaced, showing her dissatisfaction.

"Save the cheap compliments for the residents of brothels," she replied with a ferocity that slapped him in the face.

The smile faded from Drasan's face, and instead there was an expression of deep thought.

"So, what do I owe the honor of your presence?" He asked brusquely as he passed her to a chestnut mare standing nearby. He quietly hoped the girl would fall for him. He was wrong.

"I was hoping to clear up a few things," she said gruffly.

"If we have nothing in common, what would we explain?" He replied coldly, and without waiting for her answer, he turned his back.

He pulled out a clean black tunic from his saddlebag and put it on. Then he looked around the recent battlefield and headed towards one of the corpses of Ridenian soldiers, who, judging by the pulp into which his face had turned, was hit with an ax.

"By the gods, Drasan! Act like an adult instead of sulking like a child!" She tossed accusingly at him.

He stiffened for a moment and resumed his search. Regardless of her company, he took off the shoes of the corpse. He ripped the chain mail from another stiff, and metal-reinforced bracers from another. He began to drag the entire pile gathered in this way, not worrying too much about blood stains and trying to ignore the mercenary.

He knew he was acting ridiculous, but now he didn't care. Neila could say anything, but her behavior revealed that she was not indifferent to her. She tried to disguise it with harshness and spite, but he knew his thing anyway.

"Can you turn to me?" She growled, eventually losing her patience.

For a moment Drasan consciously ignored her, stroking the chestnut horse on the neck. He wondered what to say. How to dress what feels like the right words. Usually, he didn't have to say anything, the women just clung to him like bees to their honeycombs. Sometimes it was enough just to smile, and they forgave him everything. In embarrassment, he brushed his hair again.

"I saved your life," he said finally, his voice bitter after all.

Neila stood up in a fighting stance, leaning on her hips, glaring at him under a menacing frown.

"So, you were probably hoping that I would let you come between my legs out of gratitude?" She asked belligerently. "Then know that I have no intention of going to bed with you. Moreover, I could list your flaws for hours, and the greatest of them all - your self-righteous ego."

"You don't even know what I did for you." He clenched his fists as her words hurt him more than he expected.

"I know you saved my life," she said coldly. "But it doesn't change anything between us, Drasan. You better wake up, let's go to war! We can all die because of your stupid cupids! If you want to relieve yourself, find some brothel, but leave me alone!" After these quite harsh words, she turned on her heel and walked away.

Drasan stayed where he was. He had difficulty controlling himself enough not to follow her and not confess his true feelings. She had hurt him far more than if she had punched him in the face. He was not used to such treatment. Maybe it was better? Perhaps it would be easier if he put all those feelings deep in his pocket.

***

After Neila had gone a long way, she slumped to the ground and stayed that way. He was unaware of how much this conversation had cost her, and she hoped he would never find out. She realized that she had hurt the dragon severely, but she had to do it. Drasan could not afford to be occupied with cupids in his mind. Fortunately, she knew what to say to alienate him.

Gaenor was waiting for her beyond the nearby rocks. He was still in human form, which didn't make him any less terrifying. He, too, shone with his bare chest, but his nakedness did not affect her like Drasan's nakedness.

"How did it go?" He asked without preamble.

She shrugged, feeling even meaner than she was a moment ago.

"I don't think he believed me," she said flatly.

Gaenor was clearly not thrilled with the answer.

"You have to try harder," he said in that cold, emotionless voice of his.

"It's not my fault," said the mercenary. "He simply refuses to accept my words."

"You're trying too little," he drawled.

"I've already told you!" She exclaimed, forgetting who she was talking to. "I don't want to hurt him anymore! It is just as painful for me! So, don't expect me to break his heart on purpose!"

"I have to!" He hissed. "It's really very important. Drasan must not be distracted by anything, he must focus on the fight. Dhalia can take advantage of any weakness, and only he can resist her. If she finds out about you, she will use it against him and we will lose our only line of defense."

"I know," Neila gasped furiously. "You think I'm not doing everything in my power to throw him away from me? I ignore him and avoid him; despite myself I refer to him as..." She broke off, because she couldn't find the right words.

Gaenor looked at her seriously and said, slowly drawing his words:

"If you really love him, you will try to make him hate you. It's not about you anymore, it's not about me, or even about him. The game is much more at stake. Drasan is a very important figure in it, we cannot afford to lose him."

Neila was shocked by the determination in his voice. She had never seen him like this before, he was shaky. You could see, he was really scared. But she still felt the most aggrieved in all of this.

Why is she the one to sacrifice? After all, she had been trying to suppress this feeling for a long time, without much success. Besides, Drasan turned out to be a very stubborn bastard, and she didn't think he would just let it go. Perhaps she should resort to trickery?

As soon as Gaenor disappeared somewhere between the rocks, she looked longingly at the waterfall, but Drasan was not there.

He must have gone to consult with Alt'ar, she thought bitterly.

She didn't feel like it herself. Velwel and Rodian were probably there as well. Although she owed her life to the witch, she still could not develop a more intimate relationship with her. She was irritated by her cool and haughty demeanor and the fact that she was downright indecently beautiful. With her, she herself looked like a common sparrow. She wouldn't be surprised if Drasan fell in love with that one.

But that damned reptile chose me, she thought, not without a hint of satisfaction. After all, she had seen the redhead make sweet eyes at him, and he just ignored her.

It didn't change the fact that she and Drasan couldn't be together. It wouldn't work. Not only because he was a prince and she was nothing, but mostly because he was born a half-dragon. They didn't fit together, belonged to two completely different worlds, and nothing would change that.

Until now, she has not looked where she is going. She was surprised when her legs carried her exactly to the place where she had previously watched Drasan bathe. She closed her eyes for a moment, trying to recall the image. His muscular figure looked great in the splashes of clear water. The mere mention of the sight gave her a thrill of excitement. Nobody has acted on her as intensely as he has so far.

"What are you doing here?" An unexpected question was asked.

The charm was broken. Neila turned angrily and came face to face with Alt'ar.

The assassin carried two freshly slaughtered deer on both shoulders, and his wolf strutting beside him as always.

"Not your business," she growled, angry that he had pulled her out of her sweet dreams.

The leader of the Guild gave her a long look that made her skin always ache.

"This is not the time to wander alone," he said dryly. "We have to stick together."

After these words, he moved forward without even looking at her. Swearing under her breath, she followed him. Ars ran ahead, dodging between the sharp rocks. Finally, they stepped out into a large clearing where most of his men had gathered. They gathered around three small fires. They kept their horses close together, some of them tied in pairs, and a makeshift stretcher between them.

Alt'ar laid his prey on the ground and walked over to Rodian. He quietly exchanged a few hasty words with her and headed for the horses.

Neila looked around for Drasan. She found him among several killers, including Velwel. He talked and laughed, completely ignoring her. She felt a twinge of pain, but then remembered that this was the point. Gaenor sat nearby, watching her closely through narrowed eyes. She suppressed the urge to approach the half-dragon and explain herself, instead she turned towards Rodian.

The witch deliberately ignored her presence, which was in itself extremely irritating. Finally, Neila couldn't stand it and cleared her throat loudly to get her attention.

Only then did Rodian deign to honor her with a contemptuous look.

"Ah, it's you," she snorted, as if at an annoying fly. "What do you want?"

"You know I don't like you..." Neila began quietly.

The witch snorted softly at that.

"...but now I need your help..." finished the mercenary, trying with all her strength to ignore that scornful huff.

"In what?" Rodian asked, showing a shadow of interest.

Neila crumpled a curse in her mouth and glanced at Drasan, but Drasan continued to ignore her.

"Do you know any good way to discourage a man?" She lowered her voice to a whisper, because she wanted to be very discreet.

Rodian's lips curled into a nasty grimace that was probably meant to be a smile. She looked at Drasan, and her lusty gaze proved that, like most women, she was not immune to his charm.

"To this day I wonder what he sees in you," she said more to herself than to the mercenary, smiling at the same time as a cat to cream.

Neila suppressed the urge to punch her on the redhead for staring so lustfully at the young prince. She needed this monkey's help, she had to restrain herself.

"Then why not try your spells to make him stop following me," she growled through clenched teeth, wanting to get the witch's attention again.

Rodian laughed softly.

"Unfortunately, there is no spell for that, my dear. But there is one way that will work..." She paused for a moment, looking at the girl in a peculiar way, judging her.

Neila grimaced and surreptitiously looked at Drasan.

"What should I do?" She asked dispassionately.

"It's simple," said Rodian. "Men aren't too complicated creatures. Each of them works on similar principles. For him to hate you, you have to hit his male ego."

Neila stared at her, still not understanding.

Rodian gasped irritably.

"Cheat him to another, stupid!" She said. "Show, that you are not doing any harm to his advances, and he will hate you."

Neila flinched slightly at the thought of it. Where would he find a fool who would agree to something similar? The solution came faster than she expected - Velwel. Only he could help her now.

***

Hidden in a huge rock massif, the cave seemed to be a perfect hiding place. For a moment, Yarred stood undecided, eyeing her suspiciously. It might turn out to be the home of one of those big black bears. He jumped off his horse and walked closer. Maybe it was just his imagination, but inside the cavity he saw a glow of fire.

Fire meant the presence of people.

The captain retreated to his mounts, not knowing what to do. It might turn out to be just a lonely wanderer, but just as well a unit of the royal army. He patted Bruen on the neck and covered the nostrils with his hand. He didn't want to reveal his presence with a single huff of his. He moved slowly, taking his steps so as not to alert the resident of the cave. But before he got there, a tall figure appeared in the entrance, wrapped in a long cloak with a hood. His shadow hid the features of his face, and the captain was convinced it was a man.

He froze motionless.

"Why don't you come in?" The stranger had a deep, trustworthy voice. "You will surely like to eat a warm soup, and there will be plenty of space by the fire."

I don't think I have a choice, the visitor thought, and with a sigh he walked towards the brightly lit cave, dragging both horses with him.

The cave turned out to be so spacious that it could easily accommodate twenty people. A gray rampart stood by the wall opposite to the entrance. Beside him were two sacks on the ground, a folded fleece of sheep, and a wide saddle with a high pommel. This indicated that the stranger was getting ready to leave the safe hiding place.

"I was going to start tomorrow, since dawn," the answer to the unspoken question chilled the Sheardonian to the core. In an instant he guessed that the strange wanderer was a sorcerer.

Instinctively, his hand tightened on the hilt of his sword and was about to turn around when he suddenly froze, unable to move.

"Let me explain," the host asked softly. "I would not read your thoughts without necessity, but as you probably know we have a war..."

"The only question is whose side you are on, mage," Yarred drawled.

"On the right, I assure you," the man replied calmly.

"I spit on your assurances," the Sheardonian snapped softly. "Who are you? And what are you looking for here?"

"I'm here for the same reason you are here," the mage continued to speak calmly.

"Free me then," Yarred replied.

The mage sighed.

"Unfortunately... I can't, first I must make sure you're not a Ridean spy. For this, I need to read your thoughts."

"Don't you dare to rummage in my head!" Yarred yelled, straining his muscles in vain.

"I must," the mage replied firmly, and Yarred felt his hands on his temples. "This might turn out to be a bit unpleasant."

As soon as he said that, something like cold tentacles broke into Yarred's head and began searching his thoughts and memories. The cursed mage was right, the impression was not pleasant. When the alien consciousness finally withdrew from his mind, he felt a painful throb in his skull and a buzzing noise in his ears but regained the ability to move. In front of him, a stranger was rubbing his temples vigorously, muttering what sounded like curses to himself.

"Ah, I really don't like doing this when I don't have to," he said quietly.

"Who are you?" Yarred decided, following his example, rubbing his temples as well. It helped.

"I'm Alder of Roggen," the mage replied, extending his hand to him.

"Yarred of Sheardon," replied the captain, taking the hand that was offered him.

"I know who you are," Alder said calmly, and then frowned, giving his face a menacing expression. "But I don't know what you're doing here. After all, Drasan told you to sit in Antua and train King Valden."

At the sound of his friend's name, Yarred straightened and looked into the sorcerer's black eyes.

"Since the Vaya kingdom ceased to exist, Drasan cannot command me. I have the right to do what I see fit," he replied.

Alder smiled.

"You are lucky that you met me on your way. I'm traveling with the apprentice and just waiting for his return, and then I'm going south, away from the lands under Bal'zar's rule." He pointed to the prepared bags.

Yarred glanced at them briefly, asked the question that haunted him:

"Where's Drasan?"

Alder didn't answer right away. He seemed to be reflecting on what he could and could not reveal to him.

"We split up a while ago," he said finally. "Based on the rumors, I believe he is currently somewhere south of Riden. After the confusion he caused in Washmorth, the king put the army on alert, so you were very lucky on your way there that you did not come across them."

"I came across, but they didn't pay attention to me. I saw plenty of Drasan's posters on the way, though," Yarred replied, reaching for the tin bowl of steaming stew Alder was handing him.

The mage said nothing for a moment, mumbling his food in silence.

"To be expected," he said finally. "From what I've noticed, Dhalia and Bal'zar disagree on one thing. She wants to capture Drasan alive, he would prefer dead. He tried to kill him several times but failed. He probably hopes that the prize will tempt mercenary thugs who will do the black work for him."

"Why does Dhalia want him alive?" Yarred asked.

Alder shrugged.

"Nobody knows that. Perhaps she believes in the old legend of the Chosen One." He smiled sourly. "Or she just likes challenges."

Yarred frowned.

"Challenges?" He repeated, not really understanding the mage's words.

"Well, yes." Alder was clearly surprised that it was not so obvious to the captain. "Drasan resisted her spells. She had failed to possess him the way she had with Gaenor and Boris. You see, witches have used beauty for centuries to get whatever their greedy hearts desired. Usually, they succeeded because hardly anyone could resist them. An interesting fact is how they could get it." He smiled, and his eyes flashed. "Apparently it was enough that they lured the victim to their bed, and there, using the generous gifts of nature and magic, they subjected them to their will. Their gifts help them fulfill their selfish desires. In Dhalia's case it is the anticipation of future events, and throughout her many years of life she has also developed a talent for manipulating weaker minds. It seems to me that Bal'zar's natural talent, from an early age with masterful skill, influenced the thoughts and actions of selected people, prompting them to do what he wanted. Dhalia certainly wants to test his skills on Drasan. I suspect it was his resistance that made her so angry, and she is determined to break him at all costs and by all means available."

"So she wants..." Yarred swallowed.

"...make him a slave to his will," Alder finished for him. "It's obvious. Drasan is much more powerful than Gaenor. According to Dhalia, destroying such a strong gift is simply a waste."

"Ah..." commented the captain shortly. He never really asked a friend about the Kahaer experience. He suspected, however, that Dhalia did not mince her measures to break his will.

Yet the young man he had seen on that fateful night when he was captured by Boris and dragged into Kahaer differed in many ways from the young man he had met after leaving the keep. He remembered how he had accused him of treason then, and how Drasan had told him about the nightmare Dhalia had prepared for him. Then it was not easy for him to believe that the friend had resisted the obvious charm of the witch, since he himself was under the influence of her beauty.

"Beauty can be a powerful tool, especially in the hands of a woman as ruthless as Dhalia," Alder said softly, staring at the dying fire. "That's why women were forbidden to practice magic. The kings got rid of them from their courts for fear of taking control of them. Many witches were burned at the stake for treason. Those who survived were exterminated by the so-called "witch hunters." But they did not manage to wipe out all of them. There are those that hid well, waiting for the right moment. Or like Vaya that came over to our side."

"Vaya was a witch?" Yarred almost choked on a piece of chewed meat.

"Oh, yes," Alder said, tossing a piece of dried wood into the embers. Flames exploded, shooting sparks. "She was one of the first to come to our side. Some of them, of course, were put to death shortly afterwards by the "sisters" blinded by envy. Vaya survived only thanks to her unique talent for controlling animals: wolves saved her from certain death. As you probably guessed, she found herself at the court of King Avgar, and he, delighted with her beauty, took her as his wife." He looked at Yarred, who was catching his every word. "Since then, Vaya has stopped using magic, except in exceptional circumstances."

Yarred was silent for a moment. He didn't know what to think. A kingdom ruled by witches: isn't this what Dhalia wants? And the queen to whom he had sworn allegiance had that power.

But she wasn't using it – he added in his mind.

Does it matter who she was? She's dead. Another witch killed her and razed the whole kingdom to the ground. Suddenly his heart felt anger. It was Dhalia who was responsible for the slaughter in Sheardon, murdering hundreds of innocent people to anger Drasan.

But she couldn't even break it that way, he thought with vindictive satisfaction. She only made him angry.

He felt a wave of admiration for his friend again. The witch stripped him of what he loved. She killed everyone he knew and destroyed the place he had called home for so many years, and he never gave up. He could still beat her, but he needed support and Yarred knew what he should do.

***

The unexpected luxury turned out to be a huge surprise for Mara. Tharon gave her one of his chambers, and it was decorated with such splendor that for several days she could not get used to it. As a guest of the most important royal adviser, she had access to all amenities, including service.

So, one morning, when a young maid slipped into her room, she jumped to her feet, reaching for a dagger hidden under the pillow. The girl ignored her and went to the copper bathtub in the corner of the room. She poured a jug of steaming water into it.

"Good morning, lady," she said automatically, continuing her work.

"Good morning," Mara muttered as she tiptoed over to the cradle. After all, Lender was still deeply asleep.

She smiled and stroked his cheek. She had barely resisted the urge not to pick it up. She didn't want to wake him up.

Today could decide their fate. Tharon was to introduce her to the most important royal officials as the daughter of the late king.

The maid bustled about preparing her bath and clean underwear. On the great bed lay a magnificent dress of green velvet trimmed with snow-white lace at the cuffs and neckline. Mara looked at her uncertainly. Until now, she had never had the opportunity to wear such elegant clothes.

The woman helped her wash and dress. At that time, she embarrassedly remembered that she didn't even know her name. She was just opening her mouth to find out when Tharon entered the room. Noticing her in her underwear alone, he tactfully looked away. The young girl, completely ignoring his presence, chased the shocked Mara by the screen, helped her put on her dress and laced her torso tightly.

Mara stood in front of the mirror and stared at herself for a moment, not trusting her eyes. A lady with large pale blue eyes looked at her from the smooth surface above a small straight nose and a thin mouth. Her flaming red hair fell in soft waves down to her buttocks. The dress emphasized all the advantages of the figure.

Tharon dismissed the maid with a short gesture, who cursed in front of him and hurried out of the room. He himself wore a purple tunic embroidered with gold thread, and a navy blue and silver cloak with Antua's coat of arms embroidered on it fell from his shoulders. He resumed the appearance of a gray, wrinkled old man with a short-trimmed beard and unusual steel-gray eyes.

He smiled at Mara, the lines around his eyes deepening, making him look even older.

"You look delightful." He placed a kiss on her hand.

Mara blushed.

"Thank you..." she stumbled, embarrassed by the compliment.

The counselor offered her an arm. Mara accepted them, paused, and looked at the cradle.

"I'm sure the nurse will be good at it. Calia just went to get her," Tharon said soothingly.

So that's the maid's name, Mara thought, still staring at the cradle. She felt a gentle tug and moved forward in a trance.

They left the room into the corridor plunged in the twilight. Set in gilded candelabra, the narrow candles gave out very little light. Mara looked curiously from side to side, admiring the tapestries and tapestries that adorned the raw walls. Tharon led her steadfastly toward the wide staircase that led down to the great entrance hall, and further to the left of the entrance was a double gate decorated with a wood-carved image of an eagle. These in turn led to the throne room, and others to the royal library and office. They were headed there now.

As they stepped in front of that door, Mara nervously smoothed the folds of her dress and straightened, at least trying to look dignified. Tharon exceeded them without hesitation. They found themselves in a circular room, up to the ceiling, filled with heavy volumes and piles of dusty scrolls.

The other members of the Council of Elders - four men and a woman - were waiting for them there. All dressed in identical, long blue robes trimmed with gold embroidery. From all the gathered, the councilor gave Mara a long look. Even though she must have been more than forty summers long ago, she has not lost any of her beauty. The slightly harsh features of the face contrasted sharply with the large brown eyes, and there was not a single gray streak in the beautifully draped jet-black curls. The man standing closest to her had long gray hair and a beard, his face was marked with numerous lines of wrinkles, and his eyes had turned blue and pale and dim, like a blind man's. Next to him stood a dark-haired and dark-eyed young man, not much older than she was. Further on, a stout gentleman with a round, chubby face and a bushy mustache, and a bit shorter than him, a thin pale old man with intense green eyes and a short, neatly trimmed white beard.

"These are Favia, Dagorad, Avygar, Ultor, and Toreh." Tharon was pointing to the next members of the Council as he named them.

The girl made a curtsy as Tharon had taught her. Two of the four men also bowed, the others nodded slightly, staring not at her, but at the man accompanying her.

"I'd like to introduce you to Mara," Tharon said calmly, despite the rather chilly reception. "The daughter of the deceased king and the only heiress to the throne."

As soon as his words were gone, there was a tense silence. Now all eyes turned to Mara. Neither felt friendly.

Favia was the first to speak.

"We all know the king died childless," she said coldly.

"Yes," Tharon looked a little confused. "He didn't have any legal children."

"So why are you introducing this girl to us?" Asked the fat Ultor in a loud voice. "Have you forgotten that our law makes it clear that bastards have no rights to the crown?"

Mara felt her cheeks burn. Were it not for Tharon's calm and confident presence, she would most likely have burst out crying. She forced herself to stay where she was, remembering her son. After all, she was doing it all for him, not for herself.

"Mara is not a bastard," Tharon said calmly. "Her mother was Dajmira..."

"Tharon, this is ridiculous," Avygar interjected with an indulgent smile. "Dajmira died in the plague at the age of only sixteen..."

"Dajmira is not dead at all," Tharon interrupted calmly. "She left because she was forced into marriage against her will. She did not know then that she was pregnant."

His words shook Mara deeply. She couldn't believe what she was hearing. She looked at the man, searching his face for confirmation of the news, but found nothing.

"And that's what that stray told you?" Favia asked sharply, her beautiful face contorted with an angry grimace. "Do you have any evidence for that?"

"The evidence will be found," Tharon smiled. "I want a blood test for Mara," he said, folding his hands over his chest.

There was a murmur of indignant voices. All those gathered protested vehemently. Aged Dagorad has kept admirable peace. And it was he who finally raised a troubled hand to signal that he wanted to speak. Everyone fell silent.

"Tharon is right," he said in a low, barely audible voice. "We need confirmation of this girl's identity. You well know that a kingdom needs a wise and just ruler. If the blood test proves she is related, none of us has the right to defend what is due to her."

His words were silent again, perhaps the other Council members were digesting them. You could see, he enjoyed great respect, because even the proud and haughty Favia did not dare to protest.

"Okay then," Ultor said finally, tugging at his bushy mustache with his plump hand. "The girl will pass the blood test."

There were short murmurs of consent. Favia did not take her eyes off Mara, and the girl could not help feeling that she had just won over her enemies, among the most powerful people in the kingdom.

CHAPTER 12

The chestnut mare gasped angrily, surprised by the unexpected tug of reins. Drasan ignored her, looking for the source of a rustling noise in the darkness ahead that disturbed him. Ars' eyes shone in the gloom: they burned like two lanterns. The wolf trotted up to him and whimpered softly, then turned and disappeared again into the night. The half-dragon jabbed the chestnut with his heel, which made it snort again, but obediently moved forward.

Drasan rode slowly for a while, weaving between the sharp rocks. The melting snow formed muddy puddles at the bottom of the ravine, in which the tip sagged to the hocks. The prince squeezed her sides with his calves, forcing her to speed up. Mud squirted under the hoofs, but otherwise there was silence.

As soon as he had left the rock, he stopped once again. There was a glow on the horizon. There was still a long time until dawn, and besides, the glow was beaming the sky to the west.

Touched by a bad feeling, the young man dug his heels into the sides of the chestnut tree and galloped off into the glow. Driving around the bend, the mare jerked abruptly again that she sat down on her rump and slipped on the mud. The city was burning right in front of them, illuminating the surroundings so that it suddenly became as bright as day, and a pillar of smoke was beating the sky. The prince instinctively drew strength and began to sooth the fire. The burning houses gradually turned to smoking ashes. The man rode a walk between the buildings, ignoring the sneaking and puffing top.

The streets were swarming with burned corpses, the sickening odor of burnt meat in the air. All the town's inhabitants were slaughtered: men, women and children. In one of the houses the roof collapsed with a crash. The frightened chestnut tree danced and grunted. The half-dragon calmed her, speaking to her in a gentle voice and stroking her neck.

Suddenly, the wolf of Alt'ar emerged from the wreckage. He yelled softly, waved his fuzzy tail several times, and disappeared again among the burned buildings. Drasan dismounted and followed him.

Ars paused beside the huge man lying on his back in a pool of blood. To his surprise, the fat man coughed and opened his eyes, staring at him with a mixture of hope and fear. The half-dragon threw the mare's reins over some kind of beam and walked over to him. The man coughed again, and blood spurted from his mouth. Drasan looked at the rapidly expanding red stain on his chest and realized that the man was dying.

"Horsemen..." he grunted, looking into his eyes. "Black knights..." blood bubbles were coming out of his mouth along with the words.

Drasan knelt beside the dying man. Better than anyone he realized the importance of these words. The black knights of Dhalia. Racial killers sent by her to do the dirty work. Only her Doars left dead bodies and smoking rubble. He clenched his fists, feeling his anger building up.

The man gripped his clothes tightly and pulled him towards him.

"Their commander..." he grunted, spitting blood at Drasan, "...a black demon from the abyss of hell..."

Boris. Blood boiled in Drasan's veins. The werewolf fled when the scales of victory tipped over to their side. The Doars must have been waiting nearby. They burned the town down as a rule and as a warning to those who did not yet understand that whoever sheltered traitors and rebels would be put to death along with the entire family.

Vengeance for Sheardon flared up again in Drasan's chest. He wanted revenge for Vaya, for everyone he knew who had been ruthlessly murdered to throw him off balance. He wanted to hunt down the murderers and tear them to bloody shreds, burn them to ashes, and the wind would blow them away. Send straight into the abyss.

Blind fury seized him.

Only a heavy cough came to his consciousness. Suddenly he remembered where he was and looked at the man who was also staring at him.

"They wanted me to say..." he did not finish, because blood spurted from his mouth and his eyes went still.

Next to him, Ars howled softly. Drasan leaned down and closed the man's eyes with a movement of his hand, then nervously made a ceremonial gesture of farewell to the deceased and stood up. Still torn by anger, he walked over to the chestnut and with one jump he found himself in the saddle. The mare screamed as he dug his heels into her flanks and galloped towards the mouth of the ravine. He wanted to leave the smoking ashes behind him as soon as possible. He knew his thirst for revenge wouldn't leave him that soon, but he had to go as far as possible before his anger outweighed his common sense.

As expected, Alt'ar was dumbfounded at the sight of him. Drasan volunteered to go to town and bring back as much food as possible. The half-dragon hauled his mare right in front of him, but he didn't have to say anything. The sight of blood and ash-covered shoes said it all.

"They burned the city," the Guild leader said softly.

Drasan nodded. He still wasn't able to talk. Among the riders he spotted Neila's face, but she was the only one who wasn't looking at him.

"I expected this," Alt'ar added, staring at the horse's mane. "Anyone survived?" He asked after a moment, looking up.

"No," replied Drasan. His voice sounded strange, dead. "But it wasn't the army, they were Dhalia's wetboys. They slaughtered all the inhabitants and set the city on fire." He was not going to tell Alt'ar about the man who had revealed the details of the slaughter to him. Revenge belonged to him, he had to get the monster that turned his life into hell.

Alt'ar turned his horse and looked at his faithful killers. Their faces showed grim determination. Many of them probably knew the inhabitants of the city well, maybe even had good friends or beloved women among them.

"The enemy has gone too far," he rumbled with a power that surprised even Drasan. "We'll pay them back. We will show no mercy as they did not show mercy to these innocent people. We'll catch up with these monsters and slaughter them!"

The assassins screamed in a loud chorus. The neighing of the horses followed.

Alt'ar turned in his saddle. He suddenly seemed taller and more terrible to the Sheardonian than before. His eyes blazed with some inner light, now more than ever they resembled the eyes of a wolf. He looked at him with fear and admiration at the same time.

The leader of the Guild spurred his great steed up and galloped off the ground, followed by the other assassins.

Drasan did not follow them. He wasn't at all sure if he had done the right thing. Assassins were only a handful against well-trained soldiers who knew neither pity nor fear.

Gaenor rode up to him, surprisingly on horseback. It is possible that the fight deprived him of his strength, so he could not change form.

"You're going there," he didn't ask, but was stating a fact. He understood Drasan would not miss an opportunity to retaliate for Sheardon.

The half-dragon did not see fit to answer. Gaenor seemed to be the last person he would listen now. But the older dragon had no intention of stopping him.

"Let me go with you," he said calmly, his usually cool tone fading away. Drasan froze at the hint of fatherly concern in his voice.

He stared at him for a moment in silent surprise, unable to utter a word. He would never suspect Gaenor of having any feelings, especially since he himself insisted that they were alien to him. Meanwhile, he was standing there and looking at him with his terrifying, reptilian eyes that smoldered with something like understanding.

"I understand you think this is your private vendetta. Dhalia has destroyed everything you love. You must not allow your thirst for revenge to blind common sense," these words made Drasan even more dumbfounded.

Gaenor who gives him good advice in a fatherly tone?

"I'm in a hurry," said Drasan. It sounded a little too dryly, but he had to somehow dissuade Gaenor from the idea of accompanying him.

The column of riders ran over. Only Velwel remained, waiting for him with curiosity, listening to this unusual exchange of views. As Drasan was about to turn the mare back to join him, he felt Gaenor's hand clamping on his forearm like an iron vise.

"Be careful," the dragon said softly, looking into his eyes.

"I'm always," replied the half-dragon, struggling to free himself from his grasp, to no avail.

"I'm serious, Drasan," Gaenor continued to stare at him. "Maybe Dhalia wants you alive, but Boris doesn't necessarily..."

"Boris is dead now," Drasan replied stiffly. "I'll personally degut him..."

"That's what he's counting on, Drasan. He wants you, blinded by your revenge, to seek revenge. He senses a weakness in you and will take advantage of it ruthlessly." His words were so serious that the prince hesitated.

"Okay," he agreed, because he was really sick of this strange conversation. "I'll try to avoid fighting alone."

A shadow of a smile flashed across Gaenor's face. He released Drasan, who also smiled. A moment later, the mare turned and galloped in the wake of the rapidly departing Alt'ar's men, and Velwel rushed after him.

***

Boris looked at the black knight squad surrounding him. He chose only three hundred, sent the rest back to camp, but still felt he had an overwhelming advantage over the remnants of Drasan's "army".

Army - he thought the term too high-profile for this pathetic jumble. They were no obstacles to the well-trained Doars.

The demon shook its great head, impatiently digging its hoof into the muddy ground. He, too, was looking forward to an imminent battle.

From the rise where they stopped, the werewolf had a great view both of what was left of the town below, and of the mouth of the ravine from which Drasan and the gloomy remnants of a squad of assassins could emerge at any moment.

On the horizon, dawn was starting to turn gray as riders emerged from the narrow fissure. They were led not by a half-dragon, but by a tall man riding a war steed.

Boris cursed, not what he expected. Avoiding a fight felt like that self-righteous kid. So where was he?

The werewolf began to study the faces of the people emerging from the ravine even more closely. The riders, though from a distance seemed a random jumble of various colors, acted like a unit of a select army. The horses rode in fours in a tight formation, as in a parade. He did not see the prince, neither among the horses nor the wounded on a stretcher. On the other hand, he picked out the face of the girl Dhalia had mentioned among them without much trouble. She was driving in the middle of the seventh row.

At this distance, he could easily hit her with a crossbow, but Dhalia wished to capture her alive, as did the half-dragon.

During all these years of service with a witch, he undertook almost everything: he spied, recruited informants, gathered information and killed those who blocked his mistress on her way to power. He also often commanded the Doars. Just like now.

He watched the march of the warlords for a moment, stuck his spurs into the sides of the stallion and turned him towards the low grove growing on the top of the hill. Hidden among the trees, the Doars were not much different from the shadows at a distance. All in identical armor, on tall war horses with black spikers.

Only dark-colored horses were selected for the fight. Boris wasn't sure why, and he didn't really care.

The werewolf stopped in front of his commander, a tall, sullen, stern-faced man. He was the only one to wear a helmet decorated with a red plume.

"They are close. Get ready," he said calmly.

The commander nodded silently, held up his right hand. At this signal, the black knights divided themselves into two columns, each consisting of exactly one hundred and fifty horsemen. A sullen man took charge of one of them, and Boris moved towards the other. As always, he admired the discipline and obedience of the Doars. They lined up in perfect line, none extended half the length of a horse's head. Everyone drew their weapons on command. The blades glowed, reflecting the rays of the rising sun.

They waited in complete silence for the enemy to appear, staring at the ribbon of the road winding between the hills.

***

As soon as Dhalia entered the dining room, she stopped short. On the table, usually at this time of day, filled with the finest dishes of the royal kitchens, piles of books and old scrolls and a few newer maps were now piled up. Two people bent over this pile of papers: Bal'zar and... Arano.

Her throat felt unbearably dry at the sight of such well-known features. There were jugs of wine on the counter, but she did not dare to go there. She was expecting a fancy dinner, and she was sent to a war council. She was not dressed properly...

The deep red dress she put on shocked with the plunging neckline. This one was adorned with a diamond necklace, her hair falling in a gleaming cascade over her exposed back. Dressed like this, she would surely find her place in the noble society without any problems, but no one would deign to inform her that there would be no dinner.

As she stood undecided, someone finally honored her with his attention. Arano suddenly looked up and pierced her with those green eyes of his. For the first time in so many centuries, her heart sped up rapidly. The magician continued to strike with extraordinary beauty. He could even compete with Drasan in this respect, although he lacked his youthful passion and that characteristic wildness.

The man she had once had a crush on looked at her with the same indifference with which he could see a boring landscape painted by a provincial painter. In this look, she did not find a hint of warmth or love, or even hate. It remained empty, cold and dead. Maybe Arano she once knew had indeed died.

Dhalia felt slapped. Additionally, Bal'zar ignored her as well. It is as if it belonged to the elements of the decor. She forced a fake smile and, grasping the hem of her dress, made her way to the far end of the dining room, her heels tapping loudly on the stone floor.

Arano watched her indifferently from under a slightly furrowed eyebrow.

When she stepped across from the young king's seat, she expressed all the fury she had built up.

"Would you be so kind as to explain to me what is going on here?" She asked, her voice saturated with poisonous sweetness.

"We're working on a new war strategy," explained the ruler, glancing at her briefly.

"And you did not deign to inform me about it?" She hissed through clenched teeth.

"Actually, my dear..." the monarch rose with one movement, which surprised her completely. "...your presence at each meeting is not necessary. You haven't made anything concrete so far. I chose to base my tactics on facts instead of using your gut feeling," he explained in a cool, haughty tone.

"You will wander like children in the fog," said the witch contemptuously.

"It's not your concern," said the king wearily. "I would not like to remind you again who wears the crown here."

It did not escape Dhalia's attention that Arano smiled slightly.

"So, you exclude me from your dispute?" She tried to ignore the former lover.

"No," Bal'zar smiled slightly indulgently. "I just warn you not to interfere in matters not concerning you or your precious hybrid. Besides, you sent your barbarians there, who I suppose can handle a gang of robbers."

"So what are you going to do?" Dhalia didn't want to give up so easily. Bal'zar may have had an innate insight, but he was still a bastard in the crown.

"The snow is retreating. In a week I will be going to Antua." Announced the ruler. "Without a king, without an heir to the throne, they will be easy targets. Arano says it's best to strike from the south, as most of their strongholds are centered around the eastern border. Before they gather troops, I will strike at them with all my might. This is how I will deprive your reptile of another potential ally, obtaining horses and food for the army in one fell swoop."

"The Antuans will not put up much resistance," Arano said calmly. "Their strength has always been in the Midlemar. Since Valden's death, morale among the people has also declined among the local nobility and the army. General Darkhan also has the best years of his life behind him. I don't think he can have enough horsemen and archers to stand in the way of your army, my lord." The mage inclined his head slightly towards the young king. "However... as much as I admire your insight, I would advise you to hold off your attack until spring. Then it will be easier to gather both food and to bring war machines with you. Your troops will respond better to it too. I would also advise you to leave the main force at a strategic point, for example on the shores of Lake Falan. It would also be good to get Tarssen. After all, it is their largest city, and in addition, rich in loot that would strengthen the morale of your army."

"Thank you, Arano. I will consider everything you told me," Bal'zar replied, settling back in the chair and scratching his wolfhound on the great head.

Dhalia was overwhelmed with anger. It seemed as if she had been completely ignored in this plan to invade Antua, and she had taken Sheardon in just a week with the help of an army of less than two thousand. At the same time, over a thousand spread throughout the kingdom, venting the murderous bloodlust. It struck the gates of the royal city with less than a thousand-armed men without siege engines and captured them in two days. But no one praised her for doing all the dirty work, and the boy who has barely grown out of boyhood is getting praise from Arano himself! A mage who abhors violence and believes that war is evil, and that all conflicts should be resolved through peaceful negotiations.

Ha! So he is a great hypocrite who counts on not getting his hands dirty with someone else's blood, and she has always admired his sensitivity.

As she sat and eavesdropped on the discussion of the two men, Dhalia slowly plotted her thoughts to gain power and obedience. She did not count on the support of the army or the stupid people, but rather on the admiration of the young king himself. She could still creep into his favors and did not need a low-cut dress or lace underwear. Instead, she needed a plan that would show everyone that she still had to be reckoned with.

***

The next day turned out to be quite a surprise for Yarred. As soon as he opened his eyes, he realized that the sun was at its zenith, and his new companion had already started the fire and prepared a modest meal. The horses tied nearby began to pinch the grass that looked out from under the remnants of snow.

Embarrassed, the captain sprang from his bed.

His companion gave him a long, melancholy look. Only now in the daylight did the Sheardonian get a closer look at the features of his face. The sorcerer's apprentice was one of the kinds of young men who are not afraid of hard work. This was evident both in wide shoulders and in hands covered with calluses. A face with a rather deeply defined jaw and deep-set dark eyes pointed to some local robber, not an apprentice. His attire was simple, typical of local hunters. It consisted of thick woolen pants, tucked into knee-length boots, a linen shirt and a sheepskin-lined jacket. The only weapons he carried with him were a knife and a long bow and arrows made by him.

"Good morning," the young man grunted, handing him a half a loaf of slightly stale bread and a bowl of what looked and smelled like stew.

He himself sat down opposite and calmly took care of his own portion.

Captain Cordydian sighed heavily, for he understood that he would not be able to establish friendlier relations with this sullen man.

"What's your name?" He asked, at least trying to get him to talk.

"Berg," the muscle replied, without even looking up. He clearly didn't feel like arguing.

Yarred gave up trying to talk. He sat down and began to eat.

Ever since Alder had disappeared - no less strange than his taciturn apprentice - the captain had learned no more than he had guessed.

Riden was buzzing with rumors of a revolt in the south and of the vast army that the recently crowned king had rallied. The leader of the rebellion was reportedly one of the most eminent assassins on the peninsula - the famous Alt'ar. Many also spoke of the dragon that reportedly appeared over Washmorth and caused considerable damage to the city. Since the ability to sift gossip from the truth was one of his tasks, it was easy for the captain to guess who had started the little uprising. Unfortunately, he did not understand what Duke Sheardon was trying to achieve by hiring a gang of hired thugs.

As it was not the safest way to travel along the highways, Alder advised them not to lean beyond the valley. They could feel safe surrounded by forested hills, as it is easy to find a hiding place here. There was also a wild game. The reticent Berg turned out to be an excellent hunter, so they had enough to eat for now. Unfortunately, the prolonged absence of the sorcerer was beginning to raise some doubts.

Where could he go?

The nearest settlements were concentrated around the capital; therefore, they were swarming with troops, not missing a single occasion for drinking and walking. Especially since any day now the king could give the order to march. There were also those who, as a rule, and perhaps out of boredom, murdered innocent peasants and hung their bodies on roadside trees as a warning to those who would like to support the rebels.

Yarred was also disturbed by the fact that Antua could become the first target on the route of the Ridean troops, and he left his pregnant fiancée there. He trusted Mara's ability to take care of herself, after she grew up on the street. Therefore, she knew the hardships of life and knew where to seek help, if necessary. Even though he had acted in good faith for leaving her, he still couldn't forgive himself. She was left alone there with their unborn child. He should be there and take great care of her instead of taking on a mission that turned out to be impossible. Drasan could be the gods now, but they know where. And knowing his talent for attracting trouble, he was one of the last people he should look for right now. But it was too late to turn back. The roads were swarming with Ridean soldiers looking for an excuse to gut someone.

The captain was tired of being idle and hiding in corners. He wanted to fight. Take bloody retaliation for all murdered Sheardonians, for mother, father and sister who probably died during the siege. Above all, he wanted a witch. She was responsible for this massacre.

As he sat chewing and making plans, Berg suddenly stood up, took a short bow. With incredible skill worthy of the best archer, he put on the arrow and drew the string. Only then did the captain hear the muffled thud of hooves.

There was a slight hill on the road, although a rock rubble was a much better name. Defeating him on horseback, especially in the season of spring thaw, was almost suicide. So, the rider had to take a detour here.

It gave Berg exactly the advantage he needed, because the exit of the road was clearly visible from where he was standing. He could have stabbed an intruder with an arrow before the intruder realized that he was in danger.

The rider leaned out exactly where he measured the youth's arrowhead. He led his horse at a walk, carefully choosing his path through the rocks. The features of his face were indistinguishable from afar, for he wore a flowing cloak with a hood pulled over his head. Berg visibly relaxed, loosened his string and sat down, placing his bow on his lap.

"Master Alder is returning," he announced to the stunned captain.

Yarred was amazed at the young man's observation skills. He probably did not appreciate Berg. There was no doubt that, despite his many virtues, the boy didn't even have an iota of magical talent. The question itself was: why did the sorcerer take it to the term?

A young man would be a much better choice as a soldier or mercenary. He did not speak much, and his years in the service of the queen allowed the captain to conclude that the young man was or still is an excellently trained fighter. So where did he come from in the service of a mage who allegedly favored the rebels?

Before the Sheardonian had analyzed what he had observed, the rider stopped his horse and removed the hood from his head.

"Forgive me for this conspiracy," he said apologetically. "While soldiers still respect the sight of the mage, unfortunately it goes hand in hand with hostility among the common people, especially after Bal'zar imposed enormous taxes on them."

Captain Cordydian nodded. A widespread hatred of the new monarch was spreading among the Ridean like a plague. Some people dreamed in spirit that the rebels would give the young king a hard time. Others cursed and cursed Drasan for choosing to openly oppose the ruler.

"Bal'zar himself fosters revolt among the people," said Berg.

"It was a good thing I went to the settlement by myself," Alder said, pulling two heavy sacks off the horse. "It's getting harder and harder to get food. People are starving. There is an army everywhere and all you can get is a jug of thin beer, some bread and dried pork. Besides, soldiers confiscate all mounts right away. You'd be better off getting rid of that horse." He nodded toward Ernil.

Yarred frowned and opened his mouth to protest, before he could do so, the sorcerer spoke up again.

"Don't get me wrong. Your loyalty is admirable. Riden is boiling now like a beehive. To travel through a country swarming with soldiers, you need to blend in with the crowd. Otherwise, even if you are not considered a rebel, you will be forcibly drafted into the army."

"It's not just any junk," the captain drawled, indignant that someone might think of selling such a wonderful animal as Ernil. "Belongs to Drasan."

The mage fixed him with his piercing black eyes and said:

"I didn't mention the sale, Captain Cordydian. I wanted you to consider leaving the horse in Berg's care before you decide to go south yourself."

The captain realized he had no choice. To have any chance of finding the Duke of Sheardon, he had to sneak through Riden unnoticed, and such a beautiful black stallion was too conspicuous. He realized that he must leave him here for his own good.

"Will you go with me?" He asked the mage.

Alder smiled mysteriously.

"I'd like to, young man. However, I don't think I should, because as a mage who was once a royal adviser, I'm not welcome among the people. It will be safest for me if I go south in the spring and hide somewhere in the Haerall mountains."

"Aren't you afraid of being threatened by the barbarians who inhabit them?" Yarred asked.

"I don't think they are a threat to me. These people have a deep-seated respect for all forms of magic. I think they'll welcome me like theirs," replied the mage, pulling the heavy saddle off the horse and leading it towards the other mounts. "Berg has a slightly different opinion, besides, he loves these harsh lands and forests overgrowing them. In my opinion, he would feel bad among the mountains." He smiled at the student, and the student answered him with a slight contort of his lips. "If you like, you can set off tomorrow at dawn." He turned to Yarred. "Then it is relatively safe. As far as I can see, Drasan was last sighted near the southern town of Ram'ar."

"Thank you for the advice, Master, but I'd rather leave now," Captain Cordydian replied, stroking Bruen's neck.

"Of course," the mage said calmly. "I'll pack you some provisions for the road," he added, standing up and walking to the two sacks. After a moment he handed Yarred a small bundle. "Here's some bread, a few strips of dried pork, and some sheep's cheese," he explained. "It's not much, but believe me, food is at a premium these days."

Yarred nodded his thanks, picked up a heavy cavalry saddle, tossed it over the back of his bay, and tightened the girth. Ernil looked up and pricked his ears. The captain knew that the prince's mount was an extremely clever animal. He did not want to prolong his farewell, although he guessed that he was seeing the beautiful stallion for the last time.

Nevertheless, he went over to the horse to pat his neck one last time. Ernil nudged him with its mouth as if to cheer him up. Yarred understood the message and smiled slightly. He may not have been an adventurer or a hero type, but he has been doing quite well so far.

***

The desperate whimper of the infant roused Mara from her sleep. She jumped up from the bed and ran barefoot to the cradle. Lender calmed at the sight of her face and stretched out a tiny fat arm. She took him in her arms, wondering how ever he was that he was so big and strong. Only two months had passed since her arrival in An'thil, and the little boy seemed to understand more than he should. In addition, he was beginning to exhibit magical abilities, which at his age made him uneasy.

Tharon claimed that her son had a special gift to predict the future, but his visions were usually about the death of someone. It turned out to be a gift as intriguing as it was terrifying. Especially since Lender was never wrong. So far, he has predicted the death of his nurse, cook and elderly countess. Each of them found out about it as soon as the little one touched him.

These flashes, as Tharon called them, became more frequent and caused the boy severe headaches. He was then irritable and tearful.

It happened this time...

As soon as Mara hugged her son to her breast, she saw the pass and some stranger man pierced by an arrow. The vision of the future event shook her deeply. Lender had never foreseen the death of a stranger before. Usually, he must have seen someone at least once. The man's face was memorable, so she wouldn't have forgotten someone like that.

Despite the late hour, she put on one of the gowns, slipped her legs into slippers and, pressing the baby to her chest, made her way towards the study, where the royal adviser used to hang out even at night. The corridor was dimly lit, but the girl knew the way well.

She ran the short distance between her chambers and the royal office, but when she finally stopped in front of the oak door, she hesitated, hand on the doorknob. What if her fears turned out to be correct and the vision was related to someone connected with Yarred? Her future husband set off on the road six months ago, at the very beginning of winter. Maybe he was in Riden, maybe even managed to find Drasan. Despite the passage of time, Mara couldn't help feeling that her lover was in danger.

She shook off the thought, took a deep breath, and entered the office.

Tharon was sitting behind a massive desk over a pile of maps and scrolls. As soon as the girl crossed the threshold, he summoned her with a gesture.

Mara walked over, treading uneasily and pressing the baby to her chest, which, judging from her slow breathing, had fallen back to sleep. She remembered in time that she was wearing a nightgown, so she quickly covered her half-exposed breasts with the robe. As she faced the aged half-unicorn, she finally remembered the question she was about to ask him. First, she had to tell what brought her.

"Lender had another vision," she tried not to show the unease that overwhelmed her as she remembered the face of the unknown man. She took a deep breath and let out in one breath, "This time it was about a man I had never seen before, but I have the impression that his fate touched the fate of my fiancé."

Tharon looked up from the Lineland map on the table. His face did not express the unease that undoubtedly accompanied him. Lender's visions always came true.

"It's not terrible," he tried to console her. "Your son shows extraordinary clairvoyant abilities. Logically, his talent is constantly developing."

"It was different this time," she shook her head so violently that her long hair rippled. "I had a feeling it was dark." She bit her lower lip, asked the tormenting question, "Can Lender feel a bond with his father?"

Tharon looked up at her from the wire-rimmed glasses that rested on the tip of his nose.

"We can't rule it out," he said carefully. "Lender has an amazing talent, moreover magic seems to affect his development, which is why he is much smarter than most children his age. He also grows much faster. If my assumptions are correct, at the age of eight months he will be the height of a one-year-old child, and intellectually even four-year-old."

Mara understood that the king's adviser was trying to distract her from what might have happened to Yarred. She guessed he was no less scared than she was.

"I don't know what happened to me," she confessed, looking at her son's reddened face. "He seems so fragile and defenseless, having at the same time incomprehensible strength."

"You must accept that your son is extraordinary," replied the half-unicorn softly.

"Yes, it's true," she admitted, stroking the dormant toddler's flushed cheek. "Few can resist him, and yet he is only four months old."

To her surprise, Tharon got up and pushed the chair beside him aside.

"Sit down," he asked softly. "We need to talk about matters of much greater importance than your son's talent, Mara," he suddenly became serious.

The girl obeyed his instructions and looked at the closest scroll with curiosity. It turned out to be the family tree of the Middelmare family, beginning with Horst the Wise, who, according to legend, was crowned by Magot himself - king of dragons, and ending with Valden. The latter, in turn, according to the records, died childless. She realized that she had a long and hard way to prove her relationship to the recently deceased ruler.

"Mara..."

Hearing her name, the girl tore her gaze from the scroll and shifted it to the man sitting next to it.

"I think it's worth clearing up a few facts before I tell you about this old ritual you must undergo," Tharon said, his gray eyes still on her. They radiated gentleness and peace.

Mara looked at him a little confused. In fact, she was still a little worried about what was called the blood test.

"The politics here is based on three pillars," Tharon said slowly. "The first, as you know, is the enormous influence of the main noble families. You met their representatives yesterday. It is they who make up the Council of Elders and thus have great power. The second are craftsmen and merchants. Only thanks to them this country is still functioning. But we'll soon gain support among them, as Bal'zar closed the trade routes through Riden and Alikorn, and both lost it. That is why we can count on them willingly to welcome the end of this war. The next and the last one, but no less influential, is the military. Whoever has power over him can be sure that he is worthy of the throne."

"What about the common people?" Mara asked.

"The people here are very easy to please," Tharon said dismissively. "If I were you, I would be concerned with winning over those members of the Council who have not been openly hostile to you."

Mara felt her stomach tighten at the memory of Favia's cold gaze.

"What about the others?" She asked, trying not to show a tremble in her voice.

"If you mean Favia, there is a problem here, unfortunately..." Tharon was visibly confused and began to avoid her eyes. "She is the head of one of the high-ranking families. You'll have to appease her somehow."

"She hates me," Mara said shortly.

Tharon was even more confused.

"Don't assume such a dark scenario right away. She's just furious that I didn't ask her opinion. Because you see, I made a risky maneuver..." He broke off and finished much quieter, avoiding her eyesight. "...I put the Council in front of a fait accompli."

Mara took a sharp breath.

"It means that..."

"Yes, by the law of your blood, until your son comes of age, you are now ruler of Antua," Tharon finished for her.

CHAPTER 13

Drasan did not seem thrilled with the role Alt'ar had assigned him. According to the killer, his appearance would only worsen their already disastrous condition. So, he forced him to "cover the rear" with Rodian. Nothing has happened so far. The guild leader's trick was not working, and Boris was still at his post.

Meanwhile, Alt'ar's men rode at an unhurried walk, giving a wide berth what was left of the Ram'ar. Most of them seemed completely relaxed, as if she hadn't expected an attack at all.

"It looks like they won't attack until they spot you," said Rodian.

"I was going to show them off, but your boss thought it best for me to keep my side," the half-dragon replied, expressing his frustration. "Sometimes I get the impression that he treats me like a naked pig."

"You are not the only one who suffered," the witch grumbled. "I was relegated to the role of your nanny."

Drasan glared at her.

"Pay attention to the words, because I can forget that we have an alliance for the moment and accidentally push you off this hill," he drawled through gritted teeth.

"We both know they're only empty threats," she bit back, keeping her face stony. She wasn't going to let her show how much he had made her angry.

The prince smirked. Not that he didn't like Rodian, on the contrary: after what she had done for Neila, he wanted to give her a heartfelt hug. And the fact that they had both been pushed to the background by Alt'ar made him angry. In order not to lose his temper, he had to unload it somewhere.

Meanwhile, something started to happen. A single rider appeared on the adjacent hill. Even at this distance, Drasan recognized the familiar hated features - Boris.

The werewolf slowly descended, clinging to the cover in the form of a thin forest overgrowing the slope.

The prince noticed that the Alt'ar had stopped his men and was taking the lead himself.

He froze as he watched the two commanders stop a horse's length apart. He held his breath. Now it all depended on the mediatorial abilities of the leader of the Assassins Guild.

***

Alt'ar regarded his opponent with an appraising glance. Boris was not very good looking, he also lacked manners. It seemed unlikely that he was descended from the nobility. Nevertheless, he kept himself straight in the saddle, as befits an officer. The deadly odor emanating from him reminded the killer that he was dealing with a ruthless monster that would stop at nothing, just to complete the task entrusted to him. Anyway, his murderous instincts were quite common among most werewolves.

"I suppose I'm dealing with the notorious Alt'ar," he said rather than asked, not bothering to mention polite phrases. Thus, he reassured the leader of guild that he was dealing with a simpleton.

"And they probably call you Boris," the assassin replied, neither confirming nor denying the werewolf's statement.

"That's what I'm called," Boris grinned as he did so, revealing his long fangs. "And since, as is customary, we have made the necessary presentation, I will get straight to the point. You see, in spite of myself, I'm ready to make a deal. All you have to do is hand me that dragon bastard and his girlfriend, that mercenary. In return, my mistress can compensate you for any damage, purify your name, and make you a rich man."

Alt'ar dismissed the statement with a contemptuous huff. He knew there was a trick behind the smooth words. Nevertheless, he deeply admired Dhalia. She wanted Drasan, and it wasn't just that damn prophecy. The boy turned out to be so important to her that she did not choose any means to get him.

"Why is this brat so important?" He risked the question, not knowing if he would get any remarkable answer.

Boris's face tightened.

"Not your business," he growled, not trying to be polite.

The leader of the guild considered it sufficient evidence that the monster was kept on a short leash. Presumably his mistress did not tell him about all her plans. He was a useful tool for the dirty work.

"What if I say no?" He asked in a relaxed tone.

The werewolf smiled again, giving him the appearance of a nightmare figure.

"Then you will pass judgment on yourself and your people," he said in an unemotional tone. "Consider whether it is worth sacrificing your life for such a self-righteous whippersnapper."

Alt'ar smiled involuntarily, the words perfectly conveying his opinion of the Duke of Sheardon. Drasan was not an ideal ruler, and he did not possess any leadership skills. Yet he did not deserve the fate Dhalia intended for him.

"If you want a boy, you have to get past me and my people first. We are loyal to our comrades-in-arms." He replied contemptuously. "We do not abandon them to their fate, like the king of his faithful soldiers. Those who without hesitation threw themselves into the embrace of death with his name on their lips."

"He's not my king!" Boris snapped. He was losing both patience and self-control. "For the last time, please. Give me a boy and go on your way. It's not your thing what I do with him."

"Neither am I the king's subject," the assassin retorted. "Especially one like Bal'zar. I value honor, and this prevents me from leaving Drasan in your hands."

The werewolf gritted his teeth.

"If you like that way," he growled, turned his horse and rode away. Instead of climbing to the top of the hill, he stopped suddenly and looked up.

"I know you can hear me, dragon's offspring!" He screamed at the top of his throat, and the echo multiplied his utterance. "You've been hiding behind someone else's back too long! Come out and fight! I'd love to drop some of your precious blood!"

Alt'ar felt the people holding their breath. A deathly silence fell after the werewolf's words. The assassin knew that Duke of Sheardon's quick-tempered character would finally prevail over common sense.

"If you don't come down here, I will personally kill anyone who gets in my way! I will also make sure that no one gets away with their lives! You hear, cowardly reptile?!" Undaunted by the lack of answer, Boris continued the tirade, not hesitating to weave more and more sophisticated insults into it. "I'll count to ten and if you don't show up, my shooters will fill your defenders with arrows!"

The threat became real. If Drasan breaks, all they have to do is pray. That is why Alt'ar was glad to have left Rodian with the young man. She might not seem thrilled with her role, but she could always dissuade the impetuous half-dragon from trying to face the werewolf. For he had at least three hundred warriors behind his back.

***

Hearing the insults about himself, Drasan boiled with rage. Boris clearly wanted to provoke him to action, and if it were not for the presence of Rodian cooling his enthusiasm, he would certainly have vented his murderous fury. He wanted to hunt down that stinky servant of Dhalia and hurt him.

"Save yourself a little, Your Highness," muttered the witch. "We are to wait for a signal from Alt'ar."

"Don't tell me what to do!" He growled at her. He couldn't help but rage filling his hot head with thoughts of revenge.

"It's painfully predictable," Gaenor muttered, coming out unknown when behind him. "You think Boris didn't predict what you'll do? Do you think that knowing your impulsive nature does not know how to get you out of hiding?"

Drasan turned to him just as Boris screamed:

"One!"

The prince clenched his fists in helpless anger...

"Two!"

Rodian also stood behind the half-dragon's back, ready to stop him in the event of an unexpected desire to attack the werewolf from above.

"Three!"

"You want me to stand here and watch as others stick their necks for me?!" He drawled through clenched teeth.

"Four!" Boris roared.

"No! I want you to stop thinking only about yourself for a moment. This is not your private vendetta, we are all stuck up to our ears in this swamp," the witch snapped back. "We're supposed to secure the rear and not lean out until we see the agreed signal. If that's too much for you, I can always stun you. Just to make sure you don't do something extremely stupid."

Drasan let out a mirthless laugh. If he had changed, not even Gaenor would have been able to stop him.

Meanwhile, Boris patiently continued the countdown:

"Five... six!"

Drasan watched with increasing tension as the Alt'ar's men clasped up as they prepared for the battle. The Guild leader himself was admirably stoic. He seemed bored. The prince glanced at the neighboring hill. He wanted to catch the slightest movement among the trees, but he couldn't see anything.

"...seven... eight!"

Somewhere in the middle of this madness was Neila. The girl ostentatiously ignored his pleas to stay as far away from the battlefield as possible. Instead, he saw Velwell in the front row. His face showed tension as well.

"…nine... ten!"

The echo of the werewolf's last words barely faded as the first shots flew into the dense wall of Alt'ar's men. They hit the ground a foot from the next row. It was supposed to be a warning. The next ones will surely achieve their goal.

Suddenly the Guild leader yanked his sword from its scabbard and raised it high above his head. This was the signal for Drasan. The slayers dispersed, giving the archers no chance of hitting their targets.

The prince stood on the edge of the ledge and summoned power. He let it overwhelm him, creating a wild euphoria. He could jump and transform himself in flight. He was tempted to do this in front of Gaenor. Alt'ar assigned him a different task. He was supposed to operate as far from the battlefield as possible.

He focused on the pulsing power within him. What he was about to do, he knew, was risky and required all the fury he had built up over the years. So far he has mastered his power to what Gaenor used to call "basic." This in turn meant that the task would cost him much more to complete.

He took a deep breath and forced his stiff body to move. He only had a few heartbeats for that, and he couldn't be sure he would succeed. He's only done it once so far, and the finale wasn't one of the happiest in his life.

"You focus too much on yourself," Gaenor hissed in his ear. "Push back the power instead of store it."

"If it's that simple, try it yourself," retorted the prince, trying not to lose sight of the real purpose he was supposed to focus on. The problem was that setting fire to something as large as a forest on the side of a hill was not an easy task.

"I wish, Your Majesty. Though I surpass you in intellect, you are much stronger in power," Gaenor replied, not without irony.

"The problem is, I've only done it once so far, and I have no idea how to do it a second time," the half-dragon snarled. He was fed up with Gaenor and his snooty tone.

"Back then, you acted instinctively and on a much smaller scale, and now hundreds of people's lives depend on you, so you'd better focus before Boris gives his men a signal to attack," the dragon was ruthless, but maybe that was the motivation Drasan needed.

The anger released the destructive energy of the fire, and despite the melted snow everywhere, the pine grove suddenly burned as bright as a funeral pyre. The victory sparked euphoria in Drasan, which turned into an irresistible lust for destruction. He was going to burn the forest along with the people hiding in its shadow. He planned to be as ruthless as they were when they burned his beloved Sheardon.

He did not even stop when he heard the howling of people burning alive amid the crackle of breaking trees and the roar of flames. The roaring element completely consumed his soul. The lust for destruction and the urge to retaliate did not let him stop until he burned the hill to the ground. This time he felt nothing, neither the draining of his strength nor the exhaustion. He felt as if he could do it endlessly. And he liked it.

Let go, he heard Gaenor's voice in his head. The elder dragon didn't seem disgusted, just terrified.

Drasan did not want to stop. He was drunk on his own power. He had an overwhelming impression that for the first-time fire had unleashed in him what he had not even suspected for a moment - evil and the desire to wreak havoc.

Drasan, stop it immediately! Panic sounded in Rodian's voice.

He didn't want to stop. The roar of the flames sounded like a victory song. He was soothing his tormented soul.

Stop before you kill us! Gaenor roared.

His mental cry caused Drasan to open his eyelids violently. Only then did he realize what he had done.

The flames beat high into the smoke-blackened sky. The stench of burnt bodies filled the air. The element he released did not stop at destroying the enemy, and now, driven by his fury, it was gradually engulfing the entire valley. Even the snow could not stop the dragon's fire. Alt'ar's slayers huddled at the mouth of the gorge, surrounded by a semicircle of flames.

Seeing what was happening, Drasan focused his whole self on easing the hell he had unleashed, and only then did he feel the effects of the destructive energy he had brought to life. He fell to his knees and unleashed his power. Moments later he passed out.

***

He woke up feeling the gentle touch of women's hands on his face. He lay there for a moment with his eyes closed, enjoying the moment. He was afraid that if he opened his eyes, the spell would break.

"How long has he been unconscious?" The voice he heard was clearly Neila's. He liked that note of caring.

"It's been a while," Rodian replied in a slightly huffed tone. "He should be awake any minute."

"After what he did..."

"For your own sake, don't mention it," interrupted the witch. "I didn't think he had that much power. We should thank the gods that he is on our side."

Neila either missed the irony in that statement or ignored it, for after a moment she sighed heavily and still convinced she couldn't hear her, said:

"The real problem is, I can't keep him at a distance any longer." As she said that, he felt her gentle movement brushing his hair from his forehead. "I think..." She paused for a moment. "...I think I love him."

She said it with such tenderness in her voice that the prince barely resisted the urge not to open his eyes.

"Then tell him," said Rodian. There was no trace of malice in her voice. It is possible that the joint struggle helped them to get rid of old prejudices.

"I don't think it will change anything," the mercenary said grimly. "We are separated by a huge gulf that we will never be able to close."

"Your fears are unfounded. Have you forgotten how much he has done for you? If not he..."

"Yes, I know. I would be dead," the girl interrupted her irritably.

"So, what's the problem? Because probably not his age..." Rodian laughed softly. "He's so handsome, he could have every girl on the nod."

Drasan listened to this with the utmost curiosity. So Neila really loved him. But she acted as if she was afraid of the feeling. He wondered why?

"And that's the problem!" Neila burst out. "He can have any. All he has to do is look at one or send her one of those dark smiles of his. Women worship him and love him wherever he appears. I don't think I could handle such competition!" She said sarcastically.

So that's what she was afraid of? She didn't want him to hurt her. Did she realize how much he had sacrificed for her? He had lived like a monk since leaving Kahaer, ignoring even Rodian, who clearly wanted him. Neila was the only woman who drew him to her with such force that he could barely resist her.

Rodian sighed resignedly.

"You'll have to talk to him about it sooner or later," she said, got up and walked away.

He and Neila were left alone.

"You can stop pretending," Neila said, softly enough for only he to hear.

"Where did the conclusion that I'm pretending?" He still hadn't opened his eyes.

"You're a bad liar, Drasan," she replied without any malice in her voice.

He laughed softly, and before she could pull back, he wrapped his arms around her and pulled her to him. This time she did not resist. The prince opened his eyes and looked at her. She looked so much better than the last time he had seen her. The blushes returned to her cheeks, and her large blue eyes regained their former glow.

"Why don't you openly admit how you feel about me?" He asked.

"This is not the right time," she avoided his gaze.

"There may not be another one," Drasan replied in a tenacious tone.

Neila sighed in resignation, carefully disentangling herself from his embrace, and sat down next to him.

Drasan took time to figure out where they were. It turned out that while he was unconscious someone - Gaenor, no doubt - transported him to the river bank. They were far from the burned hill. The sun was just setting, so another day had passed.

"Where are the others?" He asked, wanting to break the awkward silence that fell between them.

She shrugged her shoulders.

"Alt'ar and Gaenor must have gone hunting," she replied, picking at the frayed sleeve of her tunic. "Velwel and some of Alt'ar's assassins have gone to get some provisions."

"And you?" He asked, trying to catch her eye. "Why did you stay?"

The mercenary didn't answer for a while.

"I owe you my life," she said finally. "Besides, someone had to make sure you don't do something stupid, because you see..." She hesitated, biting her lower lip. "Alt'ar managed to capture Boris."

"What?!" He exclaimed, sitting up so suddenly he felt dizzy.

"He knew you would be against it, but thought it was for the best," she explained.

Against? Drasan was furious with the leader of the killers for sparing such a creature's life. How could he do so noble to the monster who ruthlessly slaughtered an entire town?!

"Where's the punk?!" He drawled through clenched teeth, barely controlling himself.

"Before you decide to do something reckless, why not listen to me calmly first?" She suggested in a conciliatory tone.

The prince took a deep breath, forcing himself to control himself.

"Why?" He whispered, still stunned.

Neila put a finger to his lips and looked around anxiously, as if afraid someone might see them. But they were alone. The killers were getting ready to collapse the camp. Nobody paid any attention to them. As soon as she was sure none of Alt'ar's men were listening, she moved closer and whispered directly in his ear:

"Alt'ar believes the werewolf may prove to be the key to Dhalia's defeat."

Drasan sighed heavily. Well, after all, the Guild leader is a werewolf himself. Maybe he knows the methods of interrogating such twisted monsters?

"I don't think Boris said anything," he said, trying to remain calm. "He has a strange bond with Dhalia, he despises and hates her, but he is unable to resist her. And if he runs away, he'll tell her where we are and how many of us are left."

Neila smirked.

"He won't run away," she said. "Alt'ar keeps that Dhalia's mongrel on a silver chain," she added with vindictive satisfaction.

Drasan couldn't help himself. He also smiled.

The girl quickly became serious.

"I wanted to talk to you..." she confessed softly, "...about us and what we should do about it."

The half-dragon shifted uneasily. He guessed what to do next.

"You see, I've been thinking a lot about what you told me," she tried to stay calm. "And I came to the same conclusion as at the very beginning." She took a deep breath and blurted out in one breath, "We don't fit together, Drasan. Our relationship doesn't stand a chance." The prince snorted and opened his mouth to speak, but she wouldn't let him. "Please, let me finish. This is hard enough and without your comments. We are different, we come from two different worlds, and this opens up an insurmountable gulf between us." As she spoke the next words, her voice broke, and tears ran down her cheeks. "You grew up in a royal court and have power that scares me. I'm a girl from the street, an ordinary mercenary. I'm not fit for your mistress, much less a wife. You need a woman with a beauty and position like..."

"...like Dhalia," finished Drasan in an icy tone.

"You know that wasn't what I meant." She grabbed his hand and looked into his eyes. "Just think: what do I look like with you? I fit you like, like... a peacock to sparrow!" She exploded.

"You love me?" He asked suddenly, his fingers tightening on hers and staring deeply into her eyes.

She nodded, wiping her tears with the back of her hand.

"Then why should it fail?" He asked in a soft, barely audible whisper. "The only obstacle is your irrational fear of what others will say about us. I don't care about it."

"But I..."

"Please," he whispered, pressing her hand against his broad chest. "Give us a chance."

Neila stepped back, tearing herself out of his grip. His pleading gaze slowly melted the ice that had chained her heart for so many years.

"I only want you," he whispered, his face so close to her that their noses were almost touching. "Nobody and nothing will ever change that."

The mercenary smiled weakly. This time she didn't resist as he brought his mouth close to hers. He kissed her gently at first, as if asking for permission. When he met no resistance, he pulled her closer, kissing her more aggressively and passionately than ever before. When he finally pulled away, she could barely catch her breath.

Time stood still for them. They enjoyed their presence, listening to the rhythmic beating of their hearts. They wanted this moment to last forever.

"What are you afraid of?" Drasan whispered, pressing his face against her hair.

"I'm afraid it's just a dream," she whispered back. "And when I wake up, you..."

"Love me..." he muttered in her ear. "...and I will try to keep this dream never ending."

CHAPTER 14

"You called me, your..." Dhalia's smile died as it turned out that the young king was not in front of him, but... Arano.

The mage smiled broadly at her, displaying his perfect teeth.

"Hello, my dear," he said in a voice that gave her goosebumps.

The witch forced herself to smile back. In fact, she was wondering what she was doing here, in the middle of the night. When the messenger arrived, she was wearing a calf-length, thin silk nightgown, over which she had hurriedly thrown a cloak embroidered with gold thread. Even though she was not modest, she suddenly felt uncomfortable under the man's lustful gaze.

"Why did you call me here, and why did you call me so late?" She asked, trying to be polite.

Arano raised an eyebrow in daring mock surprise.

"Aren't you happy to see me?" He asked. "I expected a much warmer welcome." He took a few steps towards her.

Gods, he is so handsome! She thought, looking involuntarily from his face to his broad shoulders and well-built chest. Years of practice had done their job, Arano was still in excellent shape. Her heart suddenly sped at the memory of the old days, when they were inseparable, and she spent every night in his arms. She sighed, struggling to shake off the charm he was casting on her.

"Where did you get this from?" She asked, barely controlling the trembling of her voice. "Of course, I'm glad."

Arano smiled in that distinctive way she adored, and his eyes flashed.

"You're lying," he said. "Have you forgotten how well I know you? Don't try to use your tricks on me because I have seen you inside out a long time ago."

Dhalia stumbled back, never taking her eyes off him. It seemed impossible to know who had betrayed his family. Or maybe?

"Interesting," she admitted, crossing her arms over her chest. "Then you will probably tell me now why you called me here."

Arano laughed aloud.

"Plucky as always," he said, pointing to her chair. "So, let's sit down, because it's a longer story," he took his place in the chair opposite the fireplace usually occupied by Bal'zar, and clasped his hands together in front of him.

Dhalia perched on the edge of the chair. She was glad that she was hidden in the darkness of the dining room. In his presence, she felt like a young girl again. He always radiated strength and was able to force obedience. This is one of the reasons why she fell in love with him.

"Let's start with the day you released me," he began with an unreadable expression on his face. The witch stiffened. She hadn't expected him to mention it outright. "I don't remember much, except for the dinner together, after which I woke up in the dungeons. The next day I was to be burned at the stake, so I took the appropriate steps." He smiled slightly at his thoughts. "I bribed the prison guards by giving them what I had left," he looked into her eyes. "The necklace with my family coat of arms on it. At that time, I didn't know that I was not the only one who was betrayed. I came home and... found the ashes smoking."

The witch shifted uneasily but kept her face stony. In fact, she was wondering how Arano got out of prison, after all, bribing the guards would not have been enough for him, there was more to it.

Meanwhile, the mage continued:

"I had nothing to look for in my hometown, so I fled south. I hid among the nomadic tribes living there, called by most of the civilized inhabitants of the peninsula the uncouth barbarians. It turned out that they have a great knowledge of the magic of the ancient runes. I learned a great deal about forgotten rituals they call "summoning". The shamans there put into a trance with herbs and summoned beings from another world. They called them Ancient. It is said that in the old days they lived among us, and some of them ordered to worship themselves. When I asked about those who called themselves gods, they replied that it was forbidden knowledge. So I decided to look for references to this on my own. In one of the Normingrad libraries I found a very old scroll. According to what is written there, the Cursed were cursed not only by their race, but also by dragons and unicorns. They were stripped of their bodies and driven straight into the depths of the abyss. They were to stay there forever."

At these words, Dhalia felt sick. Cursed. She heard about them a long time ago, apparently the time of their reign is a bloody stain in the book of history. They had been driven out of this world shortly before the dragons left, and their names have been forgotten forever.

"I wanted to know more, so I decided to find the cave that my parents mentioned. It is said that the ancient creature living there knows the answers to all questions." He smiled. "I found it not easily, because no one could help me. However, I have heard rumors that in one of the coastal caves there lived a huge snake. So, I decided to check it out, and that's how I found Nephiss. It was she who gave me not only knowledge but also power. She showed how to summon a creature far more powerful than an ordinary demon. I had nothing to lose, so out of my desire to avenge my family, I agreed. The ritual turned out to be risky, in order to lure this powerful creature, I had to find myself on the brink of life and death. However, what I have gained in return since the former god entered my body is much more valuable than the life I lived before."

"You're insane..." Dhalia said, and she rose from her chair, intending to leave, but he grabbed her arm and pulled her toward him.

"On the contrary, I have never felt such clarity of mind." His eyes flashed, and he really started to look like a madman. "In that cave I died to be reborn again, and much more powerful than before."

"Arano, let me go!" She demanded firmly.

"Arano is dead," he hissed in a low, threatening voice. "He gave me his body, and I gladly accepted this gift, taking over both his thoughts and memories at the same time. The moment I entered his body, he took my place in a prison from which there is no escape."

He sat her down in the chair again, forced her to look at him, and as if nothing had happened, he continued his story:

"When I left the seaside grotto, I felt omnipotent, but with time I realized that it had a price. I needed magical energy to keep my body in shape. Otherwise, the limbs began to die." He grimaced as if it disgusted him. "Then I realized that in order to regain my former power I would have to find someone who would agree to bring my brother from the abyss. And after years of waiting, I finally found a human being determined enough to give me..."

"I don't believe you," interrupted the witch. "I prophesied myself..."

To her surprise, the Rideanian laughed aloud. His reaction sent an involuntary shiver to Dhalia.

"I don't mean that dragon bastard," he said. "No. Possession of a descendant of Magot was too risky. However, the Ridean queen, convinced that her child was dead, was different." A purple glow appeared in his eyes as he spoke. "I appeared in her dreams and gave instructions on what she should do to save the little prince. And when she did the ritual, I easily allowed my brother to penetrate the boy's body. Of course, this unfortunate woman died shortly after giving birth, and I decided to wait in hiding until the royal heir and sole heir to the throne would be old enough to serve my plans."

"Why are you telling me this?" Dhalia asked, trying to keep her voice under control.

"Because I hope that in return you will tell me everything about the one, they call the Chosen One."

***

Mara hugged the crying Lender to her chest. Recently, her son has had increasingly macabre visions. They were dominated by death, destruction and fire. He also seemed more restless and slept the nights less than usual. However, whenever she picked him up, he calmed down and fell asleep. Then the girl, instead of putting him back in the cradle, sat with him on the bed and stared at the chubby face framed with red curls, enchanted. It was as if she still couldn't believe that she had become a mother and that her son had inherited the throne of Antua.

The news that if she successfully passes the test, she will be crowned around the kingdom like wildfire. Protests broke out immediately, because under the law in force, the eldest male descendant of the deceased king could seize the throne. Tharon explained to the indignant nobility that Mara was to remain in power until her son came of age.

After announcing it publicly, Mara did not sleep well, she was too afraid that someone would stick a dagger in her heart... Besides, she did not know how to find herself in a new role, after all, she had no idea about court etiquette. Responsibility had overwhelmed her to such an extent that she began to miss the times when her only concern was earning a living. She knew she had to be strong. If not for herself, then for her son.

It turned out that not only Favia has an open hatred for her. Many of the courtiers also did not hide their indignation at the throne of a "stranger", and although Tharon was consoling her with the forthcoming blood test that would dispel any doubts about her inheritance rights, she did not feel confident. In addition, the mere fact that some foreign magician would subject her to strange tests in front of the entire court did not encourage her at all. Eventually, she would become the first queen in the history of Antua. And that would make her enemies among some of the most powerful men in the kingdom.

Yarred would probably know what to do, she thought. After all, her fiancé held the honorable position of captain of the royal guard. He has certainly participated in many important celebrations. If he had come here with her, he might prove to be an invaluable advisor in the field of inter-court relations. Fortunately, she also had Tharon. The man has been great as a royal adviser so far, so it's probably worth having him by your side. And who he really was made an involuntary shudder. She felt the same in the presence of Drasan, though in his case it seemed to be dictated by fear. After all, she had seen with her own eyes what he was capable of when he took the form of a giant reptile.

No wonder she trembled at the thought of what to do with Yarred when he found him. He had been given clear instructions as to what to do. He ignored the order of the heir to the Sheardonian throne to deliver him a letter from the queen. Will she punish him for his disobedience? She shuddered at the thought and chased her away as quickly as possible. If he had told him to come back to her, would he have done so willingly, knowing that he had failed his friend?

She shook her head.

No, Drasan will certainly not risk the possibility of one of his close companions being taken over by enemies. So, he will leave him with him. She must deal alone.

The appearance of Tharon snapped her out of her gloomy thoughts. She forced a smile on her face. She understood she would once again endure the torment of attending some boring party.

This time the royal adviser wore a scarlet tunic, trousers of the same color and a coat, the knee-length black boots were polished to a high gloss as usual. He looked great.

He bowed to her and smiled as well.

"I know this is all terribly tiresome for you," he said, not for the first time giving the impression that he could read her mind.

Mara sighed in resignation and put her son back in the cradle.

"I'll probably hear that this is one of my duties as a future queen," she said quietly.

"But… dear Mara, your coronation is just a formality. I'm sure it will happen right after the blood test."

Mara walked over to him, careful not to trip over the corner of the long dark blue dress she was wearing.

"Why are you still not telling me what this trial is about?" She frowned.

"Because I'm not allowed. This is one of the secrets known to the highest magicians in the kingdom," he replied, looking down.

"And why can't you do it?" She continued, even though she knew she would not receive a remarkable answer this time.

This time, Tharon silenced her. She realized that there was no point in further exploring the subject. She took his arm and they left the room together.

After descending the marble steps, they turned left. There was an entrance to the dungeons, and a bit behind it to one of the towers. The stark, unadorned door was guarded by two guards armed with halberds and short swords. The men bowed to them and passed without a word. Behind the gate there was a winding staircase leading steeply uphill. It turned out to be unnaturally cold there. Mara's skin, protected by a thin cloth, immediately became covered with goose bumps.

Tharon climbed the stairs, still not saying a word, until they reached another door. The man knocked softly and waited - nothing happened.

The wrinkles on the ancient Antuanian's forehead deepened, but he tapped again, a little louder this time. Only then did a low, husky voice come from behind the door:

"Who's there?"

"It's me," Tharon replied shortly.

They heard the sound of the bolt being pulled back, and after a while in the gap between the door appeared the face of an old man with furrows and deep wrinkles, resembling a prune. Lush gray hair framed the head, and a bushy mustache and beard reigned under the long nose.

"What do you want?" He asked, not trying to be polite.

"I'd like to introduce someone to you, dear Dogon," Tharon replied calmly, pushing Mara forward.

The old man looked at her with a long stare of deep-set black eyes, clearly satisfied, opened the door and let them in. He dressed in a peculiar way. Namely, he was wearing a long-striped nightgown that reached up to his completely bare feet.

"Is that the girl who is due to undergo a blood test tomorrow?" He was still looking at Mara, who felt very uncomfortable under his watchful gaze.

Tharon nodded as he walked to the window and stared impassively across the courtyard.

Meanwhile, Dagon put his wire-rimmed glasses on his long nose and, muttering something to himself, trotted off somewhere in the corner. Mara began to look around the circular room curiously. It turned out to be arranged in a rather strict, ascetic way. Except for the simple wooden bed, the only furniture was a carelessly crumbled bookcase, sagging under the weight of huge books, piles of scrolls, and a multitude of glass bottles filled with various liquids. It was there that this peculiar old man, shuffling papers and still muttering to himself, took his steps.

Finally, he pulled out an old yellowed scroll and returned to Mara with it. Only then did the royal adviser approach them, clearly much more pleased than he had been a moment ago. Dagon placed the document carefully on the stone floor and began to slowly unfold it. Then the girl noticed that it was not parchment, but a thin piece of animal skin, written entirely in neat, narrow handwriting.

Mara turned a scarlet blush. Until now, she hadn't admitted to Tharon that she couldn't read. Nevertheless, she and the men bent over ancient scripture.

"What is this?" She asked when it turned out that no one was going to explain it to her.

Dagon looked up at her and furrowed his bushy eyebrows menacingly.

"Isn't that obvious?" answered the question with a question. "It is a precious document, my lady, it is hundreds or even thousands of years old. It is possible that it dates back to the end of the dragons' rule in these lands."

"But what is it about?" Mara asked again.

"Ancient rituals," Tharon said seriously, not taking his eyes off the text.

The girl frowned. Both men ignored her completely, still bent over the scroll. Finally, her companion turned to the old man:

"Dagon, I would like to ask you for something..." He broke off, because the old man waved his hand impatiently.

"Ah, dear Culiaro," he sighed, scratching his nose. "You haven't changed anything since my youth," he sighed again, "you probably would like to hear the legend of the Chosen One."

Mara stiffened. It did not escape the keen eyes of Tharon, who sat cross-legged.

"Yes," he confirmed calmly, not taking his eyes off the girl. "And I think that I'm not the only one who will be happy to listen to it."

The sage shook his head.

"You are a dreamer, Culiaro, but good. I will tell you this fairy tale story again."

The girl with great difficulty took her eyes off the man sitting opposite her and looked at the face of the old man smiling at her with compulsion.

"Good," Dagon cleared his throat and began to speak in a much cleaner and less hoarse voice. "As you probably remember, at the end of the reign of the righteous rulers, one of the Seers foretold the reign of the dragons." He coughed softly. "She rebelled right after that, but that's a completely different story. Well, the prophecy dealt with things so fantastic that most did not believe it. The exception was a handful of fanatics." He looked significantly at Tharon, seated across from him. "It was about the Chosen One, born of the blood of a mortal woman and a mighty dragon. According to the soothsayer, it was supposed to restore the former balance and peace between the long-conflicted races." He is coughing again dry. "As I have told hundreds of fools who believed this legend to be true, it cannot be true. According to all the evidence gathered about the life of dragons, it is impossible for any of them to beget a child with a human woman. Such an unfortunate woman would not have survived the intercourse, let alone giving birth. And even if by some miracle she succeeded, what do you think would result from such a relationship?"

It all started to make sense to Mara as he spoke. After all, she had seen Drasan's transformation with her own eyes. She watched him stand in the scarlet flames to emerge from them in the form of a giant brown reptile. She looked at the adviser, and he nodded encouragingly.

She summoned her courage and looked straight into the eyes of the old sage.

"What if the legend tells the truth?" She asked. "I can even testify to it, because I saw him with my own eyes!"

Dagon frowned his bushy eyebrows.

"Really?" He asked in a slightly doubting tone. "And who is it? Maybe I met him."

Mara didn't like the tone, but she replied with her head held high.

"This is Prince Sheardon."

There was a pause as both men stared at Mara with a mixture of disbelief and doubt. It was Tharon who spoke first:

"You mean the adoptive son of Queen Vaya?" He asked, frowning. "I had the opportunity to meet him as a boy. It is true that he was exceptionally beautiful, which made me suspect that some elven blood might flow in his veins, but otherwise he seemed quite ordinary..." he was clearly confused. "...I didn't sense any supernatural abilities in him."

Mara remembered Yarred's words that Vaya would at all costs conceal Drasan's identity so that no one but Ashkan and her would ever know who he was.

"The Queen personally made sure that no one discovered the truth, and she belonged to powerful witches. I don't think she would have any problems casting complicated spells. Nobody would have guessed who Drasan was."

Tharon was silent for a moment, twisting and unraveling his long fingers.

"Maybe you're right." He said seriously. "After all, she did not tell anyone where the boy came from. Nor did I know why she named it in the long-forgotten dragon language."

"What?!" Mara exclaimed in surprise.

To her surprise, Dagon laughed hoarsely.

"What a nonsense! Few of us even remember this language. Many people name their children without having the slightest idea what their names mean in this forgotten language. This is most likely a mere coincidence. Yes, the words "dra" and "san" do have the meanings you mentioned, but that doesn't mean that this boy is actually running dragon blood."

Mara was still motionless, shocked by what she heard. Did Vaya really not know the hidden meaning of this name? Or maybe, like Dagon, she decided that no one would guess it by the name itself?

"And what does that name mean?" She asked now, really fascinated.

"Dra itself comes from the word "dragen," meaning dragon, and "san" is just "son"," Tharon hastened to explain. "The literal translation of the name Drasan means "dragon son". Let's leave the name alone and focus on the strange rumors Vaya was covering up. You will not deny, Dagon, that whenever something unusual happened, this boy was always seen around."

"Yes, I got these bizarre rumors," the old man agreed reluctantly. "But that doesn't prove he was a half dragon. There is not even a single mention of such creatures in the oldest texts."

"Is my word not enough?" Mara, who had had enough of this discussion, asked.

Her companion smiled sadly.

"Dear Mara, we've been having this discussion from the moment I found out about this boy's existence. He has always intrigued me, but I have never looked at him closely. Vaya's spells may have caused this, as you have suggested earlier..."

"But I can not only testify with a word, but also introduce him to you."

The two men looked at her simultaneously, and Mara smirked.

"You must have heard of the Riden rebellion and the army King Bal'zar is gathering around Washmorth. Well, Drasan is leading this rebellion."

Tharon smiled at her, but the aged Dagon's face remained taut and serious.

"If it is as you say, we have less time than I expected," he scratched his nose. "Storm clouds are gathering over Lineland, and a rumor of war is spreading among the people. Rumors of the dragons' return are also being heard more and more. We have to prepare for the worst."

His speech involuntarily gave Mara the goosebumps. She looked out the small barred window and shuddered at the sight of heavy storm clouds that heralded a blizzard.

***

Alt'ar's request surprised Drasan, for he persisted in the belief that the Guild leader was furious with him. Perhaps he did not intend to make it known.

"Do you know why I called you?" He asked quietly, looking the prince in the eyes.

"I suspect you wanted to talk to me about what I did," the half-dragon speculated. In fact, he was expecting a harsh reprimand. After all, he didn't fight fairly. He used his full power to destroy all these people, and he felt no remorse at all about it.

"You're right in part," Alt'ar agreed, sighing heavily. "I know you probably saved the lives of me and my people, but you did it in a way a bit... how to put it - too spectacular."

"I'm not going to regret it," replied Drasan. "Plus, I don't think you should be preaching me, werewolf," he blurted out like an insult.

Alt'ar remained stoically calm.

"I don't require this at all," he said lightly. "But despite your sad experiences, you are still very young, Drasan. You make decisions on an impulse, instead of having to think things through..."

"And that, in your opinion, explains Boris' sparing?" The half-dragon cut him off.

"Yes," Alt'ar replied, looking into the prince's glittering eyes.

"The decision is not yours," Drasan drawled. Flames began to creep down his body.

"Actually, it only belongs to me, boy," the assassin replied. "I captured him and incapacitated him, so it is no one else, and I will decide his fate."

Drasan bristled. He knew that to challenge a werewolf in full strength would be eminently stupid. He chose to back down before a fight would come, he would surely lose.

"Where is he?" He asked in a voice that, despite the sincerest intentions, still resembled the hiss of an enraged serpent.

"Until I feel that you have sufficient self-control, I will personally make sure that you cannot get close to him," the assassin replied in a voice that could bear no objection.

The prince knew there was no point in further discussion, turned on his heel to leave, and almost collided with Gaenor.

"What do you want?" He asked, not being polite.

The elder dragon smiled mysteriously.

"Let's take a walk," he suggested.

Drasan turned to Alt'ar. The werewolf's face showed nothing but impatience. He clearly looked forward to getting rid of both of them.

"I insist, Your Majesty." The Dragon was relentless.

"I wish you wouldn't call me that, Gaenor," Drasan muttered. He didn't seem too thrilled to talk to his older brother. "You forgot that my kingdom no longer exists, and therefore I'm not entitled to that title."

Gaenor shrugged.

"As you wish," he said.

The young man huffed irritably and walked forward without saying a word. He wasn't going to get into discussions about what he had done. He did not regret it in the slightest degree.

Gaenor caught up with him after a few steps. They walked in silence for a moment.

Winter has not yet said the last word, because the evening turned out to be frosty.

"Your thoughts are very chaotic," Gaenor finally said, breaking the unbearable silence.

"I didn't let you fumble with my head," growled Drasan. He did not feel in the mood for preach and he did not intend to let him be treated like a kid who had to be watched at every step.

"Unfortunately, too much is up to you now," the dragon replied, ignoring his reaction. "To get the most out of your abilities, you must learn to block your emotions and keep your mind clear. You are still too hot-tempered to control the element, and usually it takes over you."

Drasan turned to him, his anger rising.

"What do you want?" He asked quietly, involuntarily clenching his hands into fists. "Teach me and scold me?! If so, skip it, because I'm not a child and I'm not going to let myself be controlled!"

"If you are going to fight Dhalia, control your anger, try to silence it. Get cold, focused and composed," Gaenor replied, completely ignoring his reaction.

Drasan took a deep breath, feeling his muscle tension dissipate. He knew he should have better self-control but knowing wasn't enough.

"So, you're going to teach me this?" He asked much calmer.

Gaenor looked down at him with yellow eyes.

"Since this is a condition for our survival, I have no other choice. It won't be an easy task, because you're halfway…" He trailed off.

"…human," Drasan finished for him.

"Exactly. Therefore, repressing your emotions may prove much more difficult than with a purebred dragon…"

The half-dragon rolled his eyes.

"…and we don't have much time," finished the dragon calmly, ignoring the gesture.

Drasan leaned on his hips.

"And where do we start? He asked, knowing he couldn't get out of it.

"Lesson One," the dragon said slowly, pausing and turning so that they were now face to face. "I'm going to make a mental attack in a moment. Your job will be to clear your mind to the point where I won't find anything to use against you. Be warned that this could have painful consequences. Such penetration can also be very exhausting."

"I will endure," said the Sheardonian, sitting down opposite the dragon. Out of the corner of his eye, he noticed a large group of onlookers gathering around them.

"Ready?" Gaenor asked, lifting his head to stare piercingly at him.

Drasan nodded. There was an expression of grim determination on his face.

The attack turned out to be fast and extremely strong.

So strong the half-dragon didn't even have time to pick up the shield. The world in front of his eyes darkened rapidly, and pain exploded in his head. The suffering increased as Gaenor moved deeper and deeper, reaching back to his childhood memories.

You are not trying! Gaenor thundered. You're giving me a weapon!

Drasan took a deep breath and tried to clear his mind once more, but it caused a new wave of pain. He felt someone sticking thousands of white-hot needles into his brain. And suddenly everything stopped as suddenly as it had started. He woke up kneeling in the snow, the metallic taste of blood in his mouth. Velwel's worried face was in front of him. He saw no point in explaining to him what had happened.

"I'm fine," he hissed through gritted teeth, waving his hand impatiently.

Gaenor looked neither concerned nor less pleased.

"Tell me, am I dealing with a fool or an ignorant?" He asked coldly. "You didn't even try to block me."

"I didn't have enough time," Drasan said softly.

"During the fight you will not have enough of it either!" The dragon thundered, glaring at him. "The enemy will not be as polite as I am and will not inform you that he wants to attack! Now get ready!"

As soon as he had said it, he renewed his attack with even more force than before. This time a scream woke up Drasan... his own. He was lying on the ground, squirming in pain, holding his head with both hands. The pain was tremendous, as if someone were trying to rip his brain out. In front of him he could see not only Velwel, but also Alt'ar and Neila. They all stared at him with wide eyes with horror.

Drasan struggled to get up from the ground, feeling even weaker. He frantically tried to clear his mind but failed because he still felt angry at Gaenor for the torture he had inflicted on him.

"You're so weak!" He thundered, his ruthless yellow eyes staring at the half-dragon wobbling on his feet. "Dhalia will defeat you with one attack! She is much more powerful than me! You need to focus! Don't try to block me, just do it!"

"I can't!" Drasan exclaimed, his anger rising within him. He wanted to tear his opponent into billions of bloody shreds.

"Emotions," the dragon snorted. "They make you weak. They give your opponents a weapon in hand. Block them, become cold and inaccessible like a boulder. Otherwise, you will die!"

Drasan forced himself to calm down.

Clear your mind.

Pain resounded in her temples...

Clear your mind.

The image in front of his eyes blurred... only those ruthless reptilian eyes remained. He choked down his anger.

Clear the mind! I will not give you this satisfaction!

The contours slowly became clearer. He continued to defend himself, though he could feel the blood trickling from his nose. A dull pain throbbed in his temples, but he suppressed the urge to scream. Gathering all his remaining strength, he pushed Gaenor's consciousness aside, forced him to back off.

"Enough!" Neila stepped in between them and was now glare at both. "Stop it or you'll kill each other!"

Only then did Drasan realize that he was straddling, invisible energy flowing through his body in waves. Opposite him, Gaenor was grinning broadly, revealing a row of knife-sharp teeth. Even after him he could see fatigue, though he seemed ready for another attack.

He gently pushed Neila aside and walked over to the dragon, looking up at him defiantly.

"Good," Gaenor praised him. "That's what I mean. Get rid of your emotions, there is no place for them during combat."

"All right," Alt'ar said. "I think these exercises are enough for today. You both need rest, and you..." He measured Drasan with a long look. "...you need a decent bath." He added with a slight smile.

Only after looking at his reflection in the dirty puddle did the man understand the hint. He was covered in blood from head to toe. He pushed his sweat-soaked hair away from his forehead and smiled. Though he was swaying on his feet, he felt more content than ever before. He had defeated Gaenor in a silent battle of will, and he knew he had earned a little more respect among the assassins.

***

After swimming in the cold river, Drasan returned to the camp. He was still in a gloomy mood, though not because of the earlier lesson. Rather, it had to do with the brief conversation with Alt'ar. It implied that she would not let him near the prisoner until he was able to fully control himself. It looked as if he would have to be subject to the werewolf from now on. Someday in his life he would have disapproved of it, but now he had no choice. He really needed the leader of the "Assassins Guild" and the leader of the "Assassins' Guild" would not agree to anyone other than him ordering his men. He himself wondered how much concessions he had made so that only the killer would agree to cooperate with him. First, he did not expect such submission from himself.

Or at least the person I used to be, he added mentally.

However, that was not his main concern. He was worried about Yarred. His longtime friend was now alone in a hostile kingdom, and he had no way of helping him. In addition, he had not had contact with Mara for months. Her latest news turned out to be quite a surprise to him. If the former captain of the guard did become the father, then he would have to use much more judgment and stay with the mother of his offspring. Instead, he set off on an after all perilous journey deep into Riden, with a letter from the queen to hand him over. Since the prince was brought up without a father himself, he considered such a course a damn deed.

True, he hoped that his adoptive mother had included in the letter an explanation of why she had kept his true origin from him for so long. It is even possible that she will know her father's identity.

As long as he did not have the letter in his hand, Drasan was able to guess. Meanwhile, he should consider how to warn the rulers of Antua and Earden. For he had no doubt that it was these kingdoms that would become the first prey in Bal'zar's war campaign. Perhaps they are unaware of what is threatening them.

Absorbed in such thoughts, he reached the outskirts of the camp. He had an unpleasant conversation with Alt'ar. He was relieved to see him nowhere in the vicinity. He had the unpleasant feeling that everyone was watching him. Some surreptitiously, others openly.

He sighed deeply and sat down by the fire between Velwel and Neila. The mercenary fixed him with a concerned look, misreading his not very happy expression. When a bowl of steaming stew was handed him, he began to eat completely indifferent to his surroundings. Neither Velwel's incessant chatter nor the voices of the other killers reached him at all. He also closed his mind tightly to protect himself from Gaenor's questions. He did not want to share his thoughts and doubts with him. He was silently pleased with the werewolf's absence, as it allowed him to analyze the situation before talking to him.

He finished his portion and, still silent, walked away towards the river. He had been walking for some time, not really knowing where and for what, when he heard footsteps behind him. Someone was trying to catch up with him. He stopped so abruptly that the person bumped into him, nearly knocking him off his feet.

It turned out to be Neila.

He himself did not know why he was not pleased to see her. He realized that he was going to have to answer a series of rather embarrassing questions in a moment, and it made him tense even more.

But Neila was silent, studying him searchingly with large blue eyes. She was standing only inches from him. He knew he should do something, but he couldn't make the stiff muscles move.

Finally, he sighed heavily and said:

"If you're going to scold me, go ahead. I'm used to everyone here treating me more like a spoiled selfish child than a responsible adult man."

She said nothing to that. She was still looking at him with the same concerned gaze. He felt his anger building up within him, but he suppressed it, remembering that he was to train his emotional control.

"So far, I let Alt'ar lead, because he has a lot more experience than me. However, his decisions are also wrong, and my opinion is immediately questioned by everyone, they think that they know better anyway, even my best friend..." He paused, realizing that he said too much.

To his surprise, the girl smiled slightly.

"I expected you to need a conversation, but I hate self-pity," she said calmly. "For such an extraordinary man you have a disturbing tendency to exaggerate certain things."

Completely surprised by this so apt statement, Drasan stood petrified, not quite sure what to answer. Finally, he took a deep breath and let out in one breath:

"All my life I have been prepared for the role of a ruler. I was taught a lot of things, including strategy, but it never occurred to anyone to teach me how to cope with a difficult situation. I would never believe if someone ever told me that I would be someone else's subordinate. Meanwhile, now I must submit to Alt'ar, who is a wanted criminal and a werewolf."

Neila looked him in the eye.

"You only lack experience, but it was you, not Alt'ar, who was raised to heir to the throne. After all, it was you, not him, who went through all the suffering, torture and humiliation. You are much stronger than him. It's logical that you want to prove yourself as a king after years of preparation. And the truth is, being the ruler and the commander of an army is not the same thing."

He knew she was saying this only to cheer him up, but he felt pleasantly tickled anyway. Her recognition became more precious to him than all the treasures of the world.

"You are now like a brand-new sailing ship going on a voyage in unfamiliar waters and immediately hitting a storm," she continued, trying to cheer him up.

"Maybe you're right," he said with a deep sigh. "The truth is, I never wanted to be king. In my youth, I sincerely hated when my mother forced me to all these formal parties." He smirked. "I preferred the military. There, the rules turned out to be simple and I didn't have to worry that someone would poison my wine."

She laughed sincerely at the comparison.

"You may be surprised, but in my childhood, it was the same." She sat down on the boulder sticking out of the ground. He sat down beside her and, after a moment's hesitation, put his arm around her. She did not protest. "My father belonged to the exalted nobility of Riden's elite. Since my mother died without leaving him an heir, he went out of his way to marry his only daughter as best as possible." She smiled wryly. "I was presented as a breeding mare. My father eulogized what a wonderful wife and mother I will be. That's why I ran away from him and became a mercenary." She finished with a crooked smile.

"Then there are not so many differences between you and me, Neila," the young man said softly. "My mother insisted on getting married since I was eighteen, and though she never admitted it openly, she dreamed of having grandchildren. She hoped that when I settled down, I would abandon my adventurous lifestyle for the sake of my family. Now I think she just wanted to keep me with her."

"Maybe that's how she tried to protect you..." the mercenary said timidly.

Drasan nodded thoughtfully.

"Perhaps you're right," he said, pain contorted his face. "But it still doesn't justify the fact that she and Ashkan have lied to me all my life. I didn't learn the truth until I met the werewolf and Dhalia. Mother created the illusion of my future life in order to control me. She had to be absolutely sure that no one would discover my identity."

Neila sighed softly as she moved closer.

"You're probably the most complicated man I've ever met," she said, resting her head on his shoulder. "Maybe in different circumstances we would have made a beautiful pair," she added, much more quietly and perhaps only to herself.

Drasan decided it was better to leave it without comment. He just sat in silence, enjoying her closeness.

CHAPTER 15

When he entered the settlement, Yarred expected everything, just not what he found there. The irregularly spaced thatched huts looked abandoned. Livestock has also disappeared. He heard neither the screams of the playing children nor the barking of the dogs. In addition, it started to rain from the low navy-blue clouds.

The captain directed the horse to the largest building, in which he recognized the inn aptly named "Under the Three Pines". He stopped and jumped down into the slushy mud. He tied his horse and started towards the entrance. The door swung open with a loud thud and he found himself in a darkened room. It turned out to be completely empty except for the squat innkeeper and his wife who glared at him from behind a long bar. Not caring about this not-so-nice party, the Sheardonian rested his elbows on the wooden table.

"What do you want here, you stray?" Asked the host in a rather unfriendly tone.

"I've been on the road for a long time, I need some provisions for myself and my horse," the man replied, undeterred by the greeting.

"We have nothing to offer you," the fat man growled. "The royal soldiers came here two days ago and confiscated everything, including livestock and the last barrels of my finest booze. They also took the feed."

His wife nodded eagerly and added:

"I hope the king will deal with these rebels quickly. Otherwise, the war will ruin us all."

Captain Cordydian refrained from making any biting comment, instead looked around the room. Indeed, all tables and chairs had been pushed against the wall, only stairs leading to the second floor were located further. It was there that rooms for travelers were located.

"Or maybe the rebels are right?" He dared to say.

The host looked at him suspiciously with dull gray eyes and said:

"On those big announcements posted in all the villages they clearly say that if anyone helps the rebels, he will go straight to the scaffold. And for those who join them, sharp stakes await. War is, my lord, the king forcibly enrolls every healthy peasant in the army. I miraculously fooled myself, because they would have taken me too. There was a clear resentment in his voice, and for his grievances he blamed those who dared to go against the king."

Yarred sighed deeply, realizing that this could be the case anywhere. Presumably most Ridenian were too afraid of the new ruler to aid the rebels. He decided to go on, hoping to learn something new about Drasan's activities.

"Why don't you resist the tyrant who oppresses you?" he knew it was a very bold question.

Both the host and his wife stared at him.

"We are not warriors," the stocky man announced finally, straightening himself with dignity. "These rebels are said to be a bunch of murderers, bandits and other filth. Perhaps it was better that the king finally decided to exterminate them. Apparently, he gathered an army so great that no one has ever seen before."

The captain smiled to himself. The young king was very clever. It was enough to spread the rumor that the rebels were, in fact, a band of bandits. Some of this might turn out to be true. After all, according to Alder,

Drasan intended to seek out the infamous leader of the Assassins' Guild. He wondered if the common people knew that a real dragon was leading the rebellion.

"Or maybe it is completely different than you think, dear host," nonchalantly he leaned on the polished table top. "Perhaps the king is hiding some facts from you," he trailed off, pleased to see a spark of interest in the man's eyes. "Like the fact that these rebels are led by a real dragon." He watched the expression of utter surprise on the other's face with satisfaction for a moment, and, getting no answer, continued. "I will say more... The king has gathered such a large army not to face a handful of rebels, but because he himself is afraid of an attack. Some kingdoms do not support his campaign as their economies suffer. War is not in their favor, so so far, no other king has supported our reigning Bal'zar except Alikorn - who does not have a long-worthy successor for Lannor the Vengeful for a long time.

The host swallowed nervously and looked fearfully around the room, maybe he was afraid that someone would hear their conversation, he said in a whisper, leaning towards Yarred:

"If I were you, my lord, I would not speak so openly against our lord. It is true that they say that this is a kid who still has milk under his nose, but so far he has shown exceptional cruelty." Here he lowered his voice even more. "The soldiers burned down two villages only because, according to rumors, they sheltered the rebels. Hundreds of people were handcuffed and led to the capital to be hanged without any trial. They are still carrying out compulsory conscription, taking everyone not too young or too old to the war."

Captain Cordydian also leaned over and began to speak very quickly:

"It's time to decide which side you're on before it's too late. A great storm is coming, the earth will run with blood. You still have time, join those who are fighting for the righteous cause, instead of waiting for the worst."

The big man was clearly confused:

"Unfortunately, I decided not to take any side. Whether right or wrong," he muttered, wincing slightly. "This inn is all we have left. No, we'll try to wait out this storm. Whatever is supposed to be, it will be anyway."

Yarred sighed once more and became sad. For he understood that the man was right. What can a group of villagers do against an entire army? How could they know their fate was a sign of the desperation of their new ruler? After all, it was not announced that this "handful" of rebels had won three times over the royal army. It would be bad for the morale of the Rideans, who were to fight under the green banners of their own or forced will.

Nevertheless, he found out a lot. Leaving the inn "Under the Three Pines", he felt that it was worth it to deviate a bit from the road. He mounted his horse and continued on his way. For he was afraid that if he stayed in one place any longer, he would come across soldiers.

***

At dawn the next day, the killers prepared to depart. Rodian walked over to Drasan, who, along with Velwel, rode along the line of Alt'ar's men, checking that all were present. At the sight of her, he pulled the reins, setting the mare in place.

"Did something happen?" He asked in a slightly sharper tone than he intended.

The witch frowned.

"Alt'ar wants to see you," she replied harshly.

"Why didn't he come alone, just sent you?" Drasan asked.

Rodian raised an eyebrow, but she didn't comment aloud, though the half-dragon could see she wanted to. Instead, she gave him a sweet smile.

"I don't have time for your talk, Drasan, and I don't want to remind you that Alt'ar is in charge. Now forgive me, I have to prepare to open the doorway." After these words, she turned and walked away.

Drasan suppressed the anger at her tone and glanced at Alt'ar - the leader of the Assassins' Guild was not looking at him at all. He was just checking how many provisions they had left.

The half-dragon stood in front of him and, still suppressing his emotions, spoke:

"Rodian says you wanted to talk to me."

The assassin turned slowly to him, steel flashing in his eyes.

"Yes, that's what I'm going to do," he replied impassively. Nothing in his demeanor showed that he had even noticed the hint of menace hidden in a few words.

"So, I'm listening," Drasan's voice turned into a hollow growl.

Alt'ar frowned. He was not surprised by the hostile attitude of the Sheardonian.

"I know what you've been through," he began patiently. "But everyone agrees on one thing: it doesn't give you the right to be both judge and executioner. Your explosive nature and lack of self-control make it clear that you are not matured to be a leader. You act too impulsively, not thinking at all about the consequences of your actions." The assassin kept his voice calm, though there was steel in his words. "That's why we, along with Gaenor and Rodian, decided it would be best if you moved away from major decisions at all."

For a moment Drasan stood rooted to the ground. He barely mastered the urge to slap the Guild leader on that cold, emotionless face.

"So..." He broke off and cursed. "...in short, you think I'll just agree with whatever you think..." That's what he expected, but still he couldn't hide a note of regret.

"Exactly," Alt'ar growled softly, not letting him finish. "I'll say more: so far every decision you made has turned out to be wrong. You have no idea what to do. You can't even control yourself, let alone others. Should I go on?"

The half-dragon looked into his eyes, feeling cold fury overwhelm him despite his efforts to control his emotions. Out of the corner of his eye, he noticed that a large group of onlookers had gathered around them, and they were all waiting for his step.

"What are you going to do now?" Alt'ar asked, as if reading his mind. A sneering smirk appeared on his lips. "Will you throw yourself at me? My people will then tear you to pieces. Three hundred against you one. I doubt that your extraordinary talents will be enough to overcome them all."

Drasan did not answer. He felt the energy of the fire, fueled by his hot emotions, rising along with his anger. He didn't need to see his reflection to know that red flames were starting to creep up his body. He felt the same euphoria and desire to destroy his opponent as when he first summoned fire to his aid. The dragon in his mind wanted him to do it, to strike with all his power, turning Alt'ar in front of him into a pile of ash.

"Enough!" Gaenor roared, jumping between them at the last moment. Drasan's fireball hit him on the left side and slid down diamond-hard scales. The dragon growled and wagged its long tail, hitting the half-dragon in the chest and throwing a few feet back.

Drasan sprang to his feet and allowed the transformation to complete. He roared, mouth full of knife-sharp teeth wide open, then lunged at Gaenor. The elder dragon hissed furiously and slapped his long tail once more. The left side hit, and the prince roared with rage and pain. The sharp spikes crowning the enemy's tail hit an old scar. Taking the opportunity, Gaenor lunged at him, pinning him to the ground. Drasan's enormous jaw snapped an inch from his neck, but the older dragon's grasp was too tight for him to break free.

"If you don't stop, I'll make you do it in a very painful way," growled Gaenor.

Drasan froze, gave him a hateful look.

"It is for this reason that you must learn to control your emotions. Otherwise, your own stupidity will kill you," the dragon continued in a calmer tone. He let go of Drasan and, still watching him, added, "Now get out of my sight and come back only when you have cooled down."

"Don't order me," Drasan growled softly, standing up from the ground and glared at him.

"At the moment you are not thinking clearly and rationally. A short flight will do you good. Fly and come back when you're calmed down," Gaenor replied in a much softer tone.

Drasan growled angrily but obeyed. Everyone made room for him as he unfolded his massive wings and leapt into the air.

Once he was high up, so that the flowing river below turned into a shimmering pale blue ribbon, he felt his mind slowly return to equilibrium. The anger vanished, replaced by the joy of flight. He let a stream of refreshing cool air carry him for a moment, then turned south toward the Haerral Mountains. Up close, they were much taller than he had first imagined, though they were no match for the Unicorn Mountains. He flew for a time above low clouds that threatened to rain. After a moment he changed direction again, facing the wind that carried the scent of salt - the scent of the sea and freedom.

Quickly calm his mind. It made him feel very stupid because he realized what he was going to do. Attempting to kill the only ally who had so far shown great courage and devoted himself entirely to the cause now seemed to him something to be damned. He fully understood the consequence of his act. He knew he would most likely have to beg Alt'ar's forgiveness by tucking his pride deep into his pocket.

Gaenor was right, I must control my temper. As a matter of fact, Alt'ar did nothing wrong, he did as reason and experience dictated - he took command, seeing that I could not cope with it. It was my stupid pride that pushed me to attack him with my full power.

As he contemplated without controlling the direction of flight, he was surprised to find himself on the seashore. Below, gray-blue water broke against sharp rocks. He gradually lowered his flight in order to land on a high slope. He felt a strange longing, as if somewhere on the horizon there was a house he could not remember. He knew it was ridiculous because he was born here in Lineland. So where would the memories of another place come from, hidden behind an angry ocean? And yet, he couldn't deny that something was pulling him here.

He huffed, and a trickle of smoke flew from his nostrils and a gust of cool wind blew away. Drasan smiled.

I could fly away now, leaving Lineland in Dhalia's sovereignty. An image flashed into his mind, bright and clear. Neila. She was the one who kept him here. In some strange and not fully understandable way she possessed his heart and soul.

Suddenly he understood what he should do, maybe he had always known it, but part of him was rejecting the plan. Being alone he could not count on victory, but if he could convince the Eardenians and Antuanians to help, there was still a shadow of a chance. Then he would have an army almost equal to that under Bal'zar's orders. The news of his three victories may already have spread among the people of Riden. This also gave him a certain advantage, in the end most of the soldiers were forcibly drafted into the army to compensate for the losses suffered by the king in the last clashes. Perhaps they will not have that much will to fight.

He had to appease Alt'ar first. He still needed him. The leader of the Guild turned out to be not only an incomparable fighter, but also a great commander. He also knew that if the werewolf decided to leave him with him, his men would leave, and then the chances of defeating Dhalia would decrease significantly. As Gaenor said: it wasn't until he was overcome with anger that everything became clear. He already understood the nature of the mistake he was making, which could cost him more than a smudge of honor.

With that in mind, he spread his wings, catching the sharp gust of west wind, and leapt off the slope. For a moment he dived straight down to the rocky shore, only to spread its wings at the last moment and soar up again to the low deep blue canopy of the sky.

***

Velwel angrily kicked the lonely tuft of grass. He hated inaction. Unfortunately, Drasan's prolonged absence meant that he had to be stuck here, while Alt'ar sent most of his people away through the magic portal. He left twenty of the best with him. Besides them, there were also Rodian, Neila and Gaenor. The young assassin knew the Guild leader was really furious, though he hid it under a mask of indifference. Neila became no less irritable. Some time ago, he had been one of the witnesses to her discussion with Alt'ar. From the Guild leader's posture and brief brief replies, he concluded that the mercenary had done nothing.

Velwel also did not try to suppress his emotions. There were indications that the alliance with the Guild was in the balance, and there was no denying that Drasan was the only person responsible for this. After he flew away, many of the killers began to demonstrate their discontent very loudly, and some even threatened that they would not fight by his side anymore. Others seemed ready to throw his head at Alt'ar's feet. The Guild leader remained impenetrable. The young man guessed that he himself did not know what to do in this situation.

The sun was starting to sink west when one of Alt'ar's men finally noticed a dark shape flying towards them, clearly visible against the purple-pink sky. The dragon began to make slow circles over them. Finally, Velwel felt a powerful blast of air raking in great wings on his face. For a moment the reptile hovered a few feet above the ground, and a moment later it landed on it with a thud. The dozen or so horses remaining in the camp screamed with terror. Drasan folded his wings but did not immediately assume human form. Instead, he moved towards Alt'ar sitting on a lonely boulder.

The assassin didn't even flinch, just regarded him coolly, showing no sign of fear. For a moment they remained completely motionless, a huge reptile and a human. Both attitudes emanated from both calmness and determination. And suddenly the half-dragon bowed his long neck and said:

"Please accept my apology."

The Guild leader was silent, staring at Drasan standing before him without blinking an eye. Suddenly he got up and walked over to him. His face still showed no emotion, like a stone mask.

"I accept the apology," he said calmly, though his voice was ready to fight. "I have no grudge against you, Drasan, and, contrary to your judgments, I don't want to argue. Anyway, our forces are still pathetic, so this name is not adequate. I've had a long time to ask about something, and now here's a great opportunity." A forced smile appeared on his face. "Do you have any military support besides my men?"

There was a tense silence. Everyone, including Gaenor, stared at Drasan, curious about the answers. After all, he had not obtained it so far, and he was still hesitant to send envoys to Thoran or Earden. They realized that when Bal'zar got bored of this game, he would crush them like an intrusive fly. What could a handful of men do against an entire army?

"It's good that you ask that," Drasan said, and despite the reptilian form, Velwel noticed that he was not really pleased with the question. "I intend to go personally to Earden and then to Antua. I'll also try to send messengers to the peoples of the south, and also to the seaside of Noai'dir."

Alt'ar did not seem to be satisfied with that answer.

"And what's next?" He asked sharply. "It may be months before any of the kings decides to help us. We don't have any food supplies, we don't even have enough horses. My people are starting to miss their former lives. How much more do you think they will endure living as refugees? At my call, many of them abandoned their homes and families. And now there are only a handful of them left. They had seen Bal'zar's soldiers kill their comrades and friends, they learned the overwhelming advantage of the enemy, and yet they did not give in. And what is the reward for that?"

Velwel could see Drasan's restless movements, unable to answer these questions, but Alt'ar was not finished yet.

"Do you realize that this is not our fight? We are not soldiers or knights in shining armors, we will not fight for a kind word. With a good word, I will not heal the wounded, nor will I feed my people. A kind word is not worthy of the death of my best killers. Let me ask you directly: what are you able to offer us to stay by your side? Just don't talk to me about honor and a just cause. I'm sick of your smooth words and your avoidance of full responsibility. Convince me that it is worth fighting by your side and do it now while you still have the opportunity." His words hung in the air.

Drasan was still standing still. Despite his powerful form, Velwel thought that he had shrunk. He only stared at Alt'ar standing in front of him with glowing green eyes. Finally, he gasped loudly, and a trickle of smoke flew out of his nostrils.

"You are right, Altar," he said finally. "So far I have acted carelessly, and I can promise that it will change. I made many decisions too quickly and without much thought, so far, I turned out to be a rather poor commander. Perhaps it is due to my inexperience, though most of it is my stupidity and overconfidence. Too early I challenged the witch, risking this entire campaign to a disastrous defeat. There are some things I should take care of myself, rather than putting my trust in those who didn't deserve them..."

Velwel guessed who it was, because Neila repeated to him most of the words she had heard from Drasan himself. It appeared that his best friend had failed him, ignoring a direct order and deciding to join the fighters. He was well aware that for the half-dragon his insubordination was all the more reprehensible, because he had abandoned his pregnant fiancée.

Moments after Drasan's speech, there were excited whispers. Alt'ar himself was silent with an unreadable expression. He seemed to be still wondering. Finally, he straightened and looked into the eyes of the half-dragon.

"A wonderful, admirable speech, but it didn't answer my questions. To stay, I must have your assurance that my people will receive weapons and food. I cannot afford to continue to die for nothing. We are not your subjects and we have agreed to participate in this war only of our own free will. In the future, I advise you not to try to subdue people like us."

Drasan straightened up with dignity.

"You agreed to take my leadership!" He thundered.

Though the others flinched as the dragon's hot breath enveloped them, Alt'ar didn't even flinch.

"And we're back to jumping-off point again," he said in a harsh tone that clearly sounded like a shadow of a threat. "We don't serve you or anyone. We fight voluntarily, and if we decide to leave, we'll do so without asking you for your opinion. You still have a lot to learn, Drasan, especially since a great responsibility rests on your shoulders. Don't ask me to do everything for you, it's your fight first and foremost. Since you inadvertently provoked a much stronger opponent, you have to bear the consequences yourself." The Guild leader now stood nose to nose with the huge reptile. "There is one more issue regarding your attack on me. If we are to trust each other, I need your assurance that it will never happen again."

To their unspeakable relief, Drasan stepped back and lowered his massive head.

"Here you are right again. If we are to succeed, I need your help and your people's. In return, I promise to try to bridle my temper."

There was a tense silence again. All eyes turned to Alt'ar. The Guild leader remained serious.

"It's not enough," he said finally. "I'm fed up with empty promises and learned talk. You demand respect worthy of a king, so I am waiting for a proposition worthy of the title. Impress me and I will reconsider our alliance. Otherwise, don't count on my help."

Drasan digested his words for a moment. What did he have to offer now? His legacy was in ruins. Most of the subjects died. He doubted there were any valuables in the ruins of the palace. What if...

"The only thing I can offer you and your people is exemption from all charges against you. What do you say Alt'ar? Or maybe you will be satisfied with the title of Lord or Count?"

To the public's surprise, the Alt'ar burst out laughing.

"Here is the answer worthy of a true monarch. Perhaps, with time, you will mature into the role that has been assigned to you by your fate. So, let's say your proposal is an interesting pledge." Everyone clearly breathed a sigh of relief. Meanwhile, the werewolf continued, "It doesn't mean, however, that I will tolerate your childish behavior. So, you either learn to control yourself or our paths will part. Am I making myself clear enough, Your Majesty?"

Drasan looked him straight in the eye. He almost felt like a disciplined schoolboy. And while it was clear that he fully deserved such treatment, his pride had suffered greatly. But he swallowed the bitterness of the humiliation and said:

"As clear as possible."

Velwel looked at Neila standing next to her, who just shook her head, muttering under her breath something that read: "oh, men."

It began to darken all around. Alt'ar and his men were gearing up to finally collapse the camp. After a moment's hesitation, Velwel joined them while Drasan and Neila disappeared somewhere.

***

With a deep sigh of relief, Drasan shifted into human form, and irritated to discover that the flight had completely drained his energy reserves. The scar on his left side was still throbbing with sharp pain, but he tried to ignore it. In addition, the clothes he wore presented an image of poverty and despair. He stripped off his shirt, remaining in his pants. The frosty air chilled the hot skin pleasantly. He stood there for a while, letting the tension drop off him. Contrary to appearances, talking to Alt'ar was not easy at all. Drasan had to be very careful not to burst into anger, and the fact that he remained in dragon form made it difficult for him.

Behind him he heard a soft rustle of brush, but he didn't even turn around. He knew who to expect. Recently, he has become very sensitive to her presence. She smelled completely different than most women he knew: leather and horse and fire smoke. Unlike other women, she didn't use any perfume, and he liked that.

"It was a risky move," she said in a low, tense voice.

Drasan turned faster than she could react and pulled her to him, his teeth flashing white in a broad smile. She didn't protest when he kissed her, and even she kissed him back with no less enthusiasm. She pulled away quickly. Way too fast.

"Do you know where we're going, Your Majesty?" She feigned indignation, although the gleam in her eyes showed that she almost succumbed to him this time. "Alt'ar chose the Wolfwood as his hideout..."

He didn't let her finish, closing his mouth with a kiss. It was supposed to mask his surprise with what he had just heard. Sheardon then.

He was coming home...

CHAPTER 16

After hearing a short account of the mage's foray, in which he also did not remain silent about his mental conversation with Bal'zar, Berg lost himself in gloomy thoughts. The words of a longtime friend hurt him more severely than the enemy knife. It hurt his wounded pride and the fact that his hopes had failed. He felt all the worse because, according to Alder, it was only a small part of the punishment for insubordination. He did not care whether he would earn flogging or any other corporal punishment for it. He disappointed his king. Regardless of his motives, his deed remained reprehensible, which is why the young ruler gave him under the command of this cold reptile.

Alder was reluctant to encourage him to talk. After preparing a modest meal - which the young soldier flatly refused to eat - he went to bed, informing in advance that they would leave at dawn.

Berg knew that the burning remorse would keep him from falling asleep, so he started looking at the saddlebags at the horse's saddle. He focused mainly on checking the number of arrows, regardless of the darkness around him, he brushed the mount thoroughly. He then stowed the brush and the comb, and instead took the sharpener out and began sharpening the jagged blade of his knife. Work helped to calm the thoughts and was cleansing.

When he was done, he tossed a few logs into the dying embers of the fire and for a moment looked at the flames devouring the dry branches. The lack of occupation made the young Ridenian numb again, and the accusing voice of his king echoed in his mind. He did not kill the baby, although mages' spies have reported that the baby has great power. Now he knew that he had let himself be charmed by him. He tried to shake the burning guilt away, but it stubbornly kept coming back. He stayed there until dawn. Then Alder got up and started getting ready to depart.

They still had to decide what about the beautiful black stallion that the Sheardonian had left for them. Killing such a magnificent mount was out of the question, but they couldn't take it with them either. In the end, they decided that when they got there, they would leave the horse to his fate.

At the given sign, Berg rose from his seat and looked into the mage's black eyes, ready to accept his order without grumbling. The other silently pointed to all three mounts.

"Hold the horses," he commanded in a calm voice, rolled up his coat sleeves and began chanting a spell in a language unknown and incomprehensible to the young man.

Berg was not afraid of magic. He grew up in a world where it belonged to everyday life. But he noticed that as power began to pulsate in the air, the animals became alert and tense. Ready to rush to flee immediately if the need arises. The man understood that horses did not like witchcraft.

As the mage's voice grew louder, a small circular hole appeared in the pulsing air. It was a bit like a window, though its surface rippled like agitated water. Berg sensed the trembling of the animals crowding beside him and understood well the reason for their fear. The portal grew to such a size that it could easily accommodate a tall man riding a horse, and its surface ceased to be disturbed. It looked like a sheet of smooth glass now, though its edges still faintly pulsed with an unnatural glow. On the other side, the man saw the lake and the trees leaning towards it. It was a while before he realized that he was looking at Lake Silvach and the Wolfwood building on the other side of it.

"Go first!" Alder exclaimed, strangely pale in that unnatural light. "Take your horses with you, just be careful not to let any of them run away.

The young Ridenian swallowed. He had never used magical passages before and did not know what to expect. And this ignorance terrified him even more. He thought he'd rather fight an enemy twice his strength than enter the pulsating portal. Unfortunately, he had no choice but to move forward, dragging the leaning mounts behind him. He wasn't surprised by their panicky fear, for he felt the same way himself. When at last he reached the luminous gate formed - contrary to everything he believed - in the air, he took a deep breath, like a swimmer preparing to plunge into deep water, and with his eyes closed tightly entered the glass pane, pulsating with unnatural brightness.

Walking through the portal was like swimming in icy water. Berg felt the hair on the back of his neck stand on his head, suddenly he emerged on the other side and the warm rays of the rising sun fell on his face. He was still clutching the reins in his hands. He opened his eyes and took a deep breath of the cool morning air. He was on the right side of the lake, glistening in the dawn light like a spilled stain of metal. To his side he could hear the horses breathing loudly, and a circular passage shone behind him. After a moment, the mage emerged from him, and the portal flickered and vanished.

The young soldier stared dumbfounded where he had just been and turned hesitantly to Alder. He took the reins of his mount from him and, without any explanation, started towards the thicket that was piled up in front of them. Berg sensed that there was no way out: he had to follow him.

Soon the morning light faded out overwhelmed by the green twilight lying under the crowns of ancient oaks. Alder led the way, not stopping or looking back, and although Berg grew up in the woods, Berg amazed him with its vastness and density. Once in a place well-known to him, Ernil crawling beside him showed tremendous liveliness. The stallion cocked his ears, absorbing the sounds of the forest, and his movements became less tense and a strange joy pulsed from all over his body. It was as if the horse sensed its master close.

If that's true, he could betray them at any moment. And that would ruin the whole plan.

"Let him go," the mage ordered him, not for the first time having proven mind-reading skills.

Berg cut the rope without hesitation. Sable horse was just waiting for it. He sped forward into the thicket of the forest, quickly disappearing from their sight.

"If we're lucky, we're here before them," Alder said, leading the horse down a path that was trodden by animals and deeper and deeper into the green darkness.

Berg had no idea where she was leading, and he didn't care. The king gave him the order, and he, his faithful soldier, would obey it without hesitation.

The mage stopped suddenly and gestured for him to do the same. They both listened, so far, to the snorting of horses and the human voices, rather distant.

Alt'ar has arrived at the place.

***

A dull clatter of hooves on the cobblestones scared the feral dog away as it slipped deeper into the ruined buildings. Drasan jerked the reins, which was met with staunch protest from the chestnut mare, which danced, horseshoes ringing on the stones and bared her teeth on the bit. Neila cursed ugly, just as unsuccessfully trying to control the bay gelding that leapt to the side with an angry snort. The reason for the behavior of both mounts turned out to be piles of rotten bones piled up on both sides of the narrow street in the tattered remnants of clothes or in rusty armor, with the symbol of a wolf's head stamped on the chest.

The city has gone dead. All its inhabitants were either dead or retreated long ago. It was not difficult for them to guess what happened here after the protection spells were broken. Most of the stone walls surrounding them had collapsed into rubble, and half of the buildings bore traces of fire. It must have been a slaughter.

Once Drasan had managed to contain the snorting and running mare, they moved forward towards the fortress rising in the heart of the city - what was left of it. Many buildings had to be avoided by a wide arc, as the fire caused them to collapse into debris, blocking the passage. At last, they reached the shattered, blackened remains of the gate. There was a huge breach next to her, and the young man directed his mount there.

They rode into a large courtyard and saw another macabre sight. The prince knew that this image would be etched in his memory forever.

Sheardon Queen's headless corpse was strung onto a wooden stake and placed exactly in the center of the courtyard. As if that hadn't been enough, spears were stuck around with the heads of her faithful guards, including Yarred's father.

Although he had come to terms with the death of his carer a long time ago, Drasan jumped off his horse and, not believing his eyes, how hypnotized he moved in this direction. Before he got there, he sensed the work of a malevolent magic. Then he fell to his knees and howled in helpless anger. He had no doubt that Dhalia had a great time making this terrifying spectacle. Not only did it prevent him from paying tribute to the body of the woman he considered his mother, but also to bury her as was customary. This meant that his guardian's soul was imprisoned here forever.

Until now, all these views had shocked him deeply, but none of them could compare to what he saw now. The castle where he was born and raised looked at him with sad eye sockets without glass windows. The southeast wing collapsed, burying some debris beneath it. The palace gardens were destroyed and burned to the ground.

The realization that he was responsible for the death of the inhabitants of the castle and the city was the worst. It would never have happened had it not been for his unwavering confidence that they would be safe within Sheardon's confines. He ignored the danger and risked the lives of thousands of lives. He himself didn't know how he could have let it happen. He felt a hand on his shoulder - it was Neila standing next to him. She was silent, and he felt enormous gratitude for it. He did not feel like talking.

He looked at the remains of his heritage. Between the rubble of the collapsed tower, he spotted the remains of the blackened gates leading inside and started toward them. He broke through the rubble. It still bore the traces of the spell that had struck it. The double door had been broken open and part of the arch supporting it had cracked, so that it was hard to read an ancient protective spell carved in the stone. He squeezed through to the other side and entered the cool hall. The marble floor was littered with pieces of carvings and shards of shattered furniture with which defenders tried to barricade the entrance.

The strangest thing, although there were also many remains, nowhere to find a single corpse belonging to the invaders. The prince did not believe that the royal guard was not defending itself. He sensed the work of a witch here.

The half-dragon slowly and carefully moved deeper into the structure. The marble floor was marked with traces of combat, both manual and magical. Halfway down the corridor that once led to his private quarters, he found another pile of corpses in rusty armor. He pressed himself against the wall and walked sideways, trying not to break the bones. Behind him he heard Neila's cursing, but he did not slow down or look back. He wanted to see his chamber once more. The one he would abandoned long ago, on the night of his twenty-first birthday. He was not surprised to see the shattered remains of an oak door hanging sadly on one hinge. He jumped over it and gestured for the girl to leave him alone. The sight of the destruction in the room did not surprise him at all, he had time to prepare for it. Most of his collection of weapons was looted. One of his first bows, the one Ashkan gave him for his eleventh birthday, someone broke in two and tossed it in the corner.

Drasan picked it up and looked at the runes carved in it for a long time, designed to protect it from the sluggishness of time. He placed the bow on the floor exactly where he had found it and walked over to the broken mirror in which he had looked at himself so often.

Now, not a carefree, handsome young man looked at it from the glass pane, but a young man. His hair was not neatly trimmed and tied back at the nape of the neck as earlier, but tightly knotted and falling down to his back. A thick black beard framed his face, giving him a wild appearance. Even the eyes changed. They didn't have their former gleam, but now they were like the eyes of a predator ready to defend himself at any moment. The skin, once smooth, was marked today with deep lines of wrinkles, testifying to the efforts that have been made.

Drasan grimaced as he realized how much the torments of recent years had changed him. He stripped off his padded caftan and chain mail and then his shirt, stood half-naked, tensing his muscles again and again and, frowning, watching the changes to his body. And it wasn't the scar on the left side, but most of all the figure. He used to be proud of his excellent muscles, which was the result of many years of training in combat and archery. Now his body had become slimmer and consisted of nothing but muscles.

Satisfied, he dressed, and then his gaze fell on the object lying at his feet. He bent down and raised it to eye level. It turned out to be a silver folding medallion with a portrait of a beautiful woman with jet-black hair and a milky white complexion. It was not this that attracted the young man's attention, but her eyes...

Drasan gasped... her eyes looked exactly like his own. They had the olive-green color that was unusual on the peninsula. He was staring at his mother's portrait.

How did it get here? He was sure he had never seen it before. So it must have fallen out of the pocket of one of the looters who were looting the castle.

Tears of bitterness ran down his cheeks. He sat down on the broken bed, clutching the miniature portrait of his mother in his fingers like a precious treasure. He remembered all the years when he asked Vaya for stories about the mother, and she only repeated that everyone was delighted with her beauty. She never showed him the locket. She probably did not want him to be in the possession of a single likeness of his mother. Not only had she been hiding the fact that he was half a dragon from him all her life. She lied about the identity of his mother, but also made sure that he never recognized her. His gaze fell on his father's ring, and his heart felt even more sorrow.

He didn't know how much time he had spent in the room; he didn't try to hold back his tears. He didn't react when the mercenary sat down next to him and put her arm around him. Her silent presence was soothing. He really wanted to share with her everything he felt right now, but his voice stuck in his throat. Instead, he pressed his nose against her collarbone and she stroked his hair. They lasted a long time, Drasan stepped back and, with some hesitation, handed her a small portrait. She took it carefully, and as he, she brought it closer to her face, she studied it for a moment, squinting her eyes, because a single window gave little light.

"Is that your mother?" She asked finally, handing him the locket.

He nodded, because his throat was still tight.

"You got her..." She hesitated and looked at his face.

"...eyes," he finished in a hoarse whisper, not taking his eyes off the portrait.

Finally, he got up and went to the window. It used to be a view of the city and the shimmering Lake Silvach below, and beyond was the green wall of the Wolfwood. Now the view was marred by blackened houses and streets littered with the remains of residents who had enjoyed a peaceful and prosperous life for so many years.

He felt Neila's hand on his shoulder. He knew her company would not ease the pain and grief. He wanted to be alone so that he could study the latest discoveries in peace. Before he dared to tell her about it, she anticipated him.

"If you like, I'll leave you alone for now," she said. "If you need me, I'll be around."

After these words, she left, and he fell back into his thoughts.

***

Mara winced involuntarily as the maid stiffly laced the bodice of her dress. She is still not used to court fashion, aimed at emphasizing the bust and waist. It was associated with some discomfort. Learning to breathe shallower than usual turned out to be necessary here, as the corset did not allow for a deeper inhalation. For a girl who was not used to it, it meant suffering unimaginable torments. She realized that her current position required it, so she agreed to the inconvenience without complaint. And although her feet in high-heeled ankle-high boots stung excruciatingly, and every breath produced a stinging sting in her chest, she braved these inconveniences.

She surreptitiously glanced at the nurse, who swayed steadily to the rhythm of the hummed lullaby. The wrinkled old woman held her son to her breast with such tenderness and concern that tears came to her eyes.

I should be in her place, she thought painfully about it. She never expected it to be otherwise. Even in her wildest dreams, she never dreamed of becoming a queen. In addition, the sheer volume of responsibilities now terrified her so much that she wanted to sit down and cry. It was unbelievable how much her life had changed since Yarred had freed her from the cruel innkeeper. From a dirty, ragged girl she became the ruler of one of the most powerful kingdoms in Lineland.

"Done, Your Majesty," the maid said, and Mara flinched involuntarily.

"Your Majesty", this title made her shivers run down her spine. Today was to turn out to be one of the most important days in her entire life. In a moment she will appear in a room full of strangers and some unknown mage will use a magical ritual to check if royal blood flows in her veins. But that was not what made her panic. She still couldn't forget Favia's hateful look. She knew the council member would be present at the blood test, as would the rest. The awareness of having an enemy in such a significant personality only made matters worse.

After she kissed Lender goodbye, Mara headed down the straight corridor to the stairs leading down, and then down the wide hall toward the double doors guarded by halberd guards wearing blue tunics with a brown eagle. The men bowed to her and allowed her to enter the great audience hall, where many of the wealthier nobility had gathered. On a marble plinth stood a dark-wood carved throne, usually occupied by a ruler. Now the members of the Council were gathered around him, dressed in the same blue robes she had first seen them in.

As she made her way to the marble landing, the crowd parted before her, bowing their heads respectfully. Mara tried not to look at their faces, from time to time to reply with a polite nod of her head to greetings from notable people. When she got there, she bowed to the Council, and they replied the same - most of them at least. Trying not to meet Favia's cold eyes, the girl straightened and froze in anticipation.

After a while the trumpet sounded and the herald standing by the door hidden behind the platform announced:

"Lord Korav, son of Haldor the Wise, Supreme Mage of the Kingdom!"

The door swung open and a tall, bald man with piercing dark blue eyes, a hooked nose and a prominent chin ended in a pointed goatee entered the room. He wore a voluminous blood-red robe and carried a long cane in his hand. Most of the crowd, including members of the Council of Elders, bowed their heads respectfully, and Mara hurriedly did the same.

Lord Korav walked over to the marble plinth and stood beside Mara. His expression was unreadable. The close presence of the mage made the girl's body shudder an involuntary shiver. She knew he must be very old, though there was no sign of the passage of time on his body. And suddenly the mage spoke, and though he spoke very softly, his voice was audible throughout the room.

"We are gathered here to fulfill one of the most sacred rituals. For centuries, it has softened all disputes over the exercise of power over our kingdom. The power of the blood flowing through our veins is still strong." He looked at the audience. Everyone listened intently, which pleased him as he went on, "A person who takes the place of the dead king must have the power of royal blood. Because only this gives it the right to sit on this throne." He gestured with a sweeping gesture to a dark wood chair. "No one has the right to question the power of blood, because it gives strength to our kingdom and allows it to survive despite the winds of cruel fate that torment it. Today, this honor falls to me. I am to check if this girl's veins really run with royal blood." He gestured to Mara, who was holding her breath in anticipation of a murmur of disapproval, but nothing happened.

At the mage's nod, two slender striplings dressed in identical scarlet and gold tunics approached the landing. One carried a golden bowl, the other a silver-wrapped chest decorated with precious stones, made of the same dark wood as the throne. They both bowed to Lord Korav, handed the items to him, and withdrew hastily to the corner.

The mage placed a golden bowl on the landing, then opened the casket and the girl saw a dagger made of a spiral unicorn horn resting on a velvet pillow, shimmering with all the colors of the rainbow. Mara held her breath as Lord Korav carefully removed the item from inside the box, then turned to her.

"Lady, please roll up the right sleeve of your dress."

Mara did as she was told, trying not to stare at the dagger he was holding and wondering what she was going to use it for. Still, she flinched as the cool blade touched the skin on her forearm. Moments later she felt a slight twinge of pain and the blood dripping down her hand, which the mage was carefully collecting into a shallow golden vessel. When he finished, he pulled a handkerchief out of his large robe and wiped off the rest of the blood, then whispered a few words, and the wound disappeared without a trace.

Mara watched as the magician pulled out two leather pouches and poured a handful of some powder into a golden bowl from each of them. The blood in it boiled, burst into flames. They illuminated the face of the man leaning over her, thus giving it a ghastly appearance. After a moment, when the flames were extinguished, he lifted the vessel and turned it three times in his hands, first one way and then the other. Finally, he picked it up and to the girl's great amazement turned it upside down. A scarlet gem fell on his outstretched hand. The stone shimmered as if there were thousands of diamonds hidden inside. There was a loud murmur in the hall as Lord Korav showed it to the audience. It did not escape Mary's attention that Favia's eyes widened in astonishment and helpless anger.

She smiled inwardly, realizing that she had successfully passed the blood test. Most of the council members' faces showed polite disbelief, only Tharon smiling brightly at her. And when the mage placed the shining jewel on her hand, she struggled to hold back tears of joy.

Now no one will question her rights to the throne of Antua.

***

Drasan looked down the long corridor to the west wing and froze. For a moment he was convinced that it was a delusion, a reflection of light, but no! He could see it too clearly - a silvery she-wolf figure, woven from moonlight. Not really understanding his impulsive behavior, he started toward her, a thick layer of dust muffling his footsteps. The wolf lowered her head and stared at him with shining eyes. He was only an inch from her, his fingers almost touching the pale fur as it suddenly dissolved into thin air.

On the other side of the corridor, Neila was standing, staring at him with wide eyes. He realized that he must look silly, kneeling in the center of the corridor with his arm outstretched. As if he wanted to touch something invisible.

"Something happened?" She asked with concern in her voice.

He didn't answer right away. On the one hand, he was afraid that he would be considered a madman without reason, on the other, he felt the need to share with someone what he saw. He just had to know he wasn't crazy.

He got up from his knees and looked into her eyes.

"I'll tell you a secret. I warn you that this may seem pure madness to you..." He broke off, not knowing how to put his thoughts into words. The woman was now one of his closest friends. If she doesn't believe him, then the others will not also... "Sometimes... both in my sleep and in my waking hours, the Lady of the Dead appears to me."

There was a silence after his words.

Neila studied him, biting her lower lip. He knew it was hard for her to accept, after all, until she came across him, she avoided magic like fire. He understood that his conversations with the goddess of the dead must be something difficult for her to accept - in the delicate sense of the word.

"Drasan," she finally said, looking at him like never before. "I have no idea what to say. The mere knowledge of you is something extraordinary, and now this..." Suddenly she inhaled deeply and without saying a word, she pointed to something behind his back.

The prince turned to follow her gaze and froze. It turned out to be the silver she-wolf, shining with the same extraordinary glow. The same one he saw a moment ago. He realized that this time it appeared not only to him. Maybe she wanted someone to believe him. For a moment the phantom stared at him, then suddenly started down the corridor, sneaking past them and disappearing around the bend. Drasan followed her, heart pounding as suddenly something struck him. This is not a dream caused by the influx of memories of this place! After all, Vaya was called the Sheardon She-Wolf. He quickened his pace, led by the silvery glare, and after a while he ran. He could hear Neila's gasp breathing, but he didn't look back. He knew the corridor and knew where it led - to the royal chambers. Not even for a moment, without slowing down, he jumped over some debris and ran on, with a clear goal in front of his eyes.

Finally, the she-wolf stopped in front of a solid oak door. She looked at him and stepped through them. The prince knew this gate well, as a boy he would enter it many times - it led to the royal library. He took a deep breath and pressed the doorknob carved in the shape of a wolf's head. The door swung open noiselessly and he stood in a large chamber. Not everything was exactly as he remembered it. The shelves once cluttered with heavy books and piles of old scrolls now stood empty. The stone floor was littered with countless bits of glass and stains of dried ink. The enormous dark wood desk was left intact. Perhaps it turned out to be too heavy for thieves.

He heard Neila enter the room and stand behind him.

His heart beating painfully against his ribs, he walked towards the desk and froze in mid-step, seeing what was resting on it. There was a simple silver medallion decorated with the image of a wolf. He had seen the object on Vaya's neck many times. It is said that it was as old as the kingdom itself, and the rulers passed it down from generation to generation, just like the other insignia of power.

He barely believed it when he picked it up. He thought it was gone, as were most of the valuables in the palace. How the Queen's favorite item ended up in this place could not be deduced. Following the she-wolf, he hoped that she would answer many questions that haunted him, but it seemed that it was all about finding an old memento.

Eventually, not quite knowing why he was doing it, the prince hung it around his neck and left the library. He felt disappointed and cheated. He wondered how many more secrets Vaya had from him, and what she wanted to achieve by leaving this medallion to him. As he ran after the luminous, she-wolf, he hoped for more. He thought the queen would appear to him and explain everything she had hidden from him for so many years. Maybe she would even give him his father's name. Meanwhile, even more mysteries awaited him.

He was walking without really knowing where. He just wanted to leave the castle walls as soon as possible. The mercenary trailed behind him, but he didn't turn to face her or let him catch up with him. He didn't want to explain anything to her yet.

They were close to the exit when Neila caught up with him and blocked his way:

"Wait a minute, I think I need an explanation," she looked into his eyes.

Drasan glared at her:

"Get out of my way," he growled, his voice changed.

The girl flinched at the sight of his eyes - eyes with vertical pupils turned into reptilians regardless of his will - but she did not move.

"I'm not leaving here until you tell me what's going on." She announced firmly, leaning hands on her hips.

Drasan took a deep breath, trying to contain his anger overwhelming him.

"I don't know that myself," he said, forcing himself to sound calm. "And now I am asking you..."

"No," she interrupted him. "Tell me what's going on. Where did this she-wolf come from? And this medallion..."

"I said I don't know!" Drasan interrupted her, losing his patience.

"If you took it, it must mean something to you," Neila persisted.

The half-dragon's muscles tightened like tethers, and his breathing grew a little faster as he frantically struggled to control second nature.

"Please..." His voice was quite like a snarl. "Get out of my way."

The mercenary hesitated but stepped back to make way for him. Drasan walked past her and out into the courtyard, gave a short whistle, and a chestnut mare ran out from behind the bend, followed by a bay gelding. The horse trotted over to the half-dragon. Drasan grabbed the reins and was about to climb into the saddle when something else caught his attention. He pulled the chestnut tree behind him and started toward where the stables had once been. He was not sure if it was a hallucination, but it seemed to him that just a moment ago there was a figure of a silver she-wolf there.

Ignoring Neila's shouts, he stepped through the intact door into a well-known room. He slung the mare's reins over the beam and kept walking.

She came so suddenly that he flinched. For a short time she just looked at him with shining eyes, unexpectedly spoke in a voice so well known to him:

"I have very little time and although I understand that you may have many questions, I warn you: I will not answer all of them."

The mere fact that his mistress, guardian, and foster mother were here talking to him made Drasan's anger fade away, and tears came back to his eyes.

"First, I would like to apologize to you for taking so long to tell you the truth. I did it for selfish reasons, explaining it to myself for your good. Don't judge my behavior too harshly because I underestimated my opponent. Try not to make the same mistake, Drasan. Dhalia is deadly dangerous."

"Mother, I..." Drasan was surprised by a hoarse whisper that gave out, but he did not care too much, "...I'm sorry too... I should have protected you..."

To his surprise, the she-wolf showed glowing fangs, the hair on the nape of her neck bristled, and a dull growl emerged from the back of her throat.

"Don't apologize, Drasan. I myself am guilty of what happened, and don't you dare to think otherwise."

Drasan humbly bowed his head.

"Forgive me," he whispered.

The hair on Vaya's neck smoothed again.

"Don't apologize, my son. You have the right to feel angry and even hate me..." She broke off and lowered her head. "I'm here because you need help, and I'll do whatever I can to help you. First, listen to me carefully now because you must know the truth." Her eyes hardened. "The medallion only seems to have no value; it serves as the key to Sheardon's greatest treasure. It is the best weapon to fight against black magic. It will give you an advantage over witches and mages, but it will not affect higher beings. Remember the myth of King Laudas and learn from it."

Drasan opened his mouth to ask what this meant, but Vaya would not let him.

"My time is up here." She said. "Use the knowledge I have passed on to you wisely." After these words, she dissolved into thin air, leaving him alone.

He smiled involuntarily. He no longer felt so helpless and vulnerable. The medallion was supposed to show him the way to a powerful weapon that he could use against Dhalia. Though he did not fully understand the meaning of the Sheardon She-Wolf's final words, it was the first time that he believed in his victory.

CHAPTER 17

Alt'ar looked up into the black clouds and cursed. The storm was one of the last things they needed. A bright zigzag of lightning crossed the sky in response to his gloomy assumptions, followed by distant thunder. The assassin cursed again and jumped off the sheet-covered wagon in which he was painstakingly counting their meager supplies. Most of his men rushed to calm the horses. For they began to cry, terrified by the sounds of the storm. In addition, a wind arose so violent that the branches of the ancient trees creaked ominously, and time and again one of them broke with a loud crack. And then the rain poured down.

"Secure the horses!" He exclaimed, trying to drown out the howling of the gale. "We can't afford to lose even one!"

The men swiftly obeyed his command, seizing and tethering their mounts scared by the sounds of the storm. Another zigzag of lightning lit up the sky, and the wind intensified even more, slapping them with icy raindrops.

The Guild leader ran to the makeshift tent for the wounded. Rodian would be there, he knew. He was counting on it because he needed her help. One word of his would have been enough and she would have given up what she was doing at once.

"This isn't an ordinary storm?!" She exclaimed as loud as she could

"Something, or rather someone causes it, we must be careful," she added, looking the Guild leader in the eye. "Only one of us could control the weather, and if she's still alive, we're screwed."

Alt'ar frowned. He didn't like what she said. It meant even more trouble, and that was the last thing he wanted now.

"Secure the prisoner!" He shouted at his subordinates.

His men immediately rushed to get the job done.

"Are you sure?" He asked when they were alone.

"I'm not sure of anything anymore, Alt'ar." Rodian replied. "A real war begins to form from a small conflict and I don't know if I have the strength to remain a part of it." She looked down. "I've kept my abilities a secret for hundreds of years, and I can't let my true strength come out."

Alt'ar cursed but was thankfully drowned out by a loud roar.

"I won't allow it myself," he replied. "You're like a sister to me." Before she could protest, he closed her in a bear hug.

"We must warn Drasan," said Rodian, disentangling herself from his embrace. "If I'm right, we'll have to face a really difficult opponent and if we don't appreciate them, we will have lost."

Alt'ar cursed again. He was curious about the reason for the protracted absence of the brat. He doubted he would find anything of interest in the ruins of the castle. They have certainly been thoroughly looted by now. Besides, he was immensely irritated by its secrets.

Sitting there on a fallen trunk and looking at the magic element raging around him, he was still trying to find a way out of the swamp into which he got stuck. Until now, he had managed to avoid trouble, generally kept himself aloof from all conflicts. Most of the time it was good for him, but now he couldn't just back out. Too much depended on him. He also had to keep an eye on the hot-tempered and quick-tempered half-dragon.

The problem was, he had no idea of being at war. He was an assassin, not a soldier. Unfortunately, the time passed when he could stand aside and idly watch as the kings beat each other. Admittedly, he still had the opportunity to leave, no one and nothing would stop him, but somehow, he couldn't bring himself to do so.

Soaked to the skin and tormented by doubts, he looked at the black sky and cursed. In reaction to the curse, another lightning bolt flared over the forest.

***

Yarred had no idea what made him visit the herbalist's hut. The villagers insisted that the woman knew about magic, but the skeptical captain somehow didn't believe it.

He was surprised only when in the threshold of a half-ruined hut stood a dark-haired woman in her thirties with full mouth and big green eyes. Her clothes turned out to be surprisingly simple. For she was wearing a simple linen dress over which she had thrown a heavily soiled apron.

"Are you Caristo?" He stuttered, not believing his eyes.

"Depends on who you are, wanderer," the woman replied, but to the captain's relief, she stepped aside, letting him into the small room.

If people were telling the truth and this woman was actually practicing magic, the interior of her house looked surprisingly modest. There was no ornate furniture or coarse-woven rugs in it, instead there was a well-worn table and two cane chairs. There was a bed in the corner, and a fire crackled merrily in the fireplace. Various herbs hung from the ceiling, and a sloppy bookcase was stuck to the wall. It was lined with jars and bottles in neat rows. In some there was something floating!

Yarred swallowed.

The woman walked over to the table with a deck of badly worn cards.

"Tell you?" She asked in a polite tone, smiling encouragingly.

Get a grip, the captain chided himself, walked over to the table and sat on the edge of one of the chairs.

"Do you know who I am?" he looked at the herbalist in the eyes.

The woman frowned in mock embarrassment.

"Someone looking for answers," she said after a moment's thought.

The Sheardonian sighed heavily.

"In fact, I'm looking for a friend who is currently visiting these sites." He replied, choosing his words carefully.

Caristo smiled understandingly, skillfully shuffled the cards and laid them out on the table in front of her. She ran her hands over them for a moment, discovered one of them, and showed it to the captain. There was a drawing of a figure in a black cloak holding a long cane. Though her face was hidden in the shadow of a hood, it was not difficult to guess her identity.

"It's the Lady of the Dead," the woman explained, staring at the man through narrowed eyes. "Whoever your friend is, she walks by his side."

She flipped another page and shuddered. She showed it to Yarred, this time without saying a word. The explanations turned out to be unnecessary - the picture showed a pile of skulls and a spear stuck in it.

"This is a harbinger of a great war," the woman whispered, putting her card down on the table with a trembling hand next to the image of the Lady of the Dead.

Before she turned over another card, the captain knew what would be on it. This time she merely picked it up, threw it away in disgust. There was a snake in the picture.

"Danger!" She exclaimed. Her ample breasts were undulating, and her heart was beating like crazy. "Whoever your friend is, don't look for him. The moment you find him, you will also find death. He is marked by fate."

"But I have to find him," Yarred insisted, though he felt no less terrified than she was. "I have something very important to tell him."

"The cards won't help you," Caristo replied, getting up from the table and walking vigorously to the window. "But there is someone who can do it," she added, without turning to him.

"Will you take me to this person?" He asked eagerly, for he had given up hope of finding out anything.

"I'll show you the way," the herbalist turned to him, her eyes flashing. "The question is: are you ready to face real magic?"

Captain Cordydian knew instinctively that much depended on what he said now. He had to make it sound sincere.

"For my friend, I'm ready for anything," he replied, looking the woman in the eye.

She nodded.

"Fine then. I will take you to Terena but be warned: she can be unpredictable."

Yarred did not know who this Terena was and suspected that it was for his own sake he should not ask about it. Caristo tied a cloak around her neck and started to leave, he followed her. It was only as they stepped out onto the porch that he realized the sky was darkening sharply.

"It's going to be a storm. We have to hurry," the woman announced, moving into the thicket of the forest.

The captain untied his horse and followed her. He had no idea where they were going and kept stumbling over protruding roots until he finally reached the foot of a low mound, his eyes wide as he saw a round door between the tangle of roots.

"Leave your horse here," the herbalist told him, pointing to one of the trees. "You have to go alone," she stepped back.

Yarred nodded his thanks and walked slowly and hesitantly to the circular door. Before he could raise his hand to knock, they ducked in and a slight screeching voice heard him.

"Come in, young man."

The Sheardonian felt a sudden shiver run down his spine, but obediently stepped in, leaning in to avoid a collision with the low ceiling. Inside, it was dim, barely visible. He found the outline of the figure sitting in the chair with his back to the fireplace with difficulty. Though there was no fire in it, the coals glowed red and gold, giving off a remnant of heat.

Yarred paused in the doorway, unsure whether he should come any closer or wait for the woman to summon him. The long years at the royal court had taught him the right manners.

"Come closer, stranger," the woman said in a voice much clearer and clearer than a moment ago.

Captain Cordydian granted her wish, though with some hesitation.

"The herbalist Caristo said you could help me, Lady," he said, making a timid bow to her.

"Really?" Asked the old woman, lifting herself heavily from the armchair. "She told you that?"

Yarred tensed as an elderly woman approached him and stabbed him in the chest with a gnarled finger. Up close, she looked thin and bony, with a dry face marked with a web of fine lines, a prominent nose and sunken cheeks. Her eyes were blanketed with blindness.

"Royal court manners..." she muttered, more to herself than to him. "Then you are a nobleman. I can feel your horse and your long unwashed body, so you've come a long way. But you also have the smell of death behind you, so... a warrior or a mercenary... interesting..."

The captain waited patiently for the old woman to finish her dilatation before deciding to speak.

"I'm looking for a friend. I was told you could show me his whereabouts, lady."

"You say you're looking for a friend?" The woman asked, nodding her head and taking his hand.

For a while, nothing happened. A wave of violent shivers rocked Yarredem, making his stomach turn inside out. He doubled over, waiting for the nausea to pass. During this time, darkness pressed against him on all sides.

"It's interesting that you visited me just today, my lord. Just on the day of the spring solstice," the woman said. "Then magic is really strong and can work wonders. Maybe I can find your friend."

Captain Cordydian froze, unsure of what had just happened to him.

"Why can't I see anything?" He asked in a choked whisper.

"I had to take your sight from you for a moment, young man," the old woman replied softly. "The years when I seduced men with my beauty are long gone. Today I'm an old hermit for most of society, and I wish it would stay that way."

"Why?" The Sheardonian dared to ask.

"For many reasons I don't have the patience to explain to anyone," she replied tartly. "If everyone knew about my existence, I would become too much wanted. Besides, I got used to loneliness. Caristo is a good girl, she looks after me as best she can, but her potions won't change what I've done to myself."

Yarred felt uncomfortable. This woman had some deeply hidden secret. She wasn't going to share it with anyone.

"Will you help me?" He asked, not knowing if he had acted correctly in coming here.

The old woman laughed as if he were telling a good joke.

"Of course, I will help you, Captain Cordydian."

***

The stone steps turned out to be narrow and slippery. Dhalia had to be careful not to lose her balance with every step. The narrow dress she was wearing constrained her movements, and the high-heeled shoes gave little support. Even so, she followed the tall dark-haired man, not believing that it was really happening. It was more like a nightmare with no way to wake up.

Arano descended quickly and confidently. Like Bal'zar, he had made this path many times. For some time, they had spent more time in those stinking dungeons than in their own chambers.

When they got downstairs, the witch had difficulty suppressing her gag reflex. The stench became unbearable. It felt as if her body was soaking with it and she would never get rid of it. The stench of rotting flesh mixed with the sour smell of urine and feces sent a shudder of disgust.

"Why did you bring me here?" She asked sharply, wincing at the sound of the crash of a rotten bone she had accidentally crushed with her heel.

"You will see." He replied shortly, without waiting for her answer, he took a torch from its holder and, shining it on himself, moved along the narrow corridor.

Dhalia swallowed the bile flowing into her mouth with difficulty and followed him, trying to ignore the fact that her heels were getting caught in something sticky and slippery. Arano neither slowed nor stopped as the witch cursed under her breath, but she followed him nonetheless, wincing with every step.

How could she be so deceived? He promised to explain everything to her on the spot but did not mention that they were going to the dungeons. He didn't say a word at the sight of her elegant outfit, and she, stupid, tried so hard to choose her dress. She wore the one with a recently fashionable cut, tightly hugging the belly, waist and thighs, creating what tailors called a fish tail at the bottom.

The outfit was perfect for an elegant party, but it was in no way appropriate for a trip to the dungeon. If Dhalia knew where they were going, she would wear a much more comfortable outfit.

She should now plan a worthy welcome for her "sisters", whom she sincerely detested by the way. Meanwhile, she wandered around the dungeons, soaking up the stench straight from the cemetery, having a mad magician as a companion, claiming that one of the long-forgotten gods lived in his body.

Bal'zar knew this. Bloody brat! She should have cut his throat when she had the chance. She hoped that she would be able to tame his dark nature and would succumb to her powers, just like Gaenor once did. She was wrong. Recently, he not only freed himself from her influence, but in addition began to treat him as an ex-lover, whom he managed to get bored of.

There was still Drasan. The reptile turned out to be stronger than she expected. Somehow, deep within himself, he found leadership skills he had not even suspected existed. Last time he couldn't resist her, she could see all his thoughts and memories. She saw the deep bonds of friendship with Captain Cordydian and with a man named Velwel, as well as the feeling of affection for many others and the deep hatred he felt towards her. She sensed something else. A feeling that dominates everyone else. It had to be love. The prince loved a woman named Neila. She found out about it entering his mind. It was for her that he feared the most, it was for her that he felt ready to sacrifice his life and even freedom.

She felt his suffering as soon as she recognized the face of this girl, and in fact a young woman. She had the opportunity to see her through his eyes and therefore saw her quite differently. She saw a pretty person with large dark blue eyes, soft lips and full cheeks. Too long legs marred the harmonious build of his lean body. She had fair skin and dark hair, so she must have been from Riden.

Moments later, a vision struck her. It was about this girl's future, but it turned out to be related to Drasan as well. In a brief flash, she saw Neila bend down and lift a tiny child - probably a girl - with curly black hair and a round cherub's face. When the little girl opened her eyes, the witch flinched. She knew that shade of green too well to be wrong. Only one person on the entire peninsula had such eyes. It is true that the half-dragon has chosen his path, and it leads precisely to this child.

The moment she saw his future, something twitched within her. As if a long-forgotten part of her being awakened to life. She couldn't even name the feeling. For centuries she had not allowed herself to feel the emotions inherent in mere mortals. She considered them a weakness. She treated all men in her life as puppets. Neither made her feel very emotional.

"Here we are," Arano announced, snapping Dhalia out of his gloomy thoughts.

The witch looked stunned. They were in a large cave-like room. It was not this that was the biggest surprise, but the round altar in the center made of flat stone. There was a tied naked man deceptively resembling Drasan on it. Snakes twisted all over the floor!

She swayed and leaned on the shoulder of the man standing next to her.

"It can't be true..." she whispered in horror, but she couldn't take her eyes off the motionless body.

"And it's not," he smiled slightly. "It's just a fake. The true Chosen One is safe and sound, and he has also retained his freedom. We will let him enjoy it and give the illusion of an advantage by sacrificing your dear sisters, although we both know that it is you he wants." He looked at her with a twinkle in his eye.

"So why are you showing me this?" She did not hide her indignation.

"Because you'll bring him here," he explained bluntly. "I need his blood to complete a ritual that will keep me from having to draw strength from other beings. The blood of a descendant of Magot is the only thing that will give me freedom."

"Are you crazy?" She asked, feeling only disgust at the man standing by her side. "You just want to sacrifice him just like that?!"

"Did the remnants of your conscience be heard in you?" Arano sneered, looking at her contemptuously. She did not match his handsome features at all. "I have to remind you of what you wanted to do with him until recently?" He laughed derisively at her embarrassment. "Oh... no, I'm not going to kill him, not yet. But I have to keep him under control. The boy is just another pawn, this game takes place between much more powerful players. Unfortunately, he managed to mix things up and almost rain on our parade..."

"Your plans?" She repeated indignantly.

Arano looked at her without smiling.

"Oh, so he didn't tell you." He said in mock disbelief. "He just needed you to use as dragon bait. And now that you know the truth about us you have become useless. This girl would be a much better lure for a reptile. However, there will be time for everything."

"And how do you want to get to the mercenary, if he protects her?" She asked, trying not to let her voice reveal too much of her emotions. She couldn't believe it was the same man who had charmed her so much. Or was it not really anymore? "You still need me. Without me, you'll never guess when to strike to win."

"You overestimate your skills. I assure you that you are not the only seer in the world." He replied mockingly. "If you still want to remain useful, please show me your worth. Tell me where Drasan is at present, and perhaps I will keep you alive."

The witch understood that she had no choice. The clear threat in Arano's voice was enough to motivate him. She closed her eyes, so she could enter a trance. There were glimpses of future events in her mind. In them she saw Drasan and this girl constrained and chained. She also saw the shadow of death standing right behind them. She was always very close to the half-dragon.

She opened her eyes and looked at her companion.

"Drasan is near the ruins of Sheardon Palace," she announced calmly. "Happy?" She asked, looking into his eyes without a trace of fear.

Arano smiled at her.

"Let's say you managed to postpone what awaits you. Remember, however, that any attempt to disobey will force me to change my mind. It would be a pity," his gaze became more lascivious. "I have many very interesting memories about you. It is possible that I'm eager to recreate one of them."

Dhalia flinched at the mere thought. Would she go to bed with this handsome-faced monster? Never! She would kill herself sooner than let him touch her again. Luckily for her, Arano hadn't even guessed that she had only told him part of the truth. She didn't even mention a word about her vision for the baby. As if she knew she should keep it to herself.

She still hoped Boris would find out more. After all, he turned out to be an incomparable spy. He could become an irreplaceable source of information regarding Drasan's relationship with this girl. As long as he does not hope for someone else's sword.

***

Alt'ar did not know what had prompted him to visit the prisoner in such rotten weather. He was silently glad to be a werewolf, and he didn't feel the changes in his aura the way humans do. Boris sat upright under a tree to which he had been chained by a silver chain, as the assassin had instructed. At the sight of him, he smiled slightly, or perhaps rather twisted his lips in what could be considered a smile from poverty.

"Well, well, well," he said in a slightly hoarse voice. "I didn't expect you to visit me. I must admit that I am impressed with your composure. You see, you are a real master at pretending to be a human."

Alt'ar knew that Dhalia's servant wanted to make him angry, so he was not going to enter a discussion about himself.

"You are being extremely casual for my prisoner," he said, standing a few steps away from the tied werewolf.

"I don't have much to lose except my head, of course," he laughed sarcastically. "Your reptilian companion would love to cut me into pieces and toss me to the dogs. But from what I can see, he's not in charge here."

"It's true," Alt'ar admitted, surprised by Boris's quick-wittedness. After all, he thought he was a blunt muscle man, a simpleton, and a brute. Meanwhile, this one surprised him more and more. "So if you have nothing left, why don't you explain to me why Dhalia is hunting this boy so fiercely?"

Boris laughed hoarsely.

"Dhalia is your least concern. Bal'zar is a much more dangerous opponent. First, he wanted to kill your precious Chosen One, and now that he knows his possibilities, he will want to catch him alive..." He smiled, showing his fangs. "I don't want to be in that puppy's skin when he does."

"Why?" Alt'ar asked sharply. "What is it about this damned reptile that makes everyone want to get him?"

The werewolf shrugged.

"It's none of my business," he grunted. "I just had to bring him. Him and that girl she's so desperately trying to protect."

"Neila?" The assassin asked, although deep down he knew the answer. He saw Drasan follow her, like a hungry dog behind a juicy leg. So now that Dhalia could read his thoughts, she must have known about this feeling. The very thought of what she would do with her like this made him shudder.

Boris looked into his eyes.

"I'd love to experience the pleasure of watching this arrogant bastard whine for the life of his whore." He licked his lips. "And then I would enjoy playing with her even more in front of his eyes." He smiled at his thoughts, making the Guild leader even more disgusted.

"Drasan would love to degut you." He drawled through clenched teeth. "You live only because of me."

He knew this disgusting creature deserved to die, but felt that before it died, it had to get everything out of it.

"I would advise you not to express your thoughts so clearly in front of him, as it may turn out that I will not be able to save you from his sword."

The werewolf laughed hoarsely.

"I'm not afraid of death," he replied confidently. "I have stood face to face with her so many times that I would have greeted her like an old friend. Let him come and face the monster who murdered his mother, impaled the body of his beloved caretaker and feasted on the remains of her most faithful guards. Let him know that Boris, the trash and pusher of

Dhalia, would be happy to challenge him and watch his reptilian eyes fade."

"You're right. You are a monster, Boris," Alt'ar said, spitting on the ground in disgust. He turned, intent on leaving as the next words chilled him to the core.

"I'm the same monster as you, Bloody Alt'ar!" Boris exclaimed. "Only I, while murdering, do not hide my true nature and completely surrender to sensual sensations, and you are hiding in this weak human body! You are pathetic in this insistent resolution to be human! You are not human, and you never will be!"

Alt'ar had to try very hard not to turn around and crush his larynx. Thank the gods there was a sudden commotion at the edge of their encampment, giving him the perfect opportunity to break this stupid conversation. His wolf senses told him it was something to do with magic, but he had to come closer to be sure.

He ignored Boris and started running towards the new threat.

***

Lurking among the trees, Berg waited patiently for the Guild leader to leave. Freeing Dhalia's hideous minion was part of one of his tasks. It was enough to wait for the right moment and such a moment, to his surprise, was now. The werewolf was not guarded by anyone, everyone turned out to be too preoccupied with the disturbing phenomenon in the sky.

As Alt'ar vanished in the pouring rain, Berg left his hideout and walked over to the bound werewolf. The places where the chain touched the skin looked burned, but otherwise Boris appeared to be fully operational. The Ridenian knelt by the prisoner and took out his knife. Its blade fits perfectly into the lock of the silver-plated padlock. He kept moving it until something clicked in the lock.

The released werewolf did not even flinch, and Berg mentally thanked him for it. They both had to disappear unnoticed. The confusion in the rebel camp should help, but it certainly won't last long.

After completing the task, the young soldier slowly retreated into the thick bushes. He waited a moment longer, carefully observing Dhalia's servant, pleased with himself, he walked slowly towards the place where he had left his horse.

***

Looking at the strange signs in the sky, Rodian could not believe her eyes. She had only seen a similar phenomenon once in her unnaturally long life and was associated with powerful magic. Whoever had created this rift in the clouds was clearly going to open the portal. The whirlpool grew larger and the whistle of the wind intensified, and then, at the very center of this amazing spectacle, the silhouette of the horse and rider began to form. They grew and materialized at an alarming rate.

The witch was relieved to see the approaching Alt'ar. He was the only one who was able to keep a cool head, even in the face of such a situation.

"What's happening?" He asked brusquely. He was agitated, but not because of what was happening. Apparently, he was talking to Boris.

"To tell you the truth... I have no idea!" She replied, trying to shout over the howling of the wind.

And then the man burst out of the vortex first, and a moment later his horse jumped out. The unusual spectacle has ceased.

Alt'ar watched in disbelief and surprise as the man scrambled off the ground and tried unsuccessfully to tidy himself up. His horse stood nearby, ears pressed against body, eyes wide with fear.

"Where am I?" Asked the stranger, looking from face to face. He didn't recognize any of them.

"I'm the one asking the questions!" Alt'ar growled, stepping forward.

Rodian shielded him with her shield. She didn't want to risk something happening to him, even if he could pull through of any wound. In a way, she felt responsible for him.

"Tell me who you are and what you are looking for here, or we will stuff you with bolts!" The leader of the Assassins' Guild demanded in an unbearable tone.

The man was clearly frightened, as Rodian made from his suddenly pale face and bulging eyes.

"I'm Yarred Cordydian..." he choked out finally. "...former captain of the Sheardon royal guard... friend of Prince Drasan," he added, clearly feeling uneasy under Alt'ar's menacing gaze.

"Yarred Cordydian?!" Someone from the crowd called, and after a while the young assassin, always following Drasan like a shadow, pushed his way through the crowd. Velwel. "By Gods! How did you get here?!" He added incredulously.

"I'm sorry, Captain Cordydian, but I can't just trust your words," Alt'ar said, ignoring Velwel, nodding his head approvingly, thereby implying that Rodian could act.

The witch focused on the tall, pale man.

"It'll hurt a little," she said apologetically.

CHAPTER 18

Leaning over the horse's neck, Drasan yelled something to Neila galloping beside him, but his words were muffled by a loud roar. The mercenary cursed and gripped the gelding's sides tighter. The horses' hooves pounded on the treadmill, the wind whistled in their ears and splashed them with icy streams of rain. They could see the black wall of the forest in front of them. Encouraged by this view, their screams and heels urged the mounts to run even faster. Drasan was the first to find the saving thicket. They had to slow down there, because the road became much narrower. They trotted, weaving between the protruding roots and the blackberry bushes overgrowing the path. They got a wetting and cursed again and again at the weather.

The prince was leading. He knew this area as well as the interior of his own chamber. The forest was dimmed from time to time by lightning bolts across the sky. Every now and then he glanced nervously at his companion, but she was silent, staring at the horse's neck. It seemed that the shaky agreement reached in the castle ruins had now vanished without a trace. Maybe he was unnecessarily under the illusion that the girl would understand him, when in fact she took him for a freak with strange delusions.

At last they rode out into a clearing where they were greeted by a sullen group of mercenaries. It was their Alt'ar who assigned them to guard the camp. Each of them carried a heavy and menacing crossbow with a bolt on it. Seeing this, both Drasan and Neila pulled their reins and threw back the hoods of their soaked coats. The sentries lowered their weapons and pushed them beyond a barricade made of a dozen or so huge tree trunks. Behind her, another group was waiting for them. At its head, to the young man's surprise, was Alt'ar. Behind him huddled... Yarred!

At the sight of a familiar face, Drasan stiffened. He couldn't believe his eyes. Yarred shouldn't be here! The surprise passed quickly. It has been replaced by anger.

A friend he treated like a brother. One whom he trusted so much that he would not hesitate to entrust him with his own life. And he simply failed him in the world. At the same time, he committed an act of unworthy soldier, dishonorable to his family - he abandoned those whom he should protect, even at the cost of his life. He left both his fiancée and his unborn child to fate.

He forced himself to keep his cool, knowing that if he transformed himself, the former captain of the guard would be fate. He jumped off his horse and threw the reins at the stunned Neila. The girl did not even try to stop him, when the stiff step of the enraged predator moved towards the small group waiting for him. When he faced the tall, fair-haired man he so admired, he felt nothing but bitterness of disappointment.

He did not wait for his friend to say something to excuse himself, but he swung and punched him on the jaw with all his strength. The captain stumbled backward, but to everyone's surprise, he made no effort to defend himself against the enraged attacker. The people around him froze. Meanwhile, Drasan took another swing and slapped him again. The force of this blow knocked the captain back and he would probably have fallen if someone had not supported him. Blood was dripping from his split lip, and a mixture of surprise and disbelief appeared in his great blue eyes.

One of the mercenaries around them tried to pull the half-dragon away, but he jumped back holding his hand - Drasan's leather caftan was covered with bright red flames.

Yarred didn't even try to cover himself from the next blows. Finally, when one of them fell into the mud, Alt'ar decided to intervene. He walked between him and the half-dragon.

"What the hell's going on?! Why are you beating him like a disobedient dog?!" He asked irritably.

"It's none of your business," Drasan growled in response, his eyes transformed. "Now get out of my way!" He hissed in a voice no different from the hiss of an angry serpent. He looked at the fair-haired man kneeling in the mud, not hiding his anger and contempt. "Get up!" He roared, and several of the killers backed away in fear.

Yarred stood up, looking a little hesitantly at his old friend.

"Do you know what you got hit for?" The half-dragon asked, his voice low, quivering with anger.

The man didn't answer and didn't look up. Apart from the wound on his lip, his face was swollen and his clothes were covered with mud.

Thunder struck, and a moment later lightning shattered the sky.

The fury that engulfed the half-dragon after the first blow was slowly replaced by disappointment at the man, he had called his friend for years.

"I'll ask you again," he growled, clenching and opening his fists. "Do you know what I just beat you for in front of everyone?"

Yarred nodded hesitantly. Despite the rain and the penetrating cold, his cheeks burned with shame. Nobody spoke around him, though now indeed everyone was pressing together to observe the events.

Alt'ar stepped aside and, his arms crossed over his chest, watched the entire scene.

Drasan did not take his eyes off the man standing in front of him. His first anger was gone, but he was not going to let himself be considered a merciless tyrant. He had to explain to these people what he had punished the former captain of the Sheardon Royal Guard for.

"If you don't want to talk, let me explain it!" He hissed angrily, roared in a voice so loud that everyone could easily hear him. "Everyone know that the former captain of the Royal Guard, Yarred Cordydian, is standing in front of me! The one who tarnished the impeccable reputation of an elite unit dedicated to protecting members of the royal family for centuries! Not only did he ignore my direct order, he abandoned his pregnant fiancée! At other times he would have received a more appropriate punishment for this, but today I will take his honorable position as a gesture of grace." He looked at Yarred, who huddled under his gaze. Before Drasan could tirade, Neila stepped out of the crowd and...

Whap! She slapped the stunned guardsman with a flourish, leaving three streaks of blood on his face, traces of fingernails.

"The fucking knight is here!" She screamed, going for another blow, but Drasan in time grabbed her outstretched arm and turned to face him.

"Enough," he growled through gritted teeth. He looked so scary that she wasn't going to protest.

He released her and walked forward, quickly passing his friend huddled in the mud without even glancing at him.

***

Looking at her reflection, Mara was amazed at how much she had changed. Nothing of the old ragged and dirty girl is left in her. She had gotten used to the daily rituals of bathing and putting on new layers of clothes, and although the dresses turned out to be incredibly heavy, she had to admit that they looked very elegant. It was as if she had always belonged to this unknown and strange world. The flaming red hair of her servant was pinned up in an elaborate bun on which a delicate crown was mounted.

After being transferred to the royal chambers, Mara, not having had time to get used to the splendor prevailing here, was shocked. The chamber was located in the eastern wing of the castle, and from the great windows there was a view of the garden, the city below, and the vast plains and steppes. The stone floor was decorated with an intricately woven woolen carpet, while the walls, paintings in gilded frames. In one corner stood a large oak bed with a canopy and silk curtains, an intricately carved cradle next to it. There were other pieces of furniture that looked very old but just as gorgeous and gleaming with gold fittings.

Standing in front of the dressing table, Mara frowned, trying to remember yesterday.

This turned out to be a difficult task. Immediately after the coronation, all those present moved to the ballroom, where a grand reception was held. As it was a tradition, the young queen had to take part in it. She remembered that she had taken her seat at the head of the table, with the most distinguished nobility sitting around her. Their names and titles she just couldn't remember.

As everyone took their seats, trumpets sounded and servants in navy blue livery appeared, bringing dishes on gold and silver platters and trays with crystal decanters full of the best southern wine.

The newly crowned queen's eyes widened at the sight of so much food. The feast turned out to be great. However, she had to remember to behave as befitting her position. She ate in small amounts and drank only as much as the stiff etiquette would allow. Before she knew it, she was the only sober person in the room.

Others, especially men, ate and drank excessively. Soon the table was as noisy as the market. But when a band of musicians with a colorfully dressed minstrel at the head entered the podium, all the women were dragged to the dance floor, where they and the men swirled and clapped to the rhythm of a lively melody. The dances stimulated the wine-hungry revelers even more.

Mara quickly realized that she should drink and play with the others, especially when she noticed Tharon, sitting next to her, laughing and clapping to the beat. It was quickly picked up by the other members of the Council, followed by the rest of the feasters. Before she knew it, she was laughing and clapping along with the others. The alcohol, though drunk in moderation, quickly hit the head, and the smoke from the numerous incense sticks placed around it cleared the mind and disturbed the senses. The fun was in full swing. More decanters of wine were brought in, making the long-surnamed aristocrats noisy and cheerful.

She remembered the smoky interior of the tavern, where the same buzz was always reigning, and often on the wooden podium there were also musicians playing, playing lively melodies to the delight of a very tipsy crowd.

Mara didn't remember much about the later hours of the party, and it was bragging, because today she had to focus on the chores that awaited her. She had a very hard day ahead of her.

***

Drasan left the camp as far as he could. He wanted to be alone with his thoughts. Unfortunately, it turned out to be a vain hope - he sensed her presence before it materialized by his side.

You don't seem surprised by my presence, she said, smiling slightly. This time the Lady of the Dead took the form of a tall girl with pearly white skin and unusually fair hair.

He threw up his arms.

I'm slowly getting used to it, he said calmly, though her presence made him shiver.

She laughed softly, as if she had heard a good joke.

So have you come to terms with your destiny? She asked, still smiling.

I was forced to do it, he replied grimly.

You will not run away from it, Drasan, you are the Chosen One. The sooner you come to terms with it, the better. Deep down you know you can't win against it. The Lady of the Dead clearly had a blast at his expense.

I belong to you. He sighed in exasperation as he hit the tree, tearing his knuckles to the very bone. For a moment he thoughtlessly studied the wound as it was closing. You took my soul, what else do you want?!

I want you to do what I called you to do. Sent evil back to its place and restored the magic to its equilibrium. She announced bluntly, looking into his eyes.

Drasan flinched, but he met her gaze.

Don't you think it's too much for one being? He asked ironically.

If you don't, you will lose everything that is dear to you, she replied, ignoring the regret in his voice, Bal'zar represents evil in its purest form. If you do not stop him, the lands of Lineland will run with the blood of thousands of innocent people. Even the one you hate with all your heart is starting to believe it.

You mean Dhalia? He asked incredulously. But she is a cruel and ruthless witch! She and this Bal'zar are worth each other.

It is true, admitted the Lady of the Dead. It was like that until recently, but now I felt something in her heart that was missing before.

She has no heart, growled Drasan in frustration, feeling bitterness and pain. She murdered hundreds of innocent people out of revenge, desecrated the body of the woman I believed was my mother, and destroyed my home!

I can see into people's hearts and souls, Drasan, said the creature coldly, who proved far more powerful than both Dalhalia and himself. Trust my judgment as you may find that those you considered enemies will help you when you need it most. Do not judge everyone so hastily and do not be as shortsighted as your master Ashkan.

I cannot forgive Dhalia for what she did to the Sheardonians. They were innocent people, and now their bones are rotting like dogs. He said, not knowing whether to laugh or cry. I swore on what was left of the queen to avenge both her and her helpless subjects. The witch has to pay for it.

The Lady of the Dead did not react with a word or gesture to his words. For a moment she stared northward toward the land that belonged to the brawny Antuanians.

Dark clouds are gathering in the east, she suddenly announced. You don't have much time, my messenger of fate. Your destiny speaks up for you.

You mean war? He asked, although deep down he knew the answer.

The Lady of the Dead looked at him and smiled appreciatively. She didn't answer, just walked over and tightened her cool fingers on his wrist. He grimaced but did not withdraw his hand. She touched the long scar he had made himself during the desperate fight for Neila's life. She leaned down and gently kissed the place, and he felt as if someone had touched him with a hot rod.

Don't forget that you belong to me now.

Drasan knew he could not deny it. He had given up his soul to save Neila from imminent death. He pleaded with the Lady of the Dead for this, and she heard him, but not for nothing. Everything came at a price.

She disappeared as always: dissolving into thin air. And he, resigned and shattered, fell to the ground. He has become a prisoner of his own free will and now cannot back down. If Neila had realized just a little bit how much he had sacrificed for her, she would probably have been shocked. And he did it with joy, because it became his mainstay. His love for her helped him to keep the remnants of his humanity.

As soon as the storm was over, Drasan rose. He knew he couldn't spend the whole night here because they would eventually start looking for him. However, he preferred to push the entire conversation with the Lady of the Dead into the deepest recesses of consciousness. He guessed that if he kept it fresh, Gaenor would find out about his deepest secret. Only he had seen the Lady of the Dead, so he couldn't prove it.

He was walking at an unhurried pace. He knew the way, because the Wolfwood became almost a second home for him. There he spent every free moment. He liked the semi-darkness here and the deep green of the mossy trunks. The silence soothed his weary mind. He needed it to be able to sort things out, although of course it was not an easy task.

Was Dhalia going to turn out to be his ally? After all, she hated him as much as he hated her. If he could, he would have killed her without hesitating.

And yet you hesitated, a little voice whispered deep within his consciousness. You could have killed her, but you didn't.

What if Dhalia also became a mere pawn in the hands of the ruthless Bal'zar? Perhaps he was mistaken in considering her to be the most formidable opponent. After all, she could have killed him too, and many times, but she didn't. Had he misjudged her? Perhaps, like him, she felt deceived and betrayed?

The very thought of it filled him with a wave of doubt. Again, he had no idea what to do. He no longer wanted to be part of this twisted game. He needed the help of someone older and more experienced, someone like Master Ashkan. Only his old mentor gave no sign of life, which worried him seriously. He might still have enlisted the help of the sarcastic Gaenor or Alt'ar. He wondered what they would say if he told them that he had been chatting with the Lady of the Dead for a long time.

They would probably at best consider him mad, and at worst, even less so should he disregard his opinion on any subject. The only person he trusted completely turned out to be Neila. Unfortunately, he had no idea how to explain to her that he was only alive because he had given his soul to the Lady of the Dead for her. He tried to imagine her reaction to the words - to no avail. The mercenary was one of those kinds of people who rarely believed in something they couldn't see with their own eyes.

In reserve, he still had the always smiling and carefree Velwel, who always and willingly shared his thoughts with him. Unfortunately, even a friend has been glum and silent lately. Apparently, his enthusiasm had burned out in the face of the harsh reality of war life.

As the prince finally crawled to the edge of the encampment, he watched the Alt'ar men sitting by the fire, drinking beer and chatting merrily, longingly in his eyes for a moment. He could see neither Neila nor Velwel anywhere. He found it best to lie down and rest somewhere.

He replied with a polite nod of his head for few greetings, sought his bed, and, exhausted, fell on it, letting the darkness wrap itself around him like a warm veil.

***

Yarred Lyall Martius Cordydian - that was his full name, and now he was disgraced. The Cordydians were among the bravest knights. Service in the royal army became his tradition. His grandfather, Martius, also served as captain of the guard, and Yarred was proud to bear his name. It made him feel all the worse knowing that he had failed his father's expectations. And it made him so proud that his son had joined the ranks of the queen's own guard.

"There is no honor greater than serving a righteous ruler," Lyall Cordydian said over and over again. His father had the title of Lord and devoted his entire life to the military. He died in defense of the queen, the death of a true hero. And he failed not only his parents, but also those he cared about - Mara and his unborn child. Even convincing himself that he was acting in good faith did not help him fight his guilt. Drasan was right, he behaved in a manner unworthy of a soldier.

Wrestling with his thoughts, he made his way to the edge of the camp, where a portable hospital was built, for which a thick sheet was stretched between the trees, which is usually thrown over the goods carried on carts so that they would not get wet. Half a dozen beds lay there. Men with varying degrees of injury rested on them. Three of them were missing limbs - Yarred suspected they had been cut off to prevent contamination - others had faces covered with some strange green ointment, and still others looked quite healthy. They were watching him, and their expressions clearly showed that they did not understand what he was doing here. The red-haired woman, who read his thoughts, was walking among the wounded. He shuddered violently and was about to leave when she suddenly lifted her head and looked into his eyes. He froze under that scrutinizing gaze, feeling like a thief caught red-handed. He was not used to the presence of magic.

Suddenly he realized he was staring at her half-exposed breasts, so he shifted his gaze hurriedly to her face. There were flashes of amusement in the unbelievably green eyes - she must have noticed where he was staring, and it didn't bother her at all. After all, she had something to be proud of. It made him remember Mara with her thick copper hair and big light blue eyes. At least she was real. Witches kept their appearance unchanged for hundreds or even thousands of years solely through magic. Their beauty was an illusion intended to deceive men.

However, the smile of the redhead turned out to be completely and disarmingly sincere. She seemed to be really enjoying this meeting. He swallowed nervously as she approached him.

"I bet you'll gladly get rid of those cuts and bruises," she said cheerfully, and before he could protest, she pushed him inside and sat him down on one of the bunks.

"Drasan has outdone himself," she murmured, more to herself than to him, examining his pink-and-purple face and smacking disapprovingly. "Someone should give him a good bang for what he did."

Captain Cordydian was confused at the words.

"Never mind," he said, his voice slightly slurred. "I deserved it. I shouldn't have made a decision before consulting with him." He swallowed nervously,

"How would you do that? With a carrier pigeon?" She asked ironically. "The truth is, his majesty should heave a bit."

Yarred sighed heavily as the witch began to apply a thick coat of some foul ointment to his face, mumbling magic formulas.

"The problem is, he stopped himself," he replied in a grave tone, not meeting the woman's eyes. "If I were not his friend... failure to obey an order from any member of the royal family is considered treason. Drasan had every right to execute the death sentence on me, and he did not. A slap really is the mildest punishment he could ever apply."

"A slap?" The witch repeated, not believing her own ears. "He pounds yours head in and humiliated you in public! He didn't even give you a chance to explain!"

"And he had every right to do so. He is my king and I owe him obedience," the captain patiently explained, feeling compelled to defend Drasan's conduct. "Besides, he's still young and has too much hot blood."

"Eh, you royalists..." the woman muttered irritably. "That doesn't explain it at all."

Yarred was reluctant to continue arguing with this acrimonious and embittered woman. He suspected Drasan had gotten under her skin. He knew that the young prince had always had a soft spot for beautiful women, and they worshiped him. Perhaps, despite her obvious strengths, she had failed to seduce him, which was why he was getting on her nerves? By the way, it is interesting that although he lived like a monk in a stinking cell for over a year, he did not take advantage of this fact.

***

Alt'ar looked at the amber liquid in disgust, then took a long sip from the bottle. He winced and flinched as inferior booze made his throat and tongue burn. The thing turned out to be nasty and damned strong. And he didn't need to think clearly today, he wanted to get drunk. He took another sip and coughed. He felt the warm weight and knew it was Ars resting his great head in his lap. The assassin looked at him slightly blurry and scratched behind his ears. Amber eyes stared at him reproachfully, so he quickly shifted his gaze to the bottle in front of him.

How many years has passed? Sometimes he didn't want to remember it, he had no more than fifteen then. The werewolf's bite sounded like a death sentence. The monster's victims either died in agony or became bloodthirsty beasts themselves. In those days, it seemed practically impossible to survive an attack by such a creature. And what about when her adolescent fell.

He was breathing hard when he was found, and both healers and mages told his broken parents that they would spare him hours of torment by piercing his heart with a silver dagger. His mother did not agree to such a solution, which saved his life. His father, as a beast hunter known throughout the kingdom, did not want anyone to know about his transformation into a werewolf. He preferred to drive him out of the house.

Then everything happened very quickly. The first transformation turned out to be very painful. As a young werewolf, Alt'ar could not control himself and in his fury became deadly to his surroundings. Therefore, during the full moon, he hid in a remote area, where he could not harm anyone. He sat there until the moon waned again and he was a boy again. Only that they are more agile, faster and stronger than their peers. Growing up became a torture for him. Though he was no longer human, he still felt a strong attraction to the opposite sex. Unfortunately, due to his rather poor appearance, he did not have a crowd of admirers.

The first time he succumbed to an animal lust was etched in his memory for good. As a werewolf, he could be a much more active lover than most ordinary men. Due to the fact that the beast came out of him during climax, he avoided women, especially during the full moon.

One mage told him that with strong will and a lot of work, you can control the nature of the wolf. He preferred it because he still didn't have the courage to go out to meet his death. It took years for him to try to control the beast within him. During this time, he was ready to quit several times, and he would probably have done so in the end, if Rodian had not appeared in his life. It was she who explained to him that a mature werewolf does not age, and that his wounds heal three times faster than human wounds. The fact that she was a witch didn't bother him at all, and she didn't seem to mind that she was dealing with a werewolf.

It was Rodian who said that to tame the bloodthirsty beast, he must become a killer. Killing in a more human way was to alleviate its murderous nature. He became one and the best in all Riden. As a result, he now had full control of his second nature.

He looked sadly at the half-empty bottle, cursed, and took another long drink. The strong drink did its job, and Alt'ar could see through a haze. He never drank so much. He was afraid that the influence of alcohol could lead to transformation. But tonight, he made an exception: the fiftieth anniversary of the full moon, during which he became a monster. Ironically, through a crack in the wagon's canvas, a circular moon appeared.

CHAPTER 19

Drasan hissed in pain and looked down at his hand, to his surprise a small piece of glass was stuck in it. He took it out carefully and watched in fascination as the wound immediately healed. In the blink of an eye, the only thing left of it was a trace of blood. The half-dragon calmly returned to tossing the various kinds of scraps that collapsed the throne room. Impatiently, he tossed away some of the broken pieces of furniture and kicked the remains of a marble bust in the corner. Finally, he found what he was looking for. He pulled out a life-size portrait with a cracked frame. Someone had removed all the gold ornaments with a knife, but the painting was intact.

"Did you find what you are looking for?" Neila asked. She was leaning against one of the magnificent columns that supported the high ceiling.

The half-dragon snorted softly and unceremoniously tossed the image to the floor. The frame broke completely, with an ear-piercing crack that echoed through the empty hall. The prince threw away the larger pieces of wood, took out a knife and used it to cut the canvas. To the surprise of the dumbfounded mercenary inside was... a roll of parchment. The Sheardonian unrolled it to glance at the contents, then rolled it back up into a tight roll and tucked it under his coat.

Suddenly he froze motionless...

In the entrance hall, just outside the broken double doors, they heard footsteps. Drasan stood up slowly, trying not to make a noise. He looked at Neila, put his finger to his lips, and began to creep, carefully avoiding the shards of glass. Neila was stunned at first, then slowly followed him. The half-dragon stopped and cursed silently. He gestured for her to stay. She shook her head and reached for the hilt of the sword she carried on her back, like him. He cursed again, and without warning, he pulled her close to him and kissed her.

"Stay here," he asked in a whisper, and walked slowly towards the broken door, this time not looking back.

He found himself in a vast hall. It was dimly here. Luckily for him, the floor was covered with so thick a layer of dust that it effectively muffled his footsteps. He peered cautiously from behind the bend. The top landing was empty, but there must be someone downstairs in the entrance hall. Drasan reached over his left arm and tightened his fingers on the cool hilt of his sword. He extended the blade inch by inch, knowing that even the slightest murmur would echo through the empty hall and betray his presence.

Someone cursed exceptionally vile, and a moment later the half-dragon heard a rumble, reminiscent of only the noise made by a marble statue falling from the pedestal - there were a lot of stone busts in the entrance hall.

"Nothing here, Sachs, someone looted the castle a long time ago," said a man aloud.

Looters! Drasan felt anger. This is his only home, and he had to defend it from filthy robbers like these.

Then the other man, undeniably the leader, spoke up.

"Don't grumble, Fermus, we still have to check the throne room and royal chambers. There is definitely something left for us."

Rage swept through the half-dragon like a tide. He extended the blade fully and walked over to the remnants of the railing. A jump from this height would seem to break both legs. Only Drasan was not human. He leapt onto the railing, balancing on it like an acrobat, then leaned over and jumped down.

He landed with feline grace, right behind their backs. They did not have time to reach for their weapons when, with superhuman speed, he delivered only two blows with his sword. Both men fell dead. The head of one of them dropped off and rolled across the floor, his bulging eyes still expressing boundless astonishment. Drasan wiped the bloody streak from his face with utter indifference. He looked at his handiwork, coldly judging his own accomplishments. The second of the big thugs lay throwing himself in his death torments. Blood was gushing from his severed carotid artery. The prince only made one smooth cut, shortening him by a head.

Walking through the empty hall, he found the third thug guarding the exit. It seemed too simple. The man had his back to him. The prince crept up to him, and before he could react, he cut his throat with one smooth movement. The scavenger coughed, grunted, and froze. The half-dragon gently placed the corpse on the floor and continued. For he was sure he hadn't gotten to the leader yet. Blood dripped from the shining blade as he carried it with the blade pointed to the floor.

And then two strange things happened: he heard a rumbling growl from the corridor on the right, and then something large and fawn jumped, knocking him off his feet. He still managed to cover himself with his arm and it turned out to be lucky. Huge jaws clenched on his forearm like an iron vise, and a hideous crunch was evidence of crushed bones. Drasan screamed and released his sword, which fell with a clang near his head. He grabbed the neck of the enormous beast with his free hand. Briton growled furiously and jerked his great head, and the half-dragon struggled to keep from screaming. In complete silence, he fought the brown and yellow monster that held him in a powerful embrace. His muscles were tense under the short hair.

He felt a mounting panic. Fortunately, the dog was supposed to hold him down until his master arrived.

And then, somewhere behind, from the shadow of one of the columns, a familiar voice spoke:

"Well, well. Who do we have here?" The leader of the looters bent his disgusting pimple face over him. He bared yellowed teeth in a nasty smile, kicked the sword out of Drasan's reach.

"Hey, Sachs. I don't know that face, I guess?" Someone said from behind him. "Isn't that the one, there's a price on his head in Riden? That whole rebel leader?"

The man named Sachs cocked his head as he studied Drasan's face intently. He froze, terrified, and unable to move. He was afraid that if he did, the big dog would snatch his hand away.

"Here you go," he scratched at his beard covered with sparse stubble. "If you are right, we will get more gold for this bird than we would dare to dream."

His deliberations were interrupted by a loud scream, and a moment later a broad-shouldered man flew over the railing. At the top of the marble steps, a struggling couple appeared - a young woman and perhaps twenty feet tall, a neckless man almost three times her width.

Neila swirled with the grace of the ballerina, while the giant raised a great two-handed sword and made a wide swing - it hit the air. The girl made a quick dodge, curled up like an attacking snake and slapped the bully through her stomach. The man roared like a slaughtered bull and pounced on her. Then Neila made an impressive leap. Being in the air, from the scabbard on her thigh, she pulled out a small dagger and stabbed it with a flourish into the giant's thick neck. The man released his sword, grasped the protruding hilt with both hands, and suddenly flew back. There was an unmistakable crunch of a cracking skull as the giant's head hit the edge of one of the marble steps.

Neila stood on the landing, breathing heavily after the fight she fought. At that moment, she seemed more beautiful and more terrible than Drasan would have dared to imagine. Part of her hair escaped from her tight braid and ran in soft waves down her shoulders. And then the magic of that moment faded away, and he felt the cold blade of the knife against his neck.

"Drop it, bitch, because I swear, I'll slit his throat!" Sachs shouted.

For a moment, Drasan wanted to shout for her to leave him and run away. This moment was enough for her to decide. She dropped the sword from her hand, and he saw terror in her wide blue eyes. Then he felt a strong blow to the head and it was dark.

***

Mara winced as she saw the woman kneeling under the landing. Favia Amelia de Raven had to fight a fierce battle with the guards who came to capture her. Her dress was torn and her hair was disheveled. She stared at the queen with eyes full of hatred and contempt. A young dark-haired man was kneeling beside her, and four armed guards stood behind them. Unlike the Countess de Raven, he looked blankly at the floor, feeling ashamed and embarrassed.

The queen rose, and the herald on the left side of the throne unfolded the scroll and began to read:

"Countess Favia Amelia de Raven, you have been charged with treason against the crown and with the murder of Lord Dagorad de Truven and Baron Ultor de Amrall, members of the Council of Elders and High Kings..."

"They were cowards!" Favia de Raven shouted suddenly, her gaze burning madly at Mara. "I did the kingdom a favor by getting rid of this carcass!"

The young queen flinched barely noticeably but kept her face serious. She suspected that Favia would do his best to throw her off the throne. But the attack was not aimed directly at her, but at her advisers - those who had sworn allegiance to her.

Mara nodded, and the herald continued reading the accusations.

"For treason and double murder, you are hereby sentenced to death by beheading. The sentence will be carried out at dawn tomorrow."

Favia gave Maria a hateful look. Meanwhile, the herald unrolled another scroll and began reading the accusation list:

"Lord Avygar de Thrassen, for your complicity..."

"I'm begging you for a grace!" The pale man shouted suddenly, crawling to the landing and grasping the edge of the queen's gown. "I want to take advantage of the law of grace," he repeated, staring pleadingly at the face of his ruler, still like a stone mask.

The Queen raised her eyebrows and looked questioningly at Lord Tharon, who had just recently been appointed First General, on the right. At her signal, he stepped forward and glanced at a couple of prisoners, especially Lord Avigar, his predecessor. Then he transferred them to Mara and nodded.

"Lord Avigar," she said to the man huddled at her feet. "Are you aware of what you have done and plead guilty?"

Lord Avygar nodded eagerly.

"A traitor," Favia hissed, looking at the young lord as if he were something disgusting.

Mara ignored her and, never taking her eyes off Avigar, continued.

"Are you ready to humbly accept the punishment that awaits you?"

"Your Majesty, I'll do anything, anything..." the man muttered, his eyes filling with tears of gratitude.

"In that case, I will spare your life, but I take away your position on the Council and all the privileges associated with your position once and for all."

The punishment might have seemed too lenient for a crime as grave as treason, but Mara wanted to see the look of surprise and disbelief on Favia's face. The countess's eyes blazed with pure hatred. Despite her dirty and torn clothes and the heavy handcuffs tightened around her ankles and wrists, she still looked menacing.

The young queen was delighted that tomorrow this treacherous creature would say goodbye to the world once and for all.

***

The first thing Neila felt when she woke up was a terrible headache. She tried to move and found her arms twisted backwards and tightly bound, as were her legs, and a gag pressed into her mouth. She opened her eyes and saw muddy shoes only inches from her face. At first, she didn't know where she was or what actually happened. Only a moment later did the enlightenment come - she remembered the events of the last night, when she and Drasan had gone to the castle in order to find any valuables. The looters had caught up with them. She managed to hack a few, but they caught Drasan... and threatened to kill him.

A paroxysm of fear shook her. She tried to get up, but it was impossible because the rope was painfully caught in her wrists. She gave up this intention, and instead undertook to roll over to the other side. She did it only the third time. Drasan lay just behind her, just as uncomfortable. He was unconscious, and the rhythmic rise and fall of his chest indicated that he was still alive.

The mercenary breathed a sigh of relief, suddenly cringed as a spasm of vomiting ran through her body, and her head exploded with tremendous pain.

No, it is not possible! She thought in horror. Nobody ever guessed that she had any magical powers. Her talent became unnoticeable, and she was very careful to defend her secret around people like Rodian, Alt'ar, or Drasan. Yet someone sensed it and gave her this nasty, bitter-tasting specific.

She gritted her teeth to keep from crying out in pain and looked again at the half-dragon lying only inches away. There was an extremely nasty bruise on his forehead, and his right hand was wrapped in some dirty rags that had soaked completely with blood.

Why did these thugs leave them alive? After all, they managed to disarm them. What did they discover?

The answer came faster than she had expected. A shoe popped out and a foul odor of stale sweat, and tobacco exploded. The leader of the looters kicked Drasan in the side, leaned over him and screamed loud enough to wake the dead man:

"Wake up, bastard!"

Drasan's eyes flew open so suddenly that even Neila jumped.

The thug smiled, displaying nasty yellow teeth. The mercenary flinched at the sight.

The man uttered a curse and jerked Drasan into a sitting position, leaning him against the stump of a thick oak.

"So, what, Jack-the-lad? You're not so smart without your sword, are you?" He chuckled at his own joke, then turned serious after that. "I have to admit, it's a nice piece of steel, worth at least three hundred Riden crowns. But even it isn't as much worth as you are," here he looked at the young man in the eyes. "They probably already have a noose ready for you in the capital, rebel, but for some reason the king wants you alive. Who knows, maybe before the execution, the executioner will shine in your eyes with red-hot iron. For now, let's have a little chat."

The mercenary heard a thud that the thug's fist had just hit Drasan in the jaw, but the half-dragon made no sound. The menacing twinkle in his eyes showed that he was terribly furious. The prisoner wouldn't want to step in that idiot's shoes when he really made him angry. For she was sure that in a moment the ropes on his body would burn to ashes, and he himself would turn - to the complete surprise of the looters - into a living torch, and then into a giant reptile.

Neila held her breath, waiting for a sudden outburst of confusion... but nothing like this happened. Instead of the expected reaction, the Sheardonian had curled up into a ball, and a violent wave of shivers ran through his body.

***

Drasan lay on the ground for a moment, waiting for his nausea to subside. He didn't understand what happened when he tried to change: his body reacted differently than he expected - his skull exploded in a fierce burst of pain and he was shaken by a spasm of vomiting. There was a distinct bitter taste in his mouth, so he supposed he'd been vomiting earlier. He didn't have to think long about what he had been given. Gaudalum.

The mercenary standing over him was laughing, showing hideous yellow teeth embedded in blackened gums. Drasan felt the nausea return to him at the sight.

"Nothing, mage," he snorted and showed Drasan a small silver box filled with some golden powder. "You probably don't even suspect what it is?" And without waiting for an answer, he explained, "It's a drug made from Gaudalum root, just sprinkle a little on the tongue or rub it on the gums, and you feel like you can win with the whole army alone. But it works the opposite for mages." He laughed again. "They become as weak as children; their magical abilities are blocked." He licked his finger and dipped it in the brown powder, then licked it, squinting his little eyes happily.

Drasan looked at him with deep disgust. He had no idea what the man wanted from him. Unfortunately, now that he had lost not only all his weapons, but also his natural skills, he found himself at the mercy of this villain, who - he was sure of it - would hand him over to the commander of the first patrol of Riden soldiers.

"So, what, why don't we chat?" Sachs smiled and sat down on the ground opposite Drasan - the gaudalum box was closed and tucked into his pocket, his eyes sparkling, and his pupils unnaturally dilated. "I wonder why the king wants you so much alive. I don't believe in all the rebellion you're supposed to lead. There's something behind it, and I'd love to know what it is." His eyes hardened and turned cold. "There is a bad thing in Riden, the king is said to be getting ready to go to war with the rest of the peninsula. But I don't really care what our monarch thinks. On the other hand, you are clearly a splinter in his veil, but you interest me much more. A rebellious mage? Somehow, I don't belive it. No mage could handle an entire infantry squad. A handful of rebels could not be a threat to the royal army. The question is: what is it about you that his majesty is so afraid of you?"

Drasan was silent. He had to admit that the bastard turned out to be smart, though he didn't look at all.

"Ah," Sachs chuckled impatiently. "So you have a spirit of rebellion after all. And I'm not a patient. Let's try it differently, maybe I'll talk to your doll." He smiled broadly at Neila as he spoke, making the girl terrified.

Drasan struggled in vain in his bonds.

"If you touch her, I swear..."

"Oh, you can talk," Sachs blurted out, clapping his hands in mock enthusiasm. "Good, I was starting to worry that you didn't care about this girl's fate." He smiled wickedly, never taking his small glittering eyes off Drasan. "Please, this is your chance to spare her a lot of pain. Just answer my questions."

The half-dragon gave Neila a look that said, "I'm sorry, but I won't let these disgusting animals touch you," and turned to the leader of the looters.

"Okay, I'll tell you what you want to know and you let her go."

Sachs shook his head.

"No way, lover, your sweetheart is coming with us. I have decided to hand you over to the first steward I met," he said in a cold, dispassionate voice.

Drasan decided it would be best to stall and bargain for the girl's life. He didn't care anymore. He had no power over his fate anyway.

"Let her out. Then I'll reveal my identity to you," he said, his head held high as he looked the thug at the little pig eyes.

The mercenary screamed, but he didn't understand because she had a gag pressed into her mouth.

"Ah," said Sachs, completely unaware of what was going on in Drasan's mind. "You're the kind of noble bandits. Unfortunately, I'm not one of them. Because you see... I know very well how to deal with heroes like you. Are you going to talk now, should I ask your woman about it?" His gaze went back to Neila, who, like the half-dragon, was petrified with fear.

"I swear if you touch her..." Drasan growled.

"So what?" The looter asked mockingly, cutting him off in mid-sentence. "I took all your weapons, blocked your magical abilities, and chained you like a ram. The best you can do is sneeze at me, mage. You know it well."

Drasan knew. It didn't help to stifle the cold rage that engulfed him.

Sachs chuckled and nodded once more to the enormous subordinate. There was a click of breaking material. The prince didn't look, but he knew exactly what had just happened - the thug tore Neila's shirt open.

"No!" He shouted, hearing the woman struggle in the big man's embrace, resulting in another crack as the shirt finally tore to pieces.

"You have to try harder," Sachs said coldly. He walked over to the terrified half-naked girl who stopped moving for a moment; her small, pointed breasts were undulating, agitated by rapid breathing, the rag pressed against her mouth muffled a scream.

"Leave her!" Drasan shouted in panic. "I'll tell you anything you want to know!"

The thug laughed, but instead of turning around, in front of the half-dragon he licked his finger and ran it from the girl's neck through her breasts to the navel.

"I promised to tell you everything!" Drasan exclaimed, his voice mixed with cold fury and terror.

Sachs looked at him with drug-gleaming eyes.

"I don't doubt you will," he smiled wickedly. "Before I even became who I am, I served the King as a torture master for many years. I can extract information without touching a person with one finger, because everyone has a weak point and you only need to discover it. And now you will watch, mage," he paused briefly, enjoying the horror rising in the half-dragon's eyes, "as I fuck your woman. And you won't be able to do anything. This haughty bitch needs a good fuck, am I right, boys?"

The five looters chuckled. Absorbed in looking at their leader, Drasan did not notice when they surrounded them in a silent circle. Their eyes sparkled too, like bead-shaped rat eyes.

The mercenary had stopped struggling and was now held upright by the tight ties, tears streaming down her cheeks. It was the first time Drasan had seen her like this. He did not protest when someone brutally stuffed a dirty rag into his mouth, or when a noose was thrown around his neck, tying his head to a thick trunk so that he had to look straight ahead.

At one gesture from Sachs, the big thug released Neila, who collapsed to the ground at his feet. Drasan tried to close his eyes, refusing to look at it. But he couldn't do it, he realized too late that the rag had been soaked with something. His muscles tense again, but the rope held tight.

It's for nothing! This degenerate is about to rape the only woman he loves, and he can't help it.

Sachs grabbed Neila by the hair and began to drag her towards Drasan that he not misses a single detail. When he did so, he began to unbuckle the belt that held his pants... The woman lay still, staring at him with eyes wide open in terror. Meanwhile, the looter had time to take off his pants...

And when Drasan gave up hope for good, there was a whistle and a bolt hit the man in the genital area. The thug howled like a wounded animal and collapsed to the ground, tripping over his own knee-length clothes.

Another bolt hit the eye of the giant standing nearby. This one fell where he stood. The others scattered in panic, because although they looked around, they could not see the mysterious attacker anywhere.

And then a single rider jumped out of the riverside bushes, and though his face was hidden in the shadow of his hood, Drasan recognized him easily. Another bolt hit one of the escaping looters in the center of the back.

Velwel spurred his horse and set off in pursuit of the remaining thugs who had abandoned their mounts and carts loaded with looted belongings and fled from him like scared hares. As he seemed confident of his victory, a huge fawn dog leaped out from under one of the carts. The startled mare reared, and the young man fell off her back and then rolled onto her belly, barely avoiding being trampled. He still had the heavy crossbow in his hands. He hadn't had time to tighten it when the beast caught up with him. There was a crack of breaking material, and then a painful whine as Velwel slammed the crossbow on the great head. The dog backed away, not letting go of the corner of his coat. The young man aimed again, and this time he hit his nose. The dog howled in pain and released its victim. Velwel sprang to his feet, with the skill of a professional put on another bolt, took aim and shot at the head of the animal stunned with pain. Brytan fell dead.

Velwel threw the heavy, bulky weapon aside and ran to Drasan and Neila. At the sight of her naked breasts, he awkwardly looked away, took his tattered cloak off his shoulders and covered the girl with it. Only then did he remove the gag from her mouth and begin sawing the bonds. Still without looking at her, he set about freeing the prince.

When they were both released - and Neila wrapped her cloak around her like a toga - Velwel dared to speak for the first time.

"What exactly happened?" He asked, disbelief in his voice.

Drasan shrugged, rubbing his numb wrists - the shattered bone of his right forearm hadn't healed yet - and looked uncertainly at Neila. The girl continued to avoid his gaze.

There was a dull thump, and the ground trembled under their feet. For some reason, the presence of the black dragon did not surprise anyone.

Gaenor folded his wings and glanced at Drasan. It was enough to look into his eyes and it became known that he was not here by accident.

"You followed us," the half-dragon said in a voice with no resentment.

"And fortunately," Velwel said, unexpectedly defending the dragon. "If it weren't for him, we would have no idea what happened to you. These scums wanted to hand you over to the royal soldiers."

"Correction," Drasan said. "They were going to hand us over to the steward, and from there we would have gone to Washmorth."

Velwel's brown eyes grew even larger. For a moment he moved his mouth silently like a fish taken out of the water.

"But..." he finally blurted out. "How did they capture you... I mean, how could they overpower you... you are... you are..."

"I know who I am!" Drasan exclaimed, rising abruptly. "They used..." he added after a moment and stopped as he heard a groan from somewhere on the side. He looked in that direction and saw Sachs squirming on the ground, still clutching his crotch. A bolt shaft protruded from there. His eyes widened with fear at the sight of the dragon.

Drasan held out his hand, and Velwel gave him his knife without hesitation. The half-dragon walked over to the looter's writhing on the ground, who at the sight of the knife began to curse and scream alternately in fear.

"Shut up and listen!" Growled Drasan, his voice dry and cold. "Immediately with this knife, I'll cut your balls and dick, and you will do nothing..."

Sachs squirmed and screamed horribly but stopped quickly when Drasan pressed the cold blade to his throat.

"Before you interrupted me then, I wanted to promise you a long and slow death, and I always keep my word," he drawled his words slowly, to the horror of not only the man but also his companions, he grabbed his penis and cut it off with one swift movement, then threw away in disgust. The man howled, unsuccessfully trying to stop the bleeding.

Drasan got up, completely ignoring him. He was still holding the bloodied knife in his hand. He walked over to Neila and knelt beside her.

"We have to go." His voice still showed no emotion.

The girl looked at him, then glanced briefly at the knife and suddenly vomited, shaken by violent chills. Drasan embraced her and gently pulled her to his side, but she pulled away.

"No..." she moaned, still trembling all over her body. "Sorry, but I can't..." She doubled over and vomited again.

Drasan sat down nearby and waited patiently for her condition to improve. He felt pain all over his body, too, and violent shivers. The effect of gaudalum slowly faded away.

Gaenor had no intention of waiting for the young man to recover. He made a dull noise, scaring off the birds sitting in the nearby trees. Drasan gave him a gloomy look, but the dragon ignored it.

"Why don't you explain why you allowed this farce to happen?" He asked in a mocking voice.

The Sheardonian sighed.

"In other circumstances, I'd probably tell you to get out, but we've got a little problem with this." He showed him the little silver box taken from Sachs.

Gaenor snorted dismissively.

"You don't mean to tell me they beat you with that box? It's ridiculous."

Drasan shook his head, smiling sarcastically:

"The contents of this box are as dangerous to us as silver is to a werewolf. This is gaudalum, the Ridenians use it as a drug. According to my information, it increases self-confidence and causes hallucinations..." He broke off, seeing Velwel getting up and walking towards them. He stood in front of Drasan, who returned the box to him. The young man opened it and looked surprised.

"Gaudalum is forbidden," he told them after a moment. "What you are holding right now is worth a small fortune. I don't think it could..." He smiled hesitantly, but the smile quickly faded from his lips as he saw the expression on the half-dragon's face.

"Yes, I was going to explain it before I was interrupted" He looked at Velwel, who quickly looked down. "This innocent looking golden powder is able to block your innate magical abilities. Its side effects are sudden waves of nausea and headaches. Fortunately, it works for a relatively short time and after some time the symptoms of taking it disappear forever. Dhalia gave me a really huge dose of this stuff, so I know what I'm saying..." He glanced at Neila, still avoiding his gaze, trying to remove the rest of the vomit from her shoes. He decided it was pointless to ask her now about her magical abilities, so he turned to Gaenor again:

"Due to what happened, there is a change of plans. I will not go to Antua, but to Earden, and I will be accompanied by Neila and Velwel. Alt'ar is in charge." His voice hardened at the end of the sentence. For he wanted no doubts left as to his attitude towards the rebels.

"I saved your life, ungrateful puppy!" The dragon hissed; his yellow eyes narrowed into narrow slits. "I think I deserve a little gratitude! Isn't it, Your Majesty?" he uttered the last sentence with clear mockery.

"I'm grateful, but I also require complete obedience."

Gaenor snorted again, but bowed his head in an unmistakable bow:

"As you wish, Your Majesty," he said, spread his wings and leapt into the air.

Drasan watched him until he was out of sight in the low puffed clouds, then he sat down heavily and hid his face in his hands.

"I'm fed up," he said, to no one in particular. He just had to throw it out, because it was poisoning his thoughts like the worst poison.

"Wars, leadership, that despite having enormous power, I feel powerless more and more often."

Nobody dared to comment on this. Only Neila suddenly put her hand on his shoulder. He looked up to look at her. Her face was pale and her lips trembled as if she were about to cry. He wanted to hug her, cheer her up, but before he could do it, Velwel cleared his throat, wanting to draw attention to himself.

"We can't stay here too long," he told them calmly, and walked away to check the looters' cart.

Drasan watched for a moment as the young assassin rummaged through the looted valuables with grim determination, looking for what might be of use to them. A moment later he focused on Neila. The mercenary did not look at him, she preferred to join Velwel. The prince realized that she was not ready to talk and stood up. He found both his sword and the girl's entire set of weapons without much difficulty.

Neila accepted her property without a word, still stubbornly avoiding his gaze, and when he wanted to open his mouth and ask something, she gave him a painful look.

As the gaudalum action passed, the half-dragon felt his strength returning. The throbbing headache disappeared, but the violent waves of nausea intensified. He wasn't vomiting just because his stomach was empty. It wouldn't be unusual if he hadn't seen the same reaction from Neila a moment ago. The girl seemed to be recovering just like him. She ripped the shirt off some corpse, and because it turned out to be much too broad for it, she pulled on a leather caftan found on a cart, which she could tie tightly, completely hiding the delicate elevations of the breasts under it.

Considering that a few hours ago she had almost been raped - which would have resulted in a permanent injury at best and a death at worst - she had been doing quite well. Drasan watched her with slight anxiety, while admiring her self-control. A weaker woman would probably give in to despair, but not Neila.

***

Neila tried to forget the last few hours, which were a real nightmare for her. Seeing a mixture of fear, helpless anger and guilt in Drasan's eyes turned out to be worse than the prospect of becoming a toy in the hands of these sick degenerates. She knew she was going to be raped, it wouldn't be the first time she had ever been. She couldn't bear the thought of the prince witnessing her humiliation.

How could she meet his eyes now, knowing what he would see in them - guilt and pity? She never wanted to be his weakness. By falling in love with him, she broke the guiding principle of her master: "Never fall in love. Love is the invisible chains that restrict you." She knew it, but she couldn't shake it off.

It made her feel all the worse knowing that he clearly wanted to talk to her about it. The fact that taking gaudalum had revealed her secret did not help her at all. She always tried to do everything to stay away from magic. She hated her, she renounced and never wanted anything to do with her. What was she going to tell him now? "I'm sorry I didn't tell you about this, but it seemed irrelevant to me. I was afraid you would hate me for the harm Dhalia did to you." It sounded way too melodramatic and not her style at all.

She glanced at him and quickly looked away noticing that he was also watching her. She felt her cheeks burn. When was the last time she was blushing?

Drasan started toward her. So much for avoiding conversation. He stopped a few steps away from her, and she saw the question in his eerie eyes. He looked now like a dog that awaits a reprimand for his behavior.

She nodded, letting him come closer. He beamed visibly, and a hint of his old smile appeared on his lips. Neila couldn't help feeling that he was just waiting for the gesture.

"How are you?" He asked, keeping his distance.

She shrugged her shoulders. She was almost raped, how was she supposed to feel?

He was not discouraged by the lack of response from her and continued in the same contrite tone.

"I'm really sorry about this whole thing. I feel responsible for it. I shouldn't have exposed you this way."

Oh no! He really felt guilty! She didn't know what to answer. Once again, she felt awkward. Her heart pounded like a sledgehammer, and the blood rushed in her ears, drowning out all sounds. Why in the name of the gods was his presence influencing her so intensely?!

Before she could control her body, she stuck to his lips, and he kiss her back. She didn't quite understand her reaction, maybe it was the result of shock, or maybe she just missed the tender touch?

She couldn't control her emotions. Fear, determination and desire merged into one. She wanted him. She wanted so desperately that the feeling became a constant torment. If only she could feel his hot body touch again right next to her...

When he pulled her away from him, she wanted to burst into tears. She struggled to contain her emotions and looked into his eyes. She was relieved to see pure desire in them. Thanks to him, his dragon nature was revealed. He was breathing heavily, his hands on her shoulders trembling slightly. Like her, she felt that he was desperately trying to control himself.

Finally, slowly but surely, he shook his head. This did not seem to be the right time or place.

She understood.

CHAPTER 20

The appearance of the black dragon did not impress Altar. Maybe he was used to the presence of the great reptiles by now, or maybe he was just too drunk to surprise him in the slightest. There was a third bottle in front of him. This one was also largely emptied.

Gaenor stopped in front of him in his human form. The cold eyes of the reptile remained unchanged.

The leader of the Assassins' Guild looked up at him and muttered:

"What do you want again?"

The dragon looked at him with a cool, imperious gaze.

"Drasan said to tell you something," he said. "He heads for the Bregan Fortress at dawn."

"To Earden?" Alt'ar asked a bit dumbfounded. The bottle toppled as he sprang to his feet and stumbled backward. For a moment he stared at the amber liquid dripping from the table. "Why is this brat going to Earden?" He asked, trying to focus on the interlocutor, which was a blurry dark spot for him.

"How do I know?" Gaenor's voice was sarcastic for the first time. "I'm just a messenger here. And his highness felt no need to tell me why he was going there."

"But..." the killer began but stopped. Drasan took some action at last. If he succeeds in persuading the superstitious Eardenians to join the war, perhaps they will gain enough military force to repel the attack of Bal'zar's troops.

He sat up, or rather fell backward, staring at the dragon standing in front of him with slightly narrowed eyes. Slowly he realized that as a commander he should get the whole camp on his feet.

He got a terrible headache and started massaging his temples.

For nearly fifty years, he had managed to completely control the beast. And now he could feel his insides tearing at him. It wanted to get out, hunt, feel the taste of fresh blood in its mouth.

For just a moment, a ruby gleam flared in Alt'ar's eyes. It was enough for the dragon standing in front of him to step back, his smile slipping from his face.

Alt'ar laughed hysterically - the monster inside him growled hollowly. He stood up, never taking his hungry eyes from the dragon. The beast must be fed to become docile again.

Gaenor couldn't speak, he just gasped. He stared at the leader of the Assassins' Guild with wide eyes, while the other coldly assessed his chances against the dragon. If he attacked now, he might weaken him before he transforms.

"Enough!" Rodian's voice called his other half. The beast choked up.

The witch stepped between Alt'ar and his would-be victim, Gaenor seized the opportunity and hastily retreated.

"Sit down!" The order sounded.

The killer sat down. Though the beast growled rebelliously, he ignored it and looked into the woman's green eyes. He knew what he was going to hear next. He almost threw himself at the throat of one of the more powerful allies. What if he found out that he was holding Boris's captive?

"Have you lost your mind?" Rodian asked, much more gently than he had expected.

Alt'ar didn't answer. He knew it was a rhetorical question.

"With your one jump you were able to destroy what you have been working on for so long." She sighed loudly and hid her face in her hands. She was silent for a long time, and when she spoke, her voice dropped a few tones lower. "You are the alpha male, natural born leader. You tame the wolf within yourself. Still, there is a risk that..." She hesitated. "...Someday the monster will break the bonds that bind it. That's why you have to accept it." She looked into his eyes. "Altar, you must reveal that you are a werewolf."

The Guild leader was silent, slowly digesting her words. Was he to reveal his true face? How does she imagine it? Humans, dragons, and the rest of Lineland hate werewolves, and their aversion is entirely right. Few of these creatures could control themselves. The clear majority of them murdered without restraint. Werewolves did not listen to anyone unless there was one strong enough to control the actions of the entire pack.

Alt'ar had the strength to lead the pack but preferred to stay away from individuals like him. He killed those he happened to meet without hesitation. He was still looking for what had changed him among them. With no effect.

He has devoted years to perfecting his profession. He constantly honed the acquired skills until he perfected it. Killing was a remedy for his ailment, thanks to which he could tame the beast. Over the years he became a master, and other killers began to gather around him to form the nucleus of the Guild. Despite himself, he named himself their leader.

"Are you listening to me?" Rodian's question brought him back to reality.

Slowly, with an enormous effort of will, he nodded.

"You managed to gather the worst scum around you, now it's time for you to call for help from your people."

For a moment, Alt'ar stared at her in disbelief. Has she lost her mind? Was he to summon individuals similar to him? Creatures so monstrous that all felt only fear and hatred for them?

"You know it's impossible," his voice began to sound like a snarl. The beast woke up again.

"We have no choice, Alt'ar. Our chances are slim, and help is not coming. Even if Drasan would win the favor of this old fool who runs in white robes and makes offerings to his imaginary gods, we won't gain much. Bal'zar's army may be dangerously close to the borders of Antua."

"I can't do that!" Alt'ar roared, rising abruptly, his eyes shining like two rubies. "Don't ask me for it. You have no right to..." He paused, feeling the tension drop from him, though the beast still growled softly.

He sat up and put his face in his hands. He felt her hand on his shoulder, but he shook it off impatiently. He had to react, and there was only one way to do that. He had to release the beast from its cage, let it take over, hunt it. Without looking at Rodian, he began to shed his clothes, and when he stood completely naked in front of her, he took a deep breath and summoned the change.

He felt the pain, gritted his teeth, and surrendered to it completely. He could feel the bones stretching. The skin tingled as it furrowed, and the limbs grew at an accelerated pace. When the transformation was complete, he was still huddled, waiting for his heightened senses to stop bombarding him with hundreds of stimuli. Finally, he straightened and turned to look at the witch. She stared at him with a stony expression on her face.

In spite of everything, he fell on his four legs and, like an arrow, he flew into the forest.

***

Drasan was sitting on the bank of the river, his completely wet shirt clinging to his body like a second skin, emphasizing every muscle. He stood motionless with his back to her, and though she knew he could hear her, he didn't even flinch. She could stand and stare at his perfect musculature, not caring about the fact that his mouth was sure to have a smug smile.

Oh yeah... that damned bastard knew very well how he worked on women, and he could use it in an extremely perfidious way.

"Are you going to stand there and look at my back, or will you just come over and sit next to me?" He asked in a slightly hoarse voice, without even turning around.

His insolence knew no bounds!

Nevertheless, she came over and hugged herself, because the evening had turned out to be cool. He looked at her and instinctively sensing her discomfort, he insolently put his arm around her. She was about to shake them off when suddenly she felt a pleasant warmth wrapping around her like a protective shield. She also felt the distinct musky note of his scent. She took a deep breath of the air saturated with that wonderful scent and felt better at once.

She could sit like this endlessly, feeling his warm body next to her and taking in the view of the starry sky. She looked at him. Drasan was not an ideal one, and he was the curse of her life. And yet, whenever she was right next to him, she couldn't take her eyes off him. A little longer and she would have shed her protective layer by letting him in, and that seemed unthinkable. She could dream of him in her wildest dreams, but she would never ever give him what she clearly wanted. She almost succumbed to him a couple of times! He didn't even know he was very close to achieving his goal.

She glanced at him to make sure he was not looking at her and found that he was staring at the rippled water. He seemed absent, lost in thought, and strangely subdued.

"What's wrong?" She asked, unable to contain herself any longer.

He glanced at her, and there was such a heat in his eyes that she was scared. They were transformed and shone like two green torches.

"You don't even know how beautiful you are and how much you attract me..." he said in an unusual, slightly hoarse voice. His scent grew even more intense and his body hardened. "I can barely control myself when you're around."

Oh, not good, Neila thought and tried to pull away, but he pulled her close to him with a vibrating growl that made her shiver.

"When you're this close, your scent intoxicates me. I can't control myself and I'd love to take your clothes off," he confessed with such a fervor in his voice that she felt almost beautiful.

She had never even dared to dream of getting married, and certainly not someone like that. She was sure that many women would give anything to be in her place now.

She didn't protest as he leaned down and kissed her with such passion that she melted like hot wax. He was skilled at being a perfect lover, and she couldn't help it. She returned the kiss with such desperation that she could feel his hesitation. She surprised him. It only took a moment. Then his tongue resumed exploring her mouth, filling her body with a fire she had never felt before. She groaned, which filled him with wild satisfaction as he kissed her even more passionately, sliding down her neck and slowly caressing every inch of her.

Gods, how he kissed! She did not know that you can work such miracles with your tongue and mouth! It seemed so beautiful it was unreal.

He pulled her to him and sat her on his lap, kissing her with such ferocity and passion that it shook her body over and over with delightful shivers. She didn't protest as he ripped her shirt off her and began to caress her breasts with those hot, rough fingers of his. She just groaned spasmodically, and he kissed her again. She completely lost control of her own body and, before she knew it, began undulating, rubbing against his crotch. She wanted him more and more with each passing moment, and she couldn't control it.

Drasan lay down on the ground, rolled over her in one graceful movement, and with a low, sensual growl, he ran his tongue from the neck to the navel. She shuddered as another thrill of pleasure passed through her. All she could think about was that she was just at the very gates of paradise. Nobody had kissed her like that before or looked at her with such lustful eyes. Why shouldn't she give herself to him? What is keeping her from crossing this invisible barrier?

Another kiss gave her no doubt. She knew well what she wanted, and she wanted him, here and now. There will be no better opportunity to show him that he ignites her like no one else in life. She did what he completely did not expect: she slipped her pants down to the middle of her thighs. He stopped kissing her, but literally just for a moment, only to look at her with such wild lust that she forgot about the rest of the world. Those eyes literally devoured every inch of her bare skin, and there was nothing human left in them. For some reason, it excited her even more.

She didn't even have to say anything, he understood the very language of her body and entered her so smoothly that it took her breath away for a moment. Their movements became perfectly synchronized, and the waves of ecstasy literally tore a scream of pleasure from her throat. The heat she felt turned out to be the most wonderful thing she had ever experienced. She couldn't believe that she had denied herself this pleasure for so long.

As they both climaxed, she dug her nails into his back and ran over them, still kissing him passionately. At the same time, she felt incredibly happy and free, as if she had finally found her place in the world. Afterwards, she fell asleep in his arms, listening to the harmonious beating of their hearts.

***

The red-haired boy looked at his mother with large blue eyes glazed with tears. Lender was less than a year old, but he outgrew most children his age and became much smarter than them. Which was why he knowing all too well what was going on.

Mara smiled at her little son. She wore light cavalry armor consisting of a reinforced leather breastplate, chain mail, bracers and greaves. A sapphire cloak with a coat of arms embroidered in gold thread ran down her shoulders, and a red-stained red horsehair helmet under her arm. She would go off to war at any moment.

"Why can't I go with you?" He asked in a high-pitched but fluid voice.

"Because where I'm going will be too dangerous for you," Mara explained calmly, looking him in the eye. Her son showed a cleverness that was remarkable at his age. He understood everything that was said to him quickly.

Mara saw nothing unusual about this. Lender had a strong gift of clairvoyance. He often woke up screaming at night because he had terrible visions of what was about to happen. It was magic that made him such a large and incredibly gifted child.

Mara ruffled her son's hair and hugged him tightly to her breast.

"What if you don't come back?" The little boy asked in a terrifyingly serious voice.

The queen shuddered but did not release her son from her embrace.

"If I don't come back, you'll have to find strength. Many bad people are waiting for our lives, but we will not give up." She pushed the little boy away and looked at him closely. "Your father would be very proud of you."

"But Dad has left us and will never come back," Lender said seriously, looking at his mother with his large penetrating eyes. "I saw him die, Mom," he whispered in an excited voice.

Mara shuddered violently. Most of Lender's visions turned out to be frighteningly clear, sometimes the boy could sense the danger that threatened his relatives. He had been dreaming of his father's death for some time. The queen did not want to admit the thought. She could not lose him, on the other hand, the little boy was never wrong.

Don't think about it now, she scolded. You have a job to do. The lives of hundreds or even thousands of lives depend on it.

She hugged her son once more, feeling an enormous weight in her heart. He would go to war soon, not knowing if he would come back from it. She needs to become stronger than ever before.

"Be strong," she whispered to her son, pushing him away from her and wiping a lonely tear from his cheek.

"I'll try, Mother," the boy replied seriously.

***

Bruen snorted impatiently, and Yarred leaned over and patted his neck. He had crossed the river with the small reconnaissance unit he had become - they were now in lower Riden. Their task was to check if there was any enemy unit near the forest hideout.

The commander, an up-and-coming Antuanian, led a detachment near Loona's wide-spilled trough. Villages here were few and their inhabitants abandoned their homes and with all their belongings moved back into the country. He saw nothing unusual about it. War hung in the air like storm clouds. Unfortunately, the granaries were empty. Neither did they find a trace of livestock.

"Plague," the giant spat on the ground and turned the great black stallion.

They were just leaving another village. The unfortunate peasants abandoned it in a hurry. Some of the houses were burned down, probably to prevent them from becoming the property of the alleged rebels.

A small squad of ten horsemen turned their mounts back. They were going to leave this place and return to the camp. With a sudden hunch, Yarred didn't even move.

Something was in the air. Why were only those houses on the edge of the village burnt, while those in the central part remained untouched? He opened his mouth to report it when something caught his attention. He stabbed the stallion with his heel and started in that direction. The house from which the suspicious noise was heard, judging by its size, must have belonged to the head of the village council in the past. The doors and shutters were slammed shut.

Bruen croaked a warning moment before the crossbow bolt flew past the captain's ear.

"An ambush!" He exclaimed, jerking the horse up for a run and laying against his neck so that two more bullets flashed past his neck.

The killers followed his example, but not all of them did. Two of them fell off their saddles into the mud, and the frightened horses ran towards the forest. With experience as a commander, Yarred took the initiative right away.

"Disperse!" He shouted, taking air in his lungs. "Surround this house!"

The scouts quickly obeyed his command, positioning themselves around the cottage that belonged to the mayor. The firing stopped for a moment, and a hoarse scream reached them from inside the room. The door burst open and a tall Antuanian stood in the doorway, a Ridenian a head shorter than him, his legs kicking desperately by the neck.

"He's yours, Harmi," he threw the screaming man at the doorstep.

A young Noai'dirian standing near Yarred jumped off his horse and walked over to the snarling man. Judging by the sounds, the giant crushed his larynx. The others watched impassively.

Harmi, like most Noai'dirians, was short, lean, and wiry. He had incredibly large green eyes and shoulder-length dark hair. He looked inconspicuous, but he proved to be as good in combat as his comrades.

He knelt beside the Ridenian and looked him deeply in the eyes. The man could not take his eyes off him in a strange way, and a slight smile was wandering on his lips. Suddenly, something so unexpected happened that everyone flinched. The soldier laughed harshly, convulsions shook his body, and his eyes rolled into his skull. Blood spurted from his mouth and nose, and after a while he was dead.

Harmi shot his commander a worried look:

"It's not good, Boran. This looks like suicide to me," he said, rising from the ground.

The giant scowled at these words.

"So, they all committed it. Before I even touched any of them with my finger, they were already convulsing on the floor. I only managed to get this one before he put it in his mouth," as he spoke, he showed the youngster the object he was clasping in his hand.

The Noai'dirian took it from him and raised it to his eyes - it turned out to be a small ball made of clay or stone. Looking closely at it, he saw the runes burned out.

"Black magic," he hissed, and tossed it away in disgust.

Yarred froze, unable to move, unable to tear his eyes away from the slightly glistening ball rolling across the porch. Suddenly it fell under his horse's hooves. The captain swallowed, but for some reason he slipped off the saddle and picked up the strange object. It turned out to be warm and smooth to the touch, somewhat reminiscent of glass. When he put it on his hand, it turned completely black.

The killers were too busy scouring the area to notice him hiding the ball in a small leather pouch at his belt. He had no idea what he was doing it for, and when he turned around, he saw someone watching him from under a slightly frown. It was the short Noai'dirian Harmi.

The Sheardonian smiled at him, holding up a gold coin.

"It fell out of the poor man's pocket," he explained, realizing how poorly his lie sounded.

The young man looked at him suspiciously for a moment, then he approached him and began a carefree conversation:

"Bal'zar handed each of them one berry of kahm. They are extremely poisonous and grow in the Haerral Mountains. The poison spreads through the body faster than the venom of the Noai'dirian viper and is deadly." He explained, showing him a handful of small green fruits.

"Works immediately after consumption. You can chew it after cutting your tongue or crush it and pour the juice over a fresh wound."

"Why would he kill his own soldiers?" Yarred asked, for whom something like this was beyond his ken.

"So that if they fall into enemy hands, they would not say a word during the torture," Harmi replied seriously. "Anyway, they had a choice, but loyalty to the king won. They would rather die than tell us anything. I really admire their courage."

Yarred suddenly realized that he knew nothing about his companions in the squad. He made his opinion about them mainly based on appearance or accent. This was mainly because the killers could barely tolerate him. It was closely related to the public punishment imposed on him by Drasan. However, not only that.

Captain Cordydian. Or is it the former captain? He himself didn't know what to think, especially since his friend had disappeared before he handed him the Queen's letter. Since Yarred had a great deal of knowledge of the rules by which an army should govern, Alt'ar decided that he would be fit for the recon squad and assigned him there as well.

In just a few days, Yarred Cordydian realized that his friend's only armed support was the strangest jumble he had ever seen. They were mercenaries, killers and ordinary robbers. Most were quite good at sword fighting, others were able to accurately measure with a bow or crossbow. All respected Alt'ar's command.

"Where are you from?" He asked to keep the conversation going. It is worth establishing a thread of understanding with these people.

The man smiled.

"I was born in Noai'dir, but my mother was from Riden." Harmi replied, eyeing the Sheardonian carefully. "I've spent most of my life at sea as a healer. But it's not a very well-paying profession. With my medical knowledge, I have become the perfect killer." He smiled slightly. "I like this life."

Yarred understood too well. He had spent his entire life as a soldier and could do nothing else. Mara didn't get it. How could she understand that he could find no meaning in his existence in anything other than fighting? She was one of the women brought up by the brutal world of the street. He loved her with all his heart, but he couldn't bring himself to stay where it was safe while his friend struggled.

"Come on!" Came the order of their commander, who mounted his horse again. "We're going back to the camp. You need to report what we discovered here as soon as possible."

Yarred fully agreed with him. He pivoted on his heel, walked over to his horse, and climbed effortlessly into the saddle. The Noai'diran stood beside him. He hummed softly to his mount, his hand on his wounded neck. The bleeding stopped.

Yarred looked into the healer's green eyes, who nodded and grinned. The Sheardonian stood there for a moment, completely stunned. Could he have imagined, or had this man really healed his horse's wound in just a few seconds? Suddenly he realized how wrong he was in judging these people. He fought alongside them, not even knowing their names, seeing them only as murderers and convicts. Meanwhile, they turned out to be completely normal: they had families and, like him, they missed them. Why was he never interested in it? How could he become so indifferent to the suffering of others?

This war must end, he thought as he left the place.

***

"Marry me," Drasan whispered. He was lying on his back and Neila was cuddling against his chest. They had been passionately in love all night and he felt that the right moment had come.

The girl raised her head and looked into his eyes.

"If it's a joke, it's in bad taste," she said with her usual acrimoniousness.

"This isn't a joke," he murmured, rolling over and pinning her to the ground with all his weight. "Marry me, Neila. There won't be a better moment. If you wish, I'll renounce my title and become an outlaw wandering in the woods. I'll do anything but be my wife."

He felt her hesitation. He knew he couldn't rush her. For her, the decision became even more difficult than it was for him. He had put her in danger anyway. His instincts told him that she would be safest by his side, so nothing prevented them from becoming a married couple.

"Drasan, I..." She stammered, seeing his expectant gaze. "It's really, really... I don't know what to say."

"Why don't you just say you'll marry me," he offered her timidly, stretching like a cat after an exceptionally long nap. He was also fully aware that her eyes were devouring him.

"Would you please stop?" She rebuked him sharply. "Because of you, I can't concentrate."

He grinned, brushed her lips with a fleeting kiss, and stood up.

"I must hunt, my dearest," he told her with exceptional ease. "Our night together has literally strained me and I'm hungry as a bear."

She scowled at him but said nothing, which he took was a good sign.

He disappeared into the bushes in search of breakfast. He had no trouble finding his clothes, abandoned on the river bank. He got dressed, taking advantage of the invigorating chill of the early spring morning at leisure. Finally, he put on his chain mail and fastened his sword belt, because you never know who he will meet on the way.

He knew Neila needed a moment of solitude right now to calmly think things through. The hunt was an excellent excuse, considering that she would certainly not despise a bit of roast meat on her own.

Fortunately, in the riverside rushes he found a trail left by a large animal. A deer or an elk might have passed that way. In any event, such a large prey would give him the strength he needed to make a proper impression on the Eardenian king. His nose guided him south along the shore, and the smell was quite fresh. The mighty herbivore couldn't have gone far. Drasan might have transformed, but he was not going to waste his energy on it. His victim had no chance against him anyway.

The mere thought of fresh meat, which he would soon be satisfied with, overwhelmed him with a murderous frenzy of hunting. He was guided downstream by an unmistakable instinct. He was close to his target when he suddenly became aware of someone's presence at the edge of his consciousness. Someone was trying to make mental contact with him.

He growled in frustration. It might turn out to be the enemy, but something was telling him that it would simply try to breach the envelope surrounding consciousness. It was like a light brush. Reluctantly, he opened his mind, ready to block.

He was relieved to discover it was only a Rodian.

Drasan... I'm forced to give you Alt'ar's orders. You are to return to the camp immediately.

Order? What is this lousy mongrel thinking? He thought in frustration, knowing Rodian would hear it anyway. Her next words chilled his heart.

Boris escaped, and it looks like someone helped him. Alt'ar is furious. He trusted his guards.

How is it: he escaped? He asked furiously. The werewolf's escape complicated everything. He would certainly come back to Dhalia and tell her everything he had noticed or heard.

I'm as surprised as you are - the witch replied to unspoken thoughts. In any case, you must come back. She added, breaking contact without warning.

Drasan immediately turned on his heel and started back. He forgot about hunting, he forgot about his earlier proposals. How stupid and naive he was to believe that Dhalia's tentacles would not penetrate the famous Assassins' Guild. She had spies everywhere, often very close to the royal court.

Suddenly he stopped, touched by the thought that explained everything. If the witch had spies at the royal courts, perhaps they were also in Sheardon, near Vaya? Someone who knew well not only the queen herself, but also her adopted son. He knew his skills and how to outsmart him. What if it is someone in her immediate vicinity, such as a personal servant or a counselor?

Such a person could tell Dhalia about the prince's weakness for beautiful women or about his nocturnal escapades to the Wolfwood. Maybe he had even seen this vile traitor day after day and suspected nothing? Could anyone hate him that much? Most of the servants and courtiers treated him with the respect due to the heir to the throne. However, not all of them. No one would ever dare to show him open aversion or hostility.

With that thought darting in his head and haunting him, he ran to where he had left Neila. He breathed a sigh of relief when he found her safe and sound. The girl managed to get dressed and watched him with interest.

"We have to go back to the camp." He took a deep breath to calm himself. "Boris escaped, and in fact one of ours helped him with that. If I'm not mistaken, he will quickly sniff me and follow my lead, although he is more likely to report his Lady."

Even if the news shocked her, she did her best not to let it show. It convinced him that she was really tough.

"I understand you want to go now," Neila didn't ask, stating the fact. "What about Velwel?"

The half-dragon felt something icy pour into his stomach. Because of it all, he forgot about Velwel! The young killer left them alone by the river and went off to find something for dinner.

Drasan didn't wait for the fact-finding girl to get to her horse as quickly as he did. For thirty heartbeats he was in the saddle.

"We have to find him before he gets into trouble," he said, and started down the river without saying anything else.

***

Velwel cursed ugly. He had no idea why he chose to follow the river bank. His hunting skills were close to zero. He had to have an excuse to leave Drasan and Neila alone. They needed this lack of supervision to get closer to each other. He knew it. Therefore, he decided to allow his friend to take the appropriate steps.

Now, when it turned out that he had lost his way in the dense forest on the riverbank, he thought quite differently. He couldn't count on friends, and the only option left for him was to be on his way back along the same path he had come here.

Velwel was not entirely sure if it was a good plan. What if he bumps into them at the wrong time? He could spoil what he had planned.

No, he thought firmly. He will give them the time necessary to find a common language.

With that in mind, the young assassin sped his horse up and walked down the narrow muddy path along the shore covered with dense reeds and young willows.

Little did he know that someone was tirelessly following in his footsteps. He could not have known it without having a keen sense of smell or hearing. Unfortunately for him, the chestnut mare turned out to be almost deaf, so she could not warn him of the imminent danger.

The hunter, however, remained patient and calm. He knew that he would not miss the prey.

CHAPTER 21

Bal'zar cursed extremely ugly. And again, and again. He cursed and cursed, and Dhalia and Arano sat next to them, patiently waiting for the show to end. The young king had been furious since morning when a messenger returned, reporting that a reconnaissance detachment sent to the edge of this damned forest had been wiped out to his feet.

It turned out that they were valuable people, whom he manipulated without much problem, like an outstanding puppeteer with puppets. Therefore, their loss caused an attack of unrestrained anger, which resulted in the youth huddled in a pool of blood. The same one who brought the dark news. The ruler literally gutted the unfortunate.

"I'm sick of these stints," he said, sitting down and rubbing his temples. "Why don't we attack them now? We know where they are hiding, we could crush them with one well-aimed blow."

"Because I say so," Arano replied, looking into his brother's glittering eyes. "They only pretend to be weak and clumsy. But there are two dragons and a werewolf among them. The fact that they know the terrain and know where to lure the enemy army also gives them an advantage. If we attacked now, we would lose not only outnumbered but also the element of surprise. We keep Antua in check, we will soon reach the gates of the capital itself. Seizing it shouldn't be a problem, as well as capturing the queen and her bastard. Both can be quite a bargaining chip when we face this band that Drasan is leading with this warlord Alt'ar." Saying this he glanced at Dhalia, trying to provoke her to express her opinion on this subject.

The witch was silent, and no emotions could be read from her face.

Bal'zar growled in frustration. He did not seem pleased, even despite his many minor victories and the seizure of the largest city, which was also the center of commerce. The only thing that made him feel better was Alt'ar's head impaled on a spear. The leader of the Assassins' Guild got on his nerves even more than Drasan. Perhaps because he had escaped the reptile from Washmorth's trap for him. And it was no one else, and he was the one who got Dhalia's best men to be beaten. On top of that, he captured that fetid creature - Boris.

The young king did not care too much about the fate of this vile creature. Dhalia's minion was also annoying him. He was concerned about the lack of word from Alder. He would know if someone killed him. And he sent his best soldier with him.

"We can't hide behind the city walls forever," he said, trying to keep his nerves in check. "It's time to implement the plan, brother. Time to provoke the enemy to take action, offer him a tasty morsel for bait." Out of the corner of his eye he saw Dhalia quiver slightly. He smiled indulgently at the gesture. "I didn't mean you, my dear," he explained. "Your sisters are better for it. Thanks to this, we will kill two birds with one stone. Don't you think brother?" He asked Arano with the question, for in the presence of the witch the older brother would not dare to oppose him. There will be time for a serious conversation.

Dhalia got up. She clearly wanted to say something, he could see it from the look in her eyes, but she gave it up. She just pursed her lips as if to emphasize her unwillingness to participate in any further discussion.

Bal'zar's smile widened. Of course, he knew that the change in her attitude was due to a recent visit to the dungeons with his little brother. And this one, when he wanted to, could become very persuasive.

Arano sighed heavily and leaned back in his chair.

"Dragons, werewolves, it's not really a problem for any of us." He said, running a hand through his hair. "It's just that the time isn't right to reveal our true possibilities to the world. We have to wait, hide in the shadows, and act with caution."

The ruler grunted angrily, more to himself than to any of them.

"And you, my dear?" He finally turned to Dhalia, deciding to tweak her a little more. "Your unique talent can be helpful in making the right decisions."

"I can't predict the outcome of this clash," growled the witch. "Something, or rather someone, is disturbing my visions, and until I find out what the cause is, it would be prudent not to act rashly."

"Is it that overgrown lizard of yours?" Bal'zar asked mockingly. "I guess he won't stick his nose out of the woods. At least until Alt'ar won't let him. I guess the werewolf was a lot better at taming his fiery temper than you."

Dhalia laughed, but it was a laugh without cheer.

"I don't think Drasan is willingly obeying anyone's orders. It's not his style. Sooner, he himself decided that it was better keep his head down." She replied. "As for Alt'ar, I suspect he has enough cunning to understand that he will not win this war by himself. So he will look for allies in Earden."

Bal'zar's reaction to her words was quite different than she had expected.

"Do you think I'm a fool?" He asked, frowning. "You think I haven't looked through your games, witch? I warn you, don't even try to deceive me, or you will pay for it with your life."

He saw the witch huddle under his gaze. Arano must have made it clear to her who she was dealing with. And that was enough to make her lose her unwavering confidence in her usefulness.

Arano stretched slightly and yawned like a well-fed cat.

"I'm tired of your discussions," he announced, standing up and walking over to Bal'zar.

The young ruler knew what his brother would say. He could see it in his eyes.

"You can do better than that," Arano announced. "No dragon or werewolf can match you. So stop throwing yourself like a kid and start thinking. You've got a whole pile of aces up your sleeve, just pull out one of them."

For a moment Bal'zar felt like a scolded schoolboy. Unfortunately, Arano hit the nail on the head. He had many assets his enemies had no idea about. One of them turned out to be the ability to manipulate beings with weaker minds. He could make people flock to him, seeing him as their benefactor or, in extreme cases, even a god.

Arano knew this and, using the phrase "you can do more", tried to gently guide him into the correct line of reasoning. One that will bring them victory. It was a logic worthy of a true ruler. Bal'zar, on the other hand, understood that his brother would say no more and would not show him the right way. He had to make that decision himself. Instead of wading into sterile discussions, he chose to act.

He gestured to one of the members of the personal guard. The youngster turned out to be not much older than him, he probably didn't even have to use the razor yet. He stood before the king and, flapping his heels, made a low bow.

"Your Highness?"

"Emperor," Bal'zar corrected him. Out of the corner of his eye he saw the smile on his older brother's face. It was he who suggested that he use this title now. People must have seen him as a benefactor who would reduce duties and taxes and bring order to the highways.

"Where is the Antuanian army now?" He got straight to the point.

"Our spies report that most of their forces are stationed at Anthil. The queen also sent a large part to the defense of the inhabitants of the surrounding villages and larger settlements," replied the young man with admirable enthusiasm and verve.

Bal'zar chuckled under his breath. People did not need to fear him, he was to become their new savior. Although sometimes he had to introduce some order by hanging a few or even a dozen rebels, the locals praised him to the heavens for his lawfulness anyway.

"Excellent," he said, and without waiting for the traditional bow, he added, "Tell General Wilks that we're going to Anthil at dawn tomorrow."

The youngster snapped his heels and was gone.

The smug Bal'zar sank back into his chair and reached for his goblet of wine. Soon these dark beings will crawl before him just like vermin. He will take back what has always been due to him.

***

Immersed in gloomy thoughts, Velwel did not even hear the rustle of the bushes, and when he turned, it turned out that it was too late. A tall figure that looked like an inhabitant of the abyss emerged from the forest.

The killer cursed.

He recognized the creature even in the gloom between the trees.

Werewolf.

To his horror, the creature lifted its snout upwards and let out a long howl that made its hair stand up on the back of its neck. The chestnut mare neighed and reared up. Surprised, Velwel fell from her back to the ground and rolled onto her stomach. The horse's hooves, maddened with fear, missed her head an inch as it ran away. He stood up, trying to ignore the back pain. He knew he had no chance with a werewolf, but why not to try? He yanked his sword from the scabbard on his back and assumed a trained posture.

The werewolf just laughed, and it was a chilling laugh.

"You think he's coming for you?!" He exclaimed hoarsely, without waiting for an answer, he continued. "I hope so... I don't want him to miss such a show."

Velwel did not have to wonder. He knew who he meant.

Boris smiled, baring his knife-sharp teeth, and walked slowly towards him. As if he didn't have to rush, as if he were sure that no one and nothing would stop him.

Velwel didn't even try to run away. He chose to face his destiny whatever it was. He saw the monster. He saw him begin to walk towards him. He could smell the stench of him. He slowly raised the sword up to his eyes, though he knew it didn't make sense, he was already dead anyway. In his head he heard Alder's voice sounding very realistic: "A werewolf can only be killed with silver."

Where the hell should I get the silver? He thought, his eyes never leaving the monster. He noticed that a nasty scar ran through his hideous face and that he only had one eye. His hands on the hilt began to sweat violently. He knew deep down that the Lady of the Dead herself had looked for him.

Boris stepped in front of him. As a werewolf, he could be proud of his impressive height, and his muscles stood out under his thick black fur.

"Are you afraid?" He asked in a mocking voice and then he himself added: "Stupid question, I feel your fear." He laughed hoarsely, as if he had said it a good joke.

"I'm not afraid of death," Velwel said, looking into one eye, now burning like hell.

The werewolf snarled, baring long fangs all the way to his gums.

Velwel thoughtfully waited for the attack, ready to accept death as befits a warrior. The blow was not from the front as expected. Before he realized that there were two opponents, he received a massive blow to the back of the head. All he felt before he fell to the ground was a sharp pain, and then everything went dark.

***

Since he failed to convince the mercenary to stay in the camp, Drasan decided it would be safer to go with him instead of following him. He did not foresee that her company would turn out to be such a burden. He still had to answer a whole lot of ridiculous questions and repeat over and over again like a mantra that he didn't need any support at all to deal with Boris once and for all.

"What if he hurts you or Velwel?" She asked with the inquisitiveness that is characteristic only of women.

Drasan sighed heavily. He did not have the strength or the patience to explain the same to her a hundredth time, but he had no choice.

"I won't let it happen a second time," he replied. "As for Velwel, we should be glad if he's not dead yet. I know Boris and I know he has no qualms, let alone conscience. I take comfort in the thought that he might have set a trap for me."

There was a salutary silence for a moment, during which he could once again analyze the whole incident. He was sure that Velwel had not gone hunting at all. He wasn't one of the best hunters, and he usually left that plot to him or Alt'ar. He had to disappear just to give him and Neila a moment alone.

As soon as they drove into a vast clearing, he had all the questions that haunted him answered.

There was blood almost everywhere...

Drasan jumped off his horse and, with an expression of deep concentration on his face, began to examine the imprints in the damp soil.

"The blood is fresh, and it seems that it doesn't belong to a human." So Velwel is alive," he informed his companion.

Used to the sight of Neila's gore, she also jumped off the saddle. She knelt where the largest puddle had spilled, looked closely at the broken soil and the traces that looked like footprints of a giant wolf.

"The amount of blood indicates someone has bled a large animal. A deer or a horse. I deduce he dragged them on the ground, leaving a trail," she said in the tone of a seasoned tracker, raising her head to look at him. "It's a kind of crumb mark... for you."

"That is why I will continue on my own," said the prince, coming up to his horse.

Neila didn't even express a word of disagreement. She felt too shocked to say anything. He saw both fear and concern in her eyes. He was also afraid of himself, not for himself, but for Velwel.

"I'll be back," he said, trying to put as much conviction into the word as he could, and without waiting for an answer, he sped his horse away.

He drove slowly, guided by an unmistakable feeling that whatever he decided, he was still in a lost position. Gaenor warned him about Boris. In his opinion, the werewolf had been getting ready for him for a long time. Perhaps he even bent and even broke his Lady's orders.

A bloody trail led between two broad oaks and further into the forest. There it was almost impossible to ride, so the prince left his mount and continued on foot. His sense of smell told him he was close, for Boris' dead stench burning his nostrils overwhelmed all the other smells. Drasan kept walking. He trusted his nose, as well as the fact that Velwel was still alive.

He stopped only at the edge of a small clearing. He guessed the werewolf already smelled him. He had to make sure that, apart from Velwel, they were completely alone. His heart skipped a beat at the sight of his friend. He seemed unconscious and a little scarred, but he was alive.

Drasan crouched behind a massive oak trunk and waited. Like Boris, he was a patient hunter, and he could move noiselessly when needed. He knew that as soon as he moved towards his unconscious friend, the werewolf would also leave his hiding place. Instead of doing what was predicted in advance, he chose to wait for his opponent's first move.

Boris was alone. He too. The question is which of them is more patient.

Dragons are usually surprise predators, so it was not in their nature to hunt from an ambush. That is why Drasan was surprised like a hare trapped in a snare.

The werewolf crept up behind him and attacked him immediately. Drasan didn't even have time to think about drawing his weapon when he received a massive blow to the back of the head. It turned out to be strong enough to knock him to his knees. The next one would probably have stunned him, but he had rolled over the ground in time, beyond the reach of the attacker.

He tried to get up. Boris jumped to him and with an accurate kick to the side he knocked him back to the ground.

Drasan spat the blood out of his mouth and tried to rise again, but his instincts told him that it was not a very good idea.

"Did you really think I would let you trick me?" Asked the werewolf, standing in front of him with his hands on his hips. Even in his human form, he remained terrifying and deadly.

"I didn't think so for a single heartbeat," replied the prince, looking up at the monster's face, contorted by an unnatural grimace. "But I was wondering what your head would look like on the wall of my chamber when I cut it off."

Boris grinned, revealing long fangs.

"You're still haughty," he said. "You are like your mother in the last moments of her life, when she spat in my face," he added with a twinkle in his eye.

The Sheardonian didn't even flinch, despite the pain in the words. He gritted his teeth and forced himself to stare into the glowing red eye.

"Do not insult my mother's memory," he replied, trying to keep his voice under control. Inside, he was mad with rage. "We both know there is only one way it can end. This is between you and me, keep others out of it."

"Is it about that skinny boy?" The werewolf asked, the contempt in his voice making Drasan bristle. "I was going to leave him for dessert after I finished with you." He smiled again.

Drasan thought that this smile must have triggered a panic attack in his victims. But he wasn't one of the victims, not anymore. Boris could predict almost anything except his intentions.

In the blink of an eye he focused and summoned power, building a wall of fire between himself and the werewolf. It gave him a moment to think. He was still far too weak to produce anything beyond that.

The next sound he heard chilled him to the core. It turned out to be a scream, or rather an inhuman howl of a tortured man.

Boris was not alone.

"I'm afraid I don't have the patience to bear your games today," the monster snapped. "I'll give you one last chance, dragon bastard. Stop magic tricks and give up, and maybe I'll spare the boy."

Drasan growled in frustration. He had no choice but to agree to Boris' terms. He only knew one thing: it was impossible to be leaded back into the Dhalia's bloody claws. Not this time.

After a long, tense moment of silence, he lowered the flames just enough to meet Boris's face. The werewolf did not seem surprised by his reaction.

"I will give up if you swear that Velwel will go free," Drasan said.

Boris pretended to think for a moment. After this he replied:

"A tempting offer... There is, however, a tiny detail that I forgot to mention." He smiled wickedly. "A girl."

There was a muffled hiss from deep in the half-dragon's throat at that word.

"You'll get her over my dead body!" He hissed through clenched teeth.

Boris laughed hoarsely.

"I would gladly agree," he said quietly. "Unfortunately, I'm not the master of my own fate," he added, without looking at Drasan.

"Then hand it over to this bitch." The young man growled. The essence of the werewolf's words had yet to be understood. "I'd sooner kill myself than let myself be trapped again."

Little did he know that he had automatically taken a ready-to-fight stance. Flames began to crawl down his body, blood bubbling through his veins. Were it not for Gaudalum, he would have crushed Boris to dust along with all this damned forest.

The werewolf standing opposite was also bent on his legs, a snarl streaming down his throat. Suddenly he changed his mind as his lithe body sagged and his lips stretched into a nasty smile.

"You want a deal?" He asked in Dhalia's voice, glaring at the young man with his red eye. "Here you are. I propose one pure fight without magic. A duel between you and Boris. The rules are simple: the first who collapse, he loses."

"Since when do you fight clean?" Drasan asked.

"I'm just giving you a chance," Dhalia replied with a broad smile that looked gruesome on the servant she controlled. "If you win, you and your comrades will go away free. If you lose, well... Then you will voluntarily put yourself in my hands."

"What if I refuse?" Drasan asked.

Boris's lips parted in a nasty grimace.

"Then you won't even have enough of your companion to bury you."

"Then I have no choice," he replied, knowing he was trapped. Whatever he decides, Velwel will die anyway.

There's always a choice, he heard an insistent whisper. You just must do the right one.

Messenger of fate. This is who I am, he thought bitterly, reaching for his sword.

The piece of steel weighed heavily in his hand as he assumed a learned posture. Fighting has always been his element. Sword in hand, he felt the master of his fate. This time it turned out completely different.

The sword felt suddenly heavy and bulky. He had never felt anything like this before a fight. It's as if everything in him is screaming for him not to.

Meanwhile, Boris had drawn his own blade: black, dull and sinister. A heavy, two-handed sword adapted to overhead blows. The werewolf seemed to use this uncomfortable weapon like a skilled swordsman. He also got into a posture and made a few straight cuts to warm up.

Drasan felt idiotic with a weapon that, although it had always belonged to him, now seemed strange to him. Formerly deadly in his hands, now it felt as crude as a metal bar. He tried to clear his mind, as he always did before the fight, but this time his thoughts were in chaos. Starting the fight in such a state was equal to suicide.

"Ready?" Boris asked, smiling ominously.

What an idiotic question! Of course, he didn't feel ready!

Nevertheless, he swung the sword and lied for the first time before the duel:

"Ready."

It is the worst possible move, but he had no choice.

Finally, they faced each other, armed with blades. Only one could have come out of the clash alive, and they both knew it well. They began circling each other similarly to the tigers preparing to fight. Drasan moved slowly, dancing steps, foot by foot. On the other side, Boris was doing the same. Simultaneously, they raised their swords and leapt towards each other. The steel clicked loudly.

The prince did not feel himself. He barely parried the slash of that great sword. If it weren't for that, Boris would have cut him in half. He jumped back, trying to catch the old rhythm again, but the werewolf wasn't going to let him. He leapt at it, raising his sword high above his head. The young man sparred with great difficulty. The force of the blow nearly knocked him to his knees.

Drasan pushed his opponent away and whirled in a pirouette. This play turned out to be a mistake. The werewolf was quick and clever once again. He wriggled in dodging, so that the blow intended to chop off both of his legs hit the air. The unnerved prince staggered, which was enough for his opponent to deliver a nasty stab that pierced his right shoulder.

The half-dragon roared in rage and pain. Such mistakes were made in the distant past, when he fought his master with wooden sticks and the only injuries, he suffered were abrasions and bruises. Now he could only fight with his left hand. The result of the fight was a foregone conclusion.

For the first time he felt fear. If he loses - and this is more than certain - he will have to sacrifice Velwel's life or keep the contract and hand himself over to a witch. Both options seemed equally terrifying. But he couldn't give up so easily. Not if he is able to stand on his feet and raise his sword.

Boris smiled triumphantly.

"Relax, we'll finish quickly," he said.

Drasan roared in rage. Suddenly his movements lost fluidity, and the wound in his arm was slowly healing, though he still hadn't fully recovered. The monster attacked with an easy to predict roundhouse blow. The half-dragon dodged and counterattacked, but his opponent parried easily. He turned out to be too fast for him. He wanted to end this tiring fight as soon as possible and knew how. He hoped that the young man would lose his concentration for a moment, which would mean his failure.

The prince dodged again, barely avoiding the murderous blade. He jumped back and attacked once more, aiming for the legs. He wanted to end this before he completely lost his strength. So far, he hasn't even managed to scratch the werewolf. This attack has become an act of desperation. And he hit the air again. Boris did a back flip and landed in a half-squat.

The half-dragon snarled, baring his teeth.

His right arm was tugging unpleasantly. He had to do something, or he would lose. Then came the solution. Boris only had one eye, which greatly restricted his field of vision. To win, it was necessary to use this fact to your advantage.

The werewolf had the advantage of speed and strength. Drasan had only one chance to hit the spot where he would win.

With that in mind, he straightened up and resumed his posture, ignoring the pain in his arm. Boris jumped at him right away. They exchanged a few blows, the last one nearly crushing the prince's left shoulder. And then the young man spun, the blade whistled through the air, slashing his opponent's arm. The monster staggered. Though accelerated recovery had begun, the wound weakened him considerably.

And this very moment was enough for Drasan to deliver the final blow. This time he was aiming for the legs. The blade whistled ominously, slashing his left thigh. A fountain of blood spurted out, and the werewolf's knees buckled.

The fight was over.

Drasan brought the blood-dripping blade to the throat of his sworn enemy. Many years of hatred for this monster pulsed in his veins. As Boris stuck his one eye on him, Boris hesitated.

"Come on!" The werewolf encouraged him. "Finish it. My life is one great torment anyway."

The resignation in his voice made the prince regret him involuntarily. Boris did not enjoy freedom, his life belonged to Dhalia. He had no free will.

Staring at his mortal enemy, Drasan hesitated once again. He knew Boris was a beast and should be killed, but somehow, he couldn't bring himself to do it. Despite his gut burning with hatred, he was unable to deliver the final blow to this shred of living thing.

"End of the fight," he drawled through gritted teeth.

Boris didn't answer. I think he has come to terms with his fate.

Drasan lowered his sword.

"Get out!" He growled at him.

Boris looked at the prince incredulously.

"I don't want your pity," he snapped back, but his eyes were expressing otherwise. He seemed utterly amazed at the half-dragon's behavior.

"You won't get a second chance," the Sheardonian replied icily, looking away from the face of his hated enemy. The words of the Lady of the Dead rang in his ears: "You may find that those you thought where enemies will help you when you need them most."

I hope you wouldn't be wrong, he thought, wiping the sword from the blood and putting it into its scabbard.

The werewolf was still on his knees in the mud, his eyes downcast.

Suddenly they looked up simultaneously as a terrifying scream of pain broke the silence, followed immediately by a bloodcurdling howl.

"What are you waiting for? Your friend doesn't have much time," Boris growled, looking at Drasan. "I'm afraid Berg won't show him even a hint of pity. He is not controlled by anyone, and he is much stronger than I'm."

There was no need to tell the Sheardonian twice. He ran towards the place where the bloody call had come from. He prayed silently to all possible deities that it would not be too late. He got there just in time to see the huge gray werewolf bend over the hard-breathing Velwel, getting ready to deliver the final blow.

This time he did not hesitate for a moment. He jumped on the beast, intending to sink the sword into its heart. The werewolf turned towards him and grinned bloody fangs, but instead of facing him, he simply turned and fled into the forest thicket.

Drasan approached his mortally wounded friend and felt his heart sink in him.

The young man's chest was torn apart, his legs and hands protruded at a strange angle like a puppet whose strings were suddenly cut off.

For a moment he just stared at Velwell, he felt completely powerless. He was slowly realizing the terrible truth.

Even if his friend survives, he will become a bloodthirsty beast - a werewolf.

CHAPTER 22

Dusk was falling, casting deep shadows across the small clearing. Neila was sitting on a fallen log, staring blankly into space. She thought about Drasan's proposal, weighing the pros and cons. Marriage in the light of the current events seemed absurd to her. Once, having a choice between the old bastard and the young heir to the throne, she would not hesitate a moment, but now...

If she marries, she will lose what she has fought for so long - freedom. She will be his wife, and hence, queen. The very thought made her shiver. Is he able to abandon the life of a mercenary in favor of a mass of duties, including bearing children?...

No, she thought, shaking her head violently to dismiss the thought. She could remain his friend, even his lover, but not the goddamn wife! What was he thinking about making her such an idiotic offer?! Hadn't she made it clear to him that she wasn't interested in a permanent relationship?

Frustrated, she picked up one of the rocks swarming on the shore and threw it into the foaming depths. She loved him. To a hundred devils! She loved madly! Even now, his disappointed gaze haunted her. Will he forgive her if she refuses?

She was so focused on her own thoughts that she barely noticed the sudden movement in the nearby brush. As a result, she reacted only when the head, shoulders and the rest of the body of the great werewolf emerged from among the thickets. The beast stood on its hind legs and looked at it through ruby eyes. Fortunately, she had already seen Alt'ar in his shaggy form, so she was not moved by the sight.

Behind his leader, his faithful aides, including Rodian, emerged from the forest, who did not fail to send the girl a contemptuous look.

"Alt'ar asks where is Drasan?" the witch acted as an interpreter.

"He went looking for Velwel," Neila replied with a shrug. She knew this disrespectful gesture would not convince the Guild leader.

She was right.

Alt'ar growled, baring frighteningly long fangs.

"He asks why you are lying," the newcomer translated, unable to resist an ironic half-smile. "He clearly smells the two werewolves mixed with the scent of blood and fear."

Neila had no intention of bending her neck under Alt'ar's imperious gaze. She felt the werewolf tremble with suppressed anger, and knew he was pulling the string. Even so, she continued to stare into the blazing eyes.

"You're right," she said confidently. "I lied to you for your own good, Altar. Drasan is gone long enough. He rode to rescue Velwel from Boris' hands and..." suddenly she broke off, realizing what she had disregarded earlier. Two werewolves! If this turns out to be true, her lover has fallen into the trap set for him.

Her heart pounding in her chest, she glanced at Rodian.

"Drasan knew nothing of the other werewolf," she whispered in horror.

Alt'ar reacted faster than she expected. He dropped back to his paws and set off down the narrow path where the prince had disappeared.

***

The defeated Drasan sat down next to his friend, whose breath now like a hoarse rattle. He prayed to all possible deities that Velwel would turn out to be quite strong and survive. He himself did everything in his power. He treated the more serious wounds and stopped the bleeding. However, he was not a healer or a magician, and he could not estimate the young man's chances. He felt himself approaching imminent death with each frighteningly shallow breath.

Boris is gone. He couldn't find him where he left him, so it was probably a long way away. The prince returned for the horse and, having saddled him, let him loose so that he could graze calmly.

Velwel remained unconscious but was still alive. Though Drasan had wondered many times whether he should shorten his torment and cut his throat. He didn't do it just because of the familiarity he had with this talkative and somewhat irritating young man. Shit, he liked him and would have given a lot to hear his chatter again!

Gaenor was right, I'm getting too soft, he thought, remembering his hesitation at the moment he could cut one of his sworn enemies by a head. Until now, he had been fighting over it with his own thoughts.

Why didn't he do that? Boris had become a twisted monster that he would murder taking pleasure in it, undoubtedly deserving to die. Drasan saw something in his eye that prompted him to lower his sword. It is not fear or even a sense of failure, but regret. The werewolf wanted death. Deep down, he would have greeted it with relief. For him, it was an act of mercy.

For a moment he couldn't believe it. He hated Boris from the first day he saw him. Now he knew that he had never even tried to understand him. The werewolf lived the life of a slave. He was subject to someone else's whims no matter what he wanted. He hated and despised Dhalia, but he could not resist her will.

Drasan knew what that meant. He also did not choose his own fate. He was pushed down this path against his will. Like Boris, he was a pawn in the game of power.

The soft sound of huge paws steadily hitting the ground snapped him out of his reverie. Instinctively, he reached for his sword. He put it down as he sensed a familiar presence. He smiled involuntarily at the sight of a werewolf with almost white fur.

Alt'ar whined softly. There was a question in that longing note that Drasan could not answer.

The werewolf approached Velwel, who was lying motionless, and nudged him with his big nose, growled, baring long fangs, and the hair on his neck bristled.

How? There was sincere regret in the werewolf's thoughts.

Boris had a helper, Drasan replied in a hollow dull voice. They both set a trap for me. When I was fighting Dhalia's servant, the latter tortured Velwel.

To his surprise, the werewolf sat on its hind legs, lifted its muzzle, and let out a long, painful howl. It turned out to be a heart-shredding sound, for it expressed what words could not.

Drasan fell to his knees as if someone had put a heavy burden on his shoulders. Velwel did not deserve death, certainly not.

Will he survive? He asked, looking into the werewolf's ruby eyes.

I don't know, Alt'ar replied. Transformation is a long, violent, and excruciatingly painful process. If he turned out to be strong enough, he might survive. But not for free.

The words bristled Drasan's neck hair. He knew what it meant before the Guild leader had formulated his thoughts.

Young werewolves are aggressive and dangerous, and the first full moon triggers an unmanageable murderous tendency in them. Even if the boy survives, there is a high risk that I will have to kill him myself.

The half-dragon understood how heavy it had become for Alt'ar to utter these words. For him, Velwel also turned out to be more than just a companion in arms. He liked him as much as everyone else. And now that his fate was at stake, just as the prince couldn't bear the thought of never seeing the wicked gleam in his brown eyes again.

***

When Mara entered the room, all conversation ceased. Behind the cluttered desk, Tharon looked up at her over the wire glasses he was wearing.

"Things are complicated, Your Majesty," he spoke in complete silence. "Our spies report that Bal'zar's army has been sighted within two days of the city. They march very fast. I believe they will be here soon. I'm afraid we need to evacuate both you and Prince Lender to safety place."

Mara tried her best to keep the stone mask on her face, though her heart skipped a beat. Lender's visions were right. The enemy army met no resistance, because the people of Antua welcomed the usurper as their benefactor. Most of the Antuanian infantry had been literally crushed under the onslaught of tens of thousands of Bal'zar's men, who were only the front of his army. How were they going to fight such a power?

"They used the teleport?" General Niko de Valser asked quietly. A stern man with a serious, scarred face, black eyes, and typical Antuan red hair marked with numerous streaks of gray. He wore a short goatee, now tugged nervously at it.

Tharon shook his head slowly.

"They took all the major cities. They took Tarssen in just one night, swallowed up a few smaller settlements for dessert, and For Un gave up on its own. If they keep up the pace, they'll be here in less than two days." He looked at the young queen, rapidly pale. "The threat is real, Your Majesty. We have to reckon with the fact that surrendering the city is the best solution. If the reports are true, then Bal'zar does not harm the population if they themselves give up." Saying this, he tossed a few scrolls, revealing a map of Lineland in the process. He tapped his finger on the spot he had talked about earlier. He pointed them out to the others. "According to reports, the forehead of the army was here when they suddenly disappeared into thin air," he said.

Lord Korav bent so low that the tip of his hooked nose almost touched the map.

"They must have very powerful mages," he said quietly. "This puts us in a difficult position, Your Majesty. Even I'm not strong enough to face such power." He said to the queen.

The latter, in turn, took a seat at the desk and looked at her tallest mage.

"Lender saw it," she said calmly, trying to hide her emotions. "In one of his visions there appeared the disappearing army and four sisters - witches..."

"It's impossible!" Count Rokor, Ultor's successor, broke in her word. His round face, pendulous cheeks, flushed with indignation. "All the witches have been killed. It was also forbidden to train magically gifted girls. All kingdoms unanimously supported..."

"You are forgetting yourself, Count!" General Niko Valser growled softly. "You are speaking to the queen."

"Thank you, Niko," Mara said. "We've all heard about what happened to Rosher, and it was because of the witch. Doesn't that prove that there are still women of great magical talent in Lineland? Looks like we're going to have another battle with them." She paused and looked at the faces of the crowd, turned back to Niko Valser. "General?"

"Yes, Your Majesty?"

"Prepare our troops for the march. I will meet the usurper who is invading our lands." She announced in an imperative tone.

"But Your Majesty..." Tharon dared to protest. He was staring at the queen from under a frown. "Our forces are only 2,000 armed men, while

Lord Riden has tens of thousands behind him. In addition to, of course, praiseworthy courage, I'm asking you to be reasonable..."

Mara gave him a fierce look, and he fell silent.

"I'm reasonable, Advisor," she said seriously, looking at the commander of the troops. "Will the dragon balance our forces?" She asked.

"Dragon?" Valser repeated, stunned, as if he didn't believe what he was hearing.

"Yes, General. Dragon," replied the queen. "And if we're lucky, maybe even two." Her eyes turned to Count Rokor. "I expect you to take over my responsibilities when I go to war. I also mean my son's safety."

"I'll do my job," the man replied calmly.

Niko Valser opened his mouth to speak, but the queen did not let him speak.

"It was an order, General," she said coldly. "I advise you to do it as soon as possible."

The general closed his mouth and bowed low.

"As you wish, Your Majesty," he replied, and hurriedly left the library, chain mail jingling.

As soon as the door slammed behind him, Mara fluttered and looked at the members of the Council of Elders.

"We have a lot to do and an awful little time," she said, a little calmer. "So, I hope that you will help me." She sighed deeply. Suddenly she felt much older. "What I said in front of General Vasler is not all," she said slowly. "Lender saw the course of the battle, which could soon happen... It turned out to be a defeat, blood and dead bodies everywhere..." She broke off and looked at Lord Korav pleadingly. "Is it really impossible to stop these visions? It's still just a baby."

The mage shook his head.

"I'm afraid not, Your Majesty. We still know little about his gift. Some visions are hazy and incomplete, others very clear."

Like the one where he'd seen his father die, Mara thought, but she didn't dare to say it aloud. She preferred to keep it to herself, because if she did not tell anyone about it, she believed that she would be able to save him.

"Leave it alone," she said, straightening herself with dignity and pushing aside her emotions. "It's time to discuss an issue related to the coming battle."

***

Dhalia narrowed her eyes until they formed two narrow slits. Her lips were pursed, but her expression was unreadable. What the Antuan spies reported did not bode well for her plans. The red-haired brat became the new queen, and her bastard turned out to be an incredibly gifted clairvoyant. She might have cut this whore's throat when she had the chance.

Of course, now that Bal'zar had pushed her away from the current affairs, explaining that he wanted her to focus primarily on the future, she had no choice. She had to do everything to get to Drasan somehow. She had been doing poorly so far. Fortunately, she knew his greatest weakness. She knew that the great Chosen One had shown one of the worst human weaknesses - he fell in love.

He voluntarily placed a noose around his neck, it was enough to tighten it skillfully. With this girl, you can make him do anything, because love drowns out the voice of reason.

She had to act carefully. Arano couldn't find out about her plans.

***

The sight of the mutilated body was unforgettable. Neila could hardly find any resemblance to old Velwel. The one she knew. Well, she even got to like it! Drasan and Alt'ar took turns doing a sort of watch with him, communicating with gloomy looks and talking to no one.

From what she heard the whispers repeated surreptitiously among the killers, today will be the "solstice". Whatever that meant, it didn't sound very good. The mere fact that Velwel would live and turn into a bloodthirsty beast did not impress her. And so she sat in the company of monsters straight from the legends, one more made no difference.

So, what the hell were those gloomy expressions and stealthy exchanged glances supposed to mean? After all, they should be glad that the boy is alive, and his wounds are slowly, but slowly healing. And if the price for that was to run around the full moon in fur and hunt deer, what harm was it?

Drasan's silence drove her mad. Moreover, he acted as if he did not notice her.

Now, too, he was sitting in a sort of half-trance, staring unseeingly straight ahead. He had once explained to her that this condition worked for him like a nap. It regenerates your strength and allows you to build up a reserve of energy or something like that.

Something happened during the night that got everyone on their feet.

Velwel regained consciousness.

***

A light breeze gently rippled the surface of the lake, creating small waves on it. Even so, the lone rider waited intently, watching the horizon. For the first rays of the rising sun were beginning to shine. As usual, he was accompanied by a fawn alsatian, and his master was closely watching the plain ahead. It was almost entirely covered with a carpet of the first spring flowers, the name of which he did not remember.

Waiting did not give him pleasure, but he showed patience in pursuing the desired goal. At last he saw what he was looking for. The three witches were headed straight to the scarlet pavilion at the heart of the camp, with a large flag with the symbol of Riden on top of it. He recognized them by the strong magical aura they exuded around him.

Finally, he thought, pleased. Shirza did not share his satisfaction. The dog stood as taut as a string, its hair bristled, and its mouth furrowed, and a rumbling growl was coming from its throat.

One of the three sisters stepped forward, said a few words, and the growl stopped. The great wolfhound, who had so far listened only to Bal'zar, moved towards the black-haired woman, sweeping the ground with its low-lowered tail and hugging its ears. The witch bent to gently ruffle the hair on the dog's neck, straightened, her gaze went to the lone rider.

Bal'zar nudged the great war stallion with his heels and started down the slope to meet the three witches. The highest of them appeared in front of the black-haired, still scratching wolfhound. He fawned on her all the time. It seemed that the slender blonde elf was the informal leader of the group.

"Hello." She made a deep ceremonial bow. "I'm Saruviel, and these are Mariv and Anar," she introduced herself and her two companions, who also bowed.

"Hello," Bal'zar replied, dismounting from his horse. "As you probably know, until recently I was the ruler of Riden, but, as you can see, most of Antua belongs to me," He smiled slightly. "So, you can call me Emperor."

"Of course, Lord," Saruviel replied with a smile that did not cover her eyes. "With great joy we will give ourselves under your command." She added flatteringly.

Bal'zar smiled, carefully studying the expression on the elf's face. He knew she shouldn't be trusted. She resembled a poisonous viper. She tempted with a nice sight to finally sink her teeth into the ankle of an unsuspecting victim. He liked her, so he might keep her alive, and at the same time pass the death sentence on the other two.

He went with them to the great pavilion, where his headquarters was located. They passed the guards and entered the spacious tent. Even if they felt surprised at the sight of the splendor inside, they did not show it. When Dhalia saw the guests, she got up from her seat and with a broad gesture invited them inside. Saruviel was the first to come over to her and kissed both cheeks. The same movement was repeated by the other women. It did not escape the young king's remarks that this cordiality was only pretended. In fact, witches were not very fond of each other.

After this artificial greeting, it was Saruviel who spoke first:

"We bring you a gift, sister. On the way, we managed to neutralize one of Drasan's allies," saying that, the elf handed her a silk sack.

Dhalia received it with a frown, but as she opened it, her expression changed abruptly. She turned pale, but somehow managed not to pass out. Bal'zar over her shoulder saw why. The little sack contained a perfectly preserved heart. Judging by its size and light blue color, it belonged to a unicorn.

The macabre gift made him feel that Saruviel was an enemy not to be taken lightly. It took great courage and just as great a lack of scruples to cut out a unicorn's heart.

Dhalia forced a kind of crooked half-smile, carefully putting down the sack, and looked into the cold eyes of the elf smiling contemptuously. For a moment they looked at each other like two enraged cats.

Their silent struggle was interrupted by Mariv. She walked over to Bal'zar, seductively twirling her hips.

Her movements resembled the grace of a wild cat. The woman, still smiling in a formidable way, threw another "gift" at her feet. Only then did he realize that the crowd was in fact a huddled figure. Mariv stretched out her hand, materialized a fang-bladed dagger in it, and in one fluid movement she cut the bondage of the captive.

To the surprise of all those present, the captive turned out to be an elf!

A smiling Mariv crouched down beside the sobbing prisoner. She grabbed the hair on his neck and tilted his head back, exposing his throat. Without taking her defiant glare from Dhalia, she slaughtered the unfortunate man with one swift movement. Blood spilled onto the hand-knotted rug that covered the floor. The witch looked at her handiwork, brought the bloody blade to her mouth and licked the blood off it.

Bal'zar was so fascinated by this violence and ferocity that he could not take his eyes off her lithe body. It reminded him of a childhood incident when he saw an overseas snake charmer. He displayed his extraordinary talent at the royal court. He saw the man make the big sand cobra dance with only his movements. Reptile could not take his eyes off him. Mariv undoubtedly had something similarly unusual about her, some kind of magnetism that made the animals irresistible to her.

Well, maybe not only animals - he added in mind.

Mariv stood up and tossed her hair onto her back with one movement of her head. She was still looking into Dhalia's eyes, and she was still holding the gaze.

"Here's what you should do with hybrids who betray their own race," Saruviel summed up the whole incident in a voice so cold that it shivered.

Dhalia nodded, walked around the corpse so as not to stain her spotlessly clean shoes with the blood. Bal'zar knew he was only faking it. Not that she worried about the death of some unknown garbage. The look in her eyes as Mariv slaughtered this unfortunate man made it clear that she mentally saw someone else entirely in his place.

It was then that he was sure that Saruviel was the originator of the whole performance. And again, involuntarily, he felt admiration for the elf. She turned out to be a cold bitch, that's a fact. Unlike Dhalia, she had neither scruples nor conscience. She will be useful.

CHAPTER 23

The sudden commotion in their camp by no means made any impression on Yarred. They previously moved twice and are now very close to what remains of Sheardon's once-great ramparts. Captain Cordydian looked at the ruined city in pain. It was there that he grew up, there he swore to defend the city and its inhabitants to the last drop of blood, to break this promise only a week later thanks to Drasan. He disappointed him and betrayed the queen. He abandoned everything for his arrogant and self-righteous friend, who in return left him in the middle of nowhere.

Gaenor was in command in the absence of Drasan and Alt'ar. The killers didn't particularly like him, but he wasn't going to care. He walked around the camp as puffy as a peacock at mating season and looked down on everyone, which was undoubtedly aided by his height. For he had the size of two large men. Yarred, like the others, simply tried to ignore him, hoping the dragon would ignore him as well as the others.

Vain hopes.

Complaining about Drasan turned out to be Gaenor's favorite pastime. He did not miss any occasion to criticize any of the decisions of his younger brother. And Yarred, as one of his closest friends, was for him a treasury of knowledge about the prince. The dragon ostentatiously ignored the fact that the captain owed allegiance to the heir to the throne and summoned him to him as often as his leadership duties permitted. Because nothing interesting happened after Boris escaped, the reptile had an excess of free time.

So, this hustle and bustle became like salvation for Cordydian. He was glad that he would not be forced to tell stories about his ruler's turbulent youth.

"What's happening?" He asked the young Ridenian who was just passing by him.

"We're moving deeper into the woods," replied the boy, flushed with excitement. "Our scouts report that the head of Bal'zar's army is close to the capital of Antua. It is said that the remnants of the Antuan army are running towards us."

"What?!" The captain felt completely surprised. For a moment he prayed to all possible deities that this would not become true. Antua couldn't fall that fast.

The boy just shrugged.

"So, I was told," he said, joining the others who set out to break the camp.

Yarred understood that Wolfwood was like an impregnable fortress to these people. Especially that the trees grew so densely that it was impossible to drive between them with the entire army.

Ever since he joined the Liberators, as those people called themselves, he had not had the opportunity to eat properly, much less sleep, and he could dream of bathing in a tub full of hot water. As a result, his usually neatly trimmed and combed hair resembled a messy haystack, and his normally clean-shaven cheeks had clumps of sparse stubble, unlike Drasan's beard.

Now, with news of the great Riden's army sliding through the kingdom where he had left his loved ones, he would not have been able to sleep even in the king's bed. Not when they were in mortal danger. He would never forgive himself if his loyalty to the prince had been lost. He still had the sealed scroll with him, certain that it was for Drasan's eyes only. To whom else would Vaya have something important to pass on to send a messenger on the way while the city was under siege and the kingdom was ravaged by bloodthirsty Doars? So far, he hasn't had a chance to deliver a message to his friend, and it seemed unlikely that he would be able to do so any time soon.

In fact, nothing prevented Yarred from moving towards Hearen. He had to get Mara and his baby from there. The city was a day and a half away, so if he hurried, he would be able to go there and back before Drasan.

With that in mind, without telling anyone, he walked over to the horse. Bruen greeted him with a soft snort, and as Cordydian saddled him, he stood still. It was as if he understood that his master was going to sneak out of the camp quietly, taking advantage of the confusion within it.

He managed to lead the horse into the trees. There he jumped into the saddle and headed northwest, mentally praying that it would not be too late.

***

Yarred was in mortal danger - Mara knew it even without Lender's vision, she felt it with her whole self. She looked at her son sleeping in the crib. For some time now, the nightmares that had plagued him had faded away, but that, instead of calming her down, only increased her anxiety. She couldn't wait any longer, she had to leave Anthil with only three thousand spears. It was the only military resource it had in peacetime, and there was no time to recruit and train the others.

The queen's duties overwhelmed her a bit. According to the calculations of her advisers, she could not move with all her strength, she had to leave some to defend the city. She had two thousand soldiers left. She took all the magicians with her. She needed them to create a teleporter. She decided it would be safest if they appeared on the edge of

Wolfwood, away from the border with Riden. There were very few sorcerers powerful enough to do so in Antua.

"Your Majesty," Tharon entered her chambers, dressed in armor, with a helmet under his arm. "It's time."

Mara got up. She was wearing armor herself, a short sword swung at her belt, and a blue cape with Antua's brown eagle was flowing from her shoulders.

"Are your 'Eagles' ready?" She asked, although she expected an affirmative answer.

"Eagles" was the elite units responsible for protecting members of the royal family. They were selected from among the best and most distinguished soldiers.

"Yes, Your Majesty," he replied without hesitation, pride flashed across his face. "I've assigned fifty men to defend Duke Lender. The rest will go with you, lady."

The queen nodded her head and looked one last time at her peacefully sleeping son.

May you be wrong, she thought, putting on her helmet and walking out of the room.

As soon as the door closed behind her, Lender's eyes flew open. The boy got up and looked at the full moon outside the window. He couldn't explain it yet, but he knew that many of the Antuan soldiers would never return to their families.

***

After opening his eyes, Velwel wondered for a long time what had happened. The biggest surprise for him was the two mournful faces leaning over him with concern. Drasan and Alt'ar. How did they get here?

The last thing he remembered was a pain beyond imagination, as if someone were tearing his limbs with a hot iron. Then he thought for a long time that he had died and moved into the abyss. He couldn't move, and every breath was torture. And then came the fever and chills, he thought it was over again. And that's when it all ended. Pain, fever. He even regained feeling in his legs.

Miracle!

Unfortunately, it didn't stop there. It turned out that now his senses bombard his exhausted mind with hundreds of thousands of pieces of information. He could also sense the moods of the companions gathered around him. For the first time in his life, he could clearly hear not only the rhythmic beating of their hearts, but even the rushing of blood flowing through their veins, sounding like wonderful music to him. It didn't stop there! His nose told him about the close presence of a pair of deer and two small rabbits, as well as a pair of wolves hunting them. And as far as his hearing did not fool him, the distant murmurs spoke of an impending storm.

If it wasn't in a dream, it meant...

Just the thought of it made his stomach tighten in a tight loop.

I'm a werewolf, he thought, terrified and excited at the same time. Suddenly he remembered Boris' brutal companion, for whom making him suffer and listening to him scream in agony proved to be the best entertainment.

By the gods, he didn't want to become something like that! Better death already!

"Velwel? Can you hear me?" Alt'ar's soft but firm voice brought the young man back to reality.

He looked at the Guild leader, eyes wide with horror.

"Yes," he replied in a weak, slightly hoarse voice.

"Tell me: what do you feel?" The killer looked him in the eyes.

Velwel frowned. It took a while to answer that question.

"I'm not sure," he finally confessed. "My senses tell me so much information at once..."

Alt'ar nodded understandingly.

"It's natural. It takes some time to get used to... I'm interested in what your instincts tell you."

The young man nodded, focused on his own feelings again, and only then did he realize what Alt'ar was talking about. Hunter's instinct. It was he who told him that there were living creatures nearby that he could hunt. Suddenly there was also a painful void in his stomach. He groaned pitifully, which sounded more like a longing dog whine.

"I'm hungry," he confessed.

Alt'ar put a hand on his shoulder. He didn't even notice when he got up. And now his friends, including Drasan, whom he treated like a brother, stood ready with swords and bows in their hands.

"Relax," Alt'ar said, as it turned out after a moment, addressing only the half-dragon. - I'm in control of the situation.

Velwel breathed a sigh of relief only when the prince sheathed his sword and relaxed. It was obvious that he felt guilty about the whole situation. Neila was standing there with her hand on his shoulder, but he didn't even seem to notice.

So it worked! The young man thought with a sense of triumph. They approached each other. His sacrifice was not in vain.

The friend's distressed expression was saying something else entirely. Something weighed on his heart and it was not only about Velwell's new condition. He would bet his soul that it was a girl again.

***

It didn't take much time for Neila to find Drasan. He was standing alone, leaning against the trunk of one of the thicker trees, staring intently at the bright face of the moon that emerged from behind the clouds repeatedly. For some reason, she understood his condition perfectly well. He was furious with himself for allowing a similar situation at all.

"I shouldn't endanger either of you," he said deafly, without looking at her.

"Velwel knew the risks, and so did I. We are both with you of our own free will," the mercenary replied, coming closer and facing him.

The half-dragon snorted.

"Velwel is still a kid."

"Not much younger than you," she protested, hoping she would be able to reason with him a little.

"I'm different," muttered Drasan. "That's how I was born. Nothing and no one had any influence on it."

You're so stubborn, Neila thought, exasperated. She knew that the prince needed some time to get used to the new situation for him. He still hasn't recovered from his fight with Boris. She decided it was better not to pursue the topic further.

Fortunately, he decided to change it himself.

"Have you considered my proposal?" He asked in a slightly softer tone.

Oh! A slippery subject! You must be especially careful!

"Not yet," she replied.

The sincere grief in his eyes became for her like a blow to the very heart.

Gods! Why can a guy who can turn into a giant reptile look so much like an unjustly battered dog in an instant?

"You know... It's quite a big decision..." she explained lame, feeling as horrible as he looked.

"I wasn't going to rush you," he admitted, opening his big beautiful eyes a little wider. "I just hoped you made your decision."

Oh no! This cannot be done! The mercenary thought. She did not have time to prepare for this conversation.

"Drasan, I... I'm not sure if it's a good idea," she felt mean after those words. Why was it so hard for her to tell him the truth? "You're still very young..." She tried to speak without stuttering.

"My age is a really lame excuse," he said, bitterness in his voice.

"It's not even about age," the girl said defensively. "You don't know anything about me!"

He met her eyes, and for a moment his serious face was lit with the shadow of an old smile.

"I know enough," he replied.

Neila sighed deeply. She wasn't ready for this conversation.

"Actually, you know exactly what I wanted to tell you, which is not much," she said. She sat down on a fallen log and showed him the place next to her. "It's a longer story, so you'd better sit down," she explained.

Drasan looked at her with an expression of deep thought on his face but said nothing. He sat down next to him.

"My real name is Aurelia," she began. "Aurelia Roza Nimue van Midelvelt, only daughter of Baron Ricard van Midelvelt. I had given up title, family name, and even name just to keep myself from attracting attention. When my despotic father decided to marry me to twenty years older fat hog bearing the title of Count, I ran away from home. I was only fourteen." She grimaced as if the words opened the wounds that were not fully healed. "Father preferred to announce my death publicly than to admit the disgrace of my disobedience. I had no choice: I had to give up my old life. One night I ran into an elf. This one contemptuously called me "neila". I didn't know what it meant at the time, but I liked the word. From then on, I started to introduce myself like that. After a long time, I managed to find a relatively safe place for a temporary hiding place. I cut my hair and sold it for a few crowns. With the money I received, I bought myself a boy's tunic, pants and shoes. Living on the streets among other outcasts had taught me a quick and brutal lesson in survival. A few days after my escape, I almost fell victim to a rape. A young mercenary saved me. But I will never forget that night," she shuddered at the mere memory. "Fortunately for me, the mercenary turned out to be the famous Vincent of Alrunn, better known as the Bastard of Alrunn because of his infamous profession. He took me in and raised me, training me to be his successor."

Drasan nodded. Probably as everyone, he also has heard of the mercenary.

"He was said to be one of the best swordsmen on the peninsula. He knew fighting techniques that even masters like my mentor Ashkan would never dream of," he said, and the respect with which he spoke these words assured her that he admired Vincent himself and would give a lot to teach him.

Neila smiled at his excited eyes.

"I apprenticed with him for five years. During this time, I was learning various fighting techniques, as well as studying the composition of poisons necessary for the so-called "clean robots", where no one had the right to guess that the culprit died at the hand of a hired assassin. I also needed to know what to do in the event of an arrest so that the identity of my client would not be discovered. All this knowledge turned out to be nothing compared to the experience gained. Vincent was not a patient teacher and did not seem to accept that I was a woman. During murderous trainings, I often had to face much larger and heavier opponents. This was to teach me to use my opponent's force against him." She smiled aggressively. "That's what I did during our first fight. I knew that the advantage of strength was on your side, so I chose the element of surprise."

Much to her indignation, Drasan laughed softly.

"You didn't surprise me then, you just charmed me," he explained, amused by her expression. "This was the first time I saw a woman who uses a sword so efficiently. I'm used to salon beauties, afraid of getting dirty or destroying a priceless creation."

Well, it made sense, the girl thought, smiling predatory at the same time. The fight turned out to be even, so their skills remained exactly at the same level.

"I noticed your hesitation and I knocked you down," she continued, not hiding her satisfaction. "I saw in your eyes that you wouldn't hurt a woman who was going to cut you into slices. However, I cannot delude myself that they are all as chivalrous as you, and that is why I have a few more tricks up my sleeve."

The half-dragon moved closer and put his arm around her. This friendly gesture encouraged her.

"I think you understand now why I don't want to get married," she said after a moment of silence. "For me, marriage is like... a golden cage in which I will remain locked until the end of my days. I'm not ready for this, Drasan, not even for you." Tears ran down her cheeks as she said that. "I'm not ready to give up my freedom."

She thought he would hate her for it and send her to hell. Maybe then she would be free from his charm? But instead, Drasan pressed her against his broad chest and rocked her for a moment like a little baby.

"You really thought I would enslave you?" He whispered, pressing his face against her hair. "After I almost became a passive slave myself? After I told you about the pressure my mother put on me to finally settle down? I'm far from it, Neila. I would not be able to lock you in a golden cage and watch the heat in your eyes slowly fade, because it is it that gives me something to fight for." He sighed deeply. "I just thought it would keep you safe. I will make you untouchable."

His words sounded sincere and convincing, and Neila felt silly. She always envisioned marriage as a voluntary bondage. Married women were not allowed to object to their husband or to express their opinion unless his partner gave his permission. They couldn't do what they wanted. It was in this belief that she had lived all this time.

"I don't know what to say to you," she confessed, sniffing, suddenly realizing how silly it sounded. "I just need time to think about it all."

He hugged her to him, closing her in a bear hug.

"You don't need to rush," he said tenderly in his voice.

I know, she thought in distress, glad at the same time that he wasn't pushing her. In fact, she was afraid that her tardiness would only discourage him. The whole idea of marriage still seemed to be pure abstraction to her.

Gods! Make the young prince patient!

***

The next day turned out to be torture for Alt'ar. His acute senses gave him thousands of messages, and the beast remained restless. In addition, it proved impossible to avoid talking to Rodian or Velwel for a long time. He previously excused himself from feeling bad about it, but now he felt much better, though the amount of smells and sounds received had become unbearable. He already understood the young killer.

The sight of a witch heading towards him only confirmed his fears. It seemed the young man needed his help right now, when he was barely in control! The wolf at his feet snarled a warning, but did not rise from his seat, which Alt'ar took as a good sign. In some strange way, their bond deepened even more, and they could sense each other's moods.

"We need to talk," Rodian announced, and though her expression hadn't changed at all, the werewolf sensed that it wasn't just a request.

The witch sat down next to him on a fallen log.

"If you are afraid of bloodshed, I'll lead you out of the mistake: I'm not going to have a bloody slaughterhouse here just because there's a young werewolf nearby. For years I have kept the monster inside me in check, although I do not hide the fact that I like to kill. That's why I became a hired killer," he replied in a tone fueled by a slight irony.

"That's not what I'm afraid of," the woman said calmly. "I'm more concerned about the tense relationship between you and Drasan. You know he got to like the boy very much and will certainly stand up for him sooner if he loses control."

The smile faded from the Guild leader. So far, he has not thought about it.

"I know the risks, Rodian, and I think Drasan knows them too. Moreover, I do not intend to attack Velwel, unless he does it first," he replied calmly.

"And that's the problem. I'm afraid that doesn't calm him down at all. Thank the gods, the boy hasn't shown any murderous tendencies so far."

"Well..." he began in a low voice that took on a snarl tone with the growing anger. "You probably want to ask me not to fight him, while he, overcome with lust for murder, will make me a bloody pulp."

"No," said Rodian. "I would like to ask you not to provoke anything of the kind yourself."

Alt'ar snorted. Of course, how obvious it is! Nobody expected that this frail boy could turn into a bloodthirsty beast in an instant and attack whoever fell. It would be a pity if Drasan had the role of executioner.

"I'll do what I can," he said, knowing it was a lie. He knew well that after the transformation, his murderous instincts would activate and he would not be quite himself. As a werewolf, he had neither reason nor logic, which meant he would have to avoid transformation at all costs. An additional difficulty may be the mere fact of standing face to face with an angry werewolf.

His answer clearly did not satisfy Rodian, for she continued to stare at him as piercingly as if she wanted to see through him. Finally, she stood up with the clear intention of leaving, but then changed her mind.

"I trust you won't do anything stupid or reckless," she said, turned on her heel and walked away.

Alt'ar resisted the intention of catching up with her and inquiring as to what she meant. It has become irrelevant at the moment. He perfectly understood the consequences of telling the world who he was. Werewolves belonged to the outcasts of society. Most people chose death rather than change. Some hid this fact in fear that telling the truth would destroy them.

This was what made Alt'ar different from Drasan: he carried the weight of his secret himself while he was simply hidden away. The Guild leader was irritated by having to obey the orders of an arrogant bastard who was much younger than he was and had very little understanding of the command. But he had strict rules, and that included loyalty to his friends - although he had a hard time accepting it, he really liked Velwel. He became a kind of younger brother for him. He did not know how his monster would behave, but he quietly hoped that he would be able to control it.

CHAPTER 24

Anthil certainly deserved to be called the greatest city in all of Antua. It turned out to be much less extensive than Tarssen, making up for it by the fact that it was built on top of a hill with a breathtaking view of Lake Kahlim.

The greatest admiration was aroused by the Citadel itself. Located in the heart of the city and shining with white walls from a distance, with two towers protruding on the sides like stone guards.

Dhalia stopped her horse and stared at the city for a moment, captivated. According to her visions, the queen abandoned this architectural gem and headed southwest to take refuge in the shadow of the Wolfwood with the remnants of the army. There, she will probably join forces with Drasan. That wasn't what she worried about. Bal'zar sent Anar and Mariv there with ten thousand soldiers, including six heavy cavalry flags. Sam was going to join them right after taking Anthil.

The witch suspected that there would be no major problem with that. Not now that there is a minimum crew left in the city to defend its inhabitants against the invaders. Bal'zar's tactics came down to pretending to be a gracious and just ruler without harming those determined to surrender. As a rule, it worked, and this time she would probably be a benefactor as well.

Damn boy, she thought, angry with herself that she hadn't felt such a huge amount of power in the boy. She thought he was just an exceptionally gifted magician.

There was still Arano. Though she wasn't sure if she should still call him that.

As for him, she was also wrong. He just turned out to be a cold bastard. And she once considered him a visionary and admired his persistence in his pursuit of a world full of harmony. Now she knew that from the beginning he wanted to build his utopia on a pile of corpses. And to think that people thought she was a heartless monster.

Involuntarily, she glanced back at the ranks of Emperor Bal'zar's army. It was headed by the faithful Doars - brutal barbarians with no restraints. Behind them, the white banners of Alikorn flaunted, and then the weakest link, the infantry equipped with long pointed poles called pikes. Good for taking riders off their saddles. Unfortunately, after the famous Antuan ride, she did not even notice a trace, so the fight may not take place at all.

The sight of the crowd of people must have been extremely terrifying when viewed from the walls of an unprotected city. Not even half a day has passed since they stood under the hill and the city gates swung open, letting a delegation of about five passes through. A messenger was sent to her without delay.

The boy forgot his tongue at the sight of the witch. For a good few heartbeats, he just stood there and stared at her before he could even remember what he had been sent for.

Dhalia sighed. In the absence of Bal'zar and Arano, she was the commander-in-chief, and it was her part to hear what the messenger had to say.

She jumped off her horse and handed the reins to one of her bodyguards. She herself met the negotiator. The man - about fifty years old, as evidenced by the streaks of gray woven into the red hair and the wrinkles around his black eyes - also jumped off the saddle and walked towards her with the springy stride of a person who was used to giving orders to others.

So, she had General Niko Valser himself before her. What a surprise.

He made a stiff military bow.

"I'm General Niko Valser. I have come to negotiate the terms of surrender," he announced in a low bass voice.

Dhalia nodded politely.

"I understand, General," she replied, feeling an involuntary admiration for this strict man. "Of course, as Emperor Bal'zar's chief adviser, I'm prepared to accept your surrender on his behalf."

Niko nodded stiffly.

"These are the conditions under which I will surrender the city..."

***

Looking at the half-dragon curled up in a tight ball, Neila felt very lonely. He recently returned from his aerial patrol and went to sleep right away. Alt'ar took Velwel on a hunt, and they probably wouldn't come back very soon. Most of the killers were doing their own thing. She took out her daggers and, for lack of anything else, began to clean them. She paused to look at Drasan, but he still seemed to be in a deep sleep; his massive sides rose and fell to the rhythm of his calm breathing. With a deep sigh, she walked over and leaned against his side. As always, he radiated a pleasant warmth.

She still didn't know what to say to him. She did not feel ready to take on such a great commitment as to marry someone who would one day be king. In addition, he is a huge predator that scares her. Although when he was asleep, he didn't seem so scary.

She found himself staring at the gleam of flames that flickered on his scales, making them shimmer like hundreds of thousands of diamonds. It was changing so fast! In just three months it had grown, the scales hardened on its body, and a row of hard bone spines stretched from between its wings to the tip of its tail. The smallest was the width of her hand. His human form also became different. You could say he had grown firm and tighter, but that was a gross understatement to her.

She closed her eyes, remembering their night together. She remembered seeing his athletic body. Hard muscle knots were clearly visible under the scarred skin. Long matted hair and a thick beard gave him a kind of wildness. Only the eyes remained the same: so keen that with each look he looked at, she felt as if they were reaching the very bottom of her soul.

The hoof of galloping horses broke her dreams. Instinctively she reached for one of the knives. When she saw two riders riding side by side, she set it aside. Alt'ar and Velwel were returning, and judging by the delighted expression of the latter, the hunt was a success.

Neila breathed a sigh of relief. Until now, the young killer, aside from the ravenous appetite, had behaved as before. Even so, Alt'ar never took his eyes off him. This lack of visible changes clearly worried him.

Velwel, on the other hand, was in cloud nine. While running, he jumped off his horse, bounced his feet off the ground and rolled back. Still smiling from ear to ear, he caught up with his mare without much effort and mounted her again. He was clearly enjoying the new skills.

The girl felt a pang of jealousy because he accepted all changes so easily. She, even with the sincerest efforts, could not accept herself.

The young assassin returned a short time later, leading the mount behind him. He tied her next to the other horses and, smiling complacently, walked towards Neila.

His fangs flashed in the bright afternoon sun - the only sign of change so far.

"I hit the wall," he said, yawning widely, and reached for his purse. He rummaged in it for a moment to finally extract what he was looking for - one of the few bottles of booze.

He glanced at Drasan.

"Poor thing. He must be exhausted. I hear he was tired saving my life," he said, his smile fading away.

He sat down by the fire, opened the cork and sniffed the drink with distrust, took a long sip. He grimaced, shook him like a dog, and gulped again. He repeated this ritual several times.

"I'm out of practice," he explained, seeing Neila looking at him strangely.

The girl did not consider it appropriate to comment on this.

Velwel was known to peer into the bottle frequently, yet was considered one of the best killers in Riden. Recently, however, his behavior has changed. Not only was he not drinking, but he also stopped chewing his weird leaves. As a result, he became much more alert, but his killing effectiveness dropped noticeably - he began to have scruples, and that did not bode well for someone in his profession. Maybe turning into a werewolf would change that.

She has also softened recently. In the past, she did not hesitate. Anyone who stood in the way of her task had to die. When she met Drasan, everything suddenly changed: he showed her that she didn't have to do everything herself.

Sometimes it was nice to watch him fight himself. It was then like a combination of a resilient wild cat and an attacking cobra. Every move he made; every step was like a dance. Dance of death. She could then stare at him for hours.

She looked at Velwell, stretched out by the fire and getting ready for a blissful nap.

She sighed softly.

The young man opened his eyes and looked at her for a moment, reached for a bottle of golden liquor and pressed it into her hands with the words:

"Here, has a drink. You will feel better."

The mercenary glanced at him, then at the bottle, then took it carefully, took a sip, and choked. The dirtiness turned out to be damn strong. She took another two sips quickly. Her throat burned, but her body felt a pleasant numbness.

For the first time in her life, she was drunk, and worst of all, she liked it. Alcohol brought bliss, oblivion. Maybe she just found a remedy for her problems? She needed to forget for a moment who and who Drasan was not. Not fully realizing what she was doing, she approached the sleeping dragon. She nudged him lightly with the toe of her shoe.

Nothing happened. The huge reptile was still fast asleep.

Not knowing why, Neila felt annoyed, picked up a thick limb and stabbed him in the side with it. It worked. Drasan's eyes widened and there were menacing flashes in them, but they vanished as soon as he noticed the mercenary standing in front of him. He opened his mouth wide and yawned powerfully, blowing a not-so-fresh breath at them.

Neila staggered and took a few steps back. She crashed into Velwel, who grabbed her halfway and pulled her to her feet.

"Did you get enough sleep, Your Majesty?" She asked, propping her hips and looking at the prince defiantly.

The dragon looked at her with still slightly sleepy eyes and he lifted his huge body. The scales crunched softly as he began to stretch, his back curving like a cat. Suddenly it burst into flames, and when it fell, he stood before them in his human form, smiling mischievously. For some reason, he was wearing pants.

The sight of his naked torso nearly knocked Neila off her feet. Her head felt dizzy and if it hadn't been for Velwel, she would have probably landed on the ground. She narrowed her eyes and looked again, but the half-dragon still wore only baggy canvas pants.

The girl staggered towards him, trying not to get out on the way. She began to see through a fog.

He looked at her and smiled even wider. She stopped as if her legs had stuck to the ground. She saw his lips move, but didn't hear what he was saying. For her head spun, and the last thing she remembered was the dangerously approaching earth.

***

Alt'ar looked at the sun's golden disc, now partially hidden behind the trees, and jumped off his horse. All his new moon senses screamed for him to back off, but he ignored them. For some time now, wolf nature had taken precedence over humans, and now he felt a great deal of excitement. Among the hundreds of scents surrounding him, he recognized an unknown one - the smell of a strange werewolf, or more precisely of a female, wandering around.

It was for this reason that he sent Velwel back to the camp. For an unchanged young werewolf, the presence of a female could arouse over-excitement or aggression. This was the last thing they needed.

Females were sometimes more aggressive. Wolf's instinct told the guild leader that he didn't need to fear this one. She didn't come too close, from which he concluded that she was wild and had lost all her humanity long ago. It was also evidenced by the traces of large paws, impossible to confuse with anything else. Every now and then he came across the remains of uneaten carcasses, in addition so torn that it was difficult for him to guess its origin.

The horse gasped, and close to master, Ars's leg growled, baring his fangs.

He was not mistaken. She was still nearby.

It was dark in the thicket of the forest, but Alt'ar could see as well as during the day. He listened, the only thing that reached his ears was the soft rustling of leaves blown in the wind. Ars snarled a warning and fell to the ground.

Instinct worked and the assassin just in time dodged the attacker, popping out at him from among the blackberry bushes along the path.

The black and silver she-wolf landed softly on all four legs and turned, instantly renewing her attack. This time Alt'ar had managed to pull out the silver knife. The female backed away, snarling and baring her fangs. She didn't take her flaming red eyes off the Guild leader for a moment.

"I won't hurt you," he lowered the knife a little.

The female werewolf either didn't understand or simply ignored the gesture. Alt'ar decided not to lose his cold blood. At the same time, he had to keep control of the beast sitting in him, which at all costs wanted to meet his fellow man, regardless of the bared fangs and eyes burning with murder.

For a werewolf she turned out to be intriguing, for a human being at least deadly. The guild leader couldn't let her kill or hurt any of his men. He had to do what was necessary.

Suddenly the creature stopped growling and sat up. While she certainly looked much larger than the average wolf, she was otherwise no different at the moment. Still, if Alt'ar transformed itself, she might become scared and run away.

Why are you with these people? She sent him a question mentally. So she couldn't be quite wild.

What do you mean? He replied.

You are not human, she replied, her mouth twisting into something like contempt. You don't smell like a human.

What are you doing here? Alt'ar asked.

I'm curious. She replied. Two werewolves among a group of people is something unusual... I also sensed a smell unlike any other animal.

Yeah. Alt'ar sighed. He himself was used to the smell of both dragons, but for the rest of his kin it must have been something new.

The female werewolf cocked her head as she regarded him curiously.

You are the alpha. Why are you wasting your time leading the people when you could become a werewolf prince himself?

Prince of werewolves? What is she talking about?

Alt'ar managed to keep himself from a low growl. Instead, he burst out laughing.

"I don't want to become like you," he said aloud. He lifted his upper lip slightly, exposing his teeth to make sure he was understood correctly.

The wolf gave a short bark like a laugh.

Why are you rejecting your nature? In wolf form, you can become faster, stronger. Your leadership skills could help our brothers.

Alt'ar looked at the female again. It seemed thinner and had a much darker coat than Ars, but her eyes gave her away. In wolves, they were colored amber, while in werewolves, depending on the degree to which they retained a particle of humanity, they acquired the color of blood red. Besides, unlike a wolf, he could stand on two legs. In this form, they became not only stronger, faster and more agile, but also twice as dangerous. The werewolf in this form made it clear that he was ready to tear the intruder to shreds.

But this particular female did not intend to do so. In addition, she respected the law of the stronger, which placed her in a predefined position. She was also in someone else's territory and felt less confident, which was why she preferred to assume an animal form.

"What's your name?" Alt'ar asked, much more puzzled now. As the sun waned, his wolf senses clearly prevailed over human nature.

The wolf clearly relaxed because she decided to come closer.

Niue - she barked shortly, wagged her tail shyly and looked at him with glittering eyes, expecting a presentation from his side.

"I'm Alt'ar," he replied, sheathing the knife and extending his hand toward her as if he were going to stroke her.

She backed quickly beyond his reach, snarling and snapping her teeth.

Ars fell flat to the ground at this gesture, answering, baring his fangs to the edge of his gums.

"I wasn't going to hurt you," he said, both amused and embarrassed that he was acting so absurdly.

Niue stopped growling and sat down again.

You're acting weird, she stated. Why don't you change?

Alt'ar clenched his hand into fists. The suggestion seemed tempting: release the beast from its cage for one night and let it run wild. Recently, with each full moon, he felt that he was losing control of himself more and more. What if Rodian is right? What if he should come to terms with the fact that he is a werewolf? He could take an example from Velwel. The young assassin seemed delighted with what he could do, and was very good at it. It only jumps into the fur once and gets carried away by the wolf's senses. He looked at Ars, then back at Niue, a tempting thought.

***

The slender elf entered the throne room and made a deep bow.

"Your Majesty..." she began.

"Emperor," Bal'zar corrected her with a deep sigh.

Saruviel smirked. Once again he had the impression that the grimace was forced. The witch was not used to being humble.

"Emperor," she said the word as if she were trying out its sound. "According to what Dhalia told me, we got Anthil. The city surrendered before the attack began."

The ruler smiled. So far, everything has been going according to plan. The population swallowed his lies without any problems. There will be time to bring order to the mob.

"That's great news," he said, leaning back in his chair. This was one of those times when he could enjoy the advantage over people.

The elf bowed gracefully. The expression on her face was hard to read, but her eyes spoke too much. There have been many traditions describing it as the mirror of the soul.

Saruviel's soul turned out to be steeped in evil and hate.

She hated Dhalia for her beauty and position, she hated Drasan for having so empowered him by destiny, and finally she hated him for bringing everyone to their knees without even lifting a finger.

Bal'zar could read it all in the expression in her eyes. He knew how to properly channel all this hate.

"People adore you, Emperor," she said casually, studying the young man's face carefully, hoping to see a hint of approval.

"Forget these smooth words, my dear. I know perfectly well that you are not used to groveling in front of anyone, especially men," said Bal'zar, knowing he had hit the nail on the head. "What do you really want?"

The mask on Saruviel's face changed rapidly.

"I think you know well," she said, lifting her chin proudly.

"Still, I want to hear it from your lips," Bal'zar replied, crossing his arms over his chest.

Saruviel smiled, not finding even a hint of warmth in it.

"Dhalia head," she said, savoring the words as if she tasted fine wine. "Preserved intact, so that I could personally cut her pretty face and make a wine goblet out of the skull. This bitch deserved to die a thousand times after becoming the lizard's bitch, thus cheating on her sisters. After she protected that dragon bastard while she should have slit his throat."

Bal'zar laughed softly.

Her reaction proved predictable. Sure, Dhalia had to be disposed of. For now, however, he still had some use for it, and he was reluctant to give up the useful tools.

"I can promise you, in due course, you'll get her even alive and powerless." He replied, knowing he had that cold bitch in his hand. "Do what you want with her. But not now. First, she has to play her key role," after these words he turned his back to her, thus implying that this conversation is over.

Suddenly, something else occurred to him. He turned to the elf, admiring her composure in the face of such disrespectful treatment.

"I don't think you will be needed here anymore. Go to Washmorth. My spy will be there in a while to make a report. I also need someone I trust to look after one of my precious prisoners."

He knew that the witch had to be kept as far away from the battlefield as possible, and sending her back seemed the safest thing to do.

"As you wish, my lord," she replied with lofty contempt.

Bal'zar ignored the tone. He mentally congratulated himself on such a carefully thought-out plan, along with his brother he had been creating for centuries. If successful, the Linelanders will know the true wrath of rejected gods.

***

"Your Majesty..." gasped the messenger, bursting into the tent.

The queen looked up from the pile of maps and scrolls and looked at the boy. For a scout, he turned out to be very young, probably barely reaching manhood.

They were two days' fast drive from the river, and although the army's advance was slower than anticipated, they would still be there ahead of time.

She nodded her head approvingly.

"We crossed the river, but there's no one on the other side. We saw neither our allies nor our enemies. The country on the other side seems completely deserted. We even got to the edge of the Wolf Forest..."

Mara interrupted him with a gesture:

"That confirms my suspicions. Our allies are probably hiding in the forest, and the enemy somehow, perhaps even magically, keeps a cover. So, we won't be able to see them until they decide to attack," she smiled wryly. "Thank you for the report."

The messenger bowed and walked away, leaving her with her own thoughts.

There hasn't been any battle yet. Both Bal'zar's army and Drasan's troops are waiting for something. The latter probably for armed support.

She sighed and felt even more tired than ever before. She looked at the piles of reports on the condition of the army, provisions, and mounts that piled up ahead of her. She hoped Drasan had some plan to defeat the greatest army the world had ever seen.

The canvas moved aside and Tharon entered the tent. He looked just as tired.

"I have reviewed our inventory; it will be enough even for a few months. But people are a little concerned that the enemy has not shown up so far," he said, sitting down and drawing one of the maps towards him.

"That doesn't mean they aren't here," said the queen with a sigh.

"I think the appearance of the dragon would give them some courage," the adviser suggested, looking at her uncertainly.

Mara glanced at him with dark circles under her eyes - she hadn't had much sleep recently, they had been on the road for a week now, and she had to be in command of the army as commander in chief.

"Trouble is, I don't know how to contact him," she said.

"But he has to be around somewhere, right? Let's send messengers to the Wolf Forest..."

"No," snapped the queen. "I cannot risk the lives of our soldiers, it is not very safe since Vaya's death in the Forest."

"Send me over there," he offered without hesitating.

The queen looked at him closely - he was not joking. He really was ready to do it.

"Good," she conceded with a tired smile. She stood up and smoothed the folds of her dress. "But I'll go with you."

Seeing the determination on her face, Tharon dared not refuse. She was still queen after all, and her gaze was very much like that of her father's when he was going to defy him.

"Who will take over your duties at that time?" He asked.

The queen smiled.

"I think I know the right person."

CHAPTER 25

As he entered the camp, Alt'ar felt as if everyone was staring at him.

Sure, his entire torso was splattered with blood, long dried, now forming a brown scab. It wasn't his, of course. Gaining the position of alpha took the use of force. Fortunately, after he tore a dominant werewolf to shreds, the others accepted his leadership without any problems.

The pack turned out to be quite numerous for such aggressive creatures as werewolves. She had ten more individuals, including four females. Despite the strong bond he had established with them by becoming the alpha, they still preferred to stay away from people as possible. He could feel them on the edge of his consciousness.

Still heightened senses caught hundreds of sounds and smells.

Suddenly, it turned out that each person they passed had a different smell: some smelled more familiar - fire smoke, horses and sweat, others were wearing a more complicated mixture of smells. At the sight of her standing with her hands on her hips, Rodian struggled to keep from exposing her teeth in a more wolf-than-human manner.

There was a strange mixture of emotions in her - fear, surprise, and anger.

He stopped at a distance. The beast in it backed away at the feeling of magic - the werewolves hated it.

"Come on, we need to talk," she ordered, gesturing to him.

This time he didn't listen to her. Everything human about him wanted him to follow her, but the monster opposed it. He was standing still, torn between human and wolf nature.

"Alt'ar... I know it's hard, but you have to tame the beast, it can't supersede your humanity," her voice softened a little. Apparently she really cared about this conversation.

According to Alt'ar, she spoke too loudly about it. Fortunately, most of his people, accustomed to the unusual tastes of their leader, quickly resumed their previous activities. The only person focusing all her attention on him was Rodian.

"Before you scold me, listen to me first." He spread his hands in a gesture of conciliation.

"Yes," she replied deadly seriously.

Alt'ar sighed.

"You know who I am," he winced involuntarily. "You also know that I have resisted the influence of the moon for years. I locked the beast in a cage so that it wouldn't become what I hated. I was doing it because I didn't want to be a monster..." He trailed off through a shiver. "The truth is, I'm a monster and I should have come to terms with it a long time ago. I fought it, I kept it out of my mind, but it will never change anything..."

"Alt'ar, I..."

"Let me finish!" He cut her off abruptly. I've been hiding too long from myself. Maybe it's time to end this and let the world know who I really am." He shuddered violently. "A werewolf."

Alt'ar predicted the Rodian's reaction. He could see her thoughts forming words that would hurt him more than cheek to face.

"Did you even think for a moment what will happen to me?" she accused. "If you reveal your true face to the world, I too will have to shed the mask that I have been hiding for hundreds of years. When I talked about stopping hiding your true self, I meant the Guild. The people who took us in and are now like family." She didn't even realize her words cut him like knives. "We are like brother and sister to each other. We look after each other. We accepted our demons..."

"Rodian!"He shouted her name, hoping he would stop the torrent of words. "You know your secret is safe with me. No one knows your true self, and no one will think of looking for you among outcasts like the Guild. You're safe here."

"But for how long?" The witch exclaimed, trembling all over her body. "Have you ever thought what Drasan would do if he figured it out? He's a half dragon after all! It was strange that he didn't sense me, though I almost betrayed myself to him so many times."

"Drasan loves Neila," the killer said. "If it weren't for your help, she would be dead by now. He won't hurt you just by being grateful for what you did."

"I almost killed him!" She exclaimed, unable to help herself.

Alt'ar felt himself getting hot. She was right. He remembered the expression on her face all too well that day, when she was saving the girl from imminent death. Drasan turned out to be so desperate and shocked that he would never have guessed what Rodian was doing. This was the only time she had used her powerful abilities. The sight of his blood tempted her. The temptation turned out to be too strong. The witch was carried away by her cruel and twisted lust. Had he not stopped her then, she would have surely sucked the life out of him.

Rodian was the "source." She was able to store in herself enormous amounts of magical energy. Her talent was that it was enough for someone to cut themselves and she could already sense whether he was talented or not. She didn't even have to touch the victim to drain all her energy.

"That day, I felt the enormous amount of magic that Drasan had within him. A whole sea of power. I couldn't resist, especially since he himself encouraged me to take it from him," she continued in a whisper. "So, I took a little, but it wasn't enough for me. I wanted to take everything he had." She looked at him with anguished eyes. "I am extremely dangerous, Alt'ar. Many times, more dangerous than you."

"You can control yourself," he said, not for the first time cradling her to his chest. "And no one will ever hurt you. I will not allow it."

"What if Bal'zar or any of the other mages sense me? Sources are extremely rare, Alt'ar. Think for a moment what mad King of Riden would do if you had one of them at your disposal."

The Guild leader didn't have to think about it long. Rodian has been in hiding for all these centuries for a reason. Knowing that whoever could use her abilities to gain power or position kept her away from royal courts. After amassing enormous amounts of power, she could replace an entire army of mages. Infinite power locked in one person.

Therefore, Rodian considered herself a monster to whom cruel fate gave a beautiful face and undoubted charm. She was like living glue for magicians. They clung to her like bees to honey.

"I have to go, Alt'ar. Now that you come out, there will be no place for me in your world," her words hurt a lot more than he expected. "You are a natural leader. Your place is at the head of a group of humans or even werewolves."

Alt'ar sighed in resignation. He knew he couldn't convince her.

Some things change forever, he thought as he hugged the woman to his chest for the last time.

***

Drasan listened to Velwel's explanation standing before him, his expression stony. Neila was still unconscious, and it looked as though she would remain in that state at least until the alcohol had worn off.

"...I really..." stammered the young man for the hundredth time.

"Enough!" Drasan cut him off in an indisputable tone, rubbing his temples. "I don't want to listen to your explanations anymore."

Velwel lowered his head, trying to avoid his friend's accusing gaze.

The prince sighed.

He had to make a decision, take action. It was stuck so far, and it was not going to change. All he could think of now was to cross the river and go to Earden, but before that, he had a conversation with Alt'ar.

"Stay here with her," he ordered the young werewolf. "I need to speak to Alt'ar."

Velwel grinned.

"No problem, Your Majesty." He stiffened and proudly puffed out his chest. "I will watch her like an eye in my head."

The half-dragon sighed again.

"Don't call me that," he said tiredly.

"Why?" The surprised young man asked.

"Because I have not deserved it yet," he announced, turned on his heel and left without waiting for Velwel to process his words.

It didn't take long to find the Guild leader. He was sitting by one of the five fires, and as soon as he noticed him, he got up and walked away. Drasan followed him through the trees, out of reach of human ears.

Alt'ar stood under a large oak. Ironically the same one behind which the heated discussion with Neila had taken place earlier. Or should he call her Aurelia from today?

"I must go to Earden," said the half-dragon. He decided to get straight to the point. "Since I don't trust Gaenor too much, I decided it was better for me to entrust everything to you. Go back to the rest of your people and notify them of the imminent battle."

Alt'ar chuckled softly. It was a humorless snort.

"I've got news for you, too," he straightened. "Rodian is gone. We therefore lost our only line of defense. They surely have trained mages and will cover themselves with shields that will make the arrows useless, so we will be left with a frontal attack."

Drasan frowned.

"Why are you telling me this now?" He asked sharply.

Alt'ar didn't care too much.

"Let me see..." He pretended to think. "Maybe because she was gone because of you, or maybe because of your idiotic sense of duty."

"What are you talking about?!" Asked the prince. He felt completely taken aback, he tried to remember what had offended the witch so much, but he could think of nothing.

"Then maybe I will refresh your memory," the werewolf growled, mechanically showing his fangs. "The gorge on the day of our victory, when Neila was mortally wounded and you, regardless of your own safety, ordered Rodian to save her. She obeyed, almost killing you."

"What?!" The surprised young man exclaimed. He couldn't believe his ears. Rodian couldn't become that powerful!

"Rodian is the Source, Drasan." Alt'ar confessed, though it was difficult for him. "The most powerful since Malahis."

The prince frowned, trying to remember everything about the "sources." From what he remembered from Vaya's lectures on this subject, they were mages capable of storing enormous amounts of energy. Apparently, a person endowed with this talent can literally suck magic from another being, ultimately driving it to death.

If Rodian was indeed the "source," they could use it in battle against their enemies. For this, it was enough to find a few magically gifted people. They could win against Bal'zar without sacrificing a single man. The witch, he and Gaenor will have enough for an army!

"You must turn her back," said Drasan firmly.

Alt'ar crossed his arms over his chest.

"I don't know what you've imagined, but you'd better let it go," he replied.

"Why is that?" He asked sharply.

The werewolf lifted his upper lip and snarled warningly.

"That's because I can't let you do it. You will not use her as a new form of weapon. She ran away from something like that. That's why she has been hiding for the last fifty years."

Drasan did not understand. They had victory at hand. Could they crush the tyrant with one well-aimed blow, and the werewolf chose to be loyal to a witch?

"Are you going to fight me?" He asked quietly and with evident resignation.

"If I have to."

"Can you tell me why?"

Drasan felt devastated. To think that he had a "source" at hand all this time. How could he not sense it?!

"Because I know what this will lead to. No one should have access to such power. I know that Dhalia has murdered your loved ones, and all you want is bloody retaliation, but you can't just take revenge."

The werewolf is lecturing to me? It hasn't happened yet, Drasan thought wryly.

"You have no idea what I've been through," he said, forcing himself to sound calm.

"Believe me: I have," replied the killer. "Larger than you expect."

The half-dragon decided it was better not to comment. He was in complete agreement with the Guild leader. It would be unfair to use the Rodian's innate abilities, though the temptation of infinite power remained. Perhaps, with the help of a witch, he could even rebuild Sheardon and restore the kingdom to its former glory. He could then take his rightful place, as Vaya has always desired. Immediately after that, he remembered a fact that had turned his entire plan into disrepair.

You belong to me - that was the words of the Lady of the Dead. He swore to serve her to the end of his days, and in return she let Neila live.

He was tempted for a moment to tell Alt'ar about it. Perhaps he should know that Drasan was not the master of his own destiny.

He won't believe me, he thought despairingly. Nobody will believe that he made a pact with an inhabitant of the Land of the Dead.

"Since you're going to Earden," the assassin said, carefully scanning the half-dragon's face. "There is something else you should know..."

Drasan frowned. He did not want more surprises.

Alt'ar sighed heavily. He hesitated. It was obvious that what he was about to say would not come easily to him.

"I know your aversion to my kind," he said slowly, most of the words struggling through his throat. "Unfortunately, I also know that we have a slim chance of winning..."

"Let me guess," the prince drawled, cutting his words short. "Are you going to ask for help from the werewolves?"

"In fact... I already did," Alt'ar said, straightening suddenly. There was a ruby gleam in his blue eyes. "I don't see any point in hiding from members of my own kind anymore. I'm a werewolf and nothing will change that."

"And now you put me in front of a fait accompli?" Growled Drasan, baring his teeth in the process. Crimson flames began to creep over his body.

"We are all sacrificing something, Drasan," Alt'ar replied. "Maybe it's time to shake off any old prejudices. Boris is a beast, but not all werewolves are like him. Most try to live in harmony with people..."

"You mean yourself?" Asked the half-dragon in a mocking voice. "I still can't forget that son of a bitch who almost tore Velwel to shreds. Werewolves are... monsters!"

"You're one yourself too, Drasan!" Alt'ar exploded. "Bigger and much more dangerous than any werewolf!"

"At least I can control myself," Drasan replied. In fact, he felt the ground slipping from under his feet. Alt'ar was right, he was no less dangerous than he was.

"Like the last battle?" The werewolf sneered. "Don't tell me you weren't satisfied with burning all these people. You killed them in cold blood using your supernatural abilities. How does that make you different from creatures like me?"

Drasan could not find an answer to this argument. The truth was, murdering hundreds of Doars had given him more fun than it should have been. Vaya would certainly not approve of it. She adhered to the principle that everyone should not be judged equally. Would she applaud his decision to ally with the werewolves?

Unfortunately, he would never have the opportunity to ask her about it because of Dhalia. Involuntarily, he remembered the words of the Lady of the Dead: "Do not judge everyone so hastily and be as short-sighted as your mentor."

"You're right," he confessed with a deep sigh. "I'm also a monster capable of cruelty, and nothing justifies my behavior. That day, I was blinded by revenge. I couldn't think straight. The worst part is that I don't regret my act at all."

"Werewolves aren't monsters of choice, Drasan," the assassin said. "Someone once made a decision for them. Many of them loathe themselves. Some even try to starve to death because they don't want to succumb to primal instincts."

The prince understood what the killer was trying to convey to him. It may be time to let go of old prejudices.

***

The throne room at Anthil was surely a testimony to the former glory of the royal families that ruled here. The floor was covered with large slabs of multicolored marble, supporting the column's enormous glass vault - also made of this metal. They were decorated with intricate carvings of gold and silver, and alabaster statues stood in the niches. The throne itself is made of dark wood and carved.

Bal'zar looked at this interior, admiring the craftsmanship of the best masters of masonry and artists who had worked on its unusual appearance in the past. He paid particular attention to one of the wall reliefs. It depicted a scene from the past, in which the dragon king - Magot - negotiates with the barbarian nomadic people of the time, inhabiting the steppes, which are today the kingdom of Antua. He gave them the most powerful of the five artifacts - the Book of Truth. According to a legend, which, as was usually the case, contained a grain of truth, it described the history of the world from its very beginning. The following chapters were to appear over time. The first king of Antua in his ignorance decided that this treasure should be hidden so that no one could find it. And thus, the book was lost. Horst took the secret of her hiding to the grave.

By conquering Antua, Bal'zar hoped to find any clue or scrap of information that would give him a clue as to where to look for the artifact. To this end, he spent the entire afternoon in the palace library, leafing through the bloated volumes and leafing through the yellowed scrolls. He found nothing. He knew that this treasure was not hidden in the castle or in the immediate vicinity. If they did, he would sense a magical disorder.

"You called on me, brother."

Bal'zar sighed. Arano had the annoying habit of showing up at the least appropriate moment. He turned and looked at his older brother, standing in front of the dais with a carved throne placed on it.

"Yes, Arano," he smiled slightly. "I wonder how the morale of our soldiers is. So far, they have fought only a few skirmishes, and have not seen a real battle with their eyes. Do you think they won't break when they see a dragon?"

"That's not what you called me for, was it?" Arano said, tilting his head slightly.

The Emperor's smile widened. As always, the interlocutor got to the point.

"Of course not," he replied, gesturing him closer. "As you know, I have been hunting for magical artifacts for a long time. According to legend, there are five of them. It seems to me that I accidentally found one in the ruins of a city in the south."

"Is it about those old bracelets forcing you to tell the truth?" Arano sneered.

The smile faded from the young ruler's face, replaced with a scowl of fury.

"Don't mock ancient magic, brother," he said seriously. "The items you mentioned are powerful tools. Carved into metal likely to fall from the sky, and the runes are thousands of years old. So far, I have tried them on several inmates, and they have all been forced to confess the truth."

"So, what did you discover this time?" Arano asked, crossing his arms over his chest.

"I'm interested in the so-called Book of Truth." Bal'zar replied. "Mention of her even goes back to the period before the appearance of the human race."

Arano frowned, perhaps wondering where he had heard the name. The young ruler knew his older brother too well.

"Unlike you, I'm not a scientist. You managed to escape hundreds of years ahead of me. You have had the opportunity to thoroughly explore the present world, learn about the habits and prejudices of all races," Bal'zar said in a bored tone. They rolled the subject hundreds of times. "Even conquering the peninsula is entirely your idea. You have planned a big comeback. You..."

"I know what I did," Arano interrupted, looking around vigilantly to make sure no one heard it, but Shirza the wolf was left in the room. Still, he lowered his voice to a whisper. "I have made a throne for you, little brother," as he said this, he approached the young ruler closer and closer, his features hardening. The face seemed much older. "I was behind the scenes, so your hands are clean while mine is dripping with the blood of all those who stood in your way. I have cleared the path for you, my lord, because fate has given you great power, giving me intelligence and wisdom in return."

Bal'zar cringed under the stern gaze. Arano spoke the truth: he stood behind his younger brother all his life, supported him, and when the need arose, he killed those who threatened him. In return, he demanded that he allow him to take revenge. He loved him more than life, at the same time feeling a primal fear every time his true face was revealed.

"I know, brother," he said.

Then Arano embraced him and kissed him on the forehead.

"You are the ruler of these lands, the future Emperor. Don't lose sight of the true purpose of our actions," he said in a voice that crept into which a hint of brotherly tenderness crept in.

Bal'zar understood that the search for the book had to wait. However, he did not intend to completely give up on them.

***

After a somewhat stormy discussion with Alt'ar, Drasan immediately went where he had left Velwel and the unconscious mercenary. Deep down, he knew the Guild leader was right: it was time to let go of old prejudices.

Isn't that why I spared Boris' life? He asked himself.

The truth was that then pity came to him. If Dhalia got her way, it would be exactly the same. So, he concluded that killing the werewolf was useless.

He was almost there when his instincts warned him of the danger. He bared his teeth reflexively and reached for his sword. Moments later Velwel appeared at his side, silently like a ghost... fortunately in human form.

Still, his friend couldn't help but growl from deep in his throat.

Drasan gestured for silence, and moved forward with the young werewolf lurking behind him.

They both gained confidence in one...

They felt it clearly... Magic!

Its breeze bristled the prince's neck hair and gave him an unpleasant feeling that they were being watched.

Suddenly they both stopped listening. Someone was approaching. Two riders who, judging by the sounds, were leading the horses.

Drasan gestured for his companion to move from the other side. He wanted to circle unexpected intruders, and they would probably have managed to do so, had it not been for Velwela's chestnut. Upon sensing the familiar scent of her kin, the mare let out an exceptionally loud huff.

The killer cursed the cursed animal silently. The footsteps of people and horses suddenly stopped.

Drasan knew he had no choice. He drew strength and felt her wrap around him like the arms of a longing mistress. He smiled slightly at his companion. He felt reborn, pure destructive energy pulsing through his veins.

Whoever these attackers turned out to be, they were already dead.

Before the eyes of the speechless young man, he ran the sword blade on the inside of the wrist, cutting him calmly. The entire blade is in blood. The wound healed so quickly that he hardly felt any pain. He examined the sword carefully to make sure it was all in the blood and spun the miller around it to make sure. The blade hissed and flashed crimson.

The young werewolf stared blankly at the sword and at Drasan. At last understanding seized him, then his eyes glowed red. After a moment he was on his knees, bent in two, spasms of shudder shaking his body.

Here was his friend transforming into a form of fear for the first time.

While Velwel twisted in transformation convulsions, the half-dragon struggled to figure out who he was dealing with. Two people, including a weak magical aura, pointing to a very young adept. His colleague attacked the prince mentally. He felt the cold tentacles of the stranger's mind scrambling inch by inch over his cover, looking for a gap through which to penetrate inside. He decided not to wait.

"I know you guys are there!" He exclaimed as loudly as he could. "Even from here I can smell the stench of your fear! If you leave immediately, it may not be a long and very painful death!" He said it with such confidence that he terrified himself.

For a moment it seemed as if an answer would not come, two men dressed in identical flowing robes the color of blood red emerged from among the bushes. Their shaved bald heads were covered with zigzag tattoos.

The one who looked older stepped forward.

"Bold words, young man, but I do not think you have shown such great foolishness as attacking two priests on the lands of our lovingly reigning Oddon," he said in a voice as calm as he was confident.

Not a single muscle in Drasan's face twitched. He measured the speaker with a cool, haughty look, indicating that empty threats would not scare him. He did not lower his sword.

"These lands still belong to the Sheardon Wolf, if I recall," he growled.

The older man smiled dismissively.

"Your queen is dead, boy, and her lands are left without an heir to the crown. I will forgive you for this slight insult, because I see that you are a foreigner and you may not know our habits," he said in the same calm voice, sending a clear message that he has them for a bunch of idle pussies.

The half-dragon ignored the insult. Instead, he laughed aloud. For a moment he croaked like a madman, then his expression became serious and said:

"You have no idea who I am, do you?" He asked, a menacing gleam in his eyes. "I am the heir to the throne of Sheardon," he added, without waiting for an answer.

Their silent confrontation was interrupted by a wild howl. The old priest's eyes widened with fear at the sight of the curled-up young man whom he had hitherto disregarded.

The shift was almost complete, and a terrifying wolf-human combination lay on the ground. Velwel's body, as in the case of every young werewolf, was covered with clumps of brown hair, but the pointed wolf's face full of sharp teeth did not manage to fully form.

The young monster got up with some difficulty - he did not have time to get used to the new form - and took a seat at his friend's side.

"I will answer on behalf of my companion, for this one is temporarily incapable of it," said Drasan, smiling maliciously. "If you don't want trouble, you will lead us to your king. I'll only talk to him."

To his surprise, the senior priest made a kind of bow.

"Then come, my lord, with us. For it just so happened that the king is visiting the Bregan Fortress at the time," he smiled slyly.

Drasan returned the smile and sheathed his sword. He was more than ten times stronger than the old charlatan, but he waited, his head tilted slightly, like a child of curious effects.

Velwel growled hoarsely, objecting. Like the prince felt a note of falsehood in the old man's voice.

The younger priest took it as an insult. He stepped forward, purple stains appear on his face, and his black eyes radiated with hatred. He rolled up his sleeves, as if he were going to lunge at Drasan with his bare hands.

The half-dragon ignored him, his eyes never leaving the yellowed face of the older man. The man raised his hand in an imperious gesture, at which the young man stepped back, his head bowed.

"Forgive my companion, my lord," he said with unfazed composure. "The hot blood of the ancestors still flows in his veins, and the ancestors considered the sons of the moon a plague brought to this world by the evil goddess Selen," he added for the sake of explanation.

Drasan smiled slightly. He knew he was dealing with someone with a strong mind. One part of it, the more human one, rebelled against the use of force, but was now largely drowned out by the dragon's roaring, pure stream of powerful energy. He was tempted to show those sanctimonious Eardens that beside him their gods were dust.

The only thing that prevented him from doing so was the fear that he would hurt Velwel or Neila.

"I accept the apology, holy man." He said, changing his voice on purpose. "I assure you that my companion will not hurt anyone without my orders."

Velwel smiled at him, presenting a suit of sharp teeth. He probably did not realize that in this form his smile is rather terrifying than liking.

There was a gleam of triumph in the priest's cold eyes. He did not look at Velwel, but at Drasan, who accepted that gaze with unshakable calm.

"We would be glad to take you to the king," he said finally, his voice saturated with venom. "He's checking the condition of the garrison here. For we have heard that in the north the Ridenians have taken Antua and are going to rush towards us, carrying the flaming torch of peace." He smirked, showing that he didn't believe it.

The prince was seething with anger, but forced himself to keep his voice calm:

"If so, lead us to him."

The old priest bowed his head slightly in forced respect.

"I would be glad to do that," he said. "First, I'd like to know your names to make sure you aren't the Ridenian spies."

"Tell me your name and I'll tell you mine," the half-dragon replied in an icy voice.

The man muttered something under his breath, a fake smile returning to his face.

"It is undoubtedly your pleasure to meet High Priest Fidelis and his apprentice Garod," he indicated the younger man, still standing, head bowed.

To Drasan's great relief, Velwel remained calm even in the face of this reptile in human skin. It didn't seem like the time or the place to test your strength.

"I am Prince Drasan, sole rightful heir to the throne of Sheardon," the man replied, emphasizing his origin. "I am accompanied by Velwel, a hired killer and, recently, a werewolf, and Aurelia Roza Nimue van Midelvelt, my fiancée," he added with satisfaction, watching the smile fade from the old priest's face, giving way to surprise.

"In that case, I am asking for forgiveness once again, Your Majesty," he said with a little forced politeness, and once again bowed down.

"I don't want your apologies," the half-dragon drawled coldly. "Lead me to your king."

High Priest Fidelis was abruptly quieter. But he did not get rid of the cool haughtiness. He treated Drasana with the kind of distance he behaves towards the dormant beast.

The prince was perfectly fine with it. He knew little about the Eardenians other than that they had a pantheon of deities they worshiped in bizarre rituals. It so happened that soon, or more precisely on the new moon, it was the festival of Gorah - the goddess of fertility. Getting married during this holiday guaranteed the durability of the relationship and the favor of the goddess.

Drasan glanced at the still unconscious Neila. He wondered what she would say to get married just during this holiday. He did not believe in any God or even in the existence of destiny, but he felt ready for marriage. Moreover, he made this decision himself, without any persuasion of third parties. Besides, it was this new moon that was his twenty-third birthday. It seemed nothing stands in the way... except her irrational fear of marriage.

"Drasan," Velwel's voice snapped him out of his reverie.

He looked at his friend, now in human form. He also found clothes and was holding a saddled mare by the reins.

Have I been dreaming for so long?

"You didn't let me take a loose horse, so..."

"Bregan Fortress is not far away," Drasan interrupted impatiently. "I'll get there on foot."

"But Neila..." Velwel protested, he fell silent, dismayed by the gaze of his companion.

"I'll carry her in my arms," he replied, a little angry and a little amused by the young assassin's concern.

What could so light a burden to bear mean to him? In confirmation of these words, he bent to pick up the girl and froze in mid-motion. Studying her face, he felt a twinge of pain. She seemed so calm... If it hadn't been for the fact that love had hit his head comparable to good wine, he might have left her in Earden. Maybe in time she would forget about him and find happiness in the arms of another.

Hastily he pushed the thought away. Ditching Neila, whatever his intention, would remain a crime he would never forgive himself.

He lifted her limp body as gently as he could.

"We can go," he said to the two priests who waited silently.

They didn't ask about his mount or Neila's weird, incongruous outfit.

They resembled two stone statues.

Drasan passed them, impatiently moving towards the fortress looming on the horizon. Velwel trotted behind him.

The priests watched this strange procession for a while, mounted their horses and followed them.

CHAPTER 26

Yarred raced towards the line of trees on the horizon, his face pressed against the horse's mane. He hoped to reach the border before dark. He had to warn them that the enemy was getting closer. First of all, he needed to find a family.

Bruen's combat training turned out to be extremely useful this time. The bay stallion did not even slow down for a moment, thanks to which, after less than two days, the Sheardoński finally saw the first buildings.

He breathed a sigh of relief.

Only when he passed through the wide-open gate did he become speechless...

The inhabitants of the small town acted exactly as if they had not noticed that there was a war going on. In the main square, several merchants set up carts from which they sold a variety of goods. Most of the clients were women. The accompanying men and children of all ages wandering everywhere were delighted to see the richly decorated weapons and saddles.

Much of the merchandise on offer certainly came from Riden, or perhaps even from the ships that came to Alikorn.

A market during the war!

Captain Cordydian stared and couldn't believe his eyes. The Antuans looked happy and relaxed. They chatted with the Riden merchants about the prices of wine.

After a while, among the noisy crowd, Yarred saw two familiar faces - the innkeeper and his wife. He rode up to them, making his way among the screaming children.

The healer beamed at the sight of him and beckoned him over. The captain jumped off his horse and walked towards her, dragging him with him. The woman looked genuinely happy with the meeting, her husband nodded his head, puffing on a brand-new pipe.

"Hello, my boy," she called, embracing him. "How lucky it is to see you safe and sound."

When Yarred shook his amazement, all he could say was:

"Hello, lady..."

He had no idea what to say. These people cared for his fiancée in the course of his mission, which had no right to succeed. He should have stayed with her then.

"You have a beautiful, healthy son, sir," the healer announced, looking into his eyes.

"What?" Cordydian asked, mentally counting the months to come. Suddenly it felt as if the most important part of his life was missing.

How long has it been since he left Mara? Year? Two years?!

"Your fiancée gave birth many months ago," she repeated beaming, unexpectedly saddened. "I tried to stop her, explaining that traveling in her state is crazy. Unfortunately, she left here shortly after giving birth. She went to the capital, leaving this poor young man who must have lost his mind. He worked with us all winter..."

"But Mara... What happened to her?" The shocked captain asked, unable to comprehend the mass of information.

How could I have left her here all alone? If she's dead, it's only my fault, he thought to himself.

"We thought you knew, my lord..." said the interlocutor, bowing her head. "Your fiancée was crowned Queen of Antua just a few months ago. For it turned out that royal blood flows in her, and your son is heir to the throne."

"It means..." Yarred began, but the rest of the sentence somehow couldn't pass his throat.

"As far as I know, they are safe," replied the old innkeeper, looking at his wife. "But they took that lame boy," he added, lowering his voice to a whisper and glancing uncertainly from side to side. "They were taking all the soldiers. Even those who gave up without a fight."

Captain Cordydian frowned. From what he noticed; most people did not care at all about changing the ruler. Or is it a hoax to confuse the eyes? To find out what was happening here and why, he first had to find Mara.

"Thank you," he said, hugged them both goodbye and mounted Bruen.

"Gods save you." The healer placed her hand on her chest in a pious gesture.

If there are any..., thought Yarred, but he nodded politely to the woman, nudged the stallion with his heel, and strode forward, relieved to leave town.

A familiar green twilight enveloped him as he drove into the densely growing trees. He could finally breathe a sigh of relief. His relatives are safe. The only shock was the news of the coronation of Mara.

Suddenly Bruen twitched his ears and grunted softly. Vigilant to his mount's warnings, Yarred stood in the stirrups and looked around.

Nobody. As always, an ominous silence reigned in the forest.

Yarred swallowed and nudged his sides with his heels, but the stallion didn't budge. He stared nervously at the nearby bushes. With a sudden hunch, the Sheardonian glanced in that direction and froze in terror. Between the brushwood, a pair of ruby red eyes glowed.

A huge wolf, the size of a mountain bear, stepped out onto the path and snarled, grinning fangs the size of butcher's knives. His thick, almost white fur was clearly marked with patches of dried dark brown blood. It was a moment before Yarred realized there was a werewolf in front of him. He knew he would not run away. The beast would catch up with him in a few strides, and he would have no chance of fighting him.

He dismounted and let horse loose. Fortunately, he knew a thing or two about the hierarchy of werewolves. He knelt down and looked away. If he was right, the large predator would not consider him a threat and would simply ignore him. It worked because the werewolf stopped growling and sat up. In front of the stunned Yarred, he doubled over and began to transform. First, fur fell from his body, revealing bare skin, and his limbs shrank into a human shape. The face changed as well, taking on surprisingly familiar features. After a while, in the place where the hairy beast sat a moment ago, he huddled completely naked... Alt'ar!

The Sheardonian had to close and open his eyes several times to find that his eyesight was correct. Meanwhile, the leader of the Assassins' Guild brushed the remnants of wolf fur off his bare shoulders and started walking towards Yarred. The man froze, unable to move. He watched as the man approached his horse and rummaged his saddlebags, trying to find something to wear. After a while he pulled out his pants, examined them, and quickly pulled them on.

The dressed man looked at Cordydian - his eyes regained their former blue tint.

"It's interesting that I'm meeting you," he said, staring at him. His voice was a hoarse growl.

Yarred nodded, still unable to make any sound.

"Your beloved prince has gone to Earden." Alt'ar smiled in such a way that the captain's skin went numb. Only now did he realize that his teeth did not look like human teeth at all. "With any luck, he might be able to persuade old Oddon to send us military backup." He added after a moment.

The man slowly returned to reality. Alt'ar is a werewolf, and Drasan knows it well. But something was wrong, his friend hated the race after all.

"I don't understand," he confessed after a moment, looking at the killer with some dread. "Since you're a werewolf, Drasan should sense you for a mile. He hates your kind almost as much as he hates Dhalia.

The Guild leader smirked.

"I can make myself very persuasive when I choose to," he replied cryptically. "Now tell me what are you doing here, Yarred? Looks like I put you on my recon team."

At that moment, the captain remembered the village and the enemy soldiers who had committed suicide before being captured. He hastily related the events there to the killer.

"Magic suicide?" Alt'ar asked, frowning as if he were considering something.

"It appeared to be," the Sheardonian replied. "I guess they'd rather die than be captured."

"Unlikely," he said quietly. "They must have been drugged, or..." he wondered aloud. "...they were somehow induced to obey blindly..."

"Unfortunately that's not all," said Yarred. "I went to one of the towns in Antua. No sign of any battle anywhere. The soldiers are taken prisoner and taken away to no one knows where. Bal'zar took Antua without losing a single warrior. On the other hand, people are so delighted with him that instead of taking him as a usurper, they see him as a benefactor who opened the border, thus enabling free trade."

"It's impossible. After all, he crossed the line as an aggressor. I heard about how he knocked out the crew of the frontier forts in one night. He made them sleepy with magic, then slit their throats. And people see him as a "good and just ruler"?" Alt'ar clearly did not believe what he was hearing. "It stinks from afar. How had he gained their gratitude so quickly?"

"Black magic," Cordydian suggested, his face dark. "I don't see any other possibility. After all, until recently they cursed him. They will probably welcome our doom with the same joy. According to them, we are a bunch of renegades and rebels."

"It's worse than I expected," said the leader of the Guild. "Let's go to the camp. My people must be warned."

The soldier wanted to protest. Say he has to find his family first, make sure they are safe. One look into the werewolf's blue eyes made him realize a cruel truth. If he does not do something, he will always reproach himself for it.

With a deep sigh, he grabbed the horse by the reins and followed his companion, feeling his heart breaking into a thousand sharp pieces.

***

At the sight of the motionless body lying limp against the wall, staring at him with empty glassy eyes, the guard cursed. That was just what he was missing: now he would have to go for that elven witch.

Ikeron Harel was the prison warden for twenty years. By that time, he had earned a gloomy nickname. He was called a raven because whenever he appeared, someone would most likely either die or would soon be dead.

This prisoner did not sit here long enough to go mad with the darkness, the stench and the howling of others serving various sentences here. Those in small one-man cells usually lasted much longer than those in the collective. Unfortunately, this boy turned out to be much more important than the others. The pale-faced witch ordered to keep him alive at all costs. He even got more food than the others.

Raven could not have foreseen the suicide, especially when the delinquent turned out to be inventive enough to use a tin bowl for this. He had to sharpen her against a wall for several weeks. It never occurred to him that someone could use such an ordinary object for this. Swearing under his breath, he looked carefully at the corpse's face to make sure it was really the one the king had ordered to guard. Green eyes and black hair, just like the miniature Bal'zar gave him. Although the body had already cooled down, he found that the unfortunate man must have died quite recently, otherwise he would have started to stink. Besides, the rats that were not lacking here would have eaten his eyes.

Ikeron continued to curse as he walked down the hall and casually drumming on the bars with a wooden staff. He knew it was driving the prisoners crazy. After a while, a flood of curses and insults from the condemned fell upon him. Reaching the office, he sat back in a chair and reached for an underfed, cold dinner.

Before he could bring his first bite to his mouth, he saw her. Her mere appearance in the narrow corridor significantly lowered the temperature. Raven hated her as much as the other witches, but he was much more afraid. Perhaps because he has had the opportunity to see how prisoners are dealt with more than once. Unlike this cold bitch, he could be considered a benefactor.

Therefore, as soon as she came to his desk, he jumped up. This time she wore a light blue gown with a neckline so plunging that the man had to use all his willpower to keep from staring at her partially exposed breasts. Her loose hair fell in a gleaming cascade to her buttocks. It seemed he had interrupted her at some important celebration.

She smiled, or rather curled her lips in something that was supposed to resemble it. But her gaze remained just as cold.

"Lady Saruviel," Ikeron stammered, trying hard not to reveal how much he was afraid of her. "I just had for you..."

"Hush," she cut him off, bending down so low that her cleavage was right in front of his eyes.

Raven stared at the pink nipples showing through the thin material, forgetting who he was dealing with. Despite all his reluctance, he couldn't deny that he'd love to throw her on the desk and fuck her.

The elf gasped impatiently, tapping her nails on the top of the desk.

"I know your brain is busy at the moment with something completely different, but could you please just focus on my words for a moment instead of insolently staring at my tits?" Her cold, contemptuous voice brought the warden back to reality.

"Well, lady..." Raven swallowed nervously. "It seems that this magician... the one who the king ordered to guard him... he... he... he is dead."

"What?!" She exclaimed, her cool haughtiness vanishing forever, replacing places of disbelief that quickly turned to terror. "You idiot!" She slapped the man in the face so that he stumbled backwards.

Raven stood up, rubbing his cheek. There were three bloody streaks on it.

"It's not my fault," he gasped. "He cut himself with the edge of the tin pan."

Saruviel quickly recovered, and a mask of cold indifference returned to her face.

"Lead me to his cell," she ordered.

Ikeron hastened to obey. He knew that the punishment for neglecting the prisoner would not pass him by anyway, but he preferred to postpone it a bit. The walk down the dark corridor with the witch on his heels turned out to be much longer than before. So he breathed a sigh of relief when they reached the solitary cell. It was the only one to have a door made of iron with a solid lock. Previously, a werewolf was imprisoned here, which is why silver was hidden in the walls and in the door.

Raven turned the key in the lock and opened the door. Several rats scurried at the sight of them, hiding somewhere in the shadows, from which their beaded eyes glittered. The corpse was lying exactly where he had left it. As you might have guessed, the rodents went to work, as evidenced by single bitten holes in the body and eaten eyeballs.

Saruviel knelt by the body and placed both hands on it, using magic to check if the boy was really dead. But Raven knew it. He could see it in her pupils, dilated with fear - this prisoner must indeed have been one of the more important ones.

***

Bregan Fortress resembled a great block of black granite with four tall towers. It was surrounded by a high, double wall, in which the gate seemed to be the only weak point. And this one is made of thick wooden logs reinforced with iron fittings. As they got closer, Drasan noticed that the castle was indeed made of granite blocks, as was the wall.

At the entrance to the stronghold, images of animals and people were carved. The half-dragon guessed they were the figures of the Eardenian gods and their animal counterparts. From the lessons Vaya gave him, the prince remembered that Lupo - the goddess of the hearth - was in the form of a wolf, and Thar - the god of war, a bear. The bas-reliefs placed at the entrance to the city showed an eagle and a mountain lion and two unnaturally beautiful human figures.

At the sight of the priests, the soldiers guarding the gate hastily made a complicated gesture, ending it with the placing of their right hand over their heart. Drasan stopped, and so did Velwel.

High priest Fidelis stepped past them and approached one of the tall men. He exchanged a few words in Earden with him. The guard cast a suspicious glance at the guests, lingering on the unconscious Neila, and motioned them over to him.

Drasan approached him briskly.

"We want to see the king," he said in a tone that couldn't bear any objection.

The sentry looked questioningly at the high priest, and when the high priest nodded his head in agreement, he replied:

"We'll let you in as long as you allow your thoughts to be read."

The half-dragon stiffened. He went through it more than once, in every case it was associated with pain. The last time the elves had done this to him, he had vowed never to allow it again. But he had no choice, for

Bal'zar's army was getting closer and closer, and he couldn't allow another delay.

"So be it," he said, putting all his courage into that short sentence.

The man glanced uncertainly at the priest standing next to him.

"I must also ask you to surrender all your weapons," he said.

This time the prince made a short nod of his head, unbuckled his sword belt and handed it to the man, while Velwel drew off his entire arsenal, finally handing over Neila's sword.

"According to our rules, you would have to wait for me to send for a mage to examine your minds, but..." he again cast a quick glance at the high priest, "...High Priest Fidelis has agreed to do so now."

Drasan looked into the priest's black eyes, who was now smiling mockingly. As if he wanted to ask, "What are you going to do now?"

He had no choice. He let his long slender fingers touch his temples. He immediately flinched. With his presence, the priest resembled a giant worm, slowly digging a tunnel in his mind. He had to use all his willpower not to push him out of his mind. The probing stopped suddenly and the priest moved away from him, an expression of vindictive satisfaction on his face. Fortunately, the half-dragon had hidden deep down somewhere that he didn't want to show him.

Now this skinny man put his hands on Neila's temples. He stood there for a long time, eyes closed, examining her mind. After he finished, he proceeded to check the werewolf. This time it was much shorter, but the young man turned pale and stopped smiling.

"Well, yes," the high priest sighed, turning to the two guards but looking only at Drasan. "A strange jumble, but without weapons they are not particularly dangerous. I will bring them before the king."

The sentry nodded and made another gesture. The heavy gates opened inward, revealing a large paved courtyard. The high priest entered first. Behind him was his apprentice leading both horses, then Drasan with Neila in his arms, and finally Velwel, still very pale and a little confused.

Fidelis directed them not to the front entrance, but to the side - there had to be stables and barracks there. And indeed: soon two stone buildings grew up in front of them. The first looked like a horse farm. There they also left three mounts, then went straight to the second, which also housed an armory.

The priest missed this building as well. They found themselves at the rear of the fortress, where there were also similar doors covered with carvings. The high priest only looked at the men who were guarding them, and they got out of his way. Behind the high gate there was a great entrance hall with a polished granite floor, and here too, images of deities were carved on the walls.

Drasan followed the bald man, wondering if he had been wrong by trusting in his pure intentions. The damned reptile was certainly not very fond of him. Passing another door, they stood in a huge room with a glass domed ceiling. He felt a node grow in his throat.

The room was filled with nearly a hundred people dressed in identical white robes. Women's costumes differed from each other - they were tied with red sashes at the hips. In the center, in front of the marble altar, stood a tall crowned gentleman. His outfit stood out from the rest of the men - he had gold embroidery on the cuffs. Drasan guessed it was King Oddon himself.

The entry into the hall by the three new arrivals caused a commotion. The heads of the kneelers turned in their direction - their eyes sparkled and their pupils were unnaturally dilated. They marched through the center to the dais where the ruler of the Eardenians stood - only now they noticed that his white robe at the front was spattered with fresh blood, and a dead lamb rested on the altar.

Drasan swallowed nervously. Velwel was still pale and seemed to feel like vomiting. Neila hasn't woken up so far.

King Oddon stared at the strangers with a menacing glare from pale blue eyes. He turned out to be a man of truly impressive size, even for an

Earden. He had gray hair and a neatly trimmed beard. Even a loose robe could not hide his broad shoulders and muscular chest. This confirmed Drasan's belief that the man was a natural warrior.

"Your Highness," the high priest bowed deeply. "These people insisted on meeting you. They claim to be bringing bad news."

Drasan straightened and handed the unconscious Neila to Velwel. Out of the corner of his eye, he saw that his face had regained a slightly healthier color. Now it all depended on what he said. He bowed and said:

"Forgive me for this incursion, Your Majesty, but I have come here to ask for your support," he took a deep breath and continued. "Together with a handful of people loyal to me, I am trying to fight the tyrant who wants to subjugate the entire world known to us. If I fail, the world will be flooded with evil. Your sons will either perish or become slaves, and your daughters and wives will be raped many times. We can still stop it together if we go arm in arm. The hour has come for King Earden to mount his battle steed again and grasp his sword."

The monarch stared at Drasan for a long time before finally speaking:

"I have heard about your activities, as well as how your men are a bunch of assassins, mercenaries, and rogues of all kinds. Besides, what is one man against the host of gods? We are protected by a force much greater than these walls." So, saying, the king made a circle with his hand. "You may have a great army, but before the Gods you are dust."

Drasan sighed heavily. He expected this. In an instant, he released his power, letting it flow over his body. He heard muffled screams as red flames covered his body. The show was not an illusion or a juggling trick, it just wanted to show the primal energy of fire, waiting for his orders. The fire he carried within him became truer than the gods of the hosts. He smiled with satisfaction as he watched the astonishment and fear on the king's face.

"Who are you?" He asked devoutly. He certainly thought he had a real god in front of him.

The half-dragon allowed the fire to flow down his arm and formed a single ball, not much larger than an apple. He knew that the people watching him were impressed by this little display.

"Contrary to what you may think, I am not one of your gods," he said calmly. "I'm also not human. Dragon's blood flows in my veins, and what I have demonstrated to you is a small fraction of what I am capable of." As he spoke, he raised the sphere to eye level and allowed it to grow to the size of a human head. "With all my power, I am not able to face the army alone that King Riden is leading," he explained to the stunned Earden king. "That is why I need someone like you by my side, Your Majesty."

King Oddon looked thoughtful again, and when he spoke again it showed a much greater respect for the interlocutor.

"I underestimated you, Drasan, you really are a pupil of the Sheardon She-Wolf. I have always respected her, and now I can see that she has chosen a worthy successor. Bal'zar may have wiped her little kingdom off the face of the earth, but he has failed to destroy the memory of it in the hearts of the people who are still loyal to him. They came to my borders as refugees, but I can see the fire still burning in their eyes. They are waiting for someone to lead them to fight so that they can regain their country." He paused and looked the prince in the eye. "Once, when I was younger, I would have probably joined you without hesitation for a moment. Unfortunately, times have changed and whatever I decide to do, I must have the good of my kingdom in mind. So, allow me to discuss this with my advisers. As long as the gods are with you, you will be able to count on my help."

Drasan sighed. He also predicted it. He knew Oddon was a warrior before he became king, and deep down he is. Unfortunately, priests stood above the king in the kingdom of Earden. It was they who made all the major decisions, consulting with their imaginary gods. They needed long debates to take any action. And time was running out. Facing the army with a handful of people, they had virtually no chance of survival. Even with the support of the werewolves, their forces remained in a deplorable state. He needed the help of regular troops.

"You and your companions can take advantage of my hospitality. There are strict conditions in the Bregan Fortress, because it is primarily a military facility, but you can stay here as long as you like," the king said, taking his place behind the altar again.

The audience was over. Drasan bowed and, with Velwel at his side, followed the servant who was to show them the chambers.

***

The first thing Neila felt was incredibly soft. Surprised, she opened her eyes and saw that he was lying in a large bed with four columns supporting a canopy. Silk curtains hung from it.

I guess I'm still dreaming, she thought as she sat down and ran her hands over the soft sheets. She got up, opened the curtains and gasped. She was in a semi-circular chamber decorated with as much splendor as she could never afford. By the huge window opposite the bed was a huge oak desk, and next to it were shelves piled high with heavy volumes. But that wasn't what interested Neila - at the foot of the lair there was a tin tub full of steaming water, and next to it, on a small round table, on a pile of fresh clothes, a towel.

If it's a dream, a little luxury won't hurt, she thought, throwing off her clothes with relief and tossing them in a corner in disgust. She stepped into the water and reached for the soap. She sat in a warm bath for a long time, glad that no one could see her. She hardly ever had the opportunity to visit the city baths or pay for a bowl of hot water. She scrubbed herself thoroughly, washed her hair, and regretfully left the tub.

She felt reborn. She was just reaching for her clothes when there was a soft tapping. She hadn't even had time to cover herself properly when a servant walked into the room with a tray announcing a royal meal. And behind her...

Neila gasped when she saw Drasan. His appearance has changed dramatically. He looked like a real king, bathed, shaven and with a neatly trimmed stubble! When he got rid of that thick beard, he immediately looked much younger. His hair was tied back at the nape of his neck, which only added to his charm.

He strode towards her like a rooster with his chest proudly unbuttoned so that she could admire his new outfit, which consisted of a white tunic trimmed with gold trim, emphasizing his broad shoulders and muscular chest. Plus, narrow black pants and knee-high boots.

The maid set the tray down on the table and gave Drasan a fiery glare, awkwardly trying to tease him. Then she cursed in front of Neila and fled the room.

The prince smiled as if he really amused him, stepped over the threshold and closed the door.

The mercenary's heart was pounding. Drasan looked like a young god. The embodiment of her boldest fantasies. She gazed at his new image, unable to utter a word. A wave of lust flooded her again. She couldn't and didn't want to fight it, the feeling turned out to be much stronger than her.

"You're so changed," he said, his voice slightly hoarse, lustful. "You're radiant."

The heat in his gaze grew even more powerful. He closed his eyelids, and when he opened them again there was nothing human in them. You could see, he could barely control himself.

Neila released the towel and let it fall to her feet. She stood completely naked in front of him. She wanted him to take possession of her again. And so she belonged to him with all her heart and soul.

She closed her eyes, waiting for him to come over to her alone. She dreamed of the touch of his hot lips against her skin. But nothing like that happened.

Drasan simply picked up a towel from the floor and covered her bare shoulders with it.

Neila couldn't stand the tension. She started crying. She felt humiliated. How could she dream of such a man? They were united by only one night of passion together, after which he offered her something she did not even dare to dream about - marriage.

Had he changed his mind? She didn't even want to think about it, because it would be too hard for her to bear this humiliation. He didn't want her, and she was seduced by him like an idiot! She lost her head for him, and meanwhile he lost interest so easily. He was probably looking for another stupid girl!

The prince sensed the change in her mood as he pulled her to him. He hugged and rocked like a little baby until she calmed down enough to talk about the whole incident.

Neila couldn't look at him, she looked down, but he took her chin and forced her to look at him.

"Don't get me wrong," he said, still in the same hoarse voice. "I want you so much that I can hardly control myself. Please don't make what I'm going to do more difficult for me. I want to do it right..." He broke off. It was difficult for him to talk about it. "You have no idea how hard it is for me to control myself..." He took a deep breath. "Aurelia, I know I don't have much to offer, but I want to live the rest of my days with you..."

She froze, unable to move. Was he just about to reopen the proposals? Or was she still dreaming? By the gods! He wasn't kidding, he really wanted to marry her! What is she supposed to do now? He chased her into a corner and cut off the only way out.

She shivered. What was she going to say to him? Her throat was unbearably dry. Oh gods, for the first time in her life she was afraid! Isn't it idiotic to fear marriage? Especially with someone like Drasan. Hell, he's a prince, and she... Exactly. Who is she? A killer? A noblewoman who ran away from home precisely because she did not want to get married?

"I know that it is difficult for you, and believe me, for me too." He forced her to meet his eyes again. Panic seized her. How is she supposed to explain to him that she doesn't want to get married?! She never wanted to. In this respect, she differed from her peers who dreamed of getting married as little girls. Many of them would have given anything for a chance to marry a prince.

Drasan paused repeatedly, perhaps he was afraid of her reaction. In his gaze, she saw such determination as never before. Was it a matter of life or death for him?

He knelt on one knee and took her hand, and she felt her heart speed up in an instant to a gallop.

"Aurelia van Midelvelt. I love you and I promise to remain faithful to you until the end of my days. Will you do me this honor and you will be my wife?"

And what now? There is a man kneeling in front of her that every woman dreams of, including herself. If he refuses again, it will hurt him. Why is it so hard to answer this one simple question?!

Just don't cry, oh, she scolded herself, straightened, remembering that she was covered with a skimpy towel.

"Yes," she couldn't believe she had finally found an answer. "I'm gonna be your wife."

By the gods, his eyes now shine like two jewels. He resembled a child who finally got the toy they wanted. He hugged her so tightly she gasped, then kissed her. Pleasant warmth spread over her body just as his soft lips touched hers. He kissed her gently and carefully, and she literally melted in his arms. His caresses were gentle, like a touch of wind. And the moment she felt ready to go one step further, he pushed her away from him. His eyes shone with pure desire, but he made it clear that he wouldn't touch her until his wedding night.

She respected his decision.

CHAPTER 27

Velwel stood up and stretched contentedly. It's been a long time since he had the comfort of sleeping in a soft bed, not to mention the fact that yesterday he ate freshly baked meat and drank the best wine. After combing his sparse hair, he walked over to a specially prepared bowl full of warm, steaming water.

How long had he not enjoyed these kinds of luxuries?

For several years, he answered himself. Ever since he left the royal service to become a hired assassin.

He undressed to the waist and rinsed one by one his face, torso and shoulders, finally submerging his entire head in the bowl.

"Are you finished yet?" Drasan's voice rang, amusement mixed with a strange hint of irony.

Velwel turned to him, snorting and shaking himself off the water. And... he was speechless. A completely changed friend stood before him, grinning in a wide grin. Dressed in a magnificent silver tunic with a wolf's head embroidered in gold thread - the symbol of Sheardon, and the same cape flowing from his shoulders to the floor. Plus, he wore matching scarlet pants tucked into knee-length white leather boots. Only the crown was missing and he could have gone down as king.

"Come on," he muttered approvingly. "You're tarted yourself up," he added, disappearing behind the screen. Freshly washed clothes and polished leather boots awaited him there.

"After all, a man only marries once," Drasan replied, examining his reflection in the mirror.

Velwel snorted softly. Yesterday, when a friend showed up to tell him the good news, he thought he was joking. However, when he remained deadly serious, he realized that he really decided to marry, and that with the person who so far shuddered at the mere sound of the word "marriage".

"And how is the future bride feeling?" He asked, putting on his shirt and pulling a white tunic over it.

"She's a bit nervous," the half-dragon replied. It was clear from his voice that he desperately needed someone to talk to her.

"What happened? She refused to wear fancy underwear or high-heeled shoes?" Asked the amused assassin as he pulled on his boots.

"This is not funny!" The prince scolded him.

"Well, all right, all right... I'll talk to her," he replied, struggling to contain his laughter at the sight of his friend's pitiful expression.

***

Neila stood paralyzed, staring at the magnificent gown placed on the mannequin in front of her. It was a gift from the Eardenian king and was commissioned from the finest tailor. The cut was adjusted to her figure so that the outfit stretched over the curves and masked the flaws of the figure. Translucent lace cuffs started at the elbows. The back of the dress and a long white veil are also made of the same lace. The skirt is decorated with golden thread embroidery.

She closed her eyes and opened them again, but the dress stayed where it was. A maid was about to arrive to help her put on this unusual outfit and arrange her hair.

The mercenary went to the mirror, trying very hard not to trip over her own feet. When it all started, she looked at herself critically. So now she looked at the body with the same look. As usual, an ordinary girl with a long face, high cheekbones, a small snub nose and huge blue eyes stared at her. Black hair fell casually over her shoulders. She was surprised to find that some changes had taken place. The hips have become rounded, the previously thin and spindly legs have now become slender, while the formerly small and protruding breasts have become rounder.

Suddenly there was a gentle knock on the door and Neila jumped at the sound.

"P-p... please," she stammered, picking up the robe she had thrown off the floor while admiring her reflection, and hastily wrapped herself in it.

Velwel entered the room instead of the maid. At the sight of him, she breathed a sigh of relief and sat down on the bed, trying not to think about the fact that everything would change in a moment.

The young man whistled softly at the sight of the girl's wedding attire.

"But this wonder could feed a medium-sized village," he said.

The girl gave a forced laugh and looked at him.

Velwel personified all the worst qualities of a man: not only drank, but also irritated with excessive talkativeness and insolence. Its disadvantages could be enumerated endlessly, but it also had several advantages. The most important of these is definitely loyalty to friends.

"What am I going to do now?" She hid her face in her hands.

"Hey, marrying a prince is probably not so bad..." he tried to joke, but he stopped noticing the expression on her face.

"I'm serious," she said through clenched teeth. She tried very hard not to cry. "I love him, but marriage... These are eternal chains..." tears, though she tried so hard to hold them back, pressed into her eyes.

The friend knelt in front of her and took her hands in his.

"Listen to me," he looked into her eyes. "Your future awaits you down there. Consider this a new chapter in your life. A chance to be free from who you were. To start a new life."

"But I... I don't know if I can still lead a normal life," she said softly.

"There's no harm in trying," he said with a smile.

Neila cast a hesitant glance at the gorgeous gown and tried to smile, but it gave out an incomprehensible scowl.

In any moment, a corpulent maid with quite ordinary name - Gertrud - will appear. The present assassin, and the future princess, reluctantly agreed to be served. But she knew that she needed help to insert this masterpiece of tailoring.

As usual, Gertrud complains about her thin, unfinished body and chokes at the sight of broken nails. Then she'll help you put on a heavy wedding gown and take care of your poor-looking hair. Neila steadfastly refused to pin them into a fancy bun, instead they were meant to stay loose. Usually, she hid her hair under a beret or a wig, as it indicated that she was a woman, and preferred to pass for a "beautiful young man" when carrying out assignments.

"You want me to stay here?" Velwel's voice interrupted her thoughts.

She shook her head, wiping away her tears.

"Gertrud will not allow it," she said in a grave tone. "Besides, I do not want you to see me before the wedding, I have to have a spectacular entrance," she tried to smile and this time she did it much better.

Velwel realized that she wanted to be alone and tactfully retreated, closing the door behind him. As soon as he left, the maid burst into the chamber. At the sight of the girl still wrapped in a towel, she gave an impatient mumble. The plump woman got down to tidying her up. She set up the screen and unceremoniously pushed the future bride behind it. The corset was the first instrument of torture.

Humming something under her breath, Gertrud laced him as loosely as possible, which nonetheless made every breath burn as if Neila's lungs were filling with a thousand needles. The dress, which was the recent rage among the local noblewomen, turned out to be terribly heavy and eminently uncomfortable. Trying not to get out of breath and faint, the girl stood paralyzed, watching the woman deftly deal with the hooks and ties of her outfit.

As Gertrud watched her handiwork in delight, Neila couldn't help but feel that she was becoming someone else entirely. She felt as if she was wearing a whole new personality instead of a dress. Or is it just going to happen? After all, marrying Drasan will change her life forever. As his wife, she wouldn't have to earn her bread as a mercenary. After all, it is not appropriate for a princess to run with a sword...

She remembered the Sheardonian's assurance immediately. He had no intention of taking her freedom away, so he could continue to fight if he wished. She felt a little better, took a deep breath, which immediately caused an unpleasant stinging in her chest. She winced slightly, to which Getrud responded by saying:

"Ah, nothing to be afraid of. A wedding is not the end of the world yet."

The girl ignored this statement, still pondering whether she had made the right decision. Drasan seemed ready for marriage, so she did not become a whim. Was it appropriate for her to refuse a man in such a situation, who turned out to be reserved enough not to throw her on the bed when she stood completely naked in front of him?

"That young prince of yours must have delighted the whole court," the maid chattered, brushing her hair. A giant lump grew in her throat as Neila listened. "The wedding ceremony is to be held in the temple and will be presided over by the king himself. According to our custom, married under a full month in the presence of the goddess have a chance for a long, happy and prosperous life."

Does every woman feel this way before her wedding? The bride thought as she listened to the maid's endless monologue, now busy wearing equally heavy and uncomfortable jewelry adorned with sapphires and diamonds. No, definitely not, they are all happy. Why can't I relax?

"There you go," Gertrud announced happily, leading Neila to a large mirror in an ornate dark wood frame.

As soon as the ex-killer looked at it... it took her breath away. A completely different girl was looking at her from the glass. Or is it rather appropriate to say: a woman. The dress perfectly emphasized every curvature of the body and gently widened downwards, the hair flowed over the shoulders in gentle waves, and the necklace decorated with sapphires emphasized the color of the eyes.

"All right," said the maid, smiling brightly. "We'll just try on the shoes."

Neila looked uncertainly at the white high-heeled shoes she was holding.

"Oh, darling," Gertrud said, putting her shoes down with concern in her voice, took the girl by the arm and led her to the bed, where she gently sat her down. "Isn't it worth suffering a little for now?"

Drasan's exultant face flashed in front of Neila's eyes. He seemed so happy when she agreed. She smiled hesitantly at the woman, who reached for her shoes and helped her to get on her feet. The girl got up, feeling very strange. She took a step and staggered, but Gertrud caught her arm.

"Nothing difficult," she chirped as he led her across the room.

Nothing difficult?! The mercenary thought. Her feet felt as if she were walking on hundreds of high heels, every muscle trembling in silent protest. But she ignored the pain and discomfort.

I'm doing this for you, Drasan, she thought, straightening herself with dignity and taking another wobbly step.

***

The temple of the goddess Lupo was built with such incredible splendor that hardly any building could match it. The walls were made of the whitest marble and covered with intricate frescoes depicting scenes related to the goddess herself. The vault was supported by six columns, also decorated with bas-reliefs, and in the center there was an altar, on which bright rays of the moon fell through a circular opening. Two pillows are placed on the plinth under the altar. A bowl filled to the brim with what looked like blood had been placed near the dais.

Next to the altar, clad in a long scarlet-colored ceremonial robe, with his back to the entrance, stood King Oddon. And in front of him, on a snow-white plate, there were two silver goblets and a dagger with an ornate hilt.

Drasan entered the room hesitantly. He did not dare to come closer to the diptych, he stopped at one of the marble columns, decorated with an extremely realistic bas-relief depicting a beautiful woman, perhaps even the goddess herself.

"The Moon-Lovers' ceremony is an extremely important and sacred event for us," said the ruler solemnly, turning to Drasan.

The half-dragon barely stopped himself from flinching at the sight of his eyes with unnaturally dilated pupils. Yes, he had seen people in a trance and under the influence of drugs, but this was the first time he had come across anything like it in someone who was not a priest, but a king himself.

"You must have many questions," said King Oddon calmly, not noticing the duke's vehement reaction.

"I do not know your habits, my lord," replied the Prince, bowing down in the usual bow.

"It is understandable, but nevertheless it makes me surprised that, as a non-believer in gods, you decided to marry your chosen one right here." He ran his hand across the temple. "Lupo is first and foremost the mother goddess, the guardian of the hearth, especially the women themselves. Therefore, rape is punished most severely right here in Earden, for as a vessel, the goddess - a woman cannot be desecrated. With us, it is the woman who chooses her husband, and not the other way around. Only when she herself wants to give him a body, we are dealing with a sacred act of getting close."

Drasan listened to him, nodding his head and trying not to think about his past in which he had seduced more women than he could count. He had never respected one the way he respected Neila now. He often played with their feelings and did not attach too much importance to how much harm he was doing them.

"I am aware that you may disapprove of our habits. However, I can see that you respect them, or at least you respect the rules adopted here," he said these words with dignity and dignity. "You are not human, but I trust that, as in other pagan countries, at least you understand the sanctity of the wedding ceremony. You must not take her lightly. Marriage is a big step."

Drasan nodded again. What he heard sounded menacing.

Were the Eardenians not indulging in debauchery like more than half the Lineland?

Many Sheardonian husbands, though sharing a bed with the woman, delighted in making room available for a few, if not a dozen, others. Some have acted like a breeding stallion in this respect, trying to get along with as many women as possible. And so, they turned out to be much better than the rest of the inhabitants of the peninsula. For example: in Alikorn, a man became the owner of a woman as soon as he married a woman, and fathers were happy to make their daughters' bodies available for a fee. Antua has become a real den of debauchery and a paradise for adulterers, where one can fight for position and privileges through the bed.

Everything looked completely different here. Though he had previously considered the Earden a nation full of prejudice and superstition, he had to admit that some of the rules that governed here are much more civilized than in the rest of the peninsula's kingdoms. Women were treated with respect here. The men looked at their wives with love, and treason amounted to a punishment worse than death. Adulterers were castrated. Rapists were lynched, and anyone breaking the law established by gods or priests was hung or put in stocks depending on the offense. Each criminal, regardless of his position or committed crime, was severely punished.

"I will not inquire why, as a pagan, and at the same time a strange creation of nature, you decided to marry your chosen one before the Altar of the Moon in the sanctified presence of the goddess herself. But try to respect the ceremony itself," continued King Oddon, unaware that his monologue was flowing past the prince somewhere.

"I will try, Your Majesty," replied Drasan.

The king looked at him for some time with those strange eyes, he turned to the altar, thus implying that he had said everything.

Leaving the temple, Drasan felt much better, for although he did not believe in gods, throughout the entire conversation he had an overwhelming impression of someone much more powerful than himself.

***

Gods, how can you walk in such a thing! Neila thought, focusing all her attention on not stumbling over the veil that trailed behind her.

Every step and breath were torture. After climbing just a few steps down the spiral staircase, her lungs hurt, her feet stung, and the muscles in her calves and thighs burned. She held on bravely, because the presence of Velwel, walking by her side, encouraged her. Drasan was waiting for them at the entrance to the temple.

"Are you nervous?" The young killer asked her.

"No," she lied smoothly.

In fact, she hoped that as soon as she saw her lover, all the tension would dissipate. She hasn't seen him since the decision to get married. Apparently, it was related to some strange Eardenian tradition.

"You're tough, you can do it," the young man consoled her, completely unaware of her mental and physical condition.

She could become as hard as a diamond. It only worked when facing an armed enemy. And when it came to male-female contacts, all her courage and self-confidence disappeared somewhere. She loved Drasan, but still had no idea how she would react when she stood with him at the altar.

It is not known when they reached the bottom of the stairs, at the end of which a corridor led directly to the double doors of the hall where the ceremony was to take place.

Her future awaited her there. She took a deep breath and started down the stairs. Her heart pounded as she neared her goal.

And finally, she saw him. He was standing in front of the door waiting for her, and he looked even better than the last time she had seen him. His face lit up with a smile.

Despite the lack of a crown, it looked truly royal.

She smiled hesitantly, and when he offered her an arm she clung to it. At that moment she felt grateful to Gertrud who insisted on wearing a veil. Thanks to it, no one saw the blushes on her face.

"Just don't let me go," she whispered, her voice tense.

He laughed softly, but said nothing, just led her to the temple's double doors.

They entered a great hall where a large crowd of nobles and courtiers gathered. Everyone stared at them. Neila pressed against Drasan's side, feeling the hundreds of stares digging at her like a swarm of angry bees.

The girl led herself to the altar, trying not to think that everyone was staring at her.

It's just a wedding, she consoled herself mentally. It won't be long.

She lifted her head a little and looked at her partner. His face was calm and determined, but she knew it was a mask to hide terror. He was as afraid as she was.

It cheered her up.

The platform, covered with white cloth, was getting closer. They both saw the king waiting for them.

Drasan knelt in front of him, pulling Neila with him, their heads bowed as a sign of respect.

King Oddon beamed, raised his arms, and the assembled crowd fell silent.

"Marriage is both a joy and a duty to another person," with these words he looked only at the prince and his bride. "They say love is blind, but I don't believe it. Love just sees things differently." He paused, and his gaze fell on Drasana. "Get up," he ordered.

As soon as the prince obeyed, the king took Neila's hand in his big hand and helped her to stand. Then he connected her hand to that of the half-dragon.

"By the law given to me by the Gods, I declare you husband and wife!" He announced, lifting their clasped hands and showing them to all gathered.

As soon as these words were gone, the room burst into applause. Neila couldn't help but smiled brightly at her husband. Then a smile lit his serious face. Then, regardless of everything, he leaned down and gave her a passionate kiss...

***

A fifteen-year-old adolescent nervously shifted from foot to foot, waiting for the ruler to give him the floor. Finally, Bal'zar looked at him from beneath a furrowed brow and, waving his hand, commanded in a bored voice:

"Speak."

"Your Majesty..." stuttered the messenger. "...all indications are that the reconnaissance unit... the one sent to the edge of the forest. They... a group of werewolves attacked them..." he finished, moving nervously.

On the sidelines, Dhalia raised an eyebrow.

This is new. Werewolves rarely formed into herds. Most of these monsters preferred a solitary lifestyle. The group of werewolves marauding so close to their camp was a serious problem that needed to be looked at as soon as possible.

"I thought those lousy mongrels were afraid of magic. That's what your stinker told us," now the young king was speaking directly to her.

The witch's eyes narrowed dangerously. Before she could open her mouth to answer, that smart bald man Alder told her:

"Yes. But there are exceptions to this rule. One of them is the leader of the "Assassins Guild", Alt'ar." He said in a superior tone, while looking at Dhalia, wanting to provoke her.

Bal'zar bristled at the mention of that name. Alt'ar was clearly to bite him.

"And what is so special about him?" He snorted, masking his anger with contempt.

"Ah, emperor! How I regret your disregard for our common lessons," sighed the mage. "If you only listened to me more carefully, you would know that a werewolf with such leadership skills can gather around him not one pack, but from several dozen to several hundred sons of the moon. Getting rid of him should become our priority."

"Drasan is our priority," snapped Dhalia. She couldn't help herself; the bald bastard was getting on her nerves more than the crowned one.

Bal'zar smiled and nodded graciously, admitting she was right.

"It's true," he said seriously, which surprised even her. "Drasan can become a symbol for all who believe this nonsense about the Chosen One."

"This is not nonsense," growled the witch, leaping up from her chair. "You dare to doubt my clairvoyant powers, Emperor?" She pronounced the last word contemptuously.

His highness surprised her again with his balance. Even if her words struck his pride, he did not show it.

"Sit down, my dear," he ordered her in a cool voice, turning back to Alder. "Go on, master. I want to know if this shaggy simpleton is as dangerous as our reptilian friend."

The mage smiled slightly.

"He's even more dangerous, my lord," he replied. "The dragon has his weakness in girl form, and Alt'ar has none. There is nothing we can threaten him with. Plus, he's damn good at what he does..."

"That's not what I asked, Master," Bal'zar interrupted. He was clearly bored with this discussion. "I have my spies everywhere, and I know all our Chosen One's weaknesses well, but Alt'ar is a mystery to me. You say there is no weakness, and I say there must be at least one weak point to hit."

"Rodian," Dhalia said suddenly, still amazed at the young lord's insight and leadership. "He protects her. We don't know what for or why, but she's the only one who means something to him."

"Witch? This is interesting..." Bal'zar mused, leaning back a little and rubbing his thin chin. "What do we know about her?"

"Not much more than that long ago she disowned magic," the woman replied, smiling with satisfaction that she knew something the two-faced mage had no idea. "She hasn't much magic power, maybe the werewolf keeps her for other benefits." She laughed derisively.

"Or maybe, unlike you, he likes to have a permanent partner?" The ruler said, giving her a short contemptuous glance.

His words struck her like a treacherous blade.

How did that brat know about her affairs? She was careful and tried to maintain discretion. She chose only young men devoid of magical powers as lovers. Had he expected her to remain faithful to him after he had rejected her?

The Emperor looked at her carefully.

"There are no secrets to me, my dear," he told her coldly. "Have you forgotten who I really am?" His eyes flashed purple for a moment, then turned back to their normal blue color. "Who you sleep with doesn't matter to me as long as you remain loyal. What concerns me, however, is your weakness for the half-dragon. Remember, your reptilian favorite is only a tool in the hands of my jealous sister. The key to my undoing." He laughed softly, malevolently. "But I am a generous ruler, so I will give him a choice: he will succumb to me or he will die. Your love for him doesn't matter."

What is this madman raving about?! Thought Dhalia. She felt the ground slowly slipping from under her feet. She released the beast from its cage, even more terrible and dangerous than Drasan. A monster that will devour the whole world and remain insatiable. Oh, how foolish she had turned out to be naively believing that she could control him.

"Pay attention to your thoughts, viper..." murmured the young ruler, so that only she would hear it. "Otherwise, you will share the fate of your favorite. Do you think I don't know about your intrigues? About how you would happily sink a knife in my chest, treacherous bitch?" There was an expression of vindictive satisfaction on his face. "My brother told me a bit about you. I know you need to be kept an eye on you, and that is why you will stay by my side until I decide otherwise."

Dhalia forced a crooked smile to mask her cold rage.

"What about Boris?" She asked. "I am expecting his return here."

"If I were you, I'd be worried more about yourself than about that stinking minion." Bal'zar replied, stretching lazily. "He's useless to me. He is rubbish, and I have no qualms about him."

"Then you kill him on a whim?" She asked, trying to mask her disgust with a hint of irony.

"I will kill him, for example, how traitors are dealt with," replied the king, carefully watching her reaction to these words. "Don't think I haven't seen you. Boris let himself be captured at your request, right?"

She froze. How the hell did he know? That day, she sat in a magically sealed room and checked the spells for leaks three times before deciding to merge her mind with that of a werewolf. She then controlled him and forced him to lose. She must have had someone in the Liberation camp.

"I wanted a spy of my own," growled Dhalia, angry that he saw through her so quickly.

To her surprise, Bal'zar laughed out loud.

"I know what you were planning, treacherous bitch, fortunately I managed to thwart your idea," he said, still smiling. The smile chilled her to the core. "Tomorrow before dawn, I will give the order to attack and wipe the meager remnants of the Antuan army, and when I deal with them, I will chase the rebels out of the forest and kill them like pests. There will be no epic battle. By the time your favorite comes back from Earden, it'll be over. When I crush his "Liberators"," he snorted contemptuously, as if the name made him amused, "I will find him and force him to surrender. And if he doesn't bend, well… one less opponent."

"I don't know what you're talking about," said the witch, trying to pretend to be politely surprised. "Since his capture by Alt'ar, Boris has acted completely alone. He somehow got out of my control. I don't know where he is now, but I'll find out."

Bal'zar leaned toward her, a cruel expression on his face.

"Your assurances do not interest me. I require absolute obedience. Otherwise, I will make sure that you die long and slowly."

CHAPTER 28

Berg knew he had to be more careful than usual. Penetrating the Liberators turned out to be extremely easy. He pretended to be a deserter, forcibly incorporated into the Riden army, and they accepted him as theirs. The problem was that all these people, both men and a handful of women, turned out to be trained killers. So, it became impossible to blend in with the crowd. Most of the Guild members resembled characters in a nightmare. Most of them proudly displayed the scars on their shoulders and face, sometimes boasting among themselves how they had obtained them.

The greatest freak among them all was the dragon. He usually stayed aloof, rarely took part in discussions, and looked as if he was bored of it all. He was a bit like Bal'zar, though unlike King of Riden, he lacked charisma and good manners. And most importantly: he did not blindly worship the Chosen One. He did not hesitate to criticize his decisions, to call him arrogant and conceited, and even to openly oppose orders.

Most of the killers were located in the center of the camp, while others remained aloof in loose groups. Ridenian decided that it would be safer for him to join the minority. Nobody seemed surprised by this, nobody cared.

Thanks to this indifference, Berg was able to enjoy the freedom and quietly work out the structures of the Guild. He noted, among other things, that the killers follow a strictly defined hierarchy. Among them, he distinguished ten commanders who looked after small divisions of no more than twenty people.

One of them, to his surprise, was a woman named Rilia. She stood out among thugs not only by short stature, but also by an exceptionally ferocious character. Typical woman with big balls. People loved and hated her at the same time. It was hard to say no to a woman with girlish features, big green eyes and lush hair the color of a ripe cherry. At the same time, her body had almost perfect proportions. She seemed to be the embodiment of all male fantasies.

She was the only one who liked to talk to the young Ridenian and even had some kind of sympathy for him.

So even now, as he sat alone, silently chewing on his miserable meal, it was Rilia who had come over to him. With a deep sigh, she sat down next to him and stretched her legs out, crossing them at the ankles.

"Alt'ar is back," she said, not hiding that the news pleased her. "This is our leader, and I thought you might like to meet him. You may have one last chance." She added with a crooked smile. "Judging by the rumors, King of Riden has gathered a powerful army on its way to us. Tens of thousands. Do you have any idea what that means? They will crush us with mere numerical superiority. I don't know what this whole Drasan imagined himself, but for me it's just suicide. It takes a miracle to win against them."

Berg couldn't help but smile.

Alt'ar's slayers slowly became overwhelmed by the fear that the ant probably feels the second before it dies under a soldier's boot. Bal'zar had thousands of soldiers ready to fight and die for him, while the half-dragon's allies crumbled. No order will stop them. They will not be cut into slices in the name of some king. They were subordinate to no one but a werewolf. A seasoned soldier, Berg had no doubts that everyone would be scattered when his leader died.

Rilia hit the nail on the head. The liberators needed a miracle.

Still, the commotion at the edge of the camp caught his attention. The girl stood up as well, looking in that direction. And then the spy saw him.

Tall, blond with a supple but muscular body, striding dignified with a large gray wolf at his feet. He didn't look strong, his eyes betrayed him. The eyes of a patient predator.

As he passed, the Ridenian was struck by the power of that gaze, forcing him to bend his neck.

"Amazing, isn't he?" Rilia asked. In her eyes he saw respect bordering on reverence. "Too bad he despises women so much."

Berg blinked in surprise. He had thought of Rilia as a loner the whole time, only now, when he heard the longing in her voice, he realized that the girl was in love with the leader.

So this is how the power of a born alpha manifests itself, he thought, a little surprised, and a little fascinated.

"Yes," he muttered, without much enthusiasm. "Everyone seems to have great respect for him."

The girl wasn't listening. She stared at the man walking away. After a while, she followed him along with the overjoyed crowd of killers, and Berg, whether he wanted it or not, had to follow her.

***

The chamber in the north tower served one purpose only. A huge bed of dark wood was placed directly opposite the door. The bed linen was made of silk, the windows were hung with heavy velvet curtains, thanks to which there was a slight twilight here, lit by the light of a few candles set in gilded candelabras. All this in warm colors: from pink through red and gold.

Neila looked stunned by the splendor.

Drasan walked over to the bed and sat on its edge.

"It's a lovers' chamber," he said calmly. "The Eardenes believe in the magic of their first night together. According to them, it unites spouses and helps them achieve fulfillment."

The girl stared at him, feeling much more awkward than ever. The uncomfortable clothes made a pain, and the feet, in their tightly tied boots, burned. Still, she couldn't bring herself to one move.

Her husband looked calm and confident, but deep down she knew it was appearances. He didn't want to scare her.

"We don't have to do this today if you don't want to," he said suddenly, looking into her eyes. "Just one word of yours and I'll leave."

Gods! He was ready to give up her wedding night for her! She felt hot tears under her eyelids. She couldn't cry, she had to stay strong. For him.

"I don't want you to leave," she whispered without looking at him. Staring at the golden and red carpet seemed so much easier to her. "I just..." She didn't have time to finish this sentence, and he was beside her, embracing her with a tender gesture, stroking her hair and whispering soothingly in her ear:

"Like I said, we don't have to do this today. You know that I don't believe in all this nonsense about gods and I ignore stupid superstitions..."

"But I want it," she announced in a slightly pouted tone, looking up to meet his eyes. To confirm her words, she undid the bodice of her dress and pushed it off her shoulders. The heavy material fell to the floor, forming a golden and white puddle. She stood in front of him, wearing a lace petticoat just below the knee and that damned corset.

Drasan, perhaps reading her mind, with one smooth movement unlaced this gloomy torture device. He moved closer, so close that the heat emanating from his body enveloped her. The heat of hardly suppressed desire.

She let him embrace her, take possession of the body. Her husband reacted to the call exactly as she had expected. With a sudden, abrupt movement, he pulled her close to him. The first kiss turned out to be gentle, as if it needed permission for more. She handed him back with so much enthusiasm that it must have surprised him, because he suddenly pulled away.

The charm was broken.

Neila opened her eyes only to meet the gaze of green eyes. These glistened in the dimness of the room.

"I love you," he whispered and kissed her with so much passion that the whole world swirled before her eyes.

***

Drasan rose from the bed as silently as he could, so as not to wake Aurelia, still deeply asleep. He found the pants and pulled them on, leaned in to brush his lips against the cheek of his beloved, now coated with a soft blush. There seemed to be something magical about it. Maybe because he had never felt such a connection with any woman before.

Before that, it had been easy for him to leave the bedroom after an intoxicating night. Now he stood petrified, unable to take his eyes off Aurelia's body. She seemed more beautiful than ever before: her skin, hair, and lips shone with a glow that had been hidden so far. He stayed where he was, absorbing the sight and not daring to take a step so as not to disturb the peace of the moment.

Finally, as soft as a cat, he slipped out onto the small semicircular balcony to gaze up at the sky in the gray predawn light. He took a deep breath, then a second.

What is happening with me? He asked himself, closing his eyes. He tried to control the lust that was drawing him towards his sleeping wife.

He had never felt a slave to any woman before. They served him, not the other way around. It turned out completely different with Neila. From the beginning, he felt that he had a certain bond with her.

"This is love, Chosen One," the Lady of the Dead whispered, suddenly standing by his side. Today she wore a white bride's dress, complemented by a wreath of strange black flowers. "Love is nothing but slave chains."

"Not true," he replied, wondering how weak and uncertain his voice sounded. "Aurelia gives me strength. Thanks to her, I have a purpose in my life."

"On the contrary, Drasan," the Lady of the Dead laughed unpleasantly. Her black eyes flashed. "Love for this girl is your weakness and any enemy will take advantage of it without the slightest moment of hesitation. You do not understand it yet, but you will soon find out that it is a never-ending series of suffering. You can deny it, you can lie to yourself, but you can never change anything. Your mother gave her life for you because she loved you. Your guardian has sacrificed the lives of all the people to protect you. This is the true face of love."

"You are lying," drawled the prince, unable to help himself. Each of these words became a thorn in his tormented soul.

"Everyone who loves sacrifices they lives with joy, because they believe that this victim will reverse the bad fate. Didn't love make you take an oath to me?"

Drasan turned away angry with himself. He couldn't deny it because it was the honest truth. He surrendered himself to this being's command to save Aurelia from death. But as soon as he did so, he froze, unable to move, for here was his beloved standing before him, her eyes wide with fear.

"Who are you talking to?" She asked.

The prince heard a cold laugh in his mind.

He cursed under his breath. He didn't feel ready for this conversation, but in such a situation he couldn't put it off.

"It's complicated," he replied in a casual tone. Deep down, he wanted to tell her everything, though he didn't know where to start.

"We've got plenty of time," she said, pulling him back towards the bedroom.

They sat down on the bed. Drasan still did not look up. For the first time, he was afraid that he would not be able to put it into words. Finally, he took a deep breath and looked up at her.

"Hope you do realize who you got involved with?" He asked, pain in his voice.

The question surprised her completely. He could see it in her eyes but didn't wait for an answer.

"As far as I know and what I have discovered, I am a three-race half-dragon, and since my mother was from Shantar Island, I also have some elven blood. This in turn means that I can live for many hundreds of years aging more slowly than ordinary people..." He broke off, because he had no idea how to tell her about it. "I have a grim fate," he resumed the thread. "All those who are related to me in some way pay a high price for it. Sometimes they also find death. I don't quite know why this is happening." He looked at her in distress. "She even tried to get you, but I grabbed your soul from her before she took it."

For a moment the girl sat paralyzed. She clearly understood nothing of his speech.

"You mean I got hurt? It wasn't your fault," she said confidently.

"Yes, mine," he replied forcefully. "I shouldn't get you involved in this fight, or any of you. I should have chased you away while I still had the chance. Until the fate that haunts me also overtakes you."

"Drasan..." she began, but he put a finger on her lips.

"Let me finish," he asked softly. "When I found out you were dying... I just couldn't let it. I did what I had to, called the Lady of the Dead, and offered her eternal service in exchange for your life. From then on, I am, in a way, her property. She's stalking me and giving orders..." He grimaced and rubbed the scar on his forearm, the mark of a wound he'd inflicted on himself. "I thought you should know that, especially now that you've become part of my life."

The girl stared at him for a moment, expecting him to burst out laughing. But he remained deadly serious.

"So..." she began and stopped. She couldn't find the right words.

The prince understood perfectly well what he must feel now. He had been trying to tell her this for several days, but somehow, he hadn't been able to do it before the wedding. He was now relieved to have lifted a heavy burden from his heart.

"If it weren't for the fact that you are quite extraordinary yourself, I would probably think you were crazy." She finally said. "However, considering the fact that I have been staying next to creatures straight from legends for a long time, another one will not make a difference." Suddenly she looked deep into his eyes. "How long has this been going on?" She asked, there was no trace of regret in her voice, rather resignation.

Drasan withstood that look and began his story:

"I saw her for the first time after I found out about the destruction of Sheardon. She came to me when I was looking for solitude, and has been a regular visitor since then, both when awake and in dreams. Let's call it doom, malice of fate, or a whim of destiny, but in some strange way I know that he is not a flesh-and-blood creature. More than once it has made me feel it. According to her words, I must destroy Bal'zar before he reaches his goal. Otherwise, not only those I care about will die, but also those who decide to stand up to him. So, I can't back down."

"How can you be sure that the creature you talk to in your visions is exactly who it claims to be?" The girl asked skeptically. "Or is it just a trick used by Dhalia to provoke you into attacking Bal'zar?"

Drasan sighed. That's what he feared. Aurelia was one of those who believed only what was tangible and questioned everything they had not seen with their own eyes. He doubted that the Lady of the Dead would agree to reveal her presence to her. So, he had to make her believe him.

"I know you have a hard time understanding it." He began in a gentle tone. "However, for many months I have not been the master of my fate. If you question the truthfulness of my words, take a look at this." He showed her the scar on his forearm that still remained black, and its edges had an unhealthy purple hue. "Magic only leaves such traces," he explained to her. "Black magic."

She nodded her head. Her expression clearly showed that she did not understand what he was getting at.

"That day, I only thought about saving your life, only later it dawned on me what cost it happened..." He broke off, did not know how to explain it.

For lack of ideas, he removed the locket from his neck and looked at it. Despite its unusual oval shape, it had something extraordinary about it. The animal was accurately reproduced: its head was turned towards it; its tiny eyes were made of amber crumbs so that they looked alive. It was as if the wolf was staring at him. He remembered the moments when he saw the object hanging around his babysitter's neck. Vaya never left it. He remembered the few times they'd sat in the garden together and she'd told him all sorts of stories. His favorite story turned out to be "The Myth of the Courageous King of Laudas." The hero had a weapon that no magic could handle. The sword that made him invincible...

Could it be, he thought, staring at the necklace. He recalled Vaya's words: "The medallion only apparently has no value; it serves as the key to Sheardon's greatest treasure." What if she meant just... the sword of Laudas.

"Drasan?" The quiet voice of his wife sitting next to him helped him shake off his trance. He tightened his hand on the locket and looked at her with a twinkle in his eyes.

"Aurelia..." he began. "I think I just understood why Vaya left this locket for me. This is more than an ancestral memento; I feel as if I hold the key to Bal'zar's undoing in my hand."

"I'm afraid I still don't understand any of this," the girl announced, staring at him with wide eyes.

He sighed deeply. Aurelia's reaction was exactly as he had expected. He knew he couldn't explain it to her with words... she had to see it for herself.

With that resolve, he stood up and held out his hand to her.

"Come with me," he said urgently.

She took his hand, hesitated, and looked at her outfit. It consisted of a silk petticoat.

"Nobody will see us," he said, nodding toward the balcony, he sent her one of his dazzling smiles. "We'll fly."

"What?!" She asked, taking a step back. "Finally get it to your head that I'm not flying. I prefer to feel the hard ground under my feet."

Her reaction amused him.

"Flying is not so bad. This is the fastest way to travel, apart from magic portals." He said smiling to cheer her up. "If we leave now, we have a chance to reach Sheardon before dawn."

"To Sheardon?" She repeated, completely amazed. "And why do you want to go back there?"

"Because I have a feeling, I missed something important," he replied. "There must be a hiding place or a secret chamber..."

The answer was as obvious as the use of the medallion. Vaya personally showed him the entrance to the locker located... in the stable.

"The stable," he whispered, more to himself than to her. "This is where the entrance to the chamber where the sword is hidden!"

"I have no idea what you're talking about," Aurelia said, and to his surprise she smiled slightly. "But judging by the tone of your voice, it's something really important. So, fly alone, and I will wait here and try to explain your disappearance to King Oddon as best I can."

The prince looked her deeply in the eyes, leaned down and gave her a long passionate kiss.

"I love you, Aurelia," he whispered.

"And I love you," she replied. "Go now," she added with a smile, gently pushing him away from her.

"I'll be back as soon as possible," he promised, standing up.

As he stepped out onto the balcony and the cool air blew over him, he felt indescribable joy. He unleashed his power and let the flames engulf him. The transformation was coming to him as easily as breathing. He was afraid that the balcony would not bear the weight of the mighty beast, so before it completely transformed, he climbed over the railing and jumped down. Even before the end of the transformation, he unfolded his wings, still covered in flames, and took to the air.

Preparing for take-off, Drasan involuntarily tilted his head up and looked wistfully towards the balcony. He knew deep down that Aurelia would be waiting for him, but the thought of the separation made his heart ache. At last, he understood what his guardian had told him over and over again: "Love is more than just meeting your own needs. It is the desire for the presence of the other person and the pain at the thought that you might leave them someday."

CHAPTER 29

Sword of Laudas - if this is true, then Vaya has left him a weapon capable of withstanding even the most powerful magic. After all, King Laudas himself had great magical powers. Unfortunately, the legend did not explain how he came into possession of this weapon. She portrayed him as the conqueror of all evil. After the end of his reign, the sword was lost and despite the fact that many daredevils tried to find it, no one managed to find it. Where it came from, Vaya, one of the witches the hero hated, was a mystery. The artifact had been hidden for hundreds of years, and now it turned out to be within reach. It was a gift from fate.

Such thoughts obscured his joy of gliding until the shadow of the Wolfwood appeared on the horizon. He lowered the flight looking for a place where he could land, finally saw a small clearing near the lake and headed there too. Before he settled down, he focused on the transformation again, and after a short while he stood in the center of the burned-out circle. He glanced at the ruins of the castle looming in the distance, turned on his heel and started in the opposite direction. During this short flight, he had a great opportunity for reflection. He then realized that while he absolutely disapproved of Yarred's behavior, an old friend might have something very important to convey to him, perhaps even a letter from Vaya herself. He decided to find him.

He was barely between the trees and the familiar twilight enveloped him, here and there illuminated with a greenish glow. He knew Alt'ar had moved the camp closer to the city, but he wasn't sure where exactly. Mental contact with the Guild leader was too much of a risk these days, and he had little choice.

He focused, targeting a familiar consciousness.

Alt'ar - he sent a call and waited for an answer.

Drasan? The answer came faster than he expected. What are you doing here? I thought you were in Earden working on that old madman, Oddon.

I have returned because I have something to do here, replied the Prince, trying to reveal as little as possible. Don't you know where I find Yarred Cordydian?

He sensed the werewolf's surprise before it even sent him a question.

I thought that fair-haired dribbler had fallen out of favor with you? Why are you looking for him?

The half-dragon felt impatient.

Let's assume that I have a few questions for him - formulating thoughts so that no outsider could find any worth of information in them turned out to be much more difficult than he expected.

So look for him near the stream - Alt'ar sent him an image of the indicated place and terminated the connection.

The Sheardonian without delay went to the place indicated. For he knew them very well. He often went there while hunting, and also to think. A narrow path trodden by forest creatures led to it. As he walked, he pondered what he had discovered. He even considered sharing it with his old friend, but quickly dismissed the idea. Even for noble reasons, Yarred acted shamefully, leaving the pregnant fiancée completely alone. Such behavior proved that he was not worthy of his trust.

As the werewolf had said, he found the former guardsman sitting carelessly among his new companions from the reconnaissance detachment. They camped near the stream, enjoying the respite. Bal'zar's troops were still a week away, so they had nothing to do.

Seeing the prince, Yarred sprang to his feet. His companions, surprised by this reaction, began to search for its cause, and when they noticed Drasan, they politely nodded their heads and invited him to join them. They were sitting in a circle by a small fire over which a small hare was roasting. There was an open barrel next to it, from which the pungent odor of booze radiated. Each of the companions held in his hand a tin cup half full of this drink. One of them eagerly stretched him towards him, but the prince shook his head and looked at Yarred and said:

"Can we talk privately?"

His friend shrugged.

"Sure," he said, got up and followed the half-dragon into the trees.

When they were out of voice, Drasan sat on one of the fallen trunks and, looking at his companion, said:

"While I do not approve of what you did, I trust you had a good reason, and I am eager to hear an explanation."

Yarred shot him an uncertain look, looked down, and said:

"Sometime after our parting, after I discovered that Mara was pregnant, one of my former subordinates, Miral, showed up at the inn where we were staying. It turned out he was injured. So, I have made every effort to get it dressed. He had with him a letter marked with the royal seal." With that, he reached under his puffer, took out a slightly threadbare roll of parchment, and handed it to Drasan. "Its content seems to be meant for you."

Grabbing the scroll, Drasan realized this conviction, sensing a slight quiver of magic on the seal. Only a magical being could break it. Feeling his heart speed up rapidly, Drasan broke the seal, unfolded the parchment and looked at the even rows of so well-known writing. Vaya must have made it long before her death. Without delaying any longer, he began to read:

My dear son.

The moment you read these words; I will be dead. That's why I decided to write down everything you need to know that will help you win against Dhalia. You may remember how eagerly you listened to the stories of King Laudas. Well, there is also a grain of truth hidden in this myth. Namely, it's about the sword. A weapon worthy of a king, able to withstand any spell and annihilate any magical creature.

The artifact exists, although it has been hidden so that only someone worthy of its drawing can find it. I left you the key that opens the entrance to the tunnel located just below the castle, there is a secret chamber in which a chest is waiting, and in it the greatest treasure of Sheardon - King Laudas' Sword.

Knowing its power, remember to handle it with care and not betray yourself to Dhalia that you have it. Otherwise, the power of the magic blade will be the key to your defeat. Don't forget that she is a seer and keep your intentions unpredictable. The witches cannot know that you have acquired this sword, so if you encounter any of them, kill without hesitation. Even one mental summon can reveal just how powerful a weapon you have at your disposal.

I know you will be up to the challenge as always, but as always, I am warning you against over-confidence in your victory. You must appear to be weaker than in fact, because nothing emboldens enemies more than a weakened opponent.

Once again, I am asking you to forgive me for not telling you the truth. Sometimes love makes us blind to the mistakes we make.

Keep my teachings in your heart for only now will they become useful.

I have always loved you.

Your Vaya

Drasan clasped the parchment in his hand for a long time, unable to take his eyes off it. He was torn by conflicting emotions, on the one hand he felt regret and anger, and on the other, soul-rending pain, because he knew that Vaya was gone forever. This letter was a farewell and a warning at the same time. His guardian warned him against being overconfident and disregarding the enemy. She also apologized for concealing the truth about his true origins for so long. These were her last words. Knowing he was still being watched by Yarred, the prince held back his emotion. He folded the message and tucked it into his puffer jacket. Only then did he look at his old friend and said only one word:

"Thank you.".

***

After Drasan left, Aurelia returned to the bedroom. She lay down on the cool silk sheets and tried to sleep, but despite her best efforts, she couldn't forget what had happened between them.

She remembered every brush of his lips against her skin, every touch. Unlike the men she came into contact with, Drasan turned out to be a gentle and affectionate lover. And by the gods, he really saw an attractive woman in her! It was very difficult to be separated from him, for though she sensed in some strange way that he was alive and well, she couldn't bear the fact that he was away from her now.

Knowing that she would not be able to lie like this, the girl got up and went to the wardrobe - as she had expected, most of her was taken up by expensive dresses of silk, lace, and velvet. Only after a while she managed to find some forgotten pair of pants, long riding boots and a shirt, a bit too large, but after tying it around the waist with a red sash it was almost perfect. Assessing her clothes in the mirror in the corner behind the screen, she found that it looked unexpectedly well. She braided her hair in a short braid and tied it with a thong. Now she could go in search of Velwel, and knowing his habits, she was absolutely sure that she would find him in the castle's kitchen.

With that in mind, she left the tower chamber and ran down the spiral staircase. Once in the hall, she moved left, then turned right. The kitchen was below the dining room, which meant she had to find the stairs down to find it. The search did not last long, because after a while she came across one of the servants. He quickly showed her the way to the room located in the basement.

She was scarcely on the narrow steps when she reached the seductive scent of oatmeal milk and the wonderful aroma of freshly baked bread. Following the scent, she found the double doors and stepped through them without hesitating.

The kitchen turned out to be a huge room with a dozen or so tables. In the corner there were two brick ovens for baking bread, and further in the background a large hearth, over which a cauldron with lazily bubbling oatmeal hung.

One of the plump women approached Aurelia, wiping her wet hands on her apron.

"Would you like breakfast?" She demanded in a polite tone.

The girl nodded, and the cook snapped her fingers. One of the younger helpers ran up to her at this gesture.

"Take the lady to the table and pass the porridge to her," she said, still smiling brightly.

The servant girl motioned for her to sit at the table in the corner. As she had expected, she found Velwel beside him, eagerly eating his porridge, nibbling it with a large piece of bread smeared with fresh butter, and next to the bowl stood a half-empty clay mug, from which the sour smell of freshly brewed beer was heard.

The killer beamed at the sight of her and made space on the wooden bench. Aurelia sat down, and after a while one of the cook's aides placed a bowl of steaming porridge with strawberry jam on top and a plate of freshly baked cream pancakes in front of her.

Without waiting for an invitation, the girl started eating porridge, biting her pancake from time to time.

As she had expected, Velwel did not stay silent for a long time. Having finished one portion, he asked for another, and while he waited for it to cool down a bit, he looked at Aurelia.

"Well..." he began, smiling meaningfully. "How was your wedding night?"

Aurelia choked, and for a moment she couldn't help but cough.

"Once you learn the manners, work a little on your sense of tact," she said maliciously, but couldn't hide her amusement.

"Oh, come on..." Velwel broke off and belched heavily. "...we are almost like family now."

"Err..." Aurelia muttered, her mouth full of oatmeal.

Velwel patted her lightly on the shoulder and grinned.

"And where is your spouse now?" He asked, not discouraged by her lack of communication. "She must be resting after a night full of..."

He didn't have time to finish because Aurelia gave him a punch between the ribs.

"He's gone," she said shortly as soon as she managed to swallow.

The smile vanished from the young assassin's face. An expression of disbelief replaced it.

"How is it: he's gone?" He repeated bluntly.

She shrugged.

"You know him, he is unpredictable," she only stated, deciding to keep Drasan's strange behavior to herself. The less people knew about it, the better.

After breakfast finished, she got up and stretched.

"Would you like a little fencing training?" She suggested in a more relaxed tone, trying to distract Velwel from the strange disappearance of the half-dragon.

It worked, as the werewolf grinned and patted his sword hilt affectionately.

"You hit the nail on the head," he replied.

Aurelia breathed a sigh of relief. She didn't feel like explaining her partner. She knew Drasan would do as promised and return as soon as possible. She couldn't help feeling that every moment without him was more painful than before.

***

After parting ways with Yarred, the half-dragon headed straight for the ruins of Sheardon. He chose a detour so as not to expose himself to the sight of the corpses whose bones were still white in the city streets. Having got through the breach in the wall, he headed straight for the castle stables. As he crossed the remains of the burned gate, for the first time he felt a slight tingling on his skin, a sign that magic was being used somewhere nearby. Confident in the steadfastness of his senses, the prince turned towards the last of the stalls. As long as his memory did not mistake him, it was always empty.

Once inside the narrow room, the tingling intensified. He unconsciously rubbed the skin near the scar on his forearm, began to look around. At first glance, this box was no different from the others. Here, too, the floor was littered with straw. Drasan knelt down with an unmistakable foreboding, digging through her until his fingers found something like a metal hoop. When he tried to pull her, she resisted. He proceeded to part the concave until it revealed an oval recess - exactly the same shape as the medallion.

Without waiting, he removed it from his neck, placed it in the recess and twisted it slightly. He heard a soft grinding noise. He took out the locket and tried to open the passage again. This time the hatch gave way without the slightest resistance, revealing a circular opening resembling the inside of a well.

The magical pulsing intensified even more, lifting every hair on my body.

Drasan looked down. It was dark inside the opening, and it created a small ball of fire and sent it down. As expected, the passage led to an underground tunnel. The half-dragon stuck both legs into the circular hole and swung down. He hung in his arms, ignoring the protest of his tired muscles. The floor was only a few feet below him, so he jumped off, landing softly on his bent legs.

The underground passage led somewhere towards the lake. He moved cautiously down the tunnel, shining a ball of fire suspended in the air in front of him. After a dozen or so steps, the tunnel forked. Guided by the magical pulsing, Drasan moved to the left.

After a short while, he wondered what he would find at the end. Searching the castle, Dhalia did not find the entrance, because this passage has not been visited by anyone for many years. At one point he stepped back, because magic sent him vibrations so strong that he took his breath away. Whatever it was, it was very close, and it could feel his presence clearly, as if it were something like consciousness. The half-dragon enlarged the sphere, but to his surprise, a naked wall suddenly appeared where the tunnel continued. A little surprised and a little fascinated, he brushed her fingers. It turned out smooth and warm. Under his touch, it seemed to send out a gentle vibration.

Drasan concluded that whatever Vaya hid here, it was well protected against uninvited guests. With that in mind, the half-dragon scrutinized the wall carefully, and though it seemed wholly material, he realized it was an illusion. Very good, but an illusion. He entered it without hesitating, ignoring the impact of the wave of power. All he felt was a little more tingling.

As expected, the tunnel bifurcated again. This time, guided by an infallible instinct, he chose the right arm. Here the air almost sparkled with magic. Drasan decided it was safer not to use the fire and extinguished the ball. He took a moment for his eyes to adjust to the prevailing darkness, he moved on, moving with even more caution than before. For he felt an unwavering certainty that the illusory wall was a kind of warning, and that there were hidden traps beyond which someone who was not magician would not notice.

Indeed, after only a few steps, the Sheardon had barely avoided being pierced by the silver spikes hidden in the wall. Apparently, he set off one of the traps. The presence of silver clearly indicated Vaya's fears that Boris would discover the tunnel. It is possible that she planned to hide in it, but did not have time. The thought made him feel a cold fury overwhelming him.

He circled the trap and stopped, touched by another hunch. It sensed him and called him to itself. On that impulse, he moved slowly, keeping his distance from the walls, hoping he wouldn't encounter more traps. And suddenly he found another wall, this time the most material one. He recognized it by a large bas-relief depicting a wolf - the symbol of Sheardon - with exceptional realism. The eyes of the animal were made of two polished rubies and glistened slightly.

Drasan touched the sculpture for the hidden panel that opened the wall and revealed the Laudas sword to his eyes. At last, he felt what he was looking for: an oval opening into which a silver locket fitted like a key to a lock. He placed it in it and, as before, gently twisted it. As expected, the wall moved aside, revealing a hidden room to his eyes. There was a silver-wrapped chest on the floor against the wall. The prince, walking carefully, approached her and touched the lid, felt a slight tremor under his fingers. In the place where there is usually a lock, as in the previous cases, there was an oval hole to which a locket with a wolf fitted. Without waiting, he pressed it into the hole and pressed it lightly. Something clicked softly inside the clipboard.

With his heart pounding somewhere in his throat, the half-dragon opened the lid. There was only one oblong bundle inside, carefully wrapped in wolfskin. The prince picked it up, unfolded it, and sighed with delight. Despite its simplicity, the sword aroused admiration. The double-edged blade was made of an unknown type of metal with a matte sheen, while the hilt was made of silver and decorated with the image of a wolf. Fascinated, Drasan ran his thumb over the blade and was pleased to discover that it had not dulled in spite of the years. The gentle vibrations testified to the magic contained in the weapon. He picked up the artifact to examine it more closely and found that there was a row of magical runes running along the left side of the embankment.

He remembered what Vaya had said about the weapon. The sword was made of a rock that fell from the sky by an unknown blacksmith. In addition, it was enhanced with magic. Legend said nothing about how it ended up in the hands of King Laudas, who would become Sheardon's first crowned ruler. Apparently, he has set himself the goal of cleansing the kingdom of all evil. One night on his way he met a she-wolf, and not knowing what she was dealing with, he shot her with a crossbow. To his surprise, the badly wounded beast took the form of a beautiful woman. Although the hero sensed that she was a witch, he did not kill her, but took her to the castle, where he took care of her until she recovered.

At the time, Drasan thought it was such a fairy tale.

Only now did he realize how wrong he was. He never asked Vaya how old she was, although he knew perfectly well that she was a witch. Now, holding the sword in his hand, so long hidden in the basement of the castle, he felt regret. He had so many questions, never answered. For example: why did Vaya not use the magic weapon herself? After all, she knew that Dhalia would try to use her against him. Or maybe she did it because she was afraid that the sword would fall into the hands of the enemy? She preferred to pass on the knowledge of its hiding only after her death.

Drasan shook his head to free himself from these thoughts. He looked at the sword and smiled to himself. Here at last, fate smiled at him. He became the owner of a legendary weapon, perhaps changing the fate of the war.

CHAPTER 30

Entering the shadow of the wolf's forest, the prince felt like a mythical hero returning from another adventurous journey. The sword rubbing against his thigh radiated magic, making the skin tingle unpleasantly. The half-dragon didn't care. He couldn't wait for Alt'ar's face to show him the artifact.

As soon as he approached the border of the Liberation camp, he sensed someone's presence at the edge of his mind. He froze, recalled the warning in Vaya's letter to avoid mental contact. Therefore, he blocked the alien consciousness. Unfortunately, the feeling that he was being watched has not gone away.

Until finally, on the path just in front of him a figure materialized and, sensing his anxiety, reached towards the clasp of the cloak, throwing off the hood. To his eyes appeared...

"Rodian?" He asked as if he wanted to be absolutely sure it wasn't a hallucination.

"This conversation must remain between us," said the witch, wasting no time on unnecessary pleasantries.

So, it was indeed Rodian. Has she decided to come back? He had so many questions for her that he didn't know where to start.

"Alt'ar said you left," he said as an accusation, but he couldn't help himself. "If you can't help us, why are you back?"

"Alt'ar is like a brother to me, I have no one except him," confessed the witch. "I figured if I could only keep enough willpower to stay away from you, I could help defeat the three witches."

"Three?" Surprised, Drasan took a step back.

The surprised woman raised her eyebrows.

"Haven't you heard about it? After all, two of them command Bal'zar's army." She said. "They have fifteen thousand armed men with them, including over a thousand heavy cavalry and six hundred barbarian Doars."

The news made Drasan gasp. Fifteen thousand against his five hundred! It takes a miracle to face such an enormous numerical advantage. Now the words of the former caretaker have taken on a deeper meaning.

"How much time do we have?" He asked, trying not to betray the fear that was slowly taking hold of his thoughts.

"A few days," said Rodian, looking at him in horror. "There is something else you should know..."

He looked at her, unsure of what he was going to hear next.

"Some of the Antuanian troops somehow survived, there are about two thousand of them. Their queen wants to cross the river in the exact same place where Bal'zar's army will do. If they meet..."

She didn't have to finish. He knew this was their last hope of survival, at least until Oddon mobilized troops to come to their rescue. The queen needed his help.

Rodian met his eyes a second before the scarlet flames envelop his body. After he transformed, she gritted her teeth and stepped closer.

"Take care of yourself," she said.

Drasan did not answer. He surged up, soaring above the forest.

***

At the sight of the messenger rushing towards them, Queen Mara stopped her mount, and so did the accompanying bodyguard. She hadn't expected a report that soon. When the young man got close enough that she could see the horror on his face, she understood what made him hurry.

The boy stopped the tired horse in front of her.

"Your Majesty," he panted, barely gasping for breath. "The Ridenian army has reached the river and is standing right next to the ford, blocking our passage..."

Mara held her breath. This was not what she expected. If Bal'zar sent some of his forces to stop her from reaching the forest... they were doomed.

The messenger's further words chilled her to the core.

"Our scouts report that this is only a small fraction of King Bal'zar's forces. The rest are still behind us. The king decided to move at their head to finally crush all resistance."

By the gods! If true, the remnants of her army were trapped. They won't be able to get to the river, they can't even withdraw.

The frightened woman glanced at the counselor. Tharon surprisingly retained his admirable composure. Apparently nothing could have disturbed him.

"How long do we have until Bal'zar's troops arrive?" Asked the messenger.

"Not more than two days, lord," the boy replied.

"Then all we have to do is move on." He glanced at the queen. "If we're lucky, maybe we'll get to the other side." He looked at the young man, whose horse was dangling on its legs with exhaustion. "You did well, boy," he added graciously. The queen gave a little shudder, touched by a bad feeling, looked at the young man's green eyes and asked:

"What is your name?"

The boy froze at the question and inclined his head slightly.

"I am Flyn, Your Majesty. I come from the Loharo family."

"Thank you, Flyn," Mara said, giving the boy a warm smile. She knew she had seen him somewhere, and now she realized where. It was he who appeared in one of Lender's disturbingly clear visions.

A vision in which they failed.

***

As she descended the stairs, Aurelia had to be careful not to trip over the hem of her dress. She cursed time and time again, feeling the pain in her legs, unaccustomed to heels - despite her urgent requests, Gurtred refused to let her wear her favorite outfit. The explanations were of no avail, according to the old woman, such a dress is not befitting a lady.

The girl bit her tongue at the last moment so as not to curse when one of the legs slipped off the stone step. It resulted in a painful rubbing of her ankle, which made her enter the royal gardens with a slight limp.

King Oddon strolled along a row of exotic trees showered with little pink flowers. Aurelia cursed, but the big man didn't even turn around. He seemed completely lost in thought.

Instead of a flowing robe, he wore light cavalry armor consisting of chain mail, a breastplate, bracers and reinforced leather greaves. A scarlet cloak was flowing from his muscular shoulders, and a horned helmet was tucked under his arm. He also wore a short sword in an ornate scabbard at his belt.

"I find it hard to believe I'm wearing the armor again after all these years," the king said, and she felt that he was talking more to himself than to her. When he turned around, she realized he was holding her sword. "It is an excellent weapon, worthy of a real warrior."

Aurelia smiled and thanked the compliment with a polite nod, though in reality she was wondering: how did he find out about the sword? After all, she ordered him to be well hidden.

"Getting down to business," announced the ruler, abandoning the tone of polite conversation. "I'm going to support your husband's campaign.

Unfortunately, the decision to join the war is not entirely mine. My priests demand that I put Duke of Sheardon to the test." He ended his speech with a short sigh. "So, I wanted to ask you for help..." He looked deep into her eyes. "You have to convince your husband to do it voluntarily. In Earden, the priests have far more power than the king. If they do not agree to participate in this fight, I will have to bow."

So that's it, Aurelia thought, but she said something else aloud.

"I don't think it would be easy to convince him of that."

The Eardenian sighed heavily.

"And that's why I turned to you, Aurelia. I think you're the only one who can convince him." He stared at her.

"Where did this suppose come from, Your Majesty?" She asked, not without a hint of sarcasm. "I dare say that Drasan likes to walk only known paths and make decisions for reasons he knows only. Moreover, it is impossible to convince him of anything at the moment, as he left two days ago and even, I cannot tell when he will be back."

Oddon listened to her with an unreadable expression. Judging from his demeanor, he didn't seem too thrilled with what he had learned.

"Well," the king began, his jaw twitching dangerously. "We'll have to wait for him to come back," he finished, trying to keep his temper.

Feeling the anger radiating from the ruler, the girl decided that she should say something to defend her beloved.

"I think my husband had a very good reason for leaving Bregan Fortress. It seems he managed to find an artifact that could be decisive for the outcome of the war."

The king stopped abruptly and looked at her, frowning slightly.

"May you be right, my dear, because without the consent of the priests your husband cannot count on my support," he replied.

Aurelia bit her lip.

What am I doing? I have no idea about the intricacies of politics.

Drasan, as soon as you return, I will strangle you with my bare hands, she thought, but the Earden lord gave a polite smile.

"If that's all, Your Majesty, let me leave you with your thoughts." She made a slight bow.

The king nodded, unable to utter a word, and Aurelia hurried back down the alley.

Despite its austerity, Fortress Bregan had wonderful green spaces, including extensive gardens and a training ground for Eardenian soldiers. Out of curiosity, Aurelia headed in that direction.

From a distance he reached her ears, the clank of weapons and the thud of hooves. When she emerged from among the trees, she saw the large square in all its glory. Several young warriors practiced there, each armed with a sword and shield and mounted on one of the legendary Eardenian mounts.

The old balding instructor, dressed in a gray tunic and the same pants, watched the training from a distance and waved his hands every now and then, shouting orders.

The Eardenians had a swarthy complexion and dark hair cut to the shoulders. Unlike the Ridenians, their jaws were smooth with no trace of facial hair, and their eyes were lighter than most Antuans. Despite the fact that Aurelia spent a week in the Bregan Fortress, for the first time she had the opportunity to see the famous warriors and their wonderful mounts up close.

She was surprised to find that the horses bred by the hosts are much smaller than the Antuan ones and are characterized by long, slender necks ending in a small head. Their hair was short and shiny, and their manes were braided so as not to disturb the warriors during their gallop and fight. The short stature was a clear advantage, as it allowed the mounts to maintain excellent speed and maneuverability, which could prove invaluable in the fight against the heavy Riden cavalry.

For a moment, Aurelia admittedly watched one of the warriors turn their mount to strike again against the mannequin set on the other side of the field. Without slowing down the gallop for a moment, the young man drew his bow - at that time he was driving the horse with his legs - and released an arrow which, with a loud thump, plunged into the very center of the wooden shield. The flaccid steed he rode without any signal from his rider made a neat twist. Meanwhile, the warrior reached for another arrow, aimed and fired, hitting the wooden puppet in the very center of the head.

Aurelia could stand like this endlessly, observing the excellent equestrian ability of the Earden warriors. Suddenly she missed the casual male attire. Were it not for the fact that she was wearing a navy blue velvet dress adorned with loads of snow-white lace, she would have loved to practice with them.

Those times are gone forever.

The girl looked glumly at the ring she was wearing on the finger of her right hand. From the moment she agreed to become Drasan's wife, her life changed. She did not have to make a living by swinging a sword, and although the prince had not explicitly forbidden her to fight, she suspected that if he saw her with a sword in his hand, he would probably scold her sharply.

But did he act like a husband? She thought angrily. He had abandoned her here, condemning her to death out of boredom.

Aurelia found herself unable to do anything outside of the court. The ladies in Bregan fortress seemed vacant and vain to her, hung with gold and jewels in shamelessly low-cut dresses. According to her, they weren't much different from street hookers. Instead, she preferred the company of the servants. Following Velwel's example, apart from the obligatory morning training, she spent all days in the kitchen. There she did not have to explain her clumsiness and total lack of good manners.

"Oh, there you are," came a familiar voice in her ears.

Velwel looked at her from the height of his mare's saddle.

Aurelia cursed silently.

How could she allow herself to be so careless? Several of the warriors stopped training and looked at them curiously, but quickly resumed their activities.

Velwel helped her climb onto the horse's back, which she did with some difficulty. All because of that tight dress. Finally, she settled down in front of the young killer with her legs dangling to one side of the horse. The Ridenian chuckled and the chestnut tree started walking along the edge of the training ground.

"I have a strange feeling that you don't like your new life," said the friend in a tone of cordial conversation.

Aurelia sighed.

"I guess it was easier for me to lead the life of a hired assassin," she said softly. Neila didn't have to wonder if she would bring embarrassment to her behavior. Aurelia must be careful what she says and to whom, so as not to embarrass herself and her husband.

"Come on, it's probably not that bad..." The werewolf broke off at the sight of the girl's pathetic face. "Well, when Drasan returns..."

"It won't change anything," Aurelia interrupted. "I don't think he would let me fight, and that's the only thing that makes me feel really good at. I'm afraid I don't fit in with his world and I will never..." She broke off, searching for the right word.

"...a real lady," Velwel suggested, grinning in a mischievous smile. "Do not worry about it. If Drasan wanted to marry any of these twitter parrots, he would have done so, right?"

What an apt comparison! Aurelia laughed, as she suddenly pictured one of those Queen's parties where a flock of multicolored birds sat in a town of colorfully dressed ladies, shouting over each other.

"I guess you're right," she said in a much better mood.

Velwel smiled even wider, and he dug his heels into the mare's sides. She broke forward, smoothly going from walk to canter. Aurelia rested her head on her friend's shoulder, enjoying the ride, all cares forgotten for a moment. After all, she still had a lot of time to get used to her new responsibilities.

***

Marshal Conor De'Rembl stood before his king and bowed, glancing uncertainly at the witch sitting next to him. Since the woman was ostentatiously ignoring him, he found it wise not to pay attention to her.

Bal'zar looked at him, scratching behind the big wolfhound's ears.

"The enemy made a mistake," he said calmly. "Your soldiers are the wedge of my army, Marshal. Your task will be to push the remnants of the Antuan Queen's army towards the river, where our infantry is waiting for them. You will capture the queen herself and bring her to me."

The servant nodded, knowing the lord was not finished yet.

"Don't take any other prisoners. Your task is to tear your enemies to shreds. Is it clear?"

Conor De'Rembl nodded again and looked at the witch, but she still said nothing.

"Yes, Your Majesty," he replied.

Bal'zar looked at Dhalia, wondering at her strange silence.

"Since everything is clear," he said to the old marshal. "Go."

De'Rembl bowed one last time and left the command tent.

Only when his footsteps faded away somewhere in the distance did the witch turn to Bal'zar.

"In my opinion, all this bestiality is pointless, unless..." She frowned and her eyes widened. "Do you want to get him here? My trusted spies say the half dragon is in Earden..."

"Or he just wants us to think so. In my opinion, he is somewhere much closer, and I can assure you that he will come here."

Dhalia snorted dismissively. She felt fear deep inside her soul. Bal'zar turned out to be either a brilliant strategist or a madman. Not only did he make sure that the traitors themselves surround Queen of Antua, but he also made sure that they were held in the highest positions. In this way, he could sabotage the actions of the young and inexperienced ruler. In addition, he introduced a spy into the ranks of the Liberators. At a crucial moment, this man will make sure that everything goes according to plan.

In addition, he split two of the most powerful witches so that they would not stand a chance against Drasan. She will let him win only to break later with one well-aimed punch.

"Do you want to fight him?" She asked, unable to believe she had said the words aloud.

Bal'zar smiled slightly.

"How else will I distract him by giving you time to kidnap the girl?" he answered the question with a question. "Of course, that's not my main goal. For everything to go right, I must defeat him in front of his Liberators. That should have an effect on the morale of his people."

"What if he beats you?" She asked silently, chiding herself for her audacity. Drasan was quite powerful, but would he have the strength to defeat a man who considered himself a god?

"Fortunately, your favorite is honorable, so if I challenge him to a duel without using magic, he will agree without batting an eye. But..." He thought for a moment, frowning, suddenly snapping his fingers. The tent flap opened and Alder entered the tent.

This time the bald mage did not grace Dhalia with a single glance.

"You called on me, my lord," he said, bowing to the young ruler.

"Yes," Bal'zar replied, leaning back against the backrest and scratching behind the ear of the great she-wolf. "They say you are a master of illusions."

"I think the term master is highly inappropriate in this situation, Emperor," Alder said, with false modesty in his voice. "Let's say I can create a convincing illusion and hold it for a few minutes."

"It is enough for me. I need you to confuse the werewolf until I deal with Drasan. Then you will help Dhalia to steal the princess, but not so that she does not realize that it is a trick."

Dhalia opened her mouth to protest, but he silenced her with a gesture.

"It'll be better this way, my dear. The girl must come with you voluntarily or her anxiety will alert Drasan. You will take her to the designated place and create a portal to Washmorth."

Bal'zar said it all with unwavering confidence. His plan seemed to have no loophole to exploit. So, if she wanted to live, she had to be at least loyal. She might have waited for Drasan to fall asleep and warned him in his sleep, but she doubted he would believe her. He hated her as much as he hated Bal'zar.

"It is settled then," said the ruler, smiling at his evil plan. "As soon as we suppress this meaningless rebellion, I will be concerned with unifying all the kingdoms and creating a mighty empire." For a moment something like excitement mixed with madness appeared on his face.

Dhalia felt fear of this unbalanced young man. She realized that he would stop at nothing, just to make the crazy vision a reality.

***

Entering the camp, Drasan greeted the sentries, who stared at him. Then he headed for the great pavilion, no doubt occupied by the queen. He had too little time to bother with change, and besides, the form of the enormous reptile was much more respected. People moved out of his way as he barely looked at them.

Even the sentries guarding the entrance to Queen of Antua's tent let him pass without a word. Unfortunately, he couldn't just go in there.

Instead, he nodded to a passing soldier. The man's eyes widened, but he stopped obediently.

"Please tell the queen that I am waiting for her in her tent," he ordered.

The soldier turned out to be far too scared not to fulfill the dragon's request. When a pretty red-haired woman in field armor emerged from the tent, he was literally speechless.

Despite the passage of time, he recognized the face without difficulty! Mara! Older, more beautiful, but it's still her!

To his surprise, the queen propped up her hips.

"Why so long?" She asked in a haughty voice.

"I have had some important matters, Your Majesty," he replied, tilting his head slightly as a sign of respect.

At the sight of this gesture, the soldiers were dumbfounded. Many of them gaped as they looked from their queen to the huge dragon.

"I take that as an apology, Duke of Sheardon," she replied, also bowing to him. "Now to the point," she added, looking anxiously at one of her advisers. "We are trapped. We cannot go forward, because more than ten thousand armed men, including heavy cavalry, are waiting for us at the ford. Behind us, Bal'zar presses on us, who has decided to lead the attack personally. If he does, he'll just outnumber my ride. If I decide it is better to make my way to the ford, most of my soldiers will be killed. If you have a plan, please present it to us, because at the moment all we have to do is wave King of Riden the white flag."

Drasan sighed. According to him, the situation seemed just as hopeless. Alt'ar would surely find a solution. He himself did not know much about strategy, the only thing he remembered from the extremely boring lessons with General Lenard Ghoi was that the best form of defense is a pre-emptive attack. Bal'zar certainly expected the queen to retreat or capitulate, but not to attack the outnumbered enemy.

"Surrender is not an option," he said finally. "And to break through, you need a diversion. Something that will distract the enemy forces and allow you to break into the river. I'll take care of it myself. "He met Mary's eyes.

"One day," said the queen, returning his gaze. "That's all I can give you."

One day is enough, Drasan thought, knowing exactly how and what to do to give Mara the opportunity to break to the other side.

CHAPTER 31

The appearance of the werewolves caused an even greater sensation than Alt'ar's recent transformation. Some at his request took the form of giant wolves, and there were about forty of them. They walked out into the clearing carefully, growling softly and looking nervously from side to side.

The leader of the Guild, also in wolf form, was waiting for them at the very edge of the clearing. As an animal, he could boast a really impressive height. Only the bear that lived in Riden was probably as big as it was. His fur was thick and gray-white, and his eyes were red as two rubies.

Alt'ar quietly hoped the pack would not sense the dragon's scent. He asked Gaenor to get up, unfortunately, he sensed Drasan even before he lowered the flight just enough for him to see him. He had the sense to jump to the ground in human form.

Where have you been? Alt'ar asked, his eyes never leaving the werewolves, staring at the newcomer with glittering eyes. Fortunately, the prince has learned to keep his emotions in check. Otherwise, his reluctance might arouse their aggression.

I got us armed support, the newcomer replied, his inner calmness surprising Alt'ar so much that he had to look him in the eye.

A fire was burning within them. The half-dragon kept his fighting readiness, but somehow kept his temper in check enough for a bunch of werewolves not to consider it a challenge to them.

So, you've finally learned the subtle art of self-control, the assassin stated.

He answered a soft laugh that sounded quite pleasant in his mind.

Not really, but let's assume I'm making progress, he replied.

Suddenly they both fell silent, for behold, a slender female known as Niue approached them. She sat down opposite and sniffed. It seemed she was the only one, because the other werewolves kept their distance. The Guild Leader knew that the years of prejudice were doing their part, and it was not easy to join those who had previously belonged to the enemy.

Drasan gave him a knowing look.

Let me speak to them.

He cleared his throat and stepped forward.

"Hello," he said.

In response, he heard a soft grunt of approval from most of the group.

"As you probably know, I'm not human," he trailed off, watching for the reaction of the audience, but the werewolves showed nothing. "Like you, I am a two-race hybrid, half dragon and half human. Unlike you, I was born that way, but like you, I had no choice but to accept my otherness." He looked at them but saw no reaction again. "Like everyone else, I have always considered you to be mindless beasts." At the sound of these words, several of the larger males bristled and began to growl. "But..." Drasan continued, undaunted. "...When I met Alt'ar, I changed my mind about you. He made me realize how wrong I was about your kind. I never wondered what it was like to be a misfit until I found out that I was one myself..."

His speech made an impression on the werewolves. They listened to him hypnotized. Neither was going to attack the half dragon. They seemed to accept who he was without the slightest objection.

It then dawned on Alt'ar that Drasan was a born king. As you can see, he was well prepared for it. As he spoke, his eyes shone with an inner glow. The only thing missing was the experience. It seemed like a rare gem that needed polishing.

"Enough, Drasan," Rodian interrupted suddenly. She stood at Alt'ar's side more beautiful and more terrible than ever before. "Let me speak for the one who has been with me for many years," she began, glaring at the werewolves gathered around her with a fiery glance. "I know that many of you do not understand what is at stake in this war." She paused for a moment and looked questioningly at Drasan, but Drasan nodded his head approvingly. "A mighty wizard named Bal'zar wants to seize power over Lineland. He has Alikorn, Riden and Antua in his grip. If he prevails, I am afraid he will wipe your kind off the face of these lands or make them slaves to his will. I would not wish such a life for any creature. Together with Drasan and Alt'ar, we decided to fight him, and soon we will face the largest army the world has seen. An alliance between us would be of great benefit to both sides, and your new alpha knows it well." She looked at Alt'ar sitting next to him with such tenderness as never before. "He is like my brother himself, and I trust that he made the right decision. Your race studies have allowed me to discover that you would be excellent soldiers. Your wounds heal in record time, you are faster and stronger - no armor can protect against werewolf teeth and no horse will surpass him. We don't have to be enemies to each other. We need each other. I leave the decision to you."

Alt'ar stood up, a short snarl escaping his throat. Several of the werewolves whined in response, a few others got up and came closer. Neither acted aggressively, their leader sat down again.

Drasan remained motionless for a moment, staring at Rodian, he could not believe that she was there. It was then that Alt'ar understood the problem between the witch and the half-dragon. They were both powerful and understood well what awaited them if they failed to face Bal'zar. They could remain allies in the fight, but they would never be united in friendship.

The killer shared Rodian's decision. She came back because she no longer wanted to hide who she was. She knew this might be her last fight and she accepted it.

Finally, Drasan let the tension drop and he followed Alt'ar to where Yarred and Gaenor were waiting for them. They both seemed relaxed and at ease, even with so many werewolves dotted around the edge of the camp.

The dragon gave the Guild leader a short contemptuous glance and turned directly to Drasan:

"And what's our great leader's plan?"

The half-dragon ignored him and looked at Yarred. His friend withstood that gaze for only a moment.

"A wonderful speech, worthy of a true king," he muttered.

"I am not yet," replied Drasan. There was a chill in his voice. "You've regained my trust, Captain Cordydian." He said in a stiff, formal tone. "You will lead a reconnaissance group. We must make sure that no one attacks us from the flank, when we ourselves strike the main enemy forces from the front. There may be a witch in the camp," he added, seeing the Sheardonian open his mouth to protest. "If so, you must not reveal yourself. This is a reconnaissance mission, not a diversionary one. We attack at dawn, so gather your squad and go."

Yarred sprang to his feet and was about to leave, but paused to look once more at the stern face of his old friend. He was a bit like a dog that knew you were angry, and if you choked on him you could pacify him.

"One more thing, Yarred," the young man said, this time not looking at the captain. "If you fail me this time, I'll kill you."

His voice remained so cold and emotionless that it shocked even the killer who was listening to the exchange. Drasan really matured for the role assigned to him by fate. From an inexperienced young man, he turned into a responsible leader, making no exceptions for the sake of old ties.

Alt'ar glanced at Gaenor. Even the dragon noticed the change in the young prince. He looked at his fellow man now with much more respect, even some kind of admiration.

As Yarred departed, Drasan breathed deeper and visibly relaxed.

This time Rodian spoke up:

"Since we started to act instead of hiding in the forest, maybe you will finally enlighten us, what are you planning in the end?" She asked, looking at the Sheardon with defiant eyes.

The prince smiled slightly.

"In fact, my only plan is to act as a diversionary. First, we have to get Queen of Antua out of her trap, it will give us about two thousand rides. The most important thing is not to get surrounded, because then we will be crushed by mere numerical superiority."

Gaenor snorted loudly.

"And that's your brilliant strategy?" He did not hide his contempt. "From what I've noticed of us, there are a handful of us against a well-trained army."

Drasan smirked.

"Not if we surprise them," he said calmly. "Bal'zar doesn't know about my covenant with Earden, and all we need to give Oddon time to come to the battlefield. Half of the Riden's forces are recruits who don't know much about the warrior. We have only veterans; we are supported by werewolves and we have this..." To the surprise of everyone present from the scabbard at his belt, he took a large two-handed sword with a hilt decorated with a wolf's head - the Sword of Laudas.

Even more admiration was caused by the blade, suddenly glowing with an inner light and blue flames creeping along its edge.

"It's the only artifact that can kill a mage or witch and destroy any spell cast," he solemnly told them. His eyes shone like two jewels. "And this, it seems, greatly increases our chances."

Alt'ar stared at the sword in awe. He had heard so many times about the magical weapons wielded by King Laudas! A sword completely immune to magic and able to withstand any spell. And now he was there before him.

The sight of the magic weapon worked on everyone exactly as Drasan had expected. Nobody dared even touch it.

"Impossible," Rodian said, her eyes sparkling with excitement. "A real miracle happened."

Alt'ar had to agree with her. Now Drasan has risen in the eyes of everyone to the rank of a hero who will lead them to victory.

***

Yarred stopped his horse at the edge of the river and gestured to the squad to do the same. As soon as they got close enough to where he supposed a small part of Bal'zar's army had hidden from their eyes, he increased his caution. The rushes growing by the water provided a very good cover from the enemy's eyes. At his next sign, people got off their horses and hid them among the trees.

Now they had to wait for the appearance of a living soul, which he did not doubt, because they had to water their animals and draw water for themselves. And as they watched for many hours, staring at one point, suddenly a group of people sprang from the ground, walking carefully along the previously trodden path. Now they had the harder part of the task to do: follow them and perhaps get close enough to determine the actual number of enemy troops.

The prospect both excited and terrified the Sheardon. Maybe they could even do some harm by depriving them of some of their supplies. He knew it was risky and Drasan would certainly not approve of it, but Yarred had to try to fight for his lost honor.

With this in mind, he and the others followed the slowly walking group, taking care that they did not notice them. But the slaves or servants turned out to be too focused on the task to realize that they were being followed. Thanks to this, the captain was able to see how, one by one, the members of the strange procession melt into thin air.

He paused in front of the invisible barrier, expecting at least a slight blast of magic, but felt nothing. The magic shield turned out to be completely undetectable. He tried to touch her, but his hand dipped up to the elbow as if he had more than air in front of him, but water. He drew it back hastily, hoping that no one had seen anything on the other side.

His friend would probably scold him sharply for such carelessness. Yarred had come too far to worry about it now. He was overwhelmed with excitement. What glory would he have had if he killed one of the witches? He had no doubts that they were much more powerful than he was, but what was the harm to try? His name would have been repeated for centuries. What is better than eternal glory?

Suddenly, Mara's face appeared before his eyes.

What would she say if she saw him now? Would she feel proud or condemn him sharply? And his son? If he dies today, she will never know him. He will not see him grow up; he will not pass on knowledge.

He froze for a moment, hesitating between eternal glory and the desire for a peaceful life and death in his own bed. His father died in battle, as did his grandfather and great-grandfather. The Cordydians did not die of old age, they died in battle, bringing glory to the family. If he is destined to die, he might as well draw as many lives as he can.

With this in mind, he took a deep breath and entered the invisible barrier surrounding the enemy camp. He barely surfaced on the other side when he realized his mistake. It turned out. it's too late. He felt more than heard his squad loom behind him, and a moment later the curses sounded as they all realized they had fallen into a trap.

A short, dark-eyed brunette emerged from among a small group of crossbowmen, all of whom were targeting the Sheardon's chest. Clad in a mid-thigh-tight dress made of the skin of some wild cat, it looked perfect. She looked to be about sixteen, but that was a form of fact, for she really was sure she was much more than that. For they had one of Bal'zar's witches in front of them.

"Well, well, well," she choked, staring at Yarred, narrowing her eyes a little. "Captain Cordydian himself. Don't tell me you're stupid enough to think you can outsmart me?"

Yarred didn't answer. He knew he was going to die and accepted it, but he couldn't bear the thought that others would also pay for his stupidity.

The woman laughed out loud as if it were all great fun.

Her eyes glowed slightly, and her hands made some complicated gesture, after which everyone present literally turned to stone.

Captain Cordydian swallowed nervously. He couldn't move a single muscle. He had to stare at the dark-eyed woman, waiting for what she would do. The witch was clearly not going to rush. She came up to him smiling as if at the sight of the desired toy. There was something magnetic about her gaze. Even if he exerted all his willpower, he couldn't resist it.

"Now tell me what you're doing here, Yarred Cordydian." She frowned evenly.

The man felt the blood drain to his face. He realized that he was not going to die quickly. This woman is going to play with him cruelly, like a cat playing with a mouse. And then she would kill him in the most painful and cruel way. He made a decision: he would remain faithful to Drasan even in the face of torture. It will not give up and will not bend.

"I'm not telling you anything, scabby bitch," he growled through clenched teeth.

To his surprise and annoyance, the woman laughed, a ghastly laugh devoid of mirth.

"Ah, you don't have to say anything at all! Your mind will tell me everything. I will gut your brain like a fish, reaching your deepest hidden fears and cause you so much pain that you will beg for death. Do you think you are important? The one you call your friend sent you here not to stain your hands with his blood."

"You're lying!" Yarred exclaimed suddenly. "Drasan would never..."

"Be silent!" She growled, silencing him with a single gesture. "Your beloved prince is cold and cunning as a snake. He needed a gullible like you to find out if he would be flanked when he led the insane assault on Bal'zar's heavy ride himself..."

Yarred cursed violently. In his heart, he wanted to believe her words were lies. He couldn't forget the chill in Drasan's voice as he bade him farewell, saying, "If you fail me this time, I'll kill you." Had a friend really sent him here to die?

The witch was smiling just a step away from him, a long knife materialized in her hand, which she stuck in his stomach. The Sheardonian gasped in surprise, for he felt no pain even as the sadistic whore twisted the blade. She looked him in the eyes, wanting to see how the life fades away in them. When she yanked him upward, the feeling came back, and so did the excruciating pain. Despite the best of his wishes, he couldn't help but scream. Then the witch made a simple gesture, causing his voice to die in his throat as she gutted him like a fish.

A final thought flashed to his fading consciousness:

What a fool he had been to believe that his name would survive in the songs.

***

Landing in the courtyard of the Bregan fortress, Drasan had to be careful not to crush someone from the crowd of onlookers. People pressed to get as close to him as possible, and he had so little time. He couldn't afford even a second to delay. He roared deafeningly, wanting to somehow scare them away, and he started towards the iron gates, and the people fled sideways in front of him.

As he had expected, the gate swung open, and none other than high priest Fidelis stood in it. His thin lips spread into a wide smile that did not encompass the cold reptilian eyes.

"Ah, here you are," he said with mock enthusiasm. "Your Majesty," he added after a moment, bowing low.

"I want to speak to King Oddon," Drasan said bluntly.

Fidelis smiled even wider.

"The problem is, he wants you to be tested first," he replied slyly. "You see, our king..."

"Drasan!" The familiar voice made the half-dragon's heart flood a wave of gratitude.

Aurelia ran from the gardens. To his surprise, she was wearing a dress that perfectly accentuated her figure.

"I'm glad you're here! We have a problem here that cannot wait," her gaze fell on the high priest. "This reptile demanded that you be put to the test. Otherwise, he will not consent to the commencement of hostilities."

Drasan laughed, which sounded more like a hoarse murmur. This was what he expected. This priest was going to do whatever he could to delay Oddon's actions. Perhaps he was even one of Bal'zar's spies?...

"What do you want, holy man?" He asked, being polite.

Fidelis pursed his thin lips and replied:

"King Oddon asked me to bless his army. As long as you put yourself to the test, I am willing to do this."

Drasan raised his head a little, freeing her from the embrace of his young wife. He huffed, thin wisps of smoke escaping his nostrils.

"You're enjoying the moment, aren't you?" He asked with disdain.

"Yes," replied the priest, an expression of vindictive satisfaction on his face.

"Then I have no choice," replied the half-dragon. "What is this test about?"

The high priest smiled coldly, bowed and said:

"Follow me."

The prince glanced at Aurelia. Her face was disapproving, her eyes sparkled. She walked by his side until they were in front of the bronze door. So far, neither of them has been allowed in there.

The priest pushed the heavy wing open and looked at the half-dragon.

"To get in there, you have to change. Weapons are not allowed into the temple or use magic there," all these words were uttered in a sharp commanding tone. "Your wife has to stay outside."

Drasan decided he'd better listen. He changed, although it stripped him of all his strength. Then he entered the heavy gate. He heard the priest slam it shut behind him, and a soft veil covered his senses. The room pulsed with pure power, pressed against him from all sides, explored the body and mind, and penetrated the heart.

Then the disembodied voice announced:

We know who you are, messenger of fate. We know your heart, we hear your thoughts, we feel your fear.

Who are you? Asked the prince, trying to locate the source of the voice.

Something or someone laughed sharply.

We are a scrap of old times. They call us gods, spirits, ancients. In the old days, when there was no world known to you, only we existed, and we will exist even when the present reality turns to dust. Time doesn't matter to us, Chosen One.

I was to be put to the test, replied Drasan, feeling very strange.

This is your test, messenger of fate, replied the first voice. Anyone who crosses this gate is checked. Some try to hide their crimes in the hope that no one will see them. You didn't hide anything. You let us examine you to the uttermost depths of your being. You passed the test successfully.

Drasan did not know what to make of this. If these beings called themselves gods, why didn't they stop Dhalia or Bal'zar? Why didn't they support them?

Since you've been living so long... why don't you stop Bal'zar? He asked, trying to suppress his anger.

In response, he heard a loud grunt. It was like the muffled roar of an angry lion.

Although we have created the magic, we cannot influence the material world in any way. Came the answer. The creator of the one you call Bal'zar once belonged to our brothers. We drove them out of this world ages ago. His name, like the name of its creator, was to be forgotten forever. He came back hungry for revenge, and now the evil is getting stronger every day.

Drasan knew they were telling the truth. So they weren't dealing with sorcerers, but with gods, and that meant they faced unlimited power.

How to beat them? He asked, though deep down he knew there was no simple answer to this question.

We cannot be killed; we don't feel pain or the passage of time. We can be imprisoned for this. The body that the Ancient had possessed must be destroyed, but if you do not imprison it, he will find another one for himself, and his revenge will be terrible.

The young man had no choice but to believe their words, though he had no idea how to imprison a disembodied being far more powerful than he was. He was about to leave the temple when a chorus of voices resounded in his head.

Wait!

Confused, he turned around. And then an altar with a shallow bowl and a gold dagger appeared in the center of the room.

You have to pay.

How should I pay you? He asked.

Then he understood. They wanted sacrifice. Sacrifice of his blood.

Without waiting for encouragement, he rolled up his sleeve and slit his veins with a dagger. He let the liquid flow until the wound closed.

Your sacrifice has been accepted. You can go.

Drasan left the temple feeling completely exhausted. He had no doubt that this was what the old priest meant. Fidelis watched him go as he walked over to Aurelia. As always, his wife noticed that something was wrong.

"Drasan, you were only gone for a moment, and you look exhausted," she said.

The high priest walked up to them and looked the prince in the eye.

"You passed the test," he said, then turned and walked away. As soon as he was gone, the half-dragon allowed himself a moment of weakness. He cuddled up to his partner, absorbing her warmth as if they would never see each other again. He wanted this moment to last forever, but unfortunately, he could not stop the relentlessly passing time. With some effort, he moved away from the girl and said:

"I do not have too much time. I must save my strength before the fight that awaits me."

He felt disbelief radiating from her, as well as fear.

"You want to attack Bal'zar's troops," she said more than asked.

"I have no choice," he replied, pressing his face against her hair and inhaling their sweet scent for a moment. "But don't worry, I am much bigger and stronger than he expects."

To his surprise, she hugged him tightly, pressing her whole body against him. Her closeness drove his senses crazy. He wanted to make love to her so much it hurt. He wished he had so much time.

"Don't leave me here alone," she whispered unexpectedly, despair and determination in her voice.

"I won't," he assured her. With a great effort of will, he pushed her aside and walked briskly towards the Bregan Keep. He passed through the double doors without looking back. Aurelia stayed in the doorway and watched him go, and he felt a twinge of pain. He would like to have her with him, but he knew it was impossible. She could accompany him to the camp, no further.

"Drasan, finally!" King Oddon greeted him loudly.

"Your Highness." The half-dragon bowed.

The king wore splendid armor and carried a helmet under his arm. There was a wide smile on his face.

"My people are ready; we are just waiting for a decision..."

"Done!" Drasan cut him off. "Your Majesty, we have no time to waste. The battle is near. I want to lead an attack on Bal'zar's main force tomorrow, before dawn."

The king looked at him with eyes burning with the heat of battle.

"Then let's go. I will gather my troops and stand by your side for battle at dawn," he said, striking his fist on the steel breastplate.

It was enough for Drasan. He knew the king of the Earden would not fail him. Like him, he was of a people of warriors, and would not be able to accept the fact that he would stand aside while others fight for freedom.

The prince bowed again and went out into the courtyard. As expected, Aurelia was not there. But he was welcomed by Velwel fully armed.

"Drasan! Good to see you again!" He exclaimed with such enthusiasm that the half-dragon smiled inwardly again. "Are the rumors true?! No more idle waiting! Let's finally kick ass of Riden!"

"You're a Ridenian yourself," he replied, laughing.

"Only in part," Velwel shrugged slightly. "My mother was a Riden and my father was a Noai'diran."

"Yes, I'm going to provoke Bal'zar," Drasan said, suddenly serious. "And I hope my strength is enough to defeat his troops. Otherwise, we will be defeated."

"It's always worth a try," the assassin grinned.

His enthusiasm shared with Drasan. Even if they failed, it was worth a try. Because what did he have to lose except freedom? Knowing that he would spend the rest of his life slave to either Dhalia or Bal'zar terrified him far more than dying in battle. After all, he preferred to fall in the field of glory rather than to live forever with no influence on his fate.

***

The old armorer's eyes widened at the sight of the woman standing in the doorway. Aurelia pulled up her dress so as not to soil it, and quickly walked over to him.

"I need an armor," she said bluntly.

The man looked at her briefly. Then he replied, nervously nibbling on his bushy mustache:

"Lady... I don't think I have anything..." He gave her another expert glance. "...which would suit your body shape."

Aurelia sighed. She had expected such an answer.

"Give it what you got, no time to get fit. I will need chain mail, bracers, greaves and a jacket." She enumerated one by one, looking seriously at the older man.

The armorer scratched his bald head and walked away to look for something that would fit her. At that moment she felt hot breath on the back of her neck and knew who she would find behind her back:

"I knew you were coming to stop me," she said, softly enough for only he to hear her words.

Drasan shifted a little out of the shadows and replied in a gentle voice:

"You know I won't let you fight."

"I figured you'd say that," she said without turning around. She refused to meet his eyes. "Where did you get the idea that I need your permission?" She asked.

The prince laughed hoarsely.

"Because you are my wife," he replied more seriously.

She turned to him so abruptly that he stepped back.

"It's my duty to stay by your side," she said, sharper than she intended, and for the first time she noticed the pain in his eyes. "If you want to forbid me to fight, tie me up and gag me, otherwise I'll follow you everywhere," she continued, knowing her words were hurting him, but she couldn't help herself. "I can't bear the thought you died while I was sitting here embroidering the curtains. I know I can be of use to you in battle, just let me..."

"No!" He thundered with such force that she cringed, and a menacing gleam appeared in his eyes. "I will not let you risk your life unnecessarily!"

Tears of anger and bitterness stood in Aurelia's eyes.

"All right, Your Majesty," she drawled, shaking with anger. "I will do as you wish," she added, as she passed him out of the armory.

Only when she was away from him did she let tears flow from her eyes. She had known beforehand that Drasan would not allow her to fight, but she had not expected such a vehement reaction from him. She had forgotten that she had married a half-dragon who could force obedience. It is difficult to argue with a reptile that can incinerate by breath alone.

She loved him, but she was not used to being treated like this.

She started down the corridor towards the upper floors, not looking where she was going, almost colliding with Velwel on his way to the armory. The broad smile faded from his face at the sight of her.

"Something happened?" He asked with concern.

She shook her head, wiping the tears with the back of her hand.

"Nothing that I wouldn't have expected," she replied. "It's exactly like you said. Drasan will not allow me to participate in the battle."

"If that's what you expected, where did these tears come from?" He frowned.

"It's nothing," she said, quickly wiping away any tears with the lace cuff of her dress. "I just have to accept the change that has occurred in my life." She lowered her head. "I just wanted to... ah, never mind..."

Velwel looked at her, his face serious.

"I'll talk to him," he said after a moment, and there was a hint of determination in his voice. "I'll try to convince him."

"You can't do anything," Aurelia said grimly. "He won't change his mind."

"But it's worth a try." Unexpectedly, he grabbed her shoulders. "You are like a sister to me, and Drasan is my brother. I cannot stand idly by the way you both suffer."

There was such unwavering certainty in his words that Aurelia suddenly remembered the expression in the half-dragon's eyes as she poured out all her bitterness on him. She knew it hurt him.

"Do as you like," she whispered without looking at him. All she wanted to do now was find Drasan and apologize for her behavior.

Velwel walked away towards the armory. She hadn't expected her husband to be there, but she knew where to find him.

CHAPTER 32

Drasan stood alone by the river, staring at the lazy stream. The sight of the water calmed him, but also made him feel strange longing. The role of leader of the rebellion was unbearably heavy for him. So much depended on his decisions, and he felt like an inexperienced kid. So far, he has been guided by a gut feeling, which in the current situation may not be enough. If he fails, many innocent people will die.

They had to get rid of Bal'zar first. And if you accept what he heard in the temple as truth, it will be more difficult than he expected. Was he going to imprison him? But how in the name of the gods would she do that?! The cursed brat had thousands of armed men. Breaking through to it will be quite a challenge.

He couldn't think of defeat. The plan had to work. Mostly he was counting on Dhalia ordering him to be taken alive. He would then become inviolable, and therefore would have complete freedom. First, he will kill her and then try to trap this monster. The only question is: how to do it?

He looked at the water and yawned a long time. There was little time until dawn, and he could not afford even a short rest. With a deep sigh, he spread his wings and was about to leap into the air when he saw movement behind him, and a familiar voice shouted:

"Wait!"

He folded his wings and turned his head.

Aurelia jumped off her horse and ran to him. At the sight of her, he felt a twinge of pain again.

"You know I won't change my mind," he said in a low, sad voice.

She bowed her head.

"And I'm not going to ask you to," she replied. "Just let me go to the camp with you..."

"There is no time for this!" he cut off sharply.

"Let me go with Velwel and King Oddon, but don't leave me here alone." She sounded pure despair now.

The half-dragon sighed deeply. He couldn't bear her pleading look. He knew she would be much safer here than in a camp close to the front lines. On the other hand, he guessed that even his prohibition would not stop her perverse nature. He found a solution.

"Okay. You must swear to me that under no circumstances will you leave the tent. The exception is a direct attack on the camp. I will take your sword to make sure you don't go into battle against the ban."

She stiffened. He could see from her face that she didn't like it. The weapon was as valuable to her as the one he carried himself. Nevertheless, she looked into his eyes and said:

"I promise you."

Satisfied, Drasan approached her and nudged her cheek.

"I have to go," he murmured softly, his breath blowing hot at her. His heart was pounding as he suddenly realized for the first time that he might not see her anymore. He wanted to tell her how much he loved her, but instead just said, "Please don't do anything reckless."

She smiled, though tears started to run down her cheeks.

"I'll miss you too," she said softly, looking into one of his glittering eyes.

Drasan snorted, a thin wisp of smoke escaping from his nostrils. With a heavy heart, he spread his great wings, bent his legs and leapt into the air. He could feel her eyes on him, but he dared not look.

Soon he soared above the clouds and turned west. The wind was on his side, and although dusk began to fall, he could see well enough to be able to hunt. He needed meat, not only to eat, but also to gather strength for battle.

He lowered his flight far enough to observe the grassy plains beneath him, and soon spotted a herd of deer grazing. He dove vertically downward, excitement surging through him - what kind of a hunter could match him in skill now? He fell from above onto the prey he had chosen, plunging his claws into the soft flesh and grabbed her by the neck, crushing her between her powerful jaws. He tasted hot blood in his mouth and began to feast, tearing off whole chunks of juicy meat and swallowing them with delight. He sat down with a feeling like never before. He felt like a predator now, an excellent hunter.

Soon a velvet night fell in the valley, chosen to be the lair. Having satiated his hunger, he lay down in soft ferns to rest before the flight and soak up the sounds of the world around him. Somewhere from a birch grove he heard the soft hoot of an owl. He turned his head that way, but he quickly lost interest in her - she wasn't even a snack. He put his head between the ferns and closed his eyes, leaving narrow slits to observe everything that happened around him.

He lay there almost all night, breathing evenly and letting his tired muscles rest. As the stars slowly began to fade in the sky, he stood up and yawned slowly, curving his long back like a cat. He looked over the hills, flexed his legs, and launched himself into the sky. He was very close to the target, he could see the gleaming ribbon of Loona below him, and the Wolfwood on the horizon. He roared loudly and vomited a stream of fire. In the past, he would have found such behavior stupid and unreasonable, but not today.

He descended slowly, his belly almost brushing the treetops. He landed in a dedicated empty square in the center of the encampment, where there was a feverish hustle and bustle as everyone was getting ready for the coming battle. To move freely, he had to change into a human form, which he did, ignoring the shouts of surprise.

He also had to seek out Gaenor and Alt'ar, as well as Rodian.

As he expected, he first encountered his kinsman. As usual, the dragon had an impenetrable expression.

"Subtlety is probably not your strongest point," he said, unable to help himself. "Now everyone knows where to find us."

"That's what I meant," Drasan replied evasively, looking around for Alt'ar. He couldn't see anything among the crowd of people.

"If you're looking for your shaggy friend," Gaenor said softly, not trying to hide his contempt, "you won't find him here. He went to collect what was left of the recon team you sent."

Drasan petrified, staring into the dragon's eyes, but saw no falsehood in them. He was telling the truth.

"Where?" He asked, unable to say any more.

The dragon silently pointed him in the direction, and walked away muttering to himself.

Drasan moved quickly, his heart pounding. In his mind he repeated like a mantra:

Just not Yarred. Let Yarred not be there.

Before he reached the destination, his nostrils were struck by the stench of blood and, which surprised him immeasurably, of decay. The smell was coming from the stake where Alt'ar was standing with two people he did not know. As he got closer, the stench became unbearable and Drasan covered his mouth with his sleeve.

Seeing what the pile was made of, he froze in horror. It turned out that they were single body parts separated from each other with amazing precision. And on them, with the same painstaking precision, the heads themselves were arranged, and at the very top of this disgusting pyramid, stuck on a spear...

No, he thought, terrified and shocked, not wanting to admit the thought. It is impossible...

The woman with long red hair next to Alt'ar turned to face him. Her face was wet and swollen, but he recognized her anyway.

"Mara," he muttered. "What are you..."

"Actually, I could ask you exactly the same question!" She interrupted him furiously. "What were you doing when your friend was risking his life for you?! I am here because someone without scruples and conscience delivered me a letter stating that you sent him there, Your Majesty! And now I am forced to look at the desecrated corpse of a beloved man! He didn't deserve such a pointless death!... He..." Her voice broke, but she continued to stare at him with burning eyes. "He did it for you, arrogant brat!"

Drasan felt too shaken by the sight to utter a single word. He could only watch as some unknown old man hugged the tearful Mara. He himself couldn't move.

Alt'ar turned to him, his eyes burning ruby red.

"Dawn is breaking, Drasan," he said with a strange peculiar expression on his face. "The day of our death is approaching, let's not make her wait any longer," he added, passing him and walking towards the camp.

The half-dragon felt despair overwhelm him, slowly turning into a cold rage. What he saw was sick, and only he could still stop it. He choked back the pain and let anger overwhelm him. He was going to use it against his enemies.

Dawn was breaking. A dawn that would bring them death or glory, but Drasan didn't care. Nothing mattered - Vaya, Yarred and who knows how many more were killed by him. Enough of inactivity. The day of retaliation has come.

***

Marshal Riko Wiron swallowed nervously at the sight of an army marching in a tight formation in the colors of Riden. He looked at the soldiers under his command and saw in their eyes the same fear tightening his throat.

As predicted by the queen, they reached the river bank two hours after she had left them. On the other side were the wild steppes of Riden - this was where the greatest battle since the Dragon Wars was to take place. They stood separated from the enemy army by a narrow ribbon of water, waiting for the signal.

The marshal gripped the spear shaft tighter and adjusted himself in the saddle. Dawn grayed on the horizon, but he could see no one, apart from the Rift soldiers lined up in a tight line. He looked at the front row of his own soldiers again. He knew that they were also nervous, and probably only the sight of a dragon would awaken in them their dormant courage.

And suddenly there were shouts, and several of his subordinates began to show each other something on a nearby hill. Riko Wiron looked in that direction as well and froze with his mouth open - three men appeared at the top of the hill. They stood there in front of the even ranks of Riden's soldiers, as if they were going to face the entire army on their own.

***

Marshal Conor De'Rembl was one of the veterans. He had a thirty-five-year career in the royal army. That is why it was to him that the king entrusted the custody of the best heavy cavalry unit. It consisted of nine hundred selected Riden knights, clad in heavy plate armor and riding huge steeds. Each of them carried a spear that would easily pierce a charging boar.

But De'Rembl was no fool, and though there were only three men on the hill beyond which he knew was an enemy army - two horsemen and one footman - he had no doubt it was appearances. The air vibrated with magic - the witch in the rear formed a shield around his squad to protect them from a magical attack from the enemy. But he, like most people, did not trust mages.

The marshal had been standing for an hour and looked at the three motionless figures on the top of the hill. He had an explicit order to let them make the first move. He waited for at least one signal to come out that the enemy was getting ready to attack, but nothing happened. Conor De'Rembl turned in the saddle of his gray stallion called the Bold and looked at the knights standing behind him. Some horses snorted impatiently and tore the ground with their hooves. Unused to waiting because they were trained to fight.

And suddenly, as it seemed they would still be standing there, something strange began to happen on the hill. Two riders jumped off their mounts and they vanished behind the hill. What happened next would probably forever be etched in the memory of the old soldier if he had had the chance to survive to talk about it. Both men turned into living torches, and the third one crouched down and began to grow on silvery-gray fur. It only lasted a few seconds, but it still caused panic among the usually fearless soldiers. A powerful wave of magic surged through the air like a storm, crashed on the shield that protected them. Conor shaded his eyes nonetheless, and when his eyesight regained clarity, he began to blink them vigorously - as if what he saw did not reach his consciousness.

He could not see the three men on the hill, but instead there were two dragons and a werewolf. The marshal had no doubts about it, although he considered both of these creatures mythical. One of the reptiles turned out to be brown and could be as high as a medium-sized manor house. A row of sharp bone spines extended from the base of its neck to the end of its long tail. The second, smaller and black, had a long neck and a pair of horns sprouted from its head. Next to the reptiles was a creature that was a mixture of a wolf and a human. He was covered with silvery fur from the waist up, his head with a long muzzle and pointed ears was definitely wolf from the hip-line - contrary to everything De'Rembl had heard of werewolves - he had black leather pants and boots on his feet. The beast felt huge, even for a werewolf.

One of the dragons - the black one - opened its mouth and let out a loud roar. The horses, usually so bravely resisting the hustle and bustle of battle, screamed in terror, some even reared. Conor De'Rembl swallowed nervously.

So that's it. They are to face the most terrible monsters the world has ever heard of. Let it be that way.

Before the marshal could give the order to attack, the werewolf standing on the hill raised its triangular head and let out a long, terrifying howl. For a moment nothing happened, suddenly on the horizon from the side of the enemy camp the first figures, about a hundred, began to arrive. De'Rembl was about to laugh, but the smile froze on his face and turned to a look of horror: it turned out not to be humans, but werewolves. They were nothing like their kin - probably the alpha male, because that's what they called their leader, if they had one. These creatures absolutely did not resemble human beings. Many of them moved on four grotesquely elongated legs, and flaps of saliva hung from the long wolf mouths, and the red eyes showed the lust for murder.

At the command of the alpha, they all moved down the slope with incredible speed, their lithe bodies literally blurred in their eyes. The horses, so far disturbed, now panicked. Many of them tried to get rid of the heavy riders and throw them to flee. The marshal could not take his eyes off what was happening at the top. For behold, the brown dragon turned into a ball of blood-red fire, and when the flames disappeared, he reappeared in human form, clad in silver armor, and in his hand, he carried a huge two-handed sword. As he lifted it up, the blade glowed with a riot of color, wrapping the strange knight in a luminous cocoon. It turned out to be magic so powerful that De'Rembl felt fear, one he had never felt before.

The black dragon launched into the sky, spreading great membranous wings.

It all took less than a minute. Armed with long curved claws and jaws capable of crushing bones, the beasts were just in front of the stretched line of the best Riden cavalry when suddenly the magic shield around them flashed, cracking with a crack like breaking glass. Then the werewolves rushed at the marshal's men with a triumphant roar.

What happened next, even if it happened, was never to be seen by Conor De'Rembl. The last thing he remembered was a black paw rushing towards him, armed with curved claws and a monstrous screech of torn armor.

***

Drasan and Alt'ar watched the battle unfold from the top of the hill. After the half-dragon destroyed the magic shield, the werewolves began to do what they did best - spread death. No armor could stop their fangs and claws, and their magic-empowered bodies regenerated. After the death of the commander, the heavy cavalry unit broke. Many riders started to flee. The heavily armored horses trampled the front ranks of the infantry in panic, as they retreated toward the ford at the sight of the werewolves. There, in turn, waited a long line of antho-cavalry.

Above all this noise was Gaenor, tasked to chase and kill those riders who tried to flee - no horse stood a chance against a dragon.

The smell of fresh blood filled the air, driving the werewolves into a frenzy. They ripped knights to pieces as easily as if they were rag dolls.

Drasan glanced anxiously at Alt'ar from time to time. In wolf form, he became larger and more massive, but unlike his brethren, he had full control over the lust for murder.

It was this hard-and-fast control that aroused the greatest admiration in the half-dragon. He called him now a prince - prince of werewolves. He had to admit that this title fit him perfectly. After the call of the alpha sounded, tens began to flow towards him, so now there were about a hundred here, and more kept coming. Their superhuman strength and speed proved to be extremely effective - just like it is now.

The werewolves dealt with the nine hundred best tank cavalry in no time, the ace up King Bal'zar's sleeve. Drasan still wondered why he had thrown them into battle in the first battle. It seemed a suspiciously foolish move to him, even for such a young and inexperienced ruler.

Alt'ar made a low, vibrating growl - in wolf form he could not speak.

The half-dragon followed his gaze and saw four black beasts surrounding the ten remaining knights. The werewolves circled them, not attacking, though their eyes blazed ruby. It took a moment for Drasan to understand why. Inside the circle formed by the survivors, a dark-haired witch stood, swaying, chanting protective spells. The Sheardon knew he was in a deep trance - now he had his best chance to kill her.

He looked at Alt'ar standing next to him and nodded. The werewolf growled in the affirmative, once again aimed his muzzle at the overcast sky and howled. The beasts froze, then they all started toward the hill, obeying the call of the alpha.

Drasan looked at the sword. The blade had no time to taste the blood, yet it glowed as if someone had cursed it with starlight.

He knew he had to pierce a witch's heart. If there's even a grain of truth in the legend, it should kill it. He gave a long whistle, and after a while the black stallion chased him. He, too, wore silver armor consisting of a helmet and a breastplate bristling with sharp spikes. The half-dragon was in the saddle in one leap, Ernil grunted and eagerly started down the hill, gradually speeding to a gallop.

His target was in the middle of a battlefield littered with the corpses of Bal'zar's armored cavalry. The remaining riders raised their spears at the sight of him, but he did not care. As he raised his sword, he felt a blast of magic. It swam past him somewhere. The blade in his hand flamed pure scarlet, responding to the desperate attack of the hidden witch.

At the sight of the silver knight advancing on them, the eyes of the soldiers who survived the slaughter widened with fear, but did not even flinch. Drasan picked up his sword and slapped one of the defenders through his chest. The blade tore through the thick armor like paper, then burst into flesh like butter. He felt sorry for the horse, squealing in pain as the long spikes dug into his chest. The poor animal jerked, tearing its right side in panic. On the other, the half-dragon slammed his fist into the back of the head. The others scattered as Gaenor suddenly fell on them. The dragon carried two men screaming in fear into the air. Moments later, somewhere above there was a terrifying screech of tearing armor as a large reptile grabbed one of them and cut it in two. Meanwhile, the second one slipped out of his blood-slick claws and fell screaming to the ground. There he lay motionless.

But Drasan did not look into the air, for his attention was completely absorbed by the woman kneeling in the center of the circle made of flat stones. A different rune sign was drawn with blood on each of them. She was wearing absolutely nothing, and her naked skin glowed, as did her slightly slanting eyes. She held a narrow-bladed dagger in her hand, and nearby lay the dead body of a boy who had been literally gutted, judging by the wounds.

The half-dragon jumped off his horse and approached the circle, treading carefully among the torn remains. The bloody work of the werewolves made no impression on the witch. She looked at him and smiled, showing unnaturally white teeth with clearly defined pointed fangs.

Her beauty had an eye-catching primal wildness about it.

"So, you are the one they call the Chosen One, or, if you like, the messenger of fate," she said, and bowed slightly. "I'm Mariv."

The half-dragon gritted his teeth and lifted his blade slightly.

Mariv's eyes narrowed into slits, and a low growl came out of her throat. She laughed softly.

"Isn't that weird? We are both, in a sense, wild beasts locked in human flesh," she said, looking at him with a slight frown. She stood up suddenly without the help of her hands, her movements reminiscent of the grace of a wild cat. Tight muscles played under his skin.

She was provoking him, clearly wanting him to take a step and get inside the circle, but he was cleverer. He took the sword in both hands and pushed it. The air around the circle lit up, but the barrier did not break.

Mariv laughed.

"It won't work. If you want me, you have to come in here."

So, I have no choice. He took a deep breath and stepped out of the circle.

And then she jumped, taking the form of a snow leopard in the air.

Surprised, Drasan failed to raise his sword...

The panther knocked him to the ground, knocking the weapon out of his hand. He growled and tried to shake her off. He felt a set of knife-sharp claws digging into his flesh.

She wasn't trying to kill him. She played with him awaiting the appearance of the sisters. He fell into a trap because within this circle he could not change.

Knowing this, he made a desperate attempt to reach for his sword. It was only inches from his left hand, he could almost feel the tips of his fingers brush against the cool hilt. He stretched his arm all the way, his muscles stuck in silent protest, but he managed to grab it. Before Mariv realized it, the blade plunged into her body. The witch's eyes went round with terror, the fur fell back, revealing smooth skin again. Drasan pushed harder, imposing the witch on the blade. The light in the cat's eyes flickered and went out, and the body froze motionless. Drasan knew that the poison covering the blade was eating a hole in her heart.

The half-dragon effortlessly lifted the loaded woman and threw it away in disgust. There was no blood on the gleaming blade, as if the sword had absorbed it. But that wasn't what surprised him. As soon as he ripped the sword from the dead body, it began to change: the skin suddenly sagged and covered with hundreds of wrinkles, then shattered to dust, revealing bare bones. The witch was dead, there was no doubt about it.

The battle is not over yet. Soon, enraged by the loss of the armored cavalry, Bal'zar will summon more soldiers to fight.

Drasan took one last look at what was left of Mariv and gave a long whistle, summoning Ernil. The black stallion trotted up to him. The half-dragon sheathed his sword and climbed into the saddle. If the plan is successful, King Oddon will be here soon. They had to prepare for the fight, because that was just a taste of what was to come.

***

Even if her sister's death had upset Dhalia, she still did not show it. She approached it with studied indifference. Inside, Bal'zar knew he was teeming with anger and revenge.

She knew Mariv's death was part of the plan. Like the loss of heavy driving and one of the best and most experienced commanders in his army. He would have liked to go out there and pulverize everyone, but he stayed calm.

The alliance with the werewolves took him by surprise. After all, the information he got from Alder showed that Drasan hated these monsters. It is possible that he made a mistake by underestimating his opponent.

He looked at Dhalia.

"I think your pet deserves an award today. He just cleaned up the mess you made," he said.

The witch looked at him icy cold.

"Mariv's death is just the beginning," she said in a voice filled with haughty contempt. "You have released a wild beast from your cage that will not rest until we are all perched in the deepest depths of the abyss."

Bal'zar laughed derisively.

"Indeed, that's how you can put it. At least if I threw him to eat you..." he mused.

"It's not a game, you puffy brat," she growled, standing up and pointing her finger at his chest with an accusing gesture. "That's where real people die, and you don't care about death! You fancy yourself to be a god..."

"It is a small price indeed, if the prize is absolute victory," replied the young king with a nonchalant embarrassment. "Let's wait a moment longer, let all the guests come to our party."

"You're a monster!" She sat down, resigned.

Bal'zar snorted and resumed his seat in the cushioned chair.

"So are you, my dear. How many dead bodies do you have on your account? Thousands, millions? We are no different, viper, except maybe your days are numbered and your time is passing relentlessly. If you have nothing new to tell me, shut your mouth."

Dhalia fell silent obediently, and he sighed in relief. Soon all these vermin will crawl at his feet, begging for mercy.

CHAPTER 33

Returning to the hill, Drasan was surprised that no one was attacking him. Gaenor flew just above him and landed on the summit, scarlet drops of blood pearling on his black scales. There also stood Alt'ar with Rodian at his side. The witch gave him a weak smile and stepped back a little.

The first thing that struck him was the uncertainty and even fear in the eyes of his comrades-in-arms. Gaenor was the first to step forward, anger in his eyes.

"You fool!" He hissed, baring his teeth. "Look what you did!" He added, pointing him in the direction.

Drasan turned to that side and froze, unable to move. From the top of the ridge on which they stood, he had a great view of the vast plain, and as far as the eye could see, they were occupied by equal ranks of the regular army. Tens of thousands! The bulk of it was infantry, but he had noticed several thousand cavalries as well.

"Want to know what's going to happen next?" The dragon continued in a ruthless voice. "Bal'zar will take bloody revenge. For every knight killed, he'll kill ten of our people."

Drasan glared at him. This is not the time for arguments! They have come too far to back off.

"If that's the price of freedom, then I'm ready to take it upon myself," he growled, his teeth bared as well, though Gaenor was not as impressed as he expected. "We will fight to show that we can still do it. We will not show even an iota of pity, we will become as ruthless as they are."

The dragon snorted.

"Then go over there and tell your people! Send them into the cold embrace of death, for we never had the slightest chance of winning!"

"If you are such a coward, then go back to your mistress! Maybe She will accept you, but get out of my sight, for today I'd rather perish free today than live as a slave for centuries!" Drasan thundered. Anger rushed to his head; scarlet flames enveloped his body.

The black dragon hissed and was about to lunge at Drasan when a furious Alt'ar stepped between them.

"If you want to kill each other, I won't forbid! But not today, not when we may need you," he said in a calm voice, only his eyes screeched. "We can't afford to lose a single ally now."

The furious Drasan passed him by, sliding down the slope towards the ranks of assassins waiting for him, seated in their saddles, awaiting orders. A large part of the remnants of the Antuan army gathered nearby. Thanks to the subversive action of the werewolves, they managed to make their way across the river and now gathered around their queen.

The real battle would begin soon, and he didn't know what to tell them. He faced a handful against tens of thousands. They didn't stand a chance. Nevertheless, he took on a mask of calm and composure. They could not recognize that he was afraid.

He stopped the horse and jumped off its back.

"My brothers and sisters!" He roared, his voice loud enough to be heard even in the last ranks. "I think I can call you that, because today we are all equal! Today we are fighting for more than privileges, titles or lands! We fight for freedom! And if there are gods, today they will see who we really are! They will see courage, the ability to sacrifice, honor and love." As he spoke the last words, he looked at Mara, tears shining in her eyes. "We fight for those who sacrificed their lives and for those who trust that we will be able to save them from a cruel death! I myself have lost many friends! And I tell you, today is the time for your revenge! Let our swords taste the blood of oppressors who long for our defeat!"

His words were followed by a consistent roar that shook the foundations of the earth. The werewolves raised their heads and let out a terrifying howl, and the Alt'ar on the hill echoed them. Overcome by euphoria, the half-dragon allowed his body to burst into flames. The transformed, powerful reptile let out a deafening roar that was quickly picked up by the humans, werewolves and Gaenor behind the hill.

They knew they couldn't back down now. They had nowhere to. Until Oddon arrived, they had to hold the front.

With that in mind, he sprang to flight before Gaenor did the same, and behind him he heard the roar of the hooves of the Antuan steeds and the roar of a thousand throats as the Antuanians and Alt'ar's assassins followed.

At that moment, the air flickered again and an oval magic portal appeared through which the Earden riders, led by King Oddon, who were riding their great steed, poured out. Without slowing their mad gallop, the archers tautened their strings and sent a barrage of black-feathered arrows at the Ridean standing still. Neither of them managed to reach them - they all burned down before they reached their destination.

And then Drasan saw her. She was at the forefront of the enemy army. Beautiful and scary, with white hair flowing and in a black dress. Witch. Another of the three Rodian had warned him about.

Without waiting for the others, he folded his wings and ducked straight towards her. He didn't even stop when she glared at him, or when the Antuanians charging towards the Ridenians suddenly fell off their horses, as if a strong gust of wind blew them from their saddles.

The witch laughed, and then the sky darkened abruptly, covered with heavy storm clouds. A thunder rumbled so fiercely it momentarily stunned him, and the whirlwind pushed aside and threw it at his own men like a rag doll.

"The shield is too powerful!" Gaenor roared as he landed beside him and helped him to his feet. "Our attacks are useless as long as this white-haired bitch is alive! You have to kill her!"

As soon as he said it, the lightning struck the werewolves retreating in panic. She set fire to some of them and now they were running towards the forest.

There was only one way out - Laudas' sword had to be used again.

Both the Antuanians and Eardenians stopped at some distance from the magical shield while Drasan transformed again. Sword in hand, he walked over to the slightly shimmering cover. He reached deep, infusing it with a powerful charge of his own energy, raised it above his head and slammed into the magic sphere with all his strength. The visor flickered brighter but did not disappear. The half-dragon chopped and sliced, putting more and more energy into it, but nothing happened.

Eventually, just as the situation seemed hopeless, he closed his eyes and repeatedly recited the words he had used before but forgot about them. It was only when he shouted them that he gained the power needed to destroy the barrier. He raised his sword again, but this time he slashed lightly instead of it, as if dealing with a living thing.

The barrier cracked with an ear-splitting crash that drowned out the triumphant roar from the throats of the two armies behind him. Both of them fell on the enemy like a horde of furious dogs. For a moment, Bal'zar's soldiers stared at them, not understanding what had happened. Only when the first wave of enemy troops hit them and the fight began did they understand that they had no magic cover. The tall fair-haired witch curled up, pressing her hands to her temples, the destruction of the barrier caused her physical pain.

She had clearly lost control of the magic storm, for now the lightning bolts were hitting Bal'zar's army as well, causing them to panic and panic. She quickly regained her strength and chanted a spell, which made Drasan's hair bristle. Horses immediately fell under the dozens of Eardenian riders charging at her, and several more were blown from the saddles by a powerful wave of magic before they could draw their bows.

The witch raised both hands, aiming them at the black sky. Suddenly a violent wind arose, hitting the Antuanians charging at her and pushing them to the side. Then Drasan realized that he had to act. He gripped the hilt of his sword tighter and, through the ongoing battle, he moved towards the woman.

No one dared raise a sword at him or shoot a crossbow. Everyone was getting out of his way, perhaps mistaking him for a ghost. Apparently, Dhalia or Bal'zar - never mind - had ordered them not to harm him. They were supposed to catch him, not kill him. This allowed him to reach the witch, grinning, without hindrance.

"You killed Mariv," she said in an unexpectedly low and distant voice. "You won't be that easy with me, crossbreed. I've been living much longer than you."

"You will probably be relieved to see death," Drasan replied, raising his sword, flashing so brightly as if it had been woven of light.

"You have Laudas' sword." She looked at the weapon in his hand, and there was a hint of fear in her words, though her pale countenance showed no hint of fear.

A smile of complacency crept across his face. He spun the hissing sword's blade without taking his eyes off his opponent. The woman returned the smile, her eyes shone with a milky white glow and suddenly attacked his mind with such force that his knees buckled under him. He fought off the charge quickly as Gaenor had taught him, launched a counterattack. As expected, he met a resistance so strong that he felt a dull throb at his temples. He continued, enduring the pain bravely.

You won't win with me, crossbreed, he heard a voice piercing with terror in his head.

As he struggled with the witch, the indescribable clamor of battle reigned around him. Nobody doubted who had an overwhelming advantage in this clash. Both the Eardenians and the Antuanians, who had wedged themselves into the enemy army, were now falling under the blows of the Ridean on all sides. Drasan realized that if he did not end this fight soon, they would have to retreat.

Mara, riding a white mare, flashed past him. Her armor was stained with blood. She had lost her helmet somewhere, and now her long red hair was flying like a flaming banner. The sight gave him strength. He redoubled his efforts and felt his opponent's resistance weaken. In the end, he forced her to step back into himself, pushed her on the defensive.

He opened his eyes to see the woman swaying, pressing both fists against her temples. Gained a chance! In a few strides he covered the distance to her, raised his sword, and with the very tip of the blade he slapped her across her chest. A fountain of blood splattered his face, but he ignored it.

He looked into the witch's eyes, now wide with fear, and said:

"For Yarred and all those who died before him."

After these words, still smiling mockingly, he thrust his sword with all his strength, piercing her body. This time, at the moment of death, there was a blinding flash emanating from her body that quickly faded, leaving yellowed bones behind. Drasan yanked the blade from the disintegrating carcass. Then what was left of the witch immediately crumbled to dust.

The blade was still faintly smoking as, standing over the ashes of the witch, he exclaimed at the top of his throat:

"I'm coming for you, Dhalia! Get ready to die!"

He looked at the battle going on around him. No one noticed the witch's death, though their confidence had diminished somewhat as they suddenly retreated before the two hostile armies pressed on them. Gaenor flew over the field, occasionally diving down to snatch a few Rideen with him, swallowing them whole or tearing them to pieces. Arrows fired at him slid over the hard shells without doing any harm to him.

Drasan smiled, seeing that he was having a great time and thought about the werewolves. He ordered Alt'ar to stay aside unless his intervention was absolutely necessary. He had no doubts that the presence of werewolves on the battlefield would tip the tide of victory in their favor. Still, they remained dangerous beasts, and he did not believe that in the frenzy that the smell of fresh blood gave them, they would not attack everyone, no matter if they were enemy or ally.

Suddenly, he saw someone he hadn't expected to see here, and a shudder of terror shook him: Aurelia was going to stay in the camp, what was she doing on the battlefield? Regardless of what he did, he started in the direction of the red sash that usually hung around his waist flashed. To his relief, he saw Velwel at her side. As always, he operated the sword with masterful precision. Drasan made his way mercilessly with his sword until he faced his wife.

Aurelia turned faster than Velwel, noticing the angry half-dragon striding towards them. The young man turned his mare, and when he saw Drasan his jaw dropped. Access to the girl was blocked.

The Sheardonian gave him such a look that he quickly moved out of the way. Then he grabbed the reins of his wife's horse and began to drag him with him as far away from the battlefield as possible. Velwel rode slowly beside them, a cascade of mumbling explanations flowing from his mouth.

"Drasan, I... We really didn't have time... I tried to convince her to turn back. She insisted on having to see you..."

Drasan listened silently to him, though little of the gibberish reached his consciousness. The feeling that he might lose the last person he cared about shook him deeply. Aurelia didn't say a word to him, she understood that her explanations would not change anything anyway. She allowed him to pull her out of the turmoil of battle. Only when they were away from the fighting did he say to her in a voice full of anger and fear at the same time:

"You swore to me," his voice sounded strangely hollow and unfamiliar. "I trusted you would listen to me for once."

She listened to him with her head bowed, tears streaming down her cheeks. The fact that she had failed him hurt her much more than his words.

"I asked you to stay in the camp, because you are in a much greater danger than me or Velwel or anyone else," he continued in the same tone. "I can't lose you," he added, a little softer.

"Neither am I you," she whispered, still not looking at him.

"And you won't lose, I can promise you one thing," he replied, looking at Velwel. "Get her out of here. I can only trust you now."

"I will protect her even at the cost of my own life," replied the young werewolf.

Drasan sighed heavily.

"Leave us alone for a moment," he asked, his voice sounding tired.

The fight with the Lady of the Elements had released him from strength. His next duel would be death for him, but he didn't care. Where was he to fly, if not on the battlefield, amid the clash of swords hitting each other and the roar of warriors?

Only when they were alone doing Aurelia meet his eyes and only whispered:

"Sorry, do not punish Velwel for my disobedience..."

"Aurelia," he interrupted her. "You don't even realize what a great danger you are in here..." He broke off, unable to find the right words. "You will be safe with Velwel, he will take care of you, while I..."

"When you: what?" This time she cut him off, and there was a hint of anger in her voice.

He didn't answer, his heart still hammering. Maybe it was counting down the last moments of his life.

"Look into my eyes," she demanded, taking his face in both hands. He obeyed and met a gaze full of uncertainty and pain. "Promise you will come back."

"Aurelia..." he whispered.

"Promise me that, please..."

His heart was filled with pain so great he could hardly bear it.

"I promise," he said, though the lie burned his throat like venom.

Tears welled up in his wife's eyes. At the same moment Velwel rode up and held out his hand to her.

The battle was getting closer. The Ridenians slowly but inevitably pushed their opponents towards the river. Even Oddon's brave warriors fell under the blows of too numerous enemies. The result seemed a doomed.

Drasan knew he had to come up with something quickly. Otherwise, his people will lose their will to fight.

"Velwel, take my wife away from here," he ordered sharply. He walked briskly to one of the Antuan messengers, took the reins from him and climbed into the saddle himself. "And don't leave her even one step."

Velwel nodded, nodded to Aurelia, and turned with her towards the forest.

Drasan watched them cross the river for a moment, glanced at Alt'ar and nodded. Now he had no choice: he had to bring all his strength into battle.

***

It's time, Bal'zar thought, watching the battle unfold from one of the hills.

His troops pressed against the combined forces of the Liberators, driving them towards the river. He saw Drasan and Alt'ar trying to control the panicked army without success. Queen of Antua also tried to get her soldiers together. Oddon had the sense to retreat to the other side.

The Ridenians turned out to be simply too numerous, and seeing the panicked command of the enemy army, they attacked with redoubled force.

The future emperor was just waiting for it. Previously, he had watched Drasan closely and knew that the half-dragon was weak. He couldn't even change. The time is right to teach him a lesson that will make him aware of who he is dealing with.

By his side, Dhalia did not seem thrilled to see the Liberators' defeat. It was possible that she had secretly hoped that a miracle would happen that would give the rebels victory.

"The moment we've been waiting for has arrived," he said without looking at her. His attention was drawn to watching the battle unfold below. "Go and see that the girl is safe and sound in Washmorth."

The witch gave him a hateful look, but did not dare to oppose the direct order. Before she decided to leave, the young king grabbed the reins of her horse and pulled her towards him.

"And remember that if you fail me, I will feed the dogs with your heart," he deliberately stretched out each syllable. After these words, he released her and watched her drive away down the narrow path toward the place Alder had chosen.

A smug smile slowly spread across his face. He knew Dhalia didn't need better motivation.

***

After awakening, Velwel had to wonder for a long time where he was and what actually happened. The chaos around him made him realize that he must be close to the battlefield. He sat up carefully, feeling the back of his head. Dull pain made him know that someone had tried to split his skull not so long ago. Fortunately, the werewolves' inherent ability to regenerate quickly thwarted this plan.

A battle was going on around him - and - as he consciously noticed - his friends were losing. There were enough dead bodies around him to be considered one of them.

He stood up carefully, relieved that all his bones were intact. He also felt his face, which it turned out to be covered with a gigantic scab of dried blood.

How long has it been since he got hit?

Suddenly he felt the contents of his stomach rise in his throat.

Neila!

He looked around, hoping the girl was not dead. Not finding her in the pile of bodies, he sighed with relief. This turned out to be short-term happiness. The girl is gone! It could be anywhere! And he, who was supposed to protect her, was lying the gods know how long!

Damn it! he thought. Drasan will kill me. He entrusted me with the safety of his beloved woman, and I screwed up.

The devastated Velwel began to look for the mount. There was no help, he had to find a friend's wife. Dead or alive, but he had to find her.

***

After crossing the river Velwel turned southwest, still urging his horse to run faster. When he got a little away from the battle noise, he slowed down a little pace and, to Aurelia's surprise, he grabbed the reins of her tall chestnut and set both horses in place. He stood there for a while, looking around uncertainly for something, and started again, this time without letting go of her horse's reins for a moment.

He seemed strangely nervous, which worried her much more than the direction of travel. Was someone following them?

But as Aurelia turned around, she saw empty plains, and farther away was the hill where she had parted Drasan. She could still hear the sounds of battle, strangely muffled.

Touched by a bad feeling, she decided to ask:

"Where are we going?"

"To safety," the man replied shortly, but Aurelia sensed a strange excitement in his voice, in addition to a little nervousness. He couldn't wait to get there.

And suddenly the girl stiffened in the saddle and goose bumps covered her body despite the favorable temperature. She realized that she was alone. They moved away not only from the battlefield, but also from the Wolf Forest, where the camp was located. They rode along the narrow strip of Soloma. Aurelia knew the river farther south to the Haerral Mountains. The forest was on the right, but instead of turning, they continued along the shore. There was only one explanation: Velwel did not want to take her away from the battlefield. He wanted to take her away from Drasan so that he could...

"Explain to me," she tried to prevent even the slightest hint of fear from creeping into her voice. "Why are we moving away from the forest, and in addition heading towards the Riden border?"

The companion turned to her sharply, and then his features began to change. First, the hair disappeared, revealing a naked skull, the eyes turned from brown to black, and the sparse stubble turned into a pointed beard. It turned out to be Alder!

His black eyes gleamed in the dim light, like two polished opals. To her horror, he suddenly gave a harsh laugh, stopping both mounts again.

Aurelia reacted instinctively. Without waiting for his reaction, she yanked her legs out of the stirrups, jumped off her mount, landing like a cat, and ran away. Before she could take three steps, she collapsed to the ground when someone suddenly cut her legs. She wanted to run, but the same force kept her immobile.

"So, it's you..." she croaked, the metallic taste of blood in her mouth. "And he trusted you! We thought you were dead."

Alder laughed, his laugh making her creep.

"Yes, it's me," he said, walking around it slowly, checking that it hadn't been permanently damaged. "I was a spy for Bal'zar from the very beginning, and even the great Drasan did not recognize me. For who would have suspected such a mediocre mage, and moreover, obsessed with supernatural beings?" He laughed again. "Oh, that knowledge turned out to be extremely useful. Thanks to her, I discovered something that neither my master nor that whore Dhalia knew, having all the means of persuasion at his disposal. Because you see... What your loved one did go much deeper than he thinks..."

"Give it up, you wicked bastard!" Aurelia snapped, struggling in her magical bonds. "He will not give up, nothing will stop him..."

"You are wrong, my dear," the mage interrupted calmly. "There is something that will stop him and even make him submissive and humble. That person is you, dear Aurelia..."

"I'd sooner slit my veins than..."

"And you will make him suffer so much pain?" Alder interrupted, relishing to tell her. "You don't quite understand what he did by offering his love?"

"I have no idea, but you'll be sure to tell me soon," Aurelia spat blood.

Not good, she thought, a metallic taste gathering in her mouth. She must have bitten her tongue as she fell or broken one of her teeth.

"With dragons, confessing eternal love is not just reciting a formula. When a dragon decides to bond with someone, he will strive for this love even for the rest of his life."

Hearing that, Aurelia stiffened. His words had to contain at least a grain of truth, though in part, for the description was very much like Drasan's behavior towards her.

"When he reaches his goal and gets the one he loves, he will remain faithful to her for the rest of his life. And when one of you dies, the other will fall into madness from despair."

No! Aurelia thought, her chances of getting out of this situation diminishing to zero.

"I don't believe you," she growled softly, struggling in the bonds even more violently.

"It doesn't matter now." He said calmly. "You will understand when he is in danger."

"You're lying, you slimy reptile!" The girl exclaimed. "Nobody even touches him! He..."

"Nobody touched him on my orders," said a cold voice just above her.

At the same time, the magical bonds were released, and Aurelia sprang to her feet. This time she didn't try to run away. Before her stood a woman so beautiful that she could not describe her beauty in words. Her eyes betrayed her - cold and ruthless - like mountain lakes. The girl had no doubts about who she was in front of her.

"But don't worry, we're not going to kill him." She said in a voice so calm, like at a tea chat. "Alive, he will be much more useful," she smiled in such a way that Aurelia's skin chafed.

The witch walked over to her, passing Alder, who for her was only a part of the landscape.

"You're his chosen one..." she said, eyeing Aurelia with her eyes. "Well, it's not for me to judge his taste."

"What do you want, snake?" Aurelia snapped, stepping back. She met the resistance of a magic barrier.

The woman smiled.

"Nothing special, my dear," she replied, still studying her. "I feel great potential in you. You have abilities and you are blocking them, why?"

"What do you care?" The girl growled, spitting blood from her mouth and tongue checking if all the teeth are whole.

The woman was looking at her with such curiosity as if she were some very interesting specimens of an animal.

"Nothing, actually," she said with a malicious smile. "But I like to know who I'm dealing with."

"Stop the game," Alder muttered softly. "We don't have time for this."

Aurelia turned to face him; her eyes wide with terror.

At this sight, the witch smiled even wider, whispered a few words and blew something in her face. The mercenary staggered as if she was drunk, her eyesight blurred, and after a while she collapsed without feeling.

The last thing in her fading consciousness was... she was dying. She slipped back into the darkness with relief.

CHAPTER 34

Gods, why you must experience me to this degree? Drasan thought, rubbing the back of his head.

A moment ago, one of the Riden foot soldiers was briefly lucky: he managed to hit the prince in the back of the head with what looked like a gnarled club. Instead, he was pierced by a spear of one of the few Antuan horsemen.

Werewolves fought in a frenzy from the scent of blood in the air. Hundreds of dead bodies veiled the ground, and the still alive screamed excruciatingly, clutching their temples.

Only then did he realize that the Ridenians were retreating, leaving behind both dead and wounded comrades. They were making room for the high knight on the great white stallion riding towards him through the battlefield. The rider wore matte black armor that was deceptively similar to the one Gaenor wore in Dhalia's vision.

The knight stopped his horse and jumped off its back, then, perhaps reading his mind, pulled the helmet off his head. A thatch of light, almost white hair spilled out from under it. It was Bal'zar. He'd grown and tighter since the last time he'd seen him, but he had no doubts whatsoever about his identity.

The young king smiled, displaying dazzling white teeth.

"Let me change the scenery a bit to suit our duel," he said, waving his hand carelessly. The air around them flickered and after a while they stood in the sanctuary.

Drasan backed away, his footsteps echoing through the empty room.

"What are these tricks for, Bal'zar?" He asked mockingly. "Are you afraid of failure?"

In response, the young man smiled even wider, and a large sword with a matte black blade materialized in his hand.

"You overestimate your abilities, Drasan," he said, tossing an unruly strand from his forehead. "You have no chance of winning. I admire your courage. I know you are trying to save the remnants of those pathetic rebels of yours, so I will give you a chance. If you succeed, your men will walk away free, if not... Well, when I'm done with you, I'll take care of the rest of the rebels and not even your mongrel can stop me from doing it. I'll finish them off one by one before your blood has time to cool."

"You are very confident, Bal'zar," growled Drasan, reaching for his sword. "But overconfidence can be both a great advantage and a disadvantage."

They circled slowly, observing each other with such attention that they could be compared to a pair of wolves, which would be at each other's throats at any moment. Drasan held the sword at belt level with both hands, and his opponent perfectly copied this stance. It gave the prince the impression that he was looking in a mirror. This made it difficult for him to detect the adversary's intentions. So, he decided to watch the young man closely, hoping that some small gesture would betray him.

He himself tried to seem composed and confident. As an old custom, he made sparing moves, focusing on combat experience, because he did not know what to expect from a young Ridenian. The sword glistened faintly, and he concluded that Bal'zar had no intention of launching a magic attack. The young ruler wanted to defeat him in battle, where Drasan had no equal.

They were still circling, watching, when suddenly the enemy attacked with such speed that he could barely cover himself. He showered him with a barrage of blows, pushing him to the defense. Both blades collided, sending sparks. The fight seemed to be even, which surprised Drasan so much that Bal'zar skirted his veil and slashed his left shoulder. The blade cut the armor shoulder as easily as if it had been made of paper.

"A point for me," said the young ruler. "Focus, Drasan."

The Sheardonian backed away, surprised both by the cut and by the fact that blood was still oozing from the wound that should have closed.

"No magic, Drasan," Bal'zar said, smiling mockingly. "We fight as befits ordinary mortals: until one of us falls."

The prince straightened, ignoring the pain in his shoulder. He tossed the sword to his right hand and launched a desperate attack. For the first time, he disregarded his opponent, which turned out to be a fatal mistake. Bal'zar shielded himself from his blow without the slightest effort.

The half-dragon jumped back and looked at the enemy's posture once more. It seemed familiar, though he couldn't remember where he remembered it from. He had never fought anyone good before. Each blow to his rival seemed well thought-out and was designed to immobilize him, inflict as much pain as possible, but not kill him. Bal'zar played with him, knowing that Drasan would not threaten him in any way. Unless...

No magic, let the abyss engulf him, he thought enraged.

"I'd advise you not to try, Drasan," Bal'zar said quietly, reading his mind. "Fight me, but no tricks! Otherwise, I will show you a whole new dimension of pain."

His words gave Duke Sheardon a shiver. For he understood that he would not be able to win this fight, but surrender was out of the question. She'd sooner jump on her own sword.

He assumed an upright posture, lifting the blade a little higher.

"That I get," Bal'zar said, flashing the white of his teeth again. "Your master would certainly be pleased to see you fight to the end."

Drasan tried to maintain his composure as Ashkan had taught him.

Focus on the fight. Ignore his words, it doesn't matter now, he kept repeating it in his mind like a mantra.

He knew the king was trying to upset him so that he would lose his concentration and make a mistake. But he forgot one thing: Drasan had made a mistake in confronting him in an unequal fight, but it was too late to withdraw. The only thing left to do is observe the opponent and wait for his mistake.

Bal'zar smiled and attacked. To his surprise, instead of the expected cut on the right side, the opponent whirled in a pirouette and slashed him just below the knee, cutting the tendon. Drasan roared in pain and again made a desperate counterattack, trying to ignore the shooting pain in his injured leg. The constant flow of blood made him far too slow. The Ridenian, who had not taken any injuries so far, easily parried his cut. With his swing, the handle hit him in the jaw with such force that he fell to the ground.

Then he stood over him and kicked the sword from his hand. Drasan tried to get to his feet, but the ruler would not let him. He kicked him on the left side with such force that he heard the ominous click of broken ribs.

"I don't advise getting up," he growled, pointing the tip of his blade at his throat. - Haven't you had enough yet? You have no chance to win with me. It remains to admit that I am better.

"You cheat..." Drasan wheezed.

"A killer never plays clean," Bal'zar replied coldly, grasping his forearm and breaking his shoulder with one jerk.

The prince roared in pain, desperately trying to stay awake.

"You're so predictable..." He paused, leaned over, and grabbed the half-dragon by the hair on the nape of his neck. "...admit you lost, great Chosen One."

"No," growled Drasan, feeling pain all over his body. He spat blood in the Ridenian's face.

Bal'zar wiped the blood with his free hand and slammed his fist across the stomach. The blow left his opponent out of breath.

"I'd love to kill you," he said coldly, leaning over the half-dragon. "But then you wouldn't learn anything," he added, releasing him.

Drasan lay still, gasping for breath. He felt his wounds were too serious to continue the fight, while Bal'zar emerged from it without a single scratch. He wanted to say something, but choked on his own blood.

It's not good, he thought. If the blood came from the lungs, it was going to be even worse than he expected.

"All right," said the young ruler gently. "I think it's time to end this fun."

The air flickered and they were back on the battlefield.

Drasan lay motionless on his back, expecting the final blow, ending his torment. This one did not come. Bal'zar walked over to the dead Ridenian and plucked a gnarled club from his fingers. He tossed it in his hand to estimate its weight and started back toward the prince.

"If you're counting on my sister, you're just fooling yourself unnecessarily. Thanks to you, she has her hands full today," the young lord said carelessly, tossing a club in his hand.

And suddenly he swung, aiming for the right knee of the dying prince. The blow was so strong that it blinded him for a moment. The pain in shattered bones drowned out everything else. He did not remember the rest, even if it did, because he had passed out.

When he regained it, he felt someone dragging him on the ground. It was not Bal'zar. The young Ridenian did not smell like a wet dog. Drasan opened his eyes, which cost him no little effort, for his eyelids were stuck together with dried blood. He looked up and saw Alt'ar's back muscles tense. The werewolf dragged him persistently across the field, growling under his breath what sounded like a torrent of curses.

Drasan tried to move, but it caused such a great wave of overwhelming pain that he was unable to suppress a cry of disbelief.

Alt'ar looked at him, his lips curving into a sort of ironic smile.

"I never thought I'd see anything so pathetic in my long life," he said.

Drasan didn't answer, his jaw clenched with pain. He looked down and a violent shudder shook his body as he saw what was left of his right knee.

"I don't advise you to move, because judging by what I see, you got a pretty bad hit there," he was saying very seriously, and there was genuine worry in his voice. "From what I can see you have a broken shoulder, a crushed knee and a few broken ribs, one may even be broken. That bastard gave you a nice beating. We were sorry to see it, but we couldn't get to your battlefield because the spells with which he wrapped himself turned out to be too powerful."

"What about the rest?" Drasan grunted, trying not to look at his leg.

"Most of it came out unscathed. Velwel has been hit in the head and is delirious, and King Oddon has a few wounds, but not too serious. The Queen of Antuans has a broken rib and a rather deep cut on her left thigh, but Rodian is taking care of them and they will surely get out of there. Many died, at least half of the Antuans and a good number of the Eardenians."

Drasan gritted his teeth. He felt the weight of remorse. He waited too long...

"What about Aurelia?" He asked. "Is she okay? Is she safe?"

Alt'ar was silent for a moment before answering carefully, choosing his words:

"To tell you the truth, I have no idea. Velwel claims that the ground swallows her up."

Drasan struggled to keep from leaping to his feet, reminding himself in time that it was impossible.

"How..." was the only thing he managed to say.

"We have a few guesses, but they all come down to one point..." the werewolf paused for a moment. "Someone betrayed us. Someone who knew the plan well. Someone we wouldn't even suspect for a moment."

Drasan felt all the blood drain from his face. The solution became so obvious... Dhalia! Yes, it had to be her. Bal'zar distracted him, while she...

"What are you doing?!" Alt'ar growled.

Drasan realized that he was trying to get up, putting his weight on his healthy shoulder. the pain turned out to be too intense, and after a while he lay back down on the ground, out of breath. He felt completely helpless and as weak as a kitten.

"Listen to me carefully," Alt'ar said, kneeling beside him. "At the moment you cannot face anyone. Rodian will put you together, and then we'll consult with you what to do next. The Ridenians withdrew. We have time to rest a bit before the next fight."

What he was saying seemed more reasonable than going to Washmorth alone. Drasan lay for a moment, trying to remember his words to Velwel, before entrusting him with the care of Aurelia. His friend seemed strangely reticent. Why did it not surprise him then?

Someone had to hit Velwel in the head and take over his role. Someone who knew very well that this was the last person they trusted. Enough to entrust him with the protection of his beloved wife. This someone knew Drasan well and knew in advance that after Yarred's death, the young assassin was the only option.

"I need to speak to Velwel," he whispered, more to himself than to the killer leaning over him.

"Velwel is incapable of talking..." Alt'ar protested, but stopped at the sight of the half-dragon's expression. "Judging by the size of the fracture, someone tried to split his skull open. It was only the great luck of our mutual friend that he failed, but it still takes a few days before he starts talking sense."

"You don't understand," said Drasan. "Aurelia is not missing, someone abducted her..." He broke off and shook his head violently. He felt his strength draining out of him again.

"Stop talking nonsense!" The werewolf scolded him. "You better save your strength, because as far as I recall, a broken shoulder cannot be adjusted with magic..."

***

Drasan.

It became the first conscious thought that crossed Aurelia's mind as soon as she woke up. She tried to get up, but found it impossible. She opened her eyes and looked up at the high vaulted ceiling, completely plunged in darkness. Both her arms and legs were chained with padded handcuffs to the straight bunk so that she could barely move.

She looked around the circular chamber for a moment, trying to figure out where it was, but all she could think of was Washmorth or another Riden city.

She was alive, though her body was sore, as if she had been beaten with a stick. She feared for Drasan because, although she did not believe a single word from Alder, she could not help feeling that he was in mortal danger.

The screeching of a key in the lock made her stiff. The black-haired woman who had captured her entered the room. She was alone, carrying a tray of piled up food. Only this sight made the girl realize how hungry she was.

"I take it you woke up recently and you must be hungry," said the witch, setting the tray on the floor.

Aurelia felt her guts twist with hunger, but decided not to break. First, she had to find out what the woman wanted from her.

"Who are you?" She asked. It was the first obvious question to come to her mind.

The woman smiled and sat down on the edge of the bunk.

"My name is Dhalia. Drasan must have told you about me."

Aurelia felt a chill shiver. She remembered that name. Drasan mentioned them quite often both while awake and in sleep. It was she who tortured him in the Kahaer dungeons, it was she who almost led him to death.

"It's you?!" She finally choked out, anger driving out her fear. "I saw what you did to him, the scars on his body are the best testimony to that!"

Dhalia endured this little outburst stoically and after a while said:

"Listen to me carefully now, Aurelia. There is only one way to a happy ending, and we both know it. Drasan must surrender..."

"He'll never give up!" The girl screamed, feeling a kind of pride. She knew Drasan, and she knew that she would not rest until she could stop the plans of Dhalia and Bal'zar.

"Yes, I know," said the witch, her voice turning cold. "And that's why I brought you here, Aurelia. You are the only one he will listen to. For you, he will do anything. If I threaten you..."

"I don't know what you're planning, you mean bitch..." Aurelia snapped, "but don't count on me to help you. I know my husband will tear your heart out if you scratch me."

"Bold words," said the witch. "I admire your courage, but I must disappoint you. Your rebellion or your words will not change anything, because the moment I kidnapped you, I saw Drasan's decision. Your life is more important to him than his own."

"You're lying!" Aurelia snapped, though she knew in her heart it was true. She knew her lover enough to know that when faced with a choice: her life and hers, he would choose her. As soon as she realized it, tears of anger and desperation rose in her eyes. "Then I choose death," she said, feeling she was barely brave enough to utter the words.

To her surprise, Dhalia laughed.

"And are you really ready to deliver such a devastating blow to a man who loves you? Will you kill yourself and your unborn child?" Suddenly she leaned forward to meet Aurelia's eyes. "Do you want your loved one to go mad with despair? With his character, that's for sure. And when he descends into the abyss of madness, he will cease to control his powers and annihilate not only himself, but everyone around him."

"You are lying, snake!" The girl replied, but her voice was not as sure as before.

What if Dhalia is right and Drasan goes mad after her death? More than once she had seen what he was capable of when he was in full control of himself.

"You can see it's the only solution, my dear," said Dhalia mildly. "Drasan is unpredictable as both a man and a dragon. Perhaps, had he trusted me then, things would have turned out differently."

"I don't believe you," the girl replied softly. "You hurt him."

"Only because he was too stubborn to comprehend my purpose," Dhalia said coldly.

Despite her will, Aurelia felt proud. If Drasan could handle it, she could handle it too.

"Whatever you plan, I won't help you," she said calmly.

Dhalia smiled.

"I knew you were going to say that," she admitted, and got up unexpectedly.

Right at the door, she turned to her and said as she was leaving:

"Drasan withstood everything I prepared for him. We'll see how much you can take."

She left, closing the door behind her and leaving Aurelia to her thoughts. Considering the circumstances, she preferred Drasan not to come to her aid. On the other hand, she was afraid that their bond would turn out to be stronger.

***

"What did you do?" Gaenor greeted him with these words as soon as he saw his condition.

Drasan rose on his elbow and hissed in pain. Even after Alt'ar had lifted his shoulder and Rodian had dealt with the more serious injuries, he could feel the effects of a duel with Bal'zar on him.

The dragon regarded him impassively, and from his expression, Drasan concluded that it was not about a fight, but something else entirely.

"Don't look at me like that," he growled, rubbing his knee. It hurt, and though Rodian had done her best to put them back together, he knew he would not be fully functional again.

Gaenor crossed his arms over his chest.

"You bonded with this girl," he did not ask, stating the fact.

Drasan didn't answer, but his silence was enough because Gaenor snorted.

"What does it have to do with it?" He asked softly, rubbing his temples.

"What does it have to do with it?!" The dragon roared. "Do you even realize what the best you have done?! We are not like humans; we pair up for life."

"How was I supposed to know?" Drasan retorted.

"If you weren't so ignorant, I would have told you," Gaenor replied, calming down a bit.

Alt'ar, who had been listening to this exchange so far, has now decided to join the discussion.

"What is he raving about?" he asked Drasan.

"I'd like to know, too," replied the half-dragon, shifting his position a bit and wincing in pain.

"We're all curious about it," Rodian said, standing behind Alt'ar's back.

The elder dragon sighed and sat down across from Drasan.

"In the past, I probably wouldn't mind, but now..." He met Drasan's eyes. "...bonding is the stupidest thing you could do. You caused this girl irreparable harm..."

"How about a little clearer?" Alt'ar growled, a ruby gleam in his blue eyes.

"Relax, wolf, I'll get to it soon," Gaenor said, his eyes never leaving Drasan. "Well, as I mentioned before, dragons bind once in a lifetime. Unlike humans, partners remain faithful to each other until the end. Few realize that on the first night they spend together, something like sealing a relationship takes place. Since then, they have both been bound by a bond that deepens mutual feelings and care. Unfortunately, the loss of a partner is so painful that often the other half goes insane." He paused for a moment, and his eyes rested on Alt'ar. "The madness that grips the dragon after losing his other half is very much like the frenzy a werewolf bursts into when he smells blood. Except that the mad dragon is much more dangerous and very difficult to kill. Neither silver nor magic will work on him. The second dragon has to deal the killing blow. And believe me, it doesn't like it at all."

Drasan felt himself sick.

"From your expression, I assume you finally got through what you did to that unfortunate girl," Gaenor said. "Now, listen to me carefully, before you commit another stupidity. Dhalia knew where to strike, which means she was well aware of who you gave your heart to. And now he is hoping that you will grab the bait and fly to yourself, presenting yourself to it as you did on the plate."

"Our scaly friend is right," Velwel suddenly interjected. His head was wrapped in linen, but otherwise he seemed well. "If you go to Aurelia's relief, you will fall into a trap set by the witch."

"Should I leave her there?!" Drasan growled, glaring at him.

"Don't ask questions if you don't want the answer," Alt'ar replied.

"Besides, look at you," added Rodian. "You can't even stand on your own, much less fight. I couldn't completely heal your leg, you will be limping for the rest of your days. You think Bal'zar arranged you this way was just a coincidence? If so, you are wrong. Drasan, he didn't break your leg, but turned your knee into a bloody pulp. You will never regain its former efficiency in it. These things are done for only two reasons: either to immobilize an opponent or to convey something to them. In my opinion, the message is all too clear: if you try to fight him again, he will kill you."

"He cheated," Drasan growled, rubbing the painful knee again.

"It doesn't matter," Alt'ar replied seriously. "It's important that you lost this fight. Why do you insist that you can face him again? For once, silence your heart and listen to reason. In order to fight again, we must muster our strength to counterattack. And we need you for that."

"Are you suggesting that I abandon my beloved woman?" Asked the half-dragon, rising on his elbow and staring into the werewolf's eyes.

"I'm only advising you well, Drasan," Alt'ar replied calmly. "We have suffered too heavy losses to be ruined now by your chivalry."

"That's it, boys," Rodian stepped in between them, turning to Drasan, "Gaenor and Alt'ar are both right. You have no chance of retrieving Aurelia now. Washmorth is a fortress, not yet conquered, so hide your feelings deeply, because we need logical thinking now."

"I'll talk to him," Mara said, her voice so faint that Drasan turned to look at her. She looked terrible, a large part of her head was covered in a thick roll of bandages, as was her left thigh, she was also limping.

"Of course, Your Majesty," Rodian stepped back to give the queen some room.

Mara lifted her eerily blue eyes and lowered them, staring directly at Drasan.

"I know how you feel, because I feel the same," the queen said softly. "My emotions dictate to avenge Yarred's death. I know I can't handle myself. This is one of those times when we have to choose between our heart and our common sense. Please respect the sacrifice of all those who fought and died for you. For they died believing in victory. If you let yourself be captured now, you will destroy everything we fight for. You think that's what Aurelia wants?"

Her words acted as a stimulus on the half-dragon. Deep down, he knew she was right, though he didn't want to admit it out loud. He loved Aurelia and would never forgive himself if he lost her. He was aware that she was aware of the great danger of being his partner. And yet she agreed.

"I know it probably won't cheer you up," Velwel said, for the first time keeping the total seriousness. "But Aurelia would not want you to abandon everything we fight for and fly to her rescue. She's stronger than you imagine, she can handle it."

Drasan did not reply immediately. He had to think carefully about what he heard. He knew that whatever decision he made, someone would suffer. Though abandoning Aurelia would hurt him, it seemed less of a bad thing. He raised himself on one elbow, hissing in pain, and turned to everyone present:

"I made my decision."

Everyone froze, staring at him intently.

"For now, we'll retreat to Bregan Fortress to gather strength," he added, realizing that he felt a physical pain when he said each word. And suddenly he looked around for King Oddon. "Wait a minute, and where is..." He broke off at the sight of all the people gathered. "...Oddon?" He frowned.

Everyone looked at each other, but no one wanted to answer that question. Only after a while Velwel dared to speak:

"Old Oddon is considering withdrawing his troops," he said in a low, grave tone. "He suffered very heavy losses and as everyone saw you fail..." He broke off and looked down.

He didn't have to finish. Drasan realized that the sight of his devastating defeat had slightly damaged the morale of the soldiers of both armies... or was he wrong? The sight of King Oddon entering the tent did not bring the expected relief. The Lord of the Earden looked somber.

"Can we talk in private?" He asked.

"Of course," the half-dragon replied, nodding at the others who left the pavilion, sullen expressions, one by one.

The king sat down on the empty barrel opposite Drasan and sighed heavily.

"I don't know what to do, Drasan." He wasn't looking at the half-dragon. "We have suffered a devastating defeat. Many more warriors died than I expected." He looked at the Sheardonian and suddenly seemed much older. "Everyone saw you lose to Bal'zar..."

Drasan snorted softly.

"I knew it," he said calmly. "You decided that one duel was the end of the war," he added, clenching his fists in helpless anger. "And it didn't occur to you, Your Majesty, that that was the purpose of this little shit? He wanted to show you my defeat..."

"Understand, Drasan, this is not an easy decision for any of us," Oddon replied. "But maybe... maybe it'll be better if we give up."

The half-dragon froze at these words. Give up? It was not an option.

"If you want to surrender, your majesty, go ahead," he growled, rubbing his knee where the pain resurrected. "But I'm not going to spend the rest of my life as a slave. Yes!" He added at the sight of the king's face. "This is the fate awaiting me and believe me, I prefer death!"

The king sighed again.

"I thought so too," he said, standing up. "You only think about yourself, and I've lost too many really good fighters to support you any longer."

"Here I am!" Drasan exclaimed, not hiding his anger. "Come on, tie me up and hand me over to Bal'zar! He will be pleased to have one more servant!"

His screams summoned Alt'ar and the others. They rushed into the tent and looked at King Oddon standing over Drasan, sword drawn in his hand.

"You have no idea..." he growled, putting the blade to his throat "...how much a responsibility I have as king. You only put your life at stake, I have to think about thousands of subjects."

"I didn't think I'd ever say that, King Oddon... You're a coward." The half-dragon drawled. "A true warrior does not give up and pursues his goal, regardless of the consequences. Now I see that the power has changed you..."

The Lord of the Earden clenched his jaws, sheathed his sword, and turned on his heel as he strode out of the tent. Drasan watched after him, knowing that it was not over yet, and that he would have to watch every word now. He made an enemy of one of the most powerful kings in Lineland.